# The Early Revolutionary Activities of Comrade Mao Tse-tung

# THE
# CHINA
# BOOK
# PROJECT Translation and Commentary

*A wide-ranging series of carefully prepared translations of books published in China since 1949, each with an extended introduction by a Western scholar.*

Translated by Anthony W. Sariti
Edited by James C. Hsiung

Introduction by Stuart R. Schram

# *The Early Revolutionary Activities of Comrade Mao Tse-tung*

by LI JUI

M. E. SHARPE, INC., PUBLISHER, WHITE PLAINS, NEW YORK

From The China Book Project. The Early Revolutionary
Activities of Comrade Mao Tse-tung is a translation of
Mao Tse-tung t'ung-chih ti ch'u-ch'i ke-ming huo-tung,
by Li Jui (Peking: China Youth Publishing House, 1957).

# Contents

# Introduction

Stuart R. Schram

This is the only book-length biography of Mao Tse-tung ever to be published in the Chinese People's Republic. That in itself is sufficient indication of its importance as a source for the history of China in the twentieth century, and sufficient justification for the present English translation.

Why, one might ask, has so obviously useful a work not been translated previously? One major reason, which will not be apparent to the reader who glances at the smooth and accurate English text, is that the original is written in such a dull and pedestrian style as to convey the impression that it is far less interesting than in fact it is. This factor, however, has not changed since the book was first published in Peking in July 1957, and therefore cannot explain why it was not thought worth translating then, but does appear so now. In two main respects, circumstances have changed in such a way as to enhance the value of the work in Western eyes.

First and most importantly, Mao and China occupy a place today in our perception of the world as a whole which bears no resemblance at all to that commonly allotted to them two decades ago, when the academic study of contemporary China was only in its infancy, and "Communist China" was regarded by the press as a creature of the Soviet Union, of little intrinsic interest. Secondly, the book seemed in the late 1950s and early 1960s to be so crudely hagiographic that it could scarcely be taken seriously as an historical source, apart from the quotations and summaries it contains from primary materials. Experience during and since the Cultural Revolution has taught us that there are degrees of bias which leave Li Jui far behind, and make his biography of the young Mao appear by contrast as honest and sober.

# Introduction

Not surprisingly, changing perspectives on the early history of
the Chinese Communist Party and Mao Tse-tung's role in it had
led Li Jui's work to be regarded in China, by the mid-1960s, as
inadequate if not downright heretical. Visitors to Peking at that
time were told that in any case it had never been an "official" biography. Strictly speaking, that was no doubt true, but it seems
scarcely plausible that previously unknown and highly revealing
manuscript materials, including voluminous notes made by Mao
during his student days in Changsha, would have been placed in the
hands of an author not regarded as fully reliable. If Li Jui's account has now been repudiated in Peking, the explanation clearly
lies not in any failure on his part to carry out adequately the task
with which he was entrusted in 1957, but in the fact that he did not
glorify Mao enough, and above all that he attributed too important
and too positive a role to Liu Shao-ch'i. Although the praise of
Liu appears odd in today's post-Cultural Revolution perspective,
he always takes second place to Mao. Li Jui simply treats him in
the way which seemed appropriate for the Chairman's chosen suc-
cessor. In any case, the recognition of Liu's achievements, particularly in organizing the labor movement in the early 1920s, corresponds on the whole, as I shall note subsequently, to the conclusions reached in recent Western studies by authors highly sympathetic to Mao. As for the treatment of Mao, Li Jui's crime consists
in approaching him with the greatest respect, but nonetheless as an
historical personage who, however precocious, did at least learn
something in the course of the first decade of his apprenticeship
in revolution.

The title of the book refers to Mao's "activities," but in the
Marxist perspective which Li Jui seeks to adopt, practice cannot
of course be separated from theory. This is therefore a chronicle
of Mao Tse-tung's development as a revolutionary thinker, as well
as a political biography. The contribution of the book to our knowledge and understanding of Mao's early career is rather different
in the two domains of theory and practice. As far as the concrete
record of Mao's activities is concerned, it remains today the most
important single source available to us, apart from Mao's autobiography as told to Edgar Snow. As regards Mao's ideas, on the
other hand, the position has changed radically since 1957, thanks
to the discovery of complete texts of quite a number of his writings
from the years 1919-1926. Two decades ago, Li Jui's summaries
of such materials constituted the main basis for retracing several
crucial episodes in Mao's intellectual itinerary. There are a few

points for which this is still the case, but to a very large extent
Li Jui's synthesis is now of interest more as an illustration of
how, in the late 1950s, certain awkward problems were glossed
over or rationalized out of existence.

This being the case, I propose in this introduction to go over
the ground twice, stressing first the facts about Mao's life, and
then the stages in his intellectual development, and adopting in the
two cases a substantially different approach. In looking at the historical record, I shall take Li Jui's account as providing the basic
"story line," and limit myself to pointing up some of the more important and controversial issues. This seems the only practical
course, for though Li Jui's version of a great many episodes could
be questioned, it would take several pages to sort out the evidence
regarding each one of them and an introduction nearly as long as the
book itself to say all that could be said today by way of complement, on
the basis of the available primary and secondary sources.

As regards Mao's thought, on the other hand, it is possible,
thanks to the republication of several key texts in recent years,
to sketch out an overview spanning all the crucial phases in his
development, including those which Li Jui deliberately distorts
or leaves in the dark. Here, therefore, I shall take my own account as the main theme, with occasional references to Li Jui's
interpretation by way of counterpoint.

## I. Mao's Life

As already noted, this is a political biography. Since Li Jui
follows neither the old Chinese custom of deducing his hero's future career from signs and portents during infancy, nor the modern Western psycho-cultural school which relates leadership
styles to patterns of child rearing, he contents himself with a very
brief sketch of Mao's childhood and adolescence, mainly derived,
as he indicates himself, from the autobiography as published in
the authorized Chinese translation of Red Star over China. The
book begins, in effect, with Mao's arrival at the First Provincial
Normal School in Changsha in the Autumn of 1913, shortly before
his twentieth birthday.

I have already given my own account of Mao's first two decades,
and there are a number of other biographies in English.[1] In any

---

[1] The early years are covered succinctly in Jerome Ch'en, Mao and the Chinese Revolution (London: Oxford University Press, 1965), pp. 17-32. There is
also Stephen Uhalley's "Critical Biography," and Han Suyin's quite uncritical one.

case, there is nothing worthy of note in Li Jui's brief introductory
section, except for the first of several instances of selective quotation from Mao's own story in order to efface traits which do not
appear to him to be worthy of what the future Chairman's attitude
ought to have been. [2] The remainder of the book falls broadly into
three parts. Chapters 1 to 3 (minus the opening pages) deal with
the period from 1913 to 1921, when Mao was working primarily
with urban intellectuals, first in the context of various student organizations, and then in establishing the Chinese Communist Party.
Chapter 4 is devoted to Mao's participation in the labor movement
in Hunan, in the years 1921-23. Mao's activities among the peasants in 1925-27 are covered in an appendix; the intervening two
years are left out altogether.

One reason for this gap is obvious enough: during the period
from mid-1923 to mid-1925, Mao Tse-tung not only worked closely
with the Kuomintang apparatus, in the context of the First United
Front, but produced ideological rationalizations for KMT-Communist
cooperation which appeared so odd from the perspective of 1957
(not to mention that of 1977) that Li Jui preferred not to mention
them at all. But to ascribe the pattern of his book wholly to this
factor would assuredly be unfair. Li Jui's concern is to show how
Mao served his apprenticeship as a revolutionary and learned to
lead the masses in their struggles. No doubt the period 1923-25
therefore seemed to him not only potentially embarrassing, but
also in a sense irrelevant, for during these years Mao's work as
a high Kuomintang official involved him in little contact with workers and peasants. In any case, I shall not try to bridge this gap in
the story, though I will have something to say in Part II of this introduction about the development of Mao's thinking during this
"bureaucratic" period in his career.

Of the three phases with which Li Jui does deal, Mao's rediscov-
ery of the peasantry has commonly been regarded as the most important because it seemed to announce the future course of the
Chinese revolution under his leadership. Two important recent
studies of Mao and Hunan in the 1920s have sought to redress the
balance. Lynda Shaffer, in her Columbia University thesis, "Mao
Tse-tung and the Hunan Labor Movement" (submitted in 1974; distributed by University Microfilms under the number 75-5250), has,
as the title indicates, concentrated on Mao's experience as a union
organizer in 1921-23. Angus McDonald, in his thesis, "The Urban

---

[2] See below, my note to p. 6 of the text.

Origins of Rural Revolution in Republican China" (Berkeley, 1974),
has criticized what he calls the "dogmatic presaging interpretation"
of which, in his view, I and others have been guilty in stressing
Mao's work among the peasants in the mid-1920s, and argued that
"the labor and peasant movements before 1926 were weak indeed,
substantially dependent for their success on passive toleration or
active support by both government officials and some members of
the intellectual elite." [3]

Though these authors naturally seek to justify their own interpretations, they have each made a valuable contribution to our
knowledge of Mao's early career and provided much useful background material which helps to put Li Jui's account in perspective.
It is important to note, however, that they were preceded by nearly
two decades in their effort to guide people away from an exclusive
concentration on the peasantry by Li Jui himself, who relegated
this dimension of Mao's early activities to a thirty-page appendix
and concentrated on Mao's work in the labor movement and above
all on the years when, as a student and then as a teacher in Changsha, he established a network of contacts which were subsequently
to stand him in good stead precisely with those "officials and members of the intellectual elite" whose role in the Chinese revolution
of the 1920s is stressed by Angus McDonald.

Among the manuscript materials from Mao's school days on
which Li Jui draws for his account are class notes and marginal
annotations to an ethics textbook which provide unique glimpses
of his mind and personality on the eve of the May Fourth movement, but there is also an abundance of concrete information about
Mao's activities as a student leader. From these we can see that several of the traits which have continued to characterize Mao's work
style in the ensuing decades were already present sixty years ago.

To begin with, there is the attitude toward study itself: the emphasis on concrete problems and the belief that "learning and questioning were inseparable" (p. 25). Mao, Li Jui tells us, "opposed
the study of dead books and favored the study of living ones. He
wanted to read not only books with words, but also books without
words," i.e., learn from "the myriad things and events of the
world and the nation" (p. 26). [4] Traditional-style learning methods

---

[3] McDonald, "Urban Origins," pp. 271, 487, and note 96 to p. 487.

[4] There is a striking parallel here with Mao's characterization, in the original
version of his "Yenan Talks on Art and Literature" of 1942, of life itself as "natural art." See S. Schram, The Political Thought of Mao Tse-tung (New York:
Praeger, 1969), pp. 360-361.

produced only "bookworms," and even a good school such as First Normal bored Mao to such an extent that several times he was on the verge of leaving (p. 61).

Directly related to this approach to learning is Mao's attitude as a young man toward the bearers of learning, and toward authority in general. On the one hand, he repeatedly rebelled against what he regarded as the unjust exercise of authority, for example by his teacher of Chinese Yüan the Big Beard (p. 44), as he had earlier resisted the tyranny of his father. But on the other hand, he "humbly and courteously paid visits to famous scholars" (p. 25), and had the greatest respect for teachers such as Yüan, and above all for his future father-in-law, Yang Ch'ang-chi (pp. 15-21, 20-30, and Chapter 1, passim). Li Jui sums up his attitude as follows:

Comrade Mao Tse-tung was a person famous for his modesty and friendliness.

But when it came to unreasonable things, things that could not be countenanced, especially the feudal autocratic work style, Mao Tse-tung would under no circumstances give in, but would courageously resist. Two ... features of his personality had been inseparable since youth: a gentleness grounded in firmness, and a modesty that has a reverse side — when he should not yield, he made absolutely no compromise (p. 44).

With due allowances for the mildly deferential vocabulary (what Li Jui calls "firmness" others might regard as self-righteous obstinacy) this conveys a great deal of the essence of Mao's personality as we know it then and subsequently. But, apart from the question of Mao's continuing veneration for the wisdom and knowledge of his elders, expressed in his letter of 1937 to Hsü T'e-li, another of his teachers at First Normal, [5] there is the thornier issue of his view, during his school days, of the role incumbent on intellectuals, including himself.

This brings us to the real heart of the matter, as far as the significance of the pre-May Fourth period, and perhaps of the whole period down to 1927, in Mao's development is concerned. As Mao himself repeatedly said, and as virtually everyone agrees, his ideas at this time were a mixture of the old and the new, the Chinese and the foreign. In Part II of the introduction I shall try to analyze the evolving relation between these various elements. In the domain of practice, however, as well as in that of theory, the Mao of First Normal was marked by the juxtaposition of highly diverse attitudes and patterns of behavior.

---

[5] Translated in Current Background, No. 891, p. 4. For Li Jui's sketch of Hsü's personality, see p. 42 below.

As early as the autumn of 1917, Mao Tse-tung, who was then in charge of the Student Society, took the lead in establishing a night school for the workers of Changsha, to teach them reading, writing, and arithmetic. Li Jui quite rightly argues that this shows not only Mao's concern about the welfare of the workers, but his desire to bridge the gulf between the school and society (pp. 59-65). And yet, in the summer of 1919, during the high tide of the May Fourth movement, Mao still saw the students as the most important component of the "Great Alliance" of revolutionary organizations he was seeking to promote.[6] And through the whole record of Mao's activities in Changsha, before and after the May Fourth movement, contained in Li Jui's first two chapters, there runs the central and very traditional theme of the responsibility of the educated elite for the great affairs of state. Time after time this idea is conveyed, in Mao's own words or in those of his friends and associates taken from records of conversations, exchanges of correspondence, the proceedings of various student societies, diaries, and other contemporary sources.

There is nothing at all surprising in this. Patriotic youths, at a time of national crisis, were necessarily concerned to save their country from further humiliation and internal decay, and given all the circumstances in China at the time, as well as the mentality they had assimilated in the course of their studies, they could only conclude that this mission fell upon them. Such a vocation implied, of course, an ethic of responsibility. To a classmate, Mao remarked that one must be a person with ideals who, in the words of an eleventh-century saying, "put first one's concerns for the world and put last one's pleasures in it" (p. 75).

This conversation took place in the course of preparations for the establishment of the most important of all the organizations into which Mao poured his energy and capacity for leadership during his school days in Changsha: the "New People's Study Society." Both the high-mindedness and the sense of belonging to a little band of seekers for the truth which characterized Mao and his friends at this time are abundantly in evidence in Li Jui's lengthy account of the history of the society (pp. 65-78). Although it is stressed several times that Mao felt a "large number" of members were necessary if the organization were to have the necessary strength (e.g., p. 76), this did not mean that the participants were to be selected at random, still less that it was to be a mass organization.

---

[6] See below, Part II of the introduction.

Introduction

By the time of the May Fourth movement, membership had
grown to seventy or eighty, but the requirements were still, as Li
Jui remarks, "quite strict. People who were poor in their scholarship or personal character, or who had no aspirations, could not
join the Society." It did, however, include in its membership "a
group of progressive and resolute female comrades." This, as Li
Jui says, was "something other societies at the time were unable
to match" (p. 76); it was, however, typical of Mao's relatively advanced attitude toward the role of women in Chinese society, from
that day to this.

The "New People's Study Society" was the training ground and
reservoir for a large proportion of the students and teachers from
Hunan who ultimately found their way into the Chinese Communist
Party. Lynda Shaffer argues that the mentality which characterized Mao and his friends on the eve of the May Fourth movement
persisted even after the establishment of the Chinese Communist
Party, and she finds this reprehensible:

The use of united front tactics . . . should not obscure the elitist nature of the
Communist core. Membership in the New People's Study Society was by invitation only; and when this idealistic, dedicated league was converted into the Socialist Youth Corps, from which the Party membership was selected, it continued
to be elite, as well as disciplined and secret. [7]

Ms. Shaffer explains these traits by Soviet influence, rather
than by the Chinese tradition, and suggests they were transcended
by Mao as soon as he began his work among the peasantry. There
is, of course, a strong elitist strand at the heart of Leninism, but
neither Lenin's theory nor Soviet practice are marked by the emphasis on moral self-cultivation which leaps out of nearly every
page of Li Jui's account of Mao's activities down to 1921. (This
may well be one more reason for subsequent discontent in Peking
with the book.)

Before pursuing the theme of Mao's approach to leadership into
the new period which begins with the establishment of the Chinese
Communist Party, a few words are in order regarding a topic
which is dealt with at some length in Li Jui's account, but in such
a way as to obscure many of the most interesting facets. I am
referring to Mao's participation in the Hunanese autonomist movement in the summer and autumn of 1920. In June 1920, the han-lin
and future leading figure in the Kuomintang "left," T'an Yen-k'ai,

---

[7] Shaffer, "Mao Tse-tung and the Hunan Labor Movement," p. 358.

took office as provincial governor, after his predecessor, Chang
Ching-yao, a particularly brutal warlord, had been driven out by
a movement in which Mao had played a significant role (pp. 121-
134). In November, he was deposed in his turn by his subordinate
Chao Heng-t'i, who in the end did actually grant a "provincial constitution." The Hunanese autonomy movement of the 1920s was,
for the most part, an extension of the movement toward decentralization which developed during the last years of the empire. In
other words, it was directed toward increasing control of provincial affairs by gentry and merchant elites, and not toward democratic participation. For this reason, Li Jui and others writing in
Peking have always argued that Mao merely tried to make use of
the limited freedoms offered to citizens by the constitutionalist
approach in order to organize the "worker and peasant masses"
(p. 137) but did not identify himself with the autonomist cause and
had no interest in provincial self-government as such.

Given Mao Tse-tung's known strong Hunanese patriotism, this
view has always appeared somewhat improbable, but it is only recently that the availability of five important texts from among
those penned by Mao in 1920 has made it possible to grasp the substance of his thinking.[8] As regards his general approach, the opening lines of an article published on September 26 sounded notes
which had already come to be characteristic of Mao's approach to
political work. "No matter what issue is involved," he wrote, "if
there is a 'theory,' but no 'movement' arises in consequence, this
theory cannot be put into practice."[9] In another article of September 17, Mao started from the observation that there was "no government in China," and "great confusion, utter confusion" reigned
throughout the whole country. In such circumstances, order could
only emerge from the bottom up. The political and constitutional
arguments on which this conclusion was based, to which I shall return in Part II of the introduction, are not too far removed from
the impression conveyed by Li Jui (for example, pp. 137-38), except for his statement that Mao had by this time "made a thorough
study of the experience of the October Revolution." There is,

---

[8] These materials — four articles by Mao and a proposal for a constitutional
convention drafted jointly with two others — were discovered by Angus McDonald
in a rare contemporary volume in the course of research on his dissertation. He
has published the Chinese texts in Hōgaku kenkyū, Vol. 46, No. 2, pp. 90-107,
with a commentary in Japanese, and has also summarized and in part translated
them into English in Ronin (Tokyo), No. 14 (December 1973), pp. 37-47.

[9] Hōgaku kenkyū, Vol. 46, No. 2, p. 99.

however, no hint in Li Jui's account of a note such as this:

Hunanese! Our mission is indeed weighty, and our opportunity is indeed superb. We must exert ourselves, taking first the establishment of the Republic of Hunan as our objective, carrying out [there] new ideals, and creating [there] a new life. On this plot of land we will open a new heaven and a new earth, which will serve as a precursor for the twenty-seven little Chinas. [10]

Whatever elements of Hunanese particularism may have lingered in Mao's attitude at this time, there is no doubt that he was already moving to mobilize support for social change among increasingly wide strata of society. Young students and intellectuals remained, however, the backbone of the movement. This preeminent role was reflected, for example, in the importance Mao attached to the "Cultural Book Society," which he set up in July 1920, in order to remedy the "mental starvation" of young people who had no access to the "new culture" (pp. 152-57). The Changsha branch of the "Society for the Study of Marxism," established in September, also catered mainly to students, as did the two organizations Mao helped to set up at about the same time, for the purpose of sending young people to Moscow in order to learn at firsthand about the revolution (pp. 157-62, 243-49). And finally, as already indicated, the "New People's Study Society," and the other organizations in which Mao was involved, provided recruits for the Socialist Youth Corps, set up in Hunan beginning in October 1920, and finally for the Communist Party itself (pp. 162-70).

In the light of this experience, one can understand why Mao wrote in 1939, on the occasion of the twentieth anniversary of the May Fourth movement: "The whole of the Chinese revolutionary movement found its origin in the action of young students and intellectuals." But at the same time, he was rapidly coming to the conclusion that a "narrow youth movement" which did not "unite with the broad masses of workers and peasants" would in the end achieve nothing. [11]

To recognize this in principle was easy, after the barest initiation to Marxist ideas. To apply it in practice, in Chinese conditions, was another thing altogether. Diary entries by a First Normal School student recruited by Mao for the Socialist Youth League summarize his views in November 1920: "The youth now have a way out; they are implementers of socialism. They must

---

[10] Ibid., pp. 101-102.
[11] The Political Thought of Mao Tse-tung, pp. 354-355.

go into the factories themselves and work, and by awakening the consciousness of our brothers in working circles implement the remolding of society" (p. 164).

In the late summer of 1921, Mao returned to Hunan from the First Congress of the Chinese Communist Party in Shanghai and himself went, not to work in the factories, but to organize the workers in his capacity as secretary of the Hunan branch of the "Chinese Trades Union Secretariat," which had been set up at the Congress. His activities during the next two years are the subject of Li Jui's fourth chapter, and have been dealt with at even greater length by Lynda Shaffer and Angus McDonald. Li Jui's account is clear, comprehensive, and frequently enlivened with picturesque detail. I shall not here try to summarize even the main lines of the story, but limit myself to commenting on two or three controversial issues.

The most important of these, in terms of its implications regarding the value of Li Jui's book as a piece of historical research, is the question of Liu Shao-ch'i's role in leading the labor movement in Hunan, and in particular the great Anyüan miners' strike of September 1922. The contrast is flagrant indeed between the Cultural Revolution stereotype, symbolized by the "revolutionary oil painting" "Chairman Mao goes to Anyüan," and Li Jui's statement that "Liu Shao-ch'i personally took general command of the strike" (p. 206). It is obviously impossible to go into this thorny question here: I can only note the conclusions of Lynda Shaffer, who has examined the evidence in the greatest detail. Her view, with which Angus McDonald agrees, is that "Mao's ostensible leadership of the unions at Anyüan and Shuikoushan was at best long distance"; the Anyüan workers' club was founded by Li Li-san, and the strike was effectively led by Liu Shao-ch'i. [12]

Whether or not Li Jui and others writing in China in the 1950s and early 1960s took an indecent satisfaction in exalting Liu Shao-ch'i, as they were accused during the Cultural Revolution of having done, there seems little doubt that Li Jui's account of the Anyüan strike is essentially correct. This does not mean, of course, that Mao's own role in the Hunan labor movement in 1921-23 was not important, or that he did not exercise direct leadership in many instances. It is worthy of note that several of the undertakings in which he was directly involved concerned education. Thus, in the

---

[12] Shaffer, "Mao Tse-tung and the Hunan Labor Movement," pp. 162-184, 355-57. See also McDonald, "Urban Origins," pp. 310-321.

autumn of 1921, shortly after the foundation of the Chinese Communist Party, Mao took the lead in setting up in Changsha, on the premises of the Wang Fu-chih Study Society, the Hunan Self-Study University, which was to serve as a cadre school for the Party, and a "preparatory class" for students with inadequate secondary school training (pp. 170-77). In the latter half of 1922, Mao organized a highly effective and highly characteristic program which made use of the "Popular Education Movement," launched by Jimmy Yen, and its respectable connections to promote workers' education and at the same time radicalize the content of the teaching materials employed (pp. 184-87).

In his actual trade union activity, one of the strikes which Mao led most effectively, and with which (judging by the extracts from his writings quoted by Li Jui) he found it easiest to identify, was that of the typesetters on the Changsha newspapers (pp. 246-53). It is perhaps no accident that Mao also exercised personal leadership in many strikes of workers who belonged not to the emerging modern industrial proletariat, but rather to handicrafts and trades of a more traditional kind, such as the masons and carpenters (pp. 213-29), the tailors and seamsters, the pottery workers, the rickshaw pullers and the like (pp. 254-59). Here was, once again, the encounter between the new conditions, inflicted on the workers by the development of capitalism, and the old attitudes and forms of organization such as guilds and secret societies with which these categories of the urban population had hitherto defended their interests, and here Mao was in his element. Here, too, he learned something of the problems of the lumpenproletarians, drifters, and marginal men in China's transitional society before he encountered similar categories in the countryside a few years later.

One link in the chain of circumstances which was to lead Mao from the cities to the countryside was perhaps the strike of lead and zinc miners at Shui-k'ou-shan in November 1922, which gave an impetus, we are told, to the peasant movement in the area because many of the workers had only recently left the land and had many links in the villages (pp. 239-46). There is no evidence, however, that Mao had, even by early 1923, any notion of the revolutionary potential of the peasantry; indeed, he explicitly told Edgar Snow that he had acquired such awareness only in 1925.[13] Meanwhile, his experience during the next two years took him instead to Canton and Shanghai, to work in the Communist and Kuomintang hierarchies.

---

[13] Red Star over China (New York: Grove Press, 1973), p. 159.

How are we to sum up the significance of Mao's "worker" period in 1921-23 ? One obscure and controversial question of fact which I have hitherto neglected will serve to introduce the question. The labor movement had, in fact, been founded in Hunan by a group of anarchists, who set up in November 1920 the Hunan Labor Association. Mao Tse-tung at first worked with these men, of whom the most outstanding were Huang Ai and P'ang Jen-ch'üan. Huang and P'ang accompanied him on his first visit to Anyüan, in September 1921, to assess the prospects for organizing the workers there. Shortly afterward, on January 17, 1922, they were executed by Chao Heng-t'i, the military governor of Hunan, in order to intimidate the workers following the victory of a spinners' strike. [14]

Two questions are raised by Mao's association with these anarchist leaders. One is whether he succeeded, as Li Jui claims, in converting them to Marxism and persuading them to join the Socialist Youth League two months before their death. Jean Chesneaux, in his pathbreaking work on the Chinese labor movement, shows considerable skepticism about this. At the end of his account, he refers to them as "anarchist militants," and such they probably remained, though not uninfluenced by the ideas and achievements of Mao and the Communists. [15]

Whether or not Mao recruited P'ang and Huang to the Socialist Youth League is less important for our purposes than the extent to which he was influenced by anarchism at this time. I shall deal with the development of his thinking in a moment. As far as his methods are concerned, it is important to remember that the Chinese Communist Party as a whole did not even begin to grasp something of the Leninist theory of organization until 1922, and did not understand it fully and implement it effectively until well after that. As a believer in Marxism, Mao looked to the working class in 1921-23, but he did not as yet have either the theoretical or the practical understanding of the specific problems of the urban workers to compensate for the fact that he had not grown up among them. The record of his activities and achievements, as set down by Li Jui, reveals that, but it also shows how his ingenuity, imagination, and instinctive grasp of the importance of the "organizational weapon" would soon enable him to bridge the gap.

---

[14] These events are rehearsed by Li Jui in the second section of Chapter 4 (pp. 192-199). See also Shaffer, "Mao Tse-tung and the Hunan Labor Movement," pp. 110-132, and McDonald, "Urban Origins," pp. 288-308.

[15] Jean Chesneaux, Le mouvement ouvrier chinois de 1919 à 1927 (Paris and the Hague: Mouton) 1962, pp. 253, 543.

Introduction

The story of Mao's two years as a bureaucrat, omitted by Li
Jui, I shall not try to summarize here. As for his work among the
peasantry, its theoretical overtones and implications for the future
are such that it seems preferable to deal with the period 1925-27
in unified fashion, in the context of the development of Mao's
thought.

## II.  Mao Tse-tung's Thought: The First Decade

Li Jui's detailed account of Mao's life and thought begins, as already indicated, in 1913, but it is only with the publication of Mao's
first article, in April 1917, that we are able to form some systematic view of the substance of his ideas.  Li Jui mentions this article, entitled "A Study of Physical Education," but he is careful
to avoid telling his readers exactly where to find it.  At one point,
he notes that Yang Ch'ang-chi served as intermediary in submitting
an article by Mao to the magazine Hsin ch'ing-nien (New Youth);
thereafter, he twice refers to the article and quotes briefly from
it, but without indicating where it was published (pp. 18, 27, and
28-29, and notes 55 and 59 to Chapter 1).  There are indeed things
in the article which do not altogether correspond to the picture Li
Jui is trying to project of Mao, even at this early age, but there
are also many personality traits, and many strands of thought,
which can be followed through down to the present.  Any serious
discussion of the development of Mao's thought must therefore begin here.

The overriding concern — one might almost say obsession —
which runs through the whole article is anxiety lest the Chinese
people should suffer the catastrophe of wang-kuo, that is, of losing
their state and becoming "slaves without a country."  This theme,
so widespread in China in the late nineteenth and early twentieth
centuries, is vigorously stated in the opening sentences:

Our nation is wanting in strength. The military spirit has not been encouraged.
The physical condition of the population deteriorates daily. This is an extremely
disturbing phenomenon.... If this state continues, our weakness will increase
further.... If our bodies are not strong, we will be afraid as soon as we see
enemy soldiers, and then how can we attain our goals and make ourselves respected ? [16]

---

[16] The Political Thought of Mao Tse-tung, pp. 152-53.  This book contains only
extracts from Mao's 1917 article.  I have also published a complete French
translation in my monograph Mao Ze-dong, Une étude de l'éducation physique
(Paris: Mouton, 1962), and recently M. Henri Day has translated the whole text
into English in his Stockholm thesis, Mao Zedong 1917-1927. Documents.

If Mao is clearly preoccupied here with what might loosely be
called nationalist goals, was his nationalism at this time conservative or revolutionary? An obvious touchstone for deciding this
point is whether or not he saw the aim of fu-ch'iang as in any way
tied to a social and cultural revolution perceived as a necessary precondition for strengthening the nation. In fact, the article shows
us a Mao concerned with China's fate, but almost totally uninter-
ested in reform, let alone revolution.

Of the twenty-odd textual quotations, or explicit allusions to particular passages, from classical writings contained in the article,
there are a dozen to the Confucian canon; one to the Confucian
"realist" Hsün Tzu, a precursor of the Legalists, and two to the
Sung idealist interpreter of Confucianism, Chu Hsi, as well as one
to his late Ming critic, Yen Yüan. There are also three references
to Mao's favorite Taoist classic, the Chuang Tzu. The range of his
knowledge at this time was clearly very wide, for he refers in passing to obscure biographical details regarding a number of minor
writers of various periods. It is all the more striking that eleven
out of twelve references to the Confucian classics should be to the
basic core of the Four Books (six to the Analects, three to Mencius, and one each to the Ta Hsüeh and the Chung Yung). The
answer would appear to lie in the fact that he was trying to make
a few very basic points and hence chose to refer to the most authoritative texts, even if they were well known.

And yet, though there are no explicit references to social
change, nor even any suggestion that it is necessary, the article
does contain many traces of modern and nonconformist thinking,
of both Chinese and Western origin. To begin with, there is the
emphasis on the value of the martial spirit, expressed in the opening sentences quoted above, and summed up in the statement: "The
principal aim of physical education is military heroism."[17] To
justify this view, Mao hails the example of many heroes of ancient
times, and quotes from Yen Yüan, who had denounced Chu Hsi for
"emphasizing civil affairs and neglecting military affairs" (chung-

(Skriftserien för Orientaliksa Studier nr 14), pp. 21-31. This very valuable
work, which contains translations of all of Mao's writings included in volume 1
of the Tokyo edition of the Chinese text (Takeuchi Minoru, ed., Mao Tse-tung chi,
Hokubosha, 1972), together with provocative and original, though occasionally un-
convincing, commentaries, is an important contribution to our knowledge of the
young Mao and his thought. I shall have occasion to refer to it often in the remainder of this introduction.
[17] The Political Thought of Mao Tse-tung, p. 157.

wen ch'ing-wu), thus creating a harmful tradition contrary to the
teachings of Confucius, and who characterized military men as
"the incarnation of righteousness in the world."[18] Although Yen
Yüan, like the other late Ming and early Ch'ing patriotic thinkers,
took pains to identify himself with true Confucianism, their stress
on the military virtues went against the grain of the Confucian tradition, and they are, of course, today regarded as Legalists. More
importantly, Mao did not derive this strain in his own thought
simply from the accidental reading of these thinkers; like many
other Chinese in the early twentieth century, he developed his
ideas in response to circumstances similar to those which prevailed at the end of the Ming, when the unity and integrity
of the Chinese nation was threatened as a result of military
weakness.

The lessons of the nineteenth century, followed by the German
victories of 1914-16, had given new prestige to military force, and
also to physical strength, as keys to national survival. The Japanese had played a central role in transmitting these lessons to
China, both by the example of their own successes and by direct
intellectual influence, as when Ch'en Tu-hsiu, ridiculing the physical weakness and lack of courage of Chinese youth, praised the
shou-hsing-chu-i of Fukuzawa Yukichi, in the second issue of New
Youth.[19] Mao showed his receptivity to such influences by his
words in praise of bushidō.[20]

But if this enthusiasm for things military has remained a permanent trait of Mao's thinking, an even more basic theme of the 1917
article, and one which revealed more unmistakably modern influences, was that of the importance of self-awareness (tzu-chüeh)
and individual initiative (tzu-tung). He put the point in these words,
in the opening paragraph of his article:

Strength depends on drill, and drill depends on self-awareness. The advocates
of physical education have not failed to devise various methods. If their efforts
have nevertheless remained fruitless, it is because external forces are insufficient to move the heart....

If we wish to make physical education effective, we must influence people's
subjective attitudes and stimulate them to become conscious of physical education.... [21]

---

[18] Yen Yüan, Ts'un hsüeh, Book 2; Hsi-chai hsien-sheng yen-hsing lu, Book 2.
[19] Ch'en Tu-hsiu, "Chin-jih chih chiao-yü fang-chen" (The Current Orientation
in Education), Ch'ing-nien, 1915, No. 2, p. 6.
[20] The Political Thought of Mao Tse-tung, p. 153.
[21] Ibid.

The source for the idea that the key to effective action lies in first transforming the hearts of men lies, of course, partly in the Confucian tradition, as Mao indicated by quoting the precept "Chün-tzu ch'iu-chi" from the Analects.[22] But the main inspiration for passages such as this is to be found no doubt in the eclectic, and yet basically Westernizing, ideas Mao had absorbed from his reading of Hsin ch'ing-nien, and from the lessons of his ethics teacher and future father-in-law, Yang Ch'ang-chi.

Yang, who was a disciple of Kant and Samuel Smiles, as well as of Chu Hsi, taught a moral philosophy which combined the emphasis of Western liberalism on self-reliance and individual responsibility with a strong sense of man's duty to society. As Mao put it twenty years later: He "tried to imbue his students with the desire to become just, moral, virtuous men, useful in society."[23] To this end, Yang had compiled a volume of extracts from the Confucian Analects, with accompanying commentaries, to illustrate his own interpretation of "self-cultivation." The first chapter of this book took its title from the concept of "establishing the will" (li-chih), and contains the statement: "If one has an unbreakable will, there is nothing that cannot be accomplished" (p. 18).

This point, too, is strongly emphasized in Mao's 1917 article, and it corresponds to a central and persistent element of his outlook. "Physical education," he wrote, "...strengthens the will.... The will is the antecedent of a man's career."[24] In a letter he wrote to Miyazaki Toten in March 1917, with the aim of inviting him to give a speech at the First Normal School in memory of Huang Hsing, Mao described himself as a student who had "to some extent established [his] will (p'o li chih-ch'i)."[25] Arguing, in his 1917 article, the importance of persistence and of a firm will, Mao refers successively, in the space of a few lines, to Chuang Tzu and Hsün Tzu, Mencius and Chu Hsi. Both the emphasis on the importance of subjective forces, and the eclecticism in the choice of his authorities, persist in Mao's later writings.

---

[22] Ibid., p. 159.

[23] Snow, Red Star over China, p. 146.

[24] The Political Thought of Mao Tse-tung, pp. 157-58 (Mao's emphasis). This same stress on the will as the key to success persists in Mao's very latest published poem, released in Peking in January 1976, which reads, in Jerome Ch'en's translation (The China Quarterly, No. 34, 1968, p. 3): "Under this heaven nothing is difficult, If only there is the will to ascend."

[25] Or, as Mike Day translates, "to some extent disciplined" his will. (Day, Mao Zedong, p. 18) Text in Mao Tse-tung chi, Vol. 1, p. 33. For the circumstances in which this letter was written, see Day, Mao Zedong, pp. 18-20.

Two other themes in Mao's 1917 article which have implications
for the subsequent development of his thought are the value he at-
taches to movement, and the emphasis on practice rather than
mere words. On the first point, he ridicules the disciples of Chu
and Lu, who boast of their methods of contemplation and despise
physical exercise, concluding: "In my humble opinion, there is
only movement in heaven and on earth."[26] There is an obvious
element of continuity here with Mao's quite untraditional respect
for physical effort, and perhaps a link with his approach to dialectics as well. In his lectures of 1937 on dialectical materialism,
he criticized the "metaphysics of the Sung and the Ming" from the
standpoint of the "fundamental principle of dialectical materialism"
that the development of the world consists in the movement of
matter.[27]

As for the theme of practice, Mao asserts that there has been
all too much talk about physical education; "the important thing is
not words, but putting them into practice."[28] Mao's stress on
linking theory and practice has often been traced back to Wang
Yang-ming, but this is in my opinion quite arbitrary speculation;
there is not the slightest mention of Wang in any of Mao's known
writings, and no evidence that he has been influenced by him.
Among premodern Chinese sources, one of the most important
would seem to be once again Yen Yüan, who mocked at bookworms
in terms reminiscent of those used by Mao in recent years. He
described scholars as "sitting majestically in their studies, every
one of them a frail weakling, laughed at by soldiers and peasants —
what sort of behavior is this for a man?" Reading books, Yen argued, was useless unless one put into practice what one learned.[29]

More relevant to Mao's development during the years immediately after 1917 — and also more controversial — is the likely
Western (or Westernizing) source for Mao's emphasis on practice:
Hu Shih. Rather than arguing this point with reference to Mao's
ideas in 1917, it seems more fruitful to consider it in the context
of the changes in Mao's thinking on the eve of the May Fourth
movement. In 1917 and 1918, Mao acquired, as we have already
seen, very considerable organizing experience in various contexts.

---

[26] The Political Thought of Mao Tse-tung, p. 156.

[27] Ibid., pp. 187-88.

[28] Mao Zedong, Une étude de l'éducation physique, p. 52; Chinese text, included
in this volume, p. 7; Day, Mao Zedong, p. 27.

[29] For a summary of his ideas on this theme, see H. G. Creel, Chinese Thought
from Confucius to Mao Tse-tung (Chicago: Mentor Books, 1953), p. 183.

He also advanced very rapidly in his knowledge and awareness of Western ideas and of the outside world. The manuscript notes in which Mao set down his reflections about a variety of subjects, from which Li Jui quotes extensively, constitute perhaps the most important single documentary contribution in the entire volume.

I have drawn on this source in my previous writings on the subject, and Jerome Ch'en has also translated several passages from Mao's notes and put forward his own interpretation.[30] Now it will be possible for the reader who did not have the opportunity, or the inclination, to consult the original to read the whole of the passage in which Li Jui presents these materials (pp. 33-41). There are only a few points to which I want to call attention here. First of all, there is the remarkable fragment (p. 40) on dialectics, clearly revealing the Taoist influences which can still be discerned in Mao's writings of the 1950s and 1960s. Secondly, there is, side by side with continuing Confucian influences, an increasingly strong emphasis on individualism, which leads Mao in directions incompatible with tradition, as when he writes: "Wherever there is repression of the individual...there can be no greater crime. That is why our country's Three Bonds must go, and why they constitute, with religion, capitalists, and autocracy, the four evil demons of the world" (p. 38). Finally, there is the explicit assertion: "Tradition robs us of the power and courage to act upon the world; the past weighs heavily upon the present. The inability to adapt themselves to new conditions causes the death of historical institutions.... The Chinese Republic is just now in this very position" (p. 39).

Mao's horizon was further expanded by his experiences in Peking during the winter of 1918-19. As a result, when we are once again in a position to apprehend his thinking in some detail, in the article entitled "The Great Union of the Popular Masses," which he published in July and August 1919, we find ourselves confronted with a Mao who, in a great many respects, has changed almost beyond recognition as compared with the impression conveyed by his 1917 article. And yet, if we look more closely, we can perhaps grasp certain basic continuities.

I have published a full translation of this article in The China Quarterly, together with an analysis, and Mike Day has also re-

---

[30] The Political Thought of Mao Tse-tung, pp. 26-28; Ch'en, Mao and the Chinese Revolution, pp. 45-47.

cently translated and commented on it.[31] I shall therefore content myself here with pointing out some of the more significant problems, and adding a few new facts and ideas.

The most startling passage of this article is no doubt that contrasting Marx and Kropotkin:

As to the actions which should be undertaken once we have united, there is one extremely violent party, which uses the method "do unto others as they do unto you" to struggle desperately to the end with the aristocrats and capitalists. The leader of this party is a man named Marx who was born in Germany. There is another party more moderate than that of Marx. It does not expect rapid results, but begins by understanding the common people. Men should all have a morality of mutual aid, and work voluntarily.... The ideas of this party are broader and more far-reaching. They want to unite the whole globe into a single country, unite the human race into a single family.... The leader of this party is a man named Kropotkin, who was born in Russia. [32]

Understandably, this paragraph is not included in the extracts from the article reproduced by Li Jui, since it would hardly have supported the view he puts forward that "The Great Union of the Popular Masses" was "one of the most important writings" in which Mao "began to combine a Marxist-Leninist viewpoint with the concrete practice of the Chinese revolution" (pp. 111-15). The comments of the pro-Soviet communists who published a translation of this text in Japan in 1971 are equally one-sided; in their view, Mao Tse-tung was and has remained basically an anarchist, and that is the end of the matter.[33] This interpretation is, in a sense, even wider of the mark than that of Li Jui. Mao's 1919 article reflects an important stage in the process whereby he learned about the theory and practice of revolution. It was a pre-Marxist stage, but it nevertheless shows Mao already developing a feeling for the importance of organization which would very rapidly carry him beyond the limitations of the partially anarchist viewpoint expressed in the article, toward effective participation in the founding of the Chinese Communist Party.

At the same time, it must be noted that, while Mao was, in the summer of 1919, on the way to becoming a revolutionary, there

---

[31] Mao Tse-tung, "The Great Union of the Popular Masses," followed by S. Schram, "From the 'Great Union of the Popular Masses' to the 'Great Alliance,'" The China Quarterly, No. 49 (January-March 1972), pp. 76-105; Day, Mao Zedong, pp. 85-100. The Chinese text is available in Mao Tse-tung chi, Vol. 1, pp. 57-69.

[32] The China Quarterly, No. 49, pp. 78-79.

[33] Ibid., p. 91.

is not a trace of Marxist analysis in his article. Concepts such
as class struggle, dialectics, or the materialist view of history
are not even mentioned, and the very term "class" is used only
once, and then in a totally un-Marxist sense (the "classes" of the
wise and the ignorant, the rich and the poor, and the strong and
the weak). [34] If the article has a discernible philosophical basis,
this is to be found neither in Marx nor in Kropotkin, but in the
ideas of Western liberals as transmitted — and transmuted — by
certain Chinese writers of the late nineteenth and early twentieth
centuries. Among these were Yen Fu and Liang Ch'i-ch'ao, the
Hunanese revolutionary thinker and martyr T'an Ssu-t'ung, as
well as Mao's teacher Yang Ch'ang-chi, all of whom developed in
one way or another the view that spontaneous action by members
of society, unfettered by the old hierarchical bonds, would maxi-
mize the energy of society as a whole. I have dealt with these
influences, and especially with that of T'an Ssu-t'ung, in my article in The China Quarterly. One writer about whom I said little
or nothing there, and to whom I would like to devote more attention here, is precisely Hu Shih, whose influence I suggested,
a moment ago, might be discernible already in the Mao of
1917.

It has often been pointed out that Mao's articles of 1919 were
enthusiastically hailed following their publication by the Peking
weekly Mei-chou p'ing-lun. Presenting the contents of the first
few issues of Mao's Hsiang Chiang p'ing-lun, the commentator
said: "The strong point of the Hsiang Chiang p'ing-lun lies in discussion. The long article 'The Great Union of the Popular Masses'
published in the 2nd, 3rd and 4th issues ... exhibits exceedingly
far-reaching vision, and exceedingly well-chosen and effective arguments. Truly it is one of the important articles which have appeared recently." [35] What is less well known, and what I failed to
point out myself, is that the author of this comment was none other
than Hu Shih. This is the less surprising when we note that, in his
editorial for the first issue of the Hsiang Chiang p'ing-lun, Mao
said, after enumerating the progress in various domains which
had been achieved by humanity since the Renaissance (for example,
from a dead classical literature for the aristocracy to a modern,
living literature for the common people, and from the politics of
dictatorship to the politics of parliamentarianism), that in the

---

[34] Ibid., pp. 77-78.
[35] Mei-chou p'ing-lun, No. 36 (August 24, 1919), p. 4.

field of thought or philosophy (ssu-hsiang) "we have moved forward to pragmatism."[36]

Mike Day, after calling attention to this passage, goes on to argue, to my mind quite convincingly, that the title of the "Problem
Study Society" (Wen-t'i yen-chiu hui) which Mao founded in the
summer of 1919 strongly suggests that he was influenced by Hu.
Li Jui and others writing in Peking have, of course, claimed that
in the famous controversy over "Problems and Isms," Mao stood
on the side of Li Ta-chao against Hu Shih. But as Day puts it,
"Marxist or no, Hu's strictures against those who mouth ideologies
as a substitute for the hard work of investigating problems are
quite valid. Li Dazhao entirely agreed with this point, and as anyone who has read Mao knows, his opposition to dogmatism . . . is a
constant element in his character. . . ."[37]

If Mao's ideas in 1919, like those of older and more learned
men at the time, were a mosaic of many influences, his articles
had one remarkable peculiarity: they represented one of the few
attempts to put forward a general program on the basis of concrete experience of the revolutionary mass movements of the
May Fourth period. It is true that Mao's hierarchy of social categories in the total picture as he saw it was quite un-Marxist: he
attributed maximum importance to the student movement, and
relatively little to the peasants, not to mention the workers. He
also, characteristically, devoted considerable attention to women,
and to school teachers. Looked at as a whole, his vision of the
revolutionary alliance he is striving to create is not unlike that
of the "New Left" in the United States and elsewhere five to ten
years ago. The central theme of the articles is that China's renewal will come above all from the rebellion of young people,
and especially of students, against the old order. Mike Day, in
my opinion, slightly distorts the thrust of Mao's thinking by translating ch'iang ch'üan as "authority," and thus making a key sentence in Mao's fa-k'an-tz'u read: "There is no room whatever
left for the existence of authority in religion, literature, politics,
society, education, economics, philosophy, or international [rela-
tions]; all these must be toppled by the call for democracy."[38]
In my translation of "The Great Union," ch'iang-ch'üan-che is
rendered literally as "the powerful people," the connotation being,

---

[36] Day, Mao Zedong, p. 81; Mao Tse-tung chi, Vol. 1, pp. 53-54.

[37] Day, Mao Zedong, pp. 47-48. See also the note to p. 23 below, pointing out
how Li Jui has removed Mao's own acknowledgment of his debt to Hu Shih.

[38] Day, Mao Zedong, p. 81.

I think, something like "superpowers" in current Chinese usage — bad powerholders who wantonly push others around. In this context, I would interpret the term as "arbitrary and oppressive author-ity," and thus avoid letting Mao appear as a pure anarchist. There is no doubt, however, that the instrument and motive force of the reforms Mao wants to carry out lies in democratic organizations spontaneously building up from the grass roots.

The goal of the whole process will be, in Mao's view (and here he reveals himself as a true disciple of Yen Fu), not merely the liberation of the individual from the shackles of the old society, but also, and by that very fact, the strengthening and renewal of the Chinese nation as a whole. In a supremely eloquent peroration, Mao addressed his compatriots thus:

... in every domain we demand liberation. Ideological liberation, political libera-tion, economic liberation, liberation [in the relations between] men and women, educational liberation, are all going to burst from the deep inferno where they have been confined, and demand to look at the blue sky. Our Chinese people possess great inherent capacities! The more profound the oppression, the greater its resistance; since [this] has been accumulating for a long time, it will surely burst forth quickly. I venture to make a singular assertion: one day, the reform of the Chinese people will be more profound than that of any other people, and the society of the Chinese people will be more radiant than that of any other people. The great union of the Chinese people will be achieved earlier than that of any other place or people. Gentlemen! Gentlemen! We must all ex-ert ourselves! We must all advance with the utmost strength! Our golden age, our age of glory and splendour, lies before us! [39]

There is more than one echo here of Mao's 1917 article, in the emphasis on persistent efforts and a firm resolve as the keys to national resurgence. In the intervening two years, he had learned much, both from books and from experience, about the way to tap and mobilize the energies which he perceived to be latent in the Chinese people. He had, however, a great deal still to learn before he could even begin to devise a complete and effective strategy for making revolution in a country such as China.

A phase in this learning process which had hitherto only been dimly perceived has recently come to life thanks to the discovery of the materials referred to earlier relating to Mao's participa-tion in the Hunanese autonomy movement in 1920, which provide a highly suggestive complement to his analysis, in 1919, of the role of grass-roots organization in social change.

In a highly characteristic statement of his general approach to

[39] The China Quarterly, No. 49, p. 87.

political work, Mao declared that there were two kinds of movements: one involved "entering into the midst of things (ju yü ch'i chung) and setting up a concrete movement"; the other would be "set up outside, in order to promote [the cause]." Both were necessary — but, Mao warned, "...the Hunanese autonomist movement must start from the 'people.' If this present Hunanese autonomist movement is set up, but its source resides not in the 'people,' but outside the 'people,' then I venture to predict that such an autonomist movement will not be able to last very long."[40]

Two more brief quotations sum up the substance of Mao's argument about the relation between political developments at the provincial and national levels. In his article of September 17, after noting the existence of "utter confusion" in China, Mao added:

I estimate that this sort of phenomenon will last another seven or eight years.... But in the midst of this must arise a new phenomenon.... Local domination by militarists and bureaucrats will be transformed into provincial self-government by the people of every province. The people of every province, having suffered the poison of tyrannical domination by militarists and bureaucrats, will rise up and fight for freedom. From the self-determination of the Hunanese, the Kwangtungese, the Szechwanese will follow the self-determination of the people of Chihli and Fengtien. In ten or twenty years, a different army of veterans will arise, and that will be the fulfillment of the general revolution. [41]

In their proposal of October 7 for a constitutional convention, Mao and his co-authors asserted:

The self-government law the Hunanese need now is like that of an American state constitution or that of a German Staat. China is now divided into many pieces, and we do not know when a national constitution will be produced; in fact we are afraid that first every province will have to produce its own constitution, and only later will we have a national constitution. This is just like the route from separation to unification followed by America and Germany. [42]

Angus McDonald is a little unfair, in my opinion, when he castigates Mao's biographers for playing down Mao's central importance in the self-government movement of the autumn of 1920 and thus "obscuring this important learning experience." Mao's biographers could scarcely make plain what they could not apprehend on the basis of the available documentation. McDonald is quite right, however, when he notes that Mao's activities during this

---

[40] Hōgaku kenkyū, Vol. 46, No. 2, p. 99.
[41] Ibid., pp. 101-102; cf. McDonald, in Ronin, No. 14 (December 1973), p. 41.
[42] Hōgaku kenkyū, Vol. 46, No. 2, p. 103; cf. McDonald, Ronin, No. 14, p. 44.

period reveal "lines of thought that he returned to time and again
during his long career as a revolutionary leader: his emphasis on
the positive value of personal experience in [the] struggle for the
development of political consciousness among the masses; his
strong drive toward remaking China as an example for the rest
of the world's oppressed peoples; and his belief in the importance
of decentralization as crucial for development."[43] I would, however, qualify McDonald's third point by noting that if Mao believes
in the value of decentralization, he also believes in leadership.
Indeed, the emphasis, in these articles of 1920, on the need to promote the cause of revolution both from within the people and from
without can be seen as a remarkable prefiguration of the mass-
line work style which Mao was to develop twenty years later,
which combined active participation from below with firm leadership from above.

For the moment, Mao did not have a properly elaborated view
of the relation between leadership and mass response; he merely
sensed that both were necessary. It was, of course, from his experience in organizing and leading revolutionary movements that
Mao was ultimately to evolve his theories on this subject, as well
as from his participation in the central organs both of the Chinese
Communist Party and of the Kuomintang during the period of the
First United Front.

As already suggested, Mao's experience during the eventful first six
years of the Chinese Communist Party falls neatly into three segments,
which might be characterized respectively as his workers' period (1921-
23), his bureaucratic period (1923-25), and his peasant period (1925-
27). The most remarkable thing about the first two of these periods is
that, on the basis of all the available primary and secondary sources,
they appear to have been intellectually sterile. This can be explained
in part by the fact that Mao, like everyone else in the Party, was over-
whelmingly busy with the concrete organizational tasks which faced
such a new revolutionary movement in a rapidly changing situation, and
also by the need for him to digest Marxism-Leninism before he could
make use of it with any assurance. Both of these factors are real, but
in my opinion neither is as important as the fact that his experiences in
1921-25 did not grip Mao as intensely, and arouse in him the same feelings of excitement and of personal involvement, as had his participation
in the May Fourth movement and in the Hunanese autonomist movement,
and as would his subsequent work with the peasants.

---

[43] Ronin, No. 14, p. 47.

There are available, so far as I know, only two lengthy items by Mao dating from the period from the establishment of the Chinese Communist Party in July 1921 to mid-1923. The first of these, which we have in its entirety thanks to the fact that Tung-fang tsa-chih reprinted it in 1923, is of very considerable interest, but belongs in fact rather to the tail end of Mao's May Fourth period activities. It is the "Declaration on the Inauguration of the Hunan Self-Study University" which Mao wrote in August 1921 when he set up that intriguing and characteristic institution. [44] This text places, as Mao had done since 1917, the emphasis on individual initiative and self-expression in the learning process; it also echoes the articles Mao had written a year earlier on the mission of the Hunanese. But though Mao denounces vigorously the fact that "learning is monopolized by a small 'scholar clique' and becomes widely separated from the society of the ordinary man, thus giving rise to that strange phenomenon of the intellectual class enslaving the class of ordinary people," he shows as vague an understanding of what is meant by the "so-called 'proletariat'" as he had the previous winter in correspondence with his friend Ts'ai Ho-sen, when he divided the world's total population of one and a half billion into 500 million "capitalists" (tzu-pen chia) and a billion "proletarians" (wu-ch'an chieh-chi). [45]

The other text, which is available in the form of lengthy extracts, is an open letter which appeared in the Changsha Ta-kung pao on December 14, 1922, in reply to an editorial published the day before warning the workers against being too demanding and advising them to devote themselves principally to acquiring an education. It shows us a Mao whose pen — or brush — is as sharp as ever, as he mocks this "gentleman in a long gown" who preaches at the workers but has no understanding or sympathy for their problems (pp. 251-53). There is nothing at all in it, however, about the role of the working class in the revolution; nor indeed is there any explicitly political analysis.

It is, in my opinion, highly significant that Li Jui, who gives these extracts, can find nothing else of comparable length or importance to reproduce in the lengthy chapter on Mao's leadership of the labor movement in Hunan in 1921-23 which takes up nearly a third of his book, whereas there are extremely abundant citations and summaries of Mao's writings in Li's discussion of the

---

[44] Mao Tse-tung chi, Vol. 1, pp. 81-84; Day, Mao Zedong, pp. 140-143.
[45] The Political Thought of Mao Tse-tung, pp. 296-298.

period 1918-20, and again in his appendix on the peasant movement.  Clearly Li Jui shares my view that Mao's experience in
the labor movement, while it was an important element in the
training of a revolutionary, did not give rise to any original and
important theoretical insights.

Much the same can be said of Mao's "bureaucratic period,"
which Li Jui skips over altogether, for rather obvious reasons.
Mao published several articles in Hsiang-tao in the summer of
1923, the only one of any substance being that in which he argued
that "because of historical necessity and current tendencies," it
was the merchants who should play the leading role in the Chinese
revolution.[46]

No doubt Mao was simply spelling out what appeared to him to
be the implications of the newly decided alliance with the Kuomintang, and it should be remembered that this was in effect the view
expressed at the same time by Ch'en Tu-hsiu, who argued that the
turn of the proletariat had not yet come in China.  In any case,
this lone expression of Mao's strategic outlook for the years
1921-24 was entirely outside the mainstream of his strategic
thinking — though it is obviously related to the deeply ingrained
nationalist streak in his motivation evident throughout his entire
career from 1917 onward, and which manifested itself in a brief
but pungent article published in August 1923 castigating the warlord government in Peking as the "counting house of our foreign
masters."[47]

We do not have a single substantial text by Mao for more than
two years after the appearance of these articles in Hsiang-tao,
until he took up the editorship of the Kuomintang organ the Political Weekly in December 1925.  For a considerable portion of
1924, he was working in the Shanghai Executive Bureau of the
KMT, and he wrote in this capacity a number of documents which
are locked away somewhere on Taiwan. He also spoke briefly
at the First KMT Congress in January 1924 and drafted some
resolutions for submission to the KMT Central Executive Committee in February 1924.

Even in this formal context, some of Mao's utterances, brief
though they be, illustrate some of the emerging traits of his work
style and political strategy.  Thus, at the First KMT Congress, he
objected to a proposal for setting up a "research department" on

---

[46] Ibid., pp. 206-209.
[47] Ibid., pp. 209-210.

the grounds that this would have as its consequence "the separation of research from application — something which our party,
as a revolutionary party, cannot do."[48] And the resolutions which
he submitted to the CEC at its fourth meeting on February 9, 1924,
criticized the plethora of high-level cadres in Canton. The central
and provincial KMT party organizations, he declared, were "hollow organizations"; the "real organizations," which constituted
"the decisive organ for directing the activities of party members,"
were the bureaus in the cities and at an intermediate level in the
countryside (hsien or regional bureaus).[49]

Following his sojourn in Shanghai, Mao returned in the autumn
of 1924 to Hunan for a rest and began his practical apprenticeship
in organizing the peasants. When he came back to Canton, in the
autumn of 1925, to take de facto charge of the Kuomintang Propaganda Department, edit Cheng-chih chou-pao, begin lecturing at
the Peasant Movement Training Institute (which he was to head
from May to October 1926), and participate in the Second Congress
of the KMT, he had come to hold the view, from which he was
never afterward to waver, that the center of gravity of China's
revolution lay with the peasants in the countryside.

Enumerating the weak points of Kuomintang propaganda in his
report on the subject to the Second Congress in January 1926,
Mao noted: "We have concentrated too much on the cities and ig-
nored the peasants."[50] To some extent, this shift in Mao's outlook merely reflected the changing pattern of the revolution itself:
the increasing militancy of the peasantry and the activity of P'eng
P'ai and many others, as well as of Mao, in mobilizing the peasants. Only by tapping this potential, Mao had concluded, would the
revolutionary party (or parties) be able to create the force necessary to the achievement of their anti-imperialist goals — which
Mao continued to proclaim in all his writings of the "peasant
period," 1925-27. But though the Chinese Communist Party, or a
substantial fraction of it, turned its attention to the peasantry in
the mid-1920s, the case of Mao Tse-tung is unique, not only in
the obvious sense that he subsequently assumed the leadership of
a revolution which effectively encircled the cities from the countryside, but because he formulated as early as 1926 theoretical

[48] Chung-kuo Kuo-min-tang ch'üan-kuo tai-piao ta-hui hui-i-lu (Minutes of the
National Congress of the Kuomintang of China), reprinted by Center for Chinese
Research Materials, Washington, 1971, p. 47.
[49] Schram, Mao Tse-tung (Harmondsworth and New York: Penguin, 1957), p. 77.
[50] Day, Mao Zedong, p. 232; Mao Tse-tung chi, Vol. 1, p. 151.

propositions foreshadowing the future course of the Chinese revolution.

More has been written, perhaps, about the emergence of Mao's preoccupation with the peasantry than about any other single topic in the history of the Chinese Communist movement. Scholars have been handicapped, however, in understanding the genesis and significance of Mao's vision of a "peasant" revolution because they did not have access to a crucial link in the chain: Mao's article of September 1926 entitled "The National Revolution and the Peasant Movement." By way of conclusion to this survey of Mao's experience and the conclusions he has drawn from it, I propose to summarize some of the insights that flow from this text.[51]

In his article of February 1926 on the classes in Chinese society, Mao Tse-tung, while stressing the numerical importance of the peasantry, and the degree of privation — and therefore of sympathy for the revolution — prevailing in the countryside, also characterized the urban proletariat as the "main force" in the revolution.[52] Thus, even though the concept of "proletarian hegemony" was inserted in this text only in 1951, he did recognize in early 1926 the Marxist axiom that the workers would play the central role in the revolutionary process. In September 1926, he turned this axiom explicitly on its head.

His article "The National Revolution and the Peasant Movement" begins with the statement: "The peasant question is the central (chung-hsin) question in the national revolution." This, in itself, is not at all remarkable, for the upsurge of revolutionary activity in the countryside, since the middle of 1925, had forced itself on the attention of even the most urban-oriented, to such an extent that a bow in the direction of the peasant movement had become a cliché automatically included in almost every utterance of a Communist and/or Kuomintang spokesman. Mao's argument demonstrating the importance of the peasantry in terms of the structure of Chinese society was, on the other hand, very remarkable indeed.

"The greatest adversary of revolution in an economically back-

---

[51] I have discussed Mao's September 1926 article at greater length, concentrating more on a comparison between his analysis of class relations in the countryside and that of Ch'en Tu-hsiu, in my article "Mao Zedong and the role of the various classes in the Chinese revolution, 1923-1927," in The Polity and Economy of China (The Late Professor Yuji Muramatsu Commemoration Volume) (Tokyo: Toyo Keizai Shinposha, 1975), pp. 227-239.

[52] The Political Thought of Mao Tse-tung, p. 247.

ward semi-colony" he wrote, "is the feudal-patriarchal class (the landlord class) in the villages." It was on this "feudal landlord class" that the foreign imperialists relied to support their exploitation of the peasantry; the warlords were merely the chieftains of this class. Thus, as the example of Haifeng showed, the domination of the imperialists and the warlords could be overthrown only by mobilizing the peasantry to destroy the foundations of their rule. "The Chinese revolution," he wrote, "has only this form, and no other."[53]

Not only did Mao Tse-tung assert the importance of the rural forces of reaction in the old society, and of the rural revolutionary forces in overthrowing them — he went on to argue against the importance of the cities:

There are those who say that the rampant savagery exercised by the compradors in the cities is altogether comparable to the rampant savagery of the landlord class in the countryside, and that the two should be put on the same plane. It is true that there is rampant savagery, but it is not true that it is of the same order. In the whole country, the areas where the compradors are concentrated include only a certain number of places such as Hong Kong, Canton, Shanghai, Hankow, Tientsin, Dairen, etc., on the sea coast and the rivers. It is not comparable to the domain of the landlord class, which extends to every province, every hsien, and every village of the whole country. In political terms, the various warlords, big and small, are all the chieftains chosen by the landlord class.... This gang of feudal landlord chieftains ... use the comprador class in the cities in order to dally with the imperialists; both in name and in fact the warlords are the hosts, and the comprador class are their followers. Financially, 90 percent of the hundreds of millions of dollars the warlord governments spend each year is taken directly, or indirectly, from the peasants who live under the domination of the landlord class.... Hence, although we are aware that the workers, students, and big and small merchants in the cities should arise and strike fiercely at the comprador class, and directly resist imperialism, and although we know that the progressive working class, especially, is the leader of all the revolutionary classes, yet if the peasants do not arise and fight in the villages to overthrow the privileges of the feudal-patriarchal landlord class the power of the warlords and of imperialism can never be hurled down root and branch.[54]

Despite the ritual reference to the "leading role" of the working class, the implication of this passage is clearly that the real center of power of the old society is to be found in the countryside, and the real blows must therefore be struck in the countryside. This is spelled out explicitly, in startlingly bald terms, in the concluding paragraph of the article:

[53] Mao Tse-tung chi, Vol. 1, pp. 175-176.
[54] Ibid., pp. 176-177.

The peasant movement in China is a movement of class struggle which combines political and economic struggle. Its peculiarities are manifested especially in the political aspect. In this respect it is somewhat different in nature from the workers' movement in the cities. At present, the political objectives of the urban working class are merely to seek complete freedom of assembly and of association; this class does not yet seek to destroy immediately the political position of the bourgeoisie. As for the peasants in the countryside, on the other hand, as soon as they arise they run into the political power of these village bullies, bad gentry, and landlords who have been crushing the peasants for several thousand years ... and if they do not overthrow this political power which is crushing them, there can be no status for the peasants. This is a very important peculiarity of the peasant movement in China today.[55]

In other words, the workers ("at present" — but for how long ?) are merely reformists, pursuing limited benefits for themselves; they are animated, it could be said, by "trade union consciousness." The peasants, on the other hand, not only occupy a decisive position in society, so that they cannot achieve their aims without overthrowing the whole edifice of the old order; they are aware of the situation, and are deliberately waging a broad struggle, political as well as economic.

Never afterward was Mao to go so far in explicitly putting the peasants in the place of the workers as the conscious vanguard of the revolution. His Hunan peasant report of February 1927 attributed to the poor peasants the leading role in the struggle in the countryside; it did not downgrade the importance of the cities, and of the classes based in the cities, in the same graphic terms, though there are indications suggesting that he had not abandoned his position of the previous September. The famous phrase attributing 70 percent of the achievements of the revolution to date to the peasants[56] might be interpreted as relating to force, rather than to leadership, and as merely describing a temporary condition. Another passage summarizes in capsule form the analysis developed in the September article to the effect that the "patriarchal feudal class of local tyrants, evil gentry and lawless landlords has formed the basis of autocratic government for thousands of years and is the cornerstone of imperialism, warlordism, and corrupt officialdom," and adds: "To overthrow these feudal forces is the real objective of the national revolution."[57]

The proposition that the "real objective" of the Chinese revolu-

---

[55] Ibid., p. 178.

[56] The Political Thought of Mao Tse-tung, p. 252.

[57] Selected Works of Mao Tse-tung, Vol. I (Peking: Foreign Languages Press, 1965), p. 27.

tion at its bourgeois-democratic stage was to overthrow the forces of feudalism was, in itself, entirely in keeping with Lenin's thinking, and we have seen that Mao Tse-tung endeavored, in 1926-27, to employ Marxist concepts for the analysis of Chinese society, though his mastery of them was by no means complete. At the same time, he diverged sharply from Lenin, and from the essential logic of Marxism, not only by the sheer importance he accorded to the countryside, but by attributing to the peasants both the capacity to organize themselves, and a clear consciousness of their historical role.

That the peasantry, though it is an important revolutionary force, must follow the leadership either of the workers or of the bourgeoisie, and cannot play an autonomous political role, is one of the most basic political axioms of Marxism, going back to Marx himself. Ch'en Tu-hsiu was merely expressing the accepted view when he wrote, in 1923, that although the national revolution in China could not succeed without the participation of the peasants, the latter were scattered, their cultural level was low, and they were prone to conservatism. [58] Mao's theoretical contribution, in the course of the past half century, has consisted not in replacing this axiom by its opposite, but in weaving together the principle of working class leadership and his conviction that the fate of the Chinese revolution ultimately depended on what happened in the countryside.

In September 1926, Mao said, in effect, that the peasants could not emancipate themselves without emancipating the whole of Chinese society. He seemed to be investing them with a mission not unlike that which Marx attributed to the urban proletariat in the capitalist societies of the West. At the same time, as we have seen, he recognized that the workers were the "leaders of all the revolutionary classes." These two statements can be reconciled if we take the one as relating to the form of the revolutionary struggle in the immediate future, and the other as defining the long-term pattern of events — though the synthesis implied by such an interpretation would attribute to the peasants a degree of initiative scarcely compatible with Marxist tradition. Behind the problem of the peasants' role in the overthrow of the "feudal" and other reactionary classes dominating the old society there stands, however, the more fundamental issue of their role in the revolutionary transformation which must follow the conquest of power.

---

[58] Ch'ien feng, 1923, No. 2, p. 5.

This aspect of the problem, which is hinted at but not specifically evoked in Mao's article of September 1926, has been his main concern since 1949. Here the dialectic between the axiom of working-class leadership, and the postulate of a central role for the peasantry, becomes subtler, and the contradictions more difficult to reconcile. Developments after 1927, and a fortiori after the conquest of power, do not fall within the scope of this introduction, but a few brief reflections on the similarities and differences between Mao's experiences in the 1920s, and in the 1950s and 1960s, may help us to understand both the limits of his vision in the earliest years of the Party, and the insights he actually attained at that time.

I should like to suggest, to begin with, that the pattern of Mao's development in the period 1917-27, and that of his evolution in the years after 1949, bear a remarkable formal similarity. In both cases, Mao moved from an attitude deeply marked by the influence of the Chinese past to a Westernizing stance, and then back to a theoretical and practical approach to revolution rooted in Chinese realities. Mao's Westernizing phase during the May Fourth movement was, of course, marked first by the influence of Hu Shih and John Dewey, and then by a Kautskian interpretation of Marxism, whereas the "Westernizing" phase of the early 1950s was characterized rather by the imitation of the Soviet approach to building socialism. A more important difference, however, lies in the fact that in 1926-27, while Mao's instincts led him back toward the countryside as the main theatre of China's revolution, he did not at that time have either the mastery of Marxist theory, or the experience necessary to incorporate this insight into a true synthesis between Marxism and Chinese reality.

During the last two decades of Mao's life, the position was very different. Already in 1938 he had set himself the task of the "Sinification of Marxism." Though he subsequently dropped this term, Mao Tse-tung continued to state repeatedly that he was bent on fusing together the Chinese tradition and revolutionary ideas from the West, in such a way that not only the form, but the substance of Marxism would be transmuted. Perhaps the most startling manifestation of this attitude was the fact that at the very end of Mao's life, the campaign in praise of Ch'in Shih-huang and the Legalists was still going on, albeit in muted form, side by side with that for the study of the proletarian dictatorship. While the substance of both these campaigns contradicted in some respects Mao's previous utterances, and the exact degree of his responsibility for them remains a matter for debate, the simultaneous recourse to the lessons of Leninism and of the Chinese past was, and remains, a true symbol of the dual inspiration of his thought.

The slogan of the "Sinification of Marxism" was effectively abandoned in the early 1950s because Stalin took strong exception to the suggestion that others beside himself might have made important and original theoretical contributions, and it was not revived subsequently, when beginning with the Great Leap Forward the Chinese openly challenged Soviet ideological hegemony — no doubt because it might be interpreted, and was in fact interpreted by Thorez and others in 1960, to suggest that Mao Tse-tung's thought was parochial and therefore of little interest. And yet, in 1957 Li Jui concluded his biography of the young Mao precisely on this note. Quoting Liu Shao-ch'i, whose report to the Seventh Party Congress in April 1945 was at that time regarded as the most enthusiastic panegyric on Mao's theoretical achievements, and the most authoritative statement as to the significance of Sinification, Li Jui asserted that the materials presented in his book (i.e., in the body of the work, carrying the story only down to 1923), though "not sufficiently complete," demonstrated that "the Chinese Communist Party, the path of the Chinese New-Democratic Revolution, and Sinified Marxism — that is, Comrade Mao Tsetung's doctrine (hsüeh-shuo) about the Chinese revolution — all these things truly grew up on this Chinese earth of ours, after going through a schooling in Marxism-Leninism. They are Chinese things, and yet they are altogether Marxist things" (p. 277).

This is a curious statement to make about the development of Mao's thought before his discovery of the peasantry. Though Mao was a very great patriot, and enemy of foreign domination, he had taken as his aim, for example, in setting up the Hunan Self-Study University, in late 1921, to combine the form of the old Chinese academies, with their flexibility and close personal contact between pupil and teacher, with the substance of the modern knowledge taught in the Western-type schools.

Even with reference to Mao's writings of 1926-27, one cannot speak of the "Sinification of Marxism," for Mao had not as yet acquired more than the most rudimentary understanding of Marxism, and therefore could not consciously adapt the substance of Marxist theory — though he did on occasion clothe Marxist slogans in Chinese imagery, as when he told the peasants in the summer of 1925 that "Down with the imperialists" meant "Down with the rich foreigners."[59]

And yet, though Mao's explicit theoretical contribution at this time was limited, he had, as I suggested earlier, set his foot on the path which would lead him to Sinification in practice. And though he had not yet begun to modify or replace the substance of Leninism, he had already begun to have some doubts as to the validity of certain Leninist axioms in the Chinese context. Lenin had invented the "vanguard party" as the instrument by which the urban working class, or those acting in its name, transmitted orders and ideas to the backward rural masses. This system has worked — more or less — in Russia, though the hierarchical aspect has always taken precedence over the educative aspect. In China, however, its introduction would raise further problems, different from those encountered in Russia and the West, because the ideology presented as the crystallization of the historical consciousness of the proletariat was external not only to the Chinese working class, but to the society and culture of China as a whole.

As early as 1926, Mao Tse-tung, while accepting the slogan of proletarian hegemony, had begun to valorize peasant rebellion as the motive force of Chinese history, in the present as well as in the past. Thus he had begun to seek a way for combining revolutionary consciousness imported from far outside Chinese society, and a sense of mission distilled from millennia of peasant wars. Such are some of the vistas hinted at in Mao's writings of 1926-27, of which we have not yet seen the final unfolding. Li Jui's biography of the young Mao, which offers the best one-volume overview of the matrix of experience and reflection out of which these insights grew, is therefore indispensable reading not only for students of the May Fourth period and the 1920s, but for everyone interested in the Chinese revolution of the twentieth century.

---

[59] Schram, Mao Tse-tung, p. 83.

# The Early Revolutionary Activities of Comrade Mao Tse-tung

# *Preface*

The first draft of this book was written in 1952. It was published serially in Chinese Youth [Chung-kuo ch'ing-nien] in 1953, and the chapter entitled "Student Days" was considerably abridged. "Revolutionary Activities before and after the May Fourth Movement" and the other chapters were abridged to a lesser extent. Now the original scope of the first draft has been largely restored. Also, some additions have been made on the basis of newly discovered materials, and the text has undergone some revision as well.

This is a book characterized by the use of historical data. The depth of the various chapters and sections by and large was determined by the availability of source material. It is of course not a comprehensive account of the early revolutionary activities of Comrade Mao Tse-tung.

During the process of collecting data and writing the book the author has received wholehearted assistance from many comrades and concerned quarters. He would especially like to express here his deep-felt thanks to them.

"The Hunan Peasant Movement during the First Revolutionary Civil War," which has been made into an appendix, originally appeared in Study [Hsüeh-hsi], 1951, No. 9. Some slight additions have been made to this section as well.

Li Jui
January 1957

*1*

## I. BEFORE HUNAN FIRST NORMAL SCHOOL

Comrade Mao Tse-tung was born on December 26, 1893, in Shao-shan-ch'ung, Hsiang-t'an <u>hsien</u>, Hunan. Located ninety <u>li</u> [about thirty miles] from the city of Hsiang-t'an itself, Shao-shan-ch'ung was a comparatively poor and barren Hunanese village in which families bearing a few common names lived. Hsiang-t'an is a famous commercial city of Hunan, and at that time it served as the distribution center for the trade between Hunan and Canton. New modes of thought and behavior had no difficulty penetrating this area, and so Mao Tse-tung, spending his youthful years here at home, came under the influence of the Hunan modernist movement [hsin-p'ai huo-tung].

Comrade Mao Tse-tung's father was originally a poor peasant. He later became a grain and hog dealer who went on to put his surplus money into land, thus moving up the ladder from middle peasant to rich peasant. He was very strict about his children's "upbringing," and his approach was the pure product of a rich-peasant mentality. Mao Tse-tung's life before the age of sixteen was thus one of student and small farm laborer, or small farm laborer and student. At the same time, he also took on the responsibility of keeping the business accounts for his father.

When he was six years old, Comrade Mao Tse-tung began to work at odd jobs in the fields. At eight he started to study and thereafter continued to attend classes at the local private school until the age of thirteen. He was very fond of study, but the Chinese Classics, which were so difficult to understand that even the teachers could not clearly explain them, simply did not excite his interest, even though he could recite them from memory according to strict rules. To satisfy his thirst for knowledge, he became intoxicated with those "miscellaneous writings" [tsa-shu] that were considered heterodox — China's old novels. He thought of every possible way secretly to read such books as Monkey, Water Margin, and The Romance of the Three Kingdoms. 1 He read these novels avidly and, just as he did when reading for his "regular courses," added circles, dots, and other marks [of emphasis] or wrote comments in the margins. This was an excellent reading habit that has always stayed with him. His powers of memory and comprehension were great. He could recall at will the many people and events that he had read about and apply them to observations on and comparisons with real life.

From the age of thirteen to sixteen, the young Mao Tse-tung was frequently sent into the fields to do the work of an adult. He was a capable hand. An old peasant from Shao-shan who had once worked with him in the fields said: 2 While other people weeded their fields only twice, Comrade Mao Tse-tung would weed his three times, and when he saw some weeds, he would go over and pull them up. For this reason the fields that he worked produced a larger yield than the average. He also planted assorted vegetables in front of his house and on the banks of a nearby pond and kept these gardens in excellent condition. And he was an expert in feeding cattle and raising pigs. He swept the cow pens and pigstys so clean that the cows and pigs he fed never got sick.

Besides doing farm work and helping his father keep accounts, he always managed to squeeze in some time to read. He read just about every book that one could borrow there in the country. We even have today a list dating from that time that notes eleven publications, including Sheng-shih wei-yen [Words of Warning to an Affluent Age] and a copy of New People's Journal [Hsin min ts'ung-pao], that he returned to relatives and friends. In order to read these books, he often had to cover up the window with a blanket in the evening so that his father would be unable to see the light he was reading by.

One book that had a deep influence on Comrade Mao Tse-tung at this time was the above-mentioned Sheng-shih wei-yen by the Cantonese Cheng Kuan-ying, published in 1893. This book advocated a course of making China rich and powerful; China should open mines, build roads, and develop industry and commerce; it should establish a parliament and practice "limited monarchy"; it should set up newspapers, establish libraries, and raise the level of people's cultural life. These were the reformist proposals for institutional change advocated by China's old-style progressive intellectuals

4

before the Sino-Japanese War of 1894. During this period, Mao
also read some other pamphlets that called on the people to rescue
their country from destruction and to plan for its survival. It was
especially after reading a pamphlet that dealt with how the Powers
had "dismembered China" that Mao came to the correct political
concept that the "common man has a responsibility in the rise and
fall of the state." In recalling this, Comrade Mao Tse-tung himself has said:

> I remember even now that this pamphlet opened with the sentence: "Alas, China
> will be subjugated!" It told of Japan's occupation of Korea and Formosa, of the
> loss of [Chinese] suzerainty in Indochina, Burma, and elsewhere. After I read
> this I felt depressed about the future of my country and began to realize that it
> was the duty of all the people to help save it. [3]

At this time there came to Shao-shan a modernist teacher who
violently opposed superstition and advocated that the temples be
converted into schools in order to widen the people's learning.
Mao Tse-tung gave his full support to this modernist approach.

Another event that had a great impact on the young Mao Tse-tung
was the serious famine and turmoil created by the corrupt rulers
of the Manchu dynasty a few years before the Hsin-hai Revolution.*
In Changsha thousands of famine victims rioted and attacked the
government office, forcing the fu-t'ai to flee. [4] Afterward, some
"conspirators" were beheaded. The secret society of the Shao-shan
peasants, the Society of Brothers, [5] clashed with the landowners, and
the head of the organization, a blacksmith, sacrificed his life. The next
year there also occurred in Shao-shan the poor people's Get Rice
from the Rich movement. Mao Tse-tung had a deep understanding
for the circumstances of oppression and misery in which the peasants lived. He had boundless sympathy for their "rebellion."

In his own life, his firsthand experience with "rebellion" was his
opposition to his father's despotism and harsh ways. The sole reason his father had sent him to school was to make the family "pros-
per." Whenever he discovered his son studying books outside the
"orthodox perimeter," he would unreasonably curse him as "lazy"
and "unfilial." Besides arguing back armed with the facts, Comrade
Mao Tse-tung once angrily dealt with the situation by leaving home.
This defiance finally succeeded in forcing his father to yield to a
certain degree. He was most dissatisfied with his father's hoarding

---

* The Republican Revolution of 1911. Hereafter referred to as the 1911 Revolution. — Tr.

of grain and his unwillingness to sell it at regular prices the year the poor people demanded that they "get rice from the rich." Mao felt this was a very inhumane thing to do.*

Once, at the end of the lunar year, Mao Tse-tung's father had him go and collect a sum of money owed him from a hog transaction. On the way home he ran into several poor people dressed in tattered clothes, whereupon he distributed among them the money he had collected. 6

In contrast to his father, Mao Tse-tung's mother was known among friends and relatives and everyone in the Shao-shan region for her kindness, her modest and friendly demeanor, her fairness, and the pleasure she took in helping others out of their difficulties. Comrade Mao Tse-tung had a great reverence and love for his mother. (When he was studying at First Normal, he once took his mother to the home of Comrade Ts'ai Ho-sen for a short stay.) The influence of his mother in such positive virtues as his manner of dealing with people was very great. 7

At the age of sixteen, after a hard struggle with his father, Comrade Mao Tse-tung was able to study at the hsien Tung-shan Higher Primary School in Hsiang-hsiang (his mother's hometown), which was fifty li [about sixteen miles] from his home. In this school he could arrange his schedule entirely on his own. His marks were very good. It was especially his essays that won his teachers' praises. At that time Tung-shan was a modern-style primary school. It taught the Chinese Classics, but also taught natural science and introduced the "new learning" of the West. Some of the teachers had studied in Japan and wore false queues. Mao Tse-tung learned a great many new things, and his horizons were widened considerably. Besides burying himself in the study of ancient Chinese history, he also liked to study foreign history and geography and to read books like Great Heroes of the World. Of all the new books, magazines, and other writings being published at the time, what most caught his interest was the nationally circulated journal that advocated democracy and an enterprising spirit, The New People's Journal. The essays by Liang Ch'i-ch'ao, 8 "whose pen reverberated with great feeling," held great interest for him. K'ang Yu-wei 9 and Liang Ch'i-ch'ao were much admired in

---

* Li Jui here fails to add that, according to Mao's own account, while he "did not sympathize" with his father in these circumstances, he thought the "method" of the poor villagers who seized one of his father's shipments "was wrong also" (Snow, Red Star, p. 136) [S. R. S.].

the eyes of young Mao Tse-tung at this time.

Comrade Mao Tse-tung stayed at Tung-shan Higher Primary School for only one year. Because he longed for even wider vistas, he went to Changsha in 1911 and took the exam and entered the "Hsiang-hsiang Middle School in the Provincial Capital." He immediately became an avid reader of the United League [10] party paper, The People's Strength [Min li pao]. Deeply touched by its anti-Manchu commentaries and reports of revolutionary activities, Mao on his own initiative wrote an essay expressing his political views and posted it on the school wall. The Hunan of this time was a place marked by the ardent activities of the "revolutionary party," a place where a new atmosphere prevailed. Swept up by the revolutionary wave, Mao Tse-tung fearlessly cut off his own queue and mobilized other comrades to do the same to show their determination to stand up against the Manchu dynasty.

After the outbreak of the 1911 Revolution, Hunan was the first province in the country to respond [to the events in Wuhan] and declare its independence. Just at the time when the revolutionaries and the New Army [11] were raising the standard of revolt in Changsha, Comrade Mao Tse-tung decided to join the revolutionary army in Wuchang. Once the "Han banner"* had been raised over the governor's office in Changsha, Mao joined the regular New Army there as a private. In the New Army, besides training and serving army detail, Mao Tse-tung subscribed to several newspapers from Hunan and other provinces with whatever he had left from his pay. He read through these papers very carefully every day, paying special attention to, and thinking about, current political events and social problems. He established very friendly relations with the other enlisted men in his outfit, as well as with his sergeant and corporal (i.e., squad and deputy squad leaders), helped them write letters and explained the news to them. Mao was especially close to two soldiers, a mine worker and a blacksmith, and was greatly attuned to their simplicity.

During the 1911 Revolution, T'an Yen-k'ai conspired to seize the position of "tu-tu" [military governor] in Hunan.[12] Similar things were happening in other areas as well. The fruits of the great revolution that had overturned the despotic monarchy still could not but fall into the hands of those feudal forces and warlords and bureaucrats as represented by Yüan Shih-k'ai. Mao Tse-tung lost all hope for this kind of revolution. After half a year he withdrew from

---

* Han Chinese as opposed to Manchu. — Tr.

the New Army and decided to continue his studies so that he might gain new knowledge and continue searching for a way out for China.

At this time, the instruction given in Hunan schools was rather advanced. Specialist schools in industry, commerce, law and government were established one after another. Comrade Mao Tse-tung took a series of entrance examinations for some of these schools but was not satisfied with any of them. He stayed at some of them for one or two months before he withdrew. Later, ranking first among those who had passed the entrance examination, he entered the First Provincial Middle School. Because he was dissatisfied with the rigid curriculum and the antiquated regulations, however, he withdrew after a half year of study. He felt it would be better for him to read and study on his own than to enter this kind of unimaginative school, and so he took up temporary residence at the hostel for Hsiang-hsiang students (now located on Hsin-an Lane, off Cheng Street, in Changsha), where food was very inexpensive. Every day after breakfast he went to the Hunan Provincial Library at Ting-wang Tower, Liu-yang Gate, to read. He would eat a couple of shao-ping [fried pancakes] for lunch and stay until the library doors closed. This life of self-education at the library went on for more than six months, and Mao Tse-tung read a great many new books. He read [Chinese translations of] [Charles] Darwin's On the Origin of Species, Adam Smith's Wealth of Nations, [Thomas] Huxley's Evolution and Ethics, [John Stuart] Mill's Logic, [Herbert] Spencer's A Study of Sociology, John [Stuart] Mill's A Study of Ethics,* Montesquieu's The Spirit of the Laws, and Rousseau's Social Contract,13 as well as books on world geography and history, Greek and Roman classical literature and a good many other writings of the time. The translations of many of these books had been published seven or eight years before, but they had a great influence on the young Mao Tse-tung, who was thirsting for knowledge. This was especially true of Yen Fu's translation of Huxley's Evolution and Ethics,14 which expounded the evolutionary laws of natural selection and the survival of the fittest. Because this theory was diametrically opposite to the traditional Chinese notion that the "present is not as good as the past," the book was held by some at the

---

* Li Jui distinguishes between "Mu-lo," author of Logic [Ming hsüeh], and "Yüeh-han Mi-erh," author of A Study of Ethics [Lun-li hsüeh]. There is no question that the author of Logic, "Mu-lo," is John Stuart Mill. The book was translated by Yen Fu using this transliteration. However; "Yüeh-han Mi-erh" is also a transliteration used for John Stuart Mill. Exactly what Li Jui means here is unclear; perhaps he himself is confused. — Tr.

time to "venerate the people and rebel against the sovereign, venerate the present and rebel against antiquity." The dissemination of these important writings of Western bourgeois thinkers reflected the primary struggle on the Chinese cultural and ideological front before the May Fourth movement — the struggle between the new culture of the bourgeois class and the old culture of the feudal class. At that time the gentry and bourgeois reformers were all doing a lot of work to enlighten the people, propagating bourgeois socio-political theories. This was the so-called "new learning" movement. This ideology of the "new learning" had revolutionary significance in the struggle with China's feudal ideology; it served the old Chinese bourgeois-democratic revolution. Comrade Mao Tse-tung wrote in his essay "On the People's Democratic Dictatorship":

From the time of China's defeat in the Opium War of 1840, Chinese progressives went through untold hardships in their quest for truth from the Western countries. Hung Hsiu-ch'üan, K'ang Yu-wei, Yen Fu, and Sun Yat-sen were representative of those who had looked to the West for truth before the Communist Party of China was born. Chinese who then sought progress would read any book containing the new knowledge from the West. The number of students sent to Japan, Britain, the United States, France, and Germany was amazing. At home, the imperial examinations were abolished and modern schools sprang up like bamboo shoots after a spring rain; every effort was made to learn from the West. In my youth, I too engaged in such studies. They represented the culture of Western bourgeois democracy, including the social theories and natural sciences of that period, and they were called the new learning in contrast to Chinese feudal culture, which was called the old learning.*

This life of self-study, however, met with his father's opposition. Since he still had to obtain a limited amount of funds for expenses from his family, Mao Tse-tung finally took the entrance examination for the Hunan Normal School.

## II. SCHOOL AND TEACHER

In the spring of 1913, at the age of twenty, Comrade Mao Tse-tung entered Hunan Public Fourth Normal School. In the fall of the same year, Fourth Normal merged with Public First Normal, and Mao was put in the eighth class, which had altogether thirty students.

---

* Selected Works of Mao Tse-tung, IV (Peking: Foreign Languages Press, 1967), pp. 412-413. Hereafter cited as SW. — Tr.

(Students who began at Fourth Normal in the spring and those who began in the fall were put into the same year. In all, there were five classes, numbered from "six" to "ten.") Thus, in line with these regulations, Mao studied a half year longer than he otherwise would have. Altogether, Comrade Mao Tse-tung was closely connected with Hunan First Normal School for a total of eight years: During the first five and one-half years, from the spring of 1913 to the summer of 1918, he studied there. In the next two and one-half years, from the fall of 1920 to the winter of 1922, when he was engaged in extensive revolutionary activities in Changsha, he was employed as director of the primary school attached to First Normal. He also taught Chinese at First Normal.

Teacher education began in Hunan in 1902 (the twenty-eighth year of the Kuang-hsü reign of the Ch'ing) when the Ch'ing government established the "Academy for Teacher Education" at Huang-ni-chia in Changsha. Reorganization soon followed, and three circuit teachers' schools were created. The Western Circuit was located at Ch'ang-te, the Southern Circuit at Heng-yang, and the Central Circuit at the former location of Ch'eng-nan Academy outside the southern gate of Hunan on Academy Plain. Since the old circuit nomenclature was no longer appropriate after the 1911 Revolution, the students who had not yet graduated from the three circuit schools were grouped into the Advanced Normal School; the Central, Southern, and Western Circuit Schools became First, Second, and Third Normal Schools, respectively. This is the origin of First Normal.

Ch'eng-nan Academy was where Chang Nan-hsuan [15] taught during the Southern Sung dynasty [1127-1279]. It faced Chu Hsi's [16] Yüeh-lu Academy (now Hunan Normal Academy) across the river. At the peak of their teaching careers, Chang and Chu attracted several thousand students. Because of the frequent crossings of both men, the ford there became known as Chu-Chang Ford (now Wise Officials Ford, outside the southern gate of Changsha). Seven or eight hundred years, however, intervened between the Southern Sung and the eve of the May Fourth movement. The five and one-half years during which Mao studied at First Normal was precisely the period of continuous civil war, the period when Hunan was ruled over by the northern warlords three different times, when Japanese imperialists were stepping up their aggression and, on the international scene, when the two great imperialist blocs, the "Triple Alliance" and the "Triple Entente," were engaged in a great battle. As for the stupidity and brutality of the feudal ruling class and its role in fomenting a crisis of foreign aggression, however, the northern warlords were no different from the Sung Court. But in China, including Hunan, during these years, a newly arisen industrial working class had appeared. Concentrated in the neighborhood of First Normal on Academy Plain were located the few large factories in Changsha; a graphite refining works, an electric light company, and a mint. The Wuchang-Changsha train, part of the Canton-Hankow line, that formally began operations in 1917 passed behind the school day and night. By this time the li hsüeh philosophy of Ch'eng Hao and Chu Hsi had lost its luster and could no longer be of any concern to patriotic youths. The struggle between the old and new trends of thought was becoming increasingly intense throughout the country. Under attack from the New Culture movement, with the magazine New Youth [Hsin ch'ing-nien] [17] as the nucleus, the several-thousand-year-old Confucian ideology was rocked to its foundations. All progressive Chinese were ardently seeking from the West the true solutions that would save their country from destruction. Finally, on the eve of the May Fourth movement the salvos of the Russian October Revolution were heard in China.

Hunan was a backward province, a "mountain kingdom" whose way of life had stagnated. But in an age of increasingly improved communications it became a north-south corridor. Because it was backward and stagnated, feudalism had a more solid base here than in the littoral provinces. Because it had become a north-south corridor in the modern age, it could not continue in this backward, stagnant condition. Therefore, after the 1870s, Hunan became one of the areas of the most acute struggle between the new and old ideologies. The diehards resolutely rejected anything and everything that was new. For several years Tseng Chi-tse, the son of Tseng Kuo-fan, had brought public criticism upon himself by the Changsha officials and gentry because he had taken a small steamer home to attend a family funeral. Kuo Sung-t'ao was labeled a traitor by the Changsha officials and gentry because he had been China's first minister to England and had written a book entitled Shih hsi chi ch'eng [A Record of a Mission to the West] in which he called for reform. The opposition encountered in Hunan by the reformers of the 1890s was the most fierce of all provinces. But it was also precisely this province that produced the most fervent fighters for the realization of a democratic system. After the outbreak of the Sino-Japanese War in 1894, the determined Hunan reformers and future martyrs T'an Ssu-t'ung [18] and T'ang Ts'ai-ch'ang [19] called for a change of institutions to rescue China from destruction. In 1897 the Hunan governor, Ch'en Pao-chen, and the Hunan provincial judge, Huang Tsun-hsien, advocated reforms, and in cooperation with T'an and T'ang, they set up the School of Current Affairs [Shih-wu hsüeh-t'ang], inviting Liang Ch'i-ch'ao to become the General Licentiate [Tsung chiao hsi]. At the same time, they planned building railroads, opened mines, established the School for Military Preparedness [Wu-pei hsüeh-t'ang], trained militia-men, and also published the New Journal of Hunan Studies [Hsiang hsüeh hsin pao] and the Hunan Journal [Hsiang pao]. They also es-tablished the "Southern Study Society" [Nan hsüeh hui] with a mem-bership of over one thousand people and with branches in each province. T'an and T'ang used schools and societies to advance new theories and to attack the Ch'ing government. Hunan thus be-came a most forward-looking province in the country. At this time the feudal landlord scholars and great evil gentry of Hunan Wang Hsien-ch'ien [20] and Yeh Te-hui, [21] leading their diehard followers and proclaiming themselves "guardians of the Sagely Way,"* used every kind of low-handed trick in the book to carry out an unbridled encirclement campaign against the reformers, demanding that the Ch'ing government execute K'ang and Liang and forcibly expel the reformers from Hunan's borders. After T'ang Ts'ai-ch'ang's Inde-pendent Army failed in a revolt in 1900, the diehards slaughtered over one hundred Hunan reformers. Later, Huang Hsing [22] and Sung Chiao-jen [23] set up a revolutionary organization, the China Revival Society [Hua hsing hui], and in 1905 uprisings against the Ch'ing government broke out in P'ing-hsiang, Liu-yang, and Li-ling among the mine workers and peasants. The deeds of the revolution-ary heroes heartened those enlightened intellectuals and patriotic youths who remained alert, and encouraged them to stream forward to the front ranks of the struggle one after another.

First Normal was a public school free of tuition charges, and its role was to prepare primary school teachers. The children of mid-dle and upper class families who aspired to take an entrance exam-ination for a university did not enter such a school but rather en-tered an ordinary public or private middle school. It was only the students of poor families or students who, for some reason or other, did not receive financial support from their families that would strive for the opportunity to attend this school. There were many such youngsters, and so to pass the entrance exam for First Normal one had to have an excellent scholastic background. But the national situation at that time was very uncertain, there were no

* I.e., Confucianism. — Tr.

plans for anything, and the future of graduates in the field of education was by no means guaranteed. This situation forced the students to plan for their own futures before graduation. Some students gathered together according to common aspirations regarding future occupations, and others on the basis of a common purpose; there was a great deal going on.

When Comrade Mao Tse-tung entered First Normal, he fully utilized its facilities and devoted himself to the acquisition of a solid educational foundation. He not only sought the basic principles of life and solutions to saving his country but also painstakingly steeled himself. At First Normal he came across an excellent teacher who carried on the spirit of Wang Fu-chih [24] and T'an Ssu-t'ung, made friends with a group of like-minded students, and finally organized a group to work toward the common goals ahead. Recalling this period, Mao Tse-tung has said: "Incidents in my life here in the Hunan Provincial First Normal School were many, and during this period my political ideas began to take shape. And it was here that I acquired my first experiences in social action" [Snow, Red Star, p. 145]. Thus, before and after the May Fourth period and during the First Revolutionary Civil War, Hunan First Normal, with Mao as the center and [later] under his lasting influence, became the headquarters for Hunan's revolutionary intellectuals and Marxists and frequently played a leading role in the revolutionary movement of the time. The great majority of members of the New People's Study Society [Hsin min hsüeh hui], organized by Mao in 1917, were students from First Normal. Much of the earliest core of the Chinese Communist Party was also comprised of students and teachers from First Normal. Among the students were Ts'ai Ho-sen (class No. 6, whose school name was Ts'ai Lin-pin), Ho Shu-heng (class No. 1 of the training department, school name Ho Chan-hu), Ch'en Chang-fu (class No. 2, school name Ch'en Ch'ang), Lo Hsüeh-tsan (class No. 8), Chang K'un-ti (class No. 6), Li Wei-han (section No. 2, class No. 1), Kuo Liang (section No. 2, class No. 2), Hsia Hsi (class No. 16). Among the teachers were Fang Wei-hsia (beginning in 1914 he was proctor and taught natural science and agronomy) and Hsü T'e-li (from 1913 he taught ethics and education). Comrades Ts'ai, Ho, Ch'en, Lo, Chang, Kuo, Hsia, and Fang were all bravely martyred during the revolutionary struggle. [25]

Even today there are no accurate statistics on the number of Communists and revolutionary students and alumni of First Normal who were murdered by the reactionary Kuomintang government after the Horse Day Incident of May 1, 1927, [26] but according to estimates, the total number was some several dozen to one hundred people! Shortly after the school had suspended operation it moved away from the former location of Ch'eng-nan Academy. After the Kuomintang government reactivated First Normal in 1928, it maintained that the old First Normal had produced only "violent law-breakers" and "extremists." In order to "rectify the direction" and "restore custom," it even started the school all over from class No. 1 again. On the "alumni list" it deleted the glorious names of Mao Tse-tung and his comrades-in-arms. From this time onward, the school was controlled by the KMT reactionaries, and the creative spirit of the young people was almost completely smothered. At the original location of Ch'eng-nan Academy a Hunan First Middle School was created. Everyone in Hunan's educational circles knew that although there was no possibility that First Middle School would continue the revolutionary tradition of the old First Normal School, it was nevertheless the most "difficult to manage" among the middle schools during the period of the reactionary KMT control. The students there were known for "causing trouble and driving off the principal." And so the reactionary government had an aversion even to the former address of First Normal. During the great Changsha fire of 1938 the school here was destroyed, and after the Japanese surrender, the area was made into a hospital by the KMT government. Those who were not from the older generation could hardly recognize any of the traces from thirty years before.

Before and after the May Fourth period, First Normal was really a seriously managed school. This fact was related to the vitality that existed in the educational circles at the time. After the 1911 Revolution, when Ts'ai Yüan-p'ei [27] was the minister of education in the Nanking Provisional Government, he promulgated some rather innovative educational regulations. Thus under an article in its school constitution relating to educational policy, First Normal, "aside from being in accord with the educational aims established by the Ministry of Education, specifically adopts an educational policy on the basis of the latest theory of populism (i.e., democracy). Popular education is composed of three elements: (1) moral practice, (2) physical activity, and (3) social life (including general knowledge and course work) and professional training (including the exercise of one's mental faculties and activities of various student societies)." [Other guides were:] "Constantly awaken the students' awareness of our national humiliation." "Each professor should promote the principle of self-initiative." "Temporarily establish

the national language as the central core linking all courses."
Nevertheless, in the area of student control, the school still maintained a great many tedious, feudal rules. Provisions in the constitution dealing with the "deportment" of students listed thirty-five
prohibitions. For example, students were "not to conduct any business unrelated to scholarship," "not to enter any nonacademic
party or educational society," "not to involve themselves in matters outside the school and disturb the social order," "not to hold
meetings or lectures without the permission of the principal," "not
to sing vulgar songs or play vulgar music and not to purchase harmful and useless books," etc. These prohibitions directly contravened
the "educational aims" mentioned above and were owing to the fact
that the public schools were still in the hands of the conservatives.
Nevertheless, this school did offer quite a few advantages at the
time. Aside from a rich library and spacious dormitory, the school
was particularly blessed with a good, enlightened faculty, and its
graduates were welcomed in society. Thus Mao Tse-tung said: "I
never formally went to college and never studied abroad. My knowledge, my learning gained its foundation at First Normal. First Normal was a good school." [28]

In the education and training of students the role of the teacher
is immense. The personal philosophy, disposition, and actions of
a conscientious and devoted teacher often have a deep influence
upon his students. The year Comrade Mao Tse-tung entered school,
Mr. Yang Ch'ang-chi came to First Normal to teach ethics, education, and moral philosophy. [29] Mao and his close friends Ts'ai Ho-
sen, Ch'en Ch'ang, and Chang K'un-ti were greatly influenced by
Mr. Yang in their thinking, their scholarship, their life, and their
social behavior and attitudes. Speaking of the faculty of First Normal and its influence, Mao has said:

> The teacher who made the strongest impression on me was Yang Ch'ang-chi, a
> returned student from England, with whose life I was later to become intimately
> related. He taught ethics, he was an idealist and a man of high moral character.
> He believed in his ethics very strongly and tried to imbue his students with a de-
> sire to become just, virtuous men, useful in society [Snow, Red Star, p. 146].

Mr. Yang, whose style was Huai-chung, came from a family who
for generations had lived in Pan-ts'ang, in Changsha's Tung-hsiang,
and so he was also known as Master Pan-ts'ang. Since his youth he
had been fond of studying the philosophy of Ch'eng Hao and Chu
Hsi, [30] and he had studied in Japan and England for a total of nine
years. Unlike the other students studying abroad at that time, who

15

were interested in politics, economics, law, and military affairs, he devoted himself fully to the study of education and philosophy and pursued the principles of human conduct. He returned to China just at the time of the 1911 Revolution, and T'an Yen-k'ai, wanting him to become an official, offered him the post of assistant secretary of education, but he declined. The gold-plated students (those who had studied in the West) and the silver-plated students (those who had studied in Japan) were for the most part either intriguing to get an official post, campaigning for senator, or were compradors and businessmen. Even the most "unlucky" ones wanted to be university professors. Yet Mr. Yang chose the dreary position of an instructor in a normal school. Quite obviously this was because he was dissatisfied with the current situation and had his own aims and ambitions. His idea was to nurture talent for the country by beginning with education. He taught at First Normal for six years, and in 1918 he accepted an appointment at Peking University as professor of moral philosophy. He passed away in 1920. [31]

Mr. Yang was well trained in China's old culture and had in particular made a profound study of Sung-Ming li-hsüeh [rationalism]. [32] He had also absorbed the theories of Wang Fu-chih, T'an Ssu-t'ung, and Kant. [33] He had examined the social systems and customs of old European democracy, had selected, criticized, and synthesized, and thus finally created a rather progressive moral philosophy and a philosophy of life that was concerned about practice. Although philosophically he was an idealist who believed in the theory of evolution, overstressed the function of the subjective initiative, and had a moral philosophy in which the idealist element was rather preponderant, certain of his views and opinions had a very positive effect on his students. This was especially true of his spirit of seeking new thought and of putting his ideas into personal practice. His counsels to young people contained high ideals and the great ambition of reforming society and the nation, as well as a spirit of seeking truth through facts and a spirit of painstaking practice.

It was of course a great blessing for these students to have a teacher with such progressive thinking, deep learning, and estimable character in a society dominated by a decadent feudal morality and culture. The progressive youths of First Normal quite naturally all united around Mr. Yang Ch'ang-chi. Everybody was devoted to him heart and soul, and they all listened extremely attentively to him in class. After class, Comrade Mao Tse-tung and others would usually go to Mr. Yang's home to listen to him further. There they would hear about ways to pursue study, how to act in society or would seek corrections for their notes or discuss important world affairs. Mr. Yang was extremely fond of this group of young people, and he was especially fond of Mao Tse-tung.

In the diary of the martyr Comrade Chang K'un-ti this relationship between teacher and student is noted in the entries dating from August to September 1917: [34]

August 22: After dinner went to Mr. Yang's home. The teacher said that what was important in reading was carefully to read and reread, copying out the main points. One got nothing at all out of seeking to read quickly and voluminously. He also said to advance toward our ideal life and leave the writings and fame to those who come after us. Also: Do not be overly concerned with the present-day society. Again: Power does not destroy [things] completely. Also: Nurture strength gradually, then use it all at once.

September 8: Last year Teacher Yang told me: "You spend too much time in self-denial and too little in mindfulness and cultivation. You must spend more time in mindfulness and cultivation — then you will avoid suffering in your self-denial." (This was followed by Comrade Chang Kun-ti's self-criticism and resolution that in the future he should make "frugality and the clarification of ambition his primary task.") [35]

September 13: After dinner I went to Pan-ts'ang yang yü. Teacher Yang read for us from the Ta Hua chai tu-shu lu [Study Record of Great China Studio]. Afterward there was some discussion on the virtuous person's striving for reality in his work.

Amid this mutual respect, love and understanding, Mr. Yang Ch'ang-chi taught his students with all his heart. In many areas his students learned from him and even copied him with sincere respect. Comrade Mao Tse-tung and his friends were most deeply influenced by Mr. Yang Ch'ang-chi in the following areas: First was ideology, will, and ambition. Yang Ch'ang-chi had devoted a great deal of effort to the critique of the ideology of Chinese feudal culture. For example, in criticisms of the Confucian theory of the Three Bonds [san kang], he not only highly valued Wang Fu-chih's emphasis on the spirit of individual independence ("Loyalty and filial piety are not just a call for respectfully serving the sovereign and one's parents and the self-realization of one's body and mind"), but also attached particular importance to the critique made by T'an Ssu-t'ung in his Jen hsüeh [Study of Benevolence]. T'an advocated that everyone have a spirit of independent struggle. Fathers and sons, older and younger brothers could not be dependent upon one another. For a time it became a kind of custom among the students to read and study Jen hsüeh and the theories of Wang Fu-chih. Mao and his friends did so with particular eagerness. They invariably entered into their diaries and notes such things as: "T'an Liu-yang's [36] genius filled the universe and can never be extinguished." Mr. Yang further spared no effort with regard to the introduction of the new learning. After New Youth was published, he ordered several copies and sent them around to the top students of each class. Comrade Mao Tse-tung was one of those who received a copy. In addition, there were some students who took a subscription to this magazine. Mr. Yang himself wrote articles for New Youth and, furthermore, introduced an essay by Mao Tse-tung to the magazine for publication.

Mr. Yang was very much opposed to serving as a government official and to getting involved in society. He constantly counseled his students to have lofty ideals, to master an academic discipline or a craft, to work with a serious purpose, to serve society at large and not just oneself. He often said: "Destroy the 'habitual self,' realize the 'ideal self.'" Lun-yü lei-ch'ao [Notes from the Analects] was a volume he put together that dealt with self-cultivation. He had taken a certain number of significant passages from the Lun-yü [Analects] and, borrowing the words of the Confucian school, set down his own view of the universe and philosophy of life. The first chapter of the book is on "establishing the will." For example, discussing Confucius' statement that "the commander of the forces of a large state may be carried off, but the will of even a common man cannot be taken from him," he goes on to explain the meaning to the students in the following way:

With regard to himself, a person with a strong will can suppress his evil desires; with regard to society he can withstand the oppression of the powerful. Morality is the continuation of self-control; human life is unbroken competition. If one has an unbreakable will, there is nothing that cannot be accomplished.

To face difficulty and not shirk from it, to face danger and accept the challenge, this is a case of strength of will equal to strength of conscience. Since ancient times those who have died for the Way had rather die than see their will violated. Those who opposed them could only maim their bodies but could not restrain their souls. Though their ambitions might suffer a temporary setback others were ready to step into their place as soon as they fell, and in the end they succeeded in casting great influence upon the world.

Modern educationists assert that man, being part of society, should work for the interests of that society. If there arises a conflict between his own personal interests and the interests of society, he should sacrifice his own interests to the latter. Be that as it may, one may sacrifice one's interests, but one may not sacrifice one's ideological [principles]. An unwillingness to discard one's ideological [principles] is in keeping with the point that the will of a common man cannot be taken from him (from Lun-yü lei-ch'ao).

Next were study methods. The book that Mr. Yang wrote entitled Ta Hua chai tu-shu lu has not been located, and so we cannot understand in any more systematic way his insights in this area. But from some related material we can see that his approach to study stressed breadth and depth. The special features of these two aspects are summed up in the sentence: "Thoroughly understand the past and the present, merge the Chinese with the Western." The spirit of diligent and extensive learning and the undivided close study of problems that characterized Comrade Mao Tse-tung and his friends, as well as the taking of reading notes with extensive quotes and an understanding of those quotes,* were all copied from Mr. Yang.

Further, there was a stress on practice, early planning, perseverance in one's work, and caution and hard work in one's daily life. These are more things that cause one to have great respect for Mr. Yang.

When Mr. Yang spoke of personal cultivation he said:

I do not surpass others in anything, it is only that I take to heart two words especially: steadfastness and endurance, attempting to achieve success by the length of time. If other people take several years to do something, I take several decades to do the same thing, and I needn't worry about whether I will accomplish it.... I have said that if the accomplishments of a person with great talent do not come up to those of a person with somewhat less talent, we must simply look at his steadfastness and endurance (Lun-yü lei-ch'ao).

In addition, to show the importance of perseverance, he cited Darwin's development of his theory of evolution, Spencer's writing of the Principles of Ethics, and Ssu-ma Kuang's completion of the Tzu-chih t'ung-chien [Comprehensive Mirror for Aid in Government] as examples of works that took ten or twenty years to complete.

In handling affairs he advocated:

In handling any matter, one must devote one's mind to it entirely if it is to be successful and not end in failure. Man's energy has limits, and he cannot take on too many things at a time. If he does take on too many things, his spirit will be dispersed and his strength divided, with the certain result of poor work in each and every thing.... Anyone who wishes to accomplish great things in society should have far-reaching plans and make no false moves; he cannot follow his own whims unmindful of the realistic advantages and disadvantages.... In managing all things there is a definite sequence. We should proceed slowly according to the sequence and in the end there will be success. We cannot desire speed; a desire for speed will, on the contrary, result in delays.

---

* Quotes from classical literature were not always readily understood because of the language gap. — Tr.

In explaining these points of view, Mr. Yang brought up the examples of the doom of Wang An-shih's New Laws program,* as a failure due to a lack of publicizing ahead of time and to the fact that Wang carried out his ideas unrealistically, and the ill-fated T'an Ssu-t'ung's plot † against Empress Tz'u Hsi, as a failure due to the lack of careful planning.

In teaching the course on self-cultivation Mr. Yang derived his material from such books as Lü Hsin-wu's Shen yin yü [37] and Chang Tsai's Hsi ming. [38]

Mr. Yang initiated courses in art works. Under his influence, huge art work classrooms were built and were completely equipped. There were courses in metalwork, woodwork, plaster work, etc. He advocated universal education and gave support to students in setting up a night school. As for other areas, such as being cautious in words and actions, [he advocated:] Sit quietly, think silently, do not tell lies, do not get involved in lewdness, etc. As for hard work and discipline in daily life: Be diligent and sincere in one's work, have respect for manual labor, be simple in food and dress, treasure time and use it carefully, eliminate breakfast, take cold baths, take long walks and avoid useless social functions, etc. There was not one part of all this that Mr. Yang himself did not personally practice. He had a deep influence on his students, and everyone competed with each other to emulate him. Mr. Yang felt his personal duty was to train men and nourish talent. There are still some former students of First Normal who remember a couplet he once wrote on the blackboard for the encouragement of the students. The second line read: "Wish to plant big trees that can shore up the skies." Everyone felt then that he was aiming at something.

After Mr. Yang passed away, a friend of his wrote a eulogy:

The death of Mr. Yang Huai-chung [i.e., Ch'ang-chi] makes one grieve. His fondness for study, strength of will, diligence in teaching others — I look for him among my friends but there is none like him. During the months he was resting up at a Buddhist temple in the Western Hills, he continued to devote himself assiduously to study. For he lamented the state of current affairs. Angry that many of his friends were weak-willed and did not raise themselves up, he daily wrote letters to alert them and himself to their responsibilities. He then returned home for a month's rest but went back to teach at the university. Every day he would

---

* A sweeping reform program carried out by Wang when he was prime minister (eleventh century). — Tr.

† I.e., his reform program. — Tr.

personally supervise the household's hired help. In his life he never uttered hasty words or showed an agitated countenance, and when he talked with people he was only afraid that his words might offend them. [39]

To set up a lofty ideal and moral goal and tirelessly to strive to attain them so that all of one's actions are consciously guided by them shows a high degree of will power. Throughout history, all patriots and revolutionaries who have resisted oppression have, to a man, possessed this basic quality. Mr. Yang's extraordinary success was in carrying out the teaching of this kind of will power and directly influencing his students by his own personal character, his firm belief in morality, and his moral habits. If one were to say that in education everything must be established on the basis of the teacher's character, this is because the power of education can only gush forth from the living spring of man's individuality. Mr. Yang was indeed an excellent teacher whom we cherish in memory, a teacher who looked after both words and deeds, who was the same inside and out, and who was able to "be an example" and to "teach by example."

The closeness of Comrade Mao Tse-tung's relationship with Mr. Yang Ch'ang-chi is also illustrated by the fact that with her father's full approval, Yang K'ai-hui, Yang Ch'ang-chi's daughter, saw Mao over an extended period of time, and in 1921 they were married in Changsha. In many respects Comrade Yang K'ai-hui inherited her father's excellent character. In 1930 she was arrested and martyred in Changsha.

## III. INDEPENDENT THOUGHT, SELF-STEELING

In his five and one-half years at First Normal, the course of Comrade Mao Tse-tung's study was entirely different from that of the average student. This was owing to several factors. During his youth, when he attended private school and Tung-shan Higher Primary School, and later in Changsha when he was in the army and when he studied on his own, Mao had acquired a comparatively good foundation in both the "old learning" and the "new learning." In his political views he was violently dissatisfied with the current reality and favored the reform of the state. He ardently sought out new ideas, and at the same time, nourished an industrious and frugal life and work style. He made maximum use of this kind of opportunity for schooling to seek after the truths that lay behind the saving of one's country and people and also used the opportunity to steel himself and forge ahead toward this great goal.

Former fellow students and teachers of Mao who are still working today in Hunan educational circles recall Mao's study at First Normal. Without exception they all feel that a most outstanding characteristic was his ardent and tenacious love for learning.

When Comrade Mao Tse-tung was at school he arose very early. After washing up, he would go to the study room to read. After classes, he would either read in the newspaper room or go to the library to look for books. He also liked to go to the hill behind the school to read by himself or together with some of his good friends. After everyone had gone to bed, he would read in the tearoom, in the newspaper room, or in the corridors, because the lights in these areas were kept on throughout the night.

The average First Normal student was a hard worker. But Mao Tse-tung was an exceptionally hard worker. As a rule, he always had a book in hand and never engaged in idle talk or played jokes. When he talked with friends and fellow students he always talked about what he had learned from his studies and discussed problems. During his first semesters at First Normal, he rarely strolled around town on Sundays like most of the students; he would read, go with friends to nearby mountains, or take a walk along the river. Every time he did go to town he would go to Yü-ch'üan Street (a street of secondhand bookstores in Changsha) and Fu-cheng Street to buy books. He never had a lot of money to spend, but when he had some he would always buy books. His desire for knowledge was insatiable.

Comrade Mao Tse-tung always enjoyed reading Chinese literature, history, and geography and later was especially fond of philosophy. At the same time, he never stopped reading newspapers or new books and periodicals. Natural sciences were much in vogue at the time. The majority of the students did not ask questions about politics or society but were only preparing themselves for a living. Because Mao was dissatisfied with the existing conditions and had the great ambition to change society and change the nation, he had his own independent study plans.

In the preceding period, 1913 to 1915, the courses to which Comrade Mao Tse-tung had most devoted himself were Chinese literature, ethics, history, and geography. Besides studying and becoming familiar with many of the essays in the Han Ch'ang-li ch'üan chi [Collected Works of Han Ch'ang-li (i.e., Han Yü)] [40] and the Chao-ming wen hsüan [Chao-ming Selected Essays], [41] he was also fond of the works of such men as K'ung Jung, Ch'en T'ung-fu and Yeh Shui-hsin. [42] [As one who knew him at the time has recollected:] "He borrowed history books from the library. The books that he read carefully and from which he learned a great deal were Ssu-ma Kuang's Tzu-chih t'ung-chien [Comprehensive Mirror for Aid in Government] and Ku Tsu-yü's Tu shih fang-yü chi-yao [The Essentials of Geography for Reading History]. [43] Everywhere he sought out new books on history and historical material in magazines." [44] The holdings of First Normal library were rather extensive, and the library bought just about all the newly published books available. In addition, it subscribed to ten or twenty current popular magazines. A librarian became a friend of Mao's and later joined the New People's Study Society [Hsin min hsüeh hui] as one of its earliest members.

Recalling this time, Comrade Mao Tse-tung has said: "...from 1911 to 1927, when I climbed up Chingkanshan, I never stopped reading the daily papers of Peking, Shanghai and Hunan" [Snow, Red Star, p. 150]. He was extremely meticulous in reading the newspapers and especially laid stress on the study of foreign and domestic current affairs. For example, he would compare all foreign place names and names of people against maps and books and, as much as possible, find the original versions and write them down on long strips of paper. After he had gathered together a good number of these, he combined them into a booklet, which he could flip through and read at any time. Thus, he was both thoroughly familiar with and capable of analyzing the national and international state of affairs clearly and straightforwardly. When fellow students had questions on current affairs, they often came to him for answers. When no one could find him, they were sure to guess his whereabouts: "In the newspaper room."

After New Youth was published in 1915, Comrade Mao Tse-tung became its most enthusiastic reader, having been introduced to the magazine by Mr. Yang Ch'ang-chi. Mao was particularly fond of the writings of such men as Ch'en Tu-hsiu [45] and Li Ta-chao. [46] In his thinking, these men now took the place of Liang Ch'i-ch'ao and K'ang Yu-wei.* Ch'en Tu-hsiu and Wu Yu-ling [47] demolished the essays of the Confucianists. The seminal works by Li Ta-chao, such as "Ch'ing ch'un" [Spring of Youth] and "Chin" [Today],

---

* Mao in fact said that, when he began to read New Youth, he "admired the articles of Hu Shih and Ch'en Tu-hsiu very much," and that these men became for a while his models, in place of K'ang and Liang (Snow, Red Star, p. 148) [S.R.S.].

all fascinated Mao Tse-tung and his friends. They would regularly copy out whole paragraphs of the most incisive parts of these essays, put them into their own notebooks or diaries, and later add their own comments. In everyday conversations among themselves they would often explore the points of view and the questions raised in these essays. At the same time this was going on, Mao Tse-tung developed great interest in and deeply delved into the works of T'an Ssu-t'ung, Wang Fu-chih, and Kant.

Because he had liked the study of Chinese literature since youth, had read and was quite familiar with the works of Han Yü while at First Normal, and had also read widely the writings of both the new and old learning, Comrade Mao Tse-tung was quite a good writer at this time. The teacher often marked his essays "to be posted," and they were placed in the "exhibition space" for the class to read. Whether it was in the ancient style or in the more recent literary style that was easier to understand, Mao Tse-tung wrote very well. His expository and critical essays were particularly outstanding. They had content, organization, judgment, and also a character that excited interest. In their recollections, students still particularly note that Mao's essay writing was truly characterized by the saying: "As soon as the first start is made, ten thousand words immediately follow, as though delivered on horseback." He also liked poetry, but did not often compose it. When on occasion he did write it, he wrote strong, vigorous, and dazzling masterpieces, which his friends contended with one another to recite.

Another important feature of Mao Tse-tung's studying was his skill at independent thinking and critical analysis. He often said to his classmates that one must think more about the books one has read and about the problems one has met; one must digest them. For example, when Mao was studying the writings of Han Yü, he utilized the logic he had learned to evaluate them. In sections of the essays he felt were good and logical, he added many punctuation marks and circles to the words; otherwise he drew in lines and crosses and wrote marginal criticisms like: "This doesn't make sense," or, "Absurd." In the books he had read, the upper margin notations were truly numerous. There were often two or three different markings, indicative of the number of times he had read the book. Sometimes Comrade Mao Tse-tung would add a critique of his own previous remarks. When teaching moral philosophy, Mr. Yang Ch'ang-chi selected the works of German idealist philosophers. Mao then compared the ideas of these men with those of the pre-Ch'in philosophers, [48] the Sung-Ming li-hsüeh, and Wang Fu-chih, T'an Ssu-t'ung, Liang Ch'i-ch'ao, Li Ta-chao, and Ch'en Tu-hsiu. From this comprehensive study and critique, he often reached his own unique views, which were very much prized by Mr. Yang and by Mao's fellow students. Mao Tse-tung also studied with great concentration. For example, when studying history, he would temporarily put all other books aside and concentrate his efforts on collecting and reading all kinds of historical comments, old and new. He studied philosophy in the same way. Early on in school he had also industriously studied English for a time because he wanted to read foreign books firsthand. This endeavor was later upset by more important study plans and various other activities.

In addition to studying hard on his own, Comrade Mao Tse-tung had a particular habit of raising questions, believing that learning and questioning were inseparable. He commonly "exchanged knowledge" and studied problems with friends and classmates, went to Mr. Yang's quite often, and also attended lectures at the "Wang Fu-chih Study Society" [Ch'uan Shan hsüeh she]. The Wang Fu-chih Society was established in 1915. It was a place where a group of nationalistic-minded men from Hunan who were distressed by the national injury sustained by China met to discuss exclusively the learning of Wang Fu-chih. They had a public meeting and lecture every week and also ran a periodical called the Ch'uan Shan Journal [Ch'uan Shan hsüeh-pao]. [49] When Yüan Shih-k'ai proclaimed himself emperor, this was one of the places in Changsha where one could hear publicly the cries of the opposition. [50] Mao often organized his classmates to go and attend the lectures. Besides this, Mao humbly and courteously paid visits to famous scholars in Changsha, Peking, and Shanghai to learn from them, or else established lines of communication with them. Mr. Yang spared no pains to introduce Mao to these men. Comrade Mao Tse-tung got to know Li Ta-chao and Ch'en Tu-hsiu and later secured a job at the Peking University Library, all owing to the introductions of Mr. Yang Ch'ang-chi. At the time, Mao wrote a good many letters to progressive scholars. From several of these letters, discovered in Peking after the liberation of the entire country, one can see that the scope of his discussions was very broad. The subjects ran all the way from great national affairs, study methods, physical culture, philosophical thought, philosophy of life and world outlook, to a way of saving the world. In a letter of November 1915 Mao wrote very sincerely to a corresponding scholar who was erroneously reported to have been brought into the service of Yüan Shih-k'ai. Mao earnestly warned him: "Today evil forces are gaining with every passing day and justice is buried over. At this time of great crisis, scholars should be hidden from view like the dragon in his depths. They must wait for a time to act and must not be impatient to advance." From this we can see how concerned Mao was about national affairs and also that he began seriously to think about many important political questions.

Diligent study is something most people can do. Where Comrade Mao Tse-tung and his friends differed from the average person was that they not only studied diligently but were also very concerned about practice. In this they were deeply influenced by Mr. Yang Ch'ang-chi. On the other hand, they were also influenced by Ku Yen-wu, [51] Yen Hsi-chai, [52] and Wang Fu-chih; later they were influenced by New Youth. But still the most basic point was that when he studied, Mao had a clear and active goal before him, the goal of reforming Chinese society. He already comprehended then that to know and not to act was like not knowing at all. Real knowledge could only be born of practice. Only through practice could one find out whether what he knew was indeed right or wrong. If one did not go through painstaking "self-steeling," there would be no way to realize one's ambition and ideals.

Comrade Mao Tse-tung opposed the study of dead books and favored the study of living ones. He wanted not only to read books with words but also books without words. One had to "learn from the myriad things and events of the world and the nation." This he accomplished completely. For example, he attached great importance to traveling. "Ssu-ma Ch'ien saw the Hsiao and Hsiang rivers [in Hunan], he climbed Hui-chi and passed through K'unlun, looked all around at famous mountains and great rivers, and his horizons were greatly expanded." "How can one say that a traveler sees only scenery and nothing more?" [53] Mao completely agreed with these words and worked hard to follow them in action. Consequently, during the summer vacation of 1916 he took a trip through I-yang and Ning-hsiang with a friend* and made use of this opportunity to plunge into an investigation of the social conditions as a preparation for reforming society, further developing this old practice of the concerned ancients. Mao very strongly advocated a hardworking life, believing that it could be useful in forging one's will. He also conscientiously practiced in his own life the ancient sayings: "He

---

* This was Hsiao Yü, Hsiao San's brother. Both have written biographies that deal with Mao. See S. Schram, The Political Thought of Mao Tse-tung, p. 452, for a brief review of the differing interpretations by the two brothers. — Tr.

who lives in poverty is able to accomplish things," and "If one can
eat cabbage stalks, anything can be accomplished." Mao attached
great importance to physical education and advocated the overall
development of both mind and body. He had high esteem for Yen
Hsi-chai and Li Kang-chu [54] and their philosophy of integrating the
civil [wen] and martial [wu] studies: "Civil studies and martial
studies — if one is missing, how can this be the Way?" (Yen Hsi-
chai's words). Mao Tse-tung also worked very hard in this area.
Later, when he directed the Student Society [Hsüeh yu hui] he initiated various sporting activities, ball games, swimming, hiking,
etc., that were stressed in Japanese schools. He heartily con-
curred with Ch'eng Tzu's* view that "a man isn't worth talking
about if he cannot overcome the two crises of money and sex"
and also with the teaching of Mr. Yang in these areas. And so
he resolutely closed his mouth and refused to talk about trifles,
and by his example he also influenced his friends and classmates.
In sum, in his student days, Mao Tse-tung was extraordinarily tough
and strict about the demands he placed on himself and was never
content with his own knowledge or self-cultivation. At the same
time, his concentrated study of various schools of learning and his
painstaking training had the same clear starting point: to find a
way to solve China's problems and put an end to the misery of its
people, as well as to prepare himself to go into action at any time.

In addition to being fascinated by scholarly research, Comrade
Mao Tse-tung was enthusiastic about physical training and thought
that moral, intellectual, and physical culture were of equal importance. He was in favor of developing fully the "power of the mind"
and the "power of the body." He believed that the goal of physical
education was the equal development of the whole body, and that it
should aim to strengthen not only the muscles and bones, but also
the will. He was very dissatisfied with the school curriculum of
the day, which included many courses and attached no importance
to physical education. "In the educational system of our country,
required courses are as thick as the hairs on a cow. Even an adult
with a tough, strong body could not stand it, let alone those who
have not reached adulthood, or those who are weak." [55] He told his
classmates that although Yen Tzu, Chia Sheng, and Wang Po [56]
were men of great talent, they died young. Only men like Yen Hsi-
chai, who integrated civil studies and martial studies, and Ku Yen-
wu, who in his old age was still able to travel throughout the empire,

* I.e., the Sung neo-Confucian brothers Ch'eng I and Ch'eng Hao. — Tr.

27

were worthy of emulation. He also disapproved of the unrealistic nature of the physical education curriculum in school, with its stress on just form and appearances. He felt that a couple of hours engaged in mechanical physical exercise, doing a little marching, or exercising a little bit with the wooden cudgels or dumbbells, did not help as far as the health of the body was concerned. In 1917 the school had a ten-minute exercise period following the first two morning classes every day. The exercises were too mechanical and the students were all reluctant to participate. That year seven students died. At the memorial service, Mao wrote a funeral couplet filled with great satire: "Why have seven classmates died? Simply because they did not take part in the ten-minute exercise program." This lesson attracted the serious attention of all the students and faculty in the school. Later the school authorities allowed the Student Society headed by Mao to develop extracurricular activities, and at the same time they began to pay attention to the improvement of sanitary conditions. The students now all paid more attention to effective physical training. Thus, the sports activity level of First Normal students rose daily. In the all-province athletic meet of 1917 there were some sixty or seventy prize-winners from First Normal.

Comrade Mao Tse-tung often talked about the importance of physical training with his classmates. He wanted everyone to recognize clearly the correct relationship between physical education, on the one hand, and moral and intellectual education, on the other. He wanted to nurture the habit of a fondness for physical activity. Mao emphasized three points with regard to physical training. First, one must be steadfast. Regardless of the weather or the season of the year, one should continue the routine, and when one exercises, one must concentrate all one's strength. Second, one must have a spirit of self-compulsion, [57] through which one can nurture fortitude and bravery. "To wash our feet in ice water makes us acquire courage and dauntlessness, as well as audacity. In general, any form of exercise, if pursued continuously, will help to train us in perseverance." [58] Third, the types of exercise should be small in number, simple and easy to perform, and not take an inordinate amount of time. Because Mr. Yang Ch'ang-chi was fond of the theories of the Sung neo-Confucianists Chu Hsi and Lu Chiu-yüan, he advocated the method of "sitting silently" to steel one's body and mind. Ts'ai Ho-sen, Chang K'un-ti, and other comrades were very much influenced by this, and one after another they all practiced this method of "sitting silently" (Ts'ai Ho-sen's mother was also an ardent practitioner of this method). But Comrade Mao Tse-tung maintained that "there is only movement in heaven and on earth." "Man's body goes through changes every day." [59] He felt that those who were weak of body had only to be diligent in training, overcoming their incompetency, and, after a period of time, they would be able to become stronger. Conversely, people of a strong physical nature could become weak if they abused themselves without restraint. In this regard Mao showed that he would not blindly follow anyone: even if it were someone he most respected.

Not only was Comrade Mao Tse-tung a propagandist for the importance of physical education, but he was also an ardent practitioner. He combined the best points of gymnastics, boxing, and the Chinese exercise of the "eight-part tapestry" [pa-tuan-chin] into a "six-part exercise." This included jumping and striking-out movements of the hands, feet, trunk, and head. It was an exercise that developed the whole body equally. Every day when he got up and every night before he went to bed he would perform the "six-part exercise." The classroom corridors of First Normal were very wide, and after class Mao would often perform two or three "parts" of his exercise there. Sometimes, after he had been reading or writing for a long time at a sitting, he would stretch out his legs, pound his chest, and turn his neck around in order to pep up his spirits. Sometimes in the middle of the night he would wake up and run to the courtyard outside his room to do some exercise. There were other favorite methods of physical training of his:

1. A cold bath, which he never missed or skipped in any season. During the two years preceding his graduation, Mao Tse-tung organized more than twenty students who went to the well early every morning, hauled up water in the bucket, took off their clothes, doused each other with the bucketful of water, and scrubbed their whole bodies. During the rain, snow, and bitter, piercing cold winds of winter and fall, they would often go to the hill behind the school and, wearing nothing above the waist, run around rubbing their bodies. Thus the students all called this rain bathing, wind bathing, and snow bathing. Once, during a school track meet, there was suddenly a gigantic downpour. Everyone fought to get back into the building. Only Comrade Mao Tse-tung was not a bit set back. He waited until everyone had gone before he returned to the classroom, dripping wet from head to toe.

2. Swimming, an activity he had been fond of since youth. Every day after classes during the summer, the students would go in droves to the Hsiang River or the nearby Nan-hu Harbor to swim.

In 1917 when Comrade Mao Tse-tung was head of the Student Society, according to the First Normal School Record [I shih hsiao chih] there were more than eighty fellow students who joined the activities of the "swimming section." Where Mao Tse-tung and his friends, such as Ts'ai Ho-sen, differed from the other students was that they still dared swim in the Hsiang River even after the fall season began. During summer vacation when they were staying together at Yüeh-lu-shan, they would often go swimming off the end of Shui-lu Shoal at sunset. (Shui-lu Shoal is a narrow shoal in the Hsiang River between the city of Changsha and Yüeh-lu-shan.) After swimming, they either sat or slept on the beach or raced on foot and, at the same time, conversed freely about life, national affairs, and approaches to further advancement. Their bodies bathed in the clear currents beneath the evening rays of the sun, but their minds had soared to the battlefield of human life and the universe.

3. Climbing mountains, hiking in the wilds, and sleeping in the open. As a monument to the students and teachers of the school, a large exercise field was built on the slope behind the school and a "Chun-tzu Pavilion"* was erected there. Mao Tse-tung, Chang K'un-ti, and others all liked to study and have discussions in the pavilion. They often slept out in the open next to the pavilion at night. On holidays they especially liked to hike in the wilds. They often went to Yüeh-lu-shan and to the mountains on both sides of the Hsiang River. Sometimes, when they had become tired from mountain climbing, they stayed over in a temple or slept right out in the fields.

As far as cold water bathing, wind and rain bathing, and sleeping out in the open were concerned — things difficult for the normal person to do — Comrade Mao Tse-tung and his friends believed that these could train a fearless and daring spirit. Over an extended course of time, they could forge within the body an extraordinary power of resistance. They advocated the slogan "A civilized spirit, a barbarian body." One night during a thunder and lightning storm, Mao Tse-tung came to Ts'ai Ho-sen's home soaking wet — he had just run down from the top of Yüeh-lu-shan. He said he did this in order to comprehend the flavor of the sentence in the Shu-ching [Book of History] † that reads: "Being sent to the great plains at the foot of the mountains, amid violent wind, thunder, and rain, he did not go astray." Also, he took advantage of the occasion to steel his courage. During the summer vacation when the New People's

---

* Chün-tzu, the Confucian "gentleman" or "superior man." — Tr.

† Part of the "classical" literature roughly dating from the first millenium B.C. — Tr.

Study Society was created, a large group went to live at Yüeh-lu-shan, and they carried water, cooked rice, and learned to eat broad-bean rice (a large helping of broad beans and a small helping of rice cooked together). The reason Comrade Mao Tse-tung led everyone in this conscious training was that in the future, on the road of struggle to reform the state and society, they would certainly encounter a great many hardships and they had to prepare themselves before-hand. They were very familiar with and had a deep appreciation for the significance of the following statement by Mencius:

Thus, when Heaven is about to confer a great office on any man, it first exer-cises his mind with suffering, and his sinews and bones with toil. It exposes his body to hunger, and subjects him to extreme poverty. It confounds his under-takings. By all these methods it stimulates his mind, hardens his nature, and supplies his incompetencies.

Mao and his friends took their ideals very, very seriously, and at the same time persisted in every effort that was appropriate to the attainment of these ideals.

The martyr Chang K'un-ti recorded the following in his diary in August and September of 1917 with regard to this extraordinary kind of life:

August 23. In the afternoon I crossed the river to a private home at Yin-ma-t'ang at the foot of Yüeh-lu-shan. This is the ancestoral home of Ts'ai Ho-sen. After we chatted a bit, we went on an excursion to Yüeh-lu-shan. The sun was setting when we descended, so I stayed at Ts'ai's home for the night. That night I talked to Mr. Ts'ai about his daily life. When I mentioned my summer-vacation life at Ch'iao-shih's Chien-yüan Temple, Mr. Ts'ai told me with great pleasure: "I got up early every day at four-thirty and went to bed at eight-thirty every night. When I got up I would go to the peak of T'ien-ma-shan, sit silently* there and also do exercises, not coming down until nine o'clock. At ten o'clock I ate breakfast, and after breakfast would read for about two hours. In the afternoons I either did some walking or dug up wild-grown vegetables and occasionally read some books as I pleased. At four o'clock I ate lunch, and after eating I either sat silently, did some exercises, or took a walk. Every day I took two cold baths, once after I rose early in the morning and once just before I went to bed in the evening. Also, when there was violent thunder, wind, and rain I braved them and went walking. After I had done this several times, I couldn't feel the cold winds a bit. This I did for over a month. In the latter half of this year I plan to do it regularly." When I heard this I heartily agreed with him. Ts'ai was a person who steeled his will and his body. Sitting quietly was a way to train the mind. Exercise was a way to train the body. Braving the wind and rain and taking cold baths was a way of training the body and also the mind. A great man only wor-ries that he may have no body, nothing more. If the body is strong and the mind

---

* Ching-tso — the neo-Confucian approach to "steeling the body" as mentioned previously, p. 41. — Tr.

is strong, then what cannot be done? I knew that Ts'ai knew what was essential.

In the evening I again chatted with Ts'ai and soon it was time to retire. The bed consisted of two long benches with one door plank and was set up along the side of the veranda. Mr. Ts'ai said that ever since he had moved to this place to live he had never gone inside to sleep overnight.

September 16. Today it is Sunday and I walked for an hour or two with Ts'ai Ho-sen and Mao Jun-chih (Mao Tse-tung's courtesy name). After breakfast the three of us took a walk along the railroad tracks. The weather was scorching, but luckily there was a big breeze and the heat was somewhat mitigated. After we had walked over ten li we rested at a teahouse located on the side of the tracks and drank some tea to quench our thirst. After sitting for a short while we resumed our journey. In another ten-odd li we passed the village of Ta-t'o-p'u and six more li brought us to a restaurant where we rested and ate lunch. Every large bowl of rice cost fifty wen and every bowl of vegetables twenty wen. The three of us ate altogether five large bowls of rice. After we ate we rested a bit and thought about bathing in the pool behind the restaurant, but because the water was shallow and didn't even reach our thighs we didn't follow through with our idea. And so we went to the restaurant, picked up our traveling things, and were off. Less than three li away we found a deep and clear creek-dam and the three of us went bathing. Because I was not much of a swimmer, I was very cautious. After bathing we went fourteen li and reached our destination just when the sun was about to set. We ascended the mountain from the rear by the stone steps. There was the blue of the Hsiang River at the foot and the soaring grace of the mountain peak at the top. It was called Splendor Mountain [Chao-shan]. There was a temple there called Splendor Mountain Temple. There were three or four Buddhist monks in the temple, and as we had come late we wished to spend the night at the temple. At first the monks were unwilling to let us stay, and we were of a mind to spend the night in the open air in a grove of trees. Then the monks let us in, and we temporarily gave up our plans for sleeping outside. After dinner the three of us went down the front side of the mountain and bathed in the Hsiang River. After bathing we sat on the sand and talked. A cool breeze broke the heat and the sound of the waves punctuated our talks. Our joy knew of no bounds. After some time we ascended by the original path, walking and talking. We could no longer see the mountain's reflection [in the river because the sun had set]. The monks were waiting at the front gate. The starlight shone down from above and, suddenly, from amidst the deep green of the trees there arose an indistinct mist. We soon entered the temple, and the monks led us to a guest house, indicated an empty bedstead as a place for us to sleep, and lent us a small quilt. Outside the house there were a tower and a hut. We went to the small tower to take in the cool air. A strong southern breeze blew recklessly, and the three of us chatted pleasantly for hours. We talked for a long time and enjoyed it immensely.

September 23. Yesterday afternoon I went swimming with Mao Jun-chih. Afterward we went to Ts'ai Ho-sen's home at Yüeh-lu-shan. Dusk was just setting in, so we stayed there overnight.

Got up early this morning and went up Yüeh-lu-shan with Mr. Mao and Mr. Ts'ai, starting from the latter's home. We walked along the ridge of the mountain and came down after we had reached the college. There was a strong cool breeze and the air was refreshing. We air bathed and wind bathed, and our spirits were thoroughly refreshed. It seemed somehow as if we were cut off from the real world. It was eleven o'clock when we returned.

## IV. STUDY NOTES AND MARGINAL ANNOTATIONS

From the only surviving study notebook and book with marginal notations that we have today, we can see that when Comrade Mao Tse-tung was studying at First Normal he was a tireless student strong in independent thinking and critical analysis. These surviving embers hidden away by people like treasures after disaster struck appear today as "feathers of the chi-kuang."*

Mao wrote a great number of study notes, diary entries, and newspaper excerpts when he was studying at First Normal, and he accumulated a large basketful of these that was kept at his home in Shao-shan. After the "Horse Day Incident" his relatives took all his books and other literary materials together with these notes to the backyard and burned them in order to forestall reactionary persecution. There were some people who then went and saved this book of study notes and the textbook from the ashes and kept them hidden until after the liberation.

For his notes he had used a nine-column book with forty-seven pages † (ninety-four sides), making a total of over ten thousand words. The first eleven pages consist of Mao's handwritten copy of the "Li Sao" and the "Nine Songs." ‡ Noted on the text of the "Li Sao" is a précis of each section. The last thirty-six pages are headed "Classroom Record," being mainly notes on "moral self-discipline" [hsiu-shen] and "Chinese literature" and most likely taken down in 1913 or 1914 from the classes given by Mr. Yang Ch'ang-chi. If we take a look at Mr. Yang's book Lun-yü lei-ch'ao, published in 1914, and make a comparison, this guess seems correct.

The complete texts of the "Li Sao" and the "Nine Songs" were copied out without the slightest alteration, and we can thus see the depth of Comrade Mao Tse-tung's fondness for these two pieces.

---

* A mythical animal; the phrase usually refers to fragments of ancient literary works. — Tr.

† "Pages" in the traditional Chinese-style book are actually "leaves," as in a folio. Chinese is traditionally written vertically, thus the term "columns," not lines. — Tr.

‡ Two of a number of poems by Ch'ü Yüan (340?-278 B.C.) in the collection entitled Ch'u Tz'u (Songs of the South). "Li Sao" (sometimes translated as Encountering Sorrow) is an autobiographical poem that tells of the poet's failure in political life despite his outstanding qualifications. In the end the poet feels he is too virtuous to fit into this sordid world. The "Nine Songs" is a fantasy poem that eulogizes local and universal dieties. Together with "Li Sao" and others, these poems have made Ch'ü Yüan the "father of Chinese poetry," particularly of romantic poetry. — Tr.

The scope of the "Classroom Record" is very broad. In the area of scholarly essays, it touches upon the pre-Ch'in philosophers, the Ch'u Tz'u [Songs of the South], Han fu-poetry, the Shih-chi [Historical Records], the Han-shu [History of the Han], the "ancient writing" [ku-wen] movement of the T'ang and Sung dynasties, the "li hsüeh" of the Sung and Ming dynasties, and the thinkers and essayists of the late Ming and early Ch'ing dynasties. [60] In addition, in many places he discussed historical personages and political situations and occasionally also talked about foreign historical figures, such as Napoleon, Caesar, and Fukuzawa Yukichi. [61] There are also several places where he took down notes on the elements of natural science. For every chapter he read, he wrote out in separate lines the historical allusions, word meanings, main ideas, and striking sentences, occasionally mixed with critical discussions. These latter comments were not all Mao Tse-tung's own, but at least they had been selected by him and then written down. Thus, not only can we see from this information how diligent Mao was in his youth and how extensive his studying was, we can also conjecture about the starting point of his ideology. He had no desire to become a hack writer, dealing in amazing stories and anecdotes. Neither did he weary himself with the petty search for documentary evidence; on the contrary, he always studied the great principles of mind, matter, order, disorder, sageliness, unworthiness, moral self-discipline, and government. This was a preliminary yet serious attempt to create a philosophy of life.

The more salient points in these notes are the following:

1. He emphasized that one must have high ideals, that one must encourage oneself with "sagehood." He believed that one should "set up an ideal. Afterward each and every word and action should correspond with this ideal." What he here calls an "ideal" is a kind of ultimate boundary. In the notes he writes: "My boundaries must be expanded so that the universe will become one great Self." "An individual Self is small; a universal Self is great. The individual Self is that of flesh and bone; the universal Self is that of the spirit." On how to handle skillfully the question of the "great Self" and the "small Self," he admired the benevolent and upright men of antiquity:

Someone once said: "I observe that among the Superior Men [chün-tzu] of antiquity there were those who would see themselves and their families perish and yet would have no regrets.". . . There is a saying: "When a poisonous snake bites his hand, a true brave man will cut it off at his wrist. It is not that he cares nothing for his wrist, but that if he fails to do away with it he will be unable to keep his whole body alive." Benevolent men regard the world and its posterity as their bodies, and regard themselves and their families as their wrists. Only because of the sincerity of their care for the world and its posterity do they dare not care for themselves and their families. Although he or his family dies, if the world and its posterity live, then the mind of the benevolent man will be at peace. (The benevolent man eliminates the suffering of living things in the world and plans for their peace and security.)

Thus, in discussing man he started with man's moral courage. He admired the philosophy of the Confucians, related in the Lun-yü [Analects], that advocated contentment with poverty and joy in the Way. He had a great respect for Yen Tzu-ling, [62] Fan Chung-yen, [63] Ku Yen-wu, and Wang Fu-chih. He praised Wei Hsi, who went into bankruptcy and did not compromise his principles to save his family,* likening him to Chang Liang. [64]

2. Comrade Mao Tse-tung placed special emphasis on painstaking hard work and a close agreement with reality. He called for people to "work sincerely and study sincerely." Learning, too, must be sought in reality. In his notes we read: "The learning that one obtains from behind closed doors is useless. If one wants to learn from the myriad things of the world, then one must travel widely to the Nine Divisions [of ancient China] and to the Four Canopies of Heaven."[†] We read further:

If one does not do agricultural work, then one will not understand the difficulty of sowing and reaping. If one does not weave silk, then one will not understand whence clothes come.... There are two essential points with regard to emphasizing the here and now: (1) Value the self. Seek within yourself, do not place blame on others. (2) Be conversant with modern times. For example, in reading history one must emphasize the modern period because this has [some] connection with us.

He was not like those so-called "famous scholars" who pretended to despise utility. In his notes there are the following two items:

The Superior Man plans for the Way, not for food — this is meant for those who are totally absorbed with making profit, it does not mean that all scholars denigrate planning for food.... When we say one's ambition should not lie with warm clothing and adequate food, that is only directed toward establishing one's will. So far as its ultimate purpose is concerned, the Kingly Way is also merely to enable people to dress in silk and eat grain, so as to avoid cold and hunger.[‡] So how can anyone say that one cannot plan for warmth and fullness?

---

* Wei Hsi was a Ming loyalist who refused to serve the Ch'ing dynasty after the Ming had fallen. — Tr.

[†] I.e., the ends of the earth. — Tr.

[‡] The Emperor wears and eats things commensurate with his high station — silk and grain — but he does not regard them as ends in themselves and is not overindulgent. — Tr.

3. In managing affairs, he advocated resoluteness, meticulousness, and the skillful use of people's abilities.

If one is certain of one's grasp, if one can see into the matter clearly, then anything may be accomplished.... Only after understanding can one make a decision. There has never been a case where a decision followed understanding and then the matter failed; so it was with I Yin.... [65] There is one difficult thing in establishing oneself in life; it is being meticulous. If one can avoid neglect in all affairs and extend this from the small to the large, one can even attain sagehood. On the other hand, if one is not attentive to small details, a great undertaking will fail. A person who was diligent in small affairs and whom we can emulate is Duke T'ao Hsüan. [66] A person who failed in a great undertaking through the neglect of details and whom we may take as a warning is Caesar.... A virtuous minister does not consider his own abilities as such, but always gathers together the abilities of the empire.... The measuring of capacity means that eminent ability occupies official positions, not that one conceals dirt and appoints the vile.

4. In devoting one's effort, Comrade Mao Tse-tung emphasized a policy of long-term work. In his notes we read things such as:

The way of the world is that there has never been a case where one has failed to see a thing accurately, has failed to amass a great deal [of work] and yet has been readily able to accomplish a thing.... There has never been a person who lacks the strength to take on the problems of the world, lacks the vital force to withstand its hardships, and lacks the natural temperament to bear any responsibility who has nevertheless been able to accomplish great things.

In sum, from this booklet of study notes we can see to what extent Comrade Mao Tse-tung was a diligently studious and earnest-thinking youth who harbored great ambitions. He surveyed the past and present, gathered together [the philosophies of the] various thinkers and stored up everything. But because he was good at independent thinking and critical analysis, and arrived at his own unique points of view, he was able to digest, criticize, and obtain a genuine harvest from every book he read and every ideological viewpoint he encountered. This had a great bearing on the later development of his thought and work style.

In a book of about one hundred thousand words there are over twelve thousand one hundred words written in the margins. In addition, each word and sentence has circles, dots, single and double underlinings, triangles, crosses and other marks of punctuation added. This is a rare thing in the history of book-reading. This occurs in the copy of A System of Ethics [67] that Mao Tse-tung had read.

Nineteen seventeen and 1918 were the last two years that Com-

rade Mao Tse-tung studied at First Normal. It was at this time
that Mr. Yang Ch'ang-chi was teaching moral philosophy, and the
text that he used for the class was this book, A System of Ethics.
Paulsen was a nineteenth-century Kantian idealist philosopher who
had harmonized the theories of motivation [tung-chi lun] and utili-
tarianism. At that time most students had no interest in the study
of philosophy and paid little attention to lectures. There was only
a small number with Mao Tse-tung who listened intently and who
diligently took notes. Mao was extremely fond of this book and once
wrote an article entitled "Hsin chih li" [The Power of the Mind],
which was based on several points in the book that Mao had criticized and developed.* Mr. Yang had great praise for this paper and
gave it a mark of 100. Recently, recalling those days, Mao Tse-
tung has remarked:

Everything we studied at that time was idealist theory. When we occasionally
would come across materialist theories like the one in this book, though they
were not yet pure and were still dualistic philosophies of mind and matter, we
already felt a deep interest [in them] and experienced a great revelation, which
really made me lean in their direction. [68]

Comrade Mao Tse-tung's own copy of this book was preserved
by one of his former classmates, and thus we have the opportunity
to realize that the owner of this book was already a thinker who
was delving into the basic questions of philosophy.

The marginal notations in A System of Ethics are printed † in the
blank spaces at the top and bottom of the page as well as between
the columns of text. The small ones are the size of No. 7 type, and
one must use a magnifying glass to see them clearly. Most of the
notations occur in Chapter IV, "The Evil, the Bad, and Theodicy,"
and Chapter V, "Duty and Conscience," altogether coming to over
5,900 characters. The next largest number of notes occurs in Chapter VI, "Egoism and Altruism," amounting to over 1,500 characters.
Next in order is Chapter I, "Good and Bad: Teleological and Formalistic Conceptions," with more than 1,100 characters. The vast
majority of the annotations consist of Mao setting forth his own
opinions on ethics, philosophy of life, historical view, and world

---

* Li Jui fails to add that, in 1936, Mao said: "I was then an idealist, and my essay was highly praised by Professor Yang...from his idealist viewpoint" (Snow,
Red Star, p. 146) [S.R.S.].

† I.e., not the usual cursive script written by hand that would be normal for
such notes. — Tr.

view, as well as various criticisms of and elaborations on the original text. A small portion is devoted to short comments of agreement and précis of chapters and paragraphs. He ties in a great many places with Chinese history, the philosophies of Mencius, Mo Tzu, the Neo-Confucians, Wang Fu-chih, and T'an Ssu-t'ung as well as the current of thought and national affairs on the eve of the May Fourth movement. In sum, they are filled with a spirit that seeks truth and the reform of state and society.

Wherever there were places in the original text that more or less agreed with the materialist point of view, Comrade Mao Tse-tung would always add many circles.* The page comments would often say such things as "Incisive view," "Very fine point," "This is very incisive," "This view agrees with mine very much." There are a great number of places where Mao contradicts or is dubious about the original text, and we often see the following kind of notation: "Actually not so," "This is not so," "This section is not very appropriate," "This also makes me doubtful," "I don't think one should construct a theory on this point," "In the end, I feel this theory is unsatisfactory...."

Below are a few distinctive features in Comrade Mao Tse-tung's commentaries:

1. He attached importance to the "value of the individual" and stressed the liberation of individuality, the "development of individuality." The notes read:

We must develop our physical and mental capacities to the fullest.... Wherever there is repression of the individual, wherever there is a violation of individuality, there can be no greater crime. That is why our country's Three Bonds †️ must go, and why they constitute, with religion, capitalists, and autocracy, the four evil demons of the world.... If one obeys the spiritual, why can't one obey the self? The self is the spiritual — is there anything spiritual outside the self?

2. He frequently elaborated on the author's praise for "resistance" and his emphasis on the relationship between human progress and the "conflict between good and evil." Above the paragraph on page 322 ‡️ that reads, "All work, all civilization, consists in overcoming such obstacles" [i.e., "physical evils," such as natural

---

* Underlining in traditional scholarship was done by drawing small circles beside the character. — Tr.

†️ The traditional social relationships stressing the duties of prince and minister, father and son, husband and wife. — Tr.

‡️ Of the English edition. — Tr.

calamities and "all things in nature which oppose the needs and wishes of man"], he noted: "The Yellow River flows out from the T'ung Pass, and because of the resistance of the T'ai-hua Mountains, the power of the water-flow increases in ferocity. The wind blows through the Three Gorges [of the Yangtze], and because the Wu Mountains act as a barrier, the power of the wind increases in force." Also, above the paragraph on page 327 where the text reads, "All historical institutions are the product of a struggle between good and evil," Mao noted:

When we read history, we always praise the time of the Warring States, the time of the struggle between Liu Pang and Hsiang Yü, the time of Han Wu-ti's battles with the Hsiung-nu, and the time of the battles between the Three Kingdoms.* When conditions are constantly changing and when men of talent are constantly appearing — these are the times that attract people's interest.

3. He sought new thought that would change the old tradition and attached importance to the effects of thought and knowledge. Above the paragraph on page 337 that reads, "Tradition robs us of the power and courage to act upon the world; the past weighs heavily upon the present. The inability to adapt themselves to new conditions causes the death of historical institutions," Mao noted: "The Chinese Republic is just now in this very position."
Notations such as the following frequently occur in other places:

The idea that everything in ancient times was good and that everything today is bad is not only prevalent in China but also in the West.... It is wrong to say that knowledge has no influence at all on a person's attitude. It has, in fact, a great influence.... Man can make progress, can make revolutions, and can have the courage to correct his errors all because he can act in accordance with his new knowledge.

4. He emphasized facts, the here and now, and practice. To the statement that reads, " 'The light dove dividing the air in her flight and feeling its resistance, might perhaps imagine that she could succeed much better in a vacuum.' Thus Kant illustrates the necessity of the facts of experience for the activity of our understanding" (pp. 324-25), Mao noted: "Very true, very penetrating words."
From the notations below we can see to what extent Mao treated things in a concrete manner.

---

* All historical periods of great significance in Chinese history up to the fourth century A.D. — Tr.

Only after the subjective and objective [requirements] are satisfied can we call something perfect.... We must regard our duty as the putting into practice of the very best.

When we critically discuss history and say that such-and-such was good or such-and-such was bad, we are pointing to the facts of a person's goodness or badness. Once we leave the realm of fact there is no good or bad. Therefore, to think about leaving a good reputation behind for a thousand years is foolish. To admire someone else's reputation is also foolish.

We must concentrate on the realities of our experiences in this world, all the spiritual and material things we have collected through a lifetime. Any action, for example, must be carried out by exhaustive efforts on the appropriate objective facts. As for ideas, we must realize them by exhaustive efforts on the appropriate subjective facts. We have a responsibility only to our subjective and objective realities. If it is not one or the other, then we bear no responsibility.

5. Especially worth noting is that Comrade Mao Tse-tung had been enlightened by Paulsen's theory of evolution and by the progressive theories advocated by T'an Ssu-t'ung and New Youth, and already by this time he showed a precocious penchant for dialectical materialism. For example, we can find such notes as the following to Chapter IX, "Freedom of the Will":

Although we are defined and confined by nature, we are also a part of nature. Hence, nature has the power to define and confine us and we have the power to do the same to nature; although our power is slight, one cannot say it has no influence on nature.... I say: the concept is reality, the finite is the infinite, the temporal is the intemporal, imagination is thought, form is substance, I am the universe, life is death, death is life, the present is the past and the future, the past and the future are the present, the small is the great, the yin is the yang,* the high is the low, the impure is pure, the thick is the thin. To put it plainly, the myriad things are one; change is constancy.

I am the most eminent person and I am the most lowly.

From the very fragmentary quotes above we can see how fascinated Comrade Mao Tse-tung was at the time with the study of philosophy and with the investigation of basic philosophical questions. Arising out of this extraordinary spirit of broad study, penetrating research, and practice, Mao had already made some unique discoveries in the field of thought and was far above the ideological level of the average Chinese revolutionary intellectual of the time.

Although the salvos of the October Revolution had sounded between 1917 and 1918, New Youth had not immediately echoed them. 69

_____

* The two elements of the Naturalist School of Chinese philosophy which became incorporated in later Confucianism. The Naturalists saw the world as a complementary duality of negative (yin) and positive (yang) forces. — Tr.

Thus deep in the interior of China at Changsha the young Mao Tse-tung, thirsting for new ideas and new knowledge, was only able to obtain some impure materialist thought from the writings of T'an Ssu-t'ung (Jen hsüeh) and Li Ta-chao ("Ch'ing Ch'un" [Spring of Youth], "Chin" [Today], "Hsin ti, Chiu ti" [The New, The Old]) and from the dualistic philosophy of Paulsen. With regard to his own ideological situation at this time, Mao Tse-tung has said: "At this time my mind was a curious mixture of ideas of liberalism, democratic reformism, and utopian socialism" [Snow, Red Star, pp. 148-149]. But from the marginal notations in these books we can see how ardently Mao was investigating the ultimate questions of human life and of the universe. That unrestrained thinking, which aimed at breaking through the net of the old ideas, was just like a volcano about to erupt that no amount of force can stop. At the same time, Mao was no prisoner of idealism or the theory of evolution, but, rather, he critically absorbed their positive, progressive elements welding them into a weapon for the reform of China. And so it was by no means accidental that when Marxism-Leninism was brought to China, Comrade Mao Tse-tung accepted it more readily and understood it more perfectly and more profoundly than the average Chinese progressive intellectual.

## V. SIMPLE AND HUMBLE WORK STYLE, BRAVE AND DEFIANT CHARACTER

Most of the students at First Normal came from farming communities, and their life styles were comparatively simple; and Comrade Mao Tse-tung himself gained fame throughout the entire school for living simply and frugally. At that time, room and board for Normal School students were provided by the school itself. During his period of study in Changsha, Mao Tse-tung altogether spent only 160 dollars [ch'ien]. One third of that amount he used to subscribe to newspapers, the rest he used to purchase numerous books and magazines. 70 When Mao first entered Fourth Normal, the school distributed a blue woolen uniform. He wore this piece of clothing for many years. Even when it had faded and became full of holes, Mao continued to wear it. In addition to the uniform, he often wore a grey, cotton ch'ang-p'ao* (in the winter he would add

---

* The traditional "gown" worn by higher-class Chinese men, notably scholars. — Tr.

an old lined jacket inside) and a big, white pair of cotton trousers almost the entire year around. In the summer he almost never had any socks, and the cotton sandals he wore were coming apart at the seams. His bedding was normal for a Hunan peasant family; a blue, coarse, cotton wrap-around quilt in which the cotton filler was old and hard (later when he began his early revolutionary activities in Changsha Mao still wore the grey cotton ch'ang-p'ao and used this bedding). All his classmates considered him someone who especially did not "adorn his exterior."

This simple and frugal life style was not limited to the clothing Mao wore; the other aspects of his life were the same. For example, on Sundays, when students failed to return in time for dinner, they were allowed to make up their meals. But in the kitchen the rice left in the big rice pot and vegetables left in the earthenware bowls were all cold, and generally the students who returned late would get together in small groups to heat up their dishes. Only Comrade Mao Tse-tung would get some cold rice and cold vegetables, sit by himself at the table, quietly eat his meal, and then leave.

Among the teachers it was Old Hsü (Comrade Hsü T'e-li), whose simple and frugal work style had a great influence upon the students. At that time most of the faculty in Changsha taught at several different schools at the same time. There were some teachers who traveled around by three-man sedan chairs known as "yelling chairs" (so called because when the sedan chair was lifted, a yell went up from the bearers). But Old Hsü never took a sedan chair; nor did he use rickshaws.* He would often be waiting in the morning for the city gates to open so that he could go to class. He was not in the least particular about his own personal life. He wore cotton clothes and bore severe inconveniences. He taught without weariness, worked without regard to his own self, and was most desirous of assisting other people out of their difficulties. The students all worshiped Old Hsü, and Mao Tse-tung and his friends were naturally even more deeply affected by this spirit.

In October 1916 the school made the hill behind it into an athletic

---

* Interviewed in Taipei in 1963, Professor Pai Yü, a fellow student of Mao's at First Normal, confirmed that Hsü T'e-li was one of the very few teachers who was so non-conformist as to come to school on foot, but he added that Yang Ch'ang-chi in fact belonged to the affluent minority who rode in sedan chairs. (Cf. Schram, Mao Tse-tung, pp. 42-43.) Two decades later, Mao expressed his respect for Hsü T'e-li in a letter beginning: "Twenty years ago you were my teacher, you are still my teacher, and in the future you will certainly always remain my teacher" (Current Background, No. 891, p. 4; translation modified) [S.R.S.].

field and organized an extracurricular track meet, in which the entire student body and some of the faculty participated. When Comrade Mao Tse-tung carried dirt he always carried a very full load, just as conscientiously as when working at home in the fields. He would frequently carry water and perform general labor service in his bare feet. He had a great admiration for his fellow workers in the school, and his relationship with them was very good. (In 1951, when some former First Normal classmates of Mao came to Peking to meet with him, he made a special point of asking about several of his fellow workers from those days.)

For the most part, the words and actions of humble people are simple and natural, and they have confidence in their own strength. The young Mao Tse-tung already possessed this fine characteristic. "In class he was well-behaved, very proper, and very refined. He did not jump around when he walked, he did not use coarse language when he spoke, and he always sat properly in a dignified manner, thinking, and talking very little." [71] When he spoke he was free and easy; he never got flurried, never lost his temper, or spoke in sudden anger. Even in pressing and important matters he still maintained his composure. Whenever he was at a meeting, whether as chairman or just as a participant, he never spoke recklessly. And most especially he did not indulge in long, digressive, and confused speeches. (This was the most common fault of the Modernists before and after the May Fourth period.) When everyone fell to arguing in great profusion or when the disputes became violent, he would always maintain a quiet composure and listen carefully. Only after having carefully listened to all the opinions would he then speak. In the five and a half years during which he studied at First Normal, Mao Tse-tung never had a verbal clash with anyone and never joked around, but he was amicable and most willing to help others in resolving doubts and correcting erroneous ideas. The only things he normally discussed with his classmates and friends were great world and national events, the hardship of the people's life, famous people of ancient and modern times, and personal insights he had gotten from his studies. He often added a humorous note to his discussions of problems, which were fair and reasonable, and those who listened were deeply moved. This was another facet of his personality. Whoever might have pessimistic, negative thoughts would be able to take heart and pull himself together after a talk with Comrade Mao Tse-tung. Because he was doing a good deal of work while in the Student Society, Mao often preached the following principle: Before one does anything one must study the surrounding circumstances and understand them clearly and, moreover, must give much thought to failure. If one then fails, one will not become discouraged or lose heart, since one will have been mentally prepared beforehand. When Mao ran the Student Society, he did numerous things that benefited the students, but never did he claim personal credit; never did he say that a thing was his idea or that he was the one who had done it. Comrade Mao Tse-tung was a person famous for his modesty and friendliness.

But when it came to unreasonable things, things that could not be countenanced, especially the feudal autocratic work style, Mao Tse-tung would under no circumstances give in, but would courageously resist. Two external features of his personality had been inseparable since youth: a gentleness grounded in firmness, and a modesty that has a reverse side — when he should not yield, he made absolutely no compromise.

There was a teacher of Chinese language and composition called Yüan the Big Beard whose name was Yüan Chi-liu. He was a chü-jen* of the former Ch'ing dynasty. He was very strict and made the students write classical Chinese [ku-wen] after the manner of the T'ung-ch'eng school.[†] Comrade Mao Tse-tung had gotten into the habit of patterning his Chinese after the style of Liang Ch'i-ch'ao, [72] but now because of Yüan the Big Beard's opposition, Mao changed and wrote in the classical style. Yüan was very fond of this student and praised his essays as "very similar to the style of K'ung Jung." [‡] On Saturdays he would often take Mao to his own home and talk with him. In the beginning, Mao Tse-tung more or less obeyed Yüan, but later he felt Yüan was too conservative and autocratic and so opposed him. Once, just when class was beginning and Yüan was in the classroom overseeing the students' writing of an essay, Mao Tse-tung wrote the following small phrase beneath the essay topic: "First essay for (the date)." Yüan saw this and disapproved, saying: "I didn't ask you to write this phrase, so don't write it," and ordered Mao to recopy on a new page. But after

---

* A term that referred to graduates of the provincial civil service examinations. — Tr.

† The style of Fang Pao (1668-1749) and Yao Nai (1731-1815), both from T'ung-ch'eng hsien in Anhwei. — Tr.

‡ K'ung Jung (153-208) was a descendant of Confucius (K'ung Ch'iu in Chinese); "style" (pi-i) here can refer to caligraphy or to the composition from a structural point of view, but since K'ung Jung has no particular reputation as a caligrapher the latter is probably meant. — Tr.

two requests, Mao still didn't pay the least bit of attention to him. Then Yüan, fuming, came running over and tore up the sheet of paper. Mao Tse-tung then stood up and asked Yüan what he was doing and wanted to drag Yüan to the head of the school to "settle the issue reasonably." Yüan had no answer. Finally Mao wrote once more and, as before, wrote in that one small phrase. Yüan the Big Beard could do nothing.

There was another time when Yüan the Big Beard was shouting abuse at an office boy because the latter had done something wrong. Just at that point Mao Tse-tung happened by. He thought this was extremely unfair and said in a loud voice: "How can a person be so evil to bring on such cursing and screaming!" Yüan heard this and came out. Seeing that it was Mao, he didn't know what to do and so shut his mouth and stopped his cursing.

There was one classmate who had committed a minor infraction of the rules of principal K'ung Shao-shou during the national graduates' exam in literature and who was consequently punished. This student then wrote a passage on the blackboard claiming that K'ung was a person who was "fishing for praise and reputation" (at that time K'ung was pretending to be a modernist scholar). When K'ung saw this, he expelled the boy from school. Mao Tse-tung felt this was very unfair, and so he expressed his great dissatisfaction with K'ung, maintaining that he liked to "put on airs" and that he was not a sincere and honest person, thus exposing K'ung's false mask in front of all the students.

There was another classmate who had gotten engaged on orders from his parents, the other party being the niece of a middle school principal in Changsha. Comrade Mao Tse-tung was extremely opposed to the feudal marriage system, and so he went to this principal to talk sense about the matter. In the end Mao convinced him and helped this classmate annul the wedding contract.

Another thing that shook the whole school involved an attempt to oust the school principal.

In the first semester of 1915, the school's stubborn principal made a new regulation that as from the fall term every student had to pay ten yuan for miscellaneous expenses. This was not a small sum, and the students rose up in opposition. Some were of the opinion that this regulation had been proposed by the principal so that he could ingratiate himself with the government. The students thereupon started a movement to oust the principal. Someone wrote up a declaration detailing the bad personal morals of the principal. After Mao saw the essay, he felt that it had not been done quite right. If one wanted to oust the principal, his poor management of the school must be criticized. So Mao wrote an additional section, detailing how he was running the school without any plan, was ruining the young people, and he felt fully justified and confident in doing so. Everyone agreed with this essay, and people were sent that very night to the print shop to run off copies. The next morning a student who was carrying copies back to the school was discovered by the dean. The principal was greatly angered and wanted to publicly expel seventeen of the leading "troublemakers," who included Mao Tse-tung, on account of this. There was one student from the same province as the principal who squealed and said that the declaration had been written by Mao. Because of the essay's impressive power, the principal could also tell that it had come from Mao Tse-tung's hand. Later, Yang Ch'ang-chi, Hsü T'e-li, Fang Wei-hsia, and many other teachers repeatedly interceded on Mao's behalf, saying that he was an exceptional student, that his family was very poor, that he was extremely intelligent, and that one should not cause him to lose schooling. Mao was finally spared dismissal.

The young Mao Tse-tung had a deep hatred for the entire old feudal order. He despised the gentry, whose mouths were full of benevolence and righteousness, for their meanness and their falseness, and he was able to be truly courageous in cutting these old creeping vines in two and also in struggling against them.

Comrade Mao Tse-tung was very much respected by his classmates. He led everyone in a head-on struggle against the power of the warlords and, moreover, was victorious.

After 1911 the warlords fell into a free-for-all, with the north and south ranged against each other. Hunan was located directly athwart the military thoroughfare. The Peiyang warlords* planned to occupy Hunan as a base area for conquering Kwangtung and Kwangsi provinces, and the southern warlords regarded Hunan as their front line for a northern advance. Thus, for more than ten years the north and south took turns coming into Hunan. Each clique of the Peiyang Army, as well as the so-called Ch'ien, Kui, and Hsiang Armies,† came in and out of Hunan, recruiting soldiers and buying horses; "commanders" were all over the place. The vanquished burned and looted, and the victors burned and looted. The

---

* "Northern warlords" who dominated the Chinese political scene from Peking. — Tr.

† These were armies identified with Kweichou, Kwangsi, and Hunan provinces, respectively. — Tr.

ravages of the war and of the troops came in continuing waves, and the injury inflicted upon the people of Hunan was cruel in the extreme. When Comrade Mao Tse-tung was studying at First Normal he personally experienced many occasions when troops visited misery on the people, and on three different occasions he saw the military devastations of the Peiyang warlords. The first time was in 1913 when the Kuomintang's "punishment campaign" against Yüan Shih-k'ai had failed and Yüan made T'ang Hsiang-ming tuchün of Hunan. Within three years the number of people who were shot because of implication in "political cases," according to available records, came to over five thousand. (There was one middle school teacher by the name of Li Tung-t'ien who was arrested, thrown into prison, and starved to death because in his corrections of students' compositions he had censured Yüan Shih-k'ai.) T'ang Hsiang-ming was cursed by the Hunanese as "T'ang the Butcher." In 1916, after the plans of Yüan Shih-k'ai to proclaim himself emperor had failed, the Ch'ien, Kui, and Hsiang Armies joined together and forced T'ang to flee. The second time was in 1917 during the government of Tuan Ch'i-jui, when Tuan sent Fu Liang-tso to become tuchün in Hunan and the so-called "War to Protect the Constitution" broke out. [73] The third time was after Fu Liang-tso had been routed and Feng Kuo-chang issued orders for an expedition against the southern army. In the spring of 1918 the southern and northern armies staged a great battle in Hunan. In March Chang Ching-yao entered Changsha and thereafter was tuchün of Hunan for over two years. His arbitrary cruelty was even worse than that of T'ang, and he was cursed by the Hunanese as "Chang the Venomous."

Continuous years of warfare and the benighted rule of "T'ang the Butcher" and "Chang the Venomous" also meant wanton destruction for Hunan educational circles. When T'ang Hsiang-ming came, the opening of the fall semester at Fourth Normal was delayed many days. The students stayed in lodging houses and were unable to attend school. When Fu Liang-tso came, every school stopped operations, and the students were forced to return home. When Chang Ching-yao came, he quartered his troops in the schools and ruined a particularly large amount of school equipment, so that the students could not continue to study. Thus, on the one hand, these years were ones during which school education suffered [outside] interference and ideas were suppressed. On the other hand, the fact that funds for education were regularly reduced or discontinued and the schools were occupied as quarters by troops for long periods of time meant further direct damage. First Normal was located alongside the railroad, which was an important communications thoroughfare, and the dormitory was quite large and spacious. Therefore whenever there was some disturbance in Hunan, this place would invariably become an area for stationing troops. Added to this was the fact that there were elements among the students and faculty of First Normal who were dissatisfied with the government, and the warlords would often station their reinforcements there and use the occasion to crack down [on these elements]. When Comrade Mao Tse-tung was studying there, First Normal was occupied three times by large armies. The first occasion was when Yüan Shih-k'ai declared himself emperor and T'ang Hsiang-ming sent Brigade Commander Li yu-wen to garrison his troops there.[74] The second time was in 1917 when the Kwangsi army of T'an Hao-ming stationed itself there. The third time was from 1917 to 1918 when Chang Ching-t'ang's troops were stationed there. Of the three times, the third was the longest.

Following are the relevant entries from the "Important Events of the Month" section of the First Normal School Record made between November 1917 and July 1918.

November 1917: The fighting in southern Hunan is critical, and there is a great disturbance. The students have organized a garrison force for day and night patrols. Guard duty is extraordinary.

March 1918: Students were ordered to remain quiet and not to make any disturbance so that study is not obstructed. Students were ordered to reconstitute the garrison force and maintain extraordinary guard duty. There was then great disorder in the city and it was determined that we join with other schools to organize a student security force to patrol the downtown area, which ended with the arrival of the northern troops. Miscellaneous and boarding expenses were temporarily advanced by the principal. The faculty received only ten silver dollars a month for transportation expenses.

April: The inhabitants were alarmed several times one evening by the campaign in eastern Hunan. The guarding of the school by the students was exceptionally efficient and a photograph was taken as a memento. The schools were used repeatedly for the quartering of troops. Superior Primary School and Normal School were occupied in front of the dormitories and one-half of all the classrooms were eliminated. From third grade on down the students attended joint classes.

May: The funds for March, April, and May having in general not been disbursed, there were extraordinary difficulties. Each faculty member served others without salary and went to class as usual, performing cheerfully and without let-up.

June: Most of the firewood in the school yard was taken by the troops, and there is no place for training in agricultural arts. This has been an unprecedented hardship for Hunan educational circles.

July: Permission has been granted for special makeup examinations for all the fourth-year students who have not yet finished their exams because they were either assisting with troubles at home or because their way was blocked.

After August, Brigadier Commander Chang Ching-t'ang quartered his troops there for some time. The school was thrown into great disorder, and the nearby inhabitants were extremely ill at ease. Chang Ching-t'ang was the fourth younger brother of Chang Ching-yao (the names of the four Chang brothers were "Yao, Shun, Yü, and T'ang"!*) and was known as the "fourth general." When he went out, he rode in a four-man broadcloth sedan chair, and would be escorted by the long sword corps, and along the street leading to the school gates armed troops would be lined up for half a li. The few classrooms and dormitory rooms occupied by the students and faculty were very inconvenient to go to and from. But the most serious problem was that for over half a year no funds had been disbursed. Sometimes there would be one meal a day, sometimes no food at all, and they were forced to maintain a lost situation. The young Mao Tse-tung had been an eyewitness to, and had personally experienced, all of these things. The warlords' slaughtering of the people, their milking the people dry, their arbitrary cruelty — they stopped at nothing — of course incited and spurred on even more the revolutionary thought and the will to struggle of youthful patriotic stalwarts. Thus, the formation of Comrade Mao Tse-tung's idea on resisting and extirpating the warlords certainly did not take place overnight.

Although suffering the tyrannical oppression of the warlords, the Hunan masses' dissatisfaction and defiant mood grew with each passing day. Right down to the end of 1919 and the movement to Expel Chang [Ching-yao] (this movement was joined and led by Mao), the revolutionary students of Hunan were always in the very front of the action. In every patriotic action and struggle against the warlords carried out by the students of First Normal, Comrade Mao Tse-tung was the chief organizer and leader. Especially in 1917 and 1918 when he was in charge of "general affairs" in the Student Society, Mao was a leader whose reputation was fully justified. Mao's former schoolmates still accurately remember two such occasions.

In September 1915, when Yüan Shih-k'ai was preparing to become emperor, T'ang Hsiang-ming made a formal appeal for him to ascend the throne, and Yeh Te-hui and Fu Ting-i [75] organized the Hunan chapter of the Peace Planning Society [Ch'ou an hui]. All the newspapers were prohibited from publishing any articles opposing the change in the form of government. The students and some of the

---

* Four exemplary emperors of ancient China. — Tr.

faculty (such as Hsü T'e-li and Yang Ch'ang-chi) were infuriated; they talked about it day and night and intended to express their sentiments openly. At this time there was a teacher who criticized the monarchical system before the Wang Fu-chih Study Society but supported the Peace Planning Society in the school. This brought forth some questioning from the students. Deliberately dressing it in student language, Hsü T'e-li wrote a letter to this person, warning him that he should no longer engage in such double-talk. But everyone still suffered from the fact that there was no way to express sentiments of greater opposition. Under the name of the Student Society, Mao Tse-tung then reprinted the writings of Liang Ch'i-ch'ao and others opposing Yüan Shih-k'ai's scheme of declaring himself emperor, and he made them into a small pamphlet for distribution entitled: Liang Ch'i-ch'ao teng hsien-sheng tui shih-chü chih chu-chang [The Opinions of Liang Ch'i-ch'ao and Others with Regard to the Present Situation]. Public sentiment was thus greatly aroused. This is how Mao Tse-tung's classmates praised him: "All we knew how to do was to criticize surreptitiously. We couldn't think of how to go any further." Because of this incident, T'ang Hsiang-ming sent a large contingent of military police to First Normal to conduct an investigation. The students' books and baggage were all searched, but owing to the leadership of Comrade Mao Tse-tung, preparations for this had been made long beforehand with the result that the police failed to find the traces of any "troublemaking clique."

Another famous incident was when Mao Tse-tung led his fellow students and they, with their bare hands, disarmed the northern troops.

In November 1917 Fu Liang-tso was driven out by the Kui Army man, T'an Hao-ming. During the interim, when Fu had gone and T'an had not yet arrived, Changsha became a vacuum. Wang Ju-hsien's troops, of the Eighth Peiyang Division, were just making a disorderly retreat from Hsiang-t'an and Chu-chou toward Changsha, and because they were unaware that Changsha was empty, some of the troops were milling around Hou-tzu-shih River, south of First Normal, not daring to enter the city. Comrade Mao Tse-tung had had a half year's experience of regular army life, and he now led the school's student volunteer army [76] and "set up a night patrol and maintained extraordinary guard." But the arms of the so-called "volunteer army" were only a bunch of wooden practice rifles. Mao Tse-tung then made contact with the nearby branch police station, and with several of their real guns in the lead, he held the area behind the school called Miao-kao feng-shan. Timid students and faculty all hid in the courtyard of the dormitory, in the rear, not daring to make a move. The school's working personnel now all took their orders from Mao Tse-tung. He waited until Wang's defeated troops were not far away and then ordered the police to sound their rifles at the top of the hill. The rest of the students who were holding the wooden rifles shot off a great number of firecrackers, yelling in unison, "Fu Liang-tso has fled and the Kui Army has already entered the city. If you hand over your weapons there will be no trouble!" The straggling troops were unsure of the situation, and sent men into the city to negotiate. Finally they handed over their rifles. That evening the troops bivouacked on the field in front of the school, and the next day they were given money by the Chamber of Commerce before they were dispersed.

This extraordinary daring and ability to meet changing circumstances exhibited by Comrade Mao Tse-tung won the undying praise of the school's entire student and faculty population.

Having had this experience, Mao Tse-tung even more easily led his fellow students in organizing a "garrison force" in 1918 when the northern and southern troops were again engaged in battle and Chang Ching-yao's troops invaded Changsha. Mao himself was the head of this force, which guarded the entire school. Furthermore, when order was disrupted in the city and the routed troops of the southern army were looting, the "garrison force" "joined with other schools to organize a student public safety corps and patrolled the center city." During these great military disasters the student volunteer army of First Normal also organized a "Society for Aid to Women and Children" [Fu ju chiu chi hui], which went out into the streets to aid women and children who had fallen victim to the depredations of war.

## VI. HEAD OF THE STUDENT SOCIETY, RUNNING THE WORKERS' NIGHT SCHOOL

Throughout the entire period of Comrade Mao Tse-tung's study at First Normal he was revered by a great many of his teachers, friends, and fellow students. This was because he was tireless in his study and was skilled at delving into what he studied. It was because of his self-discipline and strictness, his lack of hypocrisy, his humble work style and because he had great ambition. At the same time, it was also because he was filled with a spirit of resistance to feudal autocracy and had extraordinary daring and tact.

This was particularly true after 1917 when for several terms he consecutively presided over the affairs of the Student Society. Here he showed even more a special ability to lead and create and his possession of the capacity to attract people that caused them to heartily concur with him. And so he enjoyed high prestige among the teachers and students of the entire school. His teachers thought he had "extraordinary talent," that he was a person of "imposing ability." His fellow students thought he was a "brain" and a "wizard."

There are several things we can mention that explain why Comrade Mao Tse-tung was revered by all the teachers and students of his school.

In order to devote himself single-mindedly to the study of his own books, he never paid any attention to the study of mathematics and other such courses. When he took exams in math his grades were naturally poor, but the math instructor, Mr. Wang Li-yen, still had a high regard for him because of his abilities. Once, when school had let out for vacation, Mao did not return home but stayed at Wang's house — and this was not to study mathematics. Mr. Wang even gave him room and board. Not only this but, as noted above, Mr. Yüan Chi-liu had a high regard for Mao's writing ability. Although he had been the object of this student's "disrespect" in front of everybody and finally had to bow before him, Yüan still had great respect and affection for Mao Tse-tung. When the school authorities wanted to expel Mao, Yüan the Big Beard was one of those faculty members who came out and strenuously vouched for him.

Nothing better explains the love and respect Mao Tse-tung's schoolmates had for him than the "Election of the Men of the Year" program. This was recorded in detail in the First Normal School Record of 1918.

At that time the school authorities had set up a method for examining students in their studies and in physical education that was called the "Election of the Men of the Year." The criteria and method of election were as follows:

The election criteria covered three categories: (1) Moral education: character (value modesty, esteem moral integrity, be attentive to friendships, reject enticements); self-control (maintain order, value propriety, be restrained in speech and laughter); devotion to studies (not cutting classes, diligently reviewing, a fondness for dealing with reference material); self-discipline (end extravagant desires, endure hardships); simplicity ("eat coarse food, wear coarse clothes, and use simple drink,"* esteem frugality); service (value the public good, perform one's duty diligently). (2) Physical education: daring (to go on, brave all dangers, prepare for the unusual); as well as hygiene, exercise, and athletics. (3) Intellectual education: aptitude (being able to meet changing circumstances, being meticulous in handling affairs); language (skill at public speaking, debate, conversation); as well as literature, science, and aesthetics.

The method of election was as follows: One day after classes during the semester each class of students would hold the election in their respective classrooms, each person casting at most three ballots, each ballot for one person. "On the basis of his own knowledge, each voter will enter his evaluative remarks on the ballot. Those candidates who meet more than one of the criteria may receive multiple notation on the ballot so long as they truly meet each of the criteria." Those elected were not limited to their own class, although generally students did select others from their own class since they didn't know people from other classes very well. The election recorded in the First Normal School Record was that of June 1917. The school was composed of eleven classes (in the regular and preparatory courses, from class six to fifteen and the first class of the second division), in all, more than four hundred persons took part in the "Election of the Men of the Year." To be elected, a person must have received five votes. Among the thirty-four people who were elected, Comrade Mao Tse-tung had the highest number of votes (Comrade Chang K'un-ti was fourth). As for the categories listed in the "evaluative remarks" for those elected, there were only six people who scored in both moral and intellectual education; the rest scored only in moral education, intellectual education, or physical education. In the subcategories of moral and intellectual education Mao Tse-tung also had the highest rating — he scored in six areas: respectability, self-control, literature, articulation, aptitude, and courage. The highest number of subcategories occupied by any other of those elected was only four. For example, there were only three people besides Mao who scored in respectability; there was only one person other than Mao who scored in aptitude; there was none among the others elected who scored in both language and courage. The subcategories in which the others who were elected did well were generally either literature, arithmetic, drawing, or athletics.

---

* A well-known classical quotation. — Tr.

Early Revolutionary Activities of Mao Tse-tung

After Mao Tse-tung had joined the work of the Student Society, his talent for leading the masses had even greater opportunity for systematic expression.

In the fall of 1913 First Normal created the Skills Society [Chineng hui], the aim of which was to have the students "develop the various skills of living." In 1914 the name was changed to the Self-Cultivation Society [Tzu-chin hui], and in 1915 changed again, to the Student Society. The goal of the Student Society was to "perfect morality, study education, augment knowledge, develop an occupation, steel the body, and unite the feelings [in fellowship with others]." The Student Society had a membership that included students then in school and alumni who had graduated; the teaching faculty were "supporting members." The head of the Society was the principal of the school. This, however, was in name only. In reality, the "general affairs officer" had full responsiblity. The man of primary responsibility in the Student Society, the "general affairs officer," and each department head came from the council of representatives organized by the representatives of each class of the school. According to the entries of the First Normal School Record for 1918, Mao Tse-tung bore responsibility for important work in the Student Society every semester from 1915 until he graduated in 1918. In the four semesters from 1915 to the first semester of 1917, he was the secretary (in the previous meetings a secretariat had not yet been established). From the second semester of 1917 to the first semester of 1918, he occupied the position of general affairs officer and department head of educational research. Starting with the semester that Mao became general affairs officer, the Student Society became particularly active and accomplished many, many things.

Comrade Mao Tse-tung essentially proposed two things to the full student body: scholarly study and physical training. This was related to his thinking at that time. He believed that if one wanted to rescue China from danger and reform all the old institutions, one must have high ideals, profound learning, and a strong and robust body before one could follow through and accomplish things and bear great responsibility for a protracted period of time. He hoped to foster an advance in this direction among the students through the activities of the Student Society.

This meeting of the Student Society established the following fifteen departments: educational research, public speaking, literature (divided into Chinese, English, and Japanese), caligraphy, drawing, handicrafts, music, military arts, swordsmanship, parallel bars,

54

kick ball (soccer), tennis, open field battle, athletics, and swimming. Later they planned to start a commercial department that was to be a kind of cooperative, but the school authorities did not agree to this. Previously the department heads of each department were the teachers of each subject. At this meeting of the Student Society a change was made, and the positions were now filled with students from the fourth and fifth years. This was the result of strenuous efforts on the part of Mao Tse-tung in dealing with the school. His reasoning was as follows: the fourth and fifth year students were just about to graduate, and they should develop their capacity for self-initiative and administrative affairs. If there were teachers who would give direction from the sidelines, then the students would be capable of fulfilling the duties of the department head. Representing the president of the Society, the proctor, Fang Wei-hsia, accepted this point of view. The "general affairs officer" took over control of all the work of the Student Society. According to the First Normal School Record, the first two meetings of the council passed six resolutions proposed by Mao Tse-tung that dealt with the work of the Student Society for this session: (1) collect Society dues; (2) determine the "curtain times"* (this is a technical term used at the time which refers to the activities of each department, including meetings, speeches, and research) for each department and the method by which the students would join each department, invite the teachers to participate in the various departments and decide the number of meetings per week; (3) put together a budget; (4) publish student marks and establish a Grades Exhibit Center; (5) the Society itself and every department should carefully make a work record and set up a "record of events" system; [77] (6) establish a library.

Each department invited a faculty member to assume the responsibility of mentor. For example, Mr. Yang Ch'ang-chi was the faculty member who was mentor for the educational research department. The highest number of meetings per week for any department was one, while the athletic activities varied between once and three times a week. Activity was held after classes or in the evenings. Each one of the four or five hundred students in the school joined at least one department; some joined three or four. Whenever the school authorities had an administrative meeting or a meeting dealing with educational matters, they would bring in representatives of the Student Society to participate. This highly self-governing student organization was at the time an unprecedented creation in

---

* I.e., "meeting times." — Tr.

Hunan. Leading all his classmates in the performance of many and various significant extracurricular activities through the agency of the Student Society, Comrade Mao Tse-tung to a considerable measure translated into reality his belief in the dual development of mind and body.

Not only did the activities of the various departments of the Student Society include Grades Exhibit Centers, open speech and debate meetings, scholarly research meetings on various specialized questions, and invitations to famous people to give lectures, but they also included all-school athletic meets and group swimming outings to Shui-lu Shoal. During the critical period of fighting between the northern and southern troops, as mentioned above, the Student Society also led the students in the organization of a garrison force that patrolled the school during the evening and at night.

Comrade Mao Tse-tung was very attentive to each person's strong points and was very good at utilizing the strengths of the masses, so that each person did the job that suited him best. For example, people who were good at writing and language were assigned to the literature department to work. People with an interest in education would join the educational research department. It was in line with this principle that he organized the personnel of the Student Society and the regular student body to participate in the various activities. There is one incident, still talked about today, that can explain this characteristic of Mao: There was at the time a teacher of Chinese literature who taught poorly and to whom the students were very much opposed, but he had once run a newspaper. Mao Tse-tung often went looking for him to discuss questions on current affairs and, furthermore, explained to his schoolmates that they should value this man's ability in the newspaper field. Mao would always express the following sentiment to those around him: In looking at a person, we should first look at his strengths. Everyone has his own strengths. We should all encourage and make use of a person's strengths and should not be concerned about how small or how limited those strengths might be.

As for the activities of the Student Society, we can see even better Mao's organizational ability and surefooted, meticulous work style in the following examples.

In order to bring home to everyone the importance of the "Events Record," the Student Society issued the following announcement on October 14, 1917:

At the board meeting it was decided to keep a Student Society Events Record so that there will be a record of our current affairs to serve as reference material for a later date. After a long period of time there will eventually be a great deal of material, which will be the repository of the history and achievements of this Society. This Society has been in existence for some five years. When we look back over past events we meet total obscurity, and individual human affairs have gone unrecorded and fallen into oblivion. What could be more distressing than this? Thus, this time we will keep a record. We should also trace back as far as we can remember to the past five years so that links with the present can be established. But the scope of this society is broad and its work is divided into as many as fifteen departments, some concerned with intellectual activity and some with physical activity. The circumstances are different for each department when it meets, and the meeting places are also different. If we want to have a detailed record we must divide the responsibility among many people. The Secretariat of this Society consists of just one person, and of course it is difficult for him to look after the whole situation. Moreover, he is only a bystander, and it is difficult for him to know everything about each department. It has been decided, therefore, to establish the position of Recorder. At the first meeting of each department the members will select one person to be responsible for recording all the affairs of the department so that, duties having been divided, they will be clearer, and the records, because they will be kept by those participating, will be more complete.

According to the recollections of former schoolmates, every important announcement of the Student Society was written by Mao Tse-tung personally.

Owing to the encouragement of Comrade Mao Tse-tung, the staff of the Student Society was able conscientiously to keep up this system of "Recording Events." Not only did Mao himself record, but he also corrected the records of other people. Through the three volumes of Records of the Student Society [Hsüeh-yu hui chi shih lu] and the Night School Record [Yeh hsüeh jih chih] that have fortunately survived, we can come to realize this.

The funds of the Student Society were very limited, but making precise and careful calculations, Mao Tse-tung still devised ways to squeeze out enough money to buy all the new periodicals of the day, such as New Youth, Eastern Magazine [Tung-fang tsa-chih], Pacific [T'ai-p'ing yang], Science [K'o-hsüeh], and Educational Research [Chiao-yü yen-chiu]. Furthermore, he also solicited all sorts of books from the teaching staff, students, and from people outside the school. The Grades Exhibit Center was established in the library room. The best productions of the students were treated as library books and were kept permanently. At the time the school took subscriptions to various newspapers but did not carry Popular Education Gazette [T'ung-su chiao-yü pao], a tabloid published in

Changsha that was very well received. And so the Student Society specially ordered two copies and made up a newspaper display board, which they set up on Ta-ch'un Bridge next to the school. After students in the school had read the paper they would paste it up the next day so that the night school students and the workers from the neighboring factories could read it.

In May 1917, when the school held an athletic meet, Mao Tse-tung took charge of recording the event and put out a "Special Bulletin." By himself he hawked things to eat and used the profit from this to help the finances of the Student Society. [78] There were many outdoor activities then, but there was a real lack of indoor activity. On a rainy day or in the evening, it was very depressing. But there were no appropriate rooms and also no funds. This was a very difficult problem to solve, but Mao Tse-tung thought of a way — ping-pong. The Student Society made up twelve wooden frames and twelve nets of glazed cotton, each class receiving one set. Tables were then set up in the office of the Society, in the school auditorium, in the reception room, and upstairs — a "ping-pong craze" was born.

When Comrade Mao Tse-tung was in charge of the general affairs office of the Student Society, he fully demonstrated his talent for leadership. In addition to active management, meticulous thought, and skill at organizing the masses, what was most noteworthy was his planning and creativity. He invariably thought Society matters through very carefully: such-and-such a thing should be done, such-and-such a thing should be done urgently, such-and-such a thing should be pursued with utmost effort. He always proposed constructive ideas and the way he consulted with each of the responsible members in the departments can be said to follow these mottos: "discuss matters point by point," "make a clear, orderly presentation." Everyone gladly accepted his suggestions because these suggestions were always in accord with the actual situation and the current need.

Whenever the Student Society held a plenary session or a general officers meeting, Mao Tse-tung would chair the meeting. Sometimes fellow students would hold fast to their own views and argue among themselves, unwilling to give in to each other. Mao would listen intently to the various opinions and jot down their main points. When everyone was in the midst of vehement argument he would not rashly express his own opinion, but would wait until everyone had finished making their own ideas known; then he would get up and present a summation. His summations always included the good points and excluded the poor ones; his considerations were always excellent. He was able to make a penetrating analysis of every problem and every argument, and for this reason everyone was always in hearty agreement with him. Many arguments found a solution because of his incisive and uncomplicated analysis.

Comrade Mao Tse-tung's last semester at First Normal was the first part of 1918, and he was again elected by his schoolmates as general affairs officer of the Student Society. In April the Southern Army retreated and held Heng-yang and Yung-chou. The Northern Army occupied the school, and most of the students left. Only about a hundred students remained, and all of the activities of the Student Society accordingly came to a halt. Because each class was graduated ahead of schedule, Mao handed over Society affairs to the schoolmates who were staying behind and to the president of the Society. On the last page of the "Events Record" he personally noted the events surrounding the ending of the Student Society and also especially made two proposals. One was to increase the budget of the Student Society: raise the initiation dues from fifty cents to one yuan, the yearly dues from twenty cents to one yuan; buy more books by publishing Student Society material, so that the night school will be financially independent. The second was to add a department of social relations to maintain contact with alumni, and then to organize an Alumni Association [Hsiao-yu hui], to "ponder the past and support education." He also wrote down seven detailed suggestions. This final transfer of duties for the Student Society took place on May 29, 1918. At the end of the section Mao Tse-tung solemnly signed his own name.

At the same time that Mao Tse-tung was in charge of the work of the Student Society, he was also running the night school with whole-hearted enthusiasm. This may be seen as marking the beginning of Mao's contact with the urban workers. The two faculties from the Normal School and the attached primary school had already run a night school once before during the first part of 1917, but later some of the faculty members were unable to continue the enterprise. In the second part of the year the school was taken over and run by the Student Society alone, responsibility for this falling to the educational research department.

Many students who attended First Normal at the time cannot recall in detail the events surrounding the running of this night school. All people remember is that Comrade Mao Tse-tung worked the hardest. Fortunately, however, we can now find the most reliable records of this matter in the pages of the Night School Record and the First Normal School Record of 1918. The Night School Record, like the "Events Record" of the Student Society, was a system advocated and strenuously carried out by Mao Tse-tung. Everything relating to the teaching and the management of the night school, the criticisms of teachers, the various difficulties that the school encountered, as well as the detailed regulations on handling business and advertisements for students, was entered into the Night School Record. The entries running from the beginning of November 1917, when the school first started, to the fourteenth of the month were personally recorded by Mao Tse-tung, and these are especially detailed.

According to the records of the First Normal School Record, during a meeting of the Student Society Mao advanced four reasons why the night school had to be established. The first was that based on the current national situation the nucleus of power in society was really the majority of uneducated citizens, that is, workers and peasants. Second, the system of universal education practiced in European and American society had produced results. Although the individual circumstances of all Chinese are not the same, every person should have the opportunity to receive an education. Third, it could be a practice ground for the third and fourth year students of First Normal. Fourth, it could be used to bridge the huge chasm of difference and mutual suspicion that existed between society at large and the school. Mao especially explained the significance of the fourth reason. Owing to the numerous battles between the north and south that were raging within the borders of Hunan, school finances were without the least guarantee. Moreover, the schools were constantly being occupied and even demolished by the troops, and after the students left school they could find no jobs. For this reason they were hostile to the present benighted society. Yet the rank and file masses did not understand the internal situation at the school very well, did not understand why the students often protested and demonstrated. Mao Tse-tung's ideal was that "everybody in society will be a school graduate; yet the [formal] school will be a preparing ground for the larger school which is society as a whole. Such will be the final product of a thousand years of reform and progress" (Night School Record).

Throughout the entire period, Comrade Mao Tse-tung was very dissatisfied with the current state of formal education. He felt that it restricted one's thinking and ambition, that the curriculum was too mechanical, that what was learned was useless, and that it only produced bookworms. The teachers were working just for the money, and the students were planning for their futures. The one taught according to the text; the other learned sterilely by rote memorization. Aside from the time spent in the classroom, there was very little contact between students and teachers. Thus, even in a school like First Normal, Mao was still constantly bored. One morning he told a friend: "Last night I almost quit school. I went up to the principal's office three times prepared to make a request to leave." The methods Mao Tse-tung used in running the night school demonstrated his objective spirit and creative talent, on the one hand, and his dissatisfaction with the current educational system, on the other.

The target students of the night school were primarily the workers in and outside the school itself. This was because the immediate environs of First Normal, outside Changsha's South Gate, were where the workers from a mint, a graphite refining plant, an electric light factory, and the railroad all lived. When the night school advertised for students, it made a point of issuing the notices in pai-hua* (this was quite a novelty at the time), sincerely addressing the workers:

Dear Workers, come listen to us say a few words in pai-hua: What is most inconvenient for all of you? It is, as the popular saying goes, you can't write what is said, can't read what is written, and can't add up numbers. You have to work, and there is no one to teach you — how can you learn to write a few characters or add up a few columns? Now there is an excellent way to do it — we of First Normal have set up a night school. We had a lot of students the first half of this year, we're sure some of you have heard about it. This night school has been especially created for you workers and is open from Monday to Friday. Each night there are two hours of classes. We teach writing letters and adding up accounts, both things that you gentlemen constantly have occasion to use yourselves. We give out the reading material at no cost to you. Attending classes in the evenings won't hinder your work either. If you want to come and study, we urge you to hurry within a week's time to the registry of First Normal to sign up. Some say that the times are not right and they fear they will be breaking the order for martial law — we can take care of this matter. After he begins school, each person will be given a lecture pass. If you are stopped by the military police and asked any questions, all you have to say is that you are a student of the First Normal night school and there will be no hindrance (in First Normal School Record).

But, after the notices had been posted in the streets, and some of them had even been distributed by the police, no one came to register. Later, the message was written on large pieces of paper and pasted up at prominent places in the streets, but still only nine people came to register. Mao Tse-tung then took this problem under

---

* The vernacular, as opposed to the literary, language. — Tr.

study. He felt that a night school was still an extremely rare thing in Changsha, so it was difficult for the masses to believe. Furthermore, it was not appropriate that the police department distribute the announcements. The police represented officialdom. As soon as the people looked at them they got frightened and, completely contrary to what was desired, they became even more suspicious and afraid. And so Mao organized his schoolmates to go out into the streets and launch a house-to-house mobilization. According to the Night School Record, the group carried with them over six hundred copies of the announcement and handed them out in the mint and railroad district that were near the school. They also propagandized by word of mouth. This time there was indeed some effect. After three days there were over one hundred and twenty people who had come and registered, and there were many who continued to come later asking to register. Later, owing to space limitations, registration had to be cut off. In the Night School Record Mao Tse-tung recorded this urgent demand of the workers for education in the following words: "It was like the wailing of a baby waiting to be fed."

The curriculum of the night school was divided into three areas: Chinese, arithmetic, and general knowledge. In the Night School Record it is written that "Chinese and arithmetic are associated with technical skill, general knowledge is associated with mental ability." Chinese was divided into character recognition, essays, notes, and letter writing. Arithmetic concentrated primarily on the abacus, with some stress on computation by hand. The content set up for the general knowledge section was at first very comprehensive. It included the nine topics of history, geography, science, ethics, hygiene, industry, government and law, economics, and education. Every course had its lecture notes prepared by the night school teachers themselves. The principle that underlay the lecture notes was to be "brief and to the point," and they had to have an intimate connection with the daily lives of the students. Comrade Mao Tse-tung himself took on the responsibility for the history course. He placed extraordinary importance on historical knowledge. His teaching methodology is recorded in the Night School Record:

He taught general historical trends as well as the most significant events of re-
.cent times. He thus nurtured both the students' historical point of view and their patriotism. (Before this they had obtained a lot of miscellaneous data from folk stories and from dramas; this had resulted, however, in an unsystematic historical point of view and patriotic attitude.)

In view of the fact that previously the faculty of the night school had for the most part proved incapable of continuing the operation, Mao Tse-tung made a special point of exacting everybody's agreement to several stipulations. For example, the teacher and supervisor should come to class together and come on time. The supervisor [should] adopt an attitude of strict discipline in order to establish credibility with the students. The supervisor's responsibility is to take charge of the day's nonacademic matters, such as student discipline, teaching inspection, looking after the clock and ringing the bell, as well as filling out the "daily record." Mao was extremely good at spurring on those around him through his own eagerness and in motivating people to do their work by his own positive actions.

The night school formally began on the evening of November 9. The proctor and representative of the Student Society's president, Fang Wei-hsia, was the speaker. Mao Tse-tung very carefully explained the "class orientation card" line by line to the students. The "class orientation card" was very complete and very considerate of the concrete problems of the workers. Included here were the following two lines: "When you attend class, wear whatever you like; there is no need to dress up." "This school has already made written request to the police for protection so you don't have to be worried about getting here and returning home." (At the time, fighting had just broken out between the northern and southern troops in northern Hunan.) Mao Tse-tung looked after all the affairs of the night school, both large and small, with great care and kept them in good order. For example, it is recorded in the entry for November 12 in the <u>Night School Record</u>:

After classes Mao Tse-tung made a report to the effect that there could be no disturbances and that students should attend every class. Those who missed three times would be expelled and not permitted to come back. Those who had to relieve themselves were to go to the toilet outside. When it rained, one should put one's rainwear under one's seat and look after it. Those who didn't bring any brush and ink one time should bring them the next time. Students should take home their practice paper, write on it, and bring it with them the next time for grading.... There are four kerosene lamps in the classroom and three of them are dim. When the lamps are in the corners it is quite dark in the center; another lamp should be added.

Comrade Mao Tse-tung paid special attention to the study of pedagogical improvement. The November 14 <u>Night School Record</u> reads:

After three days' experience I feel that the Chinese used is too much and too difficult. We should cut down the amount of material and should use common language (somewhere between pai-hua and the literary language). Too much is covered in General Knowledge (referring to the written word). We should use the written word less. The reading material should use a few simple sentences in pai-hua as a guide. These [should] not be given out at the beginning but after the explanations are finished they [may] be read over once and that will be sufficient. If we adopt this method in teaching current history, I feel it will be much more lively.

Because the teacher covered too much when teaching physics, the older people didn't understand and couldn't work up any interest. Thus, after class,

Mao Tse-tung made a report saying that "physics is an extremely interesting course. What has been just taught has been only the beginning. In the future we will tell you how an electric light is able to shine and how steamboats and trains are able to move so fast." This will be enough to elicit their interest in studying. This approach can be adopted completely (November 16 Night School Record).

This year the troops of Fu Liang-tso and T'an Hao-ming moved in and out of Changsha, and the situation was very unsettled. A curfew was regularly observed at night, which greatly affected the workers' attendance at night school. Later, even though the number of students attending school had gradually dropped from the figure it had been when the school began, the faculty remained on the job under the eager inspiration of Mao Tse-tung. When vacation time came around, the students were divided into three ranks and given awards.

Comrade Mao Tse-tung's last semester at First Normal was the first part of 1918. The night school was continued that semester, but the teachers and supervisors were approximately half the number they had been the previous semester so that they might concentrate on their [regular] work. Mao continued in his position of "manager." The Night School Record still contained his entries. From this book we can also learn that to enlarge the night school's influence in society and to motivate other schools to start night schools also, Mao sent news articles and essays to Popular Education Gazette, introducing the night school of First Normal. On March 19 and 20 of this year, this paper published an article entitled "Kao yeh hsüeh-sheng" [An Announcement (about) Night School Students]. This article was a detailed introduction to the experience at First Normal in night school instruction and management.

When Comrade Mao Tse-tung graduated from First Normal the many workers from the neighboring factories all knew "Mr. Mao" of the night school, and all considered "Mr. Mao" a good teacher and a good friend. Quite obviously, when Mao was studying at First

Normal the most significant result of his running the night school
was that he got his first experience in maintaining close links with
the workers and that he forged his first bonds of sentiment with the
working class. After the establishment of the Chinese Communist
Party, when Mao Tse-tung was leading the labor movement in Hunan, he put to use on a larger scale the experience gained in running the workers' night school and also became the motivating force
behind the Hunan "Popular Education" [P'ing-min chiao-yü] movement.

In 1920, at the same time that Mao was director of the primary
school attached to First Normal, he ran a "People's School" [P'ing-
min hsüeh-hsiao] next door that was sponsored by First Normal's
Alumni Association. Later, this developed into a regular school.


## VII. ORGANIZING THE NEW PEOPLE'S STUDY SOCIETY

During the period of the May Fourth movement, outstanding intellectual youths throughout the country stepped up to the front
ranks of the age and sounded the trumpet of revolution. Those
among them who had been influenced by Marxism-Leninism and the
October Revolution became by and large the earliest leaders and
the mainstay of the Chinese Communist Party. These treasures of
the [Chinese] people, though still at school, already exhibited many
extraordinary characteristics. Their courageous spirit of breaking
through all the nets [of the old customs], their great political daring, their simple work style of maintaining close links with the
masses, their individual ethic of magnanimous selflessness, as
well as their incisive new and old learning and their immense capacity for work should be an enduring example for later generations of young people to follow.

Comrade Mao Tse-tung was the most exemplary and greatest
representative of this period. When he was studying at First Normal, he had already exhibited these characteristics in a most salient manner. At the same time, his close friends at First Normal,
the revolutionary martyrs Comrades Ts'ai Ho-sen, Ho Shu-heng, Lu
Ch'ang, Chang K'un-ti, and Lo Hsüeh-tsan, were to a man the most outstanding sons of the Chinese people. They all had the most intimate connection with the early work of the Chinese Communist
Party and the early revolutionary activities of Mao Tse-tung.

In the dark of night when danger threatened on all sides, there existed a deep bond of revolutionary friendship, whose source was the common ideal and practice of struggling for the liberation of the state, society, and the people, that gave a most valuable impetus to the forward advance of the revolutionaries. Especially during the storms before the vanguard had immersed itself in the masses, this comradeship in arms had an even more special significance.

In addition to the fact that there was a common purpose and goal, the reason that Comrade Mao Tse-tung and his close friends were able finally to come together into an organization, to throw themselves together into the bosom of Marxism-Leninism, and to carry on a surefooted struggle was closely connected with the fact that they had all come from farming communities and had had comparatively close associations with the peasants. They had a deep awareness of the suffering of the people and, furthermore, all had engaged in manual labor at one time. Thus they were able to keep in close touch with the masses and with reality and could endure hard work. They had neither the bookworm air of Ch'en Tu-hsiu nor the empty work style of the average petty bourgeois revolutionary. Mao Tse-tung often remarked to his friends that if a person wanted to be firm and strong and wanted to make progress, he should study the struggle trees make against the wind and snow, how they sink roots and bear fruit. He should not learn from the flowers and grass that bow before the wind and snow and, waving back and forth, are easily moved. Mao Tse-tung was the nucleus of this corps of "sparks."* He was richer in his creative ability, his thoughts were more profound, and he possessed a more down-to-earth spirit than anyone else.

From the fragmentary material below one can see that it was certainly no accident that the five revolutionary martyrs Ts'ai Ho-sen, Ho Shu-heng, Ch'en Ch'ang, Chang K'un-ti, and Lo Hsüeh-tsan became Mao Tse-tung's earliest comrades-in-arms.

Everyone knows that Comrade Ts'ai Ho-sen was an outstanding theorist and propagandist for the Chinese Communist Party in the early period and that he was elected a member of the Central Committee at the Second Party Congress. "Long before the May Fourth movement, the rank and file progressive youths in Hunan were already full of praise for Mao and Ts'ai and made them their models." [79] Ts'ai Ho-sen was from Hsiang-hsiang hsien in Hunan. From childhood, when he looked after the cattle, when he was a

---

*An allusion to Mao's letter to Lin Piao of January 1930, entitled in Selected Works "A Single Spark Can Start a Prairie Fire" [S.R.S.].

student, when he worked in the fields, and when he learned a handi-craft, he diligently carried out a program of independent study. Af-ter he took the examination and entered First Normal, his pain-staking diligence, practical spirit, revolutionary thinking, skill at analysis, as well as his talent for writing and his serious life and work style made him similar in many ways to Mao Tse-tung. The two of them together initiated the organization of the New People's Study Society and the Diligent Work and Frugal Study in France movement [Fu Fa ch'in kung chien hsüeh yün-tung]. At the same time, they leaned toward a belief in Marxism. Chang K'un-ti's di-ary contains much information dealing with [Ts'ai].

On August 23, 1917, Comrade Chang K'un-ti crossed the river to Ts'ai's home at the foot of Yüeh-lu-shan and stayed there for three days. Before daybreak they would both go up the mountain to exercise, and during the day they wandered about the mountain. In the evening they pleasantly chatted about each other's ambition. The following is a paragraph from Ts'ai Ho-sen's conversation on the evening of the twenty-third.

Later, Mr. Ts'ai talked about his anxieties and about the proper sequence of steps to be followed in advancing forward. (1) In view of the fact that there were no special textbooks for the study of Chinese society, he thought we should study Chinese social customs from ancient times to the present, the facts surrounding their changes, and the unchanging, everlasting truths. (2) Because there was no complete historical book on China — the so-called Twenty-four Histories, the Tzu-chih t'ung-chien, etc., mostly recorded the events of the emperor and the high ministers and officials — he intended to write a history that would be the re-sult of research into the provincial [sheng] and county [hsien] gazeteers that would focus on popular society. (3) The Chinese written and spoken language are differ-ent. [We should] study ways to unite the written and spoken word to aid the exten-sion of popular education. After that, he talked about studying. Because the re-cently arrived Western European culture and China's old culture are irreconcil-able, advocates of the new culture neglect to study the old books, while conserva-tives of the old culture neglect to study the new ones. Ts'ai and I advocated that we read more new books, but that we must also study the old ones. It is not nec-essarily true that Chinese culture and all of China's institutions are correct. And it is also true that not all of the institutions and culture of Western Europe can be properly applied to China. In considering the national situation, [we should] keep the old institutions which are good and change the ones which are not good. [We should] take all the Western institutions that can be adopted and do away with those that cannot. We should decide each case equitably without any prejudice. This is something those of us who read the new and the old books should under-stand.

Let's take a look at what Chang K'un-ti has to say about his "dis-tinguished friend."

September 26: On this trip I had first thought to go to Ts'ai's house and stay one day; unexpectedly it turned out to be three. In the past few years I have only very infrequently gone to the home of any relative or friend for three days. The good thing is that one more day at the house of a distinguished friend is one more day's profit. Thus, I have nothing against staying for a long time. Next school year I plan to cross the river a few more times, which will be a few more occasions for profit.

In 1921 Comrade Ts'ai Ho-sen was deported by the French government and immediately afterward went to work in the Party's Central Committee, participating in the direction of the May 30 movement of 1925. In 1931 he was arrested in Hong Kong and extradited to Canton. The counterrevolutionary hangmen were so brutal that they actually spread out his limbs, nailed him to the wall, beat him to death in cold blood, and cut his chest and stomach to pieces.

Comrade Chang K'un-ti was born in 1894. In his youth he attended school in his native village at the I-yang-lung-chou Primary School, and he was fond of the ideas of K'ang Yu-wei and Liang Ch'i-ch'ao. Later on, because he couldn't afford to continue his schooling, he returned home and worked in the fields. In 1913 he passed the entrance examination and entered First Normal. In school his thoughts, ambition, devotion to study, and every aspect of his life were all similar in purpose and goal to those of Comrade Mao Tse-tung and [his] comrades. He was always in the front rank of the class when it came to schoolwork and moral character. In 1919 he went to France as a member of the Diligent Work and Frugal Study [program], and because he carried on revolutionary activities he was deported in 1921 by the French government along with Ts'ai Ho-sen and other comrades. After returning home, he was sent out by the Peking Party organization as a special agent for railroad work and took part in leading the "February 7" strike. During the First Revolutionary Civil War he was still in Peking doing labor work. In 1928, after the establishment of the Fifth Corps [chün-t'uan] of the Red Army, he became head of the political department and then with Comrade Ho Lung created the revolutionary base of west Hunan and west Hupei [Hsiang O hsi]. In 1930 he was courageously martyred in the area of Hung-hu in west Hupei.

There is a diary preserved in Comrade Chang K'un-ti's home that runs from July 31 to October 2, 1917. This slender diary is very rich in content. That summer he had returned home during vacation and studied at a temple. The diary breaks down roughly into the following four categories:

1. Writings that he was fond of copied in their entirety. Among these were articles such as T'an Ssu-t'ung's Jen hsüeh and "Chuang Tzu," [critical] historical commentaries by Wang Fu-chih, and articles written by Ch'en Tu-hsiu that appeared in New Youth. Also, there were [his own] occasional critical comments. For example, he criticized Jen hsüeh for advocating religion [as a method] by which to cajole the people, believing that religion was the greatest unequal, restraining, and controlling shackle in the world.

2. Notes on the Ta-Hua chai tu shu lu taken from lectures by Yang Ch'ang-chi during his frequent visits to the "Pan-ts'ang yang yü" [Yang's home] to receive instruction.

3. Personal insights from his study and various [other] thoughts. For example, the entry of August 6 reads:

Whenever any matter comes up, we must be clear on our own position and the position of the people on the opposite side. Mencius said, "The feeling of right and wrong is the beginning of knowledge." Isn't the cultivation of a true power to discriminate between right and wrong something to which we today should devote our attention even more?

August 8: Hard work is a substitute for talent. Talent is not dependable; hard work is. All human achievements have come from arduous work.

August 12: We should dispense with all learning [that serves to] "fish for praise and reputation" or curries favor with the public. We [should] devote full effort to seeking the learning that is advantageous to oneself, beneficial to the nation and to all of mankind.

September 12: Whenever I read the diary of a friend it makes me feel ashamed and embarrassed. Others change with every passing day, and their virtue and learning improve as steam rises from boiling water. Yet for myself I see no progress, and there seems to be even some regression. Jar yourself to your bones, rouse your ambition, sweep away all evil influences, strive on, call out loudly without fear, call out loudly and valiantly advance and step into the vanguard!

4. A concern with the current situation and the life of the people. There are six days of entries that criticize the Tuan Ch'i-jui government's declaration of war on Germany and that are also concerned with the domestic affairs of Chang Hsün and Fu P'i. On August 7 he wrote:

In recent days the water has been rising daily and the number of broken dikes in various hsien is very large.... The peasants work hard all year long and look forward to this time of the year. Now, because of these cruel natural disasters, they have worked the entire year in vain. Mothers scream and their children wail — it is hard for [human] feelings to bear. I wonder whether the gentlemen* of the government think of this? Not only do they put the burden of taxes on the people one day, but they "solicit contributions" from them the next.

---

* Lit. "Dukes" (kung), here meant sarcastically. — Tr.

On the ninth he wrote: "When I meet some peasants there is not one among them who is not haggard from grief and anxiety. I cannot but be saddened by all this." On the tenth he wrote again: "After dinner Mr. Hsiung came over and we had a long, leisurely talk. We thought mostly about the peasants."

The rest of his entries deal with the life of "roaming and talking of principles" with Comrades Ts'ai Ho-sen, Mao Tse-tung, and the others mentioned above. They also deal with how he trained his body, "battled with the wind and rain for a half hour or so," "slept out in the backyard," etc.

As we read this very slender diary, a youth of twenty-four years who was deeply worried about his country and about the times, who passionately loved the people, who was hardworking and disciplined, and who sought after truth seems to appear fleetingly before our eyes, as though we could hear his voice and see him standing there.

Comrade Ch'en Ch'ang's courtesy name was Ch'en Chang-fu. He was born in 1894 in Liu-yang, Hunan. He was also one of the organizers of the New People's Study Society and further, under the leadership of Comrade Mao Tse-tung, participated at the very beginning in the work of founding the Party cells in the Hunan area. When he was in primary school he used to like to stand next to the window and, as if there were no one around, practice giving speeches. Thus among all the activities he engaged in while studying at First Normal, what has left the deepest impression on people's recollections is his talent for public speaking. He had a loud and clear voice and was good at cogent argumentation. He was once head of the Student Society's debating department.* Besides this, his diligence, his strict and careful life and work style, etc., were like those of his friends. When Mao returned to Hunan in 1920 to take up the directorship of First Normal Attached Primary School, Ch'en Ch'ang also taught there. When Mao began to lead the Hunan labor movement, Ch'en was one of the primary participants. During the First Revolutionary Civil War, the Party sent him to work at Shui-k'ou-shan [80] as head of the labor union. In 1930, on his way from Shanghai to western Hunan to work in the ranks of Ho Lung, he was arrested in Feng hsien. After severe torture, Ch'en Ch'ang still refused to say a single word. Just before he was executed in Changsha he even wrote a stirring and moving speech.

Comrade Ho Shu-heng was a Hunan representative who partici-

---

* According to earlier information, there was no "debating department" (hsiung-pien pu), only a public speaking department (yen-chiang pu). Cf. p. 54. — Tr.

pated with Comrade Mao Tse-tung in the First Congress of the Chinese Communist Party. He was from Ning-hsiang, Hunan. With his father he had studied the old learning at home since childhood, on the one hand, and had spent a life of labor "carrying water and splitting firewood," on the other. At the age of eighteen he took and passed the examination to become a hsiu-ts'ai.* Already at this time he was deeply anti-Ch'ing in his revolutionary thinking. There is still preserved at his home an "eight-legged essay" † that he wrote at the time, but this eight-legged essay is one filled with defiant ideas. The title of the essay was "Han" [Drought]. It began with the following words:

> The world today is a fierce and cruel world. Its myriad inhabitants are as burned and set afire. Is this not worse than the cruelty of the drought demon? Thus amidst this invisible drought, the people lament their persecution and deprivation. Perhaps the shepherds of the people are unaware that the poisonous grass is fuming.... What crimes have the people committed that they suffer such cruel calamity that cannot be ended?

When Comrade Ho Shu-heng was studying at the Yün-shan Academy in his own hsien, he was most friendly with Comrades Chiang Meng-chou, Wang Ling-po, [81] and Hsieh Chüeh-tsai. Later, the four of them taught together at Yün-shan Primary School. In order to established a new academic atmosphere, they ran a Student Association and championed practical writing and the study of sociology and natural science. As a result, they met the opposition of conservative elements, and a struggle between the new and old learning advocates in Ning-hsiang broke out. The conservatives conspired with the local evil gentry and attacked them as "rebels." ‡ In 1912 Ho Shu-heng passed the examination and entered First Normal's department of training. When he graduated two years later, he taught at

---

* This was the lowest rung of the three-tiered civil service examination system. The examination for this degree was held at the district (hsien) level and the degree carried a number of privileges. — Tr.

† A highly formalistic structure dating from the Ming dynasty in 1487 when it was prescribed for all civil service examinations. — Tr.

‡ Lit. "great perversion and impiety," a category of crime dating from the Han dynasty (B.C. 206-221 A.D.) now generally meaning "rebel" or "traitor." — Tr.

T'an Ssu-t'ung, whose influence on Mao is underscored several times by Li Jui, turned this expression inside out and brandished it as a battle cry of revolt by those who refused to accept the servitudes of the old Confucian morality, and Mao followed his example in 1919. See S. Schram, "From the 'Great Union of the Popular Masses' to the 'Great Alliance,'" The China Quarterly, No. 49 (January-March 1972), p. 97. [S.R.S.].

Ch'u-i Primary School in Changsha. When Comrade Mao Tse-tung organized the New People's Study Society, Ho Shu-heng was the oldest of all the members. He was a short and powerful man who was honest and enthusiastic in dealing with other people and who was most willing to put out effort and most able to endure hard work. Introducing Mao to Comrade Hsieh Chüeh-tsai, he told of "how outstanding a person Mao Jun-chih was. Jun-chih says I 'can't plan things but can make decisions.' How right this is."

Shu-heng was very modest about his ability as a planner, so he was very able to accept humbly the opinions of others. But he could also be decisive and independent. Every time a dangerous situation was at hand and people were shaken and indecisive, he was able to travel his own road courageously, oblivious of other people's opposition or approval, and stand out in front of everybody. [82]

Mao would often say:

Old Shu can handle the overall situation. He is not a man for learning, but a doer.... "Ho the Mustache" was an ox, he was a heap of feeling.... [83] His passionate emotions shot out in every direction. Whomever was hit was stirred to action. This is really how Comrade Shu-heng was. His emotions were controlled by a high sense of justice. [84]

Comrade Ho Shu-heng was a direct participant in, and director of, the early revolutionary activities of Comrade Mao Tse-tung in Hunan, especially in the New Culture movement and the establishment of the Party. After the failure of the First Revolutionary Civil War, the Party sent him to the Soviet Union to study. The letters he wrote home from the Soviet Union are filled with a fearless, heroic quality, enjoining his family: "Don't beg for pity and charity from people.... Do things that are beneficial for human life.... In living, we must really live — not lead a life worse than death."

Following the start of the Red Army's Long March in 1934, Comrade Ho Shu-heng together with Ch'ü Ch'iu-pai, Teng Tzu-hui, and other comrades pulled out of the Soviet area in February 1935. They were then surrounded by the enemy. Ho was already an old man of over sixty and could no longer walk with ease. Near Shui-k'ou in Ch'ang-t'ing, Fukien, he fell down a cliff and was martyred!

Comrade Lo Hsüeh-tsan was from Chu-chou, Hsiang-t'an. He was in the same class as Comrade Mao Tse-tung at First Normal. He was short of stature and slow of speech. His sincere and sure work style and his conscientious attitude toward his studies also won him the love and respect of all his fellow students. His family still has a letter he wrote home at the end of 1918 from Peking and a postcard written to him by Mao before he went to Peking. This was the time when Mao Tse-tung was organizing the Diligent Work and Frugal Study movement. On the basis of his school experience, it was fitting that Lo engage in educational work; thus Mao counseled him that it wasn't absolutely necessary to go to France. The postcard reads [in part]:

It would not be as beneficial as engaging in educational work. First, this is your characteristic strong point. Second, you would be able to do research in areas that correspond closely with your nature, such as language and literature. Third, your educational talent would serve as a support for Society affairs (note: this refers to affairs of the New People's Study Society).

Thus, when he was attending the preparatory classes for the Diligent Work and Frugal Study expedition to France, he studied education, and later when he went to France, he engaged in educational work among the Chinese workers there. When he was in Peking, he lived with Comrade Mao Tse-tung and eight other schoolmates from Hunan who were going to France. He was also deported back to China by the French government with Comrade Ts'ai Ho-sen and the others.

After 1921, when Mao Tse-tung was leading the labor movement in Hunan, Lo Hsüeh-tsan was one of his competent assistants. He organized the very first rickshaw workers' strike in Changsha. Right down to the First Revolutionary Civil War, he was still in Changsha working in the labor movement. According to reports, he was martyred in 1930 while working in Chekiang.

During his years of study at First Normal, Comrade Mao Tse-tung had a close rapport with these consentient friends. Except for Comrade Ts'ai Ho-sen, who after two years transferred to Senior Normal School, these friends, Comrades Ho Shu-heng, Ch'en Chang, and others, became teachers in Ch'u-i Primary School and First Normal Attached Primary School after graduation in 1914, where Mao continued to keep in very close contact with them. They regularly met either at Ts'ai's home at Yüeh-lu-shan or at Ch'u-i Primary School in the city. Increasingly they felt that China's situation was deteriorating and that they had to find a way out. But first they themselves had to go and search, search for the Truth that would save China. They often quoted the credo of Ku Yen-wu that "in the rise and fall of the empire [t'ien hsia], every common man has a responsibility" and they solemnly "considered the universe as one's own responsibility."* When they corresponded, they always

_____

* A famous quote from Fan Chung-yen (989-1052). — Tr.

encouraged each other, jokingly referring to each other as "pillars and beams of talent."* To hasten toward such a goal, Mao Tse-tung felt that under no circumstances could they depend on just one person or on a few people and dawdle about. Before anything could be achieved, a large group of determined and resolute people who shared a common purpose had to be created. Thus he realized that it was far from adequate merely to organize those within the school and a small number of other determined youths. The organization should be large and powerful and had to be developed beyond the school. In the fall of 1915 he sent out his famous "Erh-shih-pa hua sheng-cheng yu ch'i shih" [Notice in Search of Friends by Mr. Twenty-eight Strokes] (the three characters Mao, Tse, and Tung that constitute Mao's name are written with a total of twenty-eight strokes). The notice was about two or three hundred characters long and, according to Mao's own recollection, the principal substance concerned "...inviting young men interested in patriotic work to make a contact with me. I specified youths who were hardened and determined and ready to make sacrifices for their country" [Snow, Red Star, p. 146]. Some people remember that the very last line of the notice ended with a quotation from the Shih-ching [Book of Songs:] "Ying goes [the birds'] cry in search of their companion's voice" [Pt. II, Bk. I, Ode V. 1, Fa Mu]. Comrade Mao Tse-tung himself stenciled and reproduced the notice, sending it out to major schools in Changsha. On the envelope was written: "Please post where everyone can see." At the time, Changsha was still a rather isolated and backward place in the interior, and this new undertaking was naturally not easily understood by the average person. Thus Mao received replies from only five or six people. Comrade Li Li-san, who was then studying at Ch'ang-chün United Middle School (now Changsha Municipal First Middle School) in Changsha was one of those who returned a letter, but no deep relationship developed at the time. When this letter was first received by Provincial Women's Normal School, there was some misunderstanding. It wasn't until later, after they had inquired at First Normal via the mailing address (c/o Ch'en Ch'ang of First Normal Attached Primary School), that the whole situation was cleared up. There was one person who had seen the notice posted in his school's registration office and who had then written a letter to Comrade Mao Tse-tung expressing a desire to strike up a friendship. Thereupon he received an answer: "[Your letter was like] the sound of

---

* A phrase from the Classics applied to able ministers of state. — Tr.

footsteps in a deserted valley; at the sound of your feet my face shone with joy," and a date was set to meet on Sunday at the Ting-wang t'ai Library. When they met, not a word of formal greeting was exchanged; Mao started right out by asking what books he had read recently and what had he written lately. Later they became very close and often exchanged their study notes. Mao always said that one should attend well to his studies and not seek after momentary wealth and honors. One should not think about becoming an official and getting rich. One must be a person with ideals, one must "put first one's concerns for the world and put last one's pleasures in it."* After this he was often asked to come walking on Sundays and sometimes also participated in group discussions. After the establishment of the New People's Study Society, this friend who had answered Mao's notice joined the Society and became one of the earliest members.

After almost a year of ferment, during which time Comrade Mao Tse-tung and his best friends constantly exchanged ideas on what they had learned from their study and talked about everyone's future and the future of society and the nation, they felt that the times had become critical, that the need for learning had become urgent, and therefore felt very deeply the need to create an organization. Recalling this situation Mao has said, "I built up a wide correspondence with many students and friends in other towns and cities. Gradually I began to realize the necessity for a more closely knit organization. In 1917, with some other friends, I helped to found the Hsin Min Hsüeh Hui" [Snow, Red Star, p. 147]. Before and after the May Fourth period, the majority of progressive, young intellectuals from Peking, Shanghai, Tientsin, Hankou and Hangchou all had some kind of spontaneous, progressive organization. For example, there was the "Altruism Society" [Li ch'ün she], organized by Yün Tai-ying and other comrades in Wuhan, and the "Awareness Society" [Chüeh-wu she], organized by Chou En-lai and other comrades in Tientsin. The great majority of these societies, in greater or lesser degree, were organized under the influence of New Youth. The New People's Study Society was the earliest example of this kind of organization, and it was the one that played the biggest role.

The formal establishment of the New People's Study Society took place the next year. On April 18, 1918, a Sunday, the meeting that established the New People's Study Society was held in the city of Ying-wan at Yüeh-lu-shan in Changsha [hsien] at the home of Com-

---

* Saying of Fan Chung-yen (989-1052). — Tr.

rade Ts'ai Ho-sen. (This house was originally built like a "grave hut"* and no longer exists. Traces, however, can still be found.) Thirteen people attended the meeting that day. Besides Comrade Mao Tse-tung, there were Comrades Ts'ai Ho-sen, Ho Shu-heng, Ch'en Ch'ang, Chang K'un-ti, and Lo Hsüeh-tsan. The meeting passed a set of bylaws that had been drafted by Mao, the main idea of which was that members should have high aspirations and work for their country and people [min tsu]. New members of the Society had to be introduced by a Society member and had to be endorsed by the advisory council. In the bylaws there were also several pro- hibitions dealing with the life style of the members. Everyone's first choice for general secretary [tsung kan shih] of the advisory council was Comrade Mao Tse-tung. He humbly declined but was fi- nally selected as vice secretary. Among the five secretaries there were Comrades Ts'ai Ho-sen and Ch'en Ch'ang. And on this day the first dues were paid. Finally, Mao said that they should continue to de- velop the membership of the Society, that only by having a large number of people would they have any great strength. The two char- acters "new" and "people" had a meaning taken from the phrase in the Ta hsüeh [Great Learning], [85] "rests in renewing the people," and the phrase that occurs in the "T'ang Hao" [86] of the Shu-ching [Book of History], "make new people." Liang Ch'i-ch'ao had also championed the "principle of renewing the people," advocating that we "supply that which is originally deficient and then renew, thereby creating a new Chinese morality, a new Chinese way of thinking and a new Chinese spirit." The two characters "new" and "people," then, suggested a kind of progressive and revolutionary meaning.

By the time of the May Fourth movement, the number of Society members had grown to seventy or eighty. The membership require- ments were quite strict. People who were poor in their scholarship or personal character, or who had no aspirations, could not join the Society. The vast majority of the members consisted of the most outstanding students of First Normal. In addition to these, there were some progressive teachers who taught at some of the primary schools in Changsha and also some faculty members and students from Chou-nan Girls' School and others, such as Hsiang Ching-yü [87] and Ts'ai Ch'ang. For the Society to include in its membership such a group of progressive and resolute female comrades was something other societies at the time were unable to match. Later, Hsia Hsi, Kuo Liang and other comrades joined the Society in succession.

---

* Usually a thatched hut in which one lives next to the grave of a parent. — Tr.

The Society generally held a meeting every week or two, and either academic problems or problems concerning current national affairs were studied. There were also reports on study and work plans and a session of mutual criticism and expression of opinions. Sometimes the discussion of a problem would last for as long as a week. Most of the time, Comrade Mao Tse-tung would chair the meeting, and at the end it was he who would conclude the discussion. At the time, everyone was dissatisfied with all things that were old, and each person was filled with a spirit of self-improvement and of self-development, as well as with an ambition to remold society and remold the world.

By no means was Comrade Mao Tse-tung satisfied with this organization alone. He felt that it was far from enough merely to handle one undertaking and he continually thought about developing outward, beyond educational circles, beyond the province, beyond the nation. He often remarked at the time that he wanted to "go outside" to do research, and seek the "new knowledge" the world had to offer. So later, when the opportunity arose to go to France as a part of the Diligent Work and Frugal Study program, he energetically directed the project. A great many members of the New People's Study Society went to France between 1919 and 1920.

Because Society members infrequently came together as a group, a monthly correspondence system was set up for the members who were abroad. In 1919, after Comrades Ts'ai Ho-sen, Chang K'un-ti, and Lo Hsüeh-tsan had gone to France, Comrade Mao Tse-tung often printed up and sent out for study the correspondence of the Society members as well as the questions that they had brought up for discussion. Altogether, three collections of correspondence came out, all edited by Mao.

The New People's Study Society had no concrete political platform or strict discipline, but as time went on ideological differences gradually emerged during the discussion and solution of problems. Before its dissolution, Society membership could be divided into the following three types: (1) the majority, who belonged to a revolutionary faction that repudiated the status quo, (2) a reform faction that acknowledged the status quo, (3) middle-of-the-roaders without any definite ideas. Around 1921, after Mao Tse-tung had formally begun to found the Communist Party in Hunan, the New People's Study Society gradually brought its activities to a halt. Most of the Society's revolutionaries became the earliest and most important mainstays of the Chinese Communist Party. In the midst of China's violent social reformation there was a small number of the Society's members who, from an inclination toward statism and other ideologies, finally became murderers for the reactionary Kuomintang party and suppressed the young people. There were also those who went completely over to the Kuomintang government to "become officials and enrich themselves."

## VIII. "NOT A PENNY IN HIS POCKET, A CONCERN FOR ALL THE WORLD"

Owing to the limitations of the period, there was no way that Comrade Mao Tse-tung could have access to Marxism-Leninism when he studied at First Normal. All he could do at this time was to absorb critically the nourishment he needed by "throwing away the dross and retaining the essence" from old European democracy, utopian socialism, dualistic philosophy, the democratic and scientific spirit championed by the magazine New Youth, and the outstanding legacy of China's national culture and her historical personages. But no matter what the circumstances were, as far as his political point of view was concerned, he had already become "definitely antimilitarist and anti-imperialist." [88] He already had the great ambition to remold society and establish a new country. He regularly talked a great deal about this aspiration and ambition with his friends, and it is recorded very often in his own diary, in his study notes, and in his correspondence with friends. It was especially after the establishment of the New People's Study Society that he studied even more systematically the great affairs of mankind and of the nation. Poking fun at him, but yet with full respect, this is how his friends described him: "Not a penny in his pocket, a concern for all the world." This appraisal was extremely accurate.

The emergency that confronted the Chinese people and Chinese nation, the tragedy that befell the people of Hunan, suffering long years in the prison of the northern warlords, made every day for the young Mao Tse-tung one of discontent, and he felt the burden on his own shoulders daily getting heavier.

As everyone knows, the five and one-half years between the spring of 1913 and the summer of 1918 during which Comrade Mao Tse-tung was studying at First Normal were the very eve of the May Fourth movement. It was a period when imperialist aggression intensified daily, when the brutal violence and internal dissension of the warlords were becoming increasingly more serious, and when the struggle between the new and old ideologies was just reaching a high tide.

By this time the imperialist nations, in accordance with the "spheres of influence" that they had carved up, had already stuck their rotten paws into every corner of China. Their naval and commercial ships were on the inner rivers, and their leased territories [89] and military troops were in the important cities. The national railroads, the customs, the important mines, and even the post office were all controlled by them. Their stores, factories, banks, and schools were spread out over the cities and the countryside. Their goods flooded in, and their adventurers and ne'er-do-wells who had come to China to get rich enjoyed the protection of "extraterritoriality." [90] Japanese imperialism took advantage of the opportunity afforded by World War I, when the other imperialist countries had no time to concern themselves with the East, to step up its all-out military, political, and economic aggression against China, planning to convert China into its own private colony.

The warlords of the northern and southern cliques thus "pulled the wolf into the house," each colluding with one or two imperialist countries to firmly establish himself. Thus China was at war year after year, suffered the ravages of the military year after year, and was beset with internal disorder that endlessly worsened.

The people of the whole country were truly living in misery and destitution. "Facts of every description prove that it is capitalist imperialism, and the feudal forces of the warlords and bureaucrats, that inflict the most misery upon the Chinese people (whether bourgeoisie, workers, or peasants)." [91]

This situation was at its worst in the province of Hunan.

Anchored in Changsha's Hsiang River were warships flying the "sun flag" [Japan], the "checkered flag" [U.S.], and the "rice-character flag" [Great Britain].* On the bank of the river were the great Western-style buildings of the foreign companies: the Sino-Japanese Steamship Co., Butterfield and Swire (British), Jardine, Matheson & Co. (British). Japanese steamship companies, banks, factories, and stores in Changsha already numbered no less than twenty or thirty. The ores of nationally famous Hsi-k'uang-shan [92] and Shui-k'ou-shan were controlled by foreign businesses. After World War I the market for metallic ore experienced a sudden and violent drop, and a large number of workers connected with the mining industry lost their jobs.

_____

* The character for rice, mi, resembles the striping of the British flag. — Tr.

The Hunan of these years was successively under the rule of the Peiyang warlords T'ang Hsiang-ming, Fu Liang-tso, and Chang Ching-yao, and it became the arena of the long seesaw battles between the northern and southern warlords. Natural disasters and the ravages wrought by bandits and soldiers followed each other year after year without end. The amount of injury and suffering the people experienced was incredible. In 1915 four rivers, the Hsiang, the Tzu, the Yüan, and the Li, overflowed their banks at the same time, creating a disaster for thirty-four hsien in the province; there were several million victims. Later on, during the three years between 1916 and 1918, the hsien bordering the lake and the Changsha district suffered incessantly from minor and major floods or from breakages in the dams and dikes. Bandits harassed the entire province, and every month there were reports of disasters in the hsien; sometimes no more than three or five hsien were involved, other times as many as nineteen or twenty were affected. In western and southern Hunan the bandits often attacked and occupied the hsien capitals. In important areas such as Changsha, Hsiang-t'an, I-yang, Ning-hsia, and Heng-yang there were also numerous bandit alarms. But the most grievous destruction of life suffered by the people still came from the ravages of the military. This was especially true during 1917-18 when Chang Ching-yao entered Hunan and a great battle took place between the north and south; the ravages of the troops reached unprecedented heights of savage cruelty. The papers were filled with the following kinds of reports:

Owing to the fighting between the north and south or to their passage and the accompanying lecherous atrocities and plunder, nine out of ten homes in Pao-ch'ing, Changsha, Li-ling, Chu-chou, Ch'ang-te, and Hsin-hua stand empty. The shop-fronts of the wealthy have also been looted so that business has stagnated. In the countryside, the price of grain and rice has risen and the victims of hunger are in a state of panic and the bandits are swarming like bees; added to this are the annual floods — the misery of the people has reached an extremity. There is for example, Wan-ch'ou village in Changsha hsien which, owing to the passage of troops that way, suffered door-to-door plundering and was robbed clean.

Even the street sweepers of Changsha were robbed. The townspeople were constantly harassed by the troops.

The Changsha city General Chamber of Commerce made an investigation of the losses sustained in the "military disaster": these included

...losses stemming from the furnishing to the troops of food, utensils, rewards, and reduced commodity prices on unpaid purchases, losses from small scale trade in rice and salt and those sustained in cashing southern currency, plus loans — altogether reaching 150,000 silver dollars.

The number of homes burned and looted by troops in the four towns of Li-ling hsien was close to ten thousand. All that is left are the temples and six hundred ruined homes.

Ch'ang-te was hit by both floods and military disasters. When the north and south began engaging their troops, the relief funds stopped. When the battle was in full swing, one force would no sooner leave than the other would come, and the bandits swarmed like bees. After the sudden swelling of the Yüan and Li rivers, every village was completely inundated and the ripe grain was given to the flooding current.

Businesses in Hsin-hua have closed down. All commodities have soared in price. Nine out of ten stores are empty. The poor and lower classes eat gruel with vegetable ends, but even so it is difficult for them to provide for themselves. The handicraftsmen cannot exist by their hired work. Ten li outside the hsien capital bandits are appearing and disappearing, recklessly plundering or taking prisoners, holding them for ransom, raping women, and burning down cottages. To the survivors of the military ravages add starvation and add disease — this is certainly an uncommon disaster the likes of which the people have not seen in several hundred years. [93]

The discipline among Chang Ching-yao's troops (the north) was particularly bad. There was a popular ballad going around then:

Floury head, floury head (meaning the northern troops who were accus-
                    tomed to eating flour products, [i.e., noodles])*
Has eaten my duck and eaten my goose,
And now my old grandmother he wants to rape!

All these things Comrade Mao Tse-tung personally saw and experienced. The clash of imperialism and the feudal warlords with the whole population, the clashes among the warlords themselves, the clash between the landowners and the peasants, the clash between the workers and the capitalists, the clash between the diehard conservatives and the progressive modernizers — all of this was reflected into the mind of the young Mao Tse-tung. Summing up the situation at the time, he said: "Day by day, conditions in the country got worse, and life was made impossible." [94]

Most of the people living in this society, including the majority of teachers and students at First Normal, could see no ray of light or hope because all around them was a curtain of darkness: "The entire province is suffering and in misery; there is not a piece of untouched land." Thus pessimism ran very deep. "China is about to perish; China is about to perish! Society has collapsed; people

---

* Southerners eat rice products. — Tr.

have lost all hope." Such sentiments could be heard everywhere.

But Mao Tse-tung and his friends were not like this at all. They were full of confidence and had a sense of responsibility about China's future. The topic of their serious day-to-day conversations was how to seek actively after the principle by which China would be saved. Although at the time they were as yet unable to have the Marxist-Leninist viewpoint or method, they were like all great prophets, always in unremitting pursuit of truth and glory. For example, "the great spirit of Russia" in the nineteenth century, Tolstoy, [95] inspired them for a time by his dreams of universal love and peace. In Chang K'un-ti's diary for the dates between August and October there are several places that record Mao's discussions on this.

On September 22, after Comrades Chang K'un-ti and Mao Tse-tung had gone swimming in the Hsiang River, they went together to the home of Comrade Ts'ai Ho-sen at Yüeh-lu-shan. Below is the entry for the twenty-third:

It was approaching dusk and we decided to stay there [at Ts'ai's home] overnight. Our conversation went on for quite a while. Mao Jun-chih said: "At the present time our people's thought [kuo-min ssu-hsiang] is narrow. How can China have a great revolutionary in philosophy and ethics like Russia's Tolstoy who would develop new thought by washing away all the old thought?" I heartily concur with his sentiments. The Chinese people are downcast, unenlightened, ignorant of themselves, and hostile to foreign ideas; it has all become a habit with them. How could there ever be anyone like Russia's Tolstoy to come along and break through the net of old ideas, develop his ideal world, carry it out in deeds, write about it in books, always with truth as his goal, looking only at truth and not for a second looking to the side. T'an Ssu-tung in the past and Ch'en Tu-hsiu today are men of great vitality. Truly, one cannot compare the common scholars of today with them. Mr. Mao also called for a revolution of the family system and of the relationships between teacher and student. What was meant by revolution was not a confrontation of arms, but the elimination of the old and the establishment of the new.

With regard to the political viewpoint that in remolding society and in remolding China it was necessary to use revolutionary means, Mao was completely correct.

In Chapter III, "Harm and Evil," of the book A Study of Ethics mentioned above, Comrade Mao Tse-tung made the following notations on the section "On Life and Death":

I once worried that our China would soon perish, but now I know this is not so. I have no doubt about setting up a new form of government, changing the national character, or improving society. But how to effectuate this change is the problem. My idea is that we must reconstruct, such that new things will come into being through destruction and will have a new being just like a baby is born from its mother's womb. It is so with the nation, with the people, and with mankind. Throughout the centuries people have raised great revolutions, constantly cleansing the old and renewing it. These are all instances of the great [cycle of] change: life/death, creation/destruction.

In a long letter to a scholar in Peking written in August 1917, Mao Tse-tung raised the fundamental question of why the world was in such confusion and what principles were to be followed to save it. He believed that one had to start from the fundamental — a search into the truths of the universe, the remolding of philosophy, and the remolding of the thought of old China. By this time, Mao Tse-tung had already awakened to the fact that old Western bourgeois democracy was incapable of solving the problem, and so he pointed out that while Eastern thought certainly failed to correspond with everyday reality, Western thought was not necessarily perfect either. Western ideologies and Eastern ideologies had both to be remolded at the same time. In order to emphasize the importance of the study and dissemination of philosophy, the letter also made a critique of the popular theory of "setting up one's ambition" [li-chih]. He maintained that in setting up one's ambition, one must first study philosophy and ethics and then make the truths derived from this study the touchstone of one's actions. Only if one swears not to stop until one has reached one's goal can we call this having ambition. If one spends ten years and fails to obtain truth, this is ten years without ambition. If one spends one's entire life and has not obtained truth, this is a lifetime without ambition. He also believed that in pursuing studies one had to do deep research and make constant progress. By no means could one lightly discuss things and make wild judgments. In order to pursue truth, one had to prepare the present self to do battle with the self of yesterday, and the future self to do battle with the self of today. Only by devoting a great deal of time to philosophy could one avoid the danger of following blindly the opinions of others; only in this way could one have one's own genuine opinion. Mao Tse-tung greatly lamented the situation at that time in which the average youth would not listen to truth, would not respond to encouragement, and did not ask the great questions of life and death but only concerned himself with the mundane struggle of existence.

What is especially worthy of note is that Comrade Mao Tse-tung and his friends possessed a thoroughly anti-imperialist and anti-feudal spirit and ardently sought after the new foreign ideologies, on the one hand, but they attached great importance to China's historical legacy and by no means blindly worshiped Western culture, on the other. Toward the old things of China and the new things of the foreign countries they fully adopted the critical attitude of historical materialism. They "did away with the dross and retained the essence," and "in considering the national situation gave no prejudice to either side." On this crucial question they were in complete disagreement with the rather widespread and erroneous view taken by some progressive people during the May Fourth period. This view was a fundamental repudiation of the legacy of the Chinese people and a preoccupation with the backward aspects of feudalism. They did not realize that the early production and culture of China's feudal society had reached a very high level, that along with the violent social changes and developments of each and every epoch, history has left us a great many precious spiritual riches. Talking about the May Fourth period later, Mao pointed out this deficiency:

Many of the leaders lacked the critical spirit of Marxism, and the method they used was generally that of the bourgeoisie, that is, the formalist method. They were quite right in opposing the old stereotype and the old dogma and in advocating science and democracy. But in dealing with current conditions, with history, and with things foreign, they lacked the critical spirit of historical materialism and regarded what was bad as absolutely and wholly bad and what was good as absolutely and wholly good. This formalist approach to problems affected the subsequent course of the movement. [96]

The areas in which there was a clear difference between the young Mao Tse-tung and the average revolutionary who came from an intellectual background were that Mao started from the very beginning, that he attached great importance to contact with the working and peasant masses, and that he sought opportunities to draw near to them to understand their situation and humbly and sincerely work for them. For example, during his summer vacation in 1916, Mao made use of the old-fashioned "travel study" [97] technique; he set out from Changsha to Ning-hsiang, passed by I-yang, and went through the peasant communities of every hsien in central and western Hunan. The purpose of this was to deeply understand the real state of affairs in each of these places relative to its society, economy, culture, and to the life of the peasants. He was the son of a Chinese peasant and had grown up from early childhood in a farming village. He had a deep affection for the peasants. Having seen for himself the tragic suffering of the peasants caused by both

natural and human disasters and the severe oppression of the landlords, how could he remain calm? How could he bury his head in
the library? This "travel study" tour became a detailed diary of
all that Mao had seen and thought along the route. When he returned
his friends all competed with each other to read it. Out of this experience also came several dispatches written for the Hunan Popular Gazette [ Hu-nan t'ung-su pao] (this paper has not yet been located).

After the Student Society started the night school, Comrade Mao
Tse-tung got the opportunity to draw near to the industrial workers
and was able to get an understanding of their living conditions and
also the causes of labor strikes. Between 1916 and 1918, workers
in the handicraft industries of Changsha one after the other demanded raises in their compensation because the cost of living had
risen too high. Primitive strike struggles occurred among such
groups as the incense makers (who made items catering to superstition), dye workers, sawyers [chü kung], stevedores (dock workers) and the workers in the Hsiang-t'an iron industry. It was especially the incident in April 1917 at Shui-k'ou-shan, when over three
thousand miners went on a general strike with a demand for a raise
in bonuses and one worker was killed, that had the biggest influence
on society. The Changsha press at the time carried quite detailed
and complete stories of this kind of thing. For Mao Tse-tung, a
person already possessed of some elementary socialist thinking,
these facts were naturally the cause of some further deep thought
on the problems of Chinese society.

With regard to how Comrade Mao Tse-tung sought after the ways
and means of solving China's problems when he was at First Normal,
this is what Comrade Hsü T'e-li once said in recalling the situation:

When Comrade Mao Tse-tung was studying at school — this was just at the time
of World War I — democratic revolutionary thought permeated the school. He
turned his attention toward the study of the reasons for the failure of the 1911
Revolution, his conclusion being that it was the fact that the Chinese intelligentsia had separated itself from the masses. For any revolution to succeed, the
intellectual leaders of the revolution must establish intimate links with the masses
of people within the country. Because he saw this point, when World War I had
just ended and I invited him to go with me to study abroad in France, he declined
my invitation. He preferred to advance his knowledge of his own country. [98]

In June 1918, Comrade Mao Tse-tung graduated from First Normal. He and some friends stayed at the "Hunan University Preparatory Office" located at Yüeh-lu-shan (i.e., the Pan-tzu Library
of Yüeh-lu Academy). They were all very poor. While they ate one
meal they would be worrying about the next. They ate boiled rice

mixed with lima beans. Barefoot or in straw sandals they went up the mountain to fetch firewood and went a great distance to get water. On the one hand they studied their books, and on the other they made plans for the future. This kind of work-study life gave everyone an added spiritual lift. Sometimes they would go for pleasure to the Ai-wan Pavilion, the Yün-lu Palace, or Emperor Yü's gravestone, which were all on the mountain. Sometimes they would go walking in Ying-wan city or on Shui-lu Shoal. Sometimes they would watch the rose hues of dusk, sometimes gaze at the bright moon. But by no means did they relax their state of mind. The future of each person and the great matters of the world awaited solution. Where would each go? Where would Hunan go? Where would China go? What methods were to be used to solve these numerous and complicated problems? Comrade Mao Tse-tung was the most disturbed. The double scroll [tui lien]* that hung inside the Yün-lu Palace read:

> From every side cloud-covered mountains strike the eye
> The grief and joy of ten thousand homes comes to mind.

It was an apt description of the way he felt. The deep penetration of imperialist power, the tyranny of the warlords, the benighted cruelty of Chang Ching-yao, the anxiety of the young people, the suffering of the great mass of workers and peasants — this whole series of problems constantly whirled around in his head. He had a burning desire to find the road that led to the thorough solution of China's problems and planned to go to the cradle of revolutionary thought — Peking.

In his poem "Changsha" how movingly Comrade Mao Tse-tung described their noble fury at the dark state of affairs in China and their optimistic self-confidence in saving the nation and the people, the picture of their lives then, and each person's ambition!

> I stood alone in the cold autumn
> As the Hsiang River flowed northward
> Toward the point of Orange Islet.
>
> I gazed upon ten thousand mountains
> Whose endless layers of forest had covered
> And dyed them red.
>
> The broad, expansive river
> Was like translucent jade, and
> A hundred boats were there,
> Contending with the current.

---

* On each scroll one stanza is written. — Tr.

Eagles strove toward the blue skies, the
Fish roamed in shallow water, and
All the creatures fought for freedom
In the frosty air.

The immensity of it all depressed me, and
I asked, "Who decides success and failure
In this great, vast world of ours?"

Hundreds of companions I had brought
With me here.
I remember those days gone by,
Those lofty months and years.

We were all young students then,
Just in the flower of youth; and
With the scholar's spirit
We signaled the moral Way.*

Pointing to the rivers and mountains,
We wrote our words in anger —
Ten thousand marquis,† and all were dung.

Do you remember when we struck the
Water in midstream
And the waves checked our flying boat?

Comrade Mao Tse-tung and Comrade Ts'ai Ho-sen called the members of the New People's Study Society together for a meeting that lasted several days to discuss their futures. At this time Mr. Yang Ch'ang-chi had already gone to Peking University to take up a teaching position and had written a letter to Mao telling them of the news that some people had started a movement to go to France under a Diligent Work and Frugal Study program and also told him about the many new things that were happening in Peking. Seeing the dark situation in Hunan, Mao Tse-tung strenuously advocated that a group of people, on the basis of need and possibility, first leave Hunan and go to Peking and such places to make connection with outside revolutionary forces there, to strengthen themselves and work for the opportunity to join the Diligent Work and Frugal Study in France program, and to understand the real facts of the Russian and European revolutions. Everyone agreed with Mao's opinion. And so Comrade Mao Tse-tung, together with Comrade Ts'ai Ho-sen and Mr. Yang Ch'ang-chi, initiated and organized the Diligent Work and Frugal Study in France movement among the progressive youth of Hunan.

---

* By criticizing current affairs in the manner of the traditional scholar-officials. — Tr.

† Mao is probably referring to the "feudal" warlords here. — Tr.

# REVOLUTIONARY ACTIVITIES BEFORE AND AFTER THE MAY FOURTH MOVEMENT

*2*

## I. ORGANIZING THE HUNAN YOUTH TO GO TO FRANCE UNDER THE DILIGENT WORK AND FRUGAL STUDY PROGRAM. FIRST TRIP TO PEKING

During World War I, French imperialism recruited more than a hundred thousand Chinese to go to France and perform labor connected with the war effort. [1] Comrade Wu Yü-chang, together with Ts'ai Yüan-p'ei and others who were studying in France at the time, created a Diligent Work and Frugal Study in France Society [Liu Fa chin kung chien hsüeh hui], whose goal was "diligence in work, study through frugality," and in addition organized the Sino-French Educational Society [Hua Fa chiao-yü hui] to direct the project. After their return home, they publicized the diligent work and frugal study idea in Peking, Shanghai and other areas calling on young people to go to France and study via this "work-study" method.

The influence of the October Revolution was just beginning to be felt in China at that time, and the theory of "sanctity of labor" was already being advocated in progressive intellectual circles. Comrade Li Ta-chao, in an essay he wrote entitled "Shu-min ti sheng-li" [The Victory of the Masses], made the following loud, urgent call: "Let it be known that the world of tomorrow will be a world of labor. We should use this tide as an opportunity to make everyone into workers; we should not use this tide as an opportunity to make everyone into robbers. All those who do not work for the rice they eat are robbers." "If we want to be a people of the world, we should be a worker of the world. Everybody, get to work!" At the time, it was impossible to go directly to Soviet Russia to study, and the proletariats of various Eastern European countries such as Germany, Austria, and Czechoslovakia were just beginning to mount their revolution, so [Chinese] went instead to France, near the

88

scene of the revolutionary high tide. This diligent work and frugal study method, where one could both work and acquire such knowledge, was naturally very attractive to all ambitious young people.

The members of the New People's Study Society and the progressive youths of Hunan First Normal and Changsha's Lien-ho Middle School were all very desirous of going abroad to develop themselves better. The poor intellectuals welcomed the diligent work and frugal study program even more. Comrade Mao Tse-tung called together the members of the New People's Study Society who were in Changsha for a discussion session. He proposed that Comrade Ts'ai Ho-sen first go to Peking, get an understanding of the overall situation and make connections; then a decision on everyone's future direction would be made.

In late June 1918, Comrade Ts'ai Ho-sen left Changsha for Peking. After he reached Peking, he sent Comrade Mao Tse-tung several letters one after the other telling of the contacts he was making in various quarters. At this time, the Diligent Work and Frugal Study in France program was still in the discussion stage, and the finances had not yet been worked out. Ts'ai Ho-sen was of the opinion that "only if we have a lot of people drawing the water will we have enough fish to eat" — one had to motivate a large number of young people to respond enthusiastically to the movement, thus forcing the initiators of the movement to accept the responsibility for its realization. But this had to be directed by someone within the country. Ts'ai Ho-sen acknowledged that only Mao Tse-tung, respected and trusted by all, was most suited for the job. Thus Ts'ai sincerely made every effort to urge Mao Tse-tung to come quickly to Peking. In the letter he also passed along the view of Mr. Yang Ch'ang-chi, whose hope it was that Comrade Mao Tse-tung would, on the one hand, study at Peking University and, on the other, take a job.

The matter that concerned Comrade Mao Tse-tung most at this time was how to construct a base for the New People's Study Society. He wrote Comrade Ts'ai Ho-sen explaining his view: "Members must be sufficiently sought after and attracted; the Society cannot be allowed to develop at random." On the basis that most of the members of the New People's Study Society were primary school teachers, he argued that they should set up several primary schools, train men of talent from the ground up, and make them a base for carrying out future revolutionary activities. Because the members of the Society had scattered in all directions, it was especially appropriate that Changsha, the area where it had been possible to establish a base, not be abandoned. With regard to studying at Peking University, Mao Tse-tung replied that the most urgent matter at present was the necessity to conduct "large-scale, unrestrained research"; Society members should map out projects and go to Russia or France or stay in Peking to study the most progressive ideologies and doctrines in the world today, get an understanding of the realities of each country, and also to select and adopt [appropriate things] for use in China.

Because of his burning desire to go to Peking and make contact with the new tide of thought and the revolutionary personages there, Comrade Mao Tse-tung finally decided to make the trip.

Just before he left, Comrade Mao Tse-tung issued appeals at First Normal, Lien-ho Middle School, and other schools; more than twenty people made this trip to Peking for the Diligent Work and Frugal Study program. At the same time, Mao made up a very comprehensive work schedule for the members of New People's Study Society who were staying behind in Hunan.

In September of 1918 Comrade Mao Tse-tung set off for Peking with Lo Hsüeh-tsan and the more than twenty others. Along the way, the responsibilities for buying tickets, taking care of the luggage, arranging for inn accommodations, and maintaining hygiene were divided up. That year the Yellow River overflowed its banks and cut the railroad line so the trains were blocked at Honan. No one had any idea what to do. Mao Tse-tung, seeking out a native of the area and making some detailed inquiries, discovered that the waters of the Yellow River came quickly but also left quickly, and that when the water had receded they would be able to travel. Taking advantage of the delay, Mao and the others visited the neighboring countryside and investigated the living conditions of the peasants.

By the time Comrade Mao Tse-tung reached Peking, there were some forty or fifty youths there who had come from Hunan; no other province had this many people representing it. This astounded the directors of the Diligent Work and Frugal Study program, and they all felt that the youths of Hunan had a great revolutionary spirit. Because the Sino-French Educational Society had not completed the preparatory work, the group was unable to go to France immediately. Unavoidably, there was some grumbling about this. Mao Tse-tung wanted everyone to be patient and wait, explaining over and over the importance of completing the preparatory work of any undertaking. After this, everyone joined the study program of the Preparatory Class for Study in France sponsored by the Sino-French Educational Society.

Trying to rent a place in Peking was not easy and living expenses were rather high, so the Preparatory Class was held in three different places. One was in Paoting, attached to Yü-te Middle School. One was in Peking, attached to Peking University. These two places were for the advanced sections. The elementary section was set up in Li hsien. The Preparatory Class placed primary stress on French; next were other subjects like drafting (this was set up to prepare people for entrance into factories) and mathematics. The training period had a one-year limit, after which time the students would go to France. The students in Li hsien lived in Pu-li village where there was an iron works that served as a practice area.

Comrade Mao Tse-tung stayed in Peking with Comrade Ts'ai Ho-sen and a small number of other people, attending to various procedures and helping people who were having problems with expenses to develop ways to raise money (at the time there was an Emigrant Workers Bureau that could extend loans). The Sino-French Educational Society wanted the students from Hunan to propose a plan for the Diligent Work and Frugal Study in France program, and they elected Comrade Mao Tse-tung to take pen in hand and write out such a plan. Broadly speaking, the plan explained the significance of the Diligent Work and Frugal Study program, called for the continued recruiting of Hunan youths to join the program, and explained how to complete all the preparatory work in China (such as acquiring a rudimentary knowledge of French) to lessen the problems that would be encountered after the students were abroad. In addition to this, Mao also proposed to send one person to France to make advance arrangements. The Sino-French Educational Society was in complete agreement with this plan. It considered the idea of sending one person first to do preparatory work to be particularly good, and so it decided to do just that. To help send the first person, Mao Tse-tung went everywhere and expended great efforts in raising money for the travel expenses, looking after the person's family at home, and getting the luggage ready.

Between 1919 and 1920 more than sixteen hundred young people from throughout the country went to France as part of the Diligent Work and Frugal Study program. The young people from the two provinces of Hunan and Szechuan were the most enthusiastic. There were many hundreds sent from Hunan. Within Hunan, it was especially with educational circles and the young students in Changsha that the Diligent Work and Frugal Study in France program became a very enthusiastic movement. There, in addition, they organized a Hunan Branch of the Sino-French Educational Society. The press, too, gave its encouragement to the movement. Comrades Ts'ai Ch'ang, Hsiang Ching-yü, and others from Chou-nan Girls' School set up a Girls' Diligent Work and Frugal Study in France Society, mobilizing the female students from all the schools to join this movement. What gave the greatest jolt to society was that Comrade Hsü T'e-li, the famous educationalist who was already forty-three years old and who had been working in Hunan educational circles for ten or twenty years, and Mother Ts'ai (the mother of Comrades Ts'ai Ho-sen and Ts'ai Ch'ang), who was already over fifty years old, were also going to France to "half-work and half-study" as "elderly students."

In 1921 Chou En-lai, Wang Jo-fei, [2] and other comrades who had gone to France under the Diligent Work and Frugal Study program organized the Socialist Youth Corps [She-hui-chu-i ch'ing-nien t'uan] (its predecessor was the Work-Study Mutual-Aid Society [Kung-hsüeh hu-chu hui]). Comrades Ts'ai Ho-sen, Li Fu-ch'un, Li Wei-han, Li Li-san, Ts'ai Ch'ang, Hsiang Ching-yü, Chang K'un-ti, and Lo Hsüeh-tsan, all from Hunan, were active sponsors and organizers of the Socialist Youth Corps. They carried on a sharp struggle with the nationalists and anarchists among the students of the Sino-French Educational Society and the Diligent Work and Frugal Study program. Among the students studying abroad and among the Overseas Chinese workers they launched a campaign of Marxist propaganda and stood against the oppression of French imperialism. At the same time, in order to seize their educational and economic rights, they led the students of the Diligent Work and Frugal Study program into a struggle against Wu Chih-hui, [3] who was keeping a tight grip on the Lyons Sino-French University, and against the reactionary forces in the Sino-French Educational Society. In the fall of 1921 Ts'ai Ho-sen, Chang K'un-ti, Lo Hsüeh-tsan, and other comrades were deported back to China by the French government on the charge that they had been preaching communism.

Comrade Mao Tse-tung did not intend to go to France; he had his own unique work and study plans. He felt that he should stay in China. When Mao Tse-tung had been studying at First Normal, he directed his attention to the reason for the failure of the 1911 Revolution. Now he realized even more clearly: for any revolution to succeed, the revolutionary intelligentsia must forge intimate links with the masses of people. Mao himself has recalled this:

"I accompanied some of the Hunanese students to Peking. However, although I had helped organize the movement, and it had the support of the Hsin Min Hsueh Hui, I did not want to go to Europe. I felt that I did not know enough about my own country, and that my time could be more profitable spent in China."  4

Comrade Mao Tse-tung lived with Comrade Lo Hsüeh-tsan and six other members of the New People's Study Society in Peking at No. 7 Chi-an East Lane, San-yen-ching, Ching-shan-tung. This was a very ordinary Peking san-ho-yüan.* The eight of them were squeezed into one small room on the eastern side of the northern set of rooms. Their material life was very harsh, but for learning new things and for their education it was extremely convenient. There were many opportunities to participate in intellectual and academic activities. They could also freely go to Peking University and attend lectures. Their teacher and friend, Mr. Yang Ch'ang-chi, still constantly looked after them and helped them. The life they led was exceptionally full and meaningful.

This is how Comrade Lo Hsüeh-tsan introduced the friends with whom he was living in a letter he wrote home: they were "all of ex-cellent character and hard-studying men, and I have great admira-tion for them. I am with them morning and night and am constantly benefited." And he made a special introduction of Comrade Mao Tse-tung: "Mao Jun-chih has expended great efforts in recruiting comrades from Changsha to come here and in organizing the Pre-paratory Class. His wisdom and scholarship are both admired by his fellow students." In the letter he also touched upon the kind of life they were leading during this period:

...as far as studies are concerned, in addition to doing the work for regular courses, we like to read journals, newspaper articles, and the latest new theo-ries. Everything else we temporarily "put on a high shelf." ...also, in Peking there was established an Academic Lecture Society [Hsüeh-shu chiang-yen hui] where we can go and study about literature, philosophy, and the sciences. The Society also extends invitations to famous people to come and give the lectures. I go there often to listen.

Recalling this period of his life, Comrade Mao Tse-tung has said:

My own living conditions in Peking were quite miserable, and in contrast the beauty of the old capital was a vivid and living compensation. I stayed in a place called San Yen-ching ["Three Eyes Well"], in a little room which held seven other people. When we were all packed fast on the k'ang † there was scarcely room enough for any of us to breathe. I used to have to warn people on each side of me when I wanted to turn over [Snow, Red Star, p. 152].

---

* A house with a courtyard flanked by rooms on three sides. — Tr.

† A cement or brick structure heated like a stove from the inside and used as a bed in winter. — Tr.

Although all that was required for a month's living was five or six dollars, Comrade Mao Tse-tung had no way of coming by this amount of money, and so he was forced to search for some job that could support him. It was then that Mr. Yang Ch'ang-chi introduced Mao to the head of Peking University Library, Li Ta-chao, and that Mao got a job there as an assistant. Mao's workroom was right next to Li Ta-chao's office (the Red Chamber-like southeast corner on the first floor of Peking University. Now both have been made into memorial rooms). "The room was filled with a rectangular conference table and many stools. Mao himself sat in front of a three-drawered table beneath the window and did his work. That year the Marxism Circle [Ma-k'o-ssu chu-i hsiao-tsu] often met in this room, seated around that conference table." 5 By the spring of 1919 the number of young Hunanese who had joined the Diligent Work and Frugal Study program had risen to over one hundred. They could all endure hardship and were all diligent workers. They had also generally made great progress in their thinking and had carved out a very good name for themselves in Peking. Comrade Li Ta-chao had great admiration for Comrade Mao Tse-tung, acknowledging him as the leader of the young people of Hunan.

On the eve of the May Fourth movement, Peking University was the meeting place for revolutionary ideas and for various new ideological currents. Communist intellectuals, revolutionary petty bourgeois intellectuals and bourgeois intellectuals all taught here and carried on all sorts of propaganda activities. New Youth, a journal championed by all of them, was the central organ of the New Culture movement. Two representative figures among them, Ch'en Tu-hsiu, an ardent advocate of democracy, and Li Ta-chao, a man who possessed the rudiments of communist thought, encouraged the young people to move bravely forward, called upon the people to fight against feudalism, and also actively disseminated a rudimentary knowledge of socialism. Comrade Mao Tse-tung made full use of the conditions afforded by Peking University to satisfy his own thirst for knowledge and extensively to absorb new ideologies and doctrines of all sorts.

When Comrade Mao Tse-tung was still in Changsha he regularly corresponded with Comrade Teng Chung-hsia (whose school name was Teng K'ang),6 who was attending Peking University to study the problem of revolution. Teng Chung-hsia was the director of the Peking University Mass Education Lecture Corps [ P'ing-min chiao-yü chiang-yen t'uan], and he was beginning to draw near the masses of workers and peasants. At this time, they became closer in their relationship.

Academic organizations among students at Peking University were particularly well developed. There were no less than sixteen or seventeen separate ones, like the Philosophical Society, the Forensic Society, the Physical Education Society, the Society for Mathematical Research, the Library Society, the Society for Journalism Research, and the New Thought Magazine Society.* In addition to regularly going to Peking University and auditing the courses he liked and continuing to maintain the old habit, dating from his days at First Normal, of going to Mr. Yang Ch'ang-chi's home with his friends to listen to Mr. Yang's lectures on philosophy and ethics infused with a materialist slant that Mr. Yang added, Comrade Mao Tse-tung also participated in the activities of the Philosophical Society and the Society for Journalism Research.

Peking University's Society for Journalism Research [Hsin-wen-hsüeh yen-chiu hui] was still quite a novelty for China at the time. It held a lecture once a week with about thirty or forty people attending. Shao P'iao-p'ing, [7] the general editor of the Capital Gazette [Ching pao], was the lecturer, and he talked about his experience in running a newspaper. There were also other people who talked about journalistic theory. For many years Comrade Mao Tse-tung had been extremely fond of reading newspapers, and Mr. Yang Ch'ang-chi had actually planned to give him an introduction for a job on one of the papers in Peking. Thus it was with great enthusiasm and interest that Comrade Mao Tse-tung joined this research society. After three months, the Society held a formal concluding ceremony.

Before the May Fourth movement China still could not obtain directly any authentic reports on the October Revolution; nor had Marxism-Leninism been introduced systematically into China. Progressive intellectuals could only go through the few inaccurate reports that appeared in the European, American, and Japanese bourgeois press to ferret out the great significance of the October Revolution. But the victory of the October Revolution was the most powerful propaganda that Marxism had. It caused the most progressive intellectuals of that time to realize the strength of the masses and caused them quickly to abandon bourgeois democratic thought and become active propagandists for socialism. In two articles published in New Youth in November 1918, "Shu-min ti sheng-li" [The Victory of the Masses] and "Bolshevism ti sheng-li" [The Victory of Bolshevism], Comrade Li Ta-chao enthusiastically sang the praises of the victory of the October Revolution, pointing out

---

*Actually, the title of this journal, one of the most important radical organs of the time, and of the society which edited it, was not Hsin ssu-ch'ao, as Li Jui has it, but simply Hsin-ch'ao (New Tide); it bore the English title The Renaissance [S.R.S.].

that this was the "first sound of the world revolution" in the twentieth century and a "bright new day for all humanity." He believed
that under the influence of the victory of the October Revolution,
the people of the innumerable nations would awaken, and that all
historical remnants — monarchy, nobility, warlords, bureaucracy,
imperialism and capitalism — would be thoroughly destroyed by
the huge current of the revolution. He called on the Chinese people
to shoulder the historical responsibility of creating this new era.
The direction the Chinese revolution should follow, as pointed out
by Comrade Li Ta-chao, had a tremendous influence on the broad
masses of students and on intellectual circles. At the same time,
such anarchist pamphlets as "Tzu-yu lu" [Freedom Record] and
"Fu hu chi" [Crouching Tiger Collection] were quite popular among
the young students of the revolution. There was also a certain market for the thought of Kropotkin [8] and Tolstoy. Certain students
from Peking University and Peking Higher Teachers College organized a secret organization to circulate and study these writings.
Thus, Comrade Mao Tse-tung also read some anarchist pamphlets
at this time and also had some contact with these students. But
Mao was already a progressive advocate of revolutionary democracy. The main current of his thinking lay more in the direction
of Marxism. This is how he summed up his thinking at this time:

"My interest in politics continued to increase, and my mind
turned more and more radical" [Snow, Red Star, p. 152].

Because he was organizing the youth of Hunan for the Diligent
Work and Frugal Study in France program, Comrade Mao Tse-tung
came to Peking, the center of the national revolution, where he had
an opportunity to widen his horizons, to absorb a great number of
new ideologies, and to begin making contact with Marxism-Leninism.
But Mao Tse-tung, who had grown up in a misery ridden farming
village and who had sought a way out from under the cruel domination of feudal warlords, could not forget Hunan, where he had lived
and struggled for twenty-five years. At that time Hunan was still
the slaughterhouse of the Peiyang warlord Chang Ching-yao, and
the people of Hunan still lived in "deep water and hot fire." Hunan
was still an extremely backward part of the interior. There were
many things to be done in Hunan. First of all, it was necessary to
organize the revolutionary youth and the "men of purpose" into a
struggle against the oppressor of the Hunan people, Chang Ching-yao.

At the beginning of 1919, after he had gone to Shanghai to see off
the first group of friends who were going to France, Comrade Mao
Tse-tung returned to Hunan.

## II. PATRIOTIC MOVEMENT OF THE HUNAN PEOPLE BEFORE AND AFTER THE MAY FOURTH PERIOD

In March of 1919 Comrade Mao Tse-tung returned to Hunan from Shanghai.* To the members of the New People's Study Society who had remained in Changsha he told of his experience in Peking and introduced to them the rough outlines of Marxism and the various branches of socialism. He also specifically talked about the situation surrounding the Russian October Revolution as he knew it. He wanted everyone to step up their study of Marxist theory. In order to solve the problem of how he would live, he taught several history courses at Hsiu-yeh Primary School. His monthly salary was just enough to support the lowest of living standards.

Comrade Mao Tse-tung continued to organize Hunan's young men of purpose into the Diligent Work and Frugal Study in France program and at the same time went a step further to associate with people who were dissatisfied with various aspects of the current situation and exchange views with them on the current state of affairs. In addition to the revolutionary youth of the various schools, he made contact with even more people in educational and journalistic circles, since by this time a great number of the members of the New People's Study Society had already gone to work in the educational world. People in the newspaper world were quite familiar with the current situation and, like those in educational circles, had been extremely critical of Chang Ching-yao's oppression from the very beginning.

During the great war of imperialism, the European and American imperialist nations temporarily eased their oppression of China because they were busy waging war, and the Chinese capitalist economy saw further development, following upon which the ranks of the Chinese working class gradually gained strength. At the same time, Japanese imperialism intensified its aggression against China, the northern and southern warlords fought incessantly, and floods and droughts came ceaselessly every year, all of which created a catastrophe of serious proportions for the Chinese people. Such being the situation, it could not help but arouse the opposition of the broad masses of the people and cause the upsurge of revolutionary conditions. Comrade Mao Tse-tung returned to Hunan on the very eve of the May Fourth movement.

---

* According to one of the students whom Mao accompanied from Peking to the boat in Shanghai, they sailed for France on March 19, 1919. Mao therefore probably got back to Changsha toward the end of the month [S.R.S.].

New hopes had arisen for the liberation of the Chinese nation as China's revolutionary intellectuals saw the collapse of three great imperialist powers, Russia, Germany and Austria-Hungary, and the weakening of two others, Britain and France, while the Russian proletariat had established a socialist state and the German, Hungarian and Italian proletariat had risen in revolution. [9]

At this time, all patriotic people in China had their eyes on the controversy at the Paris Peace Conference over the question of Shantung. Every citizen demanded the abrogation of the treasonous treaty signed by Yüan Shih-k'ai — the Twenty-one Demands. They demanded the return of their rights in Shantung that had been forcibly taken away from them by Japanese imperialism, which had taken advantage of the situation afforded by the war in Europe, and they issued a call for opposition against the traitors Ts'ao Ju-lin, Chang Tsung-hsiang, and Lu Tsung-yü. (These three men were, respectively, minister of communications, Chinese ambassador to Japan, and the director-general of the National Mint in the Tuan Ch'i-jui government. They had a direct hand in negotiating the treaty which caused China to be humiliated and to lose her rights.) Newspaper editorials and public opinion in Peking, Shanghai, and various other areas rapidly disseminated this outcry of the people.

But the stupid and corrupt government of the Peking warlords had its hands tied. Not knowing what to do at the Paris Peace Conference, it bowed to Japanese imperialism's policy of aggression. But at the same time, the government was increasing its attention to precautionary measures against the discontent of the people. First and foremost they took precautionary measures against the discontent of the students in Peking and in the various schools throughout the country.

The feelings of the Hunanese were likewise greatly aroused; the young students were especially moved. Their classrooms were in great turmoil to begin with (the troops of Chang Ching-yao were still quartered in a great number of schools, educational expenses were, as a rule, in arrears, and the faculty and the students were often insulted by the "northern troops"), and now it was even more impossible for them to study in peace.

Comrade Mao Tse-tung devoted all his attention to the development of the current situation both within and outside of China, studying the newspapers carefully every day. He was especially concerned about the direction in which the Paris Peace Conference was moving, as well as about domestic public opinion on the Shantung question and about various patriotic movements of the people.

At this time, a large number of progressive primary school

teachers were added to the membership of the New People's Study Society. Most of the student organizations of the important public and private schools of Changsha were led by members of the New People's Study Society or by progressive youths who had some connection with the Society. Comrade Mao Tse-tung was very familiar with the progressive elements in these schools and kept up regular contact with them. He very tightly organized around himself the nuclear force of the Hunan revolutionary youth. Comrade Ho Shu-heng was teaching at Ch'u-i Primary School at the time, and Comrade Mao Tse-tung often called the members of the New People's Study Society together for a meeting at his residence.

There had already been some movement with regard to the problem of forming a unified organization for the Hunan students. On May 7, 1918, Chinese students studying in Japan carried out a general strike of classes in opposition to the joint anti-Soviet "Sino-Japanese Military Mutual Assistance Conventions" secretly concluded between the Tuan Ch'i-jui government and Japanese imperialism. There were many students arrested by the Japanese police. In the nationwide upsurge of student response, the students of Hunan launched a petition movement to do away with the treaty, and in addition went further to organize a United Association of Students [Hsüeh-sheng lien-ho hui]. But it was very poorly organized and subsequently it had not played much of a role [i.e., between the time it was first organized and the time when Mao revitalized it]. Using the several important schools that had the strongest foundations as a nucleus, schools such as First Normal and Commercial Vocational School, Comrade Mao Tse-tung now feverishly pushed on with the work of revitalizing and reorganizing the Hunan United Association of Students. In contacts with the important cadres from each school, Mao pointed out that this movement should have a clear-cut anti-imperialist, antifeudal political orientation. First on the list was the struggle for full sovereignty in Shantung and opposition to the treasonous policy of the Peking warlord government; he also gave a detailed analysis of the suppression that would certainly come from Chang Ching-yao. Mao Tse-tung issued a call to everyone to rise up and meet head-on this crucial and formidable struggle.

At the end of April 1919, twenty-five thousand students from all the schools in Peking of the technical school level and above sent out a circular telegram. This circular telegram represented the joint outcry of all the patriotic people in the country: "The struggle for the return of Tsingtao will certainly fail. The seventh of

May* is near at hand, and all Chinese citizens should wake up. We hope that everyone will hold a National Humiliation Memorial Gathering on this day and cooperate in opposing the foreigners and in saving this dangerous situation."

This circular telegram had a great influence upon the young students of Hunan and upon its patriotic people.

The peace treaty concluded with Germany at the Paris Peace Conference stipulated that Japan was to take over the German rights in Shantung. This cruel fact brought unbearable humiliation to the broad masses of people. The intellectuals who had been influenced by the October Revolution and the students who were under their influence came to an even clearer recognition of this truth: only by relying on oneself and on the broad masses can one resolve one's own fate.

On May 4, 1919, launched by the students of Peking, the first great patriotic movement of the Chinese people — the May Fourth movement — broke out. As soon as the May Fourth movement began, it had, according to Comrade Mao Tse-tung,

a feature which was absent from the Revolution of 1911, namely, its thorough and uncompromising opposition to imperialism as well as to feudalism.... [10]

The May Fourth movement came into being at the call of the world revolution, of the Russian Revolution and of Lenin. It was part of the world proletarian revolution of the time. Although the Communist Party had not yet come into existence, there were already large numbers of intellectuals who approved of the Russian Revolution and had the rudiments of communist ideology. [11]

Comrades Mao Tse-tung and Li Ta-chao were the most outstanding representatives of the left-wing intellectuals of the time.

In their demonstration of May 4, five thousand Peking students and citizens loudly cried out such slogans as: "Abrogate the Twenty-one Demands," "We swear to fight to the death to retake Tsingtao," and "Boycott Japanese goods." In addition, they put Chao-chia-lou (the residence of Ts'ao Ju-lin) to the torch and gave Chang Tsung-hsiang a painful beating. On this day thirty-two students were arrested and taken away. The students of Peking had made an appeal to the whole nation.

The revolutionary storm immediately "rolled up the entire nation like a mat." † The students from Tientsin, Shanghai, Nanking,

---

* May 7 marked the fourth anniversary of the humiliating Twenty-one Demands. — Tr.

† I.e., completely overwhelmed it. — Tr.

Wuhan and from the provinces in the south, northwest, and north-east rose up in profusion to echo the patriotic actions of the Peking students. On May 7 the students in the major cities of the country held large-scale gatherings and demonstrations, unanimously giving their support to the patriotic struggle of the Peking students.

On May 19 the students of the various schools in Peking announced a strike of classes and at the same time took to the streets in ten-man groups to launch a patriotic propaganda drive.

Tuan Ch'i-jui's lackey Chang Ching-yao knew that the situation was serious and carried out a policy of tight and brutal control in Hunan: every day, the police department sent agents out to investigate the newspapers, forbidding them to print any news of patriotic movements or of dissatisfaction with the Tuan Ch'i-jui government. Also, they did not allow the newspapers to leave blank spaces where material had been censored. At the same time, they strictly prohibited students from engaging in patriotic activities. Nevertheless, this high-handed policy of Chang Ching-yao did not stem the outburst of patriotic fervor among the young students and popular masses.

Comrade Mao Tse-tung himself wrote a leaflet calling upon everyone to rise to action and distributed it in the name of the student organizations of several schools. The members of the New People's Study Society were feverishly active day and night. They mobilized the students of the various schools to prepare for a strike of classes and selected representatives for the formal establishment of the United Association of Students. Under the impetus and leadership of Comrade Mao Tse-tung, the Hunan United Association of Students finally made the formal announcement of its creation on June 3. On this first day of its existence, it issued a declaration for a strike of classes for the purpose of winning back Tsingtao. The last sentence of the declaration read: "We ask for the head of Ts'ao and Lu as their apology to the world." On this very day the entire student population of Changsha conducted a general strike of classes. Soon all the students in the province went on strike one after the other.

The United Association of Students was located at Lo-hsing-t'ien Commercial Vocational School. Its organization was divided into a Department of Criticism and Discussion and an Executive Department. (The Department of Criticism and Discussion was in the nature of a representative council, the Executive Department was the organ for day-to-day work. At the time, student organizations all over the country adopted this organizational pattern.) The chairman of the Department of Criticism and Discussion was P'eng Huang, [12] a student of Commercial Vocational School. The chairman of the Executive Department was the representative of the Student Society of First Normal. Both were members of the New People's Study Society. Sometimes Comrade Mao Tse-tung would stay at Commercial Vocational School to direct the work of the United Students on the spot.

Before June 3 the primary participants in the May Fourth movement were still young students. Because of the arrest by Tuan Ch'i-jui's government on June 3 of over a thousand students who had been speaking out on the corners of Peking streets, the anger and exasperation of the whole country was aroused even more. The student movement boiled up even higher. Under the impetus of the students, the native industrialists and commercial men of Shanghai, who had realized some gain during the boycott of Japanese goods, finally conducted a business strike on June 5. All the commercial and industrial circles of all the major cities in the country immediately went out on strike, responding to the students' patriotic movement and protesting the barbarous conduct of the Peking government. On June 5 the workers of Shanghai began a labor strike; the number of strikers during this period reached some seventy thousand people. The workers in T'ang-shan and Ch'ang-hsin-tien also rose up in response. The great Chinese working class had begun to mount the political stage.

From this time forward, the May Fourth movement became a concerted nationwide revolutionary movement of workers, students, and businessmen.

In the face of the threat posed by the nationwide strike of workers, students, and businessmen, the Peking government had no choice but to assent to the resignation of Ts'ao Ju-lin, Lu Tsung-yü, and Chang Tsung-hsiang. The ostensibly responsible men in the Pei-yang warlord clique, the Peking government cabinet, tendered their resignations in order to mollify the nation's anger. After June 12 students throughout the country began to resume classes, workers began to return to work, and businessmen began to reopen for business.

The May Fourth movement demonstrated the great might of the revolutionary masses. China's anti-imperialist, antifeudal bourgeois democratic revolution had now advanced to a new stage. The May Fourth movement had raised the curtain on China's New Democratic Revolution.

The mass revolutionary movement of the May Fourth period

ended a little later in Hunan, and it eventually evolved into the movement for the expulsion of the Peiyang warlord Chang Ching-yao.

The public organizations of various sectors in Hunan, such as the Educational Society [Chiao-yü hui], the Chamber of Commerce, etc., had already as early as May established an "Association for the Support of National Goods" [Kuo huo wei-ch'ih hui], but because it lacked the strength to mobilize the masses, the boycott of Japanese goods did not actually develop into a movement. After the founding of the United Association of Students, Comrade Mao Tse-tung led the Association into active participation in the Association for the Support of National Goods and made the boycott of Japanese goods the central task. And so the movement to boycott Japanese goods in Changsha and Hunan surged forward. The upswing of patriotic fervor among the youth could not be suppressed by Chang Ching-yao no matter what he did. The reason the Chamber of Commerce had participated in the "Association for the Support of National Goods" was really to "support Japanese goods." The United Association of Students, knowing full well the inside story on this, sent out a large number of investigators to cotton-spinning factories, paper-manufacturing plants, department stores, southern goods shops, printing shops, and glass works to conduct detailed investigations. If they turned up some Japanese goods, they sealed them up for safekeeping, setting a time limit within which they had to be completely auctioned off. The investigators patiently carried out "persuasive education" among the merchants who had secretly transported and sold Japanese goods. They tried to persuade the merchants consciously and voluntarily to make a truthful accounting of their activities. At the same time, in accordance with the regulations of the Association for the Support of National Goods, the investigators meted out punishment to those merchants who were more seriously involved by fining them, confiscating their goods, and even putting the torch to the Japanese goods in their possession. The United Association of Students forced the merchants who had joined the Association for the Support of National Goods to fulfill the promises that they had made in jest. Some dishonest merchants became as frightened as a rat seeing a cat when they saw the investigators of the United Association of Students.

The investigators of the United Association of Students mobilized the shop employees of the various firms in Changsha into active participation in the movement to boycott Japanese goods. For example, the famous Wu Ta-mao Department Store, which dealt in

Japanese goods, was expelled from the Department Store Branch of the Association for the Support of the National Goods as a result of charges brought by the employees. The patterns of resistance among the dishonest merchants were many. After the investigators had discovered secretly transported Japanese goods in their shops, some firms still would not go along with the method for dealing with this problem as determined by the Association for the Support of National Goods. In order to make an example, the Association for the Support of National Goods, the Silk Branch of that association, and the United Association of Students joined on July 7 to hold a demonstration for the burning of Japanese goods. (The press, under the domination of Chang Ching-yao, just as later under Chiang Kai-shek, was not permitted to use the word "Japanese," the newspapers only being permitted to say "certain goods," "certain cloth.") According to the press reports of the following day, the ranks of the demonstrators started out from the offices of the silk companies, holding high large banners in the lead proclaiming: "Burn Japanese Goods Demonstration," "Attention Brothers! Do Not Buy Japanese Goods!" Following this came the military ranks and the student ranks, each person carrying a roll of Japanese cloth on his shoulders. Behind them came the shop workers of the silk industry, and last came the banners of the Association for the Support of National Goods and the United Association of Students. After the ranks of demonstrators had passed through the busiest streets of Changsha, they arrived at Educational Society Plaza. The students piled the cloth they had into a great heap, poured kerosine on it, and only after the cloth had burned to ashes did the ranks of demonstrators and mass of spectators disperse.

Simultaneous with the boycott of Japanese goods, the United Association of Students and the various organizations of all circles launched a "Patriotic Saving" campaign. Cutting down on their food expenses and contributing money, the students set up "ten-man saving societies," calling on people to save for their country and prepare their material strength for a struggle with Japanese imperialism. This played a definite role in animating the patriotic anti-Japanese movement of the time.

On the basis of experiences in Peking, Shanghai and Tientsin, the United Association of Students joined with the various industrial and commercial circles to hold a meeting on July 9 and formally founded the Hunan United Association of All Circles [Ko chieh lien-ho hui] for the purpose of uniting the people of various circles on a broader scale. Participating in the meeting that established the

Association were over thirty representatives of important businesses, such as department stores, the cotton-spinning industry, the dyeing industry, steamship lines, masons and carpenters, and the porcelain industry.

At the meeting a delegation of the Association composed of twenty representatives was created. After the founding of the United Association of All Circles, with the United Association of Students as a nucleus, there was produced an Association publication whose goal was to encourage the new current of thought. The basic-level organs of the United Association of All Circles were the National Salvation Ten-Man Corps [Chiu kuo shih-jen t'uan], which was also something learned from the experiences in Peking and Shanghai. The National Salvation Ten-Man Corps were broad mass organizations; patriotic people from all walks of life joined in profusion. For example, among the faculty members from the various schools belonging to the Educational Society led by Hsü T'e-li and others, over two hundred and fifty Corps were founded. To describe the organization and development of the National Salvation Ten-Man Corps, the press of Changsha used the phrase "a wind is rising, the clouds are moving rapidly, and there is daily progress."

On the basis of over four-hundred "Ten-Man Corps," the Hunan United Association of National Salvation Ten-Man Corps Preparatory Committee [Ch'ou-pei hui] was founded on July 15, 1919. In the latter part of October came the formal establishment of the United Association of Ten-Man Corps. Comrade Mao Tse-tung's comrade-in-arms, Comrade Liu Chih-hsün, [13] was elected as the assistant general secretary of this United Association.

During summer vacation, the United Association of Students organized the students who had remained at school and founded fourteen lecture corps in Changsha that took to the street corners and went from house to house conducting patriotic anti-Japanese propaganda. Under the blazing sun the students hurried everywhere shouting their message, some becoming so tired that they spit up blood. The lecture corps often publicized the tragic destruction of Korea, how several families were forced to share one kitchen chopper* and how the Korean people were massacred. It was really a case where "those who talked spoke with tears streaming down, those who listened covered their faces and wept"! The lecture corps also often staged various new plays, such as "The Opium War," "Alas! Taiwan," and "The Tragic History of the Destruction of Korea."

---

* Indicative of extreme poverty. — Tr.

The United Association of Students already had some connection with the working masses, since a great number of schools were running night schools and had mobilized the workers to attend classes. The industrial workers of Changsha's No. 1 Cotton Mill, graphite refinery, and mint and the trade workers from various construction trades organized a propaganda team and carried on activities in conjunction with the students.

Under the impetus of the United Association of Students and the influence of the zealous tide of patriotism in Changsha, the movement for the boycott of Japanese goods very rapidly spread to every hsien of Hunan. The branches of the Association for the Support of National Goods that were set up in dozens of hsien, such as Ning-hsiang, Li-ling, and Heng-yang, were by and large organized by the Changsha students who had returned to the hsien and who had united the various circles. At the same time, students all over and people from every circle organized lecture corps. The lecture corps of I-yang, Ch'ang-te, Han-shou, and Yüeh-yang also staged various popular new plays. The lecture corps of P'ing-chiang, as well as other patriotic organizations there, were particularly active.

In the midst of the seething wave of patriotic fervor, Comrade Mao Tse-tung, in addition to attaching great importance to the organizational infracture of the masses, paid special attention to the problem of further raising the political awareness of the masses. He believed that if the ideological consciousness of the masses were not heightened and their revolutionary ardor not strengthened, then the revolutionary movement would be unable to develop any further and, once the commotion was over, there might be no results.

There was therefore an extremely pressing need to publish a journal of a high level of political thought; Comrade Mao Tse-tung thus set to work on plans for just such a journal.


## III. MANAGING EDITOR OF THE
   HSIANG RIVER REVIEW

How to make use of newspapers and how to set up and run a periodical to disseminate the new revolutionary tide of thought — these were problems that constantly occupied Comrade Mao Tse-tung's thinking after his return to Hunan.

After the May Fourth movement, when he was guiding the work

of the Hunan United Association of Students, Comrade Mao Tse-tung edited with great energy the weekly Hsiang River Review [Hsiang chiang p'ing-lun] in order to further heighten the ideological consciousness of the masses and to impel the revolutionary movement forward with even greater force. All the important articles in this periodical were written by Mao Tse-tung himself. The articles he wrote propagated a thorough and uncompromising anti-imperialist, antifeudal, antiwarlord political ideology. In them he explained with great lucidity the strategic point of view that in order to overthrow reactionary domination it was necessary to establish a people's revolutionary united front. He also interested the readers in studying current practical problems and foreign and domestic political questions, and he encouraged the people to do battle with the old thought and old habits that were obstacles to social progress. He especially sang the praises of the victory of the October Revolution and also publicized a Marxist orientation. After the inaugural number of the Hsiang River Review had been sent to Peking, Comrade Li Ta-chao acknowledged that this journal contained the most solid and profound writing in the country. And the Weekly Review [Mei-chou p'ing-lun], [14] in introducing this journal, acknowledged it as its own friend: "That, under the rule of military men, it has been possible to produce such a good brother is truly an unexpected joy." [15]

The first issue of the Hsiang River Review was published on July 14, 1919. The format of the publication was like that of the Weekly Review, the size of one newsprint sheet cut into quarters. Every number contained about twelve thousand characters, and at the top of the paper on the right-hand side were the characters: "Published in Changsha, Lo-hsing-t'ien, Hunan United Association of Students."

On the next day, the newspapers in Changsha published news of the "publishing of the Hsiang River Review":

The Hsiang River Review of the United Association of Students was published yesterday. The contents follow that of Peking's Weekly Review. It is divided into a critical review of major Western and Eastern events, miscellaneous commentary on world affairs and events in Hunan, new art and literature, etc. The paper uses the vernacular [pai-hua] throughout and is quite sparkling.

With regard to the aim of the publication of the Hsiang River Review, Comrade Mao Tse-tung said in the "Inaugural Announcement" that no power could block the present world revolutionary tide. The strongest force in the world was the united force of all the people.

The people should rally together and carry on a struggle against brute domination for their own thorough liberation. The duty of the Hsiang River Review was to study, disseminate, and push ahead the current new high tide of revolution in the world.

Around the time of the May Fourth movement, small-scale publications were as prolific as new shoots after a spring rain. The student societies of the many schools in Changsha also produced weekly periodicals published outside of the school, such as New Hunan [Hsin Hu-nan] of Hsiang-ya Medical School, Women's Bell [Nü-chieh chung] of Chou-nan Girls' School, Yüeh-yün Weekly [Yüeh-yün chou-k'an] of Yüeh-yün Middle School, Yüeh-lu Weekly [Yüeh-lu chou-k'an] of Industrial Vocational Higher School, etc. In all, there were more than ten of these periodicals. Although they dealt with the introduction of the new culture and new thought, they were mostly verbose and repetitive and lacked a point of view. The most outstanding characteristic of the Hsiang River Review was that it carried political essays written by Comrade Mao Tse-tung that contained a rudimentary Marxist point of view and unique opinions on various affairs. He reiterated and critiqued major domestic and foreign events. Facts were analyzed in a well-formulated presentation. The conclusions were invariably filled with commentary by the writer that struck at the root of the question and indicated future trends. And the writing was particularly vigorous and powerful, simple, and easy to understand. Besides long articles, there were also "Miscellaneous Commentary on World Affairs," which dealt with international problems, "Miscellaneous Commentary on Events in Hunan," which reviewed sociopolitical phenomena, and a section called "Open Discussion" [fang yen] (this was a new literary genre of the time; some were entitled "opinion record" and others "short critique"). In just a few words they expressed the inner feelings of the readers.

Two thousand copies of the inaugural edition of the Hsiang River Review were printed, and it sold out the very same day. Since a great many people continued to come to subscribe, another two thousand copies were printed. But this was still insufficient to satisfy the demand from other areas. Therefore, starting with the second number, five thousand copies of each number were printed. This was an enormous figure for the time. The students, some of the middle school faculty, and progressive people in Changsha and various places throughout Hunan, and even those in Wuhan, Kwangtung, and Szuchuan, all became the good friends of the Hsiang River Review. It was especially the ideologically progressive young students who always carried a copy of the Hsiang River Review in their pockets. After each number of the journal arrived in the reading rooms of the schools, everyone would rush to be the first to read it. The broad masses acknowledged this as a publication that spoke as a genuine representative of the people.

A great many students went out into the streets to sell the Hsiang River Review. Comrade Mao Tse-tung himself also took to the streets and sold the journal.

Although the Hsiang River Review was the publication of the United Association of Students, there were many people who wrote for it. On the evening before the journal was sent to the presses it often proved impossible to gather together all the manuscripts that had been promised. Comrade Mao Tse-tung would then write a few more articles than usual. Despite the sweltering weather and mosquitoes, he "often wrote until after midnight. In the morning, as soon as he had gotten out of bed, and with no time to wash up or eat, he would immediately go to the classroom and teach." [16] In all, almost the entire first issue, two-thirds of the second, and half of the third and fourth were written by Mao. From the writing and editing down to setting type and proofreading, Comrade Mao Tse-tung had full responsibility. At this time, Mao was still living at Hsiu-yeh Primary School. His belongings were extremely simple: one old blue mosquito net made of Chinese linen, an old sleeping mat, a few books for a pillow, and a long gown of glazed cotton which he wore regularly and which had been washed so much that it was quite faded, somewhere between blue and white.

Comrade Mao Tse-tung devoted his attention to the study of international developments. The "Review of Major Events in the West" column and most of the "Miscellaneous Commentary on World Affairs" that appeared in each issue came from his pen. For example, he wrote a long section introducing the labor strike movements of the day in England, the United States, France, Germany, and Italy. He exposed every move that was made by England, the United States and France to divide the spoils at the Paris Peace Conference. He denounced Clemenceau, Lloyd George and Wilson, [17] "who talked of nothing but equality and justice," as "a gang of robbers." In an article entitled "Te-i-chih jen ch'en-t'ung ti ch'ien-yüeh" [Painful Treaty for the Germans] (Hsiang River Review, No. 2), he pointed to the only way out for Germany in the future — she should unite with Russia, Austria, and Czechoslovakia to become a "communist republic." He also pointed out that if there were another war after World War I, it would inevitably be in the nature of a class war. The result in Europe was bound to be the success of communism in all the countries of Eastern Europe. This is how he satirized Clemenceau, the prime minister of France who thought that he himself had won the victory: Clemenceau, that old ignorant man, still holds on to that thick grayish-yellow booklet (i.e., the Paris Peace Treaty) thinking that, names having been signed on it, it is as solid as the Alps!

At this time Comrade Mao Tse-tung paid even more attention to the great events that were occurring within the country. For example, in an article entitled "Ch'en Tu-hsiu chih pei pu chi ying-chiu" [The Arrest and Rescue of Ch'en Tu-hsiu] (Ch'en Tu-hsiu had been arrested in June 1919 in Peking and was pardoned forthwith), he maintained that the most important current problem of China was not the internal disorder of the warlords but how to heighten the ideological consciousness of the people throughout the entire country, and that the scientific and democratic spirit advocated by Ch'en Tu-hsiu and others was the most appropriate for the times. Comrade Mao Tse-tung specifically gave a detailed introduction to the recent movement in Hunan. In order to get the young people of Hunan with some ambition to continue participating in the Diligent Work and Frugal Study in France program, from the second issue onward Mao Tse-tung continually printed extensive relevant correspondence that had been sent back from France by members of the New People's Study Society. To introduce patriotic student movements in Hunan (starting from the late-Ch'ing "School of Current Affairs" [Shih-wu hsüeh-t'ang]), some [material] was printed in the fourth issue. The entire first page and one-third of the second page of the first number (published on July 21) of the Supplement carried Mao's "Commentary on Major Events in Hunan" entitled "Chien hsüeh hui chih ch'eng-li chi chin-hsing" [The Founding and Operation of the Education Invigoration Society]. The Society was an academic organization with progressive significance that was organized at the time by a great number of people in Hunan's educational circles who were critical of Chang Ching-yao's rule. Every week there was one speech, and Comrades Ho Shu-heng, Hsü T'e-li, and others all joined. Comrade Mao Tse-tung supported this Society. Most of the members of this organization were active participants in the movement to Expel Chang Ching-yao. Later, during the period of domination by T'an Yen-k'ai and Chao Heng-t'i, a great many elements in the Society, these rightists of the May Fourth movement — the upper stratum of the intellectual world — gradually fell in with the new rulers and became one of the supporting pillars of the ruling class. In his later revolutionary activities, however, Comrade Mao Tse-tung maintained the relationship of an anti-imperialist, anti-feudal united front with some of this group who had some influence.

The reactionary government of that time was conducting a propaganda campaign of calumny against Marxism and against Russia's October Revolution (Marxism was called "extremism" [kuo-chi chu-i] and the Bolsheviks were called the "extremist party") and was creating a scare psychology throughout society, as if, once the "extremist party" had arrived, a great calamity would come crashing down on people's heads. The Chang Ching-yao government also spread false stories: "Oh! Hunan is in terrible straits! The extremist party has come!" Focusing on such a situation, the "Miscellaneous Commentary on Events in Hunan" said: "We would like to ask, just what is an 'extremist party'? What is 'extremism'? Can those people who wildly proclaim that the extremist party has come give an answer to these questions?" The people you point to as "extremists" are "only determined men who give their lives to save their country, determined men who struggle for their country's rights and who demand freedom from those who rule by brute force. If indeed the extremist party does come to Hunan, perhaps it will have been provoked by those who wildly proclaim that the extremist party has already come." The short "Open Discussion" section gave a clear and simple popular explanation of "Bolsheviks": "This is nothing but making people work."

The most important essay published by Comrade Mao Tse-tung in the Hsiang River Review was "Min-chung ti ta lien-ho" [The Great Union of the Popular Masses].* This historical document of the May Fourth period that had great influence throughout the entire country was run consecutively in the second, third, and fourth numbers of the journal. The thirty-sixth number of the Weekly Review introduced it in the following words: "The forte of the Hsiang River Review is its discussions. The important article entitled 'The Great Union of the Popular Masses' that appears in the second, third, and fourth numbers of this journal is farsighted in its vision and to the point in its discussion. It is certainly one of today's important pieces of writing." † At the time, the progressive journal Sunday

---

* For a translation and discussion of this document, see "The Great Union of the Popular Masses," translated by Stuart R. Schram, and Schram, "From the 'Great Union of the Popular Masses' to the 'Great Alliance,'" The China Quarterly, No. 49 (January-March 1972), pp. 76-87 and 88-105. In the following pages, where possible, Professor Schram's translation has been utilized. — Tr.

† The author of this laudatory comment was in fact Hu Shih. See above, the introduction, p. xxix [S.R.S.].

[Hsing-ch'i jih], published in Chengtu, reprinted the essay in full. Thus "The Great Union of the Popular Masses" played a positive role in the seething ferment of youth movements that took place later in Szuchuan. Down to the first anniversary of the May Fourth movement in 1920, the representatives of the national United Association of Students were still writing articles in Shanghai publications that introduced the great significance of this article written by Comrade Mao Tse-tung. During the May Fourth period, representatives of the communist intellectuals, the revolutionary petty bourgeois intellectuals, and the bourgeois intellectuals all expressed their agreement with, and admiration for, Mao Tse-tung's article "The Great Union of the Popular Masses."

In "The Great Union of the Popular Masses," one can see Comrade Mao Tse-tung's earliest strategic concept of the necessity of establishing a people's revolutionary united front. Mao Tse-tung maintained that throughout history in revolutionary movements or in movements of resistance, from religion and academe to government and society, it had been necessary on both sides of the struggle to effect a great union; the difference between success or failure would be decided on the strength or weakness of that union. Mao Tse-tung said that today the class of brute force — the joint domination of the aristocrats and capitalists — has utterly ruined the country and has made humanity suffer in the extreme. Thus there has arisen a revolution and a great union of the popular masses. Mao Tse-tung maintained that the victory of the Russian October Revolution was the victory of the great union of the popular masses. Regardless of the three "magic weapons" possessed by the aristocrats and capitalists — military power, economic power, and even "intellectual" power — in the end, their numbers are too small. If the awareness of the broad masses is heightened and the masses then join together in a huge union, the affairs of the world will be easy to handle. On the basis of his own knowledge gained from personal experience, Comrade Mao Tse-tung said that we have already had our tests. The bullets of Lu Jung-t'ing can never shoot down traitors like Ts'ao Ju-lin and his bunch. As soon as we arise and let out a shout, the traitors will get up and tremble and flee for their lives. The article pointed out that this was the method of struggle used by the oppressed peoples of the various countries in Europe. (Author's note: in 1919, aside from the Russian October Revolution which had already succeeded, the people in Germany, Austria, and Italy were just in the midst of staging revolution.) The leader who had adopted this approach to revolution was the German, Marx. "We must arise and imitate him, we must carry out our great union!" With regard to the method used for the great union of the popular masses, Mao Tse-tung believed that one should organize separately on the basis of class distinctions. The most basic would be the peasants and workers organizations. The peasants should form a united organization "in order to promote the various interests of us tillers of the soil. It is only we ourselves who can pursue the interests of us tillers of the soil." How the landlords treat us, whether the rent and taxes are heavy or light, whether our bellies are full or not, and whether we have fields to cultivate or not are all questions to whose solution the peasants should earnestly devote their efforts. In the same way, the workers should form a united organization "in order to promote the various interests of those of us workers." With regard to the questions of the level of our wages, the length of the working day, equal or unequal sharing of dividends, or the progress of amusement facilities, the workers cannot fail to seek their solution. In line with the experiences in Europe and the United States, it was also necessary for the workers to organize labor unions in every industry and trade, such as railway, mining, metal, construction, textile, tram, and rickshaw unions, and make them a base for a united organization of all the workers in the country. The rest, such as students, women, teachers..., they all should organize on the basis of their own particular interests and demands and proceed with various reforms and struggles. Comrade Mao Tse-tung said to the students: the country is about to perish, and yet they still stick up proclamations forbidding us to love our country. We must join hands with our comrades, form ranks, rise up and struggle.

Comrade Mao Tse-tung believed that the great union of the popular masses had thus to be established on the basis of making the nation's workers and peasants the mainstay and then separately organizing the people of various strata before there could be any strength, before one could victoriously carry out the revolutionary struggle.

Comrade Mao Tse-tung believed that after the victory of the Russian October Revolution the conditions surrounding China's relations with the rest of the world underwent a fundamental change. He made a penetrating analysis of the 1911 Revolution. He pointed out that this revolution was only created by a group of anti-Manchu Chinese students abroad, the Society of Brothers [Ko Lao Hui], and a few soldiers of the new armies and of the provincial forces. As a result, it only overthrew an emperor and had very little connection with the great

majority of the popular masses. Comrade Mao Tse-tung said:
When the Russian October Revolution succeeded, the whole world
was shaken. Thereafter it has been an impetus for the popular revolutionary movements in Europe and Asia, and now the great May
Fourth movement of China has occurred. The scope of the May
Fourth movement is unprecedented, and in an extremely short
space of time its banner has advanced southward, across the Yellow
River to the Yangtze, Whampoa and Hankow, Tungting Lake and the
Min River, rising up to an even higher tide. Heaven and earth are
aroused by it, and the wicked are put to flight! Through this, the
people of the entire nation are awakened! The world is ours, the
nation is ours, society is ours. If we do not speak, who will speak?
If we do not act, who will act? We must act energetically to carry
out the great union of the popular masses, which will not brook a
moment's delay!

During the May Fourth movement a great many people's organizations had been born. Although many of these associations and societies included gentry and politicians who were not members of
the masses, and although some associations and societies were
even "entirely associations of gentry or of politicians," some, like
the National United Association of Students and the All Circles National Salvation Association [Ko chieh chiu kuo lien-ho hui], were
already quite large united organizations. Comrade Mao Tse-tung
believed that this proved that the organization of a revolutionary
united front among all the people of the country was entirely possible. He said that when the emperor was in control of everything,
we were not allowed to exercise our capacities. Whether in politics,
study, society, etc., we were not allowed to have either thought, organization or practice. Now, the reality of the May Fourth movement has made clear that when the people become active, things
are more easily managed.

Comrade Mao Tse-tung was full of boundless optimism and faith
in victory regarding the future of the Chinese revolution. In the
conclusion of his article "The Great Union of the Popular Masses,"
he foretold it like this: Our Chinese people possess inherent capacities. The more profound the oppression, the greater its resistance;
that which has accumulated for a long time will surely burst forth
quickly. The great union of the Chinese people will be achieved
earlier than that of any other place or people. Our golden age, our
age of glory and splendor, lies before us!

When Comrade Mao Tse-tung was studying at school he made a

deep investigation of both ancient and modern Chinese history. He had a thorough understanding of the special traits and the precious legacy of Chinese history and of the Chinese people. He had a very deep awareness of the great revolutionary power of the Chinese people and a perfect appreciation of the revolutionary nature of the Chinese nation [min-tsu] and the Chinese people [jen-min]. He was especially conversant with the history of the heroic anti-imperialist, antifeudal struggle of the Chinese people that had unfolded since the Opium War and with the lessons to be learned from the failure of that struggle. In eighty years the Chinese people had fought with every imperialist that had committed aggression against China and had never bowed before any counterrevolutionary force. Comrade Mao Tse-tung understood very well that all that was needed was a proper leader and then the Chinese people would be perfectly capable of forming an unconquerable united force of immense power. As far back as the May Fourth movement, Mao Tse-tung clearly began to advance one of the fundamental strategies of the Chinese revolution: one must carry out the great union of the people's power and establish a popular revolutionary united front. At the same time, in his own revolutionary practice in leading the Hunan people's patriotic May Fourth movement and the movement to Expel Chang Ching-yao, as well as the Democratic movement and the New Culture movement that followed, and especially in leading the early Hunan labor movement, Comrade Mao Tse-tung creatively and brilliantly grasped one of the main secrets of this Chinese revolution — the policy of the popular revolutionary united front. With the strength of the revolutionary masses and working class as the mainstay, and using the approach of unity and struggle, he established a genuine anti-imperialist, antifeudal united front among the bourgeoisie, petty bourgeoisie, and various democratic forces.

Comrade Mao Tse-tung's article "The Great Union of the Popular Masses," written in July 1919, in which he begins to combine a Marxist-Leninist point of view with the reality of the Chinese revolution, is one of his most important pieces of writing.

The Hsiang River Review, filled with this kind of "rebel" spirit, was, of course, welcomed by the broad masses of revolutionary youth and patriotic people. From the articles written by Comrade Mao Tse-tung they derived a sense of satisfaction and power they had never known before. Many questions that they worried about were answered. There was a great widening of the people's ideological horizons, and they felt that the future was full of hope. Nevertheless, the rank-and-file conservatives in society maintained that all this was "eccentrics with their crazy ideas" (the criticism of one Changsha newspaper), that it was all "unfounded statements," "rebellion and sedition." They were most critical about the use of the vernacular language [pai-hua], attacks on Confucius, and the crusade for the sanctity of labor and the equality of the sexes. Hence, with respect to the rule of the warlord Chang Ching-yao, the Hsiang River Review did nothing less than continually throw bombs and make it known that "rebel" forces had already grown to maturity.

Chang Ching-yao had a great deal of experience in muzzling public opinion. The Hunan-Hupei Printing Company [Hsiang-O yin-shua kung-ssu], which printed the Hsiang River Review, was often visited by military men who searched the premises and caused trouble. In the beginning of August 1919, after the publication of the fifth issue of the Hsiang River Review (this issue has not yet been found), Chang Ching-yao sent the military police to close down the United Association of Students and to confiscate the Hsiang River Review. In addition, he warned the Hunan-Hupei Printing Company that in the future it would under no circumstances be permitted to undertake the printing of the journal.

With this, Comrade Mao Tse-tung and the staff of the United Association of Students moved to the Hunan University Preparatory Office at Yüeh-lu-shan and continued their revolutionary activities.

Although the Hsiang River Review published only five issues, it did play a great role in propelling forward the Hunan revolutionary movement and had rather important educational significance for the nation's broad masses of patriotic youth and revolutionary intellectuals. Comrade Mao Tse-tung himself has recalled: "After the May Fourth movement I had devoted most of my time to student political activities, and I was editor of the Hsiang River Review, the Hunan students paper, which had a great influence on the student movement in South China" [Snow, Red Star, p. 153]. For example, Comrade Hsiao Ching-kuang has talked about how he and Comrade Jen Pi-shih were influenced by the Hsiang River Review:

Comrade Pi-shih was studying in Changsha just when the wave of the May Fourth movement was spreading throughout the entire country. At this time Chairman Mao was leading and launching a broad revolutionary movement in Hunan. The Hsiang River Review, which Chairman Mao edited, had a huge revolutionary influence. It was precisely under the influence of this revolutionary movement that our revolutionary consciousness began. At that time we still did not know much about communism, but we were filled with irrepressible hatred for imperialism and the traitorous national government. The great communist Comrade Pi-shih thus began his own revolutionary activities as a determined anti-imperialist, a revolutionary warrior who opposed the traitorous government. [18]

116

When he was running the Hsiang River Review, Comrade Mao Tse-tung often discussed problems in various areas with his intimate comrades-in-arms, very desirous of attaining a correct answer to several problems. But he felt that the strength of a small number of people was limited and so, under the name of the "Society for the Study of Problems" [Wen-t'i yen-chiu hui], he sent out the "Charter for the Society for the Study of Problems" to all relevant sectors in the country. In this bulletin over one hundred and forty small and large problems in the areas of Chinese and world politics, economics, society, education, labor, the international scene, etc., were broached: How was the union of the popular masses to proceed? Could socialism be implemented? The question of workers and peasants participating in government, the question of sending large numbers of students abroad for study, questions concerning Confucius, etc. This was just at the time when Hu Shih published his article "To yen-chiu hsieh wen-t'i, shao t'an hsieh chu-i" [A Little More Study of Problems, A Little Less Talk of Isms]. This article was a stand against the dissemination of Marxism in China. Comrade Mao Tse-tung stood on the side of the fundamental point made by Comrade Li Ta-chao that "problems and isms are inseparable." Thus, the bulletin emphasized that the study of problems should be based on theories. Before studying any problem, one must make a special study of every relevant "ism." At the same time, it further explained that regardless of the dimension of the problem, it had only to be of a comparatively wide, general nature to be brought up and studied. Those that needed an on-the-spot investigation had to be so investigated. After Comrade Teng Chung-hsia had received this document, he printed its full contents in the Peking University Daily [Pei-jing ta-hsüeh jih-k'an], No. 467 (published on October 23, 1919), and added this communication:

My friend Mr. Mao Tse-tung sent over ten copies of the "Charter for the Society for the Study of Problems" from Changsha. When my friends in Peking saw it they all pronounced it very good and said there was a need for research, and each wanted a copy from me. Now all I have left is one copy, yet there is still a great number of people who want their own. Thus I have borrowed the school's daily publication to print it up in order to answer the fine thoughts of all of those gentlemen who are concerned with the solution to today's problems.

After the Hsiang River Review was shut down, the student associations of the various schools continued to publish their weekly journals as before. At that time, at the suggestion of Comrade Mao Tse-tung, there was established an independent "United Association of Student Weeklies" [Hsüeh-sheng chou-k'an lien-ho hui], each weekly sending a representative to participate. This United Association of Student Weeklies organized around Comrade Mao Tse-tung and the Hsiang River Review and held a meeting every week to discuss how to achieve uniformity in the content of their propaganda. The journal New Hunan, the weekly run by the Hsiang-ya (now Hunan Medical College) Student Association, ran into problems after the school let out for summer vacation, for there were difficulties getting people to write for it. Afterward it was directed by Mao Tse-tung. Thus, New Hunan was edited by Comrade Mao Tse-tung from its No. 7 issue until it ceased publication. New Hunan inherited the spirit of the Hsiang River Review and began a frontal attack on the brutal rule of Chang Ching-yao. After the seventh issue, every number included a longish political essay. Mao Tse-tung also wrote many articles for the journal. On a great many important problems Mao Tse-tung had already gone through a period of mental fermentation and maturation and had collected together relevant materials. He used red-ruled paper to write his drafts, and in two or three hours he could sit down and write ten or twenty pages. Very often everyone else would be standing around talking and discussing problems while he wrote his articles.

With regard to the content of New Hunan after Comrade Mao Tse-tung became the editor, New Youth gave the following introduction (Vol. VII, No. 1):

The content of New Hunan is greatly different from what it was before the seventh issue. If the reader will read the following new declaration of policy from No. 7 he will know what we mean:

The platform of principles for this journal beginning with No. 7 is: (1) social criticism, (2) ideological reconstruction, (3) introduction of learning, (4) discussion of problems. From No. 7 onward this journal, as much as humanly possible, will be run on this platform. We are not, of course, concerned with the "success or failure" [of this journal] because our belief is: "Everything may be sacrificed except principle."

If we look further at the contents of No. 7, we see many outstanding items of interest. The most important, like "What Is Socialism?" and "What Is Anarchism?," are vast and impressive articles of several thousand characters each and are very penetrating discussions. This issue also has very good criticism of New China [Hsin Chung-kuo], which has hung out a counterfeit new signboard; it contains other good articles such as "Mourning Mei-chou p'ing-lun" and "The Problem of Work and Study."

Afterward, Chang Ching-yao confiscated and shut down each and every periodical like this that was harmful to his interests. New Hunan fought until about the tenth issue and was then finally closed down. After October 1919 Mao Tse-tung again thought of using a periodical to do battle with Chang Ching-yao, but it had become completely impossible.

Nevertheless, Comrade Mao Tse-tung still used Changsha papers, such as Ta-kung pao, to continue publishing many articles and commentaries, exposing from the flanks or making frontal attacks on the benighted rule of Chang Ching-yao and the irrational feudal system.

We can cite the following incident to explain how, at the time he was leading the seething mass patriotic movement and struggling feverishly against Chang Ching-yao, Comrade Mao Tse-tung still did not slacken his attacks against the feudal clan system.

On November 14, 1919, an incident occurred in Changsha in which a new bride committed suicide in the bridal sedanchair. When the news was published, all of society was jolted. The bride's name was Chao. She was a student and was extremely unhappy with the fact that her parents had arbitrarily made the decision concerning her marriage, forcing her to marry into a rich family. All her many protestations of opposition were without effect and so, on the day of her marriage, she took a dagger and slit her throat as she rode in the bridal sedanchair. The next morning all the papers in Changsha printed the news. Some papers also published commentary on the affair, saying that the one who had died had been "a sacrifice to the reform of the marriage system."

Opposition to the cannibalistic teachings of Rites and the old moral code, together with the promotion of a new moral code, had been an important battle on the cultural and ideological front during the May Fourth period. One of the salient questions in this area at the time concerned the liberation of women and the problem of the marriage system. Beginning with New Youth, all progressive journals ardently discussed this question. Lu Hsün, especially, wrote many stirring novels and essays. This was one of the questions that hit home first of all with the broad masses of young people. Many young men and women had their own very sad histories concerning marriage. Some had even finally taken to the revolutionary road because of this. Hunan was, of course, no exception, and the journals and newspapers often discussed the question of women and marriage. Women's Bell [Nü chieh chung], the weekly published by Chou-nan Girls' School, "mostly discussed 'women's liberation,' 'women's labor,' and other such questions." [19] Mao Tse-tung wrote a great number of articles concerning the question of women for Women's Bell.

Comrade Mao Tse-tung considered this [suicide] to be a very serious affair. He believed this tragedy was created by an infinitely evil feudal society. Thus, two days after the event occurred, on November 16, Changsha's Ta-kung pao printed an article by Mao Tse-tung commenting on Miss Chao's suicide. At the same time, he called upon everybody to discuss this problem. He believed that the discussion of any theory must be accompanied by real-life events. In a space of thirteen days, between November 16 and 28, Mao published altogether nine articles in Changsha's Ta-kung pao dealing with this incident. The discussions opened by the various newspapers in Changsha on this affair became an attack against the feudal system. A great many people from educational and press circles participated in the discussions. The articles written by the young students were particularly vehement.

In his own articles, Comrade Mao Tse-tung bitterly denounced the darkness of China's feudal society and the rottenness of the marriage system, calling the bridal sedanchair a "prisoner's cart." He believed that the deceased had been murdered by her surroundings because she had no way of escaping from society or the many-layered iron net that had been constructed by the "family of the bride," and the "family of the groom." There were many commentators who blamed only the "bride's family" and the "groom's family" for taking over and deciding the matter and forcing the girl to marry. They fell short of criticisms directed at society as a whole. Comrade Mao Tse-tung pointed out: The "bride's family" and the "groom's family" did indeed bear direct guilt, but the source of evil was the society. This society could cause the death of Miss Chao; it could also cause the death of Miss Ch'ien, Miss Sun, Miss Li. It could cause the death of "females"; it could also cause the death of "males." Mao believed that the fundamental problem was the social system. If one failed to remold this old society with a revolutionary spirit, if one failed to construct a new society, then all was hopeless. Mao Tse-tung had boundless sympathy for the bride and eulogized her spirit of resistance that she "would rather die than be unfree." But Mao Tse-tung still maintained that in order to stand against the old society it was better to be killed in battle than to die by suicide. If the goal cannot be obtained, yet one determines to fight and then perishes like broken jade, this very tough and brave spirit will inspire those who come after to rise up and wage continued struggle.

On the question of marriage, therefore, Comrade Mao Tse-tung encouraged the young people to stand up and do battle with society, to take care of their own marriages, to smash resolutely the policy of parents taking over and making the decision, and thus give meaning to this suicide. He made a thorough critique of the selfishness and injustice of China's feudal, superstitious, and corrupt marriage system, the theory of "horoscopes" [to be considered in marriages], and the policies of parents "seeking a wife for the son" and "seeking a good son-in-law."

On the question of committing suicide, Comrade Mao Tse-tung made an analysis that was filled with the dialectical spirit. At the time, a number of suicides were occurring all over China, a situation which elicited commentary in public opinion circles. New Youth published special articles on this. But the essay written by Ch'en Tu-hsiu, "Tzu-sha lun" [On Suicide], [20] was basically an analysis from the bourgeois idealist point of view, a purely bookworm type of "academic inquiry" that rattled on about the phenomenon of suicide throughout world history. Comrade Mao Tse-tung's short piece entitled "Fei tzu-sha" [Against Suicide] is, on the other hand, an example of an analysis of social phenomena that conforms to the Marxist dialectical point of view. He made a rational and reasonable critique and analysis of suicide, an action of social significance, starting from the fundamental causes in current Chinese society.

## IV. LEADING THE MOVEMENT TO EXPEL CHANG CHING-YAO, SECOND TRIP TO PEKING

The broad masses of the people of Hunan were bitter about the increasing brutality of Chang Ching-yao's rule, and their hatred was ever increasing. One and all believed that "if Chang the Venomous is not rooted out, Hunan will be without hope." The young students and some people in educational circles constituted the forward ranks of this tide of anger. Comrade Mao Tse-tung made a precise estimation of the overall situation and of the anger of the masses. He gradually led the mass patriotic movement of the May Fourth period, which had taken sentiment against Japan and the traitorous government as its central theme, into a new direction, until it became a movement that took the expulsion of Chang Ching-yao as its central theme.

Why did the people of Hunan so bitterly hate Chang Ching-yao? Ever since the 1911 Revolution, after Yüan Shih-k'ai had seized governmental power and China was divided between an opposing

north and south, Hunan had been the focus of the territorial struggles between the northern and southern warlords and had turned
into a field of perpetual seesaw battle. In the seven years that followed, Hunan was ruled by Peiyang warlords three different times.
It was especially during the rule of Chang Ching-yao, one of these
warlords, that the people suffered most severely.

The Anhwei warlord Chang Ching-yao entered Hunan after the
victory of the north over the south in the battle between the Chihli-
Anhwei Alliance and the Hunan-Kwangsi Alliance. In the more than
two years that Chang Ching-yao ruled, he showed himself capable
of anything. He burned, killed, looted, searched out and milked the
people of their wealth, put able-bodied men under arrest, destroyed
education, muzzled public opinion — every stratum of society in
Hunan passionately hated him.

In December 1918 "A Letter to the Northern and Southern Authorities from the Hunan Reconstruction Society in Shanghai" summed
up the evil acts perpetrated by Chang Ching-yao since his invasion
of Hunan:

Hunan has been most grievously wounded in this military calamity; the cruelty
is without precedent in all of history. There are over one hundred thousand
"guest troops" in Hunan who rape, loot, burn and kill — they stop at nothing. To
take some egregious examples: in the Li-ling campaign the entire city was burned
down; in the Huang-t'u Ridge campaign female corpses littered the mountainside.
In addition, cities, towns, markets, and villages were burned, plundered, and
trampled underfoot, and almost no one escaped. Defeated troops and local bandits take turns wreaking destruction, and the entire province has been picked
clean of all its public and private property. There are spying and false accusations that implicate the innocent, the tyranny of the Likin Office* that seizes commercial goods; there is no guarantee that either the people's lives or their property will last from morning until night. According to reports from people just
out of Hunan, the latest situation, the anarchy in financial circles, makes one
"tremble without even being cold." After the Yü-hsiang Bank was created, the
Jih-hsin Bank was also privately set up. The market was flooded with paper currency, money was mutually exchanged, and they banded together in collusion.
Last year the Hunan Bank arranged to have 45 million strings worth of copper
Cash certificates printed in Shanghai for the purpose of calling in and exchanging
the old bills. Today not only have the old bills not been exchanged, but the old
bills that were collected and not destroyed, as well as the new bills, are both
being released together. Totaling the old and new copper certificates, we arrive
at a figure of already over 100 million strings of Cash. Furthermore, when the
paper currency is forcibly sent out to the hsien and turned into silver money,
this means several tens of thousands of dollars [yuan] for each hsien. The total
amount of ready money taken in is enormous. Military pay is not disbursed, and

---

* Set up for the collection of internal tax on goods transported. — Tr.

the paper money is never turned into ready cash. Also, they force the establishment of a minimum legal exchange rate. The banks are able to change silver at the legal rate, and the merchants are then unable to make exchanges according to this rate. Hence the officials can circulate empty pieces of paper and the merchants are unable to exchange them at a cheap rate. Also, every day several tens of thousands of strings of Cash are being minted, all creating illegal profit. Bank notes steadily increase and copper dollars steadily decrease, until both copper and silver desert the scene. The market's currency base is destroyed, the people have gone bankrupt for no [real] reason, and industries have thus been abandoned. The most grievously affected have been, first of all, food and clothing. The soldiers and civilians exchange paper money for rice [but] the merchants could not exchange the paper money for grain, and so in the end there was an undeclared merchant's strike. Not only this, but the Hsiang-t'an Customs Bureau cleverly set up passport categories and raised the salt levy, each pack of salt being assessed at double the national rate, so that the salt merchants were forced out of business and the poor people had no one to sell to them. Thus, at the present time in the Hunan capital, a picul of rice requires one hundred strings of copper Cash, and one catty of salt requires four ounces of silver. Unless people eat simply, they starve. To such an extreme of hardship have the people come. All of what has been told here has been very painful. As for the people of the "four classes"* losing their places, the decline of [trade in] commodities, and those in poverty becoming vagabonds — it is beyond description....

The crimes of Chang Ching-yao are really too numerous to mention. The above merely mentions some of his crimes. It got even worse later. For example, taxes were collected on the land two and even three years in advance. Even though they suffered tight muzzling by Chang Ching-yao, if we open up any newspaper of the time, we can still see a continuous stream of reports on the cruel acts of the "northern army" and on the bitter suffering of the people.

What every stratum of society hated first and foremost was the complete license the "northern army" had under Chang Ching-yao to inflict vexations on the people. For example, wherever the "northern army" went it always commandeered people and transportation. When it had taken many prisoners and there was no longer any use for them, they were forced to carry rifles for the soldiers. When there were too few prisoners to go around, the number of jobs was not decreased, so that they died from exhaustion along the side of the road. Just before battle, they would change into military uniforms and be made cannon fodder. When the "northern army" crossed the border, sometimes under the pretext of "cleaning up the countryside," it would always plunder and rob without restraint. Animals, from pigs and cows to chickens and geese, any kind of clothing, or any item at all could not escape it. They

---

* The traditional social strata: scholar, farmer, artisan, merchant. — Tr.

gang-raped the women, extorted money, and, if they were displeased in the slightest way, they would set fire to and burn your house. Thus, as soon as the masses heard that the "northern army" was coming, there was none who did not end up by "running in the other direction." The peasants ceased their farmwork, the merchants stopped their activity, and even on a stormy night they would go into hiding in the mountains. After the soldiers had plundered, the local bandits swarmed forth like bees. After repeated plundering like this there was often not a human shadow for miles around. Added to this were incessant and relentless natural disasters — floods, droughts, insects. Although Hunan was a rice-producing region, it had never before seen plunder on such a grand scale year in and year out.

Educational circles likewise experienced a serious trampling underfoot. Teachers received no salary for five or six months. The little financial support that was sent out to the schools was a pile of old torn bills that had dropped greatly in value. The students of the public schools were constantly cut off from their food. Thus, the teachers were forced to stop teaching, the students to leave school, and the schools to stop their operations. Several times within one year the principals of nine public schools in Changsha had jointly asked permission to submit their resignations. The troops of Chang Ching-yao occupied schools everywhere, following each other and exchanging the schools among themselves, constantly changing their living quarters. Every public school in Changsha and some of the private schools were made into permanent barracks. The "northern army" also destroyed the equipment in the rooms, used books and maps for firewood, and used the teaching aids and lab equipment for acrobatic tricks. First Normal and Provincial First Middle School suffered the most severe damage. After the May Fourth movement the "northern army" looked upon the students with particular enmity and regularly subjected them to insults.

Chang Ching-yao and his three younger brothers (Ching-shun, Ching-yü, and Ching-t'ang) were arbitrary, cruel, and debauched in the extreme. For example, when Chang Ching-yao was celebrating his birthday, the city of Changsha was under martial law for six days. He forced the principal of First Girls' School [I nü hsiao] to become his concubine, planning to buy off her family with land, which turn of events caused a great clamor of public opinion. He also publicly advocated superstition, often taking a large group of his bodyguards to Yü-ch'üan-shan to burn incense. Chang's

"Tuchün Office" became known as the "Anhwei Guildhall." It was especially the tyrannical rule, abuse of power, and venality of Chang Ching-t'ang, the "Fourth General," that was deeply and passionately hated by the people. At the time, there was a folksong going around:

> Grave and dignified, the family Chang
> Yao, Shun, Yü, and T'ang*
> First, second, third and fourth
> Tiger, leopard, jackel, wolf!

Thus, except for an extremely small number of Anfu [21] Clique elements, there was not a stratum of society in Hunan that did not passionately hate the rule of Chang Ching-yao and especially the cruelty of the "northern army."

The reason behind Chang Ching-yao's severe suppression of the students' patriotic movement was that, aside from the usual fact that he was ordered to do so by the Tuan Ch'i-jui government, it had a direct bearing on his own personal economic interests.

Ever since 1915 when Yüan Shih-k'ai accepted the Twenty-one Demands of Japanese imperialism, the boycott of Japanese goods by the Hunanese had increasingly become a widespread and extensive movement; hence the amount of Japanese goods coming into Hunan ports decreased yearly. But from 1918 to 1919 Chang Ching-yao was minting a great deal of copper money and was buying large amounts of foreign copper, most of it from Japan. During the May Fourth period the movement of the people of Hunan to drive out Japanese goods reached an unprecedented level, and although Chang used his troops to suppress it, he was unable to stop it. Thus, the Japanese merchants suffered a setback and were no longer willing to send in goods. Chang Ching-yao's copper money could not be coined, and this had a serious influence on his personal income. So shamed, Chang Ching-yao became even more infuriated.

After July 7, 1919, when the United Association of Students held the rally to burn Japanese goods, Chang Ching-yao had the student representatives of all the schools and some faculty members go to the Educational Society to hear his instructions. People who attended that meeting still remember that it was a hot day and that four of his bodyguards were fanning Chang. Wildly Chang Ching-yao shouted: "You are not permitted to march in the streets, you are not per-

---

* The first names of the Chang brothers are those of the legendary sage-kings of Chinese antiquity. — Tr.

mitted to hold meetings, you are not permitted to investigate commercial establishments. You should work hard at studying and teaching; otherwise this general will fix you!"*

In September Comrade Mao Tse-tung began his secret activities to expel Chang. With the United Association of Students as a base, he made liaison with people in educational and newspaper circles and conferred on ways to expel Chang. At the same time, he sent P'eng Huang and others to Shanghai to conduct anti-Chang propaganda and to link up with forces outside of Hunan for the expulsion of Chang.

At this time a letter arrived from a friend in Peking casting doubt on the significance of expelling Chang. He maintained that since they believed in a fundamental remolding of society, they should not pay any attention to the small problems, the minor affairs, that faced them at the moment. Mao Tse-tung wrote back and said that this was a very big and a very important matter, it was work that had to be done to attain a fundamental reconstruction, and it was a particularly effective method for changing the current circumstances.

After summer vacation, the various schools opened one after the other. Although the United Association of Students had been disbanded by a clear order from Chang Ching-yao, it continued actively to carry on with various tasks under the leadership of Comrade Mao Tse-tung, and in November 1919, it resumed public activities in a newly organized form. The "Declaration of Reorganization" of the United Association of Students said a good deal that was "pointed at the nose" of Chang Ching-yao:

After the European war ended the current suddenly changed. The right of self-rule and self-determination rests with the citizens of the nation.... The government is numb to the feelings of the people; its measures are perverse and invidious. It sets up a party that schemes for its own interests; it is befuddled and drunk; it milks people; it sacrifices the will of the people; it treats human life like weeds; it tramples on the rights of the people; it sticks the people in some dream world and does nothing but indulge its own arrogance. If things go on like this for long, how will we be able to bear the suffering to come?

The primary activity of the United Association of Students was still to inspect for Japanese goods, using this as a way to keep up the anti-Japanese patriotic movement and also to counter Chang

* According to Pai Yü's account, Chang screamed at the students: "If you don't listen to me, I'll cut off your heads!" Chao Heng-t'i himself told me in an interview of June 1963 that Chang Ching-yao "was not a man, but a wild beast" [S.R.S.].

Ching-yao. Paying no heed to Chang Ching-yao's intimidation and persecution, the United Association of Students informed every school and every circle on December 2, 1919, that it would hold another demonstration to burn Japanese goods at Educational Society Plaza. On this day the workers from the graphite refining plant and other factories as well as many shop employees participated. A large number of student investigating units came from the shops in the district of Eight-Cornered Pavilion. Dragging out a great load of Japanese cloth goods to Educational Society Plaza, they staged a burning. Just when the masses were conducting their meeting and giving speeches, Chang Ching-t'ang, the "Fourth General," rode in on horseback, bringing with him a battalion of armed troops and a "long sword corps." They tightly surrounded the students, workers, and teachers, and Chang shouted out his abuse: "This is the action of local bandits. The men are male bandits, the women are female bandits. You can't talk reason with bandits. Take care of them; let them have it!" The long sword corps immediately forced the student representatives on the stage to their knees and, while they were at it, they slapped a few students in the face.

This was a great insult to the young students of Hunan, to the educational circles of Hunan, and to the people of Hunan!

This was a flash point; the cruel and stupid Chang Ching-yao had set himself on fire.

After the students had returned to the schools they were extremely angry and felt that unbearable circumstances had reached the limit. But there were some who expressed fear and who spread a pessimistic and hopeless tone. A lively discussion unfolded among everybody, but they couldn't reach any sort of consensus.

Throughout the night Comrade Mao Tse-tung called together the members of the New People's Study Society and the main elements of the United Association of Students. He made a report on the situation and gave some concrete instructions. Mao Tse-tung analyzed the current situation for everyone: The anger of every stratum of Hunan society against Chang Ching-yao had reached an extreme. The broad masses of young students and those people in educational circles had reached the point where they could bear it no longer. Not only had the stinking name of Chang Ching-yao spread throughout Hunan, it was also known throughout the whole nation. At the same time, the two warlord cliques of Anhwei and Chihli were at each other's throats. The contradictions between Chang Ching-yao and the Chihli warlord Wu P'ei-fu, who was at the time quartered at Heng-yang, were on the increase. Feng Yü-hsiang [22] (quartered in Ch'ang-te) was also showing no friendly feelings toward Chang. In the sharpening contradictions among the warlords, Chang Ching-yao was extremely isolated and was in a precarious position. The opportunity for expelling Chang Ching-yao had fully ripened. Mao Tse-tung believed that before, when there had been individual people from educational circles who had gone outside of the province and engaged in activities to "pull out Chang" but when there had been no mass strength to act as a backing, it was only natural that such efforts had been unable to play any real role. The most important question now was to mobilize the power of the masses — first and foremost that of the entire body of students and faculty — and to make a determined struggle against Chang Ching-yao. The first step was to stage a general strike of classes and tie the strike into the expulsion of Chang Ching-yao so as to win broad sympathy in society at large. Mao Tse-tung also said that only after classes were struck could everyone concentrate their energies on the work of expelling Chang. This is how Comrade Mao Tse-tung encouraged everyone: This time Chang Ching-yao won't force us into submission. We will conquer Chang Ching-yao and will surely chase him out.

And so the cadres of the United Association of Students went into feverish action and began to foment a general strike of classes to take place within two or three days. After the news had gotten out, Chang Ching-yao, on the one hand, sent out secret agents to every school to spy to find out what was going on, and on the other, he sent out officials to threaten the authorities of all the schools, issuing strict orders to stop the strike. At this time there were two different opinions brewing among the authorities and faculty members of the schools with regard to the strike of classes. One was to submit to the illegal order, asserting that to avoid sacrificing the student's education one should advise the students to continue classes. The other approved of expelling Chang and was in sympathy with the student strike. Focusing on this situation, Mao Tse-tung established contact with the people in the "Education Invigoration Society" [Chien-hsüeh hui] and together with them persuaded the more conservative faculty members and those principals who were sitting on the fence to go along with the strike.

At the last meeting of the All School Representative Council before the strike of classes, there were still some student representatives who vacillated and who advocated only asking for a petition, not a strike of classes. There was a representative from one of the girls' schools who upbraided these students for having no patriotic feelings. Comrade Mao Tse-tung had come in person to the meeting that day and rose to support the statement of this girl student. Mao said that the struggle against Chang Ching-yao was a struggle against imperialism, against a traitorous government, and against feudalism. In normal times everyone was for patriotism, everyone was for remolding society. Now the time had come to put this into practice. The assembly that day had decisive significance for the staging of the general strike of classes.

Starting on December 6, with First Normal, Commercial Vocational, Hsiu-yeh, Ch'u-i, and Chou-nan Girls' School going first, the various schools struck classes one after another.

In less than a week the entire body of vocational schools, middle schools, normal schools, and some of the primary schools of Changsha had all struck classes together.

Representing thirteen thousand students from middle schools and above, the Hunan United Association of Students promulgated a declaration to expel Chang that read: "For every day Chang the Venomous remains in Hunan, the students will remain out of classes."

After the success of the general strike of classes, the second step was to proceed with the concrete activity of expelling Chang. By this time the situation had become more tense. Mao called together the important cadres of the New People's Study Society and the United Association of Students and also invited some people in education circles for a meeting. Everyone discussed and decided on the following procedures:

1. Organize an Expel Chang Delegation with two representatives from each school. It should split up and go to Peking, Heng-yang, Ch'ang-te, Ch'en-chou, Shanghai, and Canton to work on getting a petition signed. On the one hand, it is to spread propaganda for expelling Chang, and on the other, it is to make use of the contradictions between Chang and Wu (P'ei-fu) to bring pressure on Chang Ching-yao militarily.

2. The faculty representatives of the various schools should separately join and lead the various delegations.

3. Some people will remain in Changsha to continue organizing the students and the people of the province in activities aimed at expelling Chang. They will also be responsible for establishing contact with representatives from other cities.

Most of the personnel of the Expel Chang Delegation went their separate ways in January 1920.

The man presiding over the trip to Peking was Comrade Mao Tse-tung. Comrades Ho Shu-heng and Hsia Hsi were sent to Heng-yang.

Thus, both within and outside the province, a great, enthusiastic high tide arose for the expulsion of Chang Ching-yao. After the delegation arrived in Hankow, Comrade Mao Tse-tung drafted the proclamation calling for the expulsion of Chang, in which he enumerated Chang Ching-yao's various evil actions, and sent it to the papers in Hankow, Peking, and Shanghai. In addition, he took a picture at Wuchang's Nien-yü-t'ao bus station of more than twenty sacks of opium seeds that Chang Tsung-ch'ang was transporting to Chang Ching-yao. When this came out in the newspapers, it made Chang's name stink all the more. After the delegation arrived in Peking, it petitioned the "cabinet minister" of the Peiyang warlords. The purpose behind this was publicly to lodge charges and expose the crimes of Tuan Ch'i-jui's Anhwei Clique of warlords. Mao Tse-tung also held a mass meeting in the Hunan guildhall with a core made up of Hunan students who were studying in Peking and reported on the events surrounding the expulsion of Chang. He gained everyone's support.

Chang Ching-yao was in Changsha jumping like an ant in a hot pan. He sent down orders to investigate the situation surrounding Ho Shu-heng and the other representatives from academic circles who were part of the Expel Chang Delegation and to deal with them accordingly. He gave orders to expel the student representatives from the various schools and also gave repeated orders and instructions prohibiting all activities. The United Association of Students led the students in the adoption of various ingenious methods for carrying on their activities, for example, the organization of an acting troupe and the presentation of new plays of an antifeudal character in order to raise money for each delegation; the continued issuing of propaganda encouraging the students not to attend school; the organization of various provisional supplementary schools; the use of inns and teahouses as places to stay and carry on activities; and work on the support of national goods was secretly continued.... Chang Ching-yao's police department adopted all kinds of intimidating measures, but there was no way to suppress the student's activities completely.

Wu P'ei-fu was a big general of the Chihli Clique of warlords. When he attacked Hunan in 1918, his "military achievements" had been quite distinguished, but he was coolly and quietly sent on station to the city of Heng-yang, there to oversee T'an Yen-k'ai (T'an continued to reserve for himself a territory in southern and western Hunan of over twenty hsien); he did not obtain the position of Hunan Tuchün and governor and — his grievance against Chang

Ching-yao being of long standing — his bitter feelings steadily increased. Several times the Delegation requested Wu to send troops to expel Chang, and Wu expressed his sympathy. Taking advantage of this opportunity, Comrades Ho Shu-heng, Hsia Hsi, and others organized all middle school students in Heng-yang and, with Third Normal School as the core (Hsia Ming-han, Chiang Hsien-yün, and other comrades were the core elements of the Third Normal students), founded the Southern Hunan United Association of Students and launched a boycott of Japanese goods and other patriotic movements. In addition, they ran the weekly Hunan Tide [Hsiang ch'ao], the primary content of which was concerned with the expulsion of Chang Ching-yao. With this weekly they gave great impetus to the anti-imperialist, antifeudal, antiwarlord movements of the people of Heng-yang and southern Hunan.

At the beginning of 1920 the clash of interests between the Chihli and Anhwei warlord cliques was becoming increasingly vehement (the leaders of the Chihli Clique were Feng Kuo-chang and Ts'ao K'un; the leaders of the Anhwei Clique were Tuan Ch'i-jui and Hsü Shu-cheng), and the Chihli army stationed in Hunan was anxious to pull out and move north, there to unite forces in order to force the Anhwei army into submission. In late May 1920 Wu P'ei-fu led his troops out from Heng-yang along the Hsiang River. On May 27 he passed Changsha and proceeded directly on to Wuhan. When Wu withdrew his troops from Heng-yang he had a tacit agreement with T'an Yen-k'ai and Chao Heng-t'i: As Wu's troops retreated, the Hsiang [i.e., Hunan] Army would advance. Although the number of Anhwei troops under Chang Ching-yao was large, they had lived an easy, comfortable life for several years, were unbearably corrupt, and lacked the least shred of combative strength. Under the pressure of the advancing Hsiang Army following Wu P'ei-fu and now closing in on them, Chang's troops crumbled without a fight. On June 11 Chang Ching-yao hastily fled Changsha. On June 26 all the troops under Chang Ching-yao pulled out of Hunan altogether.

Internal discord among the warlords had brought on the early victory of the Expel Chang Movement of the people of Hunan. But, although the old warlords had gone, new warlords — T'an Yen-k'ai and Chao Heng-t'i, flying the banner of Expel Chang — had come. The troubles of the Hunan people were by no means over.

Nevertheless, the defeat and withdrawal of Chang Ching-yao was something that made people jump for joy. The Expel Chang movement had itself been a successful antiwarlord movement. It greatly strengthened the revolutionary might of the Hunan people and at the same time was an inspiration for democratic revolutionary forces throughout the entire country.

In order to lead the Movement to Expel Chang Ching-yao, Comrade Mao Tse-tung had come to Peking for a second time, thus obtaining the opportunity further to embrace Marxism-Leninism. In February 1920, after Mao had reached Peking, the announcement that the government of the Soviet Union was establishing foreign relations with China on a basis of equality had just broken through the news blackout of the warlord government. This news received the enthusiastic welcome of the Chinese people. The influence of the victory of Russia's socialist revolution was now felt more deeply and widely in China. By this time, Chinese translations had been made and published of the Communist Manifesto and other Marxist classics. Mao diligently read and studied these books and completely embraced Marxism. Recalling this important hour, Mao has said:

During my second visit to Peking I had read much about the events in Russia, and had eagerly sought out what little Communist literature was then available in Chinese. [Three books especially deeply carved my mind and] built up in me a faith in Marxism, from which, once I had accepted it as the correct interpretation of history, I did not afterwards waver. [These books were The Communist Manifesto, translated by Ch'en Wang-tao, and the first Marxist book ever published in Chinese; Class Struggle by Kautsky; and a History of Socialism, by Kirkup.] By the summer of 1920 I had become, in theory and [to some extent] in action, a Marxist, [and from this time on I considered myself a Marxist] *[Snow, Red Star, p. 155].

Marxism-Leninism provided Comrade Mao Tse-tung with the perfect weapon for a revolutionary struggle, it gave him the correct direction for the development of the revolution and thus increased and determined more than ever his faith in the revolutionary struggle.

After Comrade Mao Tse-tung arrived in Peking, he increased his contacts in every area and had especially close ties with Li Ta-chao and Teng Chung-hsia, both revolutionary comrades with a firm belief in Marxism. At the same time, he thought more deeply about various problems. He felt that many people were still just making empty talk about transformation and making empty arguments. Such pressing questions as, What was, after all, the final goal of the transformation? What methods were to be used to achieve this goal? Where was one to start work at the present time?

---

* Material in brackets has not been included by Li Jui. — Tr.

were studied in detail only by a very small number of people. Those who made any study of organization were even fewer. Mao Tse-tung wrote a continuous stream of letters to members of the New People's Study Society in Changsha, giving them a detailed report on the situation in Peking together with his own views and suggestions. He believed that there were still many, many questions in need of detailed study and that it would therefore be best to set up an organization along the lines of a self-study university to make a thorough study of the theories of Marx and Lenin, the revolutionary movements of various countries, and the many fundamental problems surrounding the transformation of China. In his letters he said that in the future they could organize a Russia Travel Team to go and study the experience of the Russian Revolution. In these letters Mao Tse-tung repeatedly explained that the New People's Study Society should be made into a militant organization with a unified ideology, that they should gather together more true comrades and become the operational base that would be necessary in the future. For these reasons, it was necessary to make a two- or three-year plan in Changsha. Mao Tse-tung was opposed to the individualistic, absentminded reveries of some members of the New People's Study Society at the time to the effect that "I want to do such-and-such a study," "such-and-such preparation," "such-and-such destruction," "such-and-such establishment." He believed that a struggle waged by the individual was a "wasted struggle," expending much effort and gaining little success; it was most uneconomical. It was necessary to discuss matters jointly, to carry them out jointly, to organize into an "allied army," into an "army of confederates" before a guarantee of victory was possible. It was necessary to strictly prohibit "wasteful struggles" and to organize an "allied army" to do battle together.

In April 1920 Mao Tse-tung went to Shanghai. T'ong Huang and the other delegates of the Expel Chang Delegation had already carried out a great deal of activity in Shanghai. They had organized a "People's News Agency" [P'ing-min t'ung-hsün she] and had published a periodical called Heaven Asks [T'ien wen]* that was devoted to exposing the evils of the Chang Ching-yao plague in Hunan. The journal also published articles dealing with the movement to Expel Chang from the province.

---

* This periodical presumably took its title from the long poem by Ch'ü Yüan, which has remained one of Mao's favorites. See his remarks of August 1964 in Mao Tse-tung Unrehearsed (London: Penguin, 1974), p. 230 [S.R.S.].

Comrade Mao Tse-tung's life in Shanghai was very difficult. He maintained regular contact by correspondence with the people in Changsha who were involved in the Movement to Expel Chang. Some people still remember the following incident:

Once, the principal of Ch'u-i Primary School pulled out a long letter from Chairman Mao to show us. The letter said he was washing clothes to support himself. Chairman Mao said that washing the clothes was not hard, but because he had to use the streetcar for pickup and delivery, the money he got from washing was wasted on transportation expenses. [23]

During the period in Shanghai, Comrade Mao Tse-tung also gathered together members of the New People's Study Society who were staying there as well as those who were preparing to go to France and held a meeting in Pan-sung Park. The meeting clearly set down the guiding principle of the Society — "to remold China and the world." In addition, the participants conducted a detailed and exhaustive discussion of the Society's operational methods, conditions for membership in the Society, procedures for entrance into the Society, etc. It decided that the Society should be located in Changsha and that Comrade Mao Tse-tung would bear the responsibility for overall liaison. With the fact in mind that at the time there were some progressive organizations in the country that were unable to avoid superficiality and that had few deep, long-range plans, Mao Tse-tung called for the Society to adopt a "latent posture," advocating that it keep its feet on solid ground, that it have "roots and leaves," that it not make a lot of racket, but rather do a little more basic work. It should not "overflow the pier." Everyone was in the closest agreement with these proposals of Comrade Mao Tse-tung.

On the day after the withdrawal of Chang Ching-yao, the Hunan United Association of Students resumed its public activities and immediately sent telegrams to all the Expel Chang Delegations, urging them to return to the province as early as possible. At the end of June and beginning of July 1920, the various Expel Chang Delegations returned.

After he had seen off another young group of Hunanese on their way to France from Shanghai as part of the Diligent Work and Frugal Study in France program, Chairman Mao Tse-tung returned to Changsha in early July.

After this, the Hunan revolutionary movement entered a new phase.

## V. UNMASKING THE WARLORD GOVERNMENT OF T'AN YEN-K'AI AND CHAO HENG-T'I

After the withdrawal of Chang Ching-yao, all strata of Hunan society were overjoyed, and they were very anxious to rid themselves
thenceforward of the malignant grasp of the Peiyang warlords. They
wanted time to catch their breath and restore their original vigor.
In 1920, after defeat of the Anhwei Clique in the battle between it
and the Chihli Clique, it was difficult for a time for the "northern
army" to make any more incursions into Hunan. Because of this,
the general opinion among informed quarters in society was that
this was a once-in-a-lifetime opportunity for "Hunanese to manage
Hunan's own affairs," to implement "Hunanese autonomy." Responding to the times, various new organizations arose. New books and
newspapers could readily be sold, and numerous representatives
of every circle expressed their opinions in the newspapers on the
current political situation. At the same time, the spread of the influence of the October Revolution to China had already gone one
step further, and a good number of people began to interest themselves in Russia and in socialism. The slogans "Practice people's
rule" [Shih-hsing min chih] (i.e., democracy; this was the expression used at the time) and "Democracy" rang out loudly. T'an Yen-
k'ai and Chao Heng-t'i, who were leading the Hsiang Army to occupy Changsha, were just then flying the banner of "Eliminate the
evil for the people." They could not help but "obey popular sentiment." They also sent out a circular telegram that proclaimed
"Hunanese autonomy" and a desire to "return the government to
the people." [24] They planned to create an ornamental facade of a
"provincial autonomy law" (or a "provincial constitution"), thereby
to maintain control within and resistance without [against the war-
lords] and to maintain a rule that was not yet stable.
When Comrade Mao Tse-tung was still in Peking and Shanghai,
he studied with P'eng Huang and others the question of how to utilize the opportunity afforded by the victory of the Expel Chang
movement in stimulating the Hunan situation to develop in a better
direction. They prepared a document entitled "Hu-nan chien-she
wen-t'i t'iao-chien shang-ch'üeh" [A Deliberation on the Conditions
of the Question of Construction in Hunan] and sent it out for discussion to every relevant person. This short document advanced certain program points, such as the abolition of warlord rule, banks
and industries run by the people, the establishment of hsien and
hsiang [township] autonomous organs, the founding of labor unions

and peasant unions, a guarantee of the people's freedom to assemble and associate, and the freedom of speech and of the press. A piece of correspondence between Mao Tse-tung and his friends in Peking specifically speaks to this point: We should be revolutionaries; we cannot be reformists. Hunan is a province of China. If the problem of China is not solved from the base, then naturally it will be difficult for Hunan to change independently. We cannot beg for meat from the tiger's mouth piece by piece. But at the moment we are already riding on the back of the tiger, and if we don't struggle for things that can be gotten through struggle, this would be wrong.

After Comrade Mao Tse-tung returned to Changsha, he launched a whole series of social movements: the province-wide United Association of Students resumed its public activity, the Society for the Study of Russia [O-lo-ssu yen-chiu hui] was founded, a Diligent Work and Frugal Study in Russia program was started, plans were made to start a Cultural Book Society, the Hunan Popular Gazette was published, the Hsiang-t'an Society for the Promotion of Education was founded. . . .

Mao Tse-tung and his comrades-in-arms, making a detailed study of the current situation, believed that the government of T'an and Chao was following a purely fraudulent policy and that the blind optimism reigning in society was cause for concern. They believed that the popular slogan of "Hunanese autonomy" had to be explained properly for the benefit of the people, but that the open atmosphere of the time provided a truly favorable opportunity to push forward with the Hunan revolutionary movement. Thus, the "Hunan All-Student Declaration of the Discontinuance of the Strike of Classes" was issued. It admonished the people to be clearly aware that there were still many problems for the future and that they should have no illusions about the ruling class. At the same time, it criticized many faculty and student representatives who had been involved in the Expel Chang movement for having abandoned the basic work of mobilizing the masses and having grown enthusiastic for the petition approach. The declaration said:

Our sacrifices this time were too great and our return particularly unsatisfactory. Furthermore, in expelling Chang we benefited from the military situation, but a different situation would exacerbate the people's misery. Henceforward we should have a more thorough awareness. . . . In every matter we must depend upon ourselves; never again must we run hither and thither seeking help and begging for food from the tiger's mouth. Such is the goal of our future work; it is also our most sincere and carefully considered declaration.

Comrade Mao Tse-tung had made a thorough study of the experience of the October Revolution and felt that the conditions for a nationwide revolution were not yet present in China. Mao and his comrades-in-arms spoke about the reasons for the success of the Russian Revolution, which stemmed primarily from the following: First of all, there was the mighty Bolshevik party led by Lenin. This party was armed with Bolshevism. It had several hundred thousand members and had made long preparation for the revolution. Next, there was a truly reliable broad mass of people. The workers and peasants, who made up eighty to ninety percent of the country's entire population, rose up at one call. At the same time, there was also the opportunity afforded by the defeat of Russia, and so in a short while it had been possible to overturn the unstable bourgeois government with one push and to sweep away the classes that opposed the revolutionary party and the revolution. Mao Tse-tung recognized that China did not yet present these conditions. At that time, China should work on constructing a base; the revolutionary forces in various areas should work hard to push forward their local democratic movements and movements of the worker and peasant masses in order to increase in strength. Some people felt that there were few people, little strength, and insufficient confidence. Mao said that nothing could ever be successful or could ever win over a majority of the people as soon as it started. The only thing necessary was for everyone resolutely and patiently to "go from what is near to what is far," from few to many, from small to large. If one remained unshaken, despite the small number of people at the present moment, then revolutionary forces would gradually grow stronger. Mao also made these proposals and this knowledge known through articles that appeared in the Changsha press.

In order to seize the opportunity, to launch an extensive democratic movement, to increase the strength of the revolution, to lead all proposals and activities onto a correct path and, in addition, to create conditions for the unmasking of the reactionary character of the T'an Yen-k'ai and Chao Heng-t'i government, Mao Tse-tung and his comrades-in-arms P'eng Huang (at this time he was still holding a post in the United Association of Students) and Ho Shu-heng gathered together a group of people from newspaper and educational circles, began the organization of an "Association for the Promotion of Hunan Reconstruction" [Hu-nan kai-tsao ts'u-ch'eng hui] and published a declaration on "Hunan Reconstruction," which they had printed in the Changsha press on July 6. The declaration stated:

# Early Revolutionary Activities of Mao Tse-tung

The reason things in Hunan are rotten to the core is that most people are incapable of self-awareness; they cannot stand up and give their opinions. If they have something to say, they don't say it; if they have an idea, they don't let it out. The militarists of the north and south have successfully taken advantage of the situation to persecute us, occupy Hunan as their own territory, and tie up the people's wealth in their own sack. We won't talk of matters past. Henceforward the essential point is that, on the negative side, nothing would be better than the abolition of the Tuchün and disarmament; on the positive side, nothing would be better than the establishment of people's rule.... What we advocate as "Hunanese self-determinationism" does not at all mean "tribalism"; neither is it localism. It is simply that the people of Hunan should take responsibility themselves for the creation of their own development. They dare not, and cannot, decline this responsibility. The enemy of creating civilization in Hunan is the warlord, the High Inspecting Commissioner of Hunan, Kwangtung, and Kwangsi, the High Inspecting Commissioner of Hunan and Hupei, the National Protection Army, the Army of National Restoration, and the Southern Expeditionary Army. The way to deal with this kind of enemy is to force him back across the Hunan border so that he will never again come within the territory of Hunan to line up against the people. The people of Hunan should freely develop their own nature and create their own civilization — this is what we mean by "Hunanese self-determinationism."

In order to prevent people from having illusions about the newly arrived rulers, T'an Yen-k'ai and Chao Heng-t'i, and also to conduct some preemptive unmasking, at the end of the declaration were demands put squarely to the government:

T'an Tsu-an (T'an Yen-k'ai's style) and Chao Yen-wu (Chao Heng-t'i's style) are the generals who expelled Chang Ching-yao; their efforts were great and their achievement lofty, and they have become local heroes. In the future we hope they will give their attention to the following: (1) Be able to observe the principle of self-determinationism and not "invite the tiger* into the house." If the tiger does get into the house, be able to resist him squarely and throw him out. (2) Be able to adhere to the principle of democracy, regard themselves as common citizens, and completely cleanse themselves of their militaristic, bureaucratic, and gentry airs. In measures they take in the future, to take the public opinion of thirty million common people as their touchstone. The most important things are to abolish the Tuchün system and troop reduction, austerity in spending, to plan actively for universal education, and to ensure that thirty million people all have the freedom of speech and of the press. These are our greatest hopes.

The announcement of this declaration elicited extremely serious consideration from all sectors. In society at large, however, views on the "autonomy movement" were still very confused. At this time, the various Changsha newspapers were printing at least one or two, and sometimes even three or four, articles every day that were concerned with the "autonomy movement." With regard to the

---

* I.e., outside warlords. — Tr.

growth of a movement, Comrade Mao Tse-tung had always called for first "creating public opinion,"* that is, one should first complete the work of ideological mobilization. From September 3 to October 3 he published ten consecutive articles in Changsha Ta-kung pao in which he discussed the so-called Hunanese Autonomy Movement and commented on what kind of a democratic government the people really did need.

Each of these articles by Comrade Mao Tse-tung, with its clear analyses, unique viewpoint, and far-reaching goal, which took the basic interests of the people as its premise, touched the hearts of the people and became the main current of the democratic ideological tide. Mao Tse-tung made a critique of various incorrect views and penetratingly explained what kind of autonomy movement Hunan really needed. He believed that this autonomy movement should make the people — the peasants who tilled the fields, the workers who performed manual labor, the merchants who shipped goods and traded, as well as the students who attentively and eagerly sought education — its mainstay. Unless it were run by the people this "autonomy" was bound to be short-lived, false, corrupt, and empty. At the time, there were those in the upper strata of the various circles who argued that government was only the affair of a small number of people from a special class, that one had to have studied law and government before one had any right to talk about it. To draft an "autonomy law" was even more of an undertaking. (For example, Hsiung Hsi-ling sent a "General Outline for Autonomy" from Peking that people criticized, saying that Hsiung had not studied law; how could he write an autonomy law?) There were also people who felt that the question of autonomy in Hunan was too big and who were afraid to say anything. Then Comrade Mao Tse-tung, taking the example of the Russian October Revolution, posed a question to these gentlemen: Russia's government is run completely by the Russian workers and peasants. Do you mean to say that Russia's workers and peasants all studied law and government? In order to open the eyes of those people who had long lived under the influence of the reactionary ruling class's orthodox ideology, Mao used extremely simple, common and clear language to say: After World War I, government moved into new hands and law took on a new aspect.

---

* There is a striking parallel here with Mao's remarks at the Tenth Plenum in September 1962: "Anyone wanting to overthrow a political régime must create public opinion and do some preparatory ideological work," Mao Tse-tung Unrehearsed, p. 195 [S. R. S.].

The government and law of yesterday is of no use today. The government and law of the future is not in the minds of those gentlemen who wear long gowns but in the minds of the workers and the peasants. They'll do just what they want to do about government, and they'll establish such laws as they like. Mao Tse-tung called on all the people to rise up and called on everyone to participate in government and law and to get involved in the great affairs of state. In his article he said: If you do not go out and discuss government and law, they will come and discuss you every day; if you do not go out and deal with government and law, they will come and deal with you every day. Mao believed that the autonomy of Hunan was an extremely simple business and was not the least bit mysterious. "The law of autonomy" must be discussed by the vast majority of the people and must be determined by them before it can be of any use. Regardless of whether one is a worker, a peasant, a merchant, a student, a teacher, a soldier, a policeman, a woman...all people have the right to speak, and they certainly should speak and be able to speak. Especially important, as Mao Tse-tung pointed out: everyone must work hard to create the reality of Hunanese autonomy, and this may even be without any "autonomy law" at all.

So that the members of the New People's Study Society should not entertain any doubts, as had been the case during the Expel Chang movement, Comrade Mao Tse-tung kept his comrades informed at all times by writing them of his own proposals and activities. In addition, he emphasized that this "autonomy movement" was merely an expedient to deal with present circumstances and was by no means a fundamental proposal. Mao Tse-tung said that if on account of this it proved possible to bring about improved circumstances in Hunan, this would be advantageous for concrete preparatory work in the future.

By this time, there were many discussions going around, and public opinion had been created in the newspapers. Nevertheless, the average person still went no further than empty discussion or still pinned his hopes on Mr. Ch'a-ling's (i.e., T'an Yen-k'ai, who was from Ch'a-ling in Hunan) "formulation of a constitution." On the one hand, Comrade Mao Tse-tung propagated the correct theory of the people's democratic movement and, on the other, actually engaged in practical movements himself. In his articles he repeatedly explained the following principle: Whenever an undertaking starts with a theoretical base yet is not followed by a movement, there is no way for the goals of the theory to be realized. Before current problems can have any significance, many people must come together and promote a movement, and a broad mass movement must take shape. He called on the three hundred thousand people of Changsha to be the first to go into action. Thus, with the United Association of Students as the backbone, all circles and organizations in Changsha held separate meetings from late September to the beginning of October 1920 and discussed the question of how to draw up a "provincial autonomy law." Comrade Mao Tse-tung became the leader of the various mass organizations.

On September 14 T'an Yen-k'ai summoned his officials and the gentry for an "autonomy assembly," which decided that ten men from the provincial government and eleven men from the Provincial Assembly would draft the "Hunan Autonomy Law." The "Provincial Assembly," which represented the landlord class, the bureaucrats, the gentry and the merchants, immediately busied itself with a meeting to discuss the drafting of the "Autonomy Law." Conniving with a gaggle of politicians, T'an Yen-k'ai and Chao Heng-t'i put on a show of being very busy about the matter. T'an wrote a letter to the "Provincial Assembly": "Your honorable assembly is the legislative organ, so it would seem that I should ask you to manage [this affair]." On the question of drafting the "Autonomy Law," a multitude of theories came forward one after the other. Some people thought that this "fundamental law" should be drafted jointly by the provincial government, the Provincial Assembly, as well as the public organizations of teachers, peasants, workers, merchants, the United Association of Students, the United Association of Journalists, etc. There were also people who thought that it should be drafted on the basis of one individual's proposal and then jointly signed. Others suggested the convening of a Changsha City People's Congress to draft it and to then hand it over to the People's Representative Assemblies of each hsien for passage. Mao Tse-tung and his comrades in arms believed that one should strike when the iron is hot and not drag the thing out. A great many "concerned" people at the time also felt that this was an opportunity that, as the saying goes, would "disappear with the slightest relaxation." Because T'an Yen-k'ai was in the midst of publicly flying the "autonomy" flag in opposition to Peiyang warlord rule, he still had to work hard at feigning his posture of "following the sentiments of the people." Mao Tse-tung believed that if one took advantage of this opportunity to pass a "Provincial Autonomy Law" and to put the "curse of a golden hoop" about the head of the "Hunan governor," it would be advantageous for the people and for propelling ahead the revolutionary movement. Thus, under the leadership of Comrade Mao Tse-

141

tung and with the members of the New People's Study Society, the cadres of the United Association of Students, and progressive people from all circles as the backbone, and with the broad masses of students as the base, people from educational, journalistic, business, legal and judicial, and political circles were united and moved to joint discussions on the concrete steps to be taken in realizing the "formulation of a constitution."

On October 4 a meeting of the United Association of All Circles took place at Changsha's General Chamber of Commerce. Everyone agreed with Comrade Mao Tse-tung that one could not adopt an approach where, although theory was perfect, procedure was too complex. It was best to call immediately a People's Constitutional Convention through the auspices of this "revolutionary government" of T'an Yen-k'ai. Not only would this make sense in the realm of theory, it was also possible in the realm of reality. The next day, the Changsha press published a joint document from Mao Tse-tung, Chu Chien-fan, [25] Ho Shu-heng, P'eng Huang, Lung Chien-kung (the chief editor of Changsha Ta-kung pao) and 372 others that totaled over 4,000 characters and that was entitled "A Proposal for the Convening of a Hunan People's Constitutional Convention by the Hunan Revolutionary Government to Formulate a 'Hunan Constitution' for Constructing a New Hunan." This document explained in detail, from both a practical and theoretical point of view, "how to realize Hunanese autonomy." First, T'an Yen-k'ai's actions in expelling Chang Ching-yao, his statements about his plans for autonomy, his convening of the convention to "formulate a constitution," and other such measures all proved on theoretical, practical, and legal grounds that he had already placed himself in opposition to the Peking "central government" (the Peiyang warlord government). Therefore, it was quite fitting and proper that the hat of "revolutionary government" be placed on the head of "Mr. Ch'a-ling." (Later T'an Yen-k'ai announced after all that he was unhappy with the designation "revolutionary.") Second, this "revolutionary government" should unite the various organizations and convene a "People's Constitutional Convention"; the people's representatives should be at least directly, equally, and universally selected, every fifty thousand people having one representative. The right of drafting and of promulgating the "Constitution" was to belong to the "Constitutional Convention." Finally, on the basis of the "Constitution," a formal assembly for Hunan and autonomous governments for the province, hsien, district, and village should be created.

At this time, the mass organization in Changsha with the most organizational power and most prestige remained the United Association of Students. On October 6 the Association sent out a letter to the various organizations, asking them each to select and send a representative for a meeting. The letter also fixed the date of October 10 for a petition march. The letter read:

Ever since the success of the Expel Chang movement, the plans of the government, the expectations of the people, and the encouragement of the newspapers have all concentrated on local autonomy. Truly, if we are unable to attain complete local autonomy, then the government will be as corrupt as before, the suffering of the people will continue as before, and there will be no way to construct a new Hunan. Thus, if we want to attain complete autonomy, this is truly the best opportunity. "When thirty thousand catties hang by a hair, the least relaxation and all is lost." If we stroll along doing nothing for months and years, it will be too late for regrets! Today, those from all strata within and outside the province who make proposals either vainly entrust themselves to empty talk, hold to their own individual opinions, or consciously just go through the motions. This is all because the great, overwhelming majority of common people are unable to express a sound, pure and forceful opinion.

The notification sent out by the Association the same day to the various schools clearly pointed out: "The double ten* demonstration of the urban population is to warn the government on the one hand and to awaken our brethren on the other, so that the People's Constitutional Convention may be realized at an early date." 26

On October 7 the delegates attending the All Circles Convention called by the United Association of Students represented an extremely wide spectrum. The various mass organizations, private, official, progressive, middle-of-the-road, and backward, had sent delegates. At the meeting there was unanimous agreement on the "double ten" petition march.

On October 8 the 436 people who had signed their names to the "proposal" (in the preceding several days the number of signers had slightly increased) held a plenary meeting at the Educational Society's Huan-teng Arena (now the site of the Hunan Provincial People's Committee Auditorium), chose Comrade Mao Tse-tung as chairman and discussed ways and means of proceeding. Those at the meeting unanimously agreed with the electoral and organizational laws for the "Constitutional Convention." They also elected fifteen representatives to petition the government on October 10.

The day for the thorough unmasking of the T'an Yen-k'ai and Chao Heng-t'i government had arrived.

---

* I.e., tenth month, tenth day — the anniversary of the Republic. — Tr.

On October 10 it rained, but the masses who came to the meeting were very enthusiastic and numbered almost ten thousand. The marchers led the way behind two red and white banners on which were written: "[We] Request the Government to Convene a People's Constitutional Convention," and "Hunanese Autonomy." There were several dozen different handbills printed up and passed out by the various organizations. The male and female students, the workers and the merchants, and the townspeople who joined the march were all thoroughly soaked, but the morale of the masses was very high. They cried out slogans along the way as they went: "Hunanese Autonomy," "Smash the Old Powers," "Dissolve the Old Provincial Assembly," "Construct a New Hunan."

When the marchers reached the "Tuchün Office," T'an Yen-k'ai received petition representatives and agreed with the views of the people without reservation.

On this day's march occurred the tearing down of the flag at the Provincial Assembly. The masses were actually already quite dissatisfied with the "government by officials" that had emanated from the old Provincial Assembly (the Provincial Assemblymen had long passed the end of their terms of office). Thus, when the marchers reached the Provincial Assembly, they cried out the slogan, "Dissolve the Old Assembly." The next day, the Changsha press reported the situation in the following words:

Everyone raised his head and looked up. The Provincial Assembly flag struck everyone's eyes. Then this concern was expressed: How was it that "yesterday's guests" were permanently attending a "never-adjourning banquet"? Not at all knowing what to do, we openly took up the question of drafting a constitution. Realizing that we should express some of our own ideas about it, someone went up to the flag and tore it down.

The next day T'an Yen-k'ai summoned the representatives of the various organizations for a meeting specifically on account of this incident involving the tearing down of the flag, and there he began to expose his hideous face. In addition, he issued a proclamation intimidating the people: "Do not easily believe what the marchers are saying or blindly follow their outrageous action. From the overall perspective it will endanger the general situation, and closer to home it will be harmful to yourselves." This is how T'an answered the accusations against the Provincial Assembly: "More pretexts to incite insults of the Assembly. If people don't wake up, if they break the law, then the government will naturally handle them according to the law." Well, this is how "Mr. Ch'a-ling" "followed the sentiments of the people" and how he "advocated autonomy"!

By this time, the T'an-Chao government already had its attention drawn to Comrade Mao Tse-tung. After the tearing down of the flag, a rumor circulated that Mao had been the one who had done the job. Later, it was said that the "Provincial Assembly" had received an informant's letter saying that Mao Tse-tung was "inviting representatives of various public organizations to the Provincial Library for a meeting and was instigating some military men to destroy the Assembly." Mao then specifically addressed a righteous and harshly worded public letter to the police department, protesting this personal libel. The letter was published on December 5 in the Changsha press.

After this mass democratic movement that truly represented the will of the people, the mask of the T'an Yen-k'ai and Chao Heng-t'i warlord government was torn away. This awakened people to the fact that one cannot beg for food from the tiger's mouth. In order to seize the rights of the people, it was necessary to depend on their own struggle; it was necessary to depend on the power of the people to strengthen themselves. At the same time, this democratic movement had great significance for the launching of the democratic alliance of the various strata and social forces in Hunan — the movement for a democratic united front. It was especially significant for establishing the mass prestige of the Marxist revolutionaries headed by Comrade Mao Tse-tung.

In the midst of this movement, a group of petty Hunan politicians who were "dissatisfied with the situation" had used the occasion to obtain some minor government posts but then turned around and started whispering and grumbling about the actions of the masses that had "gone too far." Because of this, Comrade Mao Tse-tung wrote to his comrades in the New People's Study Society that although the big shots are not necessarily that solid, the small shots are very solid indeed. We don't have to pay any attention to them. We must create another environment, engage in long-term preparation and precise planning. After our actual strength is cultivated, we will naturally see some results. This is not something we can do by writing a few articles. We must have some true comrades who will get down to some practical work.

In November 1920, after Chao Heng-t'i had driven out T'an Yen-k'ai and had seized governmental power in Hunan, he still put on an act and invited a group of men to "draft a constitution." He also organized a self-serving "investigation committee" composed of more than one hundred and fifty "people's representatives from the hsien." In April 1921, after many months of arguing, a "draft provincial constitution" was promulgated. In the confused circumstances of warlord rule at the time, this "draft" contained some rather bright spots and still attracted a good deal of attention. Mao Tse-tung mobilized the various sectors of public opinion and continued to carry on a legal struggle with the Chao government, criticizing the fundamental shortcomings of the draft. He himself wrote an article that appeared in the Changsha press on April 25, 1921, in which he pointed out that the greatest failing of the "draft provincial constitution" was that the regulations dealing with the people's rights were far from perfect, particularly the fact that there were no regulations at all dealing with the basic rights of workers. In August 1921, in the midst of his defeat in the "Aid to Hupei" war, Chao Heng-t'i hurriedly passed this "provincial constitution." On January 1, 1922, it was formally promulgated.

Utilizing the Hunan people's desire and hopes for peace, Chao Heng-t'i had opportunistically created the so-called "provincial constitution" to impose control domestically, and at the same time pushed hard the so-called "United Provincial Autonomy" in order to control the external situation, considering himself "one notch above" the other warlords. But on January 17, 1922, after he had slaughtered Huang Ai and P'ang Jen-ch'üan, who were engaged in the labor movement, the mask of "provincial autonomy" was even more thoroughly shattered both within and outside of the province. In 1922, when the Hunan labor movement entered a new high tide under the leadership of Comrade Mao Tse-tung, the "provincial constitution," promulgated by Chao Heng-t'i to hide his shame, became an advantageous weapon in the hands of Mao for carrying on a legal struggle, something Chao Heng-t'i had never anticipated.

At the same time that he was leading this democratic movement to unmask the reactionary government of T'an Yen-k'ai and Chao Heng-t'i, Comrade Mao Tse-tung was engaged in even more important activities: he was spreading Marxism, was carrying on discussions on communism among comrades, and was preparing the organizational framework for the establishment of the Chinese Communist Party — he was engaged in the work of truly laying the foundation for the Chinese Revolution.

# ACTIVITIES SURROUNDING THE ESTABLISHMENT OF THE CHINESE COMMUNIST PARTY

*3*

## I. DISCUSSIONS ON COMMUNISM AND THE ESTABLISHMENT OF THE PARTY

In his essay "On the People's Democratic Dictatorship," Comrade Mao Tse-tung has said that dating from the period following the Opium War, progressive Chinese all sought truth from the Western nations and studied the bourgeois-democratic culture of the West. He himself expended great effort in the study of these things when he was still at school. But

imperialist aggression shattered the fond dreams of the Chinese about learning from the West. It was very odd — why were the teachers always committing aggression against their pupil? The Chinese learned a good deal from the West, but they could not make it work and were never able to realize their ideals. Their repeated struggles, including such a movement as the Revolution of 1911, all ended in failure. Day by day, conditions in the country got worse, and life was made impossible. Doubts arose, increased, and deepened [SW, IV, p. 413].

This had been Mao Tse-tung's own personal experience. Ever since the end of the 1911 Revolution he had tirelessly sought the truth that would save his nation and people. He joined with his comrades and sought the correct revolutionary road. But,

The Russians made the October Revolution and created the world's first socialist state. Under the leadership of Lenin and Stalin, the revolutionary energy of the great proletariat and laboring people of Russia, hitherto latent and unseen by foreigners, suddenly erupted like a volcano, and the Chinese and all mankind began to see the Russians in a new light. Then, and only then, did the Chinese enter an entirely new era in their thinking and their life.... The salvoes of the October Revolution brought us Marxism-Leninism. The October Revolution helped progressives in China, as throughout the world, to adopt the proletarian world outlook as the instrument for studying a nation's destiny and considering anew their own problems. Follow the path of the Russians — that was their conclusion [Ibid.].

Thus in July 1920, after Comrade Mao Tse-tung had returned to Hunan from Peking via Shanghai, he did a great deal of work disseminating Marxism-Leninism. He constantly talked about Russia's very important revolutionary experience: the broad revolutionary masses, particularly the leaders of the masses, should be made to grasp this weapon of Marxism-Leninism; otherwise the revolution could not be advanced and could not be victorious. And so as soon as he returned to Changsha he set up a "Cultural Book Society" [Wen-hua shu-she] that promoted the sale of new books and periodicals throughout the entire province. At the same time, he organized the Society for the Study of Marxism [Ma-k'o-ssu-chu-i yen-chiu hui].

When Comrade Mao Tse-tung was studying at First Normal in 1918, he organized that militant revolutionary organization, the New People's Study Society. This organization in reality played the central role in leading the Hunan revolutionary forces during the May Fourth movement and the movement to Expel Chang Ching-yao. For three years this organization, under the leadership of Mao Tse-tung, had been gradually becoming purer in theory and more close-knit in organization. Through the experience of the victory of the Russian October Revolution, Comrade Mao Tse-tung appreciated more profoundly the decisive role played by a proletarian party armed with Marxism-Leninism in a revolutionary undertaking. His articles discussing the "Hunanese Autonomy movement" clearly reflect this idea: If there is no Lenin-type Bolshevik party, the victory of the Chinese revolution will be impossible. This kind of assessment is even more apparent in his correspondence with Comrade Ts'ai Ho-sen. Thus, when the Socialist Youth Corps and the Communist Cell [Kung-ch'an-chu-i hsiao-tsu] were just beginning their activities in China, Comrade Mao Tse-tung was in Hunan actively setting up the same kind of organization. Later, while leading the seething labor movement, he gave special attention to the task of establishing a party, and he set up an excellent local organization in Hunan for the Chinese Communist Party, so that the universal truth of Marxism-Leninism became closely integrated with the Chinese labor movement.

In order first to lead the members of the New People's Study Society and all comrades outside of the Society onto the correct revolutionary path together, Comrade Mao Tse-tung gathered into three collections all the letters written by Society members to each other between 1918 and the beginning of 1921 that touched upon ideology, future plans, or ways of remolding China and the world, arranged them according to subject and chronology, and had them printed and distributed by the Cultural Book Society. The first collection contained altogether thirteen letters, three of which were written by Mao. The second collection contained thirty-one letters, eight by Mao. The most important was the third collection, with seven letters. These letters were mainly discussions between Comrade Mao Tse-tung and Comrade Ts'ai Ho-sen on Communism and on the establishment of a party. These few letters are in fact magnificent announcements that proclaim the maturation and imminent birth on both the ideological and organizational plane of the Chinese Communist Party.

Comrade Ts'ai Ho-sen arrived in France at the beginning of 1920. Working day and night and using the "furiously read and furiously translate" approach, within a very short space of four or five months he had read several dozen pamphlets and had gotten a basically clear notion of every school of socialism, the great world powers, and the situation surrounding the Russian Revolution and, with this, had come to some clear-cut conclusions. At the same time that Mao Tse-tung was in Peking for his second visit, Ts'ai Ho-sen embraced Marxism-Leninism and advocated traveling the road of the Russian people. In particular, he had a rather profound appreciation for the theories of class struggle and the dictatorship of the proletariat. In August 1920 Ts'ai wrote Mao:

Recently I gathered together [some material] and made a few judgments on the various "isms." I feel that socialism is really the prescription for remolding the present world.... In the future remolding of China it will be perfectly appropriate to employ the principles and methods of socialism.... I think that we should first organize a party — a communist party — because it is the mobilizer of the revolution, the propagandist of the revolution, the vanguard and the fighting arm of the revolution. In view of the present situation in China, we must first organize a party; only after that will the revolutionary movement and the labor movement have a nerve center.... Within two years China must establish a party that has a clear-cut doctrine and appropriate methods and a party that stands in close agreement with Russia.... Some people maintain that there are no classes in China. I deny this. It is simply that because the workers and the peasants are ignorant and unaware, they consider their weariness and misery their allotted fate. One day when class awareness is born, the flame is certain to match that of Western or Eastern Europe.

Already by this time fourteen members of the New People's Study Society had gone to France, and everyone was intensively studying the various ideologies and constantly holding discussions. With a view to studying various approaches to learning, discussing the conduct of Society affairs, inaugurating "individual character criti-

cism," and expressing opinions on views of life and views of the
universe, fourteen people, including Comrades Ts'ai Ho-sen, Hsiang
Ching-yü, Chang K'un-ti, Lo Hsüeh-tsan, Li Wei-han, and Ts'ai
Ch'ang, gathered together in early July 1920 to hold a five-day
meeting. An intense argument broke out at the meeting over the
"direction of Society affairs — the approach to remolding China and
the world." Two diametrically opposed views emerged, one held by
the revolutionaries and the other by the reformists. The majority
of comrades, headed by Comrade Ts'ai Ho-sen, called for organizing a Communist Party immediately and traveling the path of Russia, emphasizing in particular a spirit of proletarian dictatorship
and internationalism (called at the time, "international style" or
"multinational unanimity class style"). The minority, headed by
Hsiao Tzu-sheng, [1] maintained that to realize a revolution that
would remold China and the world, one

cannot exchange the sacrifices of some for the general well-being of the majority. He advocates a mild revolution — a revolution that uses education as a tool,
an approach that uses unions and cooperative associations to effect reform. He
did not quite feel the Russian type (Marxist) revolution was justified but leaned
toward the Proudhon [2] type of revolution: relatively harmonious yet slow, slow
yet harmonious.

Hsiao Tzu-sheng was one of the principal sponsors of the New People's Study Society and at the time was an influential member. During the discussions some individuals agreed with his views. They
were skeptical about the experience of the Russian October Revolution and about whether "a simple prescription can cure the world's
ills."

Both sides wrote detailed letters to Comrade Mao Tse-tung, asking him to express his own views.

On December 1, 1920, Comrade Mao Tse-tung returned a long
letter to Comrade Ts'ai Ho-sen and the Society members in France
in which he "expressed profound agreement" with Ts'ai's opinion
that China had to travel the path of socialism and the path of Russia. He disagreed with the reformist approach. Mao gave a specific
example of the very same thing that had occurred in Changsha to
explain the problem: In October of that year, Bertrand Russell [3]
had come to Changsha to lecture; he "took a position in favor of
communism but against the dictatorship of the workers and peasants. He said that one should employ the method of education to
change consciousness of the propertied classes, and that in this
way it would not be necessary to limit freedom or to have recourse

to war and bloody revolution." And so among the members of the
New People's Study Society who were in Changsha, an ardent debate
also unfolded. Mao Tse-tung said he had only one criticism of Russell's idea: This is all very well as a theory, but it is unfeasible in
practice.... Education requires (1) money, (2) people, and (3) in-
struments. Now all of these are in the hands of the rulers. Those
who run the schools and the press are all capitalists or landlords
or agents of capitalists and landlords. The reason the power of education has fallen into the hands of the capitalists and the landlords
is that they have "parliaments," "governments," and the law; they
also have armies and the police and, moreover, have the banks and
the factories. They use these to safeguard their own interests and
to repress the workers and peasants. Thus, Mao wondered, if the
Communists cannot seize political power, how can they take charge
of education? To have a revolution by dependence on the educational
approach was absolutely impossible. Furthermore, the education
of the whole world at the time was purely capitalist education. To
have capitalists believe in communism through the observation of
historical development was impossible. To change people's minds
was like trying to stop something from falling; a greater force had
to be brought into play. Mao very pointedly wrote the following: No
despot, imperialist, and militarist throughout history has ever been
known to leave the stage of history of his own free will without being overthrown by the people. At the present time the proletariat
constitutes the major portion of the world's population. Because
they are already aware of the sources of their misery and are demanding an end to it, there is a demand for revolution. This has already become a fact. The fact is before us, it is indestructible, it
is a fact that, once known, should be put into practice. Thus, the
Russian Revolution and the development of the Communist Party in
various countries is a natural result.*

In September 1920 Comrade Ts'ai Ho-sen wrote a long letter to
Comrade Mao Tse-tung and brought up the following issues: the
materialist concept of history and class struggle, the mistakes of
the Kautsky revisionists, the condition of the revolutionary movements in the various countries after the founding of the Comintern,
and the difference in principles on party membership between the
Bolsheviks and the Mensheviks. At the end of the letter he presented his detailed views on the steps to be taken in the organization

---

* For extracts from the verbatim text of Mao's comments on Russell's ideas,
see The Political Thought of Mao Tse-tung, pp. 296-98 [S.R.S.].

of the Chinese Communist Party: there should be a close-knit body to study and organize propaganda; various kinds of investigations and statistics should be made and a periodical published; most important, "be strict in seeking out genuine party members and place them in the various occupations, factories, villages, and assemblies. One must openly and fearlessly establish a Chinese Communist Party on a formal basis."

Comrade Mao Tse-tung did not receive this letter until the end of 1920. He immediately returned a letter to Comrade Ts'ai Ho-sen: "The materialist historical view is the foundation of our party philosophy.... Your views in this letter are perfectly correct. There is not one word to which I do not subscribe." He also told Ts'ai that with regard to the party, organization work was already in progress. In Shanghai a publication entitled The Communist [Kung-ch'an tang] had already been published.

To disseminate Marxism-Leninism, to struggle for the establishment of a proletarian political party — the Communist Party — that was the most essential aspect of the revolutionary activities of Comrade Mao Tse-tung before the formal founding of the Chinese Communist Party.

## II. THE FOUNDING OF THE CULTURAL BOOK SOCIETY

In July 1920, when Comrade Mao Tse-tung returned to Hunan and launched a broad revolutionary movement, he did a great deal of work in the dissemination of Marxism and the New Culture movement. The event that had the most profound influence and that was intimately bound up with the establishment of the Party was the founding of the Cultural Book Society.

During his rule in Hunan, Chang Ching-yao had demolished everything that was new. He publicly promoted prayer to the spirits and the celebration of the feast of All Souls, throwing society into a mass of confusion and disorder. Comrade Mao Tse-tung believed that the dissemination of new thought and new culture was the pressing issue of the day. The experience that he brought back from Peking and Shanghai was that to do this it was necessary to establish a general organ that would promote sales of the various new publications and from which activities could be carried on.

Comrade Mao Tse-tung immediately got to work on setting up such an organ. To solve the problem of operating expenses and also to expand influence in society, he won over progressive people and well-known people from every circle, including some famous people from cultural, educational, press, and business circles, such as the principals of Chou-nan Girls' School, First Normal, and Hsiang-ya Medical School, and the head of the Changsha Chamber of Commerce. With them he jointly sponsored the founding of a Cultural Book Society. T'an Yen-k'ai was even requested to do the caligraphy for the society's sign.

On July 31 the Changsha press printed a piece entitled "Fa-ch'i Wen-hua shu-she ti lu-ch'i" [Preface to the Founding of the Cultural Book Society]. This "Preface" read:

> There is no new culture because there is no new thought. There is no new thought because there is no new study. There is no new study because there is no new material. At present, the Hunan people are starving in their minds, which is actually worse than starving in their stomachs. It is particularly the young people who are "wailing and waiting to be fed." The Cultural Book Society wants to use the quickest and simplest method to introduce the various new magazines from China and abroad so they can serve as research material for the young people and for progressive Hunan.

On August 1 a meeting of the sponsors was held at Ch'u-i Primary School. On August 20 three rooms were rented from Hsiang-ya Medical School on Ch'ao-tsung Street for the Society's headquarters, whereupon it immediately began temporary operations. On September 9 official business began. On October 22 the first deliberative assembly was called into session. Those who had contributed money were all invited to participate in this first meeting. There were altogether over thirty people who had subscribed capital to the organization. Aside from Mao Tse-tung and his comrades-in-arms Ho Shu-heng and P'eng Huang and a great many members of the New People's Study Society, it was the upper-class people from educational circles who were in the majority. The money collected by the Book Society reached an approximate figure of more than 400 yuan. Later at the second assembly it was decided to continue expanding the subscription capital to 1,000 yuan.

At the first deliberative assembly the organizational platform of the Cultural Book Society was passed. In this platform the aim of the Society, its organization, and its procedural methods were very clearly spelled out. The guiding principle was that "all worthy new publications be widely disseminated throughout the entire province and that everyone have the opportunity to read them." This platform was printed in the Changsha Ta-kung pao of July 31, 1920.

The first deliberative assembly elected one manager. To make
it convenient for Comrade Mao Tse-tung to help with the work, he
became the "special negotiator" of the Cultural Book Society. At
first there were only two salesmen, but later when business improved there were seven or eight. Comrade Ch'en Tzu-po, [4] who
was brought into the Chinese Communist Party right after it was
founded, was the first salesman. He personally sent out books and
newspapers to the various subscribers, and because of the speed
of his work, he won their confidence.

From 1920 to the spring of 1921 the Cultural Book Society had
sixty or seventy outlets for its business dealings both within and
outside the province. Business outside the province came mostly
from the Kwangtung New Youth Society, the Shanghai T'ai-tung Book
Company, the Asia East Library, the Peking University Press, the
Peking Morning Gazette, the Peking Academic Lecture Association,
and the Wuchang Mass Altruism Book Society (founded by Yün Tai-
ying). Later, business steadily increased, and all new publications
from throughout the country were sold in even greater numbers, in
particular the official publications of the Communist Party and the
Youth Corps (Guide Weekly [Hsiang-tao chou-pao], China Youth
[Chung-kuo ch'ing-nien], Vanguard [Hsien-chü]) and the Marxism-
Leninism collection published by "New Youth" Publishers. Not one
of the broad masses of Hunan's intellectual youth, revolutionary
workers, or progressive people from the various circles was without some dealing with the Cultural Book Society. The Society also
set up branch offices all over the province. From the end of 1920
to the beginning of 1921 altogether seven branch societies were
founded in the hsien of P'ing-chiang, Liu-(yang)-hsi, Pao-ch'ing,
Heng-yang, Ning-hsiang, Wu-kang, and Hsü-p'u. The people who
founded these branches were for the most part members of the New
People's Study Society and revolutionaries who had developed connections with the Communist Party or the Socialist Youth Corps
very early. Sales sections were set up in Changsha's First Normal College, First Normal Attached Primary School, Ch'u-i Primary School, and Hsiu-yeh Primary School. Some sales personnel
were also invited to come. Later, almost all places that had a
Party organization set up branch societies or representative sales
bureaus that had business with the Cultural Book Society. The Cultural Book Society itself also gave impetus to the earliest work in
establishing local Parties and local Corps.

At the time, the revolutionary youth and rank and file progressives in Hunan were hungering and thirsting for the new culture and

new thought. In the beginning the Cultural Book Society sold somewhat less than 200 different titles, over 40 different magazines, and several newspapers. Most of these were bought up as soon as they arrived. Students and those in educational circles made up the highest proportion of buyers. Because Comrade Mao Tse-tung had already begun to develop ties with the Changsha workers in 1920 and at the beginning of 1921, and because he had had contact with Huang Ai and P'ang Jen-ch'üan, who were running the labor union, a great many workers came to buy the publications. According to the second number of the "Wen-hua she she-wu pao-kao" [Report of the Cultural Book Society], 5 in the seven months following the opening of business to the end of March 1921 the books that had sold over one or two hundred copies were Ma-k'e-ssu tzu-pen lun ju-men [An Introduction to Marx's Capital], She-hui-chu-i shih [A History of Socialism], Hsin O-kuo chih yen-chiu [A Study of New Russia], Lao-nung cheng-fu yü Chung-kuo [A Workers and Peasants Government and China], and the first collection of Ch'en pao hsiao-shuo [Morning Gazette Novels]. The magazines with the biggest sales were Workers' World [Lao-kung chieh] (5,000 copies), New Youth (2,000 copies), New Life [Hsin sheng-huo] (2,400 copies), New Tide [Hsin ch'ao] and New Education [Hsin chiao-yü]. Every day 40 copies of the New Gazette of Current Affairs [Shih-shih hsin-pao] were sold, plus 45 copies of Peking's Morning Gazette [Ch'en pao]. Whenever New Youth and the other new publications arrived, an advertisement was sure to appear in a prominent place in the newspapers giving a sketch of the contents.

Owing to the expansion of business, the Cultural Book Society soon moved to Changsha's Kung-yüan-tung Street (now Chung-shan-tung Road). Later, business improved further and the Society moved again, this time to Shui-feng-ching (now the office of the China Book Publishing Company). In the long interval between its founding and the First Revolutionary Civil War, the Cultural Book Society played an extremely important role in widely disseminating Marxism-Leninism within Hunan and in giving impetus to the New Culture movement. Besides Peking, Shanghai, and later Canton, the places that sold the most new publications were the provinces of Hunan and Szuchuan.

Once an organ like the Cultural Book Society was set up, one that openly published books and other material on Marxism-Leninism, the job of ideological preparation for the establishment of a party was greatly facilitated.

As for Party organization work, the Cultural Book Society played a great role in the area of economics and communication from its inception until the failure of the 1927 Revolution. In 1920 Comrade Mao Tse-tung began to organize the Socialist Youth Corps in Hunan. From that time onward until the establishment of the Party throughout the entire province, Party expenses proved a very thorny problem. As a rule it was necessary to depend on a small number of comrades who taught and received a salary to cover living and operating costs. Sometimes, when needs could be met no longer, a loan was made from the Cultural Book Society. Because the latter was generally considered a "business organization," it was qualified to borrow money from the [local] money shops.* At the same time, the Book Society itself could support a few people (actually it could only provide expenses to support the lowest standard of living). Because the warlord government did not yet have a closely organized spy system, the Book Society was often used as the liaison office for the provincial Party committee and the Party organizations within and outside the province. From 1921 to 1923 the Party and Corps meetings were sometimes also held here. In 1924, after Chao Heng-t'i's reactionary government had become more tightly organized, the Party, for organizational safety, stopped using the Cultural Book Society as its liaison office. But when temporary financial problems arose, the Book Society was always able to take on the responsibility. (In order to solve the Party's financial difficulties, Comrade Mao Tse-tung floated shares and set up a cotton mill. Because he was unable to compete with foreign cotton, he sold out after one year.)

There is still one further point worth mentioning with regard to Comrade Mao Tse-tung's founding of the Cultural Book Society — the democratic management system that he himself had set up and his own strict overseeing and administration.

The second number of the "Society Report," published in March 1921, read:

To those members who are directly connected with our Society, those of us who manage the business have an obligation to report on the sale of our publications, etc., so that the entire membership will know the situation within the Society. Only if this is done can we consider our duty fulfilled. Chinese businesses are always secretive. Except for the inner circle, no one can get any information. This secrecy is really wrong. If a person does something upright and is pure in mind, why can't he make the draft documents public knowledge? The Cultural Book Society is an organ publicly owned by society at large; it makes no profits at all for private individuals. In order to avoid this error, we have opposed secrecy and have adopted a policy of thorough openness, a policy of fully publicizing Society affairs beyond the Society's membership.

---

* Old-style banking organizations. — Tr.

This printed "Society Report" was edited by Comrade Mao Tse-tung himself. Besides going out to subscribing members, it was also sent as propaganda to all relevant sectors of society. The content of the "Society Report" was very thorough and comprehensive. Not only did it describe in detail such things as the purpose behind setting up the Society, its history and its operational procedures, it also listed in detail and by category all monies received and currently in surplus. There was even more detailed accounting with regard to the sale of the periodicals and books: "In the first place, if we see the number of copies of a certain book sold in Hunan, we then know the influence the book has on the Hunan people. In the second place, every six months there is an accounting, and we can make a comparison of a certain book's progress in sales."

Sometimes those who were managing the finances of the Book Society failed to set a time for clearing accounts in line with the system, and Comrade Mao Tse-tung would have to come to press them and help out with the final tabulation. Some people who worked in the Book Society at the time still remember that after Mao Tse-tung came he put together the only four tables the Society had, and everyone sat down to figure out the bills. If some places were not quite up to par in the balance sheet, Mao Tse-tung would immediately show his dissatisfaction.

In 1927, during the "Horse Day Incident," the Cultural Book Society that Comrade Mao Tse-tung had founded by his own hand and that had helped a generation of young people to acquire knowledge of Marxism-Leninism was smashed by the Kuomintang reactionaries. Nevertheless, the spirit and the cause of the Book Society were glorified by the revolutionary culture organizations that came later.

## III. ORGANIZING THE SOCIETY FOR THE STUDY OF MARXISM

At the same time that he founded the Cultural Book Society, Comrade Mao Tse-tung organized the Society for the Study of Marxism [Ma-k'o-ssu chu-i yen-chiu hui] with a view toward organizing revolutionary comrades to make a close study of Marxism-Leninism. On the ideological plane, this was a precondition for the establishment of the Party.

From childhood, Comrade Mao Tse-tung was a person who attached much importance to study and a person who was himself quite capable of studying. In school his favorite subjects were history and philosophy. Very early he had engaged in the study of the various schools of socialism that had been transmitted to China. For many years he worked hard to find the correct revolutionary path. How jubilant he was when the salvos of the October Revolution sounded and brought with them Marxism-Leninism! With the greatest enthusiasm he organized his comrades and comrades-in-arms to study this universal truth.

The Society for the Study of Marxism in Shanghai, Peking and elsewhere, began organization in May 1920. At this time, "New Youth" publishers had already begun rather systematically to publish books on Marxism-Leninism.

In September 1920 Comrade Mao Tse-tung was director of First Normal Attached Primary School (the school grounds were next door to First Normal) and was elected president of First Normal's Alumni Association. Until the winter of 1922 he remained in this position. This was a definite help to him in carrying on his revolutionary activities. His comrades-in-arms Ch'en Ch'ang and others were also all teaching at First Normal Attached Primary School. First Normal was where Mao Tse-tung had begun his revolutionary activities and where he had founded the New People's Study Society. After Chang Ching-yao had hightailed it out of Hunan, the school was even more full of vigor and vitality and was one of the headquarters of Hunan's revolutionary youth. From this battleground, with its revolutionary base, Comrade Mao Tse-tung rallied comrades together and nurtured new revolutionary forces.

Those who joined the Society for the Study of Marxism were members of the New People's Study Society, the mainstays of the United Association of Students, and individual progressive teachers, numbering some several dozen altogether. The majority was alumni and students from First Normal. Comrades Ho Shu-heng, Ch'en Ch'ang, Hsia Hsi, Kuo Liang, and Hsiao Shu-fan [6] all joined. First Normal Attached Primary School and the Alumni Association (located around the corner from Hsi-yang Street below Changsha's Miao-kao feng-shan) were the places regularly used for the crowded meetings. Most of the time Comrade Mao Tse-tung chaired the meetings. By that time Mao Tse-tung had a more thorough understanding of the basic theory of Marxism-Leninism than the average person who believed in Marxism. But most important was this: from the very beginning of his revolutionary activity, Mao Tse-tung combined a study of revolutionary theory with a continuous participation in the practice of revolution. On the relationship be-

tween revolutionary theory and revolutionary practice, he had this
to say at the time: In any revolutionary undertaking one must have
an ideological base; but if no movement follows, the goal of this
theory cannot be realized. Mao Tse-tung regularly directed everyone to maintain close contact with reality in China [in general] and
Hunan [in particular] and to study the general principles of Marxism. He always opposed the study of "dead books" and was in favor
of "living books." He always opposed making books into dogma.
When he was studying the philosophy of dualism at First Normal,
he combined ancient and modern Chinese and foreign history and
trends of thought to make his own, independent critique and study.
For many years he had been an avid reader of newspapers. When
he was walking along the street he also often turned his attention
to reading public announcements [that were posted]. He was most
concerned about the current state of affairs both within and outside
China and Hunan. As a student, he went into the countryside and
made on-the-spot investigations of conditions in the villages. In
November 1920 he went to P'ing-hsiang and other hsien to conduct
an investigation of social conditions. He believed that making systematic and comprehensive study of the circumstances of one's environment was the constant duty of a revolutionary. In sum, at that
time Mao Tse-tung maintained that one had to study Marxism-
Leninism with a goal in mind and had to wed this philosophy to the
current revolutionary reality in China. This brilliant thought, ability, and practical spirit of Comrade Mao Tse-tung made him naturally the publicly acknowledged leader of those progressive elements and revolutionary young people in Hunan who believed in
Marxism.

The classical Marxist writings the Communist Manifesto and
Socialism: Utopian and Scientific and the pamphlets in the New
Youth collection "Class Struggle" and "A History of Socialism,"
were all required reading for the members of the Society for the
Study of Marxism. In addition, New Youth and the Peking Morning
Gazette were also regular reading for everyone. On November 7,
1920, the monthly The Communist, edited by the Shanghai Society
for the Study of Marxism, was secretly published. (Altogether seven
numbers of this periodical appeared. It ceased publication soon after the founding of the Party.) In this monthly was an introduction
to the history of the Russian Communist Party. Lenin's State and
Revolution was also printed, along with a number of other writings.
There also reports on the status of the Comintern and the activities of the Communist parties in Europe and America. There

were articles that criticized anarchism and also easy-to-understand articles on how to implement the theory of Marx in China. All means were used to send large batches of The Communist from Shanghai to Peking, Wuhan, and Changsha. As soon as Comrade Mao Tse-tung received this publication, he would send it around for everyone to look at. The people united around Mao Tse-tung could thus gain a further appreciation of the Communist Party and recognize more clearly that a new-style political party of the proletarian class was the fundamental guarantee for leading the revolution to victory.

Comrade Mao Tse-tung studied and read these books and periodicals with great care. As a rule, he made marginal notations in all the books he read and diligently took notes. He regularly discussed with everybody his own understandings of what he had read and compared notes with them. But what he stressed most was how, in line with the principles of Marxism, one could wage an effective revolutionary struggle in Hunan. Mao's colleagues at First Normal Attached Primary School that year still clearly remember that his bookshelves were filled with books and periodicals on Marxism. No matter where he went, he always had a book in his hands. Recalling Comrade Mao Tse-tung's diligence in reading books and his devotion to intense study, Comrade Hsieh Chüeh-tsai has said:

When in Changsha I once went to the Wang Fu-chih Study Society where Comrade Mao Tse-tung was staying, but he was not there; he was moving. Just then some people appeared who were moving out his things. (Note: He moved to Ch'ing-shui-t'ang sometime in the winter of 1921.) There was a large basket that was completely filled with notebooks. I was greatly startled. The richness of Comrade Mao's reading and his attentiveness had been responsible for this great basket of notes. [7]

At this time, First Normal was promoting the New Culture movement with great effort. From Peking and Shanghai young, progressive teachers were invited. Breaking precedent, Comrade Mao Tse-tung taught a class of Chinese (having just graduated from First Normal, he was now teaching there). Among these teachers there were some who believed in anarchism and who expended great effort in spreading anarchist thought among their students. A group of students who had been influenced by them founded a small anarchist organization. But the largest and strongest progressive organization of students at First Normal was the "Society for the Reverence of New Learning" [Ch'ung hsin-hsüeh hui] organized by Comrade Hsiao Shu-fan and others with a total membership of more than one hundred people. Comrade Mao Tse-tung endorsed their stand against anarchist thought and also conducted a campaign of criticism against this ideology in his Chinese classes. And so the dissemination of Marxism-Leninism at First Normal maintained an overwhelming supremacy from beginning to end. In the few other major schools the situation was similar.

To be able to publicize openly the October Revolution and spread Marxism-Leninism, Comrade Mao Tse-tung, Ho Shu-heng, and P'eng Huang joined with Fang Wei-hsia and other progressives from Hunan educational circles in August 1920 to initiate the organization of the Society for the Study of Russia and a Diligent Work and Frugal Study in Russia program. The abridged bylaws of the Society for the Study of Russia read:

This Society has as its aim the study of all Russian ideologies. The Society's affairs include: (1) after some results from study are seen, the publication of a Russian Collection, (2) the sending of people to Russia to make on-the-spot investigations, (3) the promotion of a Diligent Work and Frugal Study in Russia program.

At the time, under the reactionary rule of the Peiyang warlord government and Chao Heng-t'i, Marxism was falsely labeled as "extremism" and Russia was cursed as "the land of the starving people." Although the Society for the Study of Russia and the Diligent Work and Frugal Study in Russia program were unable to get a very good start, the influence of the victory of the Russian October Revolution on the broad masses of young people was really overwhelming. A great number of Hunan youth were looking abroad to find a solution to their problems; all their thoughts were on Russia, and they wanted very much to go there. Comrade Mao Tse-tung very carefully introduced a group of revolutionary youth to relevant quarters in Shanghai. After very great difficulties, these young people went to Soviet Russia to study. After they returned home, most of them became the Party's earliest and most important mainstays. For example, Comrades Jen Pi-shih, Hsiao Ching-kuang, and others, by way of Comrade Mao Tse-tung's introduction, were in the first group that went to Soviet Russia to study. Recalling the situation at this time, Comrade Hsiao Ching-kuang has said:

One day Comrade Pi-shih came in with an extremely jubilant look on his face. As soon as he entered he said to me: "I have a way!" I asked him what way, and he answered: "Go to Russia!" "Go to Russia!" What a jolt of excitement this gave me. We didn't really know much about Russia at all. Hadn't they overthrown the old society to the roots and established a new society over there ?! For youths like us at the time who were full of hatred for imperialism and the traitorous government, "to the roots" in the phrase "overthrown the old society to the roots" summed up the whole meaning of revolution. Comrade Pi-shih made up his mind without the least hesitation. Having been introduced through the revolutionary organization under the leadership of Chairman Mao, we went together to Shanghai to study Russian. It was at this time that Comrade Pi-shih and I joined the Socialist Youth Corps. 8

Besides this, Comrade Mao Tse-tung also recommended many articles from The Communist to the Changsha press for publication, such as "O-kuo kung-ch'an tang ti li-shih" [The History of the Russian Communist Party], "Lieh-ning ti li-shih" [The History of Lenin], and "Lao-nung chih-tu yen-chiu" [A Study of the Workers and Peasants System]. 9 Articles that discussed Marxism also began to appear in the newspapers. When we add to this the founding of the Cultural Book Society, we see that it wasn't until this time that the broad masses of Hunan society had some idea of what Marxism was all about.

IV. ESTABLISHING THE SOCIALIST YOUTH CORPS.
ESTABLISHING A PARTY WITH
CLOSE TIES TO THE MASSES

After Comrade Mao Tse-tung returned to Hunan, he set up regular lines of communication with the Peking Marxist organization (those in positions of responsibility were Li Ta-chao, Teng Chung-hsia, and others). In October 1920, when he received the bylaws of the Socialist Youth Corps from Peking, Mao Tse-tung began to set up in Hunan the reserve force of the Communist Party — the Socialist Youth Corps. In August 1920 in Shanghai, and then in Peking, Changsha, Canton, and Wuhan, there was founded the Chinese Socialist Youth Corps (after 1925 the name was changed to the Chinese Communist Youth Corps), which in both ideology and organization was to play a definite preparatory role in the establishment of the Chinese Communist Party.

After much study, Comrade Mao Tse-tung and his comrades-in-arms felt that a great many of the members of the New People's Study Society had already undergone a relatively long period of ideological preparation, had participated in a great number of practical revolutionary struggles, and were determined to struggle for the Marxist ideal. Thus they could join the Socialist Youth Corps

162

just for the asking. At the same time, they believed that once a corps organization existed, the historical mission of the New People's Study Society could be brought to a close. The many members of the New People's Study Society were all in full agreement with Comrade Mao Tse-tung's views. And so it was that comrades like Kuo Liang, Hsia Hsi, and Hsiao Shu-fan became the first group of members of the Socialist Youth Corps. The New People's Study Society had never experienced the constraints of a concrete political platform or strict discipline. Before and after the movement to Expel Chang Ching-yao there had been internal ideological splits. There were now a few members who, having been influenced by nationalism, or scheming for their own individual aggrandizement, disapproved of the next step of joining a corps organization. They were also disseminating all kinds of bad influence within the Society. Before long these people traveled a different road from that of the revolution; some of those in the group later became counterrevolutionaries. Such was the inevitable post-May Fourth movement disintegration of the leftist, middle, and rightist intellectuals. In an effort to put some seriousness into the original aim of the New People's Study Society and also into its spirit of collective struggle, Comrade Mao Tse-tung got everybody's agreement and announced the expulsion of these elements from the Society. In addition, in the third collection of the Society members' letters was printed "Hsin-min hsüeh-hui chin-yao ch'i-shih" [An Important Notice to the New People's Study Society], which read:

It has been almost three years since the founding of this Society. Although the form has not been perfect, the spirit has been constant. But on a number of occasions we have not been able to understand the attitude of individual members toward the Society. There are those who are involved in other affairs and cannot divide their attention. There are those whose sentiments are in perfect harmony with other organizations and who therefore have no sentiments toward this Society. There are those who make absolutely no demands on themselves for self-improvement. There are those who lack an interest in collective life. There are those whose actions are unsatisfactory to the majority of the Society's membership. With respect to people who find themselves in the situation described above, this Society maintains that although they have become Society members, there is in reality no possibility of mutual help or mutual encouragement. To keep the spirit of the Society intact, there is no alternative but to no longer acknowledge them as members.

Before the founding of the Chinese Communist Party, the New People's Study Society in reality played the leading and crucial role in the Hunan revolutionary movement. In the Society's birth and maturation, one can see that when Comrade Mao Tse-tung began his revolutionary activities he possessed a strong sense of party spirit and purposely endeavored to establish a new-style, strict, and secret revolutionary organization.

Comrade Mao Tse-tung actively sought out organization members from among the progressive students at First Normal, First Middle School, and Commercial Vocational School. A First Normal student who embraced Mao's mission to set up an organization [10] briefly recorded the events in his diary running from September to December 1920. This constitutes the most accurate record available to us today. The following are some excerpts from this diary.

September 10, 1920: Went to the Popular Education Office. The Popular Gazette will be published tomorrow. Mr. Ho (Note: Comrade Ho Shu-heng. Ho was the head of the Popular Education Office at the time.) asked me to contribute an article and I told him then and there that I would.

I returned to First Normal and that evening talked about a great many things with Tse-tung.

September 25: Yesterday brother Tse-tung came to invite me for a walk along the river with him this afternoon. When we arrived at the Cultural Book Society we saw Miss Yang K'ai-hui. It was already drizzling; Tse-tung, P'eng Huang, and myself...all we brothers braved the rain and started on our trip.... Didn't get back until ten thirty in the evening.

November 17: Received a letter from Tse-tung. He sent me ten copies of the bylaws of the Youth Corps. The aim is to study and implement the remolding of society. He made an appointment with me to meet him Sunday morning and also asked me to seek out some true comrades.

November 21: I saw Tse-tung (at the Popular Education Office). He said that he was soon going to Li-ling to investigate education and also directed that the Youth Corps should turn its attention to finding true comrades; [he said] things should go slowly, there should be no rush.

November 22: The youth now have a way out; they are implementers of socialism. They must go into the factories themselves and work, and by awakening the consciousness of our brothers in working circles implement the remolding of society.

December 2: When Tse-tung came he said that the Youth Corps should wait until Chung Fu (Note: Ch'en Tu-hsiu's alias) came before the inaugural meeting was held, that attention be given to study and implementation. He also enjoined me to find some more true comrades.

December 7: Went to the Cultural Book Society to see Tse-tung and Yin-pai (Note: P'eng Huang's courtesy name).

December 15: Received a return letter from Tse-tung [in which he said]: First Normal has never had any school spirit. You should work hard to find some key comrades and create a very good school spirit. As for the Youth Corps, work hard to find some members and, if at all possible, have a meeting this semester.

December 26: Tse-tung came. The Youth Corps will hold its inaugural meeting next week.

December 27: Tse-tung sent nine copies of The Communist.

# The Establishment of the CCP

Before the founding of the Chinese Communist Party, Comrade Mao Tse-tung had established the Socialist Youth Corps in Hunan and had developed a certain number of corps members among young students and young workers. From the diary material quoted above, we can get a glimpse of Mao Tse-tung's thinking on the establishment of a corps: one should "find true comrades," one could not be too rapid in expanding. That is to say, extraordinary attention was to be paid to the quality of the corps members, they must be admitted with the utmost care. The Socialist Youth Corps in Peking and Shanghai were a mixed bag. There were Marxists, anarchists, guild socialists, and syndicalists — it was a very confused situation. (Because of this, the Socialist Youth Corps temporarily announced its dissolution in May 1921. After a readjustment it resumed in November.) By the first half of 1923 the Socialist Youth Corps already had a large and powerful organization in Hunan. Changsha, Anyüan, Yüeh-chou, Ch'ang-te, Heng-shan, Heng-yang, Feng-yang, Shui-k'ou-shan, Hsin-ho, T'ung-kuan, P'ing-chiang, and Hsin-ning all set up local organizations of the Corps, and Corps membership approached two thousand. Looking at the country as a whole, it was in Hunan that the organization of the Corps had developed to the greatest extent. In addition, as can be seen from the place-names mentioned above, the major working districts in Hunan, such as Anyüan, Shui-k'ou-shan, Hsin-ho, Changsha, and T'ung-kuan, all set up Corps organizations.

From 1920 to 1921 anarchists were quite active in the various Changsha Middle Schools. There were some students who, influenced by anarchism, had a formless organization called the Association of Shared Happiness [T'ung lo hui] that assembled once a week for wide-ranging discussions. For the most part, these were excellent, progressive-thinking students. In order to win over these people and lead them onto the path of Marxism, and at the same time with a view toward giving some order to the lives of rank and file comrades so that their working efficiency could be raised, Comrade Mao Tse-tung proposed the organization of a Youth Association of Shared Happiness. Everyone would gather together once every Sunday to go hiking on Yüeh-lu-shan, to go sailing on the Hsiang River, to talk about various doctrines, to discuss current events, or to recite poetry. They would not stick to any fixed format but would be relaxed and happy, and could also engage in ideological education. Thus, after some time had passed, these students who had once believed in anarchist thought were in large measure gradually won over by Comrade Mao Tse-tung.

Early Revolutionary Activities of Mao Tse-tung

By 1921, owing to Comrade Mao Tse-tung's correct leadership and the training derived from the practical revolutionary struggle before and after the May Fourth movement, Hunan had an excellent foundation for the establishment of the Party along both ideological and organizational lines. This was especially true in the area of cadres. The New People's Study Society led by Mao Tse-tung had already trained a large group of intellectual cadres who were loyal to the revolutionary cause, who had close ties with the masses, and who had a simple work style; and there was already quite a number of professional revolutionaries among them. Mao Tse-tung had a full appreciation of the decisive significance that professional revolutionaries had for the establishment of a genuine working-class party. At the time, there were individual comrades with a rather low level of awareness who insisted on continuing their university careers, thinking that "if we want to make a revolution it is better to seek some more learning." Mao Tse-tung criticized this erroneous thinking, saying that only by concentrating one's heart and soul on carrying out revolutionary work could one obtain real revolutionary learning; only then could a revolution develop.

In May 1920 the initiating organ [fa-ch'i tsu] of the Chinese Communist Party — the Shanghai Communist Cell [Kung-ch'an-chu-i hsiao-tsu] — was formally set up. The Peking Cell was founded in September. After Comrade Mao Tse-tung had received notification of this from Shanghai and Peking, he immediately founded the same type of organization in Changsha. Comrade Mao Tse-tung and his close comrades-in-arms Ho Shu-heng and others proceeded with great prudence in carrying out this urgent and serious work. Mao Tse-tung considered Ho Shu-heng to be his most steadfast and reliable revolutionary comrade. In June 1921 Comrade Mao Tse-tung was informed by Shanghai that the inaugural meeting of the Party was going to be held. He then went to Shanghai with Comrade Ho Shu-heng. Comrade Hsieh Chüeh-tsai recalls their departure:

One evening, with black clouds covering a sky that was threatening rain, I suddenly learned that Comrade Mao Tse-tung and Comrade Ho Shu-heng were going to depart for Shanghai. I thought this action was quite "abrupt." They also declined to let us see them off at the boat. I later found out that they were going to attend the First Congress of the Chinese Communist Party — the congress that gave birth to the great Chinese Communist Party. 11

At the First Congress Comrade Mao Tse-tung, along with the majority of delegates, opposed the rightist legal Marxist view that the Party not lead the workers and peasants in waging struggle but be only an academic organ for the study of Marxism. At the same time, he also opposed the erroneous view of the ultra "left" that considered proletarian dictatorship the immediate goal of the Party's struggle, that opposed the waging of open, legal, revolutionary activity, and that denied intellectuals entrance into the Party. During the course of the meeting, the delegates exchanged information on the conditions for the establishment of the Party and on the status of revolutionary work in various areas. Hunan, led by Comrade Mao Tse-tung, was the province with the best foundation.

After the close of the First Congress of the Party, Comrade Mao Tse-tung was sent back to Hunan to take up the position of Party secretary for the Hunan district (at the time called the Hsiang district). Mao Tse-tung immediately developed the Party organization in Changsha. Also, in accordance with the groundwork done in each area, he established local Party organizations. Mao very carefully and on an individual basis took into the Party the most progressive elements of the original revolutionary organizations and of the Socialist Youth Corps. At the same time, he began a broad expansion of the labor movement, developing Party members from progressive elements among the workers. Starting with Changsha's First Normal, First Middle School, Commercial Vocational School, and Ya-chung Industrial School, Party members were also developed in the schools, and some schools set up branches. Starting with Changsha's Canton-Hankow Railroad, mint, graphite refining plant, No. 1 Cotton Mill, electric light company, the masons and carpenters, and the sewing and printing industries, Party members were developed from among the workers. As early as the winter of 1921-22, Party members had been developed in Heng-yang, P'ing-chiang, Anyüan, Yüeh-chou, and Ch'ang-te. Some places established Party cells.

In the fall of 1921 Comrade Mao Tse-tung personally went to Anyüan to acquaint himself with the situation there and to prepare for the expansion of work there.

Before any locality established a Party organization, Comrade Mao Tse-tung would first have to acquaint himself in detail with every aspect of the situation and with the profile of the prospective members to be recruited. He paid special attention to the strength or weakness of the groundwork among the masses. For example, during the May Fourth movement there were students in P'ing-chiang who had studied abroad in Japan, had embraced utopian socialism, and who returned home to set up factories, run workers and peasants night schools, and organize labor and peasant unions, with the result that the mass patriotic movement was greatly advanced. Students, workers, and peasants all had rudimentary organizations. Workers who had embraced crude socialism were now the heads of the labor and peasant unions. After Comrade Mao Tse-tung became acquainted with this situation, he wrote a letter with the endorsement of relevant Party members, inviting these two union heads to come to Changsha. After several extensive talks with them, he recommended the two for entrance into the Party and directed them to return to P'ing-chiang and establish a Party organization. (One of these two worker comrades was named Yü Fen-min. He was with the first group that followed Mao into Chingkang-shan in 1927. Both of these men sacrificed their lives during the Second Revolutionary Civil War.) Thus, during the period of the First Revolutionary Civil War the Party organization in P'ing-chiang had a very good base.

From the very beginning, Comrade Mao Tse-tung attached great importance to the fundamental principle for establishing a party — establish the Party among the masses and maintain intimate links with them. At that time he often spoke to his comrades about the principle behind small organizations and large movements: before there can be any mutual dependence or development, one must combine an excellent and powerful Party organization with a large-scale mass movement and mass organization.

In the winter of 1921 Comrade Mao Tse-tung sent Comrade Chang Ch'iu-jen (martyred in 1928 in Chekiang) to Heng-yang. There, with Third Normal as a foothold (Chang was an English teacher at Third Normal), he established a Corps and Party organization. On May 2, 1922, Mao personally went to Heng-yang. At the May Fourth memorial meeting prepared by Third Normal he issued important directives and also convened a meeting of the Socialist Youth Corps. Mao Tse-tung stayed in Heng-yang for about one week, daily seeking out young cadres to speak with. As a result, everyone was greatly enlightened. Among these young students, Comrade Mao Tse-tung discovered some most progressive elements, like Comrades Hsia Ming-han, Chiang Hsien-yün, and Huang Ching-yüan. After they left school they became useful cadres for the Party.

After this, about once every three months, Comrade Mao Tse-tung would personally go to Heng-yang to make an inspection tour of the work.

In the winter of 1921 the Party rented a house in Changsha outside Hsiao-wu Gate at Ch'ing-shui-t'ang to serve as both a place for Comrade Mao Tse-tung to live and also as the organ of the provincial Party committee. The meetings of the provincial Party committee were all held in this very plain and simple house (which still stands). Mao Tse-tung attached great importance to the Party's meeting system and to Party discipline. Once at a meeting someone took issue with the paying of Party dues. Mao immediately dealt out severe criticism, pointing out that this violated the basic duty of a Party member. He attached an extraordinary amount of importance to the democratic life of the Party and insisted on the system of criticism and self-criticism, using the metaphor that one takes medicine when one is ill.* When documents from the Party Center arrived, he would study them word by word and conscientiously transmit them. Most of the provincial Party committee documents and the reports to the Party center were drafted by Mao Tse-tung. Toward his comrades he was extremely humble, sincere, and concerned, just as if they were his own family members. He had great respect for the opinions of others, and when he talked he always gave the other side ample opportunity to speak, he himself listening attentively. His answers were simple, clear, succinct, and very much to the point. Day in and day out he led a simple life. He regularly went into the midst of the working masses, always saying that he could never learn enough from the workers and peasants. He worked tirelessly from dawn till dusk and was extremely efficient in his work. These work styles all deeply influenced the comrades around him.

From the first day of its establishment, the Chinese Communist Party's [most consistently] correct leader was Comrade Mao Tse-tung. He was the most outstanding representative of those who combined Marxism-Leninism with Chinese revolutionary reality. At the same time, just as Comrade Liu Shao-ch'i has said:

He is also an ordinary member of our Party, placing himself completely at the service of the Party. He is most scrupulous in the observance of Party discipline in every respect. He is the leader of the masses, yet he bases everything on the will of the people. He stands before the people as their most loyal servant and their humblest pupil. [12]

---

* The metaphor of "curing a sickness" to refer to the acknowledgment of one's errors as a necessary condition for ideological remolding was, of course, put forward once more by Mao during the Yenan Rectification Campaign of 1942-43. See, for example, Mao's speech of February 1, 1942, Selected Works, III, p. 50 [S.R.S.].

After the birth of the great Chinese Communist Party, the complexion of the Chinese revolution underwent a fundamental change. Comrade Liu Shao-ch'i has said:

Prior to the founding of our Party in 1921, the Chinese nation and people, led by their most talented representatives, had for eighty years waged successive, heroic revolutionary struggles against imperialism and feudalism. The birth of our Party was conditioned by the international and internal events which were taking place at the time it occurred. Internationally, these were principally the First World War and the Great October Socialist Revolution in Russia. Internally, they were the increasingly ferocious imperialist aggression and feudal warlord oppression, the people's revolutionary struggles, and the rise of the working-class movement following the May Fourth movement in 1919. These conditions caused Chinese revolutionaries headed by Comrade Mao Tse-tung to turn for the first time from radical revolutionary democracy to proletarian communism, thereby giving birth to the Communist Party of China.

Since its very birth, our Party has had a clear-cut class-consciousness. It has adopted the proletarian standpoint in leading the Chinese bourgeois-democratic revolution. It has combined the universal truth of Marxism-Leninism with the concrete practice of the Chinese working-class movement and the Chinese revolution, and has acquired an exemplary style of work befitting an advanced proletarian political party. All these gave a fresh complexion to the Chinese revolution. 13

Among the earliest group of intellectuals and workers recruited into the Party in Hunan by Comrade Mao Tse-tung were not only a large number of excellent top-ranking Party personnel but also a great many outstanding mass leaders, such as Comrades Ho Shu-heng, Kuo Liang, Hsia Hsi, Chiang Hsien-yün, Hsia Ming-han, Chiang Meng-chou, Ch'en Yu-k'uei, Huang Ching-yüan, Ch'en Ch'ang, Chang K'un-ti, Lo Hsüeh-tsan, Liu Chih-kou, Yang Fu-t'ao, Chang Han-fan, Liu Tung-hsüan, and Hsieh Huai-te. This finest flower of the Chinese race, these heroes of the Chinese revolution, were all bravely martyred one after another for the cause of communism. They left a legacy of everlasting glory for the Party and for the Chinese people and set an enduring example for posterity.

## V. FOUNDING SELF-STUDY UNIVERSITY. TRAINING YOUNG REVOLUTIONARY CADRES

After the founding of the Chinese Communist Party, Comrade Mao Tse-tung attached greater importance to the study of theory. In August 1921, with a view to strengthening the study of Marxist-Leninist theory among Party and Corps cadres and also to rallying the progressive intellectuals in society to study the theories of

Marx and Lenin, Comrade Mao Tse-tung, using the finances and
location of the Wang Fu-chih Study Society, founded Self-Study University [Tzu-hsiu ta-hsüeh]. Self-Study University was an ideal
that Mao Tse-tung had cherished for a very long time: to select
the best from both the ancient lecture technique and from the modern school system; to gather together comrades, to learn freely,
and to study together.

The Wang Fu-chih Study Society was set up in the first year of
the "Republic" [1911] by a group of Hunanese literary men for the
purpose of expounding on the scholarly thought of Wang Fu-chih.
Today this narrow little meeting place is still partially preserved
in its original condition. During 1914 and 1915 the Wang Fu-chih
Study Society held weekly lectures on the thought of Wang Fu-chih.
It also attacked Yüan Shih-k'ai's scheme to become emperor, and
it won general approval in society at large. When Comrade Mao
Tse-tung was studying at First Normal, he went to listen to some
of the lectures. Those who presided over the affairs of the Society
were largely teachers of the old learning. The government gave
the Society a monthly subsidy of 400 yuan. Comrade Ho Shu-heng
was a member of the Society and was on friendly terms with an enlightened old teacher who was one of the directors. At this time,
the president of the Society had definite contradictions with Chao
Heng-t'i. After getting the agreement of the Society, Comrade Mao
Tse-tung used its headquarters and the monthly stipend of 400 yuan
to found Self-Study University as the center for the Party's public
activities. Ho Shu-heng later became president of the Wang Fu-
chih Study Society.

On August 16 the Changsha press carried the "Hu-nan tzu-hsiu
ta-hsüeh tsu-chih ta-kang" [General Organizational Outline of the
Hunan Self-Study University]. The first section, "Name and Aim,"
read:

In view of the deficiencies of the present educational system, this university has
adopted the good points of both the ancient academies and modern schools. It has
adopted the method of studying various kinds of learning on one's own initiative
in the hope of discovering truth and creating human resources, so that culture
will be extended to the common people and learning diffused throughout society.
It has been set up by the Hunan Wang Fu-chih Study Society and is named "Hunan
Self-Study University." Hence, in attracting students it relies only on scholarship and does not set up [any other] qualifications. The approach to learning is
primarily free study and group discussions. The teachers are responsible for
bringing up questions and correcting notes and essays. The students do not pay
any tuition, and those who live in the dormitories pay expenses for board only.

After the bulletin of Self-Study University was out, Hunan cultural and educational circles discussed it in great profusion, calling this a strange affair and maintaining that it was an organization without foundation or support, an organization that was neither fish nor fowl. But such talk could not have the least effect on the existence or development of the school. In the very beginning Comrade Mao Tse-tung himself, his many comrades-in-arms, and some of the Party and Corps cadres were all students at Self-Study University. After Comrades Hsia Ming-han, Ch'en Yu-k'uei, [14] and others got out of school, they enrolled in Self-Study University and lived at the Wang Fu-chih Study Society. Self-Study University was equipped with a richly stocked library that gathered together all the progressive books, magazines and newspapers that could be obtained in China and provided them for everyone to read. Students regularly held symposia to discuss various questions on Marxism-Leninism. Although the number of students attracted was small, this "university" resolutely carried on and eventually played a very important role in disseminating Marxism and in raising the theoretical level of the cadres.

The intellectual youths who stayed at Self-Study University and engaged in the labor movement had to have a firm revolutionary will to withstand the condemnation of society. (For example, if one had contact with workers one was reproached for "not considering one's moral character.") Comrade Hsia Ming-han had a run-in with his big feudal landlord and big bureaucratic family and left home. When living at Self-Study University he was so poor that it was difficult for him to sustain himself. (Comrade Hsia Ming-han was martyred in 1928 at Wuhan. A poem he wrote just before he was to be executed read:

> Cutting off my head is not important
> If what I believe in is true.
> When Hsia Ming-han is killed and gone
> There'll be others to follow him too!

This poem expressed a great heroic spirit and has been repeated by people ever since that day.)

In April 1923 the Changsha press printed "Sheng ch'eng ko hsiao hsien-k'uang tiao-ch'a chi" [An Investigation of the Current Status of City Schools]. On Self-Study University there was the following report:

This school was organized for the average student who has an ambition to study but who feels that the present school system is no good or whose financial capacity is insufficient for any of the other universities. At the present time, it has only the two departments of humanities and political economy. The school emphasizes solely self-study. Except for foreign languages, there are no class periods. Each person studies freely or takes part in discussion sessions. The procedure for entrance is that each student answers six questions by correspondence. After this, he has two oral exams that determine admittance. This is quite different from normal entrance examinations. Here are the questions that have been set up: (1) What schools have you been to before? What have you done? What is the financial situation of your family and yourself? (2) In which departments do you want to study? Why do you want to study in these departments? (3) What subjects have you studied before? (4) For how many semesters do you want to study? What are your postgraduate plans? (5) Opinions on one's view of life. (6) Criticism of society, etc. At present there are twenty-four students. Every day each person writes up study notes and fills out a study work sheet. Every day he writes an essay that is read and examined by the principal in order to determine the student's mark. The best daily essay is selected for inclusion in the school's monthly publication.

The influence of Self-Study University was not limited to the province of Hunan; there were echoes in Peking and Shanghai where progressive publications introduced and praised it. For example, Ts'ai Yüan-p'ei wrote an article entitled "Hu-nan tzu-hsiu ta-hsüeh ti chieh-shao yü shuo-ming" [An Introduction to and Explanation of Hunan Self-Study University].

In 1922 Self-Study University held several public lectures on Marxist theory.

With a view to disseminating systematically the theories of Marx and Lenin and to studying and discussing the problem of the Chinese revolution, Comrade Mao Tse-tung had long thought about founding a public periodical in Hunan. Now, in the name of Self-Study University, he founded the monthly New Age [Hsin shih-tai]. The inaugural issue of New Age was published on April 15, 1923, and the first article, written by Comrade Mao Tse-tung, was entitled "Wai-li chun-tai yü ke-ming" [Foreign Powers, Warlords, and Revolution]. There were also articles like "Ho wei ti-kuo chu-i" [What Is Imperialism?] as well as translated documents like the Marxist classic Critique of the Gotha Program. In issues No. 2 and No. 4 there were the following articles: "Ma-k'e-ssu hsüeh-shuo yü Chung-kuo" [Marxist Theory and China], "Kuan-nien shih-kuan p'i-p'ing" [A Criticism of the Idealist View of History], "Kung-ch'an-chu-i ching-chi chin-hua" [Communism and Economic Progress], etc.

# Early Revolutionary Activities of Mao Tse-tung

Chairman Mao Tse-tung succinctly and revealingly analyzed China's domestic and foreign political state of affairs. He explained the principle that to counter the power of imperialism and the war-lords, the revolutionary democratic united front, with CCP-KMT cooperation as its nucleus, had to steadily increase its strength. Mao Tse-tung believed that although it was the fondest hope of in-ternational imperialism that China be completely occupied by the most benighted reactionary government, the political economic sta-tus of semicolonial, semifeudal China made it quite impossible for the Fengtien, Chihli, and Anhwei cliques and the southwestern war-lords to form a united front. Further, the result of a government that was increasingly thrown into confusion the more reactionary it grew was certain to arouse the revolutionary spirit of all the people in the country and to increase their organizational capacity. Revolutionary elements were certain to increase daily and the bat-tle line would naturally grow stronger and firmer day by day. Chair-man Mao Tse-tung said that only after the revolutionaries had fi-nally gained victory over the warlord reactionaries could we con-sider China's democratic, independent government finally achieved. The turn of events that occurred during the First Revolutionary Civil War substantiated these masterful arguments.

Comrade Mao Tse-tung regularly thus used the fundamental view-point of Marxism-Leninism in analyzing the concrete reality of the Chinese Revolution to educate the great masses of revolutionary youth and revolutionary cadres of the time.

In 1922 there was still not one school in the entire country that openly trained young revolutionary cadres, but after the May Fourth movement those youths who were inclined toward revolution and who demanded the new thought were like a rapidly flowing tide. This was particularly the case in Hunan. The standards used in attracting students to Self-Study University were rather high. They were inappropriate for the rank and file intellectual youth; they were even less capable of meeting the demands of young workers. For this reason, Self-Study University formally set up a "Prepara-tory School" [Pu-hsi hsüeh-hsiao] in September 1922 (later a junior and middle class were established), publicly called for students, and began training young revolutionary cadres for the Party. Although the courses that were set up were generally like those of any ordi-nary school — there was Chinese, English, mathematics, history, geography, etc. — the instruction in Chinese and history made full allowance for the intertwining of Marxist ideological education with problems chosen by the teacher. Ho Shu-heng, Li Wei-han, Hsia

Hsi, Chiang Meng-chou, Lo Hsüeh-tsan, Hsia Ming-han, and other comrades were all teachers in the Preparatory Class at one time or another. In a thin textbook from a continuation class in Chinese that has survived, there is a piece entitled "Kao Chung-kuo nung-min" [Address to the Chinese Peasants]. It was written on the basis of conditions in the Hunan countryside. It analyzed in detail the socio-economic circumstances of the various classes in the Hunan countryside and the reason behind the gradual concentration of land, pointing out that the only way out for the peasants was revolution and the recovery of their land from the hands of the landlords. Guide Weekly and China Youth were made required outside reading for the students of the Preparatory Class.

Among the students recruited for the Preparatory Class and the junior and middle school sections were young progressive intellectuals and young progressive workers. At the time of highest enrollment, there were over two hundred students. For example, Comrade Li Yao-jung [15] and five other young workers who at the time were working at the Kuang-Hua Electric Light Company were all students of the Preparatory Class. Every day after they finished work they hurried to the Wang Fu-chih Study Society from far away beyond North Gate to attend classes. The best students were all introduced into the Corps and Party by the teachers. In 1925 the Party organized a large group of revolutionary youths from Hunan to go to Canton. In this group were many students of the Self-Study University Preparatory Class and the later Hsiang River School [Hsiang chiang hsüeh-hsiao].

At this time the Hunan United Association of Students was also set up at Self-Study University. The positions of responsibility in the Association were held by people from Self-Study University. For example, Comrade Hsia Hsi was the person who held primary responsibility from 1922 to 1923.

Ever since he had issued a warrant for the arrest of Comrade Mao Tse-tung in April 1923, Chao Heng-t'i had been brooding over his desire to close down Self-Study University. Nevertheless, because of the old and respected name of the Wang Fu-shih Study Society and because some upper-stratum Party connections were involved, he had not gotten an opportunity to play his hand. In November of this year the Chao Heng-t'i government instigated a company of Hupei troops to station themselves at the Wang Fu-chih Study Society and set a time limit of two days for all the students to move out of the school. The Party mobilized Society members and upper-level people from educational circles to intervene with the Ministry of Education before Chao Heng-t'i was forced to cut his own face [i.e., ruin his reputation] by issuing a "handwritten edict": "Self-Study University is forthwith dissolved." Moreover, he stated to the people in educational circles that "the theories promoted by Self-Study University are heterodox; they affect public security."

The Party had long before been prepared for the reactionary measures of Chao Heng-t'i. After Self-Study University, the attached Preparatory Class, and the junior and middle divisions had been sequestered, a regular middle school run by the Hunan provincial Party committee — the Hsiang River School — formally began classes on November 24, 1923. A majority of the over two hundred students who were originally at Self-Study University now transferred to this school.

Hsiang River School had two divisions: one was the Middle School and the other the Village Normal School. The curriculum was, on its face, the same as that of other ordinary schools of the time. The principal of the school was a very early member of the New People's Study Society and a person who Comrade Mao Tse-tung felt had the most experience in running schools, Comrade Lo Tsung-han (he died of illness in 1927). For the most part, the teachers were people who had originally run Self-Study University. Comrade Chiang Meng-chou was the administrator and bore the greatest practical responsiblity. He was a very close childhood friend of Comrade Ho Shu-heng. They traveled onto the path of revolution together, starting from studying the old books, talking about justice, and engaging in the new learning. "He was about the nineteenth person in Hunan to join the Party." [16] Comrade Chiang Meng-chou's close contact with the masses, his search for truth in his work, his lack of fear in the face of difficulty, and his spirit of suffering first before others were all greatly praised by everyone.

Self-Study University and Hsiang River School were Party schools; there were no school funds, and the principal did not live at the school. Comrade Chiang Meng-chou was, in name, the administrator, but in reality he raised funds, attracted students, set up the curriculum, invited teachers, repaired the building, cooked all by himself.... The training students and comrades got from him derived from the fact that he taught a lot "by deed" and little "by word." [17]

In March of 1929 Comrade Chiang Meng-chou was murdered in Changsha. After he died, owing to the great prestige he had always enjoyed in his native home of Ning-hsiang, every circle of Ning-hsiang society participated in a great memorial service for him, the likes of which had never before been seen there. Not only did thousands of workers and peasants come to the memorial service, but people from educational circles and the local gentry who had some sense of justice also came. The memorial became a great protest of the Ning-hsiang people against the giant tide of white terror that reigned at the time.

With regard to the ideological education that Self-Study University Preparatory Class and Hsiang River School were giving their students, we can get a glimpse from the diary and essays of Comrade Ho Erh-k'ang, [18] who studied in the Self-Study University Preparatory Class and the Hsiang River School. Comrade Ho Erh-k'ang was from Hsiang-t'an, and his home was not far from Comrade Mao Tse-tung's own at Shao-shan-ch'ung. His family was very poor and he couldn't afford to go to school. Only later, after he had received some help from Mao Tse-tung, did Ho come to Changsha to enter Self-Study University Preparatory Class. Below are some fragmentary excerpts from Ho Erh-k'ang's diary and essays:

August 16, 1923: It was not until toward evening that I went to my light to read. Mr. Ho (Note: i.e., Comrade Ho Shu-heng) called me into his room and asked me about my family situation and also how it was that I wanted to come and study, what was the purpose of my studying? He then gave me a topic to write on: "My Family Background and Ambitions.". . . Actually my ambition is to live forever. At the present time China is suffering extreme ill-treatment at the hands of foreign countries. Many places have been cut away, many have been leased away, and the people who run our government are all warlords who ill-treat the people; the people are in very dire straits. When I think that our country has come to such a point, my mind is in constant turmoil and I want to make it my ambition to run China properly.

In the second semester of 1924 the topic was "Why Doesn't Everyone Believe in Communism?" In the essay I wrote, "The evolution of human society has already taught us: we cannot but travel the new path of Communism."

April 28: At the two o'clock class in Civics there was a lecture about Lenin's [idea of] national revolution.

Received a letter ordering me to organize a lecture team and go out to the city and suburbs on a lecture circuit on "May 1."

May 5: Today is the 107th anniversary of the father of Communism, Marx. In the afternoon a commemorative assembly was held at P'u-t'ien-ch'un. In addition, people had been invited to lecture on Marxist theory.

May 7: There was a great demonstration with loud cries along the route of march, proclaiming, down with Japanese imperialism, down with English and American imperialism; renounce the Twenty-one Demands.

May 29: Discussed the second chapter, "Class Struggle and Political Parties," of An Introduction to Political Economy.

# THE EARLY LABOR MOVEMENT IN HUNAN LED BY COMRADE MAO TSE-TUNG

4

## I. GOING INTO THE MIDST OF THE WORKING MASSES. STARTING TO LEAD THE LABOR MOVEMENT

During the May Fourth movement of 1919 when the center of the movement shifted from Peking to Shanghai, the principal strength of the movement also shifted from the students to the working class. The Chinese working class began to exhibit its own strength and moreover began to come under the influence of Marxism-Leninism. The political strikes of the workers in Shanghai, T'ang-shan, and Ch'ang-hsin-tien led to the rapid victory of the anti-imperialist struggle waged by all people throughout the country. "The rise in strength of the Chinese workers gave impetus to Left-wing Chinese intellectuals of the May Fourth movement and made them determined to carry on revolutionary work among the workers," [thus] "causing the Chinese labor movement and the Chinese revolutionary movement to enter a new period." [1]

As soon as the Chinese working class appeared in the Chinese political arena, it exhibited an enormous fighting strength. On the one hand, this was brought about by the international and domestic situation of the time: the victory of the Russian October Revolution and the rise of patriotic movements among a people that had been oppressed by both foreign and domestic reactionaries. But at the same time,

The remarkable militancy displayed by the Chinese working class was chiefly due to three reasons. Firstly, the Chinese working class was subjected to the ruthless oppression by foreign imperialism, and domestic feudalism and capitalism. Secondly, it is highly concentrated. Although Chinese industries are under-developed, they are highly concentrated. The total number of workers engaged

178

in modern industrial enterprises each employing more than 500 workers is very large. Thirdly, although the industrial workers are in a minority in relation to the total population, the number of proletarians and semi-proletarians of various kinds is large. If the semi-proletarians in the countryside — the poor peasants — are taken together, the proletarians and semi-proletarians constitute far more than half the total population. The oppression to which they were subjected was extremely cruel. For these reasons, the working class of revolutionary China constitutes a powerful fighting force, has formed its own strong political party, the Communist Party, and has become the leader of all the revolutionary classes of China. [2]

During the rule of the Peiyang warlords, Hunan's industry was quite backward (when Chiang K'ai-shek ruled, the situation was the same). What could be called modern business enterprises could be counted on the fingers: the rather large mines at Hsi-k'uang-shan (antimony) and Shui-k'ou-shan (lead and zinc) and, in Changsha, the spinning factory, the mint, the graphite refining plant, and the electric light company. Including the mines and the railroad, there were about twenty or thirty thousand industrial workers. Nevertheless, the several above-mentioned reasons for the formation of the militancy of the Chinese working class were also present in Hunan. The workers from Shui-k'ou-shan, the Canton-Hankow Railway, and the mint had, before the May Fourth movement and the founding of the Party, already waged struggles by striking and had shown great fighting strength. During the May Fourth movement and the movement to Expel Chang Ching-yao, the working class had also actively participated in the struggle.

Before the founding of the Chinese Communist Party, Comrade Mao Tse-tung had already begun to turn his attention to the labor movement. He did his best to draw close to the working masses and acquaint himself with the actual conditions of the laboring man's life. He often went to observe and investigate the workers' voluntary schools that had been set up by various schools and organizations. At the time, there was a "labor union" in Changsha organized by anarchists who were carrying on among the workers activities that lacked a clear-cut political direction. Comrade Mao Tse-tung paid a great deal of attention to this organization and believed that it was headed in the wrong direction. Later, after a long period of patient work and factual lessons, the activists among these Changsha industrial workers who had been influenced by anarchism were finally won over by Mao Tse-tung. The two leaders of the "labor union," Huang Ai and P'ang Jen-ch'üan, also joined the Socialist Youth Corps before they were butchered by Chao Heng-t'i.

In December 1920, Comrade Mao Tse-tung published an article

in the Changsha newspaper concerning the necessity of establishing a labor organization, pointing out that only after the workers themselves had heightened their awareness, set up a strong and firm organization, and devoted their efforts to struggle could they better their lives and raise their status. This was the only way. To achieve "liberation of labor" by depending on the compassion of the employer, by talking about the principles of humanity, or by hoping that other people would speak up for you was sheer fantasy.

On May Day 1921, the factory workers of Changsha, some several thousand people, held a demonstration, advancing the slogans "Improve Treatment" and "Strengthen Solidarity."

"In 1921 came the founding of the Chinese Communist Party and the real beginning of China's labor movement." [3] After the First Congress of the Chinese Communist Party, in a move to give open and unified leadership to the national labor movement, the "Chinese Trades Union Secretariat" [Chung-kuo lao-tung tsung-ho shu-chi-pu] was founded with Comrade Mao Tse-tung as secretary of the Hunan branch. After Mao returned to Hunan from the completion of the First Party Congress, he concentrated his efforts on leading the Hunan labor movement. Just as he himself has recalled: "I returned to Hunan and vigorously pushed the work among the labor unions" [Snow, Red Star, p. 158]. He sent key Party personnel to Anyüan, Shui-k'ou-shan, the Canton-Hankow Railway, and every important industry and handicraft industry in Changsha to initiate work among the workers. Comrade Mao Tse-tung himself took the lead in going into the midst of the working masses and disseminating the fundamental principles of Marxism among them. He personally was the secretary for many unions and directly led the workers in their strike struggles. Moreover, as a representative of the workers, he personally waged a face-to-face battle of reason with Chao Heng-t'i. Thus, from 1922 to the beginning of 1923, following the nationwide upsurge of the labor movement, the Hunan labor movement saw tremendous development. The industrial workers from Anyüan, Shui-k'ou-shan, the Canton-Hankow Railway, and Changsha together with the workers of the various handicraft industries were extensively organized and extensively waged a victorious strike struggle. In all, more than twenty labor unions were established, and the number of organized workers reached forty or fifty thousand. A great number of excellent labor cadres were nurtured during the strike struggles. In some labor union organizations there was a gradual development of Socialist Youth Corps and Communist Party members and the establishment of Corps and Party branches. The intellectual cadres that were sent to participate in and lead the labor movement thus gained much training and rapid improvement, so that the rudimentary Marxist-Leninist theory they had learned was able to be combined with the reality of the Chinese labor movement of the time.

On November 1, 1922, on the basis of victorious struggles and resolute masses, a centralized organization of workers from the entire province was founded — the Hunan United Association of Syndicates [Hu-nan sheng kung-t'uan lien-ho-hui] with Comrade Mao Tse-tung as the Association's first general secretary.

After the "February 7 tragedy," when the nationwide labor movement was at a low ebb, Hunan was the sole province where the movement still continued to develop. By 1924, it was only in Hunan that public labor unions of urban workers organized according to industry were still fully intact. Of all the mine workers in the country, it was also only those in Anyüan and Shui-k'ou-shan who were fully organized, despite the fact that later Chao Heng-t'i used every method to break the labor movement. As Comrade Kuo Liang said in his essay "Hu-nan kung-jen yün-tung ti kuo-ch'ü yü hsien-tsai" [The Hunan Labor Movement, Yesterday and Today],

Assembly and association were generally prohibited. The miners' union at Shui-k'ou-shan and many of the labor unions in Changsha were closed down. The workers were cruelly massacred, and the labor movement was dealt a heavy blow. But the revolutionary Hunan labor movement by no means suffered a setback in morale because of this; the workers did not in the least let up in their open struggles and secret associations. When the May 30 movement suddenly unfolded and the nation's working class fought a bloody hand-to-hand battle with imperialism, the Hunan workers fought in unison, and the number of organized workers rose to more than seventy thousand.

After the May 30 movement, Chao Heng-t'i intensified his persecution:

For example, the massacring of the workers at Anyüan and Shui-k'ou-shan, the dissolution of the labor unions, the arrest and imprisonment of the workers at the No. 1 Cotton Mill, and the suppression of the Changsha typesetters' strike. Under these circumstances, it was nevertheless still possible to broaden secret organization, and the number of workers participating in labor unions throughout the province rose to one-hundred and ten thousand. 4

During the Northern Expedition War, the workers of Anyüan, the Chu-chou-P'ing-hsiang Railway, the Canton-Hankow Railway, Changsha, Li-ling, P'ing-chiang, and Hsiang-t'an threw themselves into the battle and consolidated the rear area, thus making an immense contribution. At the beginning of 1927, the number of organized workers throughout the province reached four hundred thousand. After the defeat of the Revolution of 1927, the workers from Anyüan and Shui-k'ou-shan waged a fierce armed struggle. Among the worker and peasant revolutionaries that Comrade Mao Tse-tung took with him onto Chingkangshan were several hundred workers from Anyüan, Shui-k'ou-shan, and Changsha.

Thus, the idea that "the Chinese Communist Party was the offspring of the integration of the Chinese labor movement with Marxism-Leninism" is a truth that can be amply proved from the facts surrounding Comrade Mao Tse-tung's earliest work in the Hunan labor movement.

History itself explains the origin of this great transformation that was China's modern revolution: It was from the era of the May Fourth movement, after China's most advanced intellectuals like Comrade Mao Tse-tung and Comrade Li Ta-chao had aligned themselves with the labor movement, that

the Chinese proletarian political party — the Chinese Communist Party — with Comrade Mao Tse-tung as its great representative, appeared, and that the integration of Marxism-Leninism with the practice of the Chinese revolution, the concentrated representation of this being the thought of Mao Tse-tung, also appeared. This was the great turning point of all Chinese history. This was the great turning point when the Chinese people, after several thousand years of being ruled and through thirty years of struggle, gradually and completely won the ruling position for themselves. The present victories of the earthshaking New Democracy of the Chinese people started from this. [5]

Comrade Mao Tse-tung has said:

In the Chinese democratic revolutionary movement, it was the intellectuals who were the first to awaken. This was clearly demonstrated both in the Revolution of 1911 and in the May Fourth movement, and in the days of the May Fourth movement the intellectuals were more numerous and more politically conscious than in the days of the Revolution of 1911. But the intellectuals will accomplish nothing if they fail to integrate themselves with the workers and peasants. In the final analysis, the dividing line between revolutionary intellectuals is whether or not they are willing to integrate themselves with the workers and peasants and actually do so. [6]

After the May Fourth movement, Comrade Mao Tse-tung quite consciously engaged in revolutionary activity with this spirit. Mao Tse-tung had always understood very well the truth that Marx had enunciated: "The educator must first be educated." He often said: "If one wants to be the teacher of the people, one must first be the student of the people." From the very beginning of his own revolu-

tionary activity he consciously worked in accordance with this
spirit.

When Comrade Mao Tse-tung at first drew close to the workers,
he experienced a period of hard work. He often went barefoot or
wore straw sandals, wore a straw hat, and wore coarse, short trousers and jacket to facilitate his approach to the workers. For example, in order to acquaint himself with the situation of the Canton-
Hankow Railway workers, he spent many days drinking tea with
some railway and transport workers in the teashop at Changsha's
North Station. He had sincere talks with them and eventually made
friends among them.

One of the reasons Comrade Mao Tse-tung was able to merge
with the workers was that he actually succeeded in popularizing his
language. He has said: "We are revolutionaries working for the
masses, and if we do not learn the language of the masses, we cannot work well.... The mastery of language is not easy and requires
painstaking effort. First, let us learn language from the masses.
The people's vocabulary is rich, vigorous, vivid, and expressive
of real life." [7] Since his youth in the countryside, Mao had always
been on very friendly terms with the peasantry. When he ran the
night school at First Normal, he drew near to the working man.
Thus he had always been very familiar with and had attached great
importance to the rich and vivid language of the people. Now, with
a view toward launching a labor movement, he of course paid even
more attention to studying the speech of the working masses. According to the recollection of the people closest to Comrade Mao
Tse-tung at the time, his language was popular and vivid, deeply
penetrating but easy to understand, simple, clear and powerful,
rich in humor, filled with appropriate imagery, especially filled
with the character of the Chinese people and the local features of
the language, and had an unsurpassed appeal. Proof of this can be
seen in the many proclamations, handbills, and relevant writings
of the strike movements. A great number of these proclamations,
handbills, and writings were penned by Mao himself or were par-
tially revised by him.

At the time, Comrade Mao Tse-tung was physically rather weak.
His own material living standard was about the same as that of the
average worker. He often went to working-class districts and made
extensive contacts with the workers in various enterprises. The
activists among the workers also often came to the Wang Fu-chih
Study Society and other places where Mao Tse-tung lived. Having
established friendly contacts with the broad masses of working

people, Mao felt that a vast and limitless new world had opened up before his eyes. On the one hand, he developed a deep appreciation of the life, thought, feelings, and demands of the workers and, on the other, he adopted an extremely humble and respectful attitude and learned from the working masses. He encouraged himself and enriched himself with the wisdom, creativity, courage, and strength of the masses, which caused him to undergo a fundamental reconstruction in his own view of life and view of the universe, not only from a rational but also from an emotional point of view. During the earliest period of the Chinese revolution, Comrade Mao Tsetung was fundamentally different from that type of people who, like Ch'en Tu-hsiu and Chang Kuo-t'ao, sat and discussed principles, gave armchair directives and spouted Marxism. Mao Tse-tung has said: "Whether he is a true or false Marxist, we need only find out how he stands in relation to the broad masses of workers and peasants, and then we shall know him for what he is." [8] This is an immutable truth. Later, Mao talked about the change in his own thinking and feelings that occurred after his union with the peasant and worker masses:

After I became a revolutionary and lived with the workers and peasants and with soldiers of the revolutionary army, I gradually came to know them well, and they gradually came to know me well too. It was then, and only then, that I fundamentally changed the bourgeois and petty-bourgeois feelings implanted in me in the bourgeois schools. I came to feel that compared with the workers and peasants the unremolded intellectuals were not clean and that, in the last analysis, the workers and peasants were the cleanest people and, even though their hands were soiled and their feet smeared with cow dung, they were really cleaner than the bourgeois and petty-bourgeois intellectuals. That is what is meant by a change in feelings, a change from one class to another. [9]

Where does one start in organizing the workers?

In the experience of the Party organizations at Peking and Shanghai in 1921 in launching the labor movement, what came first and foremost was the founding of a night school in the working-class districts. Comrade Mao Tse-tung himself had had experience in running a workers' night school when he was studying at First Normal. Thus from the latter half of 1921 to 1922 Mao Tse-tung sent out many Party and Corps cadres to set up a number of workers' night schools among the production workers at Anyüan, on the Canton-Hankow Railway, at Shui-k'ou-shan, in Changsha and among the masons and carpenters, tailors, barbers, and rickshaw workers. In the beginning it was inevitable that the workers should harbor suspicion, that they were hesitant and not very willing to

come. Thus generally a day class for the workers' children was
first set up. Through the workers' children further contact was
made with the family elders and after the day class had established
a good reputation, it was easy to set up a workers' night school. In
the beginning, all the money for leasing the school building, for
mimeographing the texts, for paper and ink, etc., was donated by
the Party. In general when each night school was begun, it was
matched with a cadre who bore complete responsibility for the curriculum, for putting together the texts, etc., for both the day and
night school. After the labor movement was opened up on a large
scale, the number of workers attending the night schools increased
and the labor unions got organized. Only then did the unions take
over the night schools and provide all the running expenses. At
this time, the Party had to mobilize a large group of cadres to go
and serve as teachers. In some places, like Anyüan and Shui-k'ou-
shan, after successful strikes, the mining authorities were forced
to put out the money to build school buildings for the workers and
to supply the regular monthly running expenses.

Preparing the texts was a major problem. At the time, there
were no ready-made popular teaching materials containing revolutionary thought that could be used. Comrade Mao Tse-tung gave
his special attention to the solution of this problem. At first, Mao
wanted the teachers to utilize the material in the old Chinese history textbooks to explain the significance of the "sanctity of labor."
He wanted them to use the examples of the progress from living in
trees and pits* to living in reed sheds and houses with windows,
from eating hair and blood* to striking fire and cooking food, from
wrapping up in tree leaves and wild animal skins to wearing silk
and woven cotten clothes, from fishing, hunting, and raising domestic animals to agriculture and handicraft industries, from the use
of stone and iron implements to the use of machinery to explain the
significance of the sanctity of labor and to awaken the workers'
class consciousness to the injustice of the exploitation of the people by the capitalists and to the chasm of difference between rich
and poor. After the number of workers' night schools had increased,
Comrade Mao Tse-tung felt the pressing need to prepare comprehensive teaching materials.

In the latter half of 1922 there were some people from educational
circles in Hunan (among them some ideologically progressive elements) who were actively promoting a so-called "Popular Education"

---

* According to the classical texts. — Tr.

movement in preparation for opening up a large number of preparatory schools for the common people. The government, moreover, was subsidizing the venture. At this time, individual Party members with some social status participated in the leadership of the movement. Comrade Mao Tse-tung then directed them to make good use of this movement to help the Party with its task of setting up workers' night schools. In 1923 the Hunan Society for the Promotion of Popular Education [Hu-nan p'ing-min chiao-yü ts'u-chin hui] was formally founded. Well over several dozen hsien founded branch societies, and all of them had fixed financial aid. Later, under the direction of Mao Tse-tung, the Party organizations of each area also did a good job of launching labor movements and peasant movements via the use of "Popular Education."

The main problem at the time was a lack of popular textbooks. Under the leadership and encouragement of Comrade Mao Tse-tung, Comrade Li Liu-ju, who presided over the work in popular education, compiled a four-volume series entitled P'ing-min tu-pen [The Popular Reader], which was published in the Hunan Popular Gazette, and, in October 1922, published in book form. In less than a year, four editions had been published and several tens of thousands of volumes sold.

This four-volume reader was so set up that it led from the easy-to-understand to the more deep and difficult, from short essays to longer ones. Its style of language was popular, and the lessons ranged in size from just over ten to three or four hundred characters. In content, it included problems of everyday life, social culture, scientific knowledge, and major national and international events. Particularly important was that it introduced a rudimentary knowledge of Marxism and the orientation of the Russian October Revolution. For example, the lesson in Volume I entitled "The Origins of Clothing, Food, and Shelter" read in part: "Man's clothing, food, and shelter have all been created by the peasants and workers. However, these brothers who work in the fields and perform manual labor do not themselves have any good clothes to wear, enough food to eat, or houses to live in. This is just too unfair!" The lesson entitled "The Division of Labor and Mutual Aid" that appears in Volume II maintained that life in human society should follow the dictum "from each according to his ability and to each according to his deserts. One certainly cannot be like those bureaucrats, warlords, and capitalists who devour the people, who sit and take the things made by others." In Volume III, aside from such lessons as "The Rights of the People," "Equality," and "Assembly," there are two lessons concerned with organizing united associations of peasants and workers. This is how "A Letter on Meeting with Friends and Organizing a United Association of Peasants and Workers" movingly put it:

No one in the world has suffered more than we peasants and workers. Although we work desperately to create things, we ourselves do not enjoy anything at all. We are nothing but other people's beasts of burden. Unless we all quickly wake up and unite, we will be buried at the bottom of the eighteen-layer hell,* and the day of release [fan-shen] will never come.

Volume IV devotes six lessons to the introduction of the various schools of socialism and presents a simple and succinct introduction to communism — the scientific socialism founded by Marx — and to its influence on the world, as well as to the victory of the Russian Communist Party (Bolsheviks) and its basic policy. Very obviously, these four volumes of the P'ing-min tu-pen, rich in ideology and revolutionary encouragement, played a great ideologically enlightening role with respect to the broad working masses. This kind of a reader could educate the working masses to recognize their own strength, could inspire them to rise up and make revolutionary struggle, and could lead them to travel the path of Marxism and of the Russian Revolution. Some elderly comrades who were born of working-class families still recall very clearly being taught the P'ing-min tu-pen and the great influence it had on their joining the revolution.

Besides using the workers' night schools to conduct Marxist-Leninist education among the working masses and to open up their ideological consciousness, Comrade Mao Tse-tung also frequently organized those Party members and progressive people who had some social status to utilize their legitimate positions to give significant lectures to the working masses.

This method of workers' night schools was indeed the best and most effective way at the time for the revolutionary intellectuals to unite with the workers. As part of a plan, a great many intellectual cadres organized by the Hunan Party and under the leadership of Comrade Mao Tse-tung were sent out in groups among the working masses of various areas to set up night schools and to lead the labor movement. In 1922, after Comrade Liu Shao-ch'i had returned to Hunan, he participated in the leadership of the labor movement and was sent to the very important district of Anyüan for more than

---

* A Buddhist concept. — Tr.

two years to preside over the union work there. In addition, Comrades Li Li-san, Chiang Hsien-yün, Mao Tse-min, and Huang Ching-yüan went to Anyüan. Comrades Chiang Hsien-yün,* Mao Tse-t'an, and others went to Shui-k'ou-shan, while Comrade Kuo Liang and others went to the Canton-Hankow Railway, and Comrades Hsia Ming-han, Lo Hsüeh-tsan, and others went to the rickshaw workers and various other businesses. On the one hand, this dynamically launched the Hunan labor movement, and, on the other, it permitted the Party's important key members to go deeply into the midst of the lower strata from the very beginning and rapidly to remold and improve themselves. In this way, the Party and the revolutionary movement were made to advance forward on the correct and solid road — the road of the combination of the universal truth of Marxism with the reality of the Chinese revolution.

From 1922 to the beginning of 1923 there were more than ten large and small strike struggles by workers from various areas in Hunan that took place under the leadership of Comrade Mao Tse-tung. The highest number of strikers, such as those at Anyüan, approached twenty thousand, and the smallest number, such as those in Changsha's writing brush and type businesses, was two or three hundred people. The longest strikes, such as the strike of the Changsha barbers, lasted over one year. The shortest lasted from five or six to ten-odd days. All these struggles won victories; there was not one failure. The principal reason for the victories, besides the fact that they occurred during the upsurge of the nationwide strike movement, was the correctness of Comrade Mao Tse-tung's leadership.

Seen against the prevailing situation in Hunan, the enemy was very tenacious. Chao Heng-t'i was an extremely crafty and treacherous warlord with great experience in exercising domination who had entered into collusion with the Political Study Clique [Cheng-hsüeh hsi]. [10] With one hand he held up the "provincial constitution," and with the other hand he killed people. He received representatives of the workers and also arrested representatives of the workers. He orally acceded to the demands of the workers but in deed demolished these demands. Many of Chao Heng-t'i's subordinates were crafty and treacherous men like this. In addition, Anyüan and the Canton-Hankow Railway were squeezed in on all sides by the power of the neighboring provincial feudal warlords.

---

* Same characters as the Chiang Hsien-yün above — possibly a typographical error. — Tr.

Although the managers of the bureaucrat-capitalist enterprises were simple, stupid, and corrupt, they were as one in their cruel treatment of the workers. Big and small businesses in Changsha, then, were completely under feudal rule. There was not one proprietor who was not in close league with the government bureaus and who did not treat the workers with extreme, barbaric cruelty. Affairs in Hunan society were also extremely complicated and confused. The reason was, on the one hand, that Hunan had been a place where conservative power had had a strong base ever since the days of Tseng, Tso, P'eng, and Hu. [11] On the other hand, this province was right in the middle of the change brought on by the violent clash between the new and old ways of thinking. The change in people was also very mysterious. There were some people who were "Ch'in in the morning and Ch'u in the evening,"* people who had their feet in several boats at the same time. Without the ability to seize correctly the weapon of struggle that is Marxism-Leninism, and without flexible strategy and tactics, it would have been difficult to deal with this type of situation.

In the period following the May Fourth movement, the revolutionary attitudes of the Hunan workers, peasants, and student masses were the same as those of [people in] other progressive areas of the country; they were in a great upsurge. Ever since the time of the Taiping Heavenly Kingdom, Hunan had had a tradition of revolution.† Thus, mass conditions were very good.

When the enemy is strong and the masses good, the success or failure of the struggle will be decided by the leadership. During the entire strike movement, in what areas was the correct leadership of Comrade Mao Tse-tung outstandingly demonstrated? Based on the facts of the various strike struggles that we will recount below, there are in general the following several areas:

1. Going deep into the midst of the working masses, carrying out a program of maximum work, and struggling for the current, urgent interests of the masses. Ordinarily, the Party organization carried on constant political education among the workers through the night schools and also regularly carried out investigations and inquiries among the workers, thus raising mass consciousness and becoming intimately acquainted with the thoughts and sentiments of the workers.

---

* The names of two rival states during the Warring States period (eighth to third century B.C.). — Tr.

† For Ch'en Tu-hsiu's "Salute to the Spirit of the Hunanese," see Carrère d'Encausse and Schram, Marxism and Asia (London: Allen Lane, The Penguin Press, 1969), pp. 211-212 [S.R.S.].

When the time was ripe, [the Party] presented the most pressing demands of the working masses and launched the struggle, bringing home to the masses their own strength and their way out, and making them realize that only under the leadership of the Communist Party and only by their own effort in struggle could they win the rights they deserved. Thus, every struggle had clear and appropriate economic demands and political goals, and it was possible to mobilize the vast majority and even all of the masses to participate with one mind. During the struggle, the education of the masses went on uninterrupted, exposing the enemy and expanding power — the more they fought the stronger they became. Thus, with the victory of each strike struggle, not only were they able to achieve economic benefits, but also there was an immense political harvest, causing a great heightening of the working masses' class consciousness, of their confidence in struggle, and of their will to unite.

2. With every struggle there was comprehensive organizational work and full preparation. Before launching the struggle, extensive contact was always made with the masses. Ten-man teams were organized, and many places even set up labor unions first. Accurate estimates based on the facts had to be made beforehand of the relative posture of the enemy and ourselves, the changes that could occur, and the concrete peculiarities of the moment. As for the rest, strike conditions, slogans, and strike funds, they were all fully explained to the masses and everyone was mobilized to engage in preparation for the future. In sum, there was foresight and comprehensive arrangements; without a guarantee of certain victory, one does not go into battle lightly. During the struggle, then, special attention was given to training labor leaders. Because there was preparation beforehand, whenever a strike occurred in one area, the entire working class would rise up and give assistance. Production industry and handicraft industry, one business and another business, place A and place B, within the province and outside the province — they would all respond to each other's call, they would all come to each other's assistance, increasing their own will and destroying the enemy's might.

3. Correctly grasping the strategic weapon of Marxism. In every struggle [Mao] always made full use of Chao Heng-t'i's ornamental "provincial constitution," "attacking him with his own sword." He used the might of the people to force the ruling class to acknowledge its own "promises." On the other side, he brought home to the masses the ruling class's real face of deceit by exposing the contradictions between their "promises" and their actions. Putting to

use the various social forces was also very successful. For example, that so-called public organization the "Hunan Industrial General Assembly" [Hu-nan kung-yeh tsung-hui] was a hollow, bureaucratic, feudal organization (the director called himself a lawyer — but that was in name only). Comrade Mao Tse-tung directed Party members with upper class connections to mobilize progressive people to join this organization. Ordinarily, they would be brought into play to provide money for setting up night schools, and teachers would then be sent from the Party. During a strike, the bureaucratic elements and more enlightened people would be used in mediation work. Thus when the mending, textile, and writing brush industries waged a strike and finally asked the "Hunan Industrial General Assembly" to come and mediate for them, it generally proved to be to the workers' advantage. Besides this, there was a "Chinese Union" [Chung-Hua kung-hui]. This was a bureaucratic organization put together by some politicians who were allegedly promoting industry. During the strike movement this organization was also used to perform support work. Owing to Mao Tse-tung's success in winning them over, there were often ideologically progressive legislators or legislators with a relatively enlightened attitude who would make speeches from the podium of Chao Heng-t'i's Provincial Assembly supporting the workers' just actions.

Besides this, extreme importance was attached to social mobilization for strengthening prestige and power. If we examine the Changsha press of the day, we see that news and proclamations relating to each strike were being published almost continually and that the unions also often held press conferences. Before and after the strike, Comrade Mao Tse-tung would always mobilize Party cadres or would himself, under the guise of a reader, set to work and write to the newspapers in support of the workers' strike struggle. Therefore, every time there was a strike, a public opinion that was advantageous to the workers was always created.

In sum, everything was for the broad and deep mobilization of the masses, and the broad mobilization of the masses was made to serve the cornerstone.

Under the leadership of Comrade Mao Tse-tung, the early Hunan labor movement scored great accomplishments. Every strike struggle won a victory, which had a great influence on the whole country. During the high tide of nationwide strikes that took place from 1922 to the beginning of 1923, it was particularly the strikes at Anyüan, on the Canton-Hankow Railway, and at Shui-k'ou-shan that caused the high tide to surge forward with greater ferocity. In contrast with all other areas in the country at the time, [12] the outstanding characteristics of the Hunan labor movement led by Comrade Mao Tse-tung were: the organization of the labor unions was, in general, relatively healthy; there was constant work, and since ordinarily attention was paid to political education and to tackling the problem of the workers' well-being, the lower-level masses were, in general, all relatively organized. During the strike struggles, outstanding labor leaders and a large group of excellent labor cadres were trained who had a very high level of class consciousness and who were able to be completely selfless and even able to offer up their lives for the revolution. At the same time, great attention was given to the development of Party members from among the workers. Although the number of Party members who were workers was small at the time, the more important productive and handicraft industries before and after the strikes all developed Party members or established Party organizations.

## II. WINNING OVER THE ANARCHISTS HUANG AI AND P'ANG JEN-CH'ÜAN

When Comrade Mao Tse-tung began to lead the Hunan labor movement, he came upon a very difficult problem at the very outset; he had to wipe out the influence of anarchism among the workers.

In November 1920 there were two graduates of Hunan First Industrial School who organized a "Hunan Labor Union" [Hu-nan lao-kung hui] in Changsha. One of these graduates was named Huang Ai and was from Ch'ang-te in Hunan. In 1919 when he was studying in Tientsin, he actively participated in the May Fourth movement, was put in prison twice, and at the beginning of 1920 returned to Hunan. The other was named P'ang Jen-ch'üan, and he was from Hsiang-t'an, also in Hunan. He had participated in the movement to Expel Chang Ching-yao. After both of these people graduated from First Industrial School, they worked in Hunan factories and were quite well acquainted with the suffering of the workers. During the May Fourth movement they were influenced by anarchist ideology and, wishing to improve the workers' cultural and material life, joined up with some classmates, factory technicians, and workers to form the "Hunan Labor Union." The two sections of the labor union's abridged bylaws relating to "aims" and "membership" set forth the following stipulations: "Aim: reconstruct 'material life,' improve the knowledge of the workers." "Membership: all those who work with machinery or in the handicraft industry or those who have industrial training may, whether they be male or female, become members of this union after being introduced by two members."

Thus in the beginning most members of the labor union were students from industrial schools. The students from Changsha's First Industrial School, Ch'u-i Industrial School, and First Vocational School made up the basic ranks when mass assemblies were held. Later, the labor union gradually developed some union members from among the workers of Changsha's No. 1 Cotton Mill, the graphite refining plant, the masons and carpenters, and the tailor and barber businesses. Three union members made up a cell; in the very beginning, they did not set up a union for each industry; nor did they hold any cell meetings. In December 1921 when No. 1 Cotton Mill was staging a strike, the membership of the union sharply increased to four or five thousand people.

Anarchism is the pipedream of the petty bourgeoisie. It advocates extreme freedom, and wants no government, no law, no leaders. It wants to abolish all institutions involving an element of constraint; it wants to level wealth and equalize everything. Just as Lenin said, anarchists "want to abolish the state completely overnight, not understanding the conditions under which the state can be abolished." [13] But this ideology of absolute freedom and equality and no government was very much in harmony with the demands of the rank and file workers who had been eroded by petty bourgeois ideology, and particularly with the demands of handicraft workers who possessed this petty bourgeois ideology. Amidst the prevailing environment of cruel domination by the warlords, a continuing drop in real wages, and excessive exploitation by the feudal gang bosses, the masses' spontaneous feeling of resistance naturally made them easy prey for anarchist propaganda.

The only important piece of work carried out by the labor union after its founding was the launching at No. 1 Cotton Mill (the precursor of today's Yü-hsiang Cotton Mill in Changsha) of the movement for public ownership. Actually, this movement represented the interests of the local Hunan industrialists and businessmen. In 1912 No. 1 Cotton Mill was a joint venture of government and private interests.* Owing to the continuous warlord battles, however, it was never able to begin operations. Later, Chang Ching-yao leased the government stock rights to the China Realty Company,

* "Kuan-shang ho-pan" (government-merchant joint management). — Tr.

which was owned by private capital. After Chao Heng-t'i took power, he received a gift of stock from this company and continued to recognize China Realty's rights. Later, China Realty was unable to continue operation and in turn leased its stocks to capitalists from outside the province. In this way, stock rights for Hunan people were ruled out. At the same time, the company also called in people from outside the province to work as technicians and workers in the mill. Thus this company elicited the staunch opposition of some influential people in Hunan business and education circles. When the labor union raised this movement for a publicly owned mill and led the mill workers in an economic struggle against the boss of the China Realty Company, the approach naturally gained the support of people in all circles, especially those in business circles. The labor union had been a mixed bag in the first place and now, with all this happening, the complexity of its composition became even greater. A great many people who were "hanging up a sheep's head and selling dog meat" [i.e., misrepresenting themselves] now came running in.

But Huang Ai and P'ang Jen-ch'üan themselves were pure, upright, and courageous youths who had a definite anti-imperialist, antifeudal, revolutionary outlook. The China Realty Company had once tried to bribe them with a huge sum of money, but the bribe met with a stern rejection. In founding the labor union they underwent a very difficult and very heroic struggle against the China Realty Company. In April 1921 they mobilized more than two thousand workers to demonstrate at No. 1 Cotton Mill, brought the boss of the China Realty Company across the river to march, and forced him to sign an "oath" guaranteeing that he would no longer lease out No. 1 Cotton Mill. Because of this, Huang Ai was arrested by Chao Heng-t'i; he spent more than a month in jail and while there went on a hunger strike. Only later, after Chao Heng-t'i had sent in armed assistance, was the China Realty Company able to begin operations. Huang and P'ang also founded a Workers' Study Society [Kung-jen tu-shu hui] and had certain links with the working masses. They were resolute in their belief that the workers had to struggle with the capitalists. As Huang Ai once said in the Labor Weekly [Lao-kung chou-k'an], published by the union: "In the past, the enemy called for a conditional compromise with this union, but this union did not accept. This is because we know very well that there is no room for compromise between the working class and the capitalist class."

Because the labor union had a definite mass base, and because

Huang Ai and P'ang Jen-ch'üan had considerable prestige among the
workers, it was no simple matter for Comrade Mao Tse-tung to
win over the people in the union. At the time, there were some
union members who regularly cursed Marxists as "long tails," that
is, Marxists were people who advocated government. They said that
since they [the Marxists] wanted government, there was little difference between them and the warlords. Mao Tse-tung was very well
acquainted with the internal conditions of the labor union, and he
made a distinction between the authentic working masses and their
upper strata elements. Among the upper strata elements he also
made a distinction between the pure, revolutionary youths like
Huang Ai and P'ang Jen-ch'üan, and the schemers who "hung up a
sheep's head and sold dog meat." At the same time, he made a concrete analysis of the rank and file working members, distinguishing
between the genuinely progressive and the backward. Mao Tse-tung
carried out a patient program of education and persuasion among
the workers who had joined the labor union and got the progressive
elements among them to discard anarchism and believe in Marxism.
For example, he won over Jen Shu-te, a carpenter and a member
of the labor union. Jen Shu-te was a carpenter with a calm and sure
disposition and a genial attitude, and he was a person praised by all
his fellow workers. In 1921 he would often come to the Wang Fu-
chih Study Society to do part-time jobs. Comrade Mao Tse-tung
made friends with him and regularly instilled in him revolutionary
thought. He was the first Changsha worker to join the Communist
Party. Later, he often brought activist workers from among the
masons and carpenters in the labor union with him to the Wang Fu-
chih Study Society to draw near Comrades Mao Tse-tung, Ho Shu-
heng, and others and to receive Marxist education. These masons
and carpenters all felt that Mao and Ho were extremely amiable,
that what they said made a lot of sense, that they were also very
concerned about the workers' family life, and that every word they
said showed great solicitude for the workers. When they later
found out that Comrades Mao Tse-tung and Ho Shu-heng were Marxists, their prejudice against Marxism gradually dissipated. After
the 1922 strike victories of the masons and carpenters and the various [other] businesses, the progressives who had joined the labor
union now all joined the Party one after another.

Comrade Mao Tse-tung had known P'ang Jen-ch'üan earlier. They
were both from Hsiang-t'an, and their homes were only thirty or
forty li from each other. During the movement to Expel Chang
Ching-yao, P'ang had placed a great deal of trust in Mao. Mao

encouraged Huang and P'ang to resist capitalists, to resist Chao Heng-t'i, and he encouraged them to launch a labor movement. But he criticized them for waging only economic struggle, for having a labor movement policy that both lacked comprehensive organization and great, far-reaching political goals. He criticized their muddle-headed anarchist thinking that led them to consider the use of explosives and rifles to wipe out government. He criticized them for talking only about labor unions and not studying Marxism. Recalling his relationship with Huang and P'ang, Comrade Mao Tse-tung has said that in the case of the anarchists and their opposition to Marxists, "...we supported them[....] in many other struggles...[But we compromised with them, and] through negotiation prevented many hasty and useless actions by them" [Snow, Red Star, p. 158].

On the first anniversary of the founding of the labor union, Comrade Mao Tse-tung wrote an article entitled "So hsi-wang yü lao-kung hui" [What We Hope from the Labor Union] and had it printed in the Labor Weekly. Focusing on its weak points, Mao Tse-tung advanced three hopes for the labor union: One was that the goal of the labor organization should not only be rallying the laborers and using strikes to win victories for higher wages and shorter working hours, but that it should be "nurturing class consciousness and using the great unity of the whole class to plan for the fundamental interests of the whole class." Second was that the union organization have a democratically created business office with plenipotentiary powers. For the labor union to have too many officials, too many branches, and an authority too divided would be extremely unsound. The third was that in order to strengthen the workers' concept of union organization, the workers should support their own union, should prepare a strike fund, and must hand over a minimum amount of union dues. Comrade Mao Tse-tung used the fundamental slogans of Marxism, "From each according to his ability, to each according to his deserts," "The whole world belongs to the workers," and "Workers of the world, unite," to spur on the entire union membership.

In accordance with the proposals of Comrade Mao Tse-tung, the labor union reorganized and concentrated its efforts on the creation of the three departments of Secretariat, Propaganda, and Organization. It also asked Mao Tse-tung to help in the management of union affairs. Huang Ai and P'ang Jen-ch'üan were in full accord with Comrade Mao Tse-tung's proposal for a "great union of small organizations."* And so, in its last stage, the labor union set up over ten unions in such areas as civil engineering, machine-work, and printing. And the union membership paid union dues.

In the fall of 1921 Comrade Mao Tse-tung invited both Huang Ai and P'ang Jen-ch'üan to Anyüan for a week to get a firsthand acquaintance with the real conditions of the workers. Mao Tse-tung also specifically directed individual comrades to maintain regular contact with Huang and P'ang. It was probably at the end of 1921 that these two people finally joined the Socialist Youth Corps. [14] Issue No. 15 of Vanguard [Hsien-ch'ü], published by the Central Committee of the Socialist Youth Corps after Huang and P'ang had been martyred, publicly proclaimed that Huang and P'ang "were fine members of our Socialist Youth Corps and were pathbreakers for students throughout the country." With regard to their connections with the Party at the time, Comrade Teng Chung-hsia has recorded the following in his Chung-kuo chih-kung yün-tung chien shih [A Short History of the Chinese Trade Union Movement]: "In 1921, after the founding of the Hunan branch of the Communist Party, cooperation was begun with Huang and P'ang. Actually, Huang and P'ang leaned toward the Communist Party at that time, and two months before they were killed they had in fact been introduced to and had joined the Socialist Youth Corps." [15]

In January 1922 there was a general strike at No. 1 Cotton Mill over a demand for a year-end bonus. The China Realty Company bribed Chao Heng-t'i with 50,000 yuan to harm Huang and P'ang. On January 16, 1922, in the dead of night, after Huang Ai and P'ang Jen-ch'üan had discussed at the union meeting the question of arbitrating the strike with the China Realty Company, Chao Heng-t'i sent in troops who arrested the two men and took them away. Without any inquest, they were secretly taken outside Liu-yang Gate on the morning of the seventeenth and there were beheaded (Chao Heng-t'i feared stirring up the working masses and had to act promptly). On this day there was a great snowfall, and the fresh blood dyed the snow-covered ground red! Immediately thereafter, Chao Heng-t'i closed down both the labor union and its publication, Labor Weekly.

After the news of the murder of Huang and P'ang got out, Comrade Mao Tse-tung was extremely angered and exasperated and

* Note the parallel here with the "Great Union of the Popular Masses," built up out of many small unions, which Mao advocated in 1919. (See above, pp. 111-115, and the introduction, pp. xxvii-xxxi.) [S.R.S.].

immediately called a meeting, drawing up the order of battle against Chao Heng-t'i and calming down the feelings of the workers. On this day a great number of workers stopped work and cried bitterly at the doors of the labor union. In the afternoon the working masses filled village after village and district after district; overcome with extreme sorrow and anger, they spontaneously broke into the Domestic Affairs Commission and Finance Commission to express their bitter protest against the Chao Heng-t'i government. Soon thereafter, under the personal sponsorship of Comrade Mao Tse-tung, the working masses held two memorial meetings for Huang and P'ang at the Wang Fu-chih Study Society and also put out a special memorial publication. After this, January 17 of every year became a day when Changsha and many other places around the nation held a commemoration gathering for Huang and P'ang and issued a memorial publication. In January 1927 the Hunan people gave an impressive public burial to the four revolutionary martyrs Huang Ai, P'ang Jen-ch'üan, Huang Ching-yüan, [16] and Wang Hsien-tsung. [17]

At this time, Chao Heng-t'i clamped a tight news blackout on all the newspapers in Hunan and forbade the printing of any reports having to do with this affair. On the basis of his previous experience in leading the movement to Expel Chang Ching-yao, Comrade Mao Tse-tung sent people to Shanghai and other places to launch anti-Chao propaganda and, in the name of Hunan labor circles, sent a circular telegram around the country condemning the evils of Chao. He also published the details of Chao's slaughter of Huang and P'ang in the Shanghai, Canton, and Peking press. Mao Tse-tung himself went to Shanghai for a short period on account of this affair and mobilized nationally famous scholars to send telegrams and protest Chao's brutal actions. Just at that time, Chao was in the midst of waving the bogus signboard of "provincial autonomy," bluffing and deceiving the entire nation. When his "provincial constitution" had been promulgated for just sixteen days (it was promulgated on January 1, 1922) he had carried out a policy of massacre. The extensive anti-Chao propaganda movement under the leadership of Comrade Mao Tse-tung caused the little false fame that Chao Heng-t'i was intending to establish throughout the nation to be thoroughly dragged through the dust. Chao Heng-t'i was very distressed about this affair but there was nothing that he could do. From 1922 to 1923, under the leadership of Mao Tse-tung, the Hunan labor movement began to develop at a furious pace, and this was one of the reasons that Chao Heng-t'i did not dare adopt immediately a policy of slaughter once more. Later, in waging a personal verbal confrontation with Chao Heng-t'i, Comrade Mao Tse-tung still spoke in defense of Huang and P'ang and exposed Chao's murderous intrigues.

In Chung-kuo chih-kung yün-tung chien shih we read:

After Huang and P'ang were killed, the trade union movement suffered a setback. The elements of the so-called Hunan Labor Union all fled the scene, but the members of the Communist Party did not flee at all; they performed extremely arduous and painful work under the reign of this white terror. After several months they began strike struggles. [18]

Bad elements in the labor union later took advantage of the deaths of Huang and P'ang to fill their pockets with money. They were also bought by the warlords, and during the May 30 movement they became scabs to break the Shanghai strike. Another group of top people, such as Chien Ch'ü-ping [19] and P'ang Jen-chien, [20] kept up their revolutionary work under the educational influence of Comrade Mao Tse-tung and also later joined the Party. Having been the object of long and painstaking work by Mao Tse-tung and the Party, the overwhelming majority of union members in the lower strata devoted themselves to the struggle under the leadership of the Party.

The change in attitude of Huang Ai, P'ang Jen-ch'üan and by the masses of the labor union after having been educated and won over by Comrade Mao Tse-tung was the victory of Marxism over anarchism. Huang Ai and P'ang Jen-ch'üan were the earliest heroes martyred in the Chinese labor movement — they both deserve to be remembered.

## III. THE NATIONALLY FAMOUS ANYÜAN STRIKE

The strike in September 1921 of the seventeen thousand workers of the Anyüan Mines and Railway (the coal mines of Anyüan and the Chu-chou-P'ing-hsiang Railway) was the first great struggle of the Hunan labor movement under the leadership of Chairman Mao Tse-tung and was "victorious as soon as the banner unfurled." Comrade Mao Tse-tung sent Comrade Liu Shao-ch'i to take direct command of this struggle. The thoroughgoing victory of this strike, as well as its scale and accomplishments, had a profound influence on the development of the nationwide labor movement. Its influence on the Hunan labor movement and on the revolutionary movement was particularly great.

Although Anyüan was part of Kiangsi, it bordered on Hunan and was connected thereto by the Chu-chou-P'ing-hsiang Railway. For this reason it had always had very close ties with Hunan in politics and economics. In the fall of 1921, after the labor movement in Changsha had a foothold, Comrade Mao Tse-tung, with Huang Ai, P'ang Jen-ch'üan, and three others, personally came to Anyüan after having been introduced by the workers of Changsha and the Chu-chou-P'ing-hsiang Railway. Calling themselves "observers," they went down into the mines and visited the native and foreign factories and the railroad machine plant. Altogether they stayed one week. The workers of Anyüan still remember that at that time Mao Tse-tung wore an old set of clothes made of blue cotton and carried a broken umbrella on his back. His attitude was extraordinarily sincere and humble, and he made detailed inquiries into the laborers' work and families. He also talked about the advantages of studying and proposed to run a supplementary school for them. There were some workers at the time who were very much in favor of this idea. [21]

In the Labor Record [Lao-kung chi], which was edited by the Anyüan workers themselves and which described their miserable life and victorious struggle, this is how they sang of the coming of their savior: "In 1921 the mist suddenly dispersed and we saw the blue sky. A man of ability, Mao Jun-chih [Tse-tung], came from Hunan to Anyüan and proposed that a labor union be set up for us and that the world of labor unite."

The Anyüan coal mine was part of P'ing-hsiang hsien in Kiangsi, and in 1898 (the 24th year of the Kuang-hsü reign of the Ch'ing) two high officials of the Ch'ing government, Chang Chih-tung and Sheng Hsüan-huai, made a loan from Germany in the name of this kuan-tu shang-pan or "government supervised and merchant managed" enterprise (essentially bureaucratic-capitalist). They used new mining techniques and were able to extract more than 2,000 tons of coal per day, supplying fuel to the Ta-yeh iron ore mine and the Han-yang ironworks. At the same time, the Ch'ing government built the Chu-chou-P'ing-hsiang Railway for the transportation of the material. In 1907 the three enterprises were organized into the Han-Yeh-P'ing Company. Using the large loan approach, Japanese imperialism later captured complete control of the company.

During the late Ch'ing-early Republican period, the important positions, like "general manager" [tsung-pan] and "assistant manager" [pang-pan], in bureaucratic-capitalist enterprises like the so-called "government supervised and merchant managed" industries were largely filled by ignorant and uneducated officials and gentry. A large group of parasites was nurtured in these enterprises. The bureaucratic shareholders' investments in the enterprises were mostly in the nature of high interest loans. These enterprises very often relied on loans from foreign powers to maintain themselves, and in the end they gradually became industries controlled by imperialism. As for powers over construction matters, they were also largely in the hands of foreign personnel. The management of the entire enterprise was thus [characterized by] the feudal gang boss system.

The workers of the Anyüan Mines and Railway were no exception. At the very beginning they came under the oppression of imperialism, bureaucrat-comprador capitalists, and feudal forces.

At the time, the Anyüan coal mines had over twelve thousand workers, the Chu-chou-P'ing-hsiang Railway, forty-five hundred.

The equipment of the coal mine was very much below par in every respect. It was especially under the feudal contract labor system that the workers' life was pitiful. According to the recollections of some old Anyüan workers, no consideration whatsoever was given to any safety equipment in the mine shafts. Serious troubles with flooding, cave-ins, water breakthroughs, and fire often occurred. "In the morning one would go down into the shafts, and no one knew whether one would come up in the evening or not." It was very common for workers to be crushed, burned, or drowned. When a person died, [a compensation of] only 16 yuan for "interment expenses" was made.

Nominally, each foreman managed fifty workers, but in reality there were only thirty men doing the work. With thirty men doing the work of fifty, the food costs and wages of the other twenty went as "squeeze" to the foreman. A foreman could make about 150 yuan a month. At the same time, he would "show gratitude" to the overseer with about 100 yuan. The general overseer at that time, Wang Hung-ch'ing, could make 2,000 yuan every month. The foremen, overseers, and the bosses of the local secret societies also jointly set up gambling halls, opium dens, houses of prostitution, etc., in the neighborhood of the mines to squeeze the last drop of profit out of the workers.

In order to ensure a rich profit, the mining authorities and the foremen intensified their exploitation of the workers by adopting such methods as extending working hours, increasing the workload, and lowering wages as much as possible. The workers would work from twelve to fourteen or fifteen hours a day, and their wages were so low that they couldn't maintain themselves with it. Added to this was the fact that wages were regularly in arrears. The workers' food was extremely bad, and the places where they ate and slept stank to high heaven. Fifty or sixty people lived in one small room, and the beds and bedding were set up in three levels, one on top of the other. On the coldest days of the year many workers still wore tattered, single-layer clothing; much less, when a worker became ill, was there any thought to taking medicine and getting better. There was a popular saying among the workers:

> I came to Anyüan to earn some pay.
> It's two or three years now that I've had to stay.
> My old mother's at home, and I'd like to go see her,
> But I haven't got the money to pay my way!

Besides cruelly exploiting the workers, the foremen had the right to curse, beat, fine, and even fire or confine a worker whenever they felt like it. If there was the least thing that didn't please them, they would beat the workers with a cudgel or kick them. Among the overseers there were also some Germans who all went around with hardwood sticks in their hands.

The life of the workers at the Anyüan mines is a portrayal of the grievous life of the worker in semicolonial, semifeudal China.

The workers of the Chu-chou-P'ing-hsiang Railway also suffered triple oppression from imperialism, bureaucratic-capital, and feudal forces.

After Comrade Mao Tse-tung came to Anyüan and made his investigation, he felt this was virgin territory that bore unlimited potential for a labor movement. Mao Tse-tung attached tremendous importance to this place called Anyüan.

After Comrade Mao Tse-tung returned to Changsha, he immediately sent Comrade Li Li-san (whose name at the time was Li Lung-chih), who had just returned from France, to Anyüan to open up the work. Later, he sent Liu Shao-ch'i, Chiang Hsien-yün, Huang Ching-yüan, Mao Tse-min [22] and a great many other comrades to Anyüan to work. From the fall of 1922 to the spring of 1925 Comrade Liu Shao-ch'i led the work at Anyüan.

When Comrade Mao Tse-tung sent Comrade Li Li-san to Anyüan, he gave the following directive of principle: We are now working on a labor movement and must win legitimacy and stand with our feet firmly on the ground. Mao Tse-tung specifically mentioned that they should utilize the Popular Education movement of the time to carry on their activities, that they should make connections with the local gentry, and also that they should acquire legal status through the local government. And so Li Li-san came to Anyüan in the name of promoting the Popular Education movement. The result of the activities pursued in accordance with Mao Tse-tung's directive was that the hsien magistrate of P'ing-hsiang made a formal announcement of his approval of the Popular Education movement. First, Li Li-san set up a school for workers' children. Therefrom he quickly established friendly ties with the childrens' parents. After two months a workers' night school was formally founded, and Li himself became a teacher there. At that time the Hunan Party organization supplied the comrades who were working on the labor movement with 20 yuan per month; this covered the food allowances for each teacher and the operating expenses for the workers' night school. The workers themselves also gave a little money for ink and paper. The curriculum was composed of only mathematics and Chinese, and the texts were mimeographed. When the teachers conducted class they related their teaching to the lives of the Anyüan workers and carried on Marxist propaganda.

Through this kind of workers' night school, close ideological ties were forged between the teachers and the broad masses of workers. The workers gradually came to understand that they could not tolerate the oppression and exploitation of the capitalists and foremen and that everyone should join together, organize, and struggle against the capitalists, overseers, and foremen, for this was the only possible way to improve treatment, raise wages, and increase rights. After the work of the night school had been developed a step further, Comrade Mao Tse-tung dispatched a steady flow of cadres from Changsha to Anyüan. Under the training of Mao Tse-tung, the night school teachers — the cadres from the Hunan Party organization — had a simple work style and were like brothers to the workers. They attained high prestige among the working masses.

The teachers very carefully and on an individual basis developed a group of Corps members from among the workers and, after that, took the best among these Corps members into the Party. The earliest to enter the Party were Comrades Chu Shao-lien and Chu Chint'ang. The activists among the workers were organized through the ten-man team approach. Gradually, every work area of the railroad and mines, such as the coal processing tower, the coking area, and the various mine shafts, established ten-man teams, and each area produced a person who assumed general responsibility.

In October 1921 the workers of the Wuchang section of the Canton-Hankow Railway went out on strike, demanding a raise in wages and improvement in treatment. The strike lasted five days and victory was won. This was a great inspiration for the workers of the An-yüan Railway and Mines.

The year of the first high tide in the nationwide labor movement was 1922. In the first half of the year the Hong Kong sailors, the Shanghai cotton mill workers, and the Canton salt workers successively all went out on strike. The barbers and other handicraft workers in Changsha waged many strikes. This all had a great influence on the Anyüan workers.

The political consciousness of the workers gradually increased, and they began to feel the need for the formation of an overall organization. In March 1922 they began planning, and on May 1, when the nation's first labor congress convened in Canton, the "Anyüan Railway and Mines Workers' Club" [An-yüan lu-k'uang kung-jen chü-lo-pu] was founded. (At the time, all labor organizations throughout the country customarily used the term "workers' club" because in some places the foremen had organized a "union" [kung-hui], and the workers thus used this term to make the distinction.) Comrade Li Li-san was the president [chu-jen] and Comrade Chu Shao-lien was the vice president. The Club was set up in a building east of the Hupei Association of Fellow Provincials [Hu-pei t'ung hsiang hui] located on the hill right across from the Anyüan Bureau of Mines. At the time of its founding, only 300 workers joined the Club; afterward, membership rapidly increased, and on the eve of the strike, membership had risen to over seven thousand people.

After the Workers' Club had been founded, the working masses felt there was something to rely on. There was a future, and their confidence in the struggle surged to unprecedented heights. Through the black smoke and polluted vapors of Anyüan shot a ray of the dawn's light. At this time, Comrade Mao Tse-tung sent Comrade Chiang Hsien-yün to Anyüan to participate in the leadership work of the union.

When the mining authorities saw that the power of the Workers' Club was developing rapidly, they plotted to stamp it out and consequently spread rumors that the Workers' Club was a "subversive group" [luan tang] and should be dissolved immediately. They announced that they would expel Comrade Chu Shao-lien from the borders of the province, and they tried to intimidate and bribe Comrade Chiang Hsien-yün, but in all of this they failed to attain their goal. When the workers became aware of this situation, they were extremely angry. The Club quickly called a meeting of representatives and discussed countermeasures. There was unanimous agreement on using the approach of unyielding struggle.

For several months running, the authorities of the railway and the mines had been in arrears on the workers' wages by several dozen percentage points, and all the workers were extremely dissatisfied at this.

In July 1922 another component of the Han-Yeh-P'ing Company — the Han-yang ironworks — was struck, and the demand was for an increase in wages and improvement in treatment. The strike lasted five days and achieved victory. After the [Anyüan] workers heard about this, their discussions intensified.

By the beginning of September the situation at Anyüan was extremely tense. At this crucial point in time, Comrade Mao Tsetung himself came to Anyüan. Together with the comrades of the Anyüan Party branch, he studied the conditions that lay before them and felt that the time for a strike was nearly ripe. What was most important at that immediate time was to develop rapidly the membership of the Workers' Club and at the same time to engage in various concrete preparations for the strike.

With a view to winning victory in this struggle, Comrade Mao Tse-tung specifically sent for Comrade Liu Shao-ch'i to come to Anyüan and join in the leadership of the strike.

On the day before the strike the Anyüan Party organization received another directive from Mao in the form of a letter. In the letter he invoked the motto of the "certain victory of sullen troops,"* and pointed out that they had to use the most moving slogans to get all the workers to wage a just and relentless struggle. At the same time, they had also to win very extensive sympathy from society at large.

At this time the mining authorities went a step further in their intimidation. They said they were going to send troops and that the Club had to dissolve immediately. Liu Shao-ch'i discussed the situation with comrades from the Party branch and decided to make a counterattack. They raised three conditions and set a limit of three days for the railway and mining authorities to answer; otherwise the workers would go out on strike. The three conditions were (1) that the railway and mining authorities petition the Office of Administration for protection for the Workers' Club, (2) that they give a monthly subsidy of 200 yuan to the Workers' Club, (3) that the total amount of back wages owed the workers be paid within one week. Seeing the workers' unyielding attitude and the very tense situation,

---

* I.e., troops who are deeply moved must certainly be victorious. — Tr.

the authorities of both interests had no choice but to yield a step, and they acknowledged the first and second items of the full proposal. As for the third item, they pleaded current financial difficulties and said they were unable to meet the condition.

Just at this time a strike broke out once again on the Wuchang section of the Canton-Hankow Railway. On September 10 the troops that were stationed in Yüeh-chou shot some workers who were on strike. More than seventy people were wounded, six of them fatally. When the news got out it was like adding oil to the fire; the entire body of workers at Anyüan was stirred and aroused. The number of workers who joined the Workers' Club now rose to more than ten thousand.

On September 12 an emergency meeting of the Party branch was held. At the meeting Comrade Liu Shao-ch'i drew a clear picture of the situation between the enemy and ourselves as it then existed: the consciousness of the working masses had risen rapidly, and their determination to struggle was strong and powerful; the Workers' Club had very high prestige among the workers, and the vast majority of workers were already organized; the upsurge of the strike movement both within and outside the province could be a great stimulus; at the same time, the estimate was that the railway and mining authorities lacked preparation and, moreover, were internally divided in opinion. Thus the decision was made to announce the strike and to raise further conditions before both authorities. Comrade Liu Shao-ch'i personally took general command of the strike.

On the night of September 13 the Workers' Club sent out the strike order. The next day no one went to his shift in the pits, and several cars caught fire in the railway depot. But to protect the safety of the entire mining area and to prevent bad elements from taking advantage of the opportunity to cause a disturbance, the electric factory, the water pump machinery, and the fans were kept running; the workers in those places did not stop work.

On the morning of September 14 the entire mining area was plastered with eye-catching posters. "Before we were beasts of burden, now let's be men!" The workers all saw the Anyüan strike proclamation and the seventeen demands. A few days later the Changsha press also printed news of the Anyüan strike, as well as the full text of the strike proclamation and the conditions.

The proclamation was short and powerful and was written in the workers' own language. Below is the full text:

# The Early Labor Movement in Hunan

Elders, Brothers, Sisters of all circles! What a loss of humanity we have suffered from the constant beating and cursing we get from other people! Just think of it: How strenuous is our work, and how meager our wage! We cannot take our oppression any longer! We therefore demand: "Improve treatment," "Raise wages," and organize a group — the Club.

Our organization is now being undermined by people spreading rumors. Our wages are owed to us by the authorities and they do not give them to us. We have made repeated demands to the authorities, but up to now there has been no satisfactory response. There is simply no place we can turn to for help in this society.

We want to live, we want to eat. Now we are starving, we cannot keep ourselves alive, we lead a life of living death, and we have no alternative but to use the strike as a means of last resort by which to attain our demands. (Our demands are appended below.)

The conditions that we demand are extremely just and legitimate, and we will fight to the death to achieve our goal. If we don't work, all that will happen is that we will die; if we do work as we did before, as the beasts of burden of other people, this will be more painful than death. We vow to deal with [the authorities] to our last ounce of living strength. Everyone keep ranks and hold on to the end!

Elders, Brothers, Sisters of all circles! Please come to our aid. More than twenty thousand of us are waiting here for you with empty stomachs!

The seventeen demands were primarily for a guarantee of the workers' political rights, improvement in treatment, and an increase in wages.

After the strike was called, the authorities of the railway and mines were terrified and urgently asked Fang Pen-jen, the "West Kiangsi Garrison Commissioner" [Kan-hsi chen-shou-shih] to move in his troops from P'ing-hsiang. From the fifteenth of the month the entire mining area was under martial law; everywhere there were rifles, cannon, sabres, all making a great clamor. Afraid of the power of the workers, however, they did not dare suppress them. The Party organization then mobilized the workers to launch a propaganda campaign aimed at the troops, explaining the misery the workers had suffered and the goals of the strike. This kind of propaganda got immediate results, and a great many soldiers showed a sympathetic attitude toward the workers.

Seeing with their own eyes the great unity of the workers and their great fighting power, seeing that the reactionary troops of Fang Pen-jen could play no role in subjugating them, and fearing that if the strike went on too long their losses would be too great, the railway and mining authorities invited the local Chamber of Commerce to send someone out to mediate on the third day of the strike. And so representatives from three sides — the labor organization, the Chamber of Commerce, and the railway and mining authorities — held a negotiating session. The delegates of the strike team were Comrades Liu Shao-ch'i and Chiang Hsien-yün.

The strike was continued for five days. Finally, on the morning of September 18, the railway and mining authorities had no choice but to acknowledge fully the demands of the workers. The "mediators," representatives of both authorities, and the delegates from the strike team all signed on the spot.

After conferring and negotiating [by the various parties], the workers' seventeen demands were combined into thirteen, the principal substance of which was: The Club will become a union, and the railway and mining authorities will recognize the right of the union to represent the workers in all dealings with both authorities. Hereafter, both authorities should get the agreement of the union to fire a worker. To add mine shaft workers and foremen it will be necessary to ask the head of the shaft to appoint them according to their qualifications; it is forbidden for the overseer to select people privately for certain appointments (actually, this abolished the feudal gang boss system). As for an increase in wages, various kinds of workmen's insurance and welfare, etc., there were concrete regulations in line with the workers' demands.

The strike was victorious, utterly victorious. The inexpressible happiness of the workers was truly something that could never have been even dreamed of before.

After the victory of the strike came the formal founding and reorganizing of the union organization — the Workers' Club. Comrade Li Li-san was elected general director, Comrade Chu Chin-t'ang director of the shafts, and Comrade Chu Shao-lien director of the Railway Bureau. Comrade Liu Shao-ch'i was a special commissioner. The basic organization of the Club was the ten-man team. Based on the nature of the work and the locality, groups of ten people were combined into a team and the team had a "representative of ten." Every ten teams had a "representative of one hundred." Every work area had a general representative. (For example, the coking area, the coal processing tower, and each shaft had one general representative.) Each work area had an assembly of the representatives of ten and the representatives of one hundred. The highest representative assembly was the Plenary General Representatives Assembly [Ch'üan-t'i tsung-tai-piao hui-i], which met twice a month. The plenary representatives of one hundred and representatives of ten assemblies met every year or every half year. The highest day-to-day working organ of the Club was the Council [Wei-yüan-hui], composed of the various councilmen (from education, official documents, cooperation, etc.) and the secretary. The councilmen and the secretary were appointed by the Board of Directors [Chu-jen t'uan] (composed of the general director, the director of the Railway Bureau, and the director of the shafts) and approved by the Plenary General Representatives Assembly. Thus the workers' organization was quite compact.

The Club actually became the highest organ of authority in the Anyüan mining district. Every worker was issued a "membership card." All the rules passed by the Club dealing with the workers' self-discipline, such as prohibitions against gambling, fighting, etc., were followed by all workers, who now set up an unprecedented new life-style and new order of things.

The Club paid special attention to the problem of firing workers. Unless a worker had committed a particularly serious violation, the Club generally did not permit him to be fired. Whenever the two authorities wanted to add new workers or hire and fire foremen, they had to get the necessary papers from the Club before the decision could go through. The Club also decided on all questions of internal discord among the workers; the authorities, the foremen, and the officials were not allowed to participate. In times past, the judicial department of the mine district police station was like a marketplace, what with its numerous cases (suits of the workers against the labor brokers, the officials, etc.). After the strike, according to the workers, it had changed into "a Buddhist temple without the incense and paper money." The police had lost their authority completely. Later the Club even helped the police wage a struggle for an increase in wages.

In 1922 the two authorities donated funds, and a new building, one that was famous throughout the country, was built for the Workers' Club. This was the first building that ever really belonged to the Chinese working class itself.

After the victory of the strike, there was marked progress in the workers' political rights, in their working conditions, and in the treatment they received. The feudal contract labor system that had been used for twenty years by the overseers and the foremen for their extra-economic exploitation of the workers was abolished and changed to a cooperative system in which a cooperative contract was discussed and decided upon. There was a general increase in the workers' wages, regular wages were paid on holidays, and for normal rest periods no money was deducted from the worker's board. At the same time, working hours were shortened, so that those who did day work in the winter were able to come out of the shafts and still see the sun. Thus, the following year almost all the workers had new clothes made and added quilts, sleeping mats, and mosquito nets to their possessions. What was most important was that the workers rallied together and helped each other; they no longer gambled and no longer quarreled.

From the summer of 1923 to the spring of 1925 Comrade Liu Shao-ch'i was the general director of the Anyüan Workers' Club. "Director Liu" had very high prestige among the Anyüan workers. No matter where he went there were always workers who were secretly protecting him, fearing that some harm would come to him. Some old Anyüan workers remember to this day the content of the popular textbook put together for them by "Director Liu," a text that imbued them with class consciousness, Liang-ko kung-jen t'an-hua [Conversations between Two Workers].

After the victory of the strike, the fame of the Anyüan Workers' Club spread throughout the country. The Workers' Club did a great many things for the workers. The education division founded seven Workers' Preparatory Schools and also opened up a children's class during the day. Altogether, there were almost two thousand people in the day and night classes. Comrade Mao Tse-tung invited many progressive teachers from Changsha to come to Anyüan and help the Workers' Club develop the workers' cultural life. The various work areas set up a total of twelve reading areas that were open to the public day and night so that the adult workers could read over the material. A Women's Vocational Section was also set up, which specifically aimed at tackling the problem of studying culture and learning a vocational skill for working-family dependents. Every one of the textbooks was compiled by the education division itself. In addition, the Anyüan Trimonthly [An-yüan hsün-k'an] was also published.

There was also a Lecture Division that sent out a constant stream of people (mostly Communist Party cadres and teachers from the Preparatory School) to talk to the workers about domestic and foreign affairs and questions on political and economic struggles. The traveling Arts Division regularly put on new, meaningful plays for the workers.

Among all the things done by the Club, the masses cherished the consumers' cooperative most. In times past, the workers had been terribly exploited by the merchants. Several dozen money changers in street stalls would take advantage of changing copper and silver to fleece the workers. The rice merchants were the same. After the cooperative was founded, the money stalls and rice stores all collapsed. The capital of the cooperative was subsequently expanded to more than 13,000 yuan; almost every worker became a share-holder. The manager of the cooperative was Comrade Mao Tse-min.

In the winter following the victory of the strike, Comrade Mao Tse-tung again went to Anyüan to inspect the work; he personally sought out workers to talk with and acquainted himself with the change in their thinking that followed the strike, and he also partic-ipated in a meeting of the representatives of one hundred. At the meeting he reported on the status of the national labor movement and on how, in the future, they should strengthen their solidarity. Mao Tse-tung directed the Anyüan Party organization to take ad-vantage of the strike victory and develop a group of Party mem-bers — to admit into the Party the most outstanding elements among the workers who had taken part in the strike.

By 1923 the Anyüan Party organization had already established thirteen branches, even more branches of the Corps, and had founded local committees for both the Party and the Corps.

After the "February 7" tragedy in 1923, Comrade Mao Tse-tung summoned Anyüan comrades to Changsha for a meeting and made a concrete analysis of the situation "between the enemy and our-selves." He made clear that they should take a sure and stable course of action. They should not rush recklessly into a strike but should exhibit a "crouched horse and bent bow" posture, make am-ple preparation for the strike, and finally decide whether or not to use the strike measure in light of the concrete situation. Mao Tse-tung said this was the most advantageous approach, the only way that they could be invincible. In accordance with the directives of Mao Tse-tung, the Anyüan workers on the one hand sought out the mining authorities to negotiate and with stern words clearly pointed out the plotting on the part of the authorities in asking for troops to come and break up the Workers' Club, also making clear that this kind of thing was certain to provoke another strike and that the en-tire mining district would suffer ruin. On the other hand they pushed through a program of feverish mobilization among the workers, calling upon everyone to make full preparation. Hence the mining authorities were put on the defensive and in the end did not dare make a move. Thus, after the "February 7" tragedy when the na-tional labor movement moved into low tide, in the big industrial areas it was only the Anyüan labor union that endured. "It was like a workers' 'Utopia.'" [23] The workers of Anyüan staged a huge dem-onstration on May Day of this year.

The two authorities and the feudal foremen naturally harbored resentment toward the workers' victory and all along they schemed to turn the tables on them. But their subversive plots were unsuccessful owing to the workers' firm solidarity and their great capacity for struggle.

In September 1925 the general manager of the Anyüan coal mines, Sheng En-i (the son of Sheng Hsüan-huai), finally entered into collusion with the "West Kiangsi Garrison Commissioner," Li Hung-ch'eng, and had a regiment of troops sent in who dispersed the Workers' Club with arms, shot and killed the director of the Workers' Club, Comrade Huang Ching-yüan, beat to death or seriously injured more than ten workers, fired over five thousand workers and, finally, shut the coal mines down. A great many Party members and labor activists went to Canton. The Peasant Movement Training Institute [Nung-min yün-tung chiang-hsi-so], run by Comrade Mao Tse-tung, itself accounted for over thirty of them. Others joined the Whampoa Military Academy and the Political Training Department [of the Academy]. When the troops of the Northern Expeditionary Army arrived, the Anyüan workers actively participated in the battle. They organized a transport team of over two thousand men and joined the Northern Expeditionary Army by the thousands. After the "Horse Day Incident" of 1927, Hsü K'o-hsiang created the "June 5 Incident" in Anyüan and P'ing-hsiang, massacring over a thousand Communist Party members, workers, and peasants. The Anyüan workers, under the leadership of Chu Shao-lien and other comrades, then waged a direct armed struggle against the reactionaries.

After such repeated revolutionary struggles, the Anyüan workers still refused to collapse. In September 1927, when Comrade Mao Tse-tung was leading the Autumn Harvest Uprising in eastern Hunan, he visited the Anyüan workers and the peasant self-defense troops of the P'ing-chiang, Liu-yang and Li-ling region. The backbone of the Second Regiment of the First Army of the Workers and Peasants Revolutionary Army that was later organized was composed of the workers from Anyüan.

In 1928 the Anyüan coal mines came to a standstill, but a powerful secret Party organization was still preserved among the workers, and the Hunan provincial Party committee was once set up there. After Comrade Mao Tse-tung went up the Chingkangshan, his connections with the outside, his dealings with the cadres of the Party Center and the provincial Party committee, the transmission of documents, etc., all went through the Anyüan Party organization.

At the beginning of 1929 the Kuomintang reactionaries sent a heavy concentration of troops to Anyüan to carry out a campaign of cruel suppression. Comrade Chu Shao-lien and more than a hundred others were all martyred. In September 1930, when the Red Army attacked and entered Anyüan, Comrade Mao Tse-tung made a special appearance and called a mass meeting. According to the recollections of some old workers: "Comrade Mao Tse-tung said to the working masses: 'If you don't want to suffer oppression, if you want to live happy days, then there is nothing else to do but resolutely struggle against the reactionaries and follow the Communist Party!'" [24] That time more than one thousand workers joined the Red Army.

## IV. THE VICTORY OF THE CHANGSHA MASONS AND CARPENTERS IN WINNING THEIR FREEDOM TO DO BUSINESS

In October 1922, under the personal leadership of Comrade Mao Tse-tung, the more than four thousand masons and carpenters of Changsha persevered in a strike struggle of more than twenty days and won a victory that brought an increase in wages and freedom to do business. This was the first strike victory ever won by the Changsha workers. This great victory was one more step in laying the foundation for the rapid development of the Hunan labor movement, and at the same time it established the unsurpassed prestige of the Communist Party and Comrade Mao Tse-tung among the broad working masses.

This was a stirring and seething struggle, and it was extremely successful. During the course of the struggle, Comrade Mao Tse-tung's genius for leadership was manifested everywhere, as was the bravery and the tenacity of the Hunan working class as it first went into battle. There are four points about this struggle that are particularly worth mentioning: (1) The workers were internally very tightly organized. It was possible to maintain to the end a strike lasting more than twenty days, with more than four thousand masons and carpenters demonstrating and petitioning, sleeping out in the open, and even having clashes with the military police. For the decentralized workers of the handicraft industry, this was an extremely difficult thing. (2) They won the support of people from other circles. Besides the assistance of the working class both within and outside the province, they won the support of upper-level public organizations and the sympathy of various social circles.

213

(3) They made ingenious use of legal struggle. They used the petition assembly approach in their struggle, took full advantage of the "provincial constitution" promulgated by Chao Heng-t'i, etc. (4) They spread propaganda, created public opinion, and strengthened the power of the working class.

In 1919, when Chang Ching-yao was ruling Hunan, the masons and carpenters had launched a strike struggle over the question of wages. Subsequently, the Chang Ching-yao government stipulated that the daily pay of masons and carpenters would be 42 copper dollars (420 cash [wen]) and gave notice that "there will never be an increase." At the time, a silver dollar was worth only 1,400-odd cash, 420 cash being about equal to 30 silver cents. In 1922 every silver dollar could be changed for 2,100-odd cash; 420 cash was now worth only 20 silver cents. In addition, the workers' wages were paid in "bird money" (the copper certificates of the Hunan government mint had a bird printed on them), and in the black market one silver dollar could be changed for more than 300 cash. Therefore the real wages of the workers were only equal to 200-odd copper cash per day. Yet commodity prices were calculated on the basis of the silver dollar. Thus, the difficulty of the life of the workers was compounded. In June and July of this year the masons and carpenters made a universal demand for a raise in the value of their work to a daily level of 34 cents for A work (by regular workers), and 26 cents for B work (by workers who had not yet "graduated from apprenticeship"). In reality, all they were doing was converting their original salary into silver at the old market value. Nevertheless, the various street organizations, the merchants, and the gentry rose up in a wave of opposition. The hsien magistrate of Changsha, Chou Ying-kan, called a meeting of the All-City Gentry and Merchant Assembly [Ch'üan-shih shen shang ta-hui] and put up proclamations prohibiting the workmen from raising their prices, suppressing the workers' just demands as "spontaneous action contemptuous of the official decision in the case." When the masons and carpenters saw the proclamations they blew their tops, and in one evening they tore down and destroyed all the proclamations throughout the city.

In order to expose the unreasonable stand of the Changsha hsien magistrate, Comrade Mao Tse-tung first mobilized press opinion. For example, Changsha's Ta-kung pao printed an article entitled "Wo yao t'i ni mu kung-jen shuo chi chü kung-tao-hua" [I Would Like to Say a Few Just Words on Behalf of the Masons and Carpenters], which put Chou Ying-kan on the spot:

It has been several years now since Chang Ching-yao has run off, and the "provincial constitution" has been fully promulgated. Now you take the words of Chang Ching-yao and make them law — how ridiculous! In the future, when one silver dollar, as in 1916 and 1917, is exchanged for 10,000 [ cash?], will you force people to abide by the law of Chang Ching-yao and receive only 42 copper coins per day ? Then the more than four thousand masons and carpenters in the city of Changsha will have no alternative but simply to starve to death! Furthermore, in increasing housing rents, whose orders were you following anyway ? If you say you were not following orders, then why do you insist on controlling the workers by using the words of a provincial governor who has already run away ? The "provincial constitution" clearly provides for the people's freedom to do business. You complain that the cost of their work is too expensive; then just don't ask them to do any work. Why do you want to restrain them and forbid them to increase the price of their work ? [25]

The demands of the masons and carpenters for increased prices were fully justified and courageous.

At that time, the nominal organization of the masons and carpenters was the feudal guild — the Lu Pan* Temple. (The old temple was on Tung-ch'ang Street and had few workers; the new temple was on Yü-nan Street and had many workers.) The persons who held power were the feudal gang bosses, more than ten men who were "one-year managers." Each and every one of these men depended on the blood and sweat of the masons and carpenters to wax rich and fat. Their ways of exploiting the workers were many. For example, every worker was to pay membership money to the guild when he passed his apprenticeship. He also had to throw a graduation banquet. Because of this, the workers would often have to work for nothing for one or two years. New apprentices had to hand over "entrance dues." In addition, the managers operated the many shops, houses, and public property of the Lu Pan Temple, often arbitrarily making their own secret, fraudulent sales. When the masons and carpenters demanded higher prices, they began, as always, by selecting two representatives from among the "one-year managers" — the head gangster, Kuo Shou-sung, and the small gang boss, Kan Tzu-hsien (Kan was an old feudal tyrant and was executed in Changsha in October 1951) — to negotiate on their behalf with the Changsha hsien magistrate. They invited the leaders of Changsha's 256 t'uan,† the gentry, and the officials of the hsien office to a big banquet and "negotiated" for many days, with the result that Changsha hsien only permitted the current wage (42 copper dollars) to be

---

* Lu Pan was the "patron saint" of carpenters. — Tr.

† Home guard units. — Tr.

converted into silver dollars. But each worker had already contributed 50 cents for "negotiation expenses," and so the workers
started to become dissatisfied with this bunch. Later, Kuo Shou-
sung and Kan Tzu-hsien wanted the workers to contribute more
money to enable them to go and "negotiate," and the workers drove
them away.

With a view to leading the masons and carpenters in waging an
organized struggle, Comrade Mao Tse-tung personally undertook
patient work. With the leader of the masons and carpenters, Jen
Shu-te, and with the activists Ch'ou Shou-sung, Chu Yu-fu, Chang
Han-fan, Yang Fu-t'ao, and Shu Yü-lin (all of these comrades were
martyred after the Horse Day Incident; only Yang Fu-t'ao was a
mason), he planned the organization of a genuine workers organization — the Masons' and Carpenters' Union [Ni mu kung-hui]. Among
the masons and carpenters were still some remnants of anarchist
influence. For example, some workers disagreed with waging a petition struggle against the government. By this time, Comrade Jen
Shu-te had already joined the Party. Most of the activists among
the masons and carpenters had already begun to embrace Marxism
and had confidence in the leadership of the Communist Party. Through
them Comrade Mao Tse-tung educated and organized the broad
masses of masons and carpenters. He held many meetings at the
Hsiu-yeh School, the Hsiang-hsiang Guild Hall, and at the Wang Fu-
chih Study Society. The work developed very quickly. At the very
beginning the ten-man team was taken as the basic organizational
unit. After a period of two or three months, at the beginning of September, there were 108 teams that had been excellently organized,
with a membership reaching over one thousand. And then the formal organization of the Masons' and Carpenters' Union preparatory
committee took place. Mao Tse-tung himself drafted the eighteen
articles of the Changsha Masons' and Carpenters' Union Constitution. The main contents of the Constitution were: With the aim of
"improving the workers' lives and protecting the workers' rights,"
items were drafted calling for the establishment of preparatory
schools, a consumers' cooperative, health insurance, unemployment
assistance, and other necessary items. The basic organization was
the ten-man team. Every ten members would combine into one team
and would elect one representative of ten. From the Ten-Man Representative Assembly, forty-one men were to be elected to organize
a Council. The term of tenure on the Council was one year, and five
departments were set up under the Council to take care of the daily
work; General Affairs, Correspondence, Accounting, Housekeeping,

and Public Relations. Article IX of the Constitution stipulated: "The Union engages a secretary to handle all its affairs."

On September 5 the Changsha Masons' and Carpenters' Union formally opened its inaugural meeting. The meeting was held on Ts'ang-hou Street at Hsiang-hsiang Middle School. There were more than seventy representatives of ten (that day was very close to the Ancestor Festival [Chi tsu chieh], so some of the labor delegates had returned home) and over twenty guests in attendance. Comrade Jen Shu-te made a report on the preparations and very clearly explained the reasons why the union should be founded. Comrades Liu Shao-ch'i and Li Li-san both came as guests this day. At the proposal of Liu Shao-ch'i, the assembly also discussed ways and means of assisting the textile workers, who were just then striking. The assembly finally elected forty-one councilmen, including Jen Shu-te, Chang Han-fan, Shu Yü-lin, Ch'ou Shou-sung, Yang Fu-t'ao and Chu Yu-fu. Jen Shu-te was elected the director of the department of General Affairs. The union was set up in the new Lu Pan Temple on Yü-nan Street. Mao Tse-tung sent a Party cadre to take over the job of secretary.

Now that the masons and carpenters had a new organization, the disposition of forces for the struggle became firm and unyielding. On the one hand, the Masons' and Carpenters' Union strengthened the organization of the ten-man teams and prepared to set up preparatory night schools to strengthen internal education. On the other hand, they distributed handbills (at the time called "chits") throughout the city insisting on a change of wages to 34 cents [a day], expanded their social influence, and created public opinion in order to force the Changsha hsien magistrate to accept their conditions.

At the same time, Comrade Mao Tse-tung intensified his activities among the upper strata of society. For example, he made liaison with such upper-level organizations as the Chinese General Labor Union [Chung-Hua tsung-kung-hui], the After-Work Club [Kung-yü chü-lo-pu] that was affiliated with it, and the Endeavoring for Autonomy Society [Tzu-chih li-chin hui] and won their support for the masons and carpenters, getting them to admit that the demands of the masons and carpenters were fully legitimate. (There were some people in these organizations who were dissatisfied with the Chao Heng-t'i government.)

Under these circumstances, in late September, the Changsha hsien magistrate's office had no choice but to yield somewhat and post proclamations stipulating that wages for masons and carpenters would be 26 cents, 7 li, for class A work and 21 cents, 6 li, for class B work. Calculated on the basis of the market price of silver, this was an increase of a few cents. Actually, owing to the organized and extensive activities of the Masons' and Carpenters' Union as well as to the support of the above-mentioned upper-level organizations, this time there were already quite a number of street organizations, military and administrative organs, and schools that were willing to accept the wages put forward by the masons and carpenters.

After a comprehensive analysis of the various aspects of the situation and also of their subjective strength, Comrade Mao Tse-tung felt that he could issue the strike call for the masons and carpenters. Comrade Jen Shu-te and others held a meeting at Mao's place at Ch'ing-shui-t'ang and made a detailed study of the question of a strike. They all believed the time was ripe and that all preparation work had been completed. Everyone agreed with Mao Tse-tung on announcing the strike immediately. On October 5 the main cadres of the Masons' and Carpenters' Union discussed and unanimously decided on a six-point program: (1) Announce a general strike on October 6. (2) Set up a Disciplinary Team that will have the responsibility for maintaining order. (3) Send out a nationwide circular telegram asking for fair treatment. (4) Distribute handbills throughout the city and suburbs explaining the true picture. (5) Petition the Provincial Assembly. (6) Do not stop unless completely satisfactory results are obtained. Next day the strike declaration of the masons and carpenters was seen throughout the entire city of Changsha and in the press. This declaration was very short and was written in the following vivid and powerful words:

...In one day of work we manual workers do nothing but exchange a day of our life and one day's vitality for a few cash with which to raise our families and support our relatives — this is certainly not "eating idleness and crying grievances." Just take a look at the merchants who raise their prices every few days; why is it that no one opposes this? It is only when it comes to the few cash we workers make in wages for a full day's grueling work that this type of repression and destruction is suffered. We are not satisfied with the newly established prices of Changsha hsien and right now have no way to deal with the situation. All we know is that the value of one day's hard work must be so high, that's all. Although we cannot enjoy our other rights, we should enjoy our freedom to do business and freedom to work. Moreover, we are sworn to the death on this point; we will not be robbed of our rights. The only approach we take now is this: unless we get 34 cents for A work and 26 cents for B work, all of us workers will absolutely refuse to work!

The strike shook the whole city of Changsha. All construction work on public and private houses came to a halt; even the honorific arches for the provincial governor's office, the headquarters of the First Division, and the Foreign Office that were to be built for the celebration of "Double Ten" could not be put up. On the second day of the strike the entire Disciplinary Team of the masons and carpenters staged a march, carrying banners that read: "Maintain the Strike," and "We Ask the Assistance of All Circles." The Team notified all the masons and carpenters of the city to follow the single command of the union and not to act on their own. It also advised the apprentices of the woodshops in the San-t'ai Street-Fan-ch'eng Dike area not to do any work on their own. After the strike began, a Disciplinary Team was specifically organized with a view to undermining the plans of some people for utilizing the opportunity to make trouble and with a view also to wiping out the calumnies that the government then heaped upon the workers to the effect that they were "unorganized," "acted blindly," and so forth. In a move to prevent various places from asking masons and carpenters from outside areas to come and work, the Masons' and Carpenters' Union made liaison with and got the help of various groups in Ch'u-pei (i.e., Hupei), Kiangsi, and Kiangsu.

After the strike had gone on for four days, the Masons' and Carpenters' Union received a steadily increasing volume of letters from ordinary inhabitants and from military, police, school, business, and church circles, all acknowledging the masons' and carpenters' wage of 34 cents. At this time people were concerned that the weather might turn cold and rainy, and they hoped that the masons and carpenters would soon return to work. But aside from sending workers out to put up the honorific arches for the celebration of "Double Ten," the Masons' and Carpenters' Union responded to each and every other request for work, saying that each day Changsha hsien did not take back its original order would be a day when no work was done, "and there probably will be no regrets in changing to another occupation." Thereupon all concerned sectors petitioned the Changsha hsien office to rescind the order and to acknowledge the wage increase of the masons and carpenters.

On October 12 the Masons' and Carpenters' Union received a letter from the Workers' Club of Ch'ang-hsin-tien in Peking encouraging them to keep up the strike: "Don't stop until you have attained your goal." The workers from the Canton-Hankow Railway, Anyüan railway and mines, and those from other Changsha businesses such as the textile, mending, printing, and writing brush businesses all wrote letters and made declarations in support of the struggle of the masons and carpenters. In the letter from the Hunan branch of the Trade Union Secretariat [Lao-tung tsu-ho shu-chi-pu] dated October 8 we read: "We are backing you up with all our might and sincerely hope that you will organize well, maintain good order, and hold on to the end to win final victory."

On the eleventh day of the strike the letters from various organs, schools, and public and private residences urging a return to work increased and, moreover, they all acknowledged the wage rate of 34 cents. And so the Masons' and Carpenters' Union issued a warning to the Changsha hsien office: If by the seventeenth the old order had still not been recalled, they had decided to stage a march in the streets and hold a petition assembly on the nineteenth. At this time some of the "impartial gentry and merchants" came out and engaged in urgent mediation, asking the workers not to march and petition. In their letter to the Masons' and Carpenters' Union they said: "If some calamity occurs in the future, then it will be the workers who suffer most." The workers were not moved in the slightest by this kind of "well-meaning" intimidation. There was still a small group of workers, however, who feared something would happen and who harbored an illusion about mediation, so the Masons' and Carpenters' Union allowed these gentlemen to "arbitrate" for a few days. Finally it was made clear: the so-called "arbitration" was nothing more than compromise, changing the price to 30 cents per day; it was nothing more than these gentlemen throwing themselves a few banquets. At this time Kuo Shou-sung and Kan Tzu-hsien came out and started up their activities again, and so the workers refused to listen any longer to this gang of "negotiators" and "arbitrators."

On the afternoon of October 21, the Masons' and Carpenters' Union summoned more than two thousand workers to a meeting at Educational Society Plaza to ask for opinions from everybody on how to deal with the Changsha hsien office. The masses were full of anger and many people went to the podium to speak, all expressing the feeling that they would rather fight it out to the end than starve together with their parents, wives, and children. The assembly decided to petition the Changsha hsien office on the twenty-third and vowed to attain the goal of 34 cents. On the same day they also sent a public letter to Chou Ying-kan:

The strike has been on for a long time; we are unable to get food and clothing; hunger and cold press in on us from every side, [but] the will of the masses is like a solid rampart, and we petition the Honorable Magistrate for the following agreement: within the twenty-four hour period between 10:00 P.M. today and

9:00 A.M. tomorrow we ask the Honorable Magistrate clearly to acknowledge in writing the demand of the workers for a daily wage of 34 cents, which is barely enough to cover the cost of our food and clothing. Otherwise, we workers have decided to choose one thousand representatives on the twenty-third who will go to your Honorable Office to inquire into the reasons with Your Honor personally. If there is still no settlement, then we have decided that on the twenty-fourth the entire body of over four thousand workers will come to your Honorable Office and ask for the distribution of food and clothing to ward off the hunger and cold.

In closing, the letter earnestly explained:

The trip to the office on the twenty-third by the representatives and on the twenty-fourth by the entire body of workers will be civilized actions. Both will strictly observe the fundamental obligations of workers' self-discipline and the sanctity of labor. The Disciplinary Team personnel will be responsible for everything and we will not have to trouble Your Honor to quote the "police law for public order" promulgated by Emperor Yüan.* We are untiring in our concern for the maintenance of order.

On October 22 the Changsha hsien office issued an announcement prohibiting the petition; otherwise it would deal with the situation severely in accordance with the law. It also listed the names of sixteen representatives of the Masons' and Carpenters' Union, including that of Jen Shu-te, pointing out that among the workers there were some "malefactors." The workers were extremely angered, but there was also a small group of people who were wavering, fearing that another incident would break out like that of January 17 in which Huang Ai and P'ang Jen-ch'üan were murdered. Individual anarchists, then, did not favor the petition and said that a petition would never have a chance of getting results. Throughout the night Comrade Mao Tse-tung sought out Jen Shu-te, Chang Han-fan, Ch'ou Shou-sung, and others for consultation, explaining that the current objective and subjective circumstances were greatly different from those of the Huang and P'ang strike. For one thing, the workers were organized and had great power. Changsha and various other places in the country were just in the midst of strike struggles, and there was the working class of all Changsha and of the entire nation to act as a backup. At the same time, every circle in society was in sympathy with the workers. For another thing, the Changsha hsien office was very isolated. This affair did not have much direct bearing on the immediate interests of Chao Heng-t'i, and it was possible that Chao would not be as obstinate as he had been in the problem of No. 1 Cotton Mill. Finally, Mao Tse-tung inspired everyone: be

---

* Yüan Shih-k'ai. — Tr.

determined to struggle to the end and [you will] have a complete guarantee of victory; at the same time, he wanted everyone to complete the preparations so as to prevent any unexpected calamity that might by the merest chance, occur. Finally, Mao said: When we petition, we will all come. There will be a special person to take care of outside assistance. Put your minds at ease and bravely go out to fight with Chou Ying-kan to the finish.

The determination and confidence of the Party quickly spread to the workers via the representatives of ten, and everyone's boldness in struggle and confidence in victory were heightened.

At 8:00 A.M. on October 23 more than four thousand masons and carpenters gathered together at Educational Society Plaza for a report by Comrade Jen Shu-te on the goal of the petition: unless 34 cents were attained they would definitely not leave the hsien yamen. In addition, the gathering endorsed sixteen men as Petition Delegates; among their number were Jen Shu-te, Ch'ou Shou-sung, Chang Han-fan, Chu Yu-fu, Shu Yü-lin, and Yang Fu-t'ao. For the sake of the verbal struggle, the Communist Party member who was the secretary for the Masons' and Carpenters' Union was the head delegate. At this time, a great rain was pouring down but the workers, as always, were in very high spirits. They started out at 9:00 A.M. with the forward ranks waving a banner of white glazed cotton cloth reading: "The Petition Assembly of the Masons' and Carpenters' Union." On another banner was written: "We Insist on 34 Cents. If We Don't Attain Our Goal, We Won't Work!" "Oppose the Bogus Autonomy, Implement Real Autonomy."

This was the first time ever for such a huge, majestic, and powerful petition struggle by the Changsha workers. On this day Comrade Mao Tse-tung personally participated. He wore a tui-chin* and slipped into the workers' ranks.

After the ranks had arrived at the Changsha hsien office, they saw that a square table had been placed in the middle of the main entrance and that on top of the table were placed two long benches. On these benches was stuck a paper "great command." (This was a screen to hide behind used by the feudal ruling class in their suppression of disorder. When the "great command" was displayed, they could seriously punish and even kill a person.) It was easy to see that Chou Ying-kan thought to display some of his grandeur, with the idea that he could capitalize on this eventually to intimidate the workers. Guarding the main entrance was a line of troops who

---

* A single-breasted garment that buttons in front. — Tr.

would not let the working masses enter. The entire body of workers then all gathered together on the front lawn of the office. They sent eight General Disciplinary Personnel and forty [regular] personnel to guard the main gate and would not permit unauthorized personnel in or out. The sixteen delegates divided into two groups and went in to see Chou Ying-kan. Chou's attitude was unyielding as always; he maintained that the official organization had met and had settled on 30 cents, and that he was not in a position to raise or lower the figure. In addition, he arrogantly said: "You make enough to eat." The delegates thereupon totaled up the cost of living, and Chou was beaten in the argument. Later, Chou heard the masses outside yelling their slogans. He was so frightened that he went into the inner chamber and refused to leave. The first group of delegates came out and reported to the workers that the negotiations had been fruitless, and they also expressed their determination: "If the problem is not solved today, we don't leave the yamen today. If the problem is not solved tomorrow, we don't leave the yamen tomorrow." At this, the second group of delegates went in. After waiting awhile, the delegates were not seen to come out. By this time it was already well past noon. According to the recollection of workers who participated in the petition, Comrade Mao Tse-tung jumped out of the midst of the people up onto the big, round raised bed of flowers in the middle of the lawn and said to everyone: We masons and carpenters can't live from day to day because our wages are so low. It was only when this point was reached that we asked the government to increase our wages. Our first group of delegates went in and negotiated a long time without any result. Now our second group has been in there for awhile and we still don't have any news. Chou Ying-kan is cutting us off from each other. If we wait a little longer and there is still no news, let's all go to the yamen together and look for Chou Ying-kan to talk things over. After he finished talking, he led the workers in shouting out the slogans: "We Insist on Thirty-Four Cents!" "If We Don't Attain Our Goal, We Won't Leave the Yamen!" After awhile there was still no movement from inside, and so the workers rushed en masse headlong toward the yamen yelling their slogans. The troops on guard pointed their bayonets at the workers, and the workers seized two rifles. At this time an official came out of the yamen and intentionally berated the soldiers, telling them that they should not point their bayonets at people. There were also some workers who said that they shouldn't cause any trouble for the soldiers, and so the rifles were returned. But now this official lifted up the "great command" and hollered: "You are all rebels. What is all this? If you persist in this I will lose my manners." The workers' delegates thereupon went forward and argued their point: "We come empty-handed, wanting food to eat. Why do you use the 'great command' to frighten people? Who is being unreasonable!" This said, this character was at a loss for an answer. Now everyone followed the delegates and all squatted down on their heels to await the results of the talks with the second group.

Because a clash broke out between the guards and the workers around 4:00 or 5:00 P.M., Chou Ying-kan requested Chao Heng-t'i's General Headquarters to send a company of soldiers and completely encircle the workers.

With this situation the workers became more alert. An old worker who was a member of the first group of petition delegates recalls how at this time Mao Tse-tung inspired the masses:

Comrade Mao Tse-tung was in among the ranks and wanted us to carry on resolutely. He led the workers in crying out slogans. He had a whistle with him, and everytime he blew the whistle the workers would shout out sentence after sentence. The morale of the masses was raised. At this time, someone in the yamen discovered that he was the leader and came to get him. He slipped through several trees close to the wall and ran into the ranks of the workers. After the affair was over, there was one paper that said: "Every time the workers shouted out their slogans, the tiles would fly off the roof of the Changsha hsien office." [26]

It was getting near dark and no one had eaten for a whole day, so the union bought a few baskets of wheat cakes to satisfy their hunger. At this time the workers from the mint, the electric light company, and the tailor, textile, and barber businesses sent numerous representatives who brought tea and snacks with them. Some sent lanterns, toilet paper, and oil cloth* for the workers to use for sleeping out overnight. The workers were now stronger than ever.

The second group of delegates sat in the reception room of the hsien magistrate, pressing Chou Ying-kan to accept their conditions. Chou telephoned Chao Heng-t'i to ask for instructions on whether or not he could arrest the head delegate, saying that after he was shot the workers would be frightened away. Probably because of what he had learned from the Huang and P'ang incident, Chao Heng-t'i did not agree. When the delegates heard Chou telephoning Chao Heng-t'i, they said to Chou in a strong voice: "We are not afraid of the governor or of Wu P'ei-fu; do you think you people from Changsha hsien can frighten us!" At 9:00 P.M. Chao Heng-t'i

---

* For tents. — Tr.

sent a staff officer to "arbitrate." He came out and asked the workers for their opinions, and everybody cried out in one voice: "We
insist on thirty-four cents. If we don't attain our goal we won't
work!" The staff officer said: "The governor has agreed to settle
this within three days. In the meantime, why don't you all go home."
The workers once again cried out in one voice: "Unless we get
thirty-four cents, we don't leave the yamen." They kept this up until midnight — the delegates inside and the several thousand workers outside. Later, the head of the Administration Department, Wu
Ching-hung, telephoned and promised to call an assembly of public
organizations the next afternoon at two o'clock. He asked the worker
delegates to attend and said, no matter what, there would be results.
Comrade Mao Tse-tung talked it over with the delegates and temporarily agreed to this disposition of the matter. It was only now that
the workers left en masse. The workers separated and went to the
Lu Pan Temple and the Lü Tsu Temple to spend the night. By now
it was already three o'clock in the morning of the twenty-fourth.

At 10:00 A.M. on October 24 all the workers went to Educational
Society Plaza for a meeting and decided that if the assembly of public organizations brought no results, they would petition the governor's office. At two o'clock in the afternoon they sent out twelve
delegates, including Jen Shu-te, Chang Han-fan, Ch'ou Shou-sung,
Chu Yu-fu, and Yang Fu-t'ao, to the Administration Department to
sit in on the assembly of public organizations and "demand their
debt from the debtor in his own house." All of the workers then
waited for the results at Educational Society Plaza. The struggle
had entered its final stage. At this time Mao Tse-tung directed that
the goal of the struggle should turn clearly to winning the freedom
of the masons and carpenters to conduct their own business, a freedom that was clearly stipulated in writing in Chao Heng-t'i's "provincial constitution."

With a view to defeating thoroughly the reactionary government
and gaining final victory, and also because the previous evening
Chou Ying-kan had been intent on harming the head delegate, Comrade Mao Tse-tung changed places with this comrade and personally took over the position of first delegate and led the worker delegates to the Administration Department (located at the site of the
present Chung-shan Park in Changsha).

During this conference Comrade Mao Tse-tung carried a copy of
Chao Heng-t'i's "provincial constitution," using the articles in it
to argue down the head of the Administration Department, Wu Ching-
hung. An old worker recalls: Comrade Mao Tse-tung spoke for the

workers and made a clear and straightforward presentation with reason in every word. He spoke [so well] that the head of the Administration Department, Wu Ching-hung, was at a loss for words. Wu Ching-hung then asked: "What is the gentleman's name? Is he a worker?" Comrade Mao Tse-tung replied: "You, Sir, have asked about my credentials, and I reply that I am a representative of the workers. If you want to make an investigation of my background, it would be best to talk about it another time. Today, in my capacity as a representative of the masons and carpenters, I am demanding that the government settle the wage problem." After conferring for three hours there was still no result, and then a telephone call came from Educational Society Plaza: "If there are no results, then we had better come en masse to petition the office."

By this time the condition that was being discussed was not the 34-cent daily wage; it was the struggle for the "freedom to do business" based on the "provincial constitution," that is, the current wage was 34 cents, and if there were to be any change in conditions in the future and the workers wanted to raise their wages, the government would be unable to intervene. The "one-year general managers" were opposed to the freedom to do business, saying that it would undermine the regulations of the guild. The reason was that once the freedom to do business was granted there would be no one to come to the guild meetings any more; people would be able to come from the country and work at will. There were some worker delegates who expressed this misgiving. Wu Ching-hung and his group, under the pretext that there was a division of opinion among the workers, said that people were manipulating the union. Comrade Mao Tse-tung then wanted Wu to send some people to go and ask the opinion of the workers. When the officials of the Administration Department, carrying lanterns, went to Educational Society Plaza to make observations, thousands of workers were all squatting and sitting on the ground. They had not dispersed and were very orderly. As for the question of "the freedom to do business," there was no dispute at all. They returned and reported the situation to Wu Ching-hung. The delegates held fast until eight o'clock in the evening when Wu Ching-hung finally could do nothing but comply: if the masons and the carpenters would compose a petition requesting the freedom to do business, the government would grant the request. Mao Tse-tung then copied down on the spot the conversation between Wu and the delegates. Wu looked it over and stated further that the "proclamation" of Changsha hsien was null and void and that the workers had the freedom to do business. Thereupon the delegates, on the

one hand, took the record of the proceedings to Educational Society
Plaza for a report. The workers, on the other hand, wrote up a petition to hand to Chao Heng-t'i for approval.

According to the reports in the Changsha press the following day,
the full text of the "Conversation Minutes" was as follows:

> The masons and the carpenters demanded an increase in their wages to 34 cents,
> did not recognize the Changsha hsien magistrate's proclamation of the fourteenth
> of the eighth lunar month, and struck work in disagreement. This issue, accord-
> ing to the statement of the delegates from these businesses, was basically over
> the free contractual relationship between the laborer and the customer: it should
> be freely agreed upon by both parties, and unless constraint was used (this
> phrase was added by Department Head Wu) the government officials were not to
> interfere. Representing the provincial governor, the department head allowed the
> matter to be handled in conformity with the above-mentioned proposals and hoped
> that this idea would be communicated to the workers. The above was recorded in
> the Administration Department of the provincial governor's office in the pres-
> ence of the department head, Wu Ching-hung.

The "Petition to the Provincial Governor" specifically mentioned
the point that this petition demanding the freedom to do business
was "pleading oppression" in accordance with 'Article XVI of the
provincial constitution.'" (This article in Chao Heng-t'i's "provincial constitution" read: "The people have the rights to petition the
government and to request relief in times of disaster.") It also
clearly stated: "At the present time, numerous letters are arriving
from General Headquarters and from various offices, schools, and
dwellings, all acknowledging the 34-cent wage and requesting that
work begin. It is only the Changsha hsien magistrate who refuses
to decide the issue. This is really violating the 'provincial constitution' and obstructing work."

The strike struggle of the Changsha masons and carpenters to
win the freedom to do business and increase their wages that had
been maintained for nineteen days under the personal leadership of
Comrade Mao Tse-tung had gained final victory. And so the Party
organization mobilized night and day and decided to hold a celebration ceremony on the afternoon of the twenty-fifth for all the workers in the city of Changsha.

On the morning of October 25 Comrade Jen Shu-te and the others,
still led by Comrade Mao Tse-tung, went to the Administration Department and urged Wu Ching-hung to sanction the "Petition." At
noon about twenty thousand people composed of the organized working masses of No. 1 Cotton Mill, the graphite refining plant, the
electric light company, the Canton-Hankow Railway, the barbers,

the writing brush business, the tailors, the painters, and the printers and the entire body of masons and carpenters all gathered together on Educational Society Plaza to hold a ceremony celebrating the victory of the masons' and carpenters' strike and took pictures to commemorate the event. Fearing that a last minute calamity might occur with the delegates at the Administration Department, twenty thousand people set out for the "provincial governor's office" to await [the results of the meeting]. As the ranks were just coming into another village they ran into delegates who were returning to pass on the news: the "Petition," with Wu Ching-hung's "sanction," had been handed over "to the provincial governor for review." And so the ranks loudly shouted their slogans as they marched along the road from Lao-chao Wall, past Eight-Cornered Pavilion, Yao-wang Street, Hsiao-tung Street, and on to the Provincial Office. In front of the provincial office lawn they waited for all the delegates to come out and report the final results.

After Wu Ching-hung had finally affixed his seal to the document, the worker delegates discovered that in the "comments" were the words: "Their wages should be mutually settled upon at all times; the workers cannot be permitted to set the wages unilaterally." Comrade Mao Tse-tung firmly disagreed with this sentence, and with the ranks of twenty thousand waiting outside, Wu Ching-hung had no alternative but to strike out the phrase, "the workers cannot be permitted to set the wages unilaterally." With this the strike of the masons and carpenters finally won a thoroughgoing victory.

The delegates went to the provincial office lawn and reported to the working masses: Final victory had been completely won. The twenty thousand workers thunderously cheered and loudly cried out: "Long Live the Freedom to Do Business!" "Long Live Labor!" "Workers of the World Unite!" and following this set off a great many firecrackers. After this the entire group marched through the streets. When they arrived at the hsien office, the workers streamed into the main hall of the yamen setting off many firecrackers and shouting: "Long Live the Victory of the Strike!" "Down with Chou Ying-kan!" The workers were beside themselves with joy. This was a victory the likes of which the Changsha workers had never experienced before.

On October 26 the "Masons' and Carpenters' Petition Assembly" put up the announcement of the victory, which bore these concluding phrases: "From this day forward if a person does not give 34 cents we will not go to his house and work. This right of the freedom to do business was actually stipulated in the 'provincial constitution' long ago. It is only that previously there was no safeguard; now we can consider that there is a safeguard. Beginning tomorrow it will be business as usual for everybody."

This victory of the masons and carpenters inspired the workers of all Changsha and all Hunan, and the Hunan labor movement surged forward with even greater vigor. The prestige of Comrade Mao Tse-tung and the Communist Party among the working masses was raised even higher. The small number of workers who were anarchist remnants were completely won over. They felt that the strike led by Huang and P'ang had failed and that what the people from the Communist Party had said was now borne out; hence they fully believed that the Communist Party was a party that genuinely worked for the workers' interests. Following this, labor unions were founded in great profusion for all the businesses in Changsha. The barbers' strike, which had been going on for a long time without any solution, and the textile workers, who were just in the midst of their strike, both won victory under the influence of the great victory of the masons' and carpenters' strike.

After the victory of the strike, Chang Han-fan, Yang Fu-t'ao, Chu Yu-fu, and other comrades joined the Party; Shu Yü-lin and other comrades joined the Corps. Before the defeat of the Revolution in 1927, the number of Party and Corps members among the masons and carpenters of Changsha reached over three hundred. A great many of the outstanding elements among them were martyred in the revolutionary struggle! From 1926 to 1927 Comrade Chang Han-fan was head of the labor department of the Changsha city Party committee, and he was martyred in 1928. And Comrade Yang Fu-t'ao was martyred in 1928, when he was secretary of the Heng-yang Special Committee. Comrade Chu Yu-fu was martyred at the end of 1927, when he was secretary of the Changsha hsien Party committee.

## V. THE VICTORY OF THE GREAT STRIKE OF THE CANTON-HANKOW RAILWAY WORKERS

In September 1922 the workers of the Canton-Hankow Railway went through a bloody struggle and a fifteen-day strike to achieve a great victory.

This strike was a struggle that combined politics with economics. During the strike struggle the workers were very tightly organized. In the face of the warlords' policy of cruel murder and the Railway

Bureau's softening up policy, the working masses struggled bravely and never, from beginning to end, did they submit. Finally, with the assistance of the broad masses of workers inside and outside the two provinces of Hunan and Hupei, especially that of the nation's railway workers, the warlords Wu P'ei-fu and Hsiao Yao-nan had no choice but to accede completely to the demands of the workers.

The earliest railway strike in China occurred on the Canton-Hankow line. In December 1920 the construction group of the southern section of the Canton-Hankow line struck over a demand for the payment of back wages, and in March 1921 the signalmen of this line struck because of the beating the workers had received from the army. But the influence of these two strikes on the outside was slight. In October 1921 the workers on the Wuchang section of the Canton-Hankow line struck for five days for increased wages and improved living conditions, and they achieved victory. At this time Comrade Mao Tse-tung was already attaching great importance to work among railway workers and personally had spent a great deal of time in acquainting himself with the conditions on the Canton-Hankow line. In addition, he had sent some capable Party cadres to Changsha's Hsin-ho Main Station to set up a workers' night school. At the beginning of 1922 the Hsin-ho Station founded a Workers' Club. Later, with a view to strengthening the leadership of the Canton-Hankow Railway workers, the Party sent Comrade Kuo Liang to assume general responsibility. Because the strike of the Canton-Hankow line had Party leadership, it had extensive and profound influence.

Comrade Kuo Liang was from T'ung-kuan, Changsha, and when he was studying at First Normal from 1920 to 1921 he was the leader of the student movement. Already at that time he began to participate in the labor movement under the leadership of Comrade Mao Tse-tung, and his first effort was to organize the Changsha rickshaw men. His talent for drawing near the masses and for arousing them was quite outstanding. He was one of the most capable assistants in the early Hunan labor movement led by Mao Tse-tung. All the way up to the First Revolutionary Civil War he was head of the labor department of the Hunan provincial Party committee and the most famous mass leader of the Hunan labor movement. On March 29, 1928, Kuo Liang was heroically martyred in Changsha; at the time, he was the secretary of the Hunan-Hupei-Kiangsi Special Committee.

In August 1922 Comrade Kuo Liang came to Yüeh-chou. (At the time, owing to the annexations of the warlords, the Canton-Hankow

Railway was divided into two sections, Hunan and Hupei. Each section had its own bureau head. Yüeh-chou was occupied by the northern troops, and it was under the control of the Hupei section.) Owing to the very early influence of Changsha's Hsin-ho Station, in late August the Yüeh-chou Workers' Club of the Canton-Hankow line was founded. Kuo Liang himself was the Club's secretary. The Club's inaugural proclamation read:

> The workers are the source of the world's happiness, but the workers themselves can't enjoy the least bit of happiness. Now the workers have self-awareness. We workers of the Canton-Hankow line also have self-awareness. We have already drawn lessons from the flow of events. What is first and foremost in planning for the happiness of workers is that workers of the same class solidly unite. This is the first reason why we must found a Club. [27]

After the founding of the Club, a workers' preparatory school was formally created. The school contained a great deal of recreation equipment to get the workers interested in studying.

There were two things at the time that the workers of the Canton-Hankow Railway detested most and were most bitter about. First was the harsh treatment of the workers by the overseers. Second was the fact that their wages were often held back and not distributed; the prices of things were going up daily, and when the workers waited until they got hold of their money it was no longer worth anything. After a great many workers from Yüeh-chou Station had joined the Workers' Club they received the Party's class education. Added to this was the inspiration of the raging strike struggles of the workers and students from various areas and of patriotic movements. They thus strengthened their courage for struggle and demanded improved treatment and the preservation of the workers' legitimate rights.

On the Canton-Hankow line's Wuchang section there was a coach work overseer by the name of Chang En-jung. He was originally a small overseer, and because the bureau chief of the Hupei section, Wang Shih-yü, was from the same place as he was, and because he was good at flattery and toadying, he was promoted to the position of full overseer, becoming a useful henchman for Wang. This person conspired with another of Wang Shih-yü's confidants, Miao Feng-ming, who was an interpreter. (At the time since there were many foreigners among the top technical personnel of the Chinese railroads, there was a need for interpreters.) Relying on their authority, they colluded together and unscrupulously ill-treated the workers. They also bribed a group of hooligans to go around selling

opium and thus added greatly to their wealth. In addition, they intentionally caused trouble when the workers were at their jobs.
Sometimes a worker would get into a verbal brawl with one of these
hooligans, and Chang and Miao would take advantage of the opportunity to fire the worker and substitute a hooligan in his place; the
hooligan would then become even more perverse. And thus the
workers of the Canton-Hankow line utterly detested these two characters and unanimously demanded that they be dismissed from their
positions. In line with the wishes of the workers, the Yüeh-chou
Workers' Club sent up a petition to Wang Shih-yü. Wang paid no
heed to the workers' demands; on the contrary, he told Chang En-
jung to find some way to fire the "troublemakers." Thus Chang En-
jung falsely accused the workers of such things as "stealing coal"
and constantly punished, beat, or fired them. The oppression and
suffering experienced by the workers was worse than before.

With the lesson of the nationwide high tide of labor strikes and
the previous strike at the Canton-Hankow line, Wang Shih-yü was
deeply afraid of the workers' great power and resorted to every
trick in the book to undermine their unity. After the founding of
the Yüeh-chou Workers' Club, Wang instigated Miao Feng-ming
and Chang En-jung to organize a "Workers' Research Institute"
[Kung-jen yen-chiu-so] to buy off the workers and to act as a
counter to the Workers' Club. Chang and Miao intimidated the
workers saying: "If you don't join, we'll send you to the government offices for severe punishment." At the same time, they took
advantage of the feudal hometown relationship and got a small number of backward workers to join this subversive organization of
strikebreakers. The Workers' Club then once again demanded that
Chang and Miao be relieved of their positions, but as before they
could get no response. The working masses' defiant mood was
surging higher and higher. Kuo Liang believed that the great majority of the workers were demanding a strike and that the time for
waging this kind of struggle was ripe. At this time Comrade Mao
Tse-tung was leading firsthand the work at Changsha's Hsin-ho
Station. He agreed with the assessment in Comrade Kuo Liang's
report, and immediately linked up with the Wuhan Party organization and mobilized the workers of Hsü-chia-p'eng to rise up and
echo the call. He also rapidly pulled together the organization of
the Canton-Hankow Railway workers so as to facilitate action. At
the direction of Mao Tse-tung, the Yüeh-chou Workers' Club joined
with all the workers of the Canton-Hankow line in petitioning the
Ministry of Communications by telegram for an answer within three

days to the request for the dismissal of those two strikebreakers, Chang and Miao. Finally, they notified the railroad authorities that if by September 5 a completely satisfactory solution had not been achieved, they would play their last card — a strike of the entire railway line.

On September 6 the Canton-Hankow Railway Workers' Clubs from Hsü-chia-p'eng, Yüeh-chou, Changsha, and Chu-p'ing founded a United Association of Workers' Clubs [Kung-jen chü-le pu lien-ho-hui] of the entire line, set up departments of Investigation, Security, Correspondence, Inspection, and General Affairs, and prepared for the strike. The various Workers' Clubs held meetings and mobilized every worker to prepare well for the strike. To prevent the strike from being undermined, the workers dismantled the important machine parts of the locomotives and put them away; then they leisurely began to stop work. On September 9, cars were not running between Hsü-chia-p'eng and Yüeh-chou, Changsha. The repair shop had also stopped work. The Canton-Hankow Railway strike had formally begun.

Throughout, Comrade Mao Tse-tung kept a close eye on this very significant strike and maintained close contact with Comrade Kuo Liang.

The United Association of Workers' Clubs of the Canton-Hankow line raised eight demands requiring the Railway authorities' response. The main contents of the eight demands were: Chang En-jung and Miao Feng-ming were to be dismissed. The wages of the workers of the entire line, on the model of the Peking-Hankow Railway, were to be calculated monthly rather than daily for those who had worked two years (changing the short form to the long form patterned after the Peking-Hankow line), and wages were to be paid monthly with no delay. During sick leave, wages were to be paid as usual. The wages of firemen, unskilled laborers, etc., were to be increased and arrears made up. In promotions, the seniority rule should be followed. Workers were not to be punished without cause and not to be fired at will. There were other items dealing with the welfare of the workers.

News of the strike declaration rapidly traveled the length of the line, throughout the province, and to every place in the country. Besides charging Chang and Miao with their evil crimes, shedding light on the workers' poverty-ridden life, and asking the nation-wide working class and every circle to rise up and give assistance, the declaration clearly outlined the following goals of the strike:

To "free ourselves of oppression," to "support our organization," to "improve our lives," and to "raise our stature," we must strike! We are fighting purely for our own personal interests. We are fighting for our survival, we are fighting for our stature, and we are sworn to fight to the death to attain our goal! Fellow workers! Bravely and resolutely struggle for life amidst death; all lies with our power of unity and struggle! Let us all unite and struggle as one against the enemy who is oppressing us!

After the strike began, the workers of Changsha's Hsin-ho Station sent a special petition to Chao Heng-t'i with a view to dividing the ruling class. In the petition they pointed out that the troop trains were running normally in Hunan and asked Chao not to interfere. The reason they did this was that there was a contradiction between Chao and the Hupei "Tuchün," Hsiao Yao-nan, that went back to the days in 1921 when, after the failure of the "Aid to Hupei" war that Chao had launched in an effort to grab up some Hupei territory, the Chihli [Peiyang] troops occupied Yüeh-chou and remained there. Under the directions of Comrade Mao Tse-tung, the Hsin-ho Station strike organization made very good use of this contradiction to win Chao Heng-t'i over to a position of neutrality in this strike movement. After a few days of the strike, the bureau head of the Hunan section of the Canton-Hankow Railway went to Hsin-ho Station to talk, stating that "neither this bureau nor the Hunan government has any intention of violently oppressing anyone," and moreover, that during the strike, wages would be paid as usual. Subsequently, Chao Heng-t'i also sent a staff officer to Hsin-ho Station to mediate and get the workers to return to work early. The Workers' Club wrote an answering letter, saying: "If the eight conditions are assented to in the morning, the trains will be running in the evening; we will certainly not violate our orders."

The just cries of the Canton-Hankow Railway workers immediately gained the sympathy of all workers throughout the country. The various labor organizations in Wuhan and the Club of the southern section of the Peking-Hankow Railway immediately sent special deputies to Hsü-chia-p'eng to lend a helping hand with the work. Also, the workers of the "Workers' Research Institute" were urged to reform, not be hoodwinked any longer by the strikebreakers, and to return to the workers' own ranks.

After the strike began, the Workers' Clubs of the various areas guarded the locomotives and equipment in shifts in order to prevent them from being damaged. A great many workers kept watch in the machine shop and did not sleep all night, patrolling back and forth so that bad elements who wanted to destroy the shop or get the workers into trouble wouldn't get the slightest opportunity. Individual foremen, moved by this great spirit of the workers, secretly helped them in carrying off some equipment and parts. Imperceptibly, the ranks of the workers expanded and became firmer.

After two days of the strike the locomotives lay motionless on the tracks like dead snakes.

On the one hand, Wang Shih-yü requested a company of troops to come to Hsü-chia-p'eng and crack down on the strike; on the other hand, he took over the running of the trains through the use of backward workers who had been instigated by Chang En-jung and Miao Feng-ming to join the "Workers' Research Institute." He also sent in an armed escort. On the evening of September 10 several hundred striking workers and the women and children of their families lay down on the tracks, preventing the trains from running. Wang Shih-yü commanded the troops to kill them, and as a result more than one hundred workers were wounded, over thirty seriously, more than ten jumped into the water and disappeared, and nine people were arrested. After the Yüeh-chou workers found out that the cars had begun to run and were coming, under the leadership of Comrade Kuo Liang they flooded onto the railway tracks on the morning of the eleventh to obstruct the passage of the train. In their hands they held banners reading: "Chang and Miao Are Utterly Vicious," "Expel the Two Bandits," "We Demand Our Just Rights"; and they all lay down on the tracks. Kuo Liang was the first bravely to lie down, and he lay in the foremost position. The train was forced to stop. Wang Shih-yü personally hurried up to the scene in a handcar and gave commands from behind the train. Beating his chest and stamping his feet, he forced the workers to start the train, screaming out like a mad dog: "Hurry up and get that train moving! If you crush these bastards to death, I'll take full responsibility." The worker who was running the locomotive moved it forward a few feet and then immediately backed up a few feet. He knew that the people who were lying down on the tracks in front of him were his own class brothers. Wang Shih-yü had no choice but to send a telegram to Hsiao Yao-nan asking him to send the "Northern Army" that was stationed at Yüeh-chou to come and crack down on the workers. Hsiao Yao-nan thereupon immediately assented. But the soldiers of the "Northern Army" sympathized with the workers and would not agree to kill them. Wang Shih-yü then gave them a huge banquet and told them: "Don't worry! I will take responsibility for everything." In addition, he bribed two company commanders with 12,000 yuan. The company commanders then ordered the troops under them to open fire, and the soldiers, forced against their wills, "closed their eyes and thrust wildly" at the working masses that continued to lie on the tracks. For a time the sound of the workers' slogans was mixed with the sound of the rifles. Over seventy people were wounded on the spot (later six died from serious wounds), some heads were split open, and some arms and legs were hacked off; some people had all their limbs hacked off. Many of their family members quickly ran in to save them and were also shot and killed. After the massacre had stopped, the "Northern Army," under the instigation of Wang Shih-yü, arrested Comrade Kuo Liang and more than thirty other activists, taking them in custody to the Wuchang army prison. Well over two hundred railway workers were either killed, wounded, or arrested at Hsü-chia-p'eng and Yüeh-chou.

After the workers at Hsin-ho Station got the news of the Yüeh-chou tragedy, they became extremely angered and immediately sent a telegram to the Ministry of Communications demanding the removal of Wang Shih-yü. At the same time, they telegraphed the Hsü-chia-p'eng Workers' Club to swear to the death and hold on to the end. They also sent three representatives to the Hsü-chia-p'eng Workers' Club to lend a helping hand with the work.

The following day a worker representative from Yüeh-chou was sent to Hsin-ho Station to give a detailed report on the cruel massacre suffered by the Yüeh-chou workers. He also explained that although the Yüeh-chou Workers' Club was still occupied by the "Northern Army," the workers had by no means ceased their activities. On the one hand, they were taking care of fellow workers who were having difficulties, and on the other hand, they were sending people to Wuhan and various other places to establish liaison. The worker representative said in conclusion: "Under the knives and guns of the enemy the broad ranks of the working people have united even more staunchly than before!" At this same meeting the workers of Hsin-ho Station sent a wire to various unions, newspapers, and organizations throughout the country asking for their assistance.

On the afternoon of this day Comrade Mao Tse-tung directed the various Changsha labor union organizations to join with the public organizations and representatives from various circles to hold an emergency session and to come to the aid of the striking workers of the Canton-Hankow Railway. They decided on the spot to send a circular telegram throughout the country in the name of the various Hunan labor organizations, proclaiming the case against Hsiao Yao-nan. They sent a deputy to console the workers at Hsü-chia-p'eng and Yüeh-chou and the striking workers on the Canton-Hankow Railway line, encouraging them to hold on to the end. They distributed leaflets notifying the workers of Changsha and of all Hunan of the events surrounding the strike and tragedy and mobilized various kinds of assistance for the Canton-Hankow Railway workers. The telegrams to the various labor organizations read:

> Even Japan's treatment of Korea and England's treatment of India were not as cruel as this.... We must bring down the vicious and ferocious warlords! Working class friends of the whole country! If the lackeys of this bunch of warlords — the bureau heads and the overseers who oppress the workers — are not stamped out, the workers will never see the light of day! Everyone unite and stamp out this bunch of bloodsucking strikebreakers!

The United Association of Workers' Clubs of the Canton-Hankow Railway immediately wired a public announcement to the whole country and presented four conditions to the railway authorities: (1) Pull back the troops that are cracking down on the workers. (2) Get rid of and punish Wang Shih-yü. (3) Relieve distressed fellow workers and workers' families. (4) Fully grant the conditions brought forward by the workers. Under the leadership of the Wuhan United Association of Labor Organizations [Wu-han kung-t'uan lien-ho-hui], the Wuhan workers issued a call to the nation's workers to rise up and give assistance to the striking railway men of the Canton-Hankow Railway. The declaration they sent out read:

> The Wuhan United Association of Labor Organizations recognizes that this is a matter of the entire working class and is not just that of some of our fellow workers of the Canton-Hankow line. It is the shame and disgrace of the whole working class, not just that of some of our fellow workers of the Canton-Hankow line. Thus the whole working class must find a solution to this problem. The Wuhan United Association of Labor Organizations has determined that the various organizations come to the aid of this strike with effective strength. Fellow workers of the Canton-Hankow Railway! Bravely and resolutely hold on to the end; be stubborn and unbending in the face of endless difficulties. We are sworn to exhaust every effort to be your reinforcements!

The Wuhan United Association of Labor Organizations and the Peking-Hankow southern section Workers' Club also informed Hsiao Yao-nan of "the decision for a general strike if there is not a completely satisfactory solution within three days."

When Hsiao Yao-nan got this notice he panicked and made an urgent telephone call to Wang Shih-yü. He cursed him roundly, telling him he should not have brought on this kind of disaster and ordering him to take care of the matter by himself. According to the press reports of the time: "When Wang Shih-yü received this telephone call he forthwith sank insensible into his chair, the sweat pouring down like rain."

Wang Shih-yü then changed direction and treated the workers with measures intended to soften them up. He invited the workers to dinner, sent them presents, sent the wounded workers to the hospital, and personally went to "make inquiries after their health." At the same time, he tried to induce the workers to return with [the promise of] double pay, thinking that the workers, because of their economic straits, would certainly be unable to hold on for long. But the workers were completely unmoved by this despicable trick and were unanimously determined to stick it out to the end.

The Canton-Hankow Railway United Association of Workers' Clubs daily received no less than several dozen letters and telegrams of support from throughout the country. Contributions from the various areas also came in unceasingly. The Anyüan Workers' Club sent a special delegate with an assistance fund, the workers of the Changsha businesses were in the midst of mobilizing contributions, the Wuhan United Association of Labor Organizations raised 1,000 yuan, the Peking-Hankow Railway Chiang-an Workers' Club lent a helping hand with 500 yuan.... Thus the striking workers were able to get relief payments of 10 cents per day for living expenses. Everyone's determination became even firmer.

The strike was maintained, and on September 22, under the leadership of Party organizations of the nation's entire railway system, more than one thousand worker-representatives were summoned from the Lung-hai, Cheng-chou, Ch'ang-hsin-tien, and Canton-Hankow railways for a meeting at Hankow, where the decision was made that if by the twenty-fifth there was still no solution, they would ally with the strike and echo the call. They also prepared for the organization of a suicide squad of two hundred people. The strike unrest was on the verge of spreading throughout the country's entire railway network.

Only now did the Ministry of Communications of the Peking government become frightened, and without delay on September 24 it sent a vice minister to the general headquarters of the Canton-Hankow Railway at Hsü-chia-p'eng to invite the workers to negotiate. Wang Shih-yü was forced to acknowledge the demands of the workers, but then he immediately changed his tune again.

On September 27 the entire body of workers from the Peking-Hankow and the Canton-Hankow railways sent a telegram to Wu

P'ei-fu, informing him that if he did not give a satisfactory answer to the workers' demands within forty-eight hours, they would all go on strike. The next day, seeing that he could not resist the might of the workers, Wu P'ei-fu had no choice but to accede completely to the eight demands originally put forward by the workers.

Comrade Kuo Liang and the workers who had been arrested were set free. Chang En-jung and Miao Feng-ming, who had suppressed the workers, were removed. Every demand of the workers was met. The great strike of the Canton-Hankow Railway workers, which had been waged at great cost, had now achieved complete victory.

On September 28 the worker-representatives of the Hsin-ho Station Workers' Club took an early train back to Changsha. The workers all rushed down to the train station to welcome them, setting off firecrackers and loudly proclaiming their victory all along the way. The workers from Hsü-chia-p'eng, Yüeh-chou, Hsin-ho, and every place along the Canton-Hankow line held huge celebrations.

After Comrade Kuo Liang had returned to Changsha, a great number of railway workers and their families came to pay their respects.

On the foundation of this victory, Comrade Mao Tse-tung personally led the workers of the Canton-Hankow Railway in founding a unified labor organization. On November 1, 1922, the Workers' Clubs from Hsü-chia-p'eng, Chu-p'ing, Hsin-ho, and Yüeh-chou sent representatives who, under the direction of Comrade Mao Tse-tung, gathered together in Changsha at Hsin-ho Station and formally founded the Canton-Hankow Railway General Labor Union [Yüeh-Han t'ieh-lu tsung-kung-hui]. This was the earliest unified organization of railway unions in the country. It was located at Hsin-ho, Changsha.

## VI. THE VICTORY OF THE GREAT STRIKE OF THE WORKERS AT SHUI-K'OU-SHAN

The strike of over three thousand workers at the lead and zinc mines of Shui-k'ou-shan in Ch'ang-ning that occurred in November 1922 broke out under the influence of the victory of the Anyüan strike that had taken place in September of the same year. The Party sent Chiang Hsien-yün and other comrades from Anyüan to help develop the work at Shui-k'ou-shan, which action played a decisive role in the victory of this strike.

Just as in Anyüan, the victorious strike at Shui-k'ou-shan had an immense influence on the whole country.

Between 1917 and 1920 the workers at Shui-k'ou-shan had waged several brave struggles against the mining authorities on behalf of the workers' welfare and over demands for the payment of back wages, and they had called two strikes. But because there was no Party leadership and because the goals of the struggles were not clear-cut, the workers got the worst of it. Nevertheless, the facts finally taught the workers: "If we want to exist, our only alternative is to unite and carry on struggle!" Deep within the thoughts of the workers were buried the seeds of "defiance."

At the time, the life at Shui-k'ou-shan was very hard: wages were very low, and the average worker got only a few cents a day. A high wage was but 10-odd cents. The mining authorities also often held back wages and owed them in arrears. The exploitation by the feudal gang bosses was extreme. The conditions and equipment were very substandard, and workers were often injured and even met violent deaths. These conditions were generally similar to those at Anyüan.

According to the recollection of a comrade who participated at firsthand in this strike struggle, [28] in 1922 when news of the swelling tide of the nationwide labor movement spread, there were excited discussions among the Shui-k'ou-shan workers, and in all of this what had the most influence on them was the strike victory at the Anyüan Railway and Mines. Everyone had a mind to carry on a struggle and win their rights, but in view of the history of several previous struggles, there was also some hesitation, a feeling that they had to learn from Anyüan, that they had to find some people to come and help. Just at this time an Anyüan worker came to Shui-k'ou-shan, and became very well acquainted with the activist and machinist Comrade Liu Tung-hsüan. As soon as he came he began talking to the workers about how great the power of the Anyüan Workers' Club was and about how it worked for the welfare of the workers. He also told everyone about the events surrounding the struggle of the Anyüan Railway and Mine workers and about the victorious outcome of the struggle.

When the workers of Shui-k'ou-shan heard this they were extremely excited and longed for the same thing, hoping that someone would also come there to lead them in establishing a Workers' Club. The activists of the previous strike struggles then gathered together and discussed the situation; they decided to send a person to Anyüan to establish contact and ask the Anyüan Workers' Club to send out a man to lead the workers of Shui-k'ou-shan in the founding of a Workers' Club. Everybody chose Liu Tung-hsüan to go because he had relatives working at Anyüan. Some people in the machine shop collected together the money for his traveling expenses.

Arriving at Anyüan, Comrade Liu Tung-hsüan was introduced by his relatives and, full of enthusiasm, saw Comrades Liu Shao-ch'i and Li Li-san. They immediately agreed to send people to Shui-k'ou-shan to lend a hand with the work. They also explained to Liu Tung-hsüan: "Because we are busy with work here we cannot spare any time to go to Shui-k'ou-shan ourselves." Liu Tung-hsüan immediately wrote a letter to the workers at the mines and told them to prepare to receive the representatives.

At the beginning of October 1922 Comrades Chiang Hsien-yün and Hsieh Huai-te, and four other Anyüan worker-comrades (all activists in the strike struggle) came to Shui-k'ou-shan.

Comrade Chiang Hsien-yün was one of the most outstanding cadres of the Party during the First Revolutionary Civil War period. He was a student of Heng-yang's Third Normal School, and during the May Fourth movement he was the student leader there. In 1922 when Comrade Mao Tse-tung went to Heng-yang to establish the Party, Chiang was in the first group to be admitted and thereafter was sent by the Party to Anyüan to engage in labor work. At the end of 1923, after the second strike at Shui-k'ou-shan had been suppressed with armed force by Chao Heng-t'i, Chiang Hsien-yün went to Canton and entered the Whampoa Military Academy. During his study at Whampoa and in the fighting at Tung Chiang his extensive ability in military and nonmilitary areas stood out. During the Northern Expedition fighting, Comrade Chiang Hsien-yün, who was regimental commander of the Fourth Army of the Northern Expeditionary Army, distinguished himself for bravery and military ability. In 1927 he was martyred in battle on the front lines in Honan.

Comrade Hsieh Huai-te was from Pai-kuo in Heng-shan, Hunan, and he was working in the Anyüan coal mines in 1908. After the failure of the First Revolutionary Civil War he organized the Anyüan workers in an armed attack on P'ing-hsiang and Li-ling. After being arrested in January 1928 he was martyred.

After Comrade Chiang Hsien-yün and the others arrived at Shui-k'ou-shan, they proceeded with the work of mobilizing and organizing the workers, taking groups of ten men to form teams in line with the experience at Anyüan. At that time the workers of Shui-k'ou-shan often sought out Chiang Hsien-yün and the others to discuss the situation and to ask questions. On one day several hundred people came. Chiang Hsien-yün took advantage of these opportunities to make speeches to the workers, telling them to strengthen their solidarity and to keep up the struggle against the forces of darkness. He spoke with great fervor and excitement and was extremely moving. Every word had a bearing on the workers' own personal interests. After the workers had finished listening, their enthusiasm for struggle soared to new heights.

In late October the Preparatory Bureau for the Shui-k'ou-shan Lead and Zinc Mines Workers' Club was founded. Comrade Chiang Hsien-yün was the chairman of the Bureau, and Comrade Liu Tung-hsüan was the vice chairman. After the founding of the Preparatory Bureau, work became more intense and went on all day and all night. Within ten short days, the preparations for the Workers' Club were basically completed. By this time representatives of ten, representatives of one hundred, and general representatives had been created from among the workers, and a workers' Disciplinary Team had been set up. The Workers' Club also printed up and sent out a large supply of propaganda material and feverishly prepared for the strike. Chiang Hsien-yün led everyone in the study of struggle countermeasures. At the same time, he established liaison with the Heng-yang Party organization; as soon as the strike began, Heng-yang would mobilize various forms of assistance.

After all the preparations had been properly made, the struggle broke out. Representing the workers, the Workers' Club presented twelve demands to the Bureau of Mines, demanding an increase in wages, improvement of living conditions, and the right to organize a union. Moreover, they made accusations against the bureaucratic-capitalists for oppressing and exploiting the workers. The Bureau of Mines at first paid no heed to this, and the Workers' Club immediately called the strike. The head of the Bureau of Mines, Chao Ming-ting, was so frightened that he ran off to Changsha.

After Chao Ming-ting had gone to Changsha, Chao Heng-t'i sent one of his regimental commanders and a staff officer under him to bring Chao Ming-ting back to Shui-k'ou-shan with plans to crack down on the workers with armed force. From the first Chao Heng-t'i's Third Mixed Brigade Independent Artillery Company had been occupying Shui-k'ou-shan and now the thought was to utilize this force to deal with the workers. But, owing to the leadership of Comrade Chiang Hsien-yün, the workers had some time before this already carried out work among the soldiers and officers of this company in a move to win them over. The workers and soldiers usually got along well anyway, and so during the strike not only did this company fail to help the mining authorities crack down on the workers, it maintained a sympathetic attitude toward them.

After the strike call of the Shui-k'ou-shan workers was issued, the telegrams of support from Changsha, Anyüan, T'ang-shan, Shanghai, Han-yeh-p'ing, and Heng-yang's Third Normal College were plastered all over the walls of the Club. Every new telegram received further stimulated the workers' will to struggle.

Chao Ming-ting and the others saw that the momentum was increasingly moving in the wrong direction and so had no alternative but to send someone to negotiate and calm down the situation. In line with the wishes of the workers and the conditions of the Anyüan workers' strike, the Workers' Club increased the number of demands to twenty-one. The main contents were: an increase in wages; implementation of an eight-hour work schedule; no wages withheld during leaves for marriages, deaths, or illness; disability insurance; no shifts on Sunday, Commemoration Day or New Year's Day; wages paid monthly; the freedoms of assembly, association, and speech for the workers; a children's school set up for the staff and workers; recognition of the legal status of the Workers' Club; etc. The worker-representatives also clearly stated that there was no room for any rewriting of these conditions. In the face of the immense power of the workers, the Mining Bureau had no alternative but to acknowledge each and every one of the demands. With this, the stirring and seething strike that the workers of Shui-k'ou-shan had maintained through the first half of November achieved thorough victory.

According to the recollection of an old Shui-k'ou-shan worker,[29] they took off the following day and held a celebration. The peasants from all around Shui-k'ou-shan came to take part — altogether there were over ten thousand people there. After the celebration a march was held, and the workers and farmers loudly shouted along the route: "Long Live the Victory of the Strike!" "Long Live the Workers and Peasants!" "Down with Corrupt Officials!" "Down with the Warlords!"

On the following day all the workers went to work and the Workers' Club published a back-to-work declaration. This mimeographed declaration of victory was kept and has been preserved to the present day. Here is the full text:

Victory! Victory! Now we can breathe, now we can save ourselves. We declare a return to work.

Before it was "The Workers Are Beasts of Burden," now it's "Long Live the

Workers!'"* But the price we extracted through this strike is only to be considered the first victory, the first step in the solution of our miserable lives. We
must go on and seek a second, a third...victory, take a second, a third...step in
dispelling the misery of our lives. [All] Fellow Workers! Let us work hard to
keep our organization — the Club — and we will never fear failure!

In this strike there were many areas in which the lieutenant and all his fellow
soldiers of the Independent Artillery Company of the Third Mixed Brigade as well
as the director of the hospital helped us. We also received assistance from all
circles. We respectfully express our deep and sincere gratitude to them!
Thank you!

Our strike has been victorious! Let us give three cheers:
Long Live the Workers!
Long Live the Workers' Club!
Long Live the Power of World Proletarian Solidarity!

A few of the most outstanding labor leaders, like Comrade Liu
Tung-hsüan, joined the Party after the strike. (In 1928 when Liu
Tung-hsüan was in charge of Party work in Ch'i-yang, he was ar-
rested and martyred.)

After the victory of the strike, there was a universal wage increase for general work, metal casting, work in the shafts, processing, and transport. In general, work followed the eight-hour
system. There was a marked change among the staff and the foremen in their attitude toward the workers. There was a very great
improvement in the material life of the workers, and they had political rights that they had never enjoyed before. The Club immediately set up a school, the building for which was paid for by the
mining authorities. They also gave a monthly sum of 200 yuan for
normal operating expenses. From Changsha Comrade Mao Tse-
tung sent a principal and teachers, among whom was Comrade
Mao Tse-t'an, [30] who was fresh out of the Preparatory Class at
Self-Study University.

Because the vast majority of Shui-k'ou-shan workers had come
from the countryside and had intimate links with the villages there,
after the victory of the great strike in 1922 they also gave impetus
to and organized the struggle of the Yüeh-pei Peasants' and Workers' Association [Nung-kung hui] in Heng-shan. At the beginning of
1923 the Party sent Comrades Liu Tung-hsüan and Hsieh Huai-te
to their hometowns in Yüeh-pei and Pai-kuo, both in Heng-shan, to
open up work among the peasants. There were a great many peas-

---

* Mao was to make use of exactly the same play on words five years later, with
reference to the peasants. See "Report on an Investigation of the Peasant Movement in Hunan," in Selected Works, I, p. 31 and note 10 to this passage [S.R.S.].

ants here who worked at Shui-k'ou-shan. When the peasants heard about the strike struggle at Shui-k'ou-shan and about the role played by the Club, they were all very excited. The Yüeh-pei Peasants' and Workers' Association (the addition of the word "workers" was to show the mutual bond between them and the organized workers at Shui-k'ou-shan) was soon founded. Very quickly the membership reached over one hundred thousand. Under the leadership of the Peasants' Association, seething struggles were launched for purposeful rice-buying to stabilize prices and prohibiting landlords from exporting rice and cotton, and struggles also began to be fomented for the lowering of rent and interest rates. Pai-kuo was Chao Heng-t'i's hometown. In the fall and winter of 1923 Chao had twice used arms in quelling the peasant movement, and in both cases bloody incidents had broken out. The Yüeh-pei Peasants' and Workers' Association was the earliest peasant union organization founded in Hunan and the earliest to wage a great struggle against the landlords there.

After the victory won by the Shui-k'ou-shan workers in 1922, the treatment of the workers improved on every front. This naturally had a deep influence on the income of the mining authorities and Chao Heng-t'i. Chao thus made up his mind to suppress the Shui-k'ou-shan labor movement. In December 1923 Chao sent Pin Pu-ch'eng, accompanied by a battalion of troops, to Shui-k'ou-shan to become bureau head. As soon as the troops arrived they occupied the Workers' Club. At the time, the workers were just in the midst of preparations for celebrating the anniversary of the victory. Provoked by the troops, the workers rose up and struggled, and one person was shot to death and several others wounded. All the workers then went on strike. With a repressive military force of one battalion behind him, Pin Pu-ch'eng closed down the Workers' Club, dismissed over one thousand workers, and forced Chiang Hsien-yün and other comrades to leave Shui-k'ou-shan. The Party organization went completely underground.

In 1924 the workers at Shui-k'ou-shan once again rose up in economic struggle but without result. Such was the situation until 1926 when the Party secretly sent Comrade Ch'en Ch'ang to Shui-k'ou-shan to revive the work. After the Northern Expeditionary Army had entered Hunan, Comrades Chiang Hsien-yün and Liu Tung-hsüan returned to Shui-k'ou-shan, and the Workers' Club was organized anew. Under the leadership of the Party, the flames of revolution at Shui-k'ou-shan reached their highest point after the Horse Day Incident; over ten thousand workers and neighboring peasants disarmed the mine police and proceeded to arm themselves with their weapons. Over three thousand workers and peasants descended the mountain and attacked the hsien capital of Ch'ang-ning. But because they lacked experience in military struggle, they were defeated. At the beginning of 1928 there were again over two hundred workers who twice disarmed the mine police, descended the mountain, and launched guerrilla warfare. These troops participated in the southern Hunan rebellion and became the foundation of the Independent Regiment of the Red Army's Fourth Army. It was precisely at this time, March 1928, that the local reactionary militia of the Kuomintang surrounded Shui-k'ou-shan and carried out a campaign of frenzied burning, looting, and slaughter. Close to two hundred workers were killed and over forty arrested.

Just like that of the Anyüan workers, the brave struggle of the Shui-k'ou-shan workers occupies a glorious page in the history of the Chinese labor movement from the very earliest time when Comrade Mao Tse-tung first led the Hunan labor movement to the early period of the Second Revolutionary Civil War.


## VII. A LESSON FOR "MR. LONG ROBES," WHO STOOD ON THE WORKERS' HEADS AND PICKED FAULT WITH THEM

In 1922 the highest monthly wage for any Changsha type-machinist or typesetter was 8 yuan; the lowest was only 4 yuan. These men worked on the average about eleven or twelve hours a day. It was particularly the typesetters, who primarily worked at night, who were in dire straits. Thus the print workers had been demanding an increase in wages and a shortening of the workday for quite some time.

Comrade Mao Tse-tung himself had once run a periodical and ordinarily had close contacts with the newspaper offices. He was thus most aware of the life the print workers led and had a thorough knowledge of their suffering. In the latter half of 1922, during the high tide of the Hunan labor strikes, Mao Tse-tung personally helped over three hundred print workers set up a Type-Machinists' and Typesetters' Union [Ch'ien-yin huo-pan kung-hui] and served for a time as union secretary.

On November 21, 1922, the Type-Machinists' and Typesetters' Union sent representatives to invite the proprietors of the various printing companies to negotiations, proposing an eight-hour workday for the type-machinists and typesetters, an increase in the wages of regular typesetters to 12 yuan a month, and the separate establishment of reasonable wage standards for various other workers and various kinds of contract work. The union specifically sent a very polished letter to the press, stating:

> The press presides over public discussion, has sympathy for labor, and has always been in hearty agreement with it. The fellow workers of our union hand-set the type for every paper; this is the small task we do for you. Our association is deep and our feelings naturally intimate. We have, as a matter of course, sent to you the demands this Union has raised before the various companies dealing with an increase in wages and improvement in treatment. We hope that your direction of the public discussion on this matter will lead to the speedy attainment of our reasonable demands. [31]

After the print workers of Chao Heng-t'i's official newspaper, the Hunan Daily [Hu-nan jih-pao], had raised their demands before the Secretariat of the Chao government, the government only agreed to increase the monthly wage by one yuan; the length of the workday would remain the same as before. When the other entrepreneurs saw the government act in this fashion they naturally followed suit. The workers were all very angered, and so decided to go out on strike. The union cadres went to find Comrade Mao Tse-tung, and he felt that they could strike. At the same time, he specifically urged them to complete full preparations, particularly for the feeding and lodging of the workers once the strike was on. This was the only way the strike could be maintained.

And so on November 25 the print workers declared their strike.

The day after the print workers went on strike not a paper could be seen in Changsha. This shocked society more than if several businesses had gone on strike.

According to the recollection of an old typesetter who participated in this struggle:

> At that time the heads of the bogus provincial government thought that work would only stop for two or three days and that we would be unable to keep up because of difficulties with food and shelter. Thus, in the beginning, they paid no attention. They never in their lives guessed that we were relying on Comrade Mao Tse-tung's far-seeing directives and had long ago prepared against this eventuality. There was no problem at all with the feeding and housing of the over three hundred print workers in the city. After the strike had been on for eight or nine days, when the bogus provincial government bosses saw that we had still not resumed work, they became frightened. They then proceeded to show their ferocious faces. On the one hand, they sent their lackeys, the military police, to

come and force us to resume work; on the other hand, they joined with the entrepreneurs of the various print shops to frighten and threaten us with the possibility
of sending materials to Hsiang-t'an for printing. At the time, some of the workers, afraid of the power of the bogus military police and also fearing that the "officials" and the entrepreneurs were really going to send things to Hsiang-t'an for
printing, broke their own rice bowls and began to waver. The Type-Machinists'
and Typesetters' Union quickly reported this situation to Comrade Mao Tse-tung.
He immediately told everyone: "To keep up the struggle is to win victory! If we
compromise midway, we can never again think of achieving victory. Although the
bogus military police are forcing us to resume work, all that is needed is for us
to maintain our effort and they won't be able to do anything. As for sending all
the material to Hsiang-t'an to be printed, this is, as a matter of fact, quite impossible; moreover, the workers in Hsiang-t'an would not accept it." Only after
this did those workers who were wavering regain their stability, and our strength
was firmer than before. [32]

The strike of the print workers continued for half a month, which
is another way of saying that the people of Changsha did not see
their local newspapers for half a month. All of society was mur-
muring complaints. The editing and publishing departments of the
various newspapers were pushing the proprietors of the various
printing companies very hard. But the proprietors of the printing
companies all took the provincial government's attitude as their
guide. The bigwigs in Chao Heng-t'i's yamen saw with their own
eyes that intimidation was not the way. No matter what, this no
newspaper situation could not go on, and for this reason there was
no choice but to ask the Type-Machinists' and Typesetters' Union
to send representatives for negotiations. As a result, the conditions
raised by the workers were fully accepted. The other printing companies naturally had to follow suit.

This print workers' strike was maintained for altogether seventeen days, and in the end it achieved a thorough victory. The workers were extremely happy and the prestige of the union was en-
hanced.

After the print workers returned to work on December 12, every
newspaper was published on the thirteenth as usual. At this time,
however, an incident occurred that was detrimental to the interests
of the workers.

Changsha's Ta-kung pao published a "current affairs review" article on December 13 entitled "Yin shua kung-jen pa-kung hou ti
chi-chü-hua" [A Few Words Following the Print Workers' Strike].
It was signed "Tun" and was written by the paper's editor-in-chief,
Li Pao-i. In his "current affairs review" the editor-in-chief first
"criticized": "We are not saying that this strike of the print workers

was without cause; we only feel that there was no necessity to strike." Following this he gave his great instructions to the workers. His attitude was extremely arrogant, and he fully exhibited the stinking, haughty behavior of a spokesman for the ruling class. He said: "I advise the print workers in the future to pay utmost attention to fundamental learning.... It is absolutely necessary to place heavy emphasis on learning so as not to be talked into anything by someone or become the victim of someone else's ideological experiments. Once you have a suitable store of learning, then and only then can you avoid various weaknesses." This old bigwig of an editor considered the weaknesses of the workers to be:
(1) "A lack of common sense." He considered the workers' demand for an earlier deadline in the handing in of copy a lack of common sense. (2) "They do not maintain order." He opined that "one must have learning before one can nourish and care for one's character, before one can carefully maintain order." He was very concerned that "in the future the workers will find it very difficult to avoid taking this victory for granted and will start raising a big clamor. The number of people is steadily increasing and they are becoming more and more heterogeneous. Although there might be numerous representatives acting as disciplinary personnel, I fear it will be impossible to maintain the victory." The third weakness of the workers was even more extraordinary: "They are ignorant of hygiene." This bigwig editor, using the example that students "also have a long working period every day," went on to claim that because the students "exercised, they are able to steel their bodies," and he followed this up by blaming the print workers for "getting sick from overwork" because they "had not engaged in any sports activities." Lastly, he had a "Labor Movement Theory" that was exactly the same as that of Chao Heng-t'i and Wu P'ei-fu: "I earnestly advise you workers — if you want the ability to be independent, you must not have any obvious weaknesses. If you want to be free from weaknesses, you must obtain suitable knowledge. Knowledge comes from learning, and so one must place great emphasis on learning. And how does one obtain learning? One must immediately enter a preparatory school and every day, come what may, one must squeeze out one or two hours to attend classes and to exercize." He further gave "earnest advice to those engaged in the labor movement." If one were not satisfied with the strike victory and the organization of a union, "the result can only promote the bad habit of workers clamoring and causing society to become more unsettled." This bigwig editor's conclusion was: "The only proper

course is to pay attention to the promotion of workers' education and [so] avoid the above-mentioned weaknesses."

The line of argument taken by the editor-in-chief of Changsha's Ta-kung pao was extremely popular among people of the middle and upper classes generally, and among those in educational and cultural circles. Sometimes these people waved the flag of "sympathy with labor," but when the workers began to get really active, when the labor movement was steadily developing, especially when their own personal interests were injured, their fox tail — their real face of hostility toward the labor movement — would immediately break out into the open. Normally, Comrade Mao Tse-tung maintained a certain contact with these people, and during the revolutionary movement and labor movement always won their assistance or neutrality as much as possible. He did not engage in direct face-to-face struggle against them when it was not necessary. But this "current affairs review" of Changsha's Ta-kung pao was no simple matter. This was not to be compared with the police station picking someone up and flogging him; it was not to be compared with Chao Heng-t'i publishing his "instructions." This was a "public statement" by a newspaper and journalist who ordinarily advertised themselves as "pleading for the life of the people." Particularly important was that Changsha's Ta-kung pao was at the time a paper that in a certain sense represented the local "spirit of the people." In the past during the rule of T'ang Hsiang-ming and Chang Ching-yao the paper had been oppressed many times because it had been fair-minded. It usually adopted an attitude of rather active support for the New Culture movement and mass patriotic movements. It also often published news of the current labor movement and sometimes even expressed a certain degree of sympathy for the workers. In the area of individual relations, ever since the May Fourth movement, Comrade Mao Tse-tung's relationship with the newspaper had been relatively close. Not only did he often write or introduce articles for the paper and help in arranging material, he sometimes also filled in for the reporters. He had also maintained a certain friendship with a good number of responsible people on the inside. The employees of this newspaper also knew that Mao Tse-tung was right in the midst of devoting his full efforts to work in the labor movement. Thus this "current affairs review," particularly the few sentences at the end, "earnest advice to those engaged in the labor movement," had been unquestionably published with a specific aim in mind. What was important was that this depraved argument calumniating the workers had a general representative character and had a definite impact on society. Thus, Comrade Mao Tse-tung thought a sharp exposure and rebuttal had to be given this "current affairs review" that had appeared in Changsha's Ta-kung pao, that was hostile to the labor movement, and that had tried to assume the attitude of a preacher. Mao believed that this high-class intellectual who "wore the long robe"* and arrogantly stood on the workers' heads pointing out their faults, and who in reality spoke for the ruling class, had to be taught an earnest and severe lesson.

On the very next day, December 14, 1922, the Changsha Ta-kung pao had no choice but to box its own ears and publish an article penned by Comrade Mao Tse-tung entitled "Ch'ien-yin huo-pan kung-hui chih 'Ta-kung pao' chi-che hsun-shu" [A Letter to Ta-kung pao's Journalist Tun from the Type-Machinists' and Type-setters' Union].

The letter first pointed out that this journalist was "putting on a long robe and warning us workers." Following this it said: the workers, peasants, and students in society seem to be "those instructed by people nowadays," while "the gentlemen from the long robe society" were "instructing people" with "great knowledgeism and great studyism." Since both sides were interested in protecting their own interests, the workers and peasants could not help but protect themselves by "showing what they can do." The letter said very politely and solemnly: The workers and peasants are not at all unwilling to be instructed by other people; it was only that in "instructing people" the following three points should be followed:

1) We wish that the people who instruct us could stand on our level and instruct us, be able not to act as our superintendent but to come down and be our friends. They should never again open their mouths and say "you workers," "lack of common sense," "not maintain order," "becoming more and more depraved," "we are giving faithful counsel to you workers," "you are promoting the workers' bad habit." They should be saying: "All of us...." That would be fine! Sir, can you really and sincerely help us and give us faithful counsel? Well then, we very much would like to clasp hands with you, and we ask you to stick out your hand quickly. Let there be no more "you" or "we." It seems somehow that "we" means "the officials" and that "you" means the "little people who should drop dead."

2) We wish that the people who instruct us would be able to investigate the facts clearly and not secretly injure us. Even less should they despise people's character. For example, if we say that your honorable newspaper receives so many pieces of gold from some private individual every month, can you admit it? We ask you moreover: you said "not again (the word 'again' was struck out by our fellow-workers when they were setting the type) be pushed into anything by some-

---

* The traditional dress for the gentry-literati. — Tr.

one, not be the victims of somebody else's ideological experiments" — what have you, sir, actually ever seen to justify saying such a thing? What kind of evidence do you have, after all, that justifies saying such a thing? We beg you to hurry up and give us an early response. We wish even more that the newspaper reporters would stick to the facts a little more when they speak. . . .

3) We wish that the people who instruct us would be able to lower their bearing and really and truly instruct us. It is quite correct that what we workers need is knowledge. We workers are very desirous of having educated people come forward and be our true friends. You, sir, say that we are being pushed into things by someone, that we are someone's victims and you "pity" us. Then you should be our real and true guide. We wish very much that you could take off your long robes, resign from your position as great editor, and help us in the labor movement. At the least, you should be a true labor educator and never again stand on the sidelines as a spectator saying such things as "I thus further give faithful counsel to those engaged in the labor movement, you . . . ! " Sir, we only acknowledge as good friends those who are able to sacrifice their own positions and endure hunger and hardship to work for the interests of the great mass of us workers. Can you, sir, honor us by your visit? Please, quickly take off your long robes!

**Finally, with regard to the question of what methods the workers had to use to obtain the opportunity to study and exercise, the letter read:**

We won't talk right now about the problem of night work. We ask you, though, where is the time for the workers to attend preparatory school? Do you mean to say that they know how to be in two places at once? Moreover, how many preparatory schools are there in the city of Changsha? How many workers are there in the city of Changsha? We ask you to make a detailed investigation of this and then we'll talk about it. We admit now that unless we shorten our working hours we will be unable to have an opportunity to study; unless we unite ourselves and establish our own preparatory schools we will be unable to have a place to study. We want to shorten the working hours, and the boss pays no attention; we want to unite, and other people undermine us. Thus we must have a movement; there is nothing else we can do. We want to support study, which is in our interest, and other people tell us that we shouldn't; we want to invite people to come and guide us and be our true friends and teachers, and other people say this is "being pushed by people into doing things," "being someone else's victim," and further that we engage in "ideological experiments." Fine, so then we invite those people who were doing all the talking — and they want to wear their long robes and cannot come. Sir, please come and help us think up a better approach to acquiring some knowledge! So that we won't have to be instructed by people forever!

As for working at night, you say that as far as the principles of health are concerned, there is no problem. Correct! People who edit the paper work at night. Officials, politicians, and senators also all work at night. Why are you nice and fat? We work not only at night, we also work in the day. We can't sleep until afternoon, and we don't have meat to eat. The health of laborers is often impaired because of deficiencies in nutrition or because of overwork. The way to save the situation, on the workers' side, is simply to sleep and rest; do you know that? If you want us manual laborers to do one, two, or three hours of exercise and sporting activity after we have exhausted our strength, aren't you really asking for our lives? These two problems that you raise — night work and exercise — cannot be answered in just a few words. We won't go into it fully right now but we give this advice: you have really been reading too many books! We would like to invite you to come and have a taste of working together with us.

The struggle of the Type-Machinists' and Typesetters' Union against the editor-in-chief of the Changsha Ta-kung pao that was led by Comrade Mao Tse-tung was a very good class education for the broad working masses, especially for the Party cadres and revolutionary intellectuals. From the very beginning of his revolutionary activities, Comrade Mao Tse-tung grasped with genius the fundamental Marxist method of class analysis. Already as early as 1922 in this struggle against Tun, the journalist for Changsha's Ta-kung pao, Mao perceived and understood the tendency of middle class people and their spokesmen to run toward the right; hence in the New Democratic [phase of the] revolutionary movement, he adopted this correct policy with regard to their two-faced nature: a policy of uniting with [the national bourgeoisie] insofar as it "tended to side with the revolution and a policy of criticizing it insofar as it vacillated and was prone to compromise. This policy of criticism was another form of struggle." [33]

Later, in his article "Analysis of the Classes in Chinese Society," Comrade Mao Tse-tung said:

The present world situation is such that the two major forces, revolution and counterrevolution, are locked in final struggle.... The intermediate classes are bound to disintegrate quickly, some sections turning left to join the revolution, others turning right to join the counterrevolution; there is no room for them to remain "independent." [34]

With the gradually strengthening reactionary rule of Chao Heng-t'i and the vigorous development of revolutionary strength, a great number of the representative elements in intellectual circles who originally exhibited a certain revolutionary character during the movement to Expel Chang Ching-yao, those top figures from educational and press circles and from society at large, gradually fell into the arms of Chao Heng-t'i. At the beginning of 1927 when the Hunan labor and peasant movement was entering its highest tide, a bigger and deeper split occurred within the Hunan middle class. Blocs like Changsha's Ta-kung pao joined the counterrevolutionary organization organized by the leader of the Kuomintang right wing, Liu Yüeh-chih, called the "Leftist Society" [Tso she], and became thoroughly counterrevolutionary propaganda organs.

## VIII. THE STRIKE OF THE CHANGSHA TRADE WORKERS

Changsha was a city of commerce and handicraft industry. There were a hundred or so handicraft and manual trades in the city. Aside from the longshoremen, the most numerous workers were the masons and carpenters, rickshaw men, and textile workers. The other trades had at most several hundred, or several dozen workers. Thus, Comrade Mao Tse-tung and his comrades-in-arms expended a great deal of effort in carrying out continuous work among these handicraft workers.

Hitherto, the Chinese handicraftsmen had a kind of feudal, superstitious guild organization. (For example, the masons and carpenters worshiped Lu Pan and the tailors worshiped the Yellow Emperor.) The workers, apprentices, and the owners of every business were all mixed together in this guild organization; hence power within the guild was naturally in the hands of the owners and the feudal gang bosses (the "one-year managers") who represented the interests of the owners. The guilds had a great many strict feudal regulations that were used to exploit the workers and the apprentices on the inside, and on the outside, to safeguard the monopoly of the guild. Every year on the god's birthday, the workers were all required to enter the temple, burn incense, and kowtow. Thus, the superstitious belief in the power of the god together with the guild consciousness tightly bound the handicraftsmen like two big locks and chains. From time to time the workers had waged struggles over wage increases, etc. For example, from 1916 to 1918 the masons and carpenters, the dye workers, the sawers, the longshoremen, and the incense and writing brush workers in Changsha had all staged spontaneous strikes for an increase in wages, but in the end they were never able to escape the mediation of the guild.

For this reason, to organize the handicraftsmen whose hands were tied by the feudal guild and to wage a struggle for their collective interest was a very difficult business.

In 1921 Comrade Mao Tse-tung began activities among the Changsha handicraftsmen. He personally went to acquaint himself with the situation, sought workers with whom to talk, set up a night school, and did a great deal of propaganda education and organizational work. For example, Mao Tse-tung became a teacher in the rickshaw workers' night school. The workers were all very close to him and showed great respect for him. At the same time, Mao sent a group of cadres to the various important businesses to help the workers organize unions and to lead the strike struggle. For example, he sent Comrade Ch'en Tzu-po to lead the strike of the textile workers, and he sent Comrade Chang Han-fan to lead the strike of the tailors. After Comrade Lo Hsüeh-tsan had returned home from France he was sent to work among the rickshaw workers. Thus, the workers from the various handicraft industries were able to incite a stirring and seething struggle and achieve victory.

In connection with this situation, Teng Chung-hsia has written the following in his Chung-kuo chih-kung yün-tung chien shih [A Short History of the Chinese Trade Union Movement]: "The latter half of 1922 was the most active period of the Hunan strike tide. Almost the entire body of handicraftsmen and coolies went out on strike; moreover, this was an allied strike that united all the small workshops and stores in the entire city. The strikes were generally successful." 35

The central problem for the broad masses of handicraftsmen at the time was that their real wages had dropped by more than half, and it was difficult to earn a living that could support even one person. This had come about because the copper yuan had dropped in value (it had sunk more than 50 percent in its silver exchange rate compared with five or six years before) and commodity prices had risen, while at the same time wages were still paid according to the old number of copper yuan. Furthermore, these wages were generally paid out in "bird money," whose comparative value was steadily decreasing. There were some businesses whose working hours were excessively long and where the workers suffered horribly. After the workers gradually gained awareness, they actively demanded an increase in wages (with a change to calculation according to the current silver dollar) and better treatment.

From 1922 to 1923 the most influential and most powerful of all the strikes by the handicraftsmen and manual workers was that by the masons and carpenters discussed above. In addition to this there were the following:

1. The barbers. In the fall of 1921 the barbers had begun a struggle for the freedom to do business, an increase in wages, and an equal distribution of the public capital between them and the proprietors. The struggle was maintained for more than a year. The public capital had originally been formed by the barbers, who amassed the capital; beginning in 1909 it fell into the hands of the proprietors. On October 9, 1922, over five hundred barbers from the city of Changsha staged a massive strike, waging a brave and tenacious struggle against the feudal, barbaric proprietors and

their supporters — the Changsha hsien office and the Police Bureau. The strike was kept up for more than twenty days and finally, under the influence of the strike of the masons and carpenters, a solution was obtained: The New Shop of Seven Families [Ch'i chia hsin tien], a joint enterprise of the barbers which had been closed down by the Changsha hsien office, reopened by itself and obtained the freedom to regulate its own business; the barbershop proprietors also had to change wages from a thirty-seventy split to a forty-sixty split (the workers getting forty percent and the proprietors sixty).

2. The tailors and seamsters. The workers in Changsha's ready-made clothing shops staged their very first strike in June 1922 and achieved victory, their wages being increased to 28 cents a day. The six hundred and fifty workers in the made-to-order clothing shops (where wages were computed on a piece-work basis, different from the tailors of the ready-made clothing shops, who were generally paid on the basis of monthly work) struck from September 29 to October 3 of the same year and won the victory to have their wages paid in silver money.

3. The textile workers. Beginning on August 23, 1922, a strike began among over one thousand workers scattered throughout more than one hundred and ten small and large plants. With an unyielding struggle they broke the stiff resistance of the fifty-two factory "alliance," struck for thirteen days, and achieved victory. All wages were to be calculated on the basis of the silver dollar.

4. The writing brush workers. On November 14, 1922, the Changsha writing brush workers staged a general strike, making demands for an increase in salary, making it illegal to fire workers without authority, and four other items. The strike was maintained for forty days. There was finally a split within the ranks of the proprietors, and negotiations with the union were held; the workers' demands were met on December 23, when an agreement was signed.

5. The rickshaw workers. The life of the Changsha rickshaw workers was particularly miserable. This was because the rickshaw proprietors often raised the rent on the rickshaws and because military requisitions were excessive. Comrade Mao Tse-tung personally taught in the rickshaw workers' night school and also sent Comrade Lo Hsüeh-tsan to lead the work. Hence on October 8, 1922, the hard-to-organize rickshaw workers formally founded the Changsha Rickshaw Union [Ch'ang-sha jen-li-ch'e kung-hui]. The development of the labor movement at the time made the rickshaw workers feel deeply that organization had to be tightly unified before one could do anything. In March 1923 the proprietors once

more raised the rickshaw rent. If the workers were to hand over the rickshaw rent every day, they would be unable to maintain themselves. In a move to demand a decrease in the rickshaw rent, the workers launched a strike and petition. Under the leadership of Comrade Kuo Liang, general secretary of the United Association of Labor Organizations, and Comrade Lo Hsüeh-tsan, they won an initial victory. In August 1923 the battle between T'an Yen-k'ai and Chao Heng-t'i turned the vicinity of Changsha into a battlefield, and the rickshaw men were forced to abandon their profession to serve the military; they had nothing to rely on for a livelihood and their lives were insecure. Kuo Liang and Lo Hsüeh-tsan led the Rickshaw Union to petition the government, and in the face of the just and brave demands of the union, the Police Department was forced to issue a proclamation stating that thereafter there would no longer be any military requisition. Subsequently, the Association of Richshaw Companies [Ch'e kung hui] (the organization of the rickshaw proprietors) had no choice but to eliminate part of the rent for the carts.

6. The pottery workers of T'ung-kuan. In December 1922 the Changsha hsien office sent an official to T'ung-kuan (some sixty li from Changsha) to raise the pottery tax and also to close down the Potters' Inn, which the workers had set up themselves. Because they wanted to live, the workers furiously protested this regulation. They selected and sent a representative to Changsha to ask Comrade Kuo Liang to come and lead this struggle of protest against the increase in the tax and against the illegal closing down of the Potters' Inn. Kuo Liang came to T'ung-kuan and pointed out that the action of the Changsha hsien office violated the "provincial constitution." The struggle was launched in conformity with the "provincial constitution" and was utterly justified. Comrade Kuo Liang then led the workers in preparing for the organization of a union. On the one hand, a petition was sent to the Changsha hsien office requesting that the regulation increasing the tax be rescinded. This petition was drafted by Comrade Mao Tse-tung, and it made full use of the articles in the "provincial constitution." This came on the heels of the strike victory of the Changsha masons and carpenters and the strike victories of the various Changsha businesses; the hsien magistrate, Chou Ying-kan, was still a nervous wreck and could only write on the petition: "To encourage self-regulation, we give our permission," and he revoked the regulation that had increased the tax. The pottery workers of T'ung-kuan were victorious.

The Changsha workers from all the various trades had organized in the midst of stirring and seething strike struggles. Some unions had first organized and then struck; some struck first and then organized; some struck and organized at the same time. Because of the correct leadership of the Party and of Comrade Mao Tse-tung, and because there was strong organization, the workers' awareness rose very quickly and the strike and struggle of every trade was courageous and determined. To express their determination to struggle, when they first began to strike, the barbers decided: if incidents of arrest or death occur during the strike, the entire body of workers will take on the responsibility of giving relief to the injured party and will demand an indemnity from the proprietors. During the strike the cruel and fanatic proprietors beat the leaders of the Disciplinary Team on the head with big iron hammers and afterward continued to beat separately three other Team members one by one. The hsien office seized people on every side, forcing the workers to begin work. There were two Disciplinary Team members who were held for four days after they had been beaten. These acts of oppression increased the workers' anger and their determination to struggle. The protest letter sent by the barbers to the Changsha hsien office stated: "We are extremely angered and indignant over this malicious action; the more you beat people the more you consolidate our unity." In plenary session they unanimously decided: "We would rather starve to death than start work." To maintain the struggle during their strike, the textile workers had sent out ten representatives to preside over the strike work. The great majority of the remaining workers scattered throughout the countryside to harvest rice or find some other work, determined to hold on until the end. These are all examples of the brave and resolute struggles that were being waged at the time.

During the stirring and seething struggles not only did the workers of the various trades in Changsha organize on their own accord, but also, under the unified leadership of the Party (later under the unified leadership of the United Association of Labor Organizations) they brought into full play a fraternal class affection. "Proletariat of the world, unite" became their most popular slogan. The strikes of the various trades were mutually supportive. For example, when the tailors went out on strike, the workers of all the businesses in Changsha sent a profusion of letters of support. Warning the tailor shop proprietors, the masons and carpenters said: "You should understand a little better that times have changed. The solidarity of the workers' organizations is much firmer. You can apply any kind of pressure or intimidation you want. Unless the tailors get their increase in wages, it's no go! We venture to counsel you to acknowledge their demands...." [36] After the victory of the T'ung-kuan pottery workers' protest over the tax increase, more than three thousand pottery workers formally founded a union. Unions from various places in Hunan, such as Shui-k'ou-shan and Anyüan, and the Changsha unions at the mint, the cotton mill, of the rickshaw workers, and of the masons and carpenters, all sent representatives to participate in this huge assembly. On this day there were more than twenty bands composed solely of workers, and there were three hundred gongs. This huge assembly was a stirring review of the great unity of the Hunan workers.

Because during the strikes the workers of the various businesses in Changsha received continuous training, their organization was strengthened, and their awareness was raised, the Party developed some Party members here. Some trades established Party organizations. For example, at the beginning of 1923 T'ung-kuan established a branch of the Party and the Corps. Because Party leadership was strong here right up to the First Revolutionary Civil War, the T'ung-kuan Potters' Union [T'ung-kuan t'ao-yeh kung-hui] was one of Hunan's most famous labor organizations. It enjoyed a good reputation and trained a great number of outstanding labor cadres. Later, during the long period of white terror rule under the Kuomintang, the T'ung-kuan Party organization was not wiped out. On the eve of the War of Resistance against Japan, T'ung-kuan was the only place doing work in the Hunan white area that still preserved a Special Committee organization.

## IX. THE FOUNDING OF THE ALL-HUNAN UNITED ASSOCIATION OF LABOR ORGANIZATIONS. ARGUING FACE TO FACE WITH CHAO HENG-T'I

Under the direct leadership of Comrade Mao Tse-tung, the Hunan, and especially the Changsha, labor movement reached a high tide in the latter half of 1922. By October, fourteen unions had been formally established throughout the province: the Anyüan Railway and Mines Workers' Club, the Shui-k'ou-shan Lead and Zinc Mines Workers' Club, the Canton-Hankow Railway's Yüeh-chou Workers' Club and Changsha Workers' Club, as well as the Changsha Masons' and Carpenters' Union, Machinists' Union [Chi-hsieh kung-hui], Rickshaw Union, Type-Machinists' and Typesetters' Union, Lithographers' Union [Shih-yin kung-hui], Barbers' Union, Tailors' Union, Writing Brush Union, Textile Workers' Union, and Shoe-makers' Union [Hsüeh-hsieh chi-shih kung-hui], with a total number of some forty thousand organized workers. Aside from the Shoe-makers' Union, all the workers who were organized had experienced severe strike struggles and had won victories. A group of outstanding labor cadres had been nurtured during the process of the strike struggles and a great number of labor activists had burst upon the scene. Party members were developed in a great many of these unions. Except for a small number of unions, such as those at Anyüan, the Canton-Hankow Railway, Shui-k'ou-shan, and the Rickshaw Union, where the Party had sent cadres who were still shouldering the primary responsibilities, there were some unions with responsible people who were already new Party members, having been developed from among the workers. Hence the organ that had originally led the Hunan labor movement — the Trade Union Secretariat, Hunan Branch — was completely incapable of corresponding to this new situation. By this time Wuhan had already founded a centralized organization for the workers: The Wu-han United Association of Labor Organizations (this was the first regional centralized labor organization in the country).

Comrade Mao Tse-tung actively planned the founding of an all-Hunan centralized labor organization to facilitate the centralized leadership of the Hunan labor movement and to launch this movement on a wider scale.

On November 1 the Canton-Hankow Railway General Labor Union [Yüeh-Han t'ieh-lu tsung kung-hui] held its inaugural meeting at Changsha's Hsin-ho Main Station. This meeting was personally chaired by Comrade Mao Tse-tung. Every labor union in the province sent delegates to participate. After the inaugural meeting of the Canton-Hankow Railway General Labor Union was opened, the labor delegates from the Chu-chou-P'ing-hsiang Railway proposed the founding of an All-Province United Association of Labor Organizations, and the representatives of the various unions were unanimous in their approval of this idea. And so an All-Hunan United Association of Labor Organizations Representative Assembly was then called. On that day representatives from the Canton-Hankow Railway General Labor Union, the Canton-Hankow Railway's Yüeh-chou and Changsha unions, the Anyüan Railway and Mines Workers' Club, and from Changsha's Masons' and Carpenters' Union, Barbers' Union, Rickshaw Union, Tailors' Union, and Writing Brush Union, all participated. Comrade Mao Tse-tung attended the meeting

as a representative of the Canton-Hankow Railway General Labor
Union. Other representatives who participated were Kuo Liang,
Chu Shao-lien, Jen Shu-te, Chang Han-fan, and other comrades.
Mao Tse-tung was chosen chairman of the assembly. The assembly formally proclaimed the founding of the All-Hunan United Association of Labor Organizations [Hu-nan ch'üan-sheng kung-t'uan
lien-ho-hui] and also decided that "all production unions and professional unions (Note: this referred to such manual workers'
unions as those of the tailors, textile workers, barbers, etc.) are
qualified to join this United Association."

After the conference Comrade Mao Tse-tung drafted the abridged
bylaws of the All-Hunan United Association of Labor Organizations.
At the second representative assembly of the various labor unions
held on November 5, Mao Tse-tung was elected the general secretary [cheng tsung-kan-shih] of the All-Hunan United Association of
Labor Organizations Directorate. Comrade Kuo Liang was the vice-
general secretary, and Comrades Jen Shu-te, Lo Hsüeh-tsan, Chu
Shao-lien, and Chu Chin-t'ang were directors and vice directors of
the various departments. At the same time, a declaration was published that informed the whole nation: the centralized organization
of all workers throughout the province of Hunan — the All-Hunan
Association of Labor Organizations — has been founded. Workers
throughout the province held celebrations on behalf of this event.
This was the second regional centralized labor organization of the
time.

The address of the United Association of Labor Organizations
was set up at 8 Pao-nan Street (across from the present Changsha
Municipal School of Government; the original building has been demolished). This was an ordinary private house of one story, three
rooms wide. The middle room was rather large and could be made
to serve for meetings. Across, but not directly opposite, was Lu
Pan Temple — the address of the Masons' and Carpenters' Union.

From this time forward the Hunan labor movement had its own
open General Headquarters. The workers all felt that there was
something to rely on right behind them. Whenever an important
problem had to be solved, they would say: "Go get the United Association of Labor Organizations," "Follow the orders of the United
Association of Labor Organizations." When the workers of the writing brush industry, the rickshaw men, or the print workers would
stage a strike and clash with the Police Department or with the entrepreneurs, or if they would come under intimidation or be ordered to return to work, they would always justly and bravely answer

their opponents: "We only take orders from the United Association of Labor Organizations!"

In the spring of 1923 the Hunan labor movement continued to surge forward. Workers' clubs were founded one after the other in the big factories that contained one or two thousand workers — the Changsha mint, graphite refining plant, and No. 1 Cotton Mill. By April and May newly organized unions in Changsha included the Teahouse Workers' Union [Ch'a-chü kung-hui] (i.e., those who worked in the teahouses), the Electric Light Union [Tien-teng kung-hui], the Garbagemen's Union [Fen ma-t'ou kung-hui], the Longshoremen's Union [Lo ma-t'ou kung-hui] (i.e., the transport workers), the Sales Clerk's Union [Tien-yüan kung-hui], the Paint-ers' Union [Yu-ch'i-chiang kung-hui], the Coppersmith Union [T'ung-chiang kung-hui], the Boatmen's Union [Hua-fu kung-hui], the Postal Union [Yu-wu kung-hui], the Grain Huskers' Union [Nien-ku kung-hui], the Watermen's Union [Shui-fu kung-hui] (people who carried river water and sold it), and the Foreign Union [Yang-wu kung-hui] (staff and employees in foreign businesses). Unions were also founded at the Hsin-hua Tin Mine and the Hsiang-t'an Manganese Mine. The number of unions that had joined the United Association of Labor Organizations by this time already reached more than thirty.

When the Peking-Hankow Railway's February 7 tragedy occurred, the United Association of Labor Organizations called upon the Hu-nan working class to rise up and lend assistance. It issued declara-tions, solicited contributions, held memorial meetings, exhibited the bloody clothes of those who had died, and also staged a huge demonstration and march of twenty thousand people in protest against the brutality of Wu P'ei-fu.

The All-Hunan United Association of Labor Organizations headed by Comrade Mao Tse-tung was the battle command headquarters of Hunan's broad working masses that had been established by them after a brave, victorious struggle, and its high repute in leadership was deeply implanted in the heart of every worker. The United As-sociation of Labor Organizations was struggle, it was victory, it was the unyielding solidarity of the working class, it was the wise and correct leadership of the Communist Party and of Comrade Mao Tse-tung.

During the May Fourth period the banner of the Hunan revolution-ary movement was the Hunan United Association of Students under the actual leadership of Mao Tse-tung. After 1922 and right down to the eve of the Northern Expeditionary Army's entry into Chang-sha in 1926, it was the All-Hunan United Association of Labor Or-

262

ganizations that, with unprecedented might, raised high the flag of the Hunan mass revolutionary movement. During this time all the mass revolutionary organizations throughout the province united around the United Association of Labor Organizations, which was under the direct leadership of Mao Tse-tung. Although legal status for the United Association of Labor Organizations had never been granted by the Chao Heng-t'i government, it had very great prestige among the masses and was, de facto, a legal organization all along. Although Chao Heng-t'i later dared to close down Self-Study University, he never openly closed down the United Association of Labor Organizations.

After Comrade Mao Tse-tung left Hunan in April 1923, Comrade Kuo Liang succeeded him as general secretary. After the Northern Expeditionary Army entered Changsha, the All-Hunan United Association of Labor Organizations changed its name to the All-Hunan General Labor Union [Ch'üan-sheng tsung-kung-hui] with Kuo Liang succeeding to the post of Committee chairman.

The first important matter of business that came up after the founding of the All-Hunan United Association of Labor Organizations, the first great struggle, was the acute face-to-face confrontation between, on the one side, twenty-three representatives of eleven labor organizations belonging to the United Association of Labor Organizations who were personally led by Comrade Mao Tse-tung and, on the other side, the Chao Heng-t'i government and Chao Heng-t'i himself. This took place during the three days of December 11, 12, and 13, 1922.

During the surging high tide of labor strikes, the Chao Heng-t'i government (from the Changsha Hsien Police Department and Internal Affairs Bureau to the Provincial Governor's Office and the Provincial Assembly) was thrown into great disorder and confusion trying to cope with the situation, and it was on the defensive everywhere. Before one swell had subsided another one rose up. One day one union sent up a petition and the following day another came to petition. If the government used the soft line approach, the workers didn't fall for it. If it used the hard line approach, they would hold on even tighter and could not be made to quit the scene. Once, the Provincial Assembly was convened, and when the discussion got around to the problem of strikes, one assemblyman accurately reflected the anxiety of the Chao Heng-t'i government. He said: "There is not five minutes of peace and quiet today in Hunan society. From now on I'm afraid there'll be no more quiet and peaceful days ever again!"

Ever since the victory of the masons' and carpenters' strike struggle, the Chao Heng-t'i government had been gradually making inquiries to find out about this affair of Comrade Mao Tse-tung and the group of intellectual "extremists" who were leading the labor movement. Comrade Mao Tse-tung's name loomed particularly large in this investigation.

Therefore Chao Heng-t'i actively tried to crack down on the workers' strike movement and deal with this group of "extremists" of student origin.

In November and December 1922, during the high tide of the labor strikes of the Changsha rickshaw men, print workers, and writing brush workers, the Chao Heng-t'i government spread many rumors. The gist of these calumniatory rumors was that there was a group of specialists in waging strike movements, and they were an "extremist faction" hired by other people; if the government killed somebody the strikers would pay a 500-yuan pension, which money came from outside; the strikers were all promoting anarchism, they wanted to overthrow the present government. In addition, the government let the word go around that it would adopt severe repressive measures against the workers in order to intimidate the working masses.

At this time new problems continually arose. For example, Changsha's Western District Police Office suddenly took down the association placard of the Rickshaw Union; Changsha hsien prepared to close down again the New Shop of the Seven Families opened by the barbers; there was a clash between the student wing (originally students of First and Ch'u-i Industrial Schools) of the Machinists' Union and the workers and apprentices; there was a clash between the feudal gang bosses of the old Tailors' Union (the Office of the Yellow Emperor) and the workers; the strike of the writing brush workers had still not been terminated, etc.

The working masses were extremely angered and upset about these rumors and new provocations. But there was a small number of backward elements who began to waver, fearing the outbreak of a new incident like that of Huang Ai and P'ang Jen-ch'üan, and although the United Association of Labor Organizations had already launched activities on a wide scale, Chao Heng-t'i had not yet formally permitted it to register and acquire legal status. In order to clarify the thinking of the masses and to encourage further the fighting will of the workers, Comrade Mao Tse-tung, after some thought, felt that he had to struggle hard and take the initiative, that there had to be a face-to-face confrontation with the Chao Heng-t'i government and with Chao Heng-t'i himself. The Party convened a meeting of the primary cadres who had responsibility in the labor movement. They all felt that the situation was very urgent, that there should be no more procrastinating. The method decided on was to send out representatives from the United Association of Labor Organizations and the various labor unions to formally seek out the Changsha hsien magistrate, the head of the Police Department, the head of the Administration Department, and Chao Heng-t'i himself for talks. The struggle method would be to "attack his shield with his own sword," to clutch Chao Heng-t'i's "provincial constitution" in their hands and move in for the attack. The objective of the talks was to make it impossible for Chao Heng-t'i to do anything but publicly reiterate his own "assent" to the important questions concerning the attitude toward the treatment of workers and the freedoms of assembly and association. Moreover, advantage would be taken of the situation to settle some concrete, controversial matters.

And so Comrade Mao Tse-tung, in his capacity as general secretary of the United Association of Labor Organizations, headed a delegation of twenty-three people representing the various labor unions, which included Kuo Liang, Jen Shu-te, Lo Hsüeh-tsan, Chang Han-fan, Ch'ou Shou-sung, and other comrades and on December 11, 1922, staged a great meeting with the hsien magistrate, Chou Ying-kan, and chief of the Police Department, Shih Ch'eng-chin; on the twelfth he met with the head of the Administration Department, Wu Ching-hung, and on the thirteenth with Chao Heng-t'i himself.

On December 13 and 14 the Changsha press published the news of the meeting. The news was all rather sketchy and was not always accurate. For this reason, the All-Hunan United Association of Labor Organizations made a written report of the proceedings of the three-day bilateral talks. On December 15 the Changsha press published the Association's statement, which was entitled: "The True Picture of the Negotiations between the Representatives of the Various Labor Organizations and Governor Chao, Administration Head Wu, Police Chief Shih, and Changsha Hsien Magistrate Chou." Society thus became aware of the real facts surrounding this affair, and this played a definite role in the development of the labor movement.

After explaining the object of participating in these talks and what transpired in their course, the statement pointed out that

# Early Revolutionary Activities of Mao Tse-tung

the items in the negotiations fell roughly into ten categories: (1) A request that the government express its attitude toward working circles. (2) The question of the freedoms of assembly and association. (3) A clear expression of the attitude of working circles. (4) Working circles and the government should regularly get together to avoid misunderstandings. (5) A proposal for the setting up of a joint labor-management tribunal. (6) The question of the Rickshaw Union. (7) The question of the Barbers' Union. (8) The question of the Writing Brush Union. (9) The question of the Machinists' Union. (10) The question of the Tailors' Union.

(The material quoted below is from the original text of the statement.)

With regard to the first item, under the intense face-to-face questioning of Comrade Mao Tse-tung, Chao Heng-t'i, Wu Ching-hung, Shih Ch'eng-chin, and Chou Ying-kan had no choice but to make the following affirmation:

The government adopts a policy of complete protection toward the workers and has no intention of suppressing them. In the numerous strikes that have occurred recently there has been no government intervention, which fact is proof of its position. Governor Chao and Administration Head Wu further state that although the government has heard of a great many things, such as a general allied strike, it has considered these unfounded rumor and has never employed any suppressive measures.

Chao Heng-t'i also brought up the incident of Huang Ai and P'ang Jen-ch'üan and still baselessly described this piece of cruel brutality as "unavoidable." He charged Huang and P'ang with the fabricated crime of "buying rifles and being in league with local bandits" and slyly went on to say that this was directed against Huang and P'ang,* not labor circles. Comrade Mao Tse-tung immediately retorted:

What you say about Huang and P'ang buying rifles and being in league with local bandits as well as their instigating the strike at the mint is all false. There were a couple of people killed on the workers' side and a couple of unions that were closed down; this was certainly damaging. But they did not stop their necessary activities because of this.

---

* Interviewed in June 1963, Chao Heng-t'i recalled with considerable glee, "I killed a couple of fellows called Huang and P'ang." (Wo sha-tiao i-ko hsing Huang, i-ko hsing P'ang.) Evoking his face-to-face encounters with Mao Tse-tung in the early 1920s (which he naturally depicted in a light rather more favorable to himself), he added: "People often ask me why I didn't kill Mao too, when I had him in my power." "Well," I inquired, "why didn't you?" Chao smiled a quizzical smile as he produced his punch line: "I didn't know he was going to turn out to be so formidable." (Wo pu shao-te t'a hui pien-ch'eng na-mo li-hai.) [S.R.S.].

266

# The Early Labor Movement in Hunan

With respect to the question of assembly and association, Comrade Mao Tse-tung took up Chao Heng-t'i's "provincial constitution" and pointed to the articles, saying:

With respect to association, the officials have often refused permission, always saying that people must first register before they can form a society. They are unaware of Article XII of the "provincial constitution": "The right of the people to associate freely and assemble peacefully without arms, insofar as this does not conflict with the criminal code, shall not be restricted by any special ordinance." There is no regulation whatsoever stipulating that people must get the approval of the officials before they associate. If it is necessary to get approval before people can associate, then the officials can have great freedom in granting sanction, the "provincial constitution" can be very freely interpreted, and Article XII of the "provincial constitution" has been thoroughly rescinded.

Mao Tse-tung also brought up the question of assembly:

It is the same with assembly. Recently during assemblies there have often been detectives who have come and obstructed things in every way or, finally, armed police have been used to break up the assemblies. They are unaware that the "provincial constitution" provides for complete freedom for the people to assemble peacefully without arms and stipulates that the government should not interfere at its own whim.

Chao Heng-t'i, Wu Ching-hung, Shih Ch'eng-chin, and Chou Ying-kan thus had no choice but to admit: "The 'provincial constitution' is, of course, in full force." But they brought up the question of "so long as the people obey the law, the government will naturally not interfere" as a pretext to encroach upon the people's freedom. Therefore, when he was in the Administration Department, Comrade Mao Tse-tung got into a sharp argument with Wu Ching-hung over the question of the law. Mao Tse-tung used bourgeois legal theory to best Wu Ching-hung in the argument. Mao said:

In times past the government often had reasons for interfering in the freedoms of assembly, association, and the press. It often drew up legal plaints on the basis that a certain assembly, association, or publication might in the future violate the criminal code and that it was not in conformity with the actual intent of the law. If, before the people even begin any activity, the government intervenes only on the basis of the intent (which is, moreover, speculation), then almost anything can be labeled as "might in the future" violate the criminal code, and there is nothing with which the government cannot interfere.

And so "Department Head Wu said that there are two schools of thought on law — the theory of motive and the theory of action. At the present time the law indeed adopted the theory of action; nevertheless, when and if a motive might lead to an occurrence of some illegal action, the government would be forced to intervene." Mao Tse-tung then said: "Unless the people directly violate the law in their actions, there really should be no intervention." He also adduced some articles of law from England and France as proof of his argument. Wu Ching-hung was at a loss for an answer.

During the negotiations, Comrade Mao Tse-tung clearly expressed the attitude of the workers:

What the workers want is socialism because socialism is really beneficial to them. But at the present time this is still difficult to attain in China. Present-day politics, of course, is based on the principle of democracy. With regard to the official announcements that workers often promote anarchism, this completely contradicts the facts; the workers do not at all believe in anarchism because anarchism is very much against the interests of the workers. Recently there have been many movements among the workers aimed at relieving their own suffering; this is the so-called labor movement. But none of this has gone beyond the three issues of an increase in wages, a reduction in working hours, and the improvement of treatment.

The Chao, Wu, Shih, and Chou crowd did indeed have a "deep and extreme hatred" for anarchism that "did not want any government," but as to what kind of a thing socialism was, they were completely in the dark. Therefore they "all considered it quite proper for the workers to adopt this attitude." The comical thing was that "the two department heads, Wu and Shih, said that socialism was a progressive doctrine and that in the future it could certainly be attained." At the same time, they came out with words that represented their true feelings: "Magistrate Chou advocated that labor and management not fight against each other but that they yield to each other so as to avoid bringing about great damage to society. Governor Chao also said that the development of industry should be the main concern at the present time, and he exhorted the workers to endure a little suffering." With regard to the opinions of Chou and Chao in protecting capitalists, Mao Tse-tung in his turn humorously remarked: "If the government really has a responsibility, it is to get the capitalists and shopowners to make a lot of concessions, and then the workers will be unlikely to clash with them any more."

The problem of the Rickshaw Union was discussed at the Police Department. Comrade Mao Tse-tung explained:

The Changsha Rickshaw Union was organized in conformity with Article XII of the "provincial constitution" with over eighteen hundred members, and it is very well organized. Now the Western District Police Station has suddenly taken down the Union placard. On their orders were written the words "established the union on their own without authority." In addition, they were abusive in language and made a deafening racket; police department officials broke tables and smashed chairs, uttered insulting language, and didn't have the least respect for the workers' dignity. There was talk abroad that the owners and the police department officials were banding together and engaging in corruption — we don't know whether this is accurate or not. All the unions are extremely exasperated, thinking that if the placard of one union could be taken down, the same thing could be done to all and that the danger was really serious. Moreover, this action was a complete violation of Article XII of the "provincial constitution."

The facts were all there; there was no way to escape. Shih Ch'eng-chin had no choice but to feign amazement, saying that he had never given such an order at all. He then acknowledged that as soon as the papers arrived for registering the Rickshaw Union, they would be approved.

With regard to the problem of the Barbers' Union,

At the Changsha hsien [office] and the Administration Department the representatives pointed out the various abuses in this case and also pointed out that the original decision violated the provision in the "provincial constitution" for the freedom to regulate business. The old corrupt practice was to be abandoned; the forty-sixty split was the most equitable for all. Magistrate Chou granted an end to the application of the original decision. After the provincial office had changed the original decision the affair could be finished. He also allowed bail to be extended to the workers who had been arrested. Department Head Wu denied that there was a recent directive to the effect that Changsha hsien execute the original decision and said that he didn't know anything about this at all. (One can see the great abuses in this case.) It was then permitted to handle the situation in accordance with a bill passed by the Provincial Assembly; if the bill did not arrive, then labor circles were to send up a petition asking to change the unreasonable original decision and the matter would be handled and finished immediately.

As for the rest, the writing brush workers' strike dragged on without settlement, and there was a small number of gang bosses who caused trouble in the Machinists' Union and the Tailors' Union, the result of which were some disputes in which the Changsha hsien [office] and the Administration Department were forced to "permit the case to be handled in accordance with the actual facts of the situation."

In the face of Comrade Mao Tse-tung's correct arguments and firm stand, the Chao Heng-t'i government suffered a thorough defeat in these "negotiations." This three-day confrontation between two hostile classes — the rulers and the ruled — amply demonstrated the great wisdom and the fearless spirit of despising the enemy possessed by Comrade Mao Tse-tung and the Chinese working class.

After the news of the victory of the United Association of Labor Organizations in these "negotiations" had gotten around, the broad working masses deeply felt: Truth and justice are on our side; we will certainly win. Hence the workers' courage and confidence in struggle soared higher. The various circles in society also felt that the power of the working class was so great that it had to be respected.

According to some news that got out not long after, Chao Heng-t'i said to his lieutenants: "If another Mao Tse-tung comes to Hunan I'm finished!"

Although at this time Chao Heng-t'i did not yet dare launch an unbridled crackdown on the labor movement or the mass revolutionary movement, he had long been scheming to injure Comrade Mao Tse-tung. In April 1923 Chao Heng-t'i issued a warrant for the arrest of the "extremist" Mao Tse-tung. Not until he had leisurely arranged the overall work of the Party in Hunan and the "arrest warrant" had been out for half a month did Mao Tse-tung leave Hunan and head for Shanghai.

In the spring of 1923 in a move to recover Lü-hsun and Darien and also to repudiate the Twenty-one Demands, the nationwide people's anti-Japanese movement entered a new upswing. Before he left Hunan, Comrade Mao Tse-tung had arranged this piece of work. Headed by the United Association of Labor Organizations, and in combination with the United Association of Students, the Educational Society, and the Chamber of Commerce, the Hunan All-Circle Foreign Affairs Reinforcement Association [Hu-nan ko-chieh wai-chiao hou-yüan hui] was founded on April 5; Comrade Kuo Liang was elected chairman, and Hsia Hsi, Hsia Ming-han, and other comrades held positions of primary responsibility. Thereupon various places throughout the province, particularly Changsha, launched a stirring and seething movement on an unprecedented scale aimed at breaking off economic relations with Japan. Thus occurred the nation-shaking "June 1" tragedy (on June 1 Japanese sailors landed in Changsha and shot and killed one worker and a primary school student). Chao Heng-t'i toadied to the foreigners in the affair, suppressed the mass patriotic movement, closed down the Foreign Affairs Reinforcement Association, and also issued warrants for the arrest of Kuo Liang, Hsia Hsi, Hsia Ming-han, and other comrades. From "Red" May to September 1923 Chao Heng-t'i issued warrants for the arrest of "extremists" on seven separate occasions. (The order in which Chao Heng-t'i listed "extremists" was: (1) anarchists, (2) Communists, (3) Marxists!)

In Shanghai Comrade Mao Tse-tung participated in the leadership work of the Communist Party Central Committee and at the same time continued to direct the Hunan Party organization in launching the struggle against Chao Heng-t'i. After this, when the Chinese Revolution had entered the period during which cooperation began between the Kuomintang and the Chinese Communist Party and during which the First Revolutionary Civil War occurred, Mao Tse-tung embarked upon the immense task of establishing a nationwide revolutionary united front. At the end of 1924 Mao Tse-tung once again returned to Hunan, set to work on the study of Hunan village conditions, and led the peasants' revolutionary struggle, establishing a firm foundation for Hunan's great peasant movement. In the meantime, Chao had issued another warrant for Mao Tse-tung's arrest, and so Mao went to Canton. In 1925 and 1926 Mao Tse-tung presided over the famous National Peasant Movement Training Institute in Canton and worked hard to train cadres to lead the peasant struggle.* Aside from "Analysis of the Classes in Chinese Society," which he wrote at this time, one of the other most important Marxist-Leninist writings was his "Chao Heng-t'i ti chieh-chi chi-ch'u ho wo-men tang-ch'ien jen-wu" [Chao Heng-t'i's Class Base and Our Present Task], which was based on his experience in leading the revolutionary movement in Hunan. This was published in Hunan as a small pamphlet. This piece of writing has not yet been found. According to people who read it at the time, the article analyzed Chao Heng-t'i's social basis as that of the feudal landlord class; the task at that time was to organize the peasants and proceed with the revolutionary struggle.

As everyone knows, in December 1926, just at the critical hour when the stirring and seething Hunan peasant movement was being attacked by the Kuomintang reactionaries and being criticized by the Ch'en Tu-hsiu opportunists, Comrade Mao Tse-tung came to Hunan and launched an on-the-spot investigation. On the basis of incontrovertible facts and a creative Marxist spirit he raised the slogans, " 'What a mess' means very good" and " 'Riffraff' (the slanderous name applied by the reactionaries to the peasant

---

* As explained in more detail below (note to p. 283), Mao ran the Institute only from May to September 1926, though he lectured there beginning in the autumn of 1925 [S.R.S.].

activists — author) means the vanguard of the revolution,"* directly inspiring and guiding the Hunan peasant movement to advance to a higher stage.

After the right wing opportunist leadership of Ch'en Tu-hsiu led the great 1927 Revolution to its grave, Comrade Mao Tse-tung relied on the foundation of the Hunan labor movement and peasant movement that he had laid to organize the first revolutionary militia of workers and peasants, and on Chingkangshan set the "spark" of the Chinese Revolution.*

---

*Allusion to Mao's article of 1930, referred to on p. 66 above. — Tr.

# CONCLUSION

Already during his youth and school days, Comrade Mao Tse-tung harbored the great ambition of liberating the Chinese people and worked hard to find the path for realizing this ideal. He deeply and critically studied Chinese and foreign doctrines and ideologies that had a bearing on the realization of this great ideal. At the same time, he made every effort in his own actions to engage in all sorts of meaningful, practical activities. From the beginning when he had first come in contact with Marxism-Leninism he was the outstanding representative of the great and brilliant tradition of the Chinese people, and without the least reservation he closely combined this universal truth with his own practical, revolutionary struggle and "raised the ideology of the Chinese nation to an unprecedented height and showed to the suffering Chinese nation and people the only correct and clear road toward complete liberation — the road of Mao Tse-tung." [1]

The revolutionary activities in Hunan from 1918 to the beginning of 1923 were the point of departure for Comrade Mao Tse-tung's leadership of China's great New Democratic Revolution. Mao Tse-tung's work during this period has great significance for the revolutionary task of the Chinese people in the present era, for the combination of Marxism-Leninism with the Chinese Revolution.

In his book Lun tang [On the Party], Comrade Liu Shao-ch'i says: "The road marked out by Comrade Mao Tse-tung is most correctly and most fully representative of the history of our Party and the contemporary revolutionary history of the Chinese nation and the Chinese people." [2] Thus, the early revolutionary activities of Comrade Mao Tse-tung at that time represented the history of the birth of our Party and represented the correct revolutionary direction of the Chinese working class and the Chinese people.

The early revolutionary activities of Comrade Mao Tse-tung

273

began with his leadership of the students' patriotic movement, the movement to expel the warlords, the people's democratic movement, and the New Culture movement, that is, they began with the leadership of anti-imperialist, antifeudal people's revolutionary movements. After completely embracing Marxism-Leninism, Mao Tse-tung kept in close touch with the working masses body and soul and gave exceedingly forceful leadership to the labor movement. Leading the revolutionary cadres of intellectual origins to go among the working masses, he inculcated Marxism-Leninism into the working class, resolutely struggled with all his heart and soul for the interests of the working masses, aroused the class consciousness of the broad working masses, organized them, and waged a victorious struggle, thus opening up a brand-new path for the Chinese revolution. On a foundation that combined the labor movement with Marxism-Leninism, Mao Tse-tung first established in Hunan a firm, strong Party intimately linked with the masses.

In his early revolutionary activities, Comrade Mao Tse-tung correctly pointed out the path of China's New Democratic Revolution through his own revolutionary practice; this path was, according to the formula he later set forth: an anti-imperialist, antifeudal revolution of the broad masses of the people under the leadership of the proletariat. As soon as he began his revolutionary activities, Mao Tse-tung identified the deadly enemy of the Chinese people as imperialism and the feudal forces, particularly imperialism. Moreover, from his own concrete revolutionary practice, from the lessons of China's recent revolutionary history, and from the theories of Marxism-Leninism, he very clearly recognized that the responsibility for leading this revolution fell completely on the shoulders of the proletariat. Although at that time Mao Tse-tung had not yet directly engaged in the peasant movement, he by no means overlooked the basic strength of the peasant masses; moreover, during the process of launching the violent struggle against the warlord Chao Heng-t'i, he gradually came to deeply recognize that in order to destroy thoroughly Chao Heng-t'i's social base it was necessary to rely on the might of the broad peasant masses. Therefore, from the end of 1924 on he began to devote all his efforts to leading the peasant movement.

Because he started from China's concrete circumstances and was skilled at accurately weighing the balance of the various social forces in the revolution, from the very beginning of his revolutionary activities Comrade Mao Tse-tung made the establishment of a broad popular revolutionary united front one of the fundamental policies of the Chinese Revolution. In his revolutionary activities at that time, especially the labor movement, Mao Tse-tung paid utmost attention to revolutionary strategy and was extremely skilled at capitalizing on every small split in the enemy camp and at finding allies for himself. Mao Tse-tung waged an extensive campaign vis-à-vis the middle class and the broad urban petty bourgeoisie, to win them over and make them allies, isolating the enemy to the maximum.

Although the membership of the Hunan Party organization that Mao Tse-tung was leading at the time was very small (it was nevertheless one of the largest local Parties in the country), the quality was very high: it was a completely modern, proletarian party, born in the long mass revolutionary movement and labor movement and set up according to the Marxist-Leninist principles of Party-building. From the revolutionary struggle and the cadres Mao Tse-tung led, we can see that the Party organization Mao was instrumental in establishing had a great many excellent work styles. For example: it maintained the principle of serving the people; it was established in the midst of the masses and maintained intimate links with them; it attached extraordinary importance to the study of Marxist-Leninist theory and paid attention to the ideological aspects of Party-building; within the Party there was a democratic life and a commitment to discipline; and Party members all had a high degree of class consciousness. Above all, under the direct influence of Mao Tse-tung the great majority of Party cadres all had a practical and realistic work style characterized by close contact with the masses.

Owing to China's historical circumstances and the infancy of the proletariat,

Our Party had neither sufficient ideological preparation in Marxism-Leninism before its foundation nor adequate time after its foundation for the propagation of theory, for it immediately immersed itself in turbulent, practical, revolutionary struggle. For these reasons, our Party suffered for a long time from inadequate Marxist-Leninist ideological schooling. [3]

But from the beginning of his revolutionary activities, Comrade Mao Tse-tung attached prime importance to the propagation of theory, ideological education, and ideological leadership. Even though the number of classical Marxist-Leninist writings that were translated and available in China was extremely small at that time, and even though the understanding of these writings among the revolutionaries was still shallow and even contained some incorrect concepts, Mao Tse-tung still firmly grasped the most fundamental principles of Marxism-Leninism and, moreover, creatively utilized these principles in his own practical activities. The limited documentary material available today is sufficient enough for us to see how Mao paid attention to the work of propagating theory. With regard to the analysis of the national and international situation, the theory and policy of the revolutionary united front, and the policy and strategy of the labor movement, Mao arrived at his own profound and unique Marxist viewpoints. Naturally, Mao's writings at this time were still works of a youthful Marxist, not yet a fully mature Marxist. Nevertheless, this was precisely the fountainhead of the victory of the Chinese revolution and the great beginning of Mao Tse-tung's theoretical preparation for our Party and for the Chinese people.

"Comrade Mao Tse-tung's greatest achievement in the Chinese revolution was that he correctly and vigorously combined the universal truth of Marxism-Leninism with the concrete practice of the Chinese revolution, solving a whole series of problems for the revolution." [4] Because of the extremely distinctive nature of Chinese historical and societal development, to adapt Marxism to China, to use the Marxist standpoint and approach to settle all the various problems of the modern Chinese revolution was, as Comrade Liu Shao-ch'i has said,

a unique and difficult task.... This can never be accomplished, as some people seem to think it can, by memorizing and reciting Marxist works or just by quoting from them. It requires the combination of a high degree of scientific and revolutionary spirit. It requires profound historical and social knowledge, rich experience in guiding the revolutionary struggles and skill in using Marxist-Leninist methods to make an accurate and scientific analysis of the social and historical objective conditions and their development. It further requires boundless and indefatigable loyalty to the cause of the proletariat and of the people; faith in the strength, creative power and future of the masses; skill in crystallizing the experiences, will and ideas of the masses and their application in mass work. It is only thus that original and brilliant additions to Marxism-Leninism can be made, on the basis of each specific period of historical development and the concrete economic and political conditions in China. It is only in this way that it has been possible to express Marxism-Leninism in plain language, easily understood by the Chinese people, to adapt it to a new historical environment and to China's special conditions and to turn it into a weapon in the hands of the Chinese proletariat and all laboring people. [5]

During the period of his early revolutionary activities, this is precisely the way in which Comrade Mao Tse-tung brilliantly and successfully proceeded with the particularly difficult undertaking of Sinifying Marxism. His method of working and his method of thinking was the unification of theory with practice. At all times and places he linked up with the practice of the current revolution and made a concrete analysis of the surrounding concrete social conditions. This was using what he himself later often called the "fundamental viewpoint of Marxism — the method of class analysis" — to study and judge the objective situation and to investigate and concentrate the experience of revolutionary practice in order to find a work method and direction.

This method was that of the creative Marxist, as Comrade Stalin said in his famous article for Lenin's fiftieth birthday: "These people do not seek instruction and direction from similar historical events or historical phenomena, they seek instruction and direction from the study of their surroundings. When they work they do not use quotes or set phrases as a foundation, but rather make their foundation out of actual experience. They use experience to examine every step of their own work, and in the midst of their own mistakes they learn and teach others to construct a new life. Therefore in the work of these people, words and actions are always at one, and the theory of Marx is fully ensured of its own vigorous revolutionary strength." [6]

When Comrade Mao Tse-tung began his revolutionary activities, he heavily emphasized the role of Party leadership, on the one hand, and he always heavily emphasized the strength of the masses, particularly the great creative power of the masses, on the other. Hence,

in every phase of work he stood in the most important and most forward post, "buried his head in work," did not engage in clamor and hubbub, made the most contact with reality, linked up with the masses on the broadest scale, had the most concern about the revolution, had the most profound thoughts, neither had the "bookworm" habit of the Ch'en Tu-hsiu variety nor the foppishness of others. Thus, ever since the creation of the Party he has been our Party's most outstanding Bolshevik representative. [7]

The material presented in this book on the early revolutionary activities of Comrade Mao Tse-tung is naturally not sufficiently complete, but from it we can readily see that the Chinese Communist Party, the path of the Chinese New-Democratic Revolution, and Sinified Marxism — that is, Comrade Mao Tse-tung's doctrine [hsüeh-shuo] about the Chinese revolution — all these things truly grew up on this Chinese earth of ours, after going through a schooling in Marxism-Leninism. They are Chinese things, and yet they are altogether Marxist things.

Long live Comrade Mao Tse-tung, the great leader of the Chinese people, the organizer and leader of the victory of the Chinese Revolution!

# *Appendix*

THE HUNAN PEASANT MOVEMENT
DURING THE FIRST
REVOLUTIONARY CIVIL WAR

On the eve of the founding of the Chinese Communist Party and during its early period, Comrade Mao Tse-tung engaged in extensive and intensive revolutionary activities in Hunan. These included the student movement, the movement to expel the warlords, the New Culture movement and, especially after 1921, the labor movement and peasant movement, to which he devoted a great deal of effort. During these movements, Mao Tse-tung established and developed the organization of the Communist Party and the Socialist Youth Corps and trained a large group of outstanding revolutionary cadres, so that the young Chinese Communist Party built up a very good mass foundation in Hunan and also created a simple and honest revolutionary work style. This was one important reason why the Hunan peasant movement was able to unfold dynamically during the period of the First Revolutionary Civil War.

Ever since the days of the T'aiping Heavenly Kingdom [1853-1864], Hunan had been one of the great arenas of the struggle between the revolutionaries and the counterrevolutionaries. In every period there appeared a typical struggle between modernization and reaction, there appeared representative personalities of every revolutionary type and every counterrevolutionary type. Thus the Hunanese had a rich revolutionary experience, and the reactionaries of Hunan had a rich counterrevolutionary experience. During the First Revolutionary Civil War, Hunan was the center of the nationwide peasant movement; it was one of the most active areas of the nationwide struggle between the revolutionaries and the counterrevolutionaries. The development of the Hunan peasant movement had a bearing on the development of the entire revolution. At this most crucial moment, Comrade Mao Tse-tung arrived in Hunan, and from January 4 to February 5, 1927, he made on-the-spot investigations of the situation of the peasant movement in the five

278

hsien of Hsiang-t'an, Hsiang-hsiang, Heng-shan, Li-ling, and Changsha and wrote his famous "Report on an Investigation of the Peasant Movement in Hunan."

## THE RISE OF THE HUNAN PEASANT MOVEMENT UNDER THE LEADERSHIP OF COMRADE MAO TSE-TUNG

In his early revolutionary activities, Comrade Mao Tse-tung had already begun to direct his attention to the solution of China's peasant problem. At the beginning of 1923, under the leadership of Mao Tse-tung, the Hunan Party's local organizations had already begun to lead the peasant movement.

With a view to training youthful revolutionary cadres, Self-Study University, founded by Comrade Mao Tse-tung, set up the Preparatory Class in September 1922. In the Chinese course of the Preparatory Class, instruction comprised, in particular, essays on the peasant question written in light of the Hunan situation. These essays made detailed analyses of the socio-economic conditions of the various classes in the Hunan countryside and of the reasons behind the gradual but steady concentration of land and the increasing bankruptcy of the peasants, pointing out that the only way out for the peasants was to rise up and struggle and take back the land from the hands of the landlords.

At the beginning of 1923, Comrades Liu Tung-hsüan and Hsieh Huai-te, who were engaged in union work in the Shui-k'ou-shan mining area, were sent by the Party to their respective homes of Yüeh-pei and Pai-kuo in Heng-shan to open up work among the peasants. There were many peasants in this area who worked at Shui-k'ou-shan. When the peasants heard them describe the Shui-k'ou-shan strike struggle and the role of the Workers' Club, they were all quite excited. Not long thereafter, the Yüeh-pei Peasants' and Workers' Association [Yüeh-pei nung-kung hui] was founded. This was the earliest peasant association founded in Hunan and also the first to carry on a great struggle against the landlords.

Pai-kuo was the home of Chao Heng-t'i. Most of the fields here were owned by the Chao family and its relatives and acquaintances. The peasants suffered severe exploitation and ill-treatment. Aroused by the propaganda of Comrades Liu and Hsieh, and in alliance with them, the peasants of Yüeh-pei carried out secret activities. After a half year of work the union approach was adopted, and organization proceeded on the basis of ten peasant households forming one group [hsiao-tsu]. Representatives of ten and representatives of one hundred were set up, and then a general regional representative was created. By this time, Heng-shan had already established the Socialist Youth Corps. Under the leadership of the Party, the inaugural meeting of the Yüeh-pei Peasants' and Workers' Association was held in mid-September 1923. There were more than ten thousand peasants from the surrounding area who attended the meeting and who elected seven people, including Liu Tung-hsüan and Hsieh Huai-te, as councilmen, Liu and Hsieh being chairman and vice chairman of the Council respectively.

According to the piece written by Comrade Teng Chung-hsia that appeared in Chinese Youth [Chung-kuo ch'ing-nien], No. 12, January 3, 1924, entitled "Chung-kuo nung-min chuang-k'uang chi women yün-tung ti fang-chen" [The Condition of the Chinese Peasants and the Direction of Our Movement]:

The meeting passed the following resolutions: (1) a resolution on how to improve the life of the peasants, (2) a resolution on the attitude of this assembly toward the government, (3) a resolution on village education, (4) a resolution on how to improve the life of the village women. In addition, a declaration was made as follows: "Honored and beloved fellow peasants! We occupy one of the four classes of scholar, farmer, artisan, and merchant. But on the level of people's rights, aside from crying out about misery and injustice, bewailing our cold and hungry status, working day and night so that our sweat is like heavy rain, we have nothing! Study? — only people with money can attend school. Live in a house? — when we go into a better house the owner suspects that we have come to steal and pick pockets! Eat? — when a bad harvest year rolls around we pull out our money and there is no grain to be bought. What about clothes? — the foreigners have raised the value of Chinese cotton and have taken it all away so that we must go without a stitch and cannot spin cotton and make cloth. As for the rest, like those people who have become officials and enriched themselves, they presume upon official position and authority to force peasants to sell their land to them. As for those people who become officials and want to make money, they frequently collect taxes in advance. Foreign countries secretly cause the Chinese warlords to fight against one another and throw their troops into action everywhere so that one day we are pressed into service and the next day we are sent out as runners; we are also the ones who are struck and beaten along the road! The foreigners send their goods to China and render valueless the things we used to produce with our own hands! The reason we suffer all sorts of oppression today is that we forgot that the power of unity was our weapon, and as a result we never stood up to the enemy. Now we know: if we want to rid ourselves of our misery there is no alternative but for everyone to unite!"

After the founding of the Peasant Association, representatives were sent out in every direction to conduct propaganda and awaken the class consciousness of the peasants. The number of those joining the Association quickly increased to over one hundred thousand.

The Peasant Movement in Hunan

Under the leadership of the Peasant Association, a struggle was
vigorously launched for publicly regulating the price of rice and
for prohibiting the landlords from exporting grain and cotton. Originally the price of grain had been three pecks per yuan; later the
price was depressed to four pecks per yuan. At the same time, a
struggle for the lowering of rents and interest payments began to
ferment. The landlord bloc, headed by the Chao Heng-t'i family,
straightaway bought off the Heng-shan hsien office. In mid-October
the hsien office sent in troops to surround the Peasant Association,
and a full ten thousand peasants rushed to its assistance. The troops
opened fire, killing one peasant and wounding many more. Moreover, nine people who held positions of responsibility in the Peasant Association, including Liu Tung-hsüan and Hsieh Huai-te, were
seized and taken away. This was precisely the time when the battle
between T'an Yen-k'ai and Chao Heng-t'i broke out. T'an's troops
occupied Heng-shan, and Liu, Hsieh, and the seven others were all
released. After the battle came to a close on November 25, Chao
Heng-t'i once again moved in a battalion and set fire to the Peasant
Association headquarters as well as to the homes of people holding
positions of responsibility in the Association and the homes of a
great many other peasants. In addition, four peasants were beaten
to death and more were injured. Over seventy peasants were seized
and taken away. In 1926, as soon as the Northern Expeditionary
Army arrived in Heng-shan, a huge memorial service was held for
the Yüeh-pei peasants who had been martyred.

In the spring of 1925,* Comrade Mao Tse-tung returned to Hunan
from Shanghai and stayed in his hometown for a very short time.
Here, while recuperating from an illness, he set to work on the
peasant movement. Mao Tse-tung associated with a great number
of the peasants, acquainting himself with their life and their demands. There were some peasant activists who were accustomed
to fighting injustice and who had often launched spontaneous struggles against the landlord militia guard [ti-chu t'uan-pao]. Mao Tse-
tung established very close ties of friendship with them so that they
very quickly became genuine peasant leaders. And so, within several months, a great many village peasant associations were organized in Mao's home district of Shao-shan and Yin-t'ien-ssu. The
peasants began to understand the principle behind "Down with the

---

* The exact date when Mao gave up his functions in the Shanghai Executive Office of the Kuomintang and returned to his native village for a rest is difficult to
determine in the light of conflicting reports, but it was almost certainly in the
autumn of 1924 rather than in the spring of 1925 [S.R.S.].

Warlords." Mao Tse-tung gave a popular explanation of the slogan "Down with Imperialism" as "Down with the Rich Foreigners" so that the peasants would embrace it more easily. The peasant associations began struggles for prohibiting landlords from exporting grain, for equalizing grain prices [to eliminate speculation coming from good and bad harvests], for an increase in the wages for farm labor, as well as for a reduction in rents. Clashes frequently erupted between the associations and the landlords and powerful gentry. Therefore the landlords communicated with Changsha city, wanting Chao Heng-t'i to come and arrest Comrade Mao Tse-tung. The peasants passed on this information and at the same time, because of the developing revolutionary situation, Mao left for Canton.

In August 1926 this affair was specifically mentioned in the "Hsiang-t'an nung-min hsieh-hui ti-i-tz'u ch'üan-hsien tai-piao ta-hui hsüan-yen" [Declaration of the First All-<u>Hsien</u> Congress of Hsiang-t'an Peasant Associations].

The organized peasant masses of all areas have experienced bitter struggle and great sacrifice. Although they are under the iron boot of Chao Heng-t'i and suffer the severe armed oppression of the local bullies, evil gentry, Home Guard, and landlords, the organization of the peasant associations secretly remains and, moreover, has carried out many struggles. For example, the peasants of Shao-shan and Chu-t'ing have had their leaders arrested by the Chao government three times for making minimal economic demands — the movement for the equalization of rice prices and the prohibition of exports. These leaders have also been repeatedly picked up by the Home Guard Bureau [T'uan-fang chü] and falsely accused of being bandits. Mao Tse-tung, a Kuomintang Central Executive Committee member, [1] was almost arrested on suspicion of inflaming the peasants.

The Shao-shan branch of the Communist Party was also established at this time by Comrade Mao Tse-tung himself. This branch played an important role during the First Revolutionary Civil War.

The Shao-shan peasants, who had received their education directly from Comrade Mao Tse-tung himself, trained and produced many mainstays for the peasant revolution and many cadres for the Party beginning in 1925 with the establishment of the peasant association. An example is the revolutionary martyr Comrade Mao Fu-hsüan, who was originally an agricultural laborer who had never gone to school. Mao Fu-hsüan was personally trained by Mao Tse-tung, who took him to the Changsha schools to be a janitor and to do half-work and half-study; afterward Mao took him to the Anyüan coal mines to participate in the labor movement. He returned to the Hsiang-t'an area during the First Revolutionary Civil War to carry on with the peasant movement. Because of this, Mao Fu-hsüan became an able speaker and writer and an extremely capable person and was, moreover, one of the leaders revered by the peasants. After the failure of the 1927 Revolution, Comrade Mao Fu-hsüan remained in Hunan and Shanghai to carry out secret work for the Party. In 1933 he was murdered in Nanking at Yü-hua-t'ai by the Kuomintang reactionaries.

During the Yenan days Chairman Mao once talked about Comrade Mao Fu-shün. He said: "For a comrade of peasant origins to study and work as hard as he did and to go right on shouldering the responsibility of the work of a provincial Party committee member was a very difficult thing." As for the others, like the revolutionary martyrs Mao Hsin-mei, Chiang Yu-k'ung, and P'ang shu-chu, they were all Shao-shan peasant cadres personally trained by Chairman Mao. [2]

Comrade Mao Tse-tung's large-scale training of cadres for the First Revolutionary Civil War, the Chinese peasant movement, and the revolutionary movement took place after he had gone to Canton to run the "Peasant Movement Training Institute."

In 1925, when Comrade Mao Tse-tung was in Canton, he took charge of the sixth [session of the] "Peasant Movement Training Institute."* There were more students than before, altogether 327 people, including students from 19 provinces, with Hunan, Kwangsi, Szuchuan, Hupei, Honan, and Shantung having the most. At this time the Hunan Party organization mobilized a large group of Party members, Corps members, and revolutionary youth to go to Canton for training. Some entered the "Peasant Movement Training Institute." Many more entered the "Political Training Class" (the head of which was Comrade Li Fu-ch'un). In this class Comrade Mao Tse-tung talked about the "Peasant Question." Most of the graduates from the political training class became political cadres in the Northern Expeditionary Army.

At the Peasant Movement Training Institute Comrade Mao Tse-

---

* The Sixth Session of the Peasant Movement Training Institute in fact took place from May to September, as is attested by the very document to which Li Jui refers in note 6 below. For the reasons behind Li Jui's deliberate obfuscation of the historical record, see Schram, Mao Tse-tung, pp. 83-91. This particular fiction has now been abandoned in China; a recent article correctly states: "From May to September 1926, Chairman Mao ran the Peasant Movement Training Institute in Canton, and himself assumed the post of principal; from March to June 1927, he once again ran the Central Peasant Movement Training Institute in Wuhan." (Wang Shao-p'u and Wu Yün-hsiang, "Chi Kuang-chou, Wu-han nung-min yün-tung chiang-hsi-so" [Reminiscences of the Peasant Movement Training Institutes in Canton and Wuhan], Hsüeh-hsi yü p'i-p'an [Study and Criticism], 1976, No. 3, p. 54) [S.R.S.].

tung taught such courses as "The Question of the Chinese Peasants" and "Village Education." In his teaching Mao Tse-tung forged close links with the realities of the Chinese villages. "He talked about the Ox Prince temple and the three potato rice, [3] things with which the students were familiar but from which they were unable to derive any principles. Thus the students listened and were extremely interested and extremely enlightened." Mao Tse-tung also wanted something from the students:

These were the conditions in the villages under which everyone lived, the conditions of the inhabitants and the land, the mode of life, the people's origins, how so-and-so got rich, how so-and-so became poor, how much official (public) land there was in the village, who managed it, who worked it, the rent...he would also analyze these and use the results as teaching material for the students. [4]

At that very time the Tung-chiang peasant movement, led by Comrade P'eng P'ai, [5] was vigorously developing. Comrade Mao Tse-tung organized the entire student body of the Training Institute to go to Hai-feng to observe and practice. "After the students had embraced the various theories, they personally entered the revolutionary peasant mass, investigated its organization and witnessed its life with their own eyes, all of which had an enormous influence on their determination to work for the peasant movement." [6]

In teaching, Mao Tse-tung made his deepest impression on people when discussing the analysis of the various classes in Chinese society. Students of the time can still recall today: He drew a great number of diagrams on the blackboard to explain the circumstances of the classes in Chinese society. Concretely and symbolically and on the basis of the economic position of each class and its attitude toward revolution he explained who were the friends of the revolution and who were the enemies, as well as what changes in attitude toward the revolution would occur in each class during the process of the revolution itself. Mao Tse-tung's article "Analysis of the Classes in Chinese Society" appeared in 1926 in the second issue of The Chinese Peasant [Chung-kuo nung-min] published in Canton. In this essay Mao pointed out:

Our enemies are all those in league with imperialism — the warlords, the bureaucrats, the comprador class, the big landlord class and the reactionary section of the intelligentsia attached to them. The leading force in our revolution is the industrial proletariat. Our closest friends are the entire semiproletariat and petty bourgeoisie. As for the vacillating middle bourgeoisie, their right wing may become our enemy and their left wing may become our friend — but we must be constantly on our guard and not let them create confusion within our ranks. [7]

Like "Report on an Investigation of the Peasant Movement in Hunan," this great document represented the correct road of the Chinese Communist Party during the First Revolutionary Civil War and openly opposed the right-wing opportunism of Ch'en Tu-hsiu. At the time, Ch'en Tu-hsiu refused to permit the organ of the Chinese Communist Party to publish this essay. During the First Revolutionary Civil War this article became the textbook in the training classes for the masses and cadres throughout Hunan and in reality guided the thought and actions of the broad revolutionary masses and revolutionary cadres.

Owing to the development of events, a group of students from Hunan who had received this clear-cut class and strategic education from Comrade Mao Tse-tung in the "Peasant Movement Training Institute" returned to Hunan without waiting to graduate. Called special commissioners for the Peasant Movement of the Provincial Kuomintang Party, most of them were sent out to work in the areas bordering the railroad. As soon as they began work they traveled onto the correct path because they had gained under Comrade Mao Tse-tung and Comrade P'eng P'ai some practical experience in mobilizing peasant masses. They began by making inquiries into the poverty and misery of the lower class, and after they had established liaison with a considerable number of activists, they founded village peasant associations. Only after two or three villages had founded peasant associations was a district [ch'ü] leadership organ set up (the leadership organs for the hsien were generally not started until after the Northern Expeditionary Army had entered Hunan). At the time, the primary elements of the peasant associations were the poverty-stricken peasants and some of the poverty-stricken rural intellectuals. These intellectuals were mostly primary school teachers who had long since been in contact with members of the local Communist Party. The emergence of this situation was, naturally, not accidental. This was owing to the generally high quality of the many revolutionary cadres trained and produced by Mao Tse-tung — from the organization of the New People's Study Society to the organization of the Socialist Youth Corps and the Communist Party, through the development of the Hunan revolutionary movement, as well as during the training class in Canton. Thus the foundation of the lower-level mass movement was very correct.

Before the Northern Expeditionary Army entered Hunan, the work launched during the peasant movement was primarily in the areas of propaganda, education, and organization. There were also some small-scale economic struggles. The work of the peasant associations was done secretly in places where the strength of the reactionaries was great. There were a great number of places where the work was semi-open or completely open. For example, the peasant movement in I-yang was carried out openly. In 1926 on the Yüan-hsiao festival day [the fifteenth of the first lunar month] a "Peasants Grievance Corps" of over ten thousand people carrying lanterns went to the hsien government office to petition, demanding "the abolition of excessive taxes and contributions," etc. A contingent blazed the trail with sixteen shooting stars (torches), and the peasants brought their oxen to the "Great Hall" of the hsien yamen and said to the hsien magistrate: "We can't afford even to feed our oxen any longer."


## THE SITUATION IN HUNAN ON THE EVE
## OF THE NORTHERN EXPEDITION

After the "May 30 tragedy" of 1925 occurred, a new anti-imperialist, antiwarlord high tide arose in Hunan among the revolutionary masses and further paved the way for welcoming the Northern Expedition.

With the Communist-led "Society for Avenging Shame"* [Hsüeh ch'ih hui] as their nucleus, the masses of the various circles united and launched various kinds of struggles. Changsha and other places launched such mass movements as labor strikes, market strikes, classroom strikes, demonstrations, movements to break off economic relations with England and Japan, and movements for the promotion of national goods and the recovery of Ta-chin wharf (the wharf at Changsha that the Japanese had leased by force). The center of the movements was in Changsha, but there was also a large number of mass patriotic struggles in various other hsien. For example, from December 1925 until February of the next year there was the famous mass patriotic movement of P'ing-chiang, during which people refused to land English kerosine. Chao Heng-t'i adopted steamroller tactics against these mass revolutionary movements and proclaimed throughout Changsha that "those who propagate extremism will be beheaded." Thereupon the Hunan Regional

---

* This organization had been formed on June 2 at a meeting convened by the leadership of the Student Union and the Federation of Labor Organizations. See McDonald, "Urban Origins," pp. 380-381 [S. R. S.].

Committee of the Communist Party (i.e., the provincial committee) actively mobilized the masses, united all the anti-Chao forces, and launched the movement to Expel Chao Heng-t'i.

On the eve of the Northern Expedition, therefore, Hunan was already in a state characterized by the saying: "Strong winds foretell the coming storm." The Chinese Communist Party had already established two local committees, [one] in southern Hunan (Hengyang) and [one] in western Hunan (Ch'ang-te), and it had a fairly strong organizational base among workers, peasants, and students. The number of organized peasants in the whole province climbed to over four hundred thousand; the number of peasant masses who were under the direct influence of the Communist Party was over one million. The number of organized workers under the leadership of the All-Hunan United Association of Labor Organizations reached one hundred and ten thousand people. Most of the students from schools of the middle level and above were organized and had already experienced many revolutionary struggles. With the direct participation and help of the Communist Party, seventeen hsien seats already had Kuomintang organizations, including a provincial Party branch. The vast majority of these organizations was led by Communist Party members and revolutionaries — the then left wing of the Kuomintang. The rightists were in an inferior position. (In Hunan, the Communist Party was organized first, then came the Kuomintang organization.) At the beginning of 1926 the Hunan Provincial Committee of the Communist Party also sent men to the various departments of the Chao government [to find those] who were then leaning toward the revolution, to proceed with work on a united front, and to persuade them to rise up and expel Chao and join the Northern Expedition.

Between the end of 1925 and the beginning of 1926 there were two bloody incidents that had an enormous influence on the provincial revolutionary movement.

The first incident was the killing of the president of the Anyüan Workers' Club, Huang Ching-yüan. Ever since the strike victory of the Anyüan mines in September 1922 and the founding of the nationally famous Workers' Club, the sovereignty of the mining authorities had diminished and they had been scheming day and night to dissolve the workers' organization. In September 1925 the mining authorities conspired with the Kiangsi troops, and a regiment was sent in the name of "opposing the expansion of communism." More than five thousand workers were fired, and the Workers' Club was dissolved by armed force. More than seventy workers were arrested, including the president of the Workers' Club, Huang Ching-yüan. There were several clashes between the workers and the soldiers, and more than ten workers were killed or wounded. Finally, work at the mines was stopped, and more than eleven thousand workers were thrown completely out of work. Anyüan immediately became a world of terror. The labor organizations from Changsha and elsewhere, as well as the masses of various circles, initiated a large-scale movement to aid the Anyüan workers. On October 16 Huang Ching-yüan was finally executed by a firing squad. This is how the press recorded the incident: "Right before he was to be punished, Huang asked, without changing his countenance: 'What [is my] crime?' The officer in charge responded: 'Do you still want to overthrow imperialism!' Huang cried out loudly: 'Down with imperialism!' 'Restore the Club!' 'It doesn't matter if Huang Ching-yüan dies!'" Huang's corpse was then forcibly abducted by the workers and transported through Li-ling to Changsha. In Changsha, over one thousand of the masses carried the coffin, setting it to rest on Educational Society Plaza. On October 26 a memorial service was held with several thousand people attending.

The second incident was the killing of the Chu-chou (part of Hsiang-t'an <u>hsien</u>) peasant leader, Wang Hsien-tsung. Wang Hsien-tsung was a mechanic from Chu-chou. In 1925 he joined the Communist Party and organized the peasant association and led the peasant movement in his native town. That year the harvest had been poor. The landlords, powerful gentry, and dishonest merchants hoarded and speculated, causing the price of grain to soar, and the peasants were destitute. And so the Communist Party called on the masses of every area to launch a relief and rescue movement. Wang Hsien-tsung led the peasant masses of Chu-chou in various struggles against the landlords, such as the movement for an equalization of rice prices. Thus, the landlord gentry Wang Hsiao-ta and others despised him and falsely accused him of being a bandit chief. He was arrested by the Home Guard Bureau and thrown into prison, where he suffered all sorts of beatings aimed at getting a confession from him. But they could get nothing out of him. Afterward, Wang Hsiao-ta and the others bought off the artillery battalion of Yeh K'ai-hsin's occupying army, and in late November Wang Hsien-tsung was murdered at San-men city. When he was about to die for his righteous cause, Wang selflessly called out to the peasants: "Peasants, unite and smash the local bullies and evil gentry!" When the peasants, workers, and student masses got the news, they held a succession of memorial services, protested to the Chao

Heng-t'i government, expanded revolutionary propaganda, and carried forward the peasant movement.

The Huang Ching-yüan and Wang Hsien-tsung incidents, following on the heels of each other, gave the Hunan masses a profound education; the masses were more aware than ever of the warlords' cruelty, and they went a step further in unfurling the struggle for the welcoming of the Northern Expedition. Thereupon the Hunan Provincial Committee of the Chinese Communist Party immediately began preparations for leading the masses in practical action to expel Chao Heng-t'i. Chao Heng-t'i, for his part, intensified his oppression of the masses' revolutionary activities. Headed by the Hunan provincial branch of the Kuomintang (the great majority of the leaders, like Hsia Hsi and Kuo Liang, were Communist Party members and left-wing Kuomintang members) and in liaison with the various mass organizations of Changsha, the founding of a people's organization that would be in the nature of an interim government was in the making during February and March 1926. On March 9 a huge gathering of a full ten thousand townspeople was summoned to Educational Society Plaza. The streets were filled with posters such as "Down with Chao Heng-t'i," and "Oppose United Provincial Autonomy." The assembly unanimously passed the "Twenty-four Proposals for Dealing with the Hunan Authorities in the Future" presented by the provincial Party branch, and founded a "Hunan People's Ad Hoc Committee" [Hu-nan jen-min lin-shih wei-yüan-hui], electing nine people from labor, commercial, and educational circles as committeemen. The first proposal of the twenty-four was "Down with Chao Heng-t'i." Among the rest were "Ask the Nationalist government to launch a northern expedition," "Organize a government that represents the will of the people," "Make the Hunan troops punish Wu P'ei-fu with a military expedition," "Abolish excessive taxation and contributions," "Open up all organizations closed by Chao Heng-t'i," "Improve treatment of workers and peasants," etc. The marching masses demonstrated in front of the gates of the Chao government and shouted out the slogan: "Down with Chao Heng-t'i!"

In the face of this tremendous pressure by the masses, the "Hunan governor," Chao Heng-t'i, fled Changsha on March 13.

After Chao Heng-t'i had fled, in May, Chao's subordinate Yeh K'ai-hsin, with the help of Wu P'ei-fu, counterattacked Changsha. The troops of T'ang Sheng-chih, already part of the Canton Revolutionary Government, were forced to retreat and hold Heng-yang. The peasant associations from all over Hunan then launched a movement to expel Yeh K'ai-hsin. Although Changsha was under the vicious oppression of Yeh K'ai-hsin, the revolutionary masses, with the workers as the mainstay, were still actively preparing to arm themselves directly and to welcome the Northern Expeditionary Army.

## THE SEETHING AND STIRRING AGRARIAN REVOLUTIONARY MOVEMENT

The Hunan masses awaited the arrival of the Northern Expeditionary Army as one longs for clouds and a rainbow during a great drought. As soon as the Northern Expeditionary Army entered Hunan, the Chinese Communist Party, through various Kuomintang branch parties, the peasant associations, and the workers' and students' organizations, mobilized the broad masses of workers, peasants, and students to participate firsthand in the battle and to offer every kind of assistance. The Northern Expeditionary Army started out from Heng-yang on July 5, 1926, and attacked simultaneously on every route. On the eighth, Hsiang-hsiang was taken; on the ninth, Li-ling; on the tenth, Hsiang-t'an; on the twelfth, Changsha and Ning-hsiang; on the sixteenth, I-yang — it was truly [like] an autumn wind sweeping away the falling leaves and a power like splitting bamboo. The fact that at the time the Northern Expeditionary Army itself was a progressive, revolutionary military force and the fact that the troops under the command of the Pei-yang warlords were decadent were two important reasons for the quick victory of the Northern Expedition, but an even more fundamental reason was the assistance given by the broad masses of peasants and workers. It was because of the participation of the peasants and workers that the several campaigns within the borders of Hunan, such as those at Li-ling, Changsha, Lin-hsiang, and Yüeh-chou, were attended by such extremely small losses and gained such great victories. Besides taking a direct hand in the fighting and intercepting scattered troops, they enthusiastically participated in other areas, such as serving as guides, carrying letters, transportation, bearing stretchers, sweeping for mines, sending food, comforting the troops, as well as agitation and the spreading of leaflets on the battlefield.

An example of this is the famous Independent Regiment of the Fourth Army led by Comrade Yeh T'ing in the Li-ling-Ssu-fen Campaign:

# The Peasant Movement in Hunan

On July 11 the Northern Expeditionary Army began to divide into three routes and launch its attack. We had over three hundred people from the People's National Salvation Regiment (composed of workers and students) and the Peasant Militia who were deployed in the area of the Li-shan Bund and Ssu-fen. When the Northern Expeditionary Army entered the area, the enemy was holding the Iron River [T'ieh chiang], and from the Ssu-fen Bridge a machine gun was sweeping the river. The boats in the river had all been seized by the enemy, and the Northern Expeditionary Army had no opportunity whatsoever to cross. At this time our militia deployed on a high piece of ground behind the enemy lines and carried out a surprise raid. At the first one or two cannon shots the enemy did not move. The militia then used shotguns and spears and made a direct attack on the enemy line, repeatedly waving the flag of the revolutionary army on all sides to destroy the enemy's morale. At this point, the enemy troops switched their attention to the militia, and the Northern Expeditionary Army then took advantage of the situation to divide into two [columns] and cross the river. While they were crossing the river, the enemy troops were still holding the line tightly and not retreating. Not until later when the Northern Expeditionary Army troops made a bold attack from the Ssu-fen Bridge and the militia attacked from both sides was the enemy beaten back and put to flight. One regimental vice commander, two battalion commanders, four company commanders, and three or four hundred soldiers were taken prisoner. One regimental commander and two battalion commanders were killed, and two or three hundred discarded rifles were taken. The Independent Regiment of the Fourth Army lost only two company commanders and ten-odd soldiers. [8]

## Again, the P'ing-chiang campaign offers an example:

Our army began its attack at dawn on August 19. The peasants brought along with them all kinds of old-fashioned weapons, hoes, and shovels and were of great help in surrounding Pai-shih Ridge. They braved the bullets and made a bold attack, courageously ascending the mountain, and the enemy troops were thrown into great confusion. The number of arms they took was countless. They killed a great many of the enemy and also penetrated to Ch'ing-shui Ridge, more than thirty li from Pai-shih Ridge. The enemy soldiers retreated step by step, and the dead filled the roads (the artillery and small-arms ammunition that were taken were, for the most part, given to our troops). Because the peasants had been overzealous in their attack, thirteen were lost in battle. The enemy troops who were stationed at Chin-k'ang and San-tu hurriedly fled because the front line broke and was overrun. The peasant Tseng, seeing a fleeing soldier carrying a rifle on his back, immediately pursued and attacked him with his carrying-pole. The soldier opened fire and hit Tseng in the abdomen, but Tseng, oblivious to the pain, continued to attack furiously with his carrying-pole, eventually taking the rifle off the soldier and shooting him to death. Because Tseng had been overzealous in his efforts, he also collapsed and died. There were at least two hundred enemy troops killed by the masses in this battle. Their fierceness, their courageous spirit, and their huge sacrifice was evident throughout. In addition to reporting on news and the correspondence of the enemy, the Communications Corps organized by the peasants also made boats from door panels and [other] wooden materials and ferried our troops across the river to Pai-hu Port, with the result that the enemy troops had no time to retreat and were disarmed. The Detective Corps spied out the enemy situation; over ten of its number either were killed or taken captive. One of the members, Li Ch'un-sheng, a worker, reconnoitered the rebel brigade commander Lu Yün (a general under Wu P'ei-fu), escaped to the Hsiao-ts'ao Temple on Hsia-hsi Street, and reported that we were surrounded for attack — Lu committed suicide because of this. The work of the Guide Corps was most outstanding when our troops were guided by Heng Ch'a to cross the Shih-tzu Cliffs. We arrived in the hsien seat at North Street. The enemy was still unaware of us, so that his entire army was taken prisoner without an escape. The Transport Corps had people who transported things several dozen li and those who transported things of their own accord and asked for no compensation. The Propaganda Corps, in addition to actively spreading propaganda, distributing leaflets, and making posters, accompanied our troops to the front lines to conduct propaganda campaigns, to encourage our fighting spirit and morale, and to issue calls to the masses. The Morale Corps sent up tea, water, rice, and gruel to the firing line and comforted the soldiers. The Deception Corps was deployed over mountains and valleys and set up pine tree cannon and shotgun explosives, setting them off at intervals. Sometimes their screaming and drum-beating would wreak havoc with the enemy troops. The Demolition Corps destroyed the enemy's electric power lines, destroyed his bridges, and cut off his lines of retreat. [9]

The rapid attack and occupation of Changsha and the maintenance of order throughout the city derived its force from the direct participation of the workers in the battle. On July 8, after the Northern Expeditionary Army had begun its general attack, the working masses of Changsha, under the leadership of the United Association of Labor Organizations, prepared for an uprising within the city in response to the Northern Expeditionary Army. Because the enemy troops were enormous in number and because the masses themselves lacked weapons, the uprising was unsuccessful. On July 9 Yeh K'ai-hsin fled, and the people of Changsha became panicky. The United Association of Labor Organizations organized over one thousand workers into a Security Corps and kept guard over the various important roads in and around the city, maintaining order within the city itself. Later, the great majority of the ruthless troops under the command of Yeh K'ai-hsin who were retreating from Hsiangt'an to Changsha were disarmed by the workers' Security Corps, some workers being injured in this action. Actually, the working class of Changsha at this time was already in possession of some arms. The workers asked the Northern Expeditionary Army's Eighth Army whether they could keep these arms or all join the Eighth Army, but both requests were refused and the Eighth Army disarmed them. There was a small number of rifles not handed over that later became the weapons base for the Changsha workers' Disciplinary Team.

In lending assistance to the Northern Expeditionary Army, the Hunan working masses organized a large number of Transport Corps to help with logistics. The city of Changsha alone had a Transport Corps of three or four thousand people organized by the United Association of Labor Organizations. The Transport Corps organized by the workers at Anyüan and Chu-p'ing also contained more than a thousand people each.

After the Northern Expeditionary Army entered Hunan, there was a tremendous development of both the labor and peasant movements. From consciously giving impetus to and participating in the Northern Expedition, the peasants rapidly moved toward the development of their own organization — the peasant association — and went further to raise their own personal and urgent political-economic demands on their own initiative. And they went even further to demand the rights of participation in and management of the government. According to the reports from the hsien in Hunan in November 1926, those that had already set up hsien peasant associations were the twenty-eight hsien of Changsha, Hsiang-hsiang, Liu-yang, Hsiang-t'an, Heng-yang, Ning-hsiang, I-yang, Ch'a-ling, Nan-hsien, Li-hsien, Han-shou, Heng-shan, Ch'i-hsien, Lan-shan, Tz'u-li, P'ing-chiang, Li-ling, Pao-ch'ing, Lin-hsiang, Feng-yang, Lin-hsien, I-chang, Yüeh-yang, Ch'ang-te, Hsin-ning, Hua-jung, Sui-ning, and Lin-wu. Places that founded bureaus for preparation of hsien peasant associations were the nineteen hsien of Wu-kang, Yüan-chiang, Hsin-hua, Yung-hsing, Ju-ch'eng, Chia-ho, Hsü-p'u, Lu-ch'i, Lin-li, T'ao-yüan, Chih-chiang, Ma-yang, An-hsiang, Ch'eng-pu, Hsiu-hsien, Hsin-t'ien, Ch'ang-ning, An-hua, and Ling-hsien. Special districts were the fifty-li radius outside Changsha and the Chu-chou-P'ing-hsiang Railway. The communications areas were Ling-ling, Tao-hsien, An-jen, Kuei-tung, Tzu-hsing, Tung-an, and Ning-yüan. In sum, there were 462 regional peasant associations and 6,867 village peasant associations with a total membership of more than 1,367,000.

We can see from the above that the development of the peasant movement was centered in the Hsiang River valley. The various hsien bordering the lake (Tung-t'ing Lake) and located in the valley of the Tzu-shui [Tzu River] were next. Within the borders of Hunan these areas had always been important as far as military and political matters were concerned, and they constituted the base area for support of the Northern Expedition.

In Comrade Mao Tse-tung's article "Report on an Investigation of the Peasant Movement in Hunan," the stirring and seething conditions of the agrarian revolution in Hunan at the time are narrated in great detail, with great vigor, and with great enthusiasm. Let us look at the peasants' revolutionary dictatorship of the time, as movingly described by Mao Tse-tung:

The main targets of attack by the peasants are the local tyrants, the evil gentry and the lawless landlords, but in passing they also hit out against patriarchal ideas and institutions, against the corrupt officials in the cities and against bad practices and customs in the rural areas. In force and momentum the attack is tempestuous; those who bow before it survive and those who resist perish. As a result, the privileges which the feudal landlords enjoyed for thousands of years are being shattered to pieces. Every bit of the dignity and prestige built up by the landlords is being swept into the dust. With the collapse of the power of the landlords, the peasant associations have now become the sole organs of authority and the popular slogan "All power to the peasant associations" has become a reality. Even trifles such as a quarrel between husband and wife are brought to the peasant association. Nothing can be settled unless someone from the peasant association is present. The association actually dictates all rural affairs, and, quite literally, "whatever it says, goes." Those who are outside the associations can only speak well of them and cannot say anything against them. The local tyrants, evil gentry and lawless landlords have been deprived of all right to speak, and none of them dares even mutter dissent.... In short, what was looked down upon four months ago as a "gang of peasants" has now become a most honorable institution. Those who formerly prostrated themselves before the power of the gentry now bow before the power of the peasants. No matter what their identity, all admit that the world since last October is a different one [In SW, I, pp. 25-26].

In the areas of economics and politics, the struggles waged by the peasants against the local bullies and evil gentry were resolute and vehement. At the same time, the peasants also did a good deal of work in improving customs and in economic and cultural construction. In sum, the Hunan peasants, under the leadership of the Communist Party, performed work in the following three areas:

1) Economic struggle: (a) rent reduction, (b) reduction in interest payments, (c) reduction in mortgage payments, (d) substitution of new leases, (e) equalization of rice prices, prohibition against exports, (f) abolition of all the extraeconomic exactions of the landlords, (g) confiscation of the property of local bullies and evil gentry, establishment of a peasants' bank, etc.

2) Political struggle: (a) bring down the local bullies and evil gentry: reckon the accounts, issue fines, "wear the high hat" and go into the countryside organizing trials, punish with the death penalty on a grand scale individual local bullies and evil gentry (there were up to twenty or thirty thousand people executed at the Yü-ch'ih-hua meeting in Changsha); (b) bring down the old militia system and give all authority to the peasant associations; (c) oppose

excessive taxation and contributions; (d) Participate in hsien government. In hsien where the power of the peasant association is great the hsien government should follow the orders of the peasant association almost exclusively; (e) dissolve the Home Guard Bureau and seize their rifles; (f) defy the illegal troops; (g) wipe out the local bandits, etc.

3) Other work in antifeudal struggle and rural construction: improvement of customs, like the prohibition against gambling and opium, the elimination of foot-binding, and the abolition of superstition; work, like the establishment of schools, the repairing and building of roads, and the building of embankments.

In the very short space of a few months more than one million members of the peasant associations, with peasants and farm laborers as the mainstay, propelled a full ten million of the peasant masses to turn the villages upside down. In places where the strength of the peasants was great, all feudal domination was smashed to pieces and all power was truly with the peasant associations. People of all social classes were drawn into this change, and people of every kind and description were compelled to bare their real faces completely in the presence of this agrarian revolution.

## COMRADE MAO TSE-TUNG AT THE ALL-HUNAN PEASANTS' AND WORKERS' CONGRESS

The All-Hunan Peasants' Congress and All-Hunan Workers' Congress met simultaneously in Changsha on December 1, 1926, in order to make further headway in "eradicating the evils carried over from feudalism, in overthrowing the warlord government, in consolidating the rear of the Northern Expedition, in ensuring the power of the revolution, and in satisfying their own needs," and also to sum up experience, to exchange information on conditions in various places, and to make a decision on the guidelines and steps for future work. This was an event that set the entire province astir. Every place that had worker and peasant revolutionary organizations held celebrations on behalf of this event. The Peasants' Congress had 170 representatives from 52 hsien and two special regions, representing a total of over 1.3 million members. The Workers' Congress had 175 representatives from 52 regional and industrial unions representing over 320,000 members.

The Congresses met for a total of twenty-six days. During the first few days, they met in joint session, heard reports, and then split up into separate meetings to discuss the proposals. The Peasants' Congress passed a total of thirty-three draft resolutions. Each of the questions dealing with the interests of the peasants and the agrarian revolution was included. The most frequent proposals concerned the questions of tenancy, the Home Guard, the local bullies and evil gentry, and the arming of the peasants for self-defense. The Congress fully supported the peasants in the use of revolutionary measures to wage political and economic struggle. The Congress passed important proposals on lowering rent, lowering mortgages (or doing away with mortgages), prohibiting high interest, abolishing the Home Guard, and organizing a peasants' Self-Defense Militia. In addition, it specifically emphasized the importance of unifying and centralizing the strength of the peasants and suggested the founding of an All-China Peasants' Association (the All-China Peasants' Association was founded in May 1927 in Wuhan with Comrade Mao Tse-tung as chairman*). Both Congresses formally created a provincial leadership organ for the peasants and workers. The majority of the people elected for positions of responsibility were members of the Communist Party.

During the meetings of the Congresses, the representatives raised numerous charges against the local bullies, evil gentry, and strikebreakers of their areas, demanding that the government deal with them according to the law. On January 4, 1927, the Hunan Special Court for Judgment of Local Bullies and Evil Gentry was founded. Special courts for the various hsien were formally set up at the same time. For the most part, the committee chairmen of the peasant associations and the labor unions, the branch Party standing committee, and the hsien magistrate took responsibility for organization.

The most significant thing that happened during these sessions of the Congresses was the attendance by Comrade Mao Tse-tung and two important talks that he gave. Because of Mao Tse-tung's long and deep association with the Hunan revolutionary movement, he enjoyed great prestige among the revolutionary cadres and revolutionary masses throughout the province. Thus, when both Congresses convened and heard that Mao Tse-tung was coming to the Hunan-Hupei area to investigate the peasant movement, they sent a telegram asking him to come and lead them personally. In mid-

---

* The Chairman of this Association was in fact Mao's old acquaintance from Changsha, T'an Yen-k'ai. See Schram, Mao Tse-tung, pp. 102-103 [S.R.S.].

December the news of Mao's return to Changsha got out. The representatives were overjoyed and formally convened a welcoming meeting for him. The welcoming announcement read:

Mr. Mao Tse-tung has gained preeminent merit in his work in the revolution. He has put particular emphasis on the peasant movement. Last year he returned to Hunan and in the area of Shao-shan, Hsiang-t'an, was active in the peasant movement. Except for the Yüeh-pei Peasants' Association, this was the first peasant movement in the province. Later, Chao Heng-t'i learned about this and plotted to put an end to Mr. Mao's life. Mr. Mao found out about these plans and made his way to Canton. Now the revolutionary military forces are expanding vigorously toward the north, and last month Mr. Mao went to the Yangtze River area to investigate the status of the peasant movement for the purpose of developing the nationwide peasant movement and establishing a revolutionary base. When the Congress convened it sent a telegram asking Mr. Mao to return to Hunan to exercise leadership over everything.

On the afternoon of December 20 the Congresses jointly welcomed Comrade Mao Tse-tung at the Educational Society's Huanteng Auditorium. Many people came on their own to listen, and even the upper floors of the building were all packed. According to the extract in the Congress Bulletin [Ta-hui jih-k'an], Mao Tse-tung said primarily that the central problem of the national revolution was the problem of the peasants. No matter whether it was bringing down imperialism, the warlords, the local bullies and evil gentry, or whether it was wanting to develop industry and commerce, all these necessarily depended on the solution of the peasant question.

On December 28 the All-Hunan Peasants' and Workers' Congresses held a joint closing ceremony and again asked Comrade Mao Tse-tung to talk on the problems of the revolutionary united front. According to the reports in the Hunan People's Gazette [Hunan min-pao] that appeared the next day, Mao Tse-tung pointed out in his lecture that on the counterrevolutionary side there was already an international, nationwide and provincewide united front organization, and that the revolutionary side should have the same kind of united front with which to oppose them. He severely denounced the calumny about the peasants, namely, that this was a "lazy peasants' movement," and he denounced the reactionary theory that "until imperialism is brought down, there should be no internal troubles." He said that in the past during the period of warlord government it was only the landlords who were permitted to wage struggles against the peasants for raising rent and interest. Was it "creating trouble" now when the peasants demanded from the landlords a slight lowering of the rent and interest? He pointed out that the people who only permitted the landlords to wage struggles against the peasants and did not permit the peasants to wage struggles against the landlords stood on the side of imperialism and were against the revolution; they were people who were undermining the revolution. He also specifically mentioned the fact that although at the time Hunan was ruled by the "Nationalist government," it was in reality ruled by the "Nationalist government" and Chao Heng-t'i together, for although Chao was no longer in Hunan, his evil remained — local bullies, evil gentry, and corrupt officials still had great power in Hunan.

After the representatives attending the Congress had heard Mao Tse-tung's talk, their concept of, and stand in relation to, the necessity of waging a resolute struggle against the counterrevolutionaries was more clear-cut, and they all felt that there was now more certainty in the areas of work method and strategy.

Later facts proved that the two speeches Comrade Mao Tse-tung gave before the All-Hunan Peasants' and Workers' Congress played a very great role in motivating the Hunan peasant movement into a more extensive and more penetrating development.

## THE REVOLUTIONARY-COUNTERREVOLUTIONARY STRUGGLE ON THE PEASANT QUESTION

The peasants' revolt disturbed the gentry's sweet dreams. When the news from the countryside reached the cities, it caused immediate uproar among the gentry.... From the middle social strata upward to the Kuomintang right-wingers, there was not a single person who did not sum up the whole business in the phrase, "It's terrible!" Under the impact of the views of the "It's terrible!" school then flooding the city, even quite revolutionary-minded people became downhearted as they pictured the events in the countryside in their mind's eye; and they were unable to deny the word "terrible." [10]

The landlords and evil gentry, the Kuomintang right-wingers, the reactionary officers in the Northern Expeditionary Army, as well as all those gentlemen who were critical of the peasants' throwing off the feudal yoke launched out on a counterrevolutionary propaganda offensive, creating every manner of "theory" and rumor to discredit the peasant movement.

The first "theory" to appear was that "the peasants are happy." For example, after Chang Shih-chao [11] returned to Hunan, he delivered a speech in Changsha in which he noted that on his return to China from Europe he had seen peasants living in broken-down thatched houses who nevertheless displayed great happiness. Not until then did he realize that the Chinese spirit and the spirit of the West were fundamentally different. He thus advocated that we "establish the nation [kuo] on the basis of the peasants," and maintained that if everybody returned to the villages, "the internal disturbances would die down of their own accord." This "theory" was promoted and expanded by a great many people at the time, who said that "the peasants plow the fields to eat. They eat the fruit of their own labor and are pleased and happy," or "they know nothing about order and disorder, take no part in promotions or demotions, but the mind of the peasant is the most peaceful and happy." There were also some people who wrote letters to the Hunan Popular Gazette, saying that the peasants were not in misery, and who counseled the newspaper not to write articles spreading the idea that the peasants were in misery. There was still another theory: "the peasants know nothing." This held that all the peasants knew how to do was to "act blindly" and that they were "inadequate to accomplish anything but more than enough to spoil everything."

The reactionary propaganda that subsequently had the most influence was the slander that the peasant movement was a "movement of the riffraff, a movement of the lazy peasants." It held that the peasants' movement for a reduction in rent and interest payments was a "manifestation of laziness," and that it "promoted a lazy-peasant doctrine" that would then "block the development of agricultural production." At the time, no one dared say publicly that the peasant associations could not be set up, and so some people seemed to retreat a step to say: "The peasant associations can be set up, but the people who are doing the work right now are no good; they should change these people!" [SW, I, p. 29]. Actually, the rank-and-file peasant associations of the time were firmly in the hands of the poor farm laborers; the peasants themselves had risen up and taken control. Yet in the eyes of the local bullies and evil gentry, those peasants who dared rise up and rebel were, of course, all "riffraff."

Another very vicious theory was that the movement "obstructs the collection of taxes," and that "it affects the Northern Expedition." P'eng Kuo-chün and other Kuomintang right-wingers yelled the loudest. At the time, P'eng was inspector of the Yüeh-chou Pass. They said that the decrease in the tax yield in Hunan was owing to the fact that the peasants had "gone too far." "People with money all fled to the cities — to Hankow or to Shanghai. The taxes could not be collected." "If the tax income does not do well, there will be no way to get military supplies. We cannot throw away the Northern Expedition on account of the peasants." The intention here was to press the big hat of obstructing the Northern Expedition down over the peasants' heads. That there were financial difficulties in Hunan and that the taxes were in decline at the time is, indeed, a fact (it had always been so ever since the days of Chao Heng-t'i). But the real reasons behind the financial difficulty were: (1) The enormous corruption of tax officials, who helped themselves to the pickings, and the merchant gentry who contracted for the "public debts" and "loans." (2) Finances were not unified; for example, "guest troops" could "borrow funds" at will. (3) Industry was in decline owing to the war. One principal approach the peasants took in waging their economic struggle was the "prohibition and equalization" scheme. The purpose was to ensure the people's food supply by preventing the landlords and rich peasants from sending their grain out of the province and by prohibiting them from hoarding and speculating and raising the price of grain at will. The peasant associations made a detailed investigation and got control of all the rice from the various hsien to equalize the areas of surplus and deficiency. This policy was carried out very meticulously. When the Northern Expeditionary Army bought up rice, the peasant associations took full responsibility. The peasant associations initiated a widespread movement to "save on food to help the troops" and guaranteed the supply of food to the front. Later, the Provincial Peasants' Congress passed a resolution and finally did away with the prohibitions. The reactionaries, however, used this opportunity to launch a great wave of propaganda saying that the peasants were "undermining social order" and "creating havoc in the rear of the Northern Expedition."

Besides this, every kind and manner of rumor was spread. For example, Canton in 1926 was filled with the rumor that the Nationalist government had composed a "communist program" called the "three-three-three-one system." Another was the "four-four-two system." That is, the grain harvested from the field would be distributed as follows: 30 percent to the landlord, 30 percent to the tenant, 30 percent to the Party and 10 percent to the peasant association. The other system saw 40 percent going to the landlord and the tenant, and 20 percent going to the Party. Now this "communist program" — the "three-three-three-one system" and the "four-four-two system" — had come to Hunan. There were still other rumors that the peasant associations were set up for the purpose of conscripting troops: "All those who join the peasant associations will become part of the Northern Expeditionary Army." Aside from these, there were rumors such as "communism [means] wives in common [kung-ch'an kung-ch'i], and they exercise naked." Even in Shanghai and Tientsin there was this rumor: "Hunan is already communized."

This propaganda offensive of the reactionaries played a considerable role and was quite capable of eliciting middle-class sympathy. For example, the rank-and-file "middle-of-the-roaders" of the Kuomintang were now vacillating more than ever and became yes-men to the reactionaries, arguing that the peasants should only participate in the work of the revolution (meaning that they should only expend their effort) and should not have their own personal economic and political demands; they should not carry out class struggle in the villages. They said that the peasant movement could develop, but that it should not engage in any actions that were "off the track"; it should not engage in "reckless action." They said that the peasants were "without knowledge," that the peasant movement was being used by other people. It even went so far that some people followed this with the cry that the peasant movement was "the action of local bandits." They wanted to "do away with the peasant movement," "at least put some limits on the peasant movement."

The various organizations of the Chinese Communist Party throughout Hunan waged a great many struggles against this reactionary propaganda. On the propaganda front, besides publishing many reports on the status of the peasant movement and on the cruel murder of the peasants by the local bullies and evil gentry in the Hunan People's Gazette and the Hunan Popular Gazette, almost every number of The Warrior [Chan-shih] (the organ of the provincial Party committee) carried articles refuting the wild theories [described above] and exposing the activities of the Kuomintang right wing and the counterrevolutionaries. In the beginning of March 1927 there was also published a pamphlet entitled Hu-nan nung-min yün-tung wen-t'i lun-wen chi [Collected Essays on the Question of the Hunan Peasant Movement]. The March 5 issue of The Warrior began to serialize Mao's "Report on an Investigation of the Peasant Movement in Hunan," which thoroughly settled accounts with the counterrevolutionary propaganda of the reactionaries.

Besides concentrating their reactionary propaganda efforts in the cities, the landlord reactionaries launched a terrible campaign

of vicious attack and slaughter in villages and small towns everywhere.

From July to September 1926, when the Northern Expeditionary
Army was advancing victoriously, there had as yet been no great
struggles in the rural areas, and the destructive activities of the
reactionaries were not yet too bad. High-ranking officers in the
Northern Expeditionary Army were still "issuing orders of encouragement" in regard to the peasants' enthusiasm for participating
in the battle, and society too was full of praise and approbation.
But by October, after the fire of the peasants had been concentrated
in an attack against the local bullies, evil gentry, and lawless landlords, the numerous reactionary forces in the countryside rapidly
collected together and launched a frenzied and bloodthirsty counterattack; in places where the power of the peasant association was
weak the reactionaries launched preemptive attacks.

The most widespread offensive stratagem used by the reactionaries in the various areas was to utilize the old Home Guard forces
to massacre the peasants openly. The rural Home Guard Bureaus
were the landlords' militia. During the warlord days they constituted the real locus of political power in the countryside and were
the organs that directly ruled the peasants. Arresting and killing
peasants had long been commonplace for the heads of these bureaus.
For example, the great tyrant of Ning-hsiang, Yang Chih-tse, ran
a Home Guard unit for several years and killed over four hundred
peasants. There was widespread use of brutal torture by the Home
Guard of every hsien. Once a peasant entered the "Bureau" he
would either meet death or become a cripple. At this time in places
where "the rifle had not yet replaced the carrying-pole" the Home
Guard either directly or indirectly was in a position antagonistic
to the peasants. After the Northern Expeditionary Army arrived,
there were incidents in which the Home Guard shot peasants, a
rather early example occurring in mid-August 1926 when the re-
signed head of the T'ung-wen Home Guard in Ning-hsiang instigated
the members of the Guard to shoot the committee chairman of the
village peasant association, Mei Tz'u-ch'eng, and several other
peasants. After September this sort of incident steadily increased.
Below are some examples excerpted from the Hunan People's Gazette and The Warrior that provide a glimpse of the landlords'
frenzied attacks:

The local bully of Kuei-yang, a certain Lei, conspired with the assistant head
of the Home Guard, P'eng Jen-shou, and the strikebreakers Li Jung-ch'en and

Liu Tung-p'u to send Home Guard troops to beat the special commissioner of the provincial Party, Ho Han, the secretary of the peasant association, Liu Chi-yüeh, and dozens of other Party members and workers. They secretly arrested over twenty Party members and visited destruction on the hsien Party branch, the peasant association, and the hsien labor union and organized an illegal Party branch, peasant association, and labor union (Hunan People's Gazette, November 10, 1926).

Wang Jih-te, member of the Yu-hsien Peasant Association, Eastern Region, joined a great number of his fellow-peasants in going to question the head of the Home Guard in his area, Wang Tse-min, because he had used the occasion of a [local] fete to sell [the rights to set up] gambling [stalls]. Because this ran counter to his interests, Wang then led a force of several dozen armed Home Guards and surrounded all the responsible committee members of the hsien Party branch, the peasant association, and the labor union, and set to robbing and killing them. All their household belongings were completely destroyed and Wang Jih-te was brutally executed (Petition of the Chia-ho Peasant Association as reported in the Hunan People's Gazette, December 31).

The bureau head of the Yüeh-yang Home Guard, Chiang Tzu-lin, burned down the village, demolished six or seven houses, and massacred a large number of peasants (Petition of peasant representatives as recorded in the Hunan People's Gazette, December 28).

The Home Guard Bureau of Li-hsien, Northern Region, smashed the village peasant association, arresting and shooting to death a number of peasants. The bureau head of the Three Eastern Regions conspired with local bandits to kill one peasant and arrest more than twenty, fining them more than 400 yuan.

On December 20 all the follow-peasants of the regional peasant association of Ch'üan-chiao-chen, I-yang, participated in the inaugural meeting of the Eighth Regional Party Branch. The bureau head of the said region was normally very hostile to revolutionaries. On this day, just when all the peasants, Party members, and masses passed in front of the regional headquarters, the peasant association was labeled an outlaw band and the bureau head instigated the Home Guard troops to open fire, killing the peasant Liu Shao-ch'iu and seriously wounding Yüan Yao-jen, Hu Ching-fu, and several others. In addition, they smashed and destroyed a decorated sedan-chair and the funeral picture of the director [i.e., Sun Yat-sen] that had been set up (Hunan People's Gazette, December 30).

The local bully from south Hunan, Ch'en Po-ch'un, in league with the Home Guard, dispersed the peasant association with armed force. In An-hua it was discovered that the local bandits had slaughtered over three hundred peasants. The commander of the Security Force for eastern Hunan, Lo Ting, for no reason executed Lo Chen, the chairman of the Peasant Association Committee of Yu-hsien, Eastern Region. It is a proven fact that all this was plotted by the local bullies and evil gentry (The Warrior, January 14, 1927).

The twenty-two friendly villages of Ch'a-ling summoned a meeting for March 16 to change their organization into a peasant association. The evil gentry Huang Cho-fu, Fan Kuan-jui, and Fan Kuei-shan hired several dozen hooligans, conspired with the Home Guard Bureau head, Lo Chao-hung, and surrounded the chairman of the organization, Fan Kuei-jung, and beat him. Fan suffered dozens of knife wounds and died. They then burned his corpse with kerosine (The Warrior, January 14, 1927).

What was this P'eng Po-kai incident that aroused the "implacable anger" of the Kuomintang right wing at the time? In February 1927 the peasant masses from T'ung-wen-chen in Hsiang-hsiang took the famous local bully and evil gentry P'eng Po-kai in custody to the hsien [office] for punishment. Before this was accomplished, P'eng bribed ninety hooligans to use swords and clubs to break him out along the way. The peasants wrestled with the hooligans in self-defense and then killed P'eng.

In areas where the strength of the peasant association was great, the Home Guard either gradually lost its ruling effectiveness or dissolved itself on its own initiative. Then the local bullies and evil tyrants would join hands with the local bandits and launch an attack against the peasant association.

The local bullies and evil gentry of An-hua conspired with the local bandits and killed over two hundred peasants. In the archives of the Provincial Peasant Association almost every nine out of ten reports deal with the local bullies and evil gentry joining up with the bandits, drinking cock's-blood wine, pointing to Heaven and swearing "Down with the peasant association. Death to the special commissioners." [12]

In the more out-of-the-way cities and towns the reactionaries also organized every kind and manner of open rebellion and even armed violence. For example, on December 1, 1926, the reactionaries of I-chang took advantage of the celebration of the convening of the All-Hunan Peasants' and Workers' Congress to make up some false peasant association membership cards and got some hooligans and backward peasants to march in the streets. Headed by the Home Guard Bureau, they smashed up the First Regional Peasant Association and tried to beat confessions out of the Association's cadres. On December 3 the commander of the Ju-ch'eng Merchant Security Corps [Pao shang tui] and the head of the Home Guard Bureau led a huge armed force and laid seige to the provincial Party branch, confiscated postal and cable communications, and put the entire city under martial law. In October 1926 on the anniversary of the Revolution the reactionaries of Lei-yang bribed some riffraff who, usurping the name of the masses, smashed the Miscellaneous Tax Bureau and the Transportation Tax Bureau. In Lan-t'ien, An-hua, there also occurred tragedies resulting from the armed violence of the reactionaries. Because their employees had organized a labor union and set up a consumers' cooperative, and because the dishonest merchants felt this was against their interests, they established liaison with the local bullies and evil gentry, bought off the director of the Merchant Corps and, on the third anniversary of Lenin's death, dispatched armed soldiers to prevent the masses' demonstration. At Hung-shui Ridge they fired on the masses, killing three peasants and wounding several dozen people. Following this they also destroyed all the revolutionary organizations and organs in the town of Lan-t'ien.

Besides every description of brutal attack, the landlord reactionaries also set in motion every kind and manner of intrigue and subversion against the peasant movement. For example, they organized bogus peasant associations and bogus progressive organizations by utilizing clan relationships. They bribed riffraff to infiltrate the peasant associations and create trouble among the peasants. They fought their way into and controlled the lower echelon Kuomintang party branches. They joined in league with the reactionary officers within the Northern Expeditionary Army and utilized all the remaining mechanisms of the old regime. At the time, the landlord class in just about every area had reactionary organizations that went under different names. For example, in Heng-yang there was the "White Party" [Pai-hua tang — lit., "Whiten" Party] (organized by the landlord tyrant Liu Mo-seng when he was recruiting new troops for the Northern Expeditionary Army in Heng-yang. Afterward, Liu was publicly judged and executed by the Heng-yang masses). There was the "Property Protection Party" [Pao ch'an tang] in Hsiang-hsiang, Hsiang-t'an, Ning-hsiang, and I-yang. There was the "Property Protection Society" [Pao ch'an hui] in Ch'i-yang. Besides the appearance of the "Three Loves Party" [San ai tang] in Li-ling, there was also the so-called "Dog Beating Society" [Ta kuo hui], which viciously maligned the peasants. There were a great many hsien magistrates who, when the forces of reaction lifted their heads, openly stood on their side. For example, after the most reactionary evil gentry of Hua-jung's An-chi Dike area, Ch'en Tso-mei, was beaten to death by the peasant masses, the hsien magistrate, Wang Pin, sent the Home Guard soldiers and the Emergency Corps [Ching-pei tui] to smash the peasant association, injuring a great many peasants. Subsequently, he further asked a battalion of the Defense Corps stationed in Yüeh-yang to come and give the peasants a demonstration of their power — the homes of many peasants were smashed and destroyed. Another example: after the hsien magistrate of Ch'en-hsien, Hsiung Shih-feng, was bribed, he released the local bullies and evil gentry who had been arrested. By this time, reactionary officers had already begun to appear in the Northern Expeditionary Army who publicly stood on the side of the landlord gentry who oppressed the peasants. After the well-known boss of the feudal gentry, Yeh Te-hui,* was executed, Hunan's local bullies and evil gentry were greatly aroused and, one after the other, they forced their way into the Northern Expeditionary Army, a great number of them enlisting in the forces under Ho Chien, the most powerful reactionary of all.

During the revolutionary period between 1926 and 1927 the Hunan peasants killed only a small number of tyrant bosses in their movement to bring down the local bullies and evil gentry — people like Ning-hsiang's Liu Chao and Yang Chih-tse, Hsiang-t'an's Yen Jung-ch'iu, and Hua-jung's Mei Shih. All told, throughout the entire province there were no more than several dozen people directly executed by the peasants. Nevertheless, from the fragmentary material mentioned above we can see that the slaughter of the peasants by the tyrannical landlords and counterrevolutionaries was more than several score that number!

The urban and rural reactionary wing at the time — the local bullies and evil gentry, the lawless landlords, the dishonest merchants, the strikebreakers, the reactionary officers in the Northern Expeditionary Army, the remnant forces of Chao Heng-t'i, the Kuomintang right wing — and the other counterrevolutionaries had as their nerve center the Kuomintang right-wing clique headed by Liu Yüeh-chih (i.e., Liu Mei-chai, the tyrannical landlord of Heng-shan who, in April 1950, was executed by the People's Government). At the time, Liu was the head of the provincial Kuomintang Peasant Department. He had both authority and power, which made things very convenient for him.

After the reorganization of the Kuomintang in 1924, a great crowd of those elements who had in the past presumed upon their Party affiliation to engage in private business and wax rich by rising in the bureaucracy remained within the Party. For this reason the Kuomintang split into a three-way political division of left, center, and right. In 1926, after Chiang Kai-shek unleashed the counter-revolutionary coup d'etat of March 20, the right-wing reactionaries once again raised their heads, and the new right-wing bloc headed by Chiang Kai-shek and Tai Chi-t'ao, the "Society for the Study of Sun Yat-sen-ism" [Sun Wen chu-i hsüeh-hui] (the old right-wing bloc had been the Western Hills Conference [Hsi shan hui-i]),

---

* Yeh Te-hui was Hunan's leading Confucian scholar; he was shot on March 5 on the Educational Plaza in Changsha after a public trial. For a sketch of his personality and social role, see McDonald, "Urban Origins," pp. 554-555 [S.R.S.].

spread out everywhere. At the beginning of 1926 when the Kuomintang had just moved into open activity in Hunan, the right-wing elements of the "Western Hills Conference" and the "Society for the
Study of Sun Yat-sen-ism" joined in league with Chao Heng-t'i and
followed his direction, launching every kind of attack, subversion,
and mutiny against the revolutionary Hunan branch of the Kuomintang. They published malicious notices in the press about their
"repudiation" of the Hunan Party branch. In Ch'ang-te's Second
Normal School an armed conflict occurred between elements of the
"Society for the Study of Sun Yat-sen-ism" and some left-wing students. There was also an incident in which the special commissioner of the provincial Party was arrested. After the Northern
Expeditionary Army entered Hunan, the workers' and peasants'
mass movement surged upward, and the power of the Kuomintang's
revolutionary wing saw tremendous development, the right wing
temporarily not daring to launch openly any counterrevolutionary
activities. In August 1926 Chiang Kai-shek came to Changsha. There
he saw that the revolutionary power of the masses was too strong,
that the Northern Expeditionary Army within the borders of Hunan
was still unable to secure the area for him, and that Communist
Party members and left-wing elements held power in the provincial
Party apparatus, and so on the surface he was as full of praise for
the Communist Party as possible and said that he would protect the
Hunan Party branch. Not long thereafter he secretly led his exceedingly undisciplined First Army, [linked to] his family clique, from
Chu-chou to Kiangsi.

In January and February 1927 the Hunan peasant movement had
already entered a turbulent stage, while at the same time, Chiang
Kai-shek was just in the midst of brewing up his counterrevolutionary revolt and organizing a nationwide counterrevolutionary front.
The problems of moving the capital to Nan-ch'ang, dissolving the
municipal Party branch in Canton, reorganizing the Hunan and Hupei provincial Party branches, as well as the problem of the Kuomintang "moderates" joining hands with the Japanese and Chang
(the Feng-tien warlord, Chang Tso-lin), all followed each other in
quick succession. The line about "exterminating the radical forces
within the Kuomintang" had already been disseminated everywhere.
All these things instigated the right-wing bloc of the Hunan Kuomintang to launch an organized and planned attack against the revolution and bring about the so-called "Leftist Society" incident.

The boss of the Kuomintang right wing and the landlords' "Property Protection Party" was Liu Yüeh-chih. Other key figures were

important members in the provincial and municipal Party branches of the time, Wang Feng-chieh, Li Yü-yao, Mao Mao-hsün, Ch'en Chia-jen, and Wang Ch'üan. Liu Yüeh-chih used his power of office to hold back the telegram sent from the provincial Party that recommended moving the capital to Wuhan. He proposed a reorganization of the Hunan provincial Party and expressed his "extreme grief and indignation" at the Ning-hsiang peasants' killing of the tyrant P'eng Po-kai. The primary activities of Liu Yüeh-chih's "Leftist Society" were naturally taken up with subverting the peasant movement that was directly injuring Liu's personal interests and position. This group of Kuomintang members had in the past called themselves "reformists" and "moderates," but when they saw the flames of the revolution flare up they cunningly thought to use the "tactics of seduction" and took the name of "Leftist Society," hoping to "mix up the fish eyes with the pearls" [i.e., things that look alike but are really different].

On December 12 the landlord and head of the "Peasant Department," Liu Yüeh-chih, publicized in the newspapers his program for a peasant movement that would protect the landlord class — "The Plan for the Peasant Movement." In this he openly opposed class struggle in the rural areas and labeled the members of the peasant association "local villains and hooligans." He wanted the peasants and the landlords to "bind together their feelings," to "put forth all their efforts for the increase of agricultural production and progress in the improvement of agriculture." He advocated that should the peasant associations of the various levels under the control of the Kuomintang not "adhere to discipline," they should "individually be reorganized, investigated, and punished." These "plans" of Liu Yüeh-chih were applauded by all counterrevolutionaries and hailed by the middle-of-the-roaders. The local bullies and evil gentry of the countryside had long since responded to the actions of Liu Yüeh-chih and rose up en masse to join the Kuomintang, previously considered a "red" organization. They thought to make use of the power and authority of the Kuomintang to intimidate the peasant associations. At this time a slogan emanated from the broad peasant masses: "People with money join the Nationalist [Party]; people without money join the peasant [associations]."

In its issue no. 35 the organ of the Hunan provincial committee of the Chinese Communist Party, The Warrior, published an article entitled "Ho wu Tso she" [What Kind of a Thing Is the Leftist Society?]. This article thoroughly unmasked the schemes of Liu Yüeh-chih. In the same number an article entitled "I-feng wei-fa ti hsin chih Liu Mei-chai hsien-sheng" [An Unsent Letter to Mr. Liu Mei-chai] pointed at Liu's nose and said:

You eat by collecting rents, and have, in fact, the kind of status characterized by the saying: "When at court an official, out of office a member of the gentry." Your relatives and old friends are middle and small landlords. The only reason you have come forward to make revolution is that you were menaced by Chao Heng-t'i and had no alternative. Your circumstances today are better than they were before. All you worry about is that you still have problems in maintaining and developing your family's [income from] rents in excess of 300 tan. Naturally you devise ways to maintain your own privileges and those of your relatives and old friends.

The reactionary wing under Liu Yüeh-chih openly launched its attack. If this counterrevolutionary activity were not resolutely put down it would, naturally, be very disadvantageous for the revolutionary situation that was then on the upsurge. Therefore the provincial and municipal Kuomintang Party branches that had Communist Party members and leftists as their mainstay decided to investigate and deal with the "Leftist Society." The residences of eight people, including Liu Yüeh-chih and Wang Feng-chieh, were searched by the municipal Bureau of Public Safety. Liu and the others were permanently expelled from the Party and their territories of activity, the three schools of San-hsiang, Ch'un-te, and Ch'en-kuang, were closed down. At that time, however, Liu and the others were not taken away for investigation and punishment. On February 27 the Organization Department of the provincial Kuomintang Party branch issued "Ch'a-chou tang-nei tsu-tang chih t'ung-kao" [An Announcement of an Investigation into the Internal Organization of the Party]. This document called on the Party branches of every level and the entire body of comrades to heighten their vigilance, to conduct close reconnaissance, and to wipe out thoroughly every counterrevolutionary action of the "Leftist Society" whenever one occurred.

Although Liu Yüeh-chih had been brought down, his "theories" — to avoid "disorder" in the countryside through peaceful construction, to use the Kuomintang to limit the actions of the peasants — were still very influential among a considerable number of people, including the Kuomintang middle-of-the-roaders. Nor could the activities of the "Leftist Society" outside the hsien be stopped completely. In Nan-hsien and Hua-jung hsien a great number of lower-level Party branches of the Kuomintang were still controlled by the evil gentry and landlords. Because of the Kuomintang's development to the right throughout the country, before the "Horse Day

Incident" the work of attacking the Kuomintang right wing and the
work of the peasants in bringing down the local bullies and evil gentry developed hand in hand. Later, in early May, the revolutionary
Hunan Party branch of the Kuomintang once again summoned an all-
province assembly to set Party affairs in order and to wipe out the
elements of the "Leftist Society."

## THE "REPORT ON AN INVESTIGATION OF
## THE PEASANT MOVEMENT IN HUNAN" AND A
## NEW STAGE OF THE HUNAN PEASANT MOVEMENT

Comrade Mao Tse-tung's "Report on an Investigation of the Peasant Movement in Hunan" is the most important document of the
Chinese Communist Party dating from the First Revolutionary
Civil War period. It is the crystallization of the correct ideological road within the Party represented by Mao Tse-tung. In accordance with the direct and dramatic struggle and life of the Hunan
peasants during the great revolutionary storm as well as the general tenets of Marxism, Mao drew scientific conclusions to direct
the advance of the entire revolution. In this report Mao Tse-tung
pointed out that the peasant question was the decisive question for
the entire Chinese revolution, that before one could achieve victory
in the revolution it was necessary to arouse the masses fully, to
organize them, and to depend on them. Although his correct views
at the time were completely rejected by the right-wing capitulationist bloc led by Ch'en Tu-hsiu, thus causing the failure of the Revolution, it was a tremendous inspiration for the Hunan agrarian revolutionary movement just in the midst of its great upsurge. The
broad masses of the Hunan Communist Party and the revolutionary
masses fully embraced the leadership of Comrade Mao Tse-tung
and turned their backs on the traitorous ambitions of Ch'en Tu-
hsiu, impelling the Hunan agrarian revolutionary movement to a
new stage — the stage of organizing and arming, of plunging deeply
into the struggle, and of solving the land question.

By April 1927 the membership of the peasant associations
throughout Hunan Province had already reached 5.18 million. According to reports from the various areas, the status of peasant
association organizations stood as follows:*

---

* It is interesting to compare these figures with the more detailed statistics
for the situation as of November 1926 given by Mao in the original version of
his Hunan report, translated in Day, Mao Zedong, pp. 348-350 (Mao Tse-tung chi,
Vol. 1, pp. 222-225) [S. R. S.].

| Membership | Hsien |
|---|---|
| 600,000 | Heng-yang |
| 300,000+ | Hsiang-t'an, Hsiang-hsiang, Liu-yang, P'ing-chiang |
| 200,000+ | Changsha, Li-ling, Ning-hsiang, Heng-shan, I-yang |
| 100,000+ | Han-shou, Hsiang-yin, Yüeh-yang, Lei-yang, Ch'ang-te, An-hua, Ch'en-hsien, Yu-hsien, Hua-jung, I-chang, Nan-hsien |
| 50,000+ | Ch'a-ling, Pao-ch'ing, Hsin-hua, Li-hsien |
| 10,000+ | An-jen, Sui-ning, Lu-ch'i, Chia-ho, Yüan-chiang, T'ao-yüan, Lin-wu, Tz'u-li, Ch'ang-ning, Hsin-t'ien, Kuei-tung, Tzu-hsing, Ling-hsien, Hsin-ning, Kuei-yang, Ju-ch'eng, Lin-hsiang, and [two] suburban regions |
| less than 10,000 | Chih-chiang, Ma-yang, Ling-ling, Ch'eng-pu, Ning-yüan, Tao-hsien, Hsü-p'u, An-hsiang, Lan-shan |

Among these hsien thirty-five had founded hsien peasant associations and sixteen had founded peasant association preparation bureaus, completely integrated under the leadership of the Provincial Peasant Association.

By this time the peasants had made the land question the first item on their agenda. The farm laborers brought forth the slogan of "equalizing distribution of rented land," the broad masses of poor peasants urgently demanded the distribution of the land, and in some places they spontaneously surveyed the land and began to distribute it. For example, the village of Hsia-ning in the vicinity of Changsha was one of the very first areas to put this into practice. The peasants distributed the land according to the population, but they used an approach that was not altogether correct: an adult received land that would produce eight tan of grain, minors were given four- or six-tan land. The peasants generally all had spears, and there was not one among them who didn't ardently plan to steal rifles from the Home Guard. The bulk of the reactionary arms of the Home Guard in Hsiang-t'an, P'ing-chiang, Heng-yang, I-yang, Liu-yang, and Ning-hsiang was seized by the peasant masses. The Peasants' Self-Defense Army founded a "Regular Corps." At the same time, de facto political power in the villages had already come into the hands of the peasant associations. The peasants also went a step further and demanded that they be allowed to run the hsien government. Because they had had the previous period of revolutionary experience, the peasants raised their vigilance on a wide scale against the landlord reactionaries. However, the mass movement was developing too quickly, and the Party leadership was totally incapable of keeping up with it. Specifically, the cadres were insufficiently prepared. Thus, the base of the mass movement at this time was not sufficiently consolidated.

On April 10, under the leadership of the members of the Communist Party and genuine left-wing elements, the provincial Kuomintang Party branch issued "Kao ch'üan sheng nung-min shu" [A Letter to the Peasants of the Province]. This proclamation very clearly pointed out that the objectives of the peasant movement were: (1) not only to bring down the local bullies, evil gentry and landlords, but specifically to bring down the feudal system upon which the existence of the local bullies and landlords depended; (2) not only to reduce rent and interest payments, but to solve the land question; (3) the peasants must acquire political power in the villages and also organize a peasants' self-defense army to crack down on the local bullies, evil gentry, lawless landlords, and all counterrevolutionaries.

By the beginning of May the Communist Party committees of Changsha, Ch'ang-te, and Heng-yang had already made preparations, and each had founded an armed Workers' and Peasants' Division, but they were by no means able to effect rapidly any firm organization. Before the "Horse Day Incident" the arming of peasants in the various areas was still very much a hit-and-miss affair; also, in a great number of areas the power of the old Home Guard had not been fully eliminated.

Overall, then, we can say that the time for a decisive battle with the counterrevolutionaries had gradually ripened. But within the revolution there existed this contradiction: On the one hand, the broad masses had been vigorously and dynamically mobilized, the power of the revolution had surged to unprecedented heights, the revolutionary masses, with the power of the peasants as the mainstay, were in favor of launching the most resolute and most fearless revolutionary actions to oppose all reactionary classes and, moreover, the counterrevolutionary camp was by no means stable and firm; the strength of the revolution surpassed that of the counterrevolution. On the other hand, however, the ranks of the Communist Party itself were very insecure. They had no experience, especially no experience in armed struggle. The leadership of the Party had fallen far, far behind the masses and still did not understand how to rally the strength of the thousands upon thousands of revolutionary masses or how to arm them to deal with possible unexpected events and win the victory of the Revolution. Lenin said:

With reformists, Mensheviks, in our ranks it is impossible to achieve victory in the proletarian revolution, it is impossible to retain it.... On the eve of revolution, and at a moment when a most fierce struggle is being waged for its victory, the slightest wavering in the ranks of the Party may wreck everything, frustrate the revolution, wrest the power from the hands of the proletariat: for this power is not yet consolidated, the attack upon it is still very strong [emphasis in the English edition]. [13]

Although at the time Hunan was a province that was able to receive directly the influence of Comrade Mao Tse-tung's correct line, this was true only to a certain degree and, moreover, mainly among the broad masses. The Party leadership in Hunan was unable to stand thoroughly and resolutely on the side of Mao Tse-tung's correct line. On the contrary, it could not help but be influenced by the right-capitulationist leadership of Ch'en Tu-hsiu, and thus, under the sudden onslaught of the counterrevolution, the Party leadership displayed vacillation and weakness and was unable to organize immediately the strength of the masses to launch out on any effective resistance against the counterrevolution.

## THE "HORSE DAY INCIDENT" AND ITS LESSON

In March 1927 the reactionary wing of the Kuomintang, headed by Chiang Kai-shek, launched a series of massacres: on March 11 it murdered the committee chairman of the Kiangsi General Labor Union, Ch'en Tsan-hsien; after Chiang Kai-shek himself came to Chiu-chiang on March 17 and to An-ch'ing on March 23, he immediately organized a secret agent force of hooligans to attack all revolutionary organs of the area and created a reign of white terror; after the Szechuan warlord, Wang Ling-chi, had been brought over by Chiang Kai-shek, he embarked on a great massacre at the Chungking Congress of the Masses on March 31, creating the "March 31 tragedy." After the "April 12" counterrevolutionary coup d'etat in Shanghai, with the Northern Expeditionary Army that was directly commanded by him and that was under his influence and the right wing of the Kuomintang as his backbone, Chiang Kai-shek actively engaged in the preparation for a huge massacre of revolutionaries on a nationwide scale. There was not a reactionary wing in any part of the country that did not embrace his "inspiration" and intensify its bloody, conspiratorial activities. In April and May the Hunan reactionaries were actively engaged in paving the way with propaganda, wildly spreading rumors, saying that everything in the countryside was communized, that at such-and-such a time all people over forty years old would be killed off by the Communist Party, etc. The rumors were particularly bad in the Northern Expeditionary Army. It was said that the monthly salary that the soldiers sent home to their families was being confiscated and distributed by the peasant associations and that the families of the officers all had their property confiscated. (In actual fact the bringing down of the local bullies and evil gentry only hit the families of Northern Expeditionary Army officers individually. For example, Ho Chien had his father-in-law beaten only once,* and the son-in-law of T'an Yen-k'ai had only been sent out to collect some donations.) In mid-May the troops led by Ho Chien began a series of slaughters in Hunan. At that time the chairman of the Lin-hsiang Peasant Association Committee, Li Chung-ho, was brutally murdered. On the eighteenth the chairman of the Ch'ang-te Suburban Peasant Association Committee suffered the "slow death." On the night of the nineteenth the troops of Ho Chien occupied the labor union and the peasant association of I-yang and disarmed the Peasants' Self-Defense Army and the workers' Disciplinary Team. On the morning of May 21 the troops of Hsiung Chen-lü, who served under the command of Ho Chien, surrounded all revolutionary organizations in Ch'ang-te. The workers' Disciplinary Team and others rose up in resistance and were met with a hail of machine-gun fire. More than eighty Communist Party members and revolutionary fighters were murdered that day.

At ten o'clock in the evening of May 21, Hsü K'o-hsiang, regimental commander of the Thirty-fifth Army that was stationed in Changsha under the command of Ho Chien, suddenly surrounded and attacked the Provincial General Labor Union, the Provincial Peasant Association, the Provincial Kuomintang Party Branch and Party School, and all revolutionary organs and carried out a night-long slaughter. The workers' Disciplinary Team swiftly entered the fray but was unable to turn back the attack of the reactionaries. There is no telling the number of people murdered that night.

With the counterrevolutionary coup of "Horse-Day," the broad revolutionary masses were immediately aroused to fury. Coura-

---

* Not surprisingly, Ho Chien himself was not consoled by the fact that his father-in-law had been beaten "only once," though when he spoke up against a radical land policy he couched his remarks in terms of its divisive effects on the army. Schram, Mao Tse-tung, p. 103 [S.R.S.].

geous Communist Party members organized fully one hundred thousand peasant troops in the hsien neighboring Changsha, took up all kinds and varieties of weapons (among them a good number of rifles), and advanced troops on Changsha from all directions. After exterminating a portion of the enemy troops around Changsha at I-chia Bay and other places, they surrounded the city on May 30. On the basis of a comparison between the enemy and ourselves at the time (Hsü K'o-hsiang's regiment had only one thousand rifles), this troop advance could have been victorious. But in the last few minutes the leadership of the provincial committee of the Communist Party in Hunan was unable to place resolute faith in the masses and depend upon them. On the contrary, it fell under the influence of Ch'en Tu-hsiu's right-opportunism and his fear that this "would bring on confusion in the entire political situation." The attack plans against Changsha were shamefully rescinded.* The majority of the peasant force thus retired from the field; there were only two Corps which happened not to have received the order and which rapidly attacked the city. After a courageous battle they were overwhelmed and defeated, and they retreated. The result of this general retreat was to scatter the ranks of the revolutionary masses and to fan the evil flames of the counterrevolution. After a few days, the reactionaries continued their massacres on a province-wide scale.

This was one of the major historical turning points in the failure of the 1927 Revolution.

In connection with the concrete situation in Hunan before and after the Horse Day coup and with the lesson of the coup, one of the people who held a position of responsibility in the Hunan Provincial Peasant Association at the time, the revolutionary martyr Comrade Liu Chiu-hsün, wrote an article in 1928 which contained the following description:

We knew the coup was coming before it occurred and all along had a plan for a counterattack. But although the Communist Party of that time was still good in organization, it was a peacetime party, it had no experience in struggle, it was unable to cope with circumstances surrounding this struggle, and the plans were merely counterattack plans, not plans for an active attack with foreknowledge of the coup. Thus, when the coup broke we were all helter-skelter and confused, and our plans all met with failure. There was only one plan for several neighboring

---

* Li Jui of course fails to mention that the order to cancel the attack on Changsha, and curb other "peasant excesses," was given by Mao himself, on instructions from Stalin [S.R.S.].

hsien in the area of Changsha that envisioned an attack on Changsha on May 31. At the same time, over ten thousand worker and peasant volunteer corps members were stationed at a place called Chiang-yü within the thirty-li vicinity of Hsiang-t'an. But because of a lack of appropriate command talent, the force was consequently destroyed to a man. Because responsible people at the provincial level were unaware of the real situation in Wuhan and because they also heard that the Kuomintang Central Committee had sent someone to Hunan to negotiate and to explain the misunderstandings, they felt they shouldn't move, and they told the peasant volunteer corps from the various areas who had agreed to attack Changsha to stop their actions, changing course in midstream and losing face that would be difficult to overcome later. At the time, because word traveled too slowly, the troops at Liu-yang had already started marching, and thus occurred the heroic action of the afternoon of May 31 when the Workers' and Peasants' Army of Liu-yang unilaterally attacked Changsha. Although it failed, this courageous struggle is worth our remembrance.

We can say that the overall reason for the failure of this uprising was that it had been poisoned by opportunism. At the time, a letter to all the peasants of the province had gone out in the name of the Interim Business Office of the Provincial Peasant Association that proposed the confiscation of the landlords' land and a crackdown on the local bullies and evil gentry. Although these empty words were on paper, they could not be carried out resolutely. One reason was that they paid sole attention to military action, such as attacking the cities, and gave no attention to the foundation work for this. Another reason was that although the letter advocated a general confiscation and distribution of land to the peasants (it did not advance any slogans about confiscating the land of the great landlords who had holdings of over one hundred mou*), it did not advance any concrete approaches, so that the peasants had no way to begin. Although it advocated a crackdown on the local bullies and evil gentry, the peasants of the time had not yet suffered the great "rural clean-up" and massacre that followed the Horse Day Incident, and they felt that this kind of action was just too extreme, and they couldn't bring themselves to do it. Although the broad masses of people had been developed, although the various hsien had tens and tens of thousands of people gathered together, although all the provisions had been collected from the various areas and those who had not yet joined, the concentration were in their home areas attending to the maintenance of martial law, there was no good organization or good leadership, particularly no experience in armed uprisings. The result was failure....

Although the Hsiang-t'an uprising failed, various hsien continued to rise up. The Communist Party still entertained illusions about the Kuomintang, with the result that it did not want to adopt publicly a policy of revolt. In a long letter of over a thousand words, Kuo Liang asked for the organization of a guerrilla force in the countryside and for the implementation of the movement to bring down the local bullies and evil gentry and confiscate the land, but he was prevented [from doing this]. [14]

During the First Revolutionary Civil War the courageous struggles of the members of the Communist Party and the revolutionary masses were very heroic and moving. The revolutionary storms

---

* 6.6 mou = 1 acre. — Tr.

with the power "to move mountains and drain seas" that occurred in Hunan and other places were difficult for the enemy to withstand. Nevertheless, the Chinese Communist Party at the time was still in its infancy, and history was not yet ripe for the correct revolutionary line of Comrade Mao Tse-tung — the integration of Marxism-Leninism with the realities of China — to win a decisive position of leadership within the Party. The right-opportunist leadership of Ch'en Tu-hsiu led to the inability of the revolutionaries to organize at this critical hour a powerful counterattack against the counterrevolutionaries, and so the revolution sank into defeat and failure.

Summing up the reasons behind the failure of the First Revolutionary Civil War, Comrade Mao Tse-tung has said:

But after all, ours was then still an infant Party, it lacked experience concerning the three basic problems of the united front, armed struggle and Party building, it did not have much knowledge of Chinese history and Chinese society or of the specific features and laws of the Chinese revolution, and it lacked a comprehensive understanding of the unity between the theory of Marxism-Leninism and the practice of the Chinese revolution. Hence in the last phase of this stage, or at the critical juncture of this stage, those occupying a dominant position in the Party's leading body failed to lead the Party in consolidating the victories of the revolution and, as a result, they were deceived by the bourgeoisie and brought the revolution to defeat. [15]

# Notes

## 1. STUDENT DAYS

1.  Hsi-yu chi ["Monkey" or "Journey to the West"] is a mythical novel by Wu Ch'eng-en written in the sixteenth century (Ming dynasty) which is replete with lies and illusions. In the book the "demons [shen mo] all have human feelings, and the bogeys [ching mei] are also conversant with human ways." The novel particularly builds up the heroic figure of Sun Wu-k'ung as brave, optimistic, clever, defiant, and strong. The San kuo chih yen-i [Romance of the Three Kingdoms] is an historical novel written in the fourteenth century (late Yüan and early Ming dynasties) by Lo Kuan-chung that he based on the ancient San kuo chih [Record of the Three Kingdoms] by Ch'en Shou and on popular tales. It relates the military and political struggles between the kingdoms of Wei, Shu, and Wu at the end of the Han dynasty. Shui-hu chuan ["The Water Margin" or "All Men Are Brothers"] is the famous Chinese novel that describes peasant warfare (during the Northern Sung dynasty). According to tradition, it was written in the fourteenth century by Shih Nai-an.

2.  Li Chi, Mao Tse-tung t'ung-chih shao-nien shih-tai ti ku-shih [Tales from Comrade Mao Tse-tung's Youth].

3.  Edgar Snow, Red Star over China [(New York: Grove Press, 1973), p. 136. Originally published by Random House, 1938]. Hereafter all material relating to the recollections of Comrade Mao Tse-tung is taken from this book. [Li Jui quotes from the authorized Chinese translation of this work, entitled Hsi-hsing man-chi, originally published in 1937, and recently reprinted in Hong Kong. There is no evidence that this, or any of the other published Chinese translations, was checked by Mao, and Snow's English text must therefore be regarded as the definitive version of Mao's story. (The working text in Chinese, corrected by Mao at the time — Red Star, p. 107 — has apparently been lost.) — S.R.S.]

4.  An official title in the Ch'ing government. This was the provincial governor [hsün-fu]. He had all civilian and military authority in a province.

5.  The Ko Lao Hui (as well as the Ch'ing pang and the Tsai-li hui) was a secret society of the people that took shape at the beginning of the Ch'ing dynasty. It comprised mainly bankrupt peasants, unemployed handicraftsmen, and vagabond proletariat. During China's feudal age elements of this kind often joined together on the basis of religious superstition to form various organizations that went under different names for the purpose of obtaining mutual assistance in their social life. Also, under certain conditions, they launched struggles and stood up

319

against the landlords and bureaucrats who oppressed them. But the peasants and handicraftsmen were unable to depend on this backward organization for a solution to their problems. This kind of backward organization frequently allowed itself to be used by the landlords and powerful gentry, thus becoming a reactionary force.

6. Liu Liu-wen, "Wo so chih-tao ti Mao Tse-tung hsien-sheng erh san shih," [Several Matters I Know Regarding Mr. Mao Tse-tung], Hsin Hua jih pao [New China Daily], September 8, 1945.

7. Comrade Mao Tse-tung's mother passed away in 1919. In his "Funeral Ode for Mother" Mao wrote:

> My mother had many excellent virtues, the first was her universal love.
> This love included relatives and friends, both near and distant.
> Her compassion and kindness moved the hearts of everyone.
> The power of her love came from true sincerity.
> She never lied or was deceitful.
> . . . . . . . . . . . . . . . . . . . . . . . . . .
> In reasoning and judgment her mind was clear and accurate;
> Everything she did was done with planning and with care.
> . . . . . . . . . . . . . . . . . . . . . . . . . .
> When we were sick she held our hands, her heart full of sorrow;
> Yet she admonished us saying, "You should strive to be good."

(This text was saved by a teacher from Mao Tse-tung's young days.)

8. Liang Ch'i-ch'ao (1873-1929) was from Hsin-hui, Kwangtung. He was a second degree graduate [chü jen] of the civil service examinations during the Kuang-hsü years [1875-1908] of the Ch'ing. After the defeat of China in the Sino-Japanese War, he followed his teacher, K'ang Yu-wei, in advocating "modernization" and was, with K'ang, a leading figure in the 1898 Reform Movement. After the 1911 Revolution, he switched from being a member of the Monarchist Party [Pao huang tang] to a high-level politican with the northern and southern warlords. His theory of "new people" advocated European-American democratic thought. Throughout his life, he managed and founded several periodicals. His writing was very biting and rich in power to arouse people, and he had a tremendous influence on the rank and file young intellectuals during the late Ch'ing period.

9. K'ang Yu-wei (1858-1927) was from Nan-hai, Kwangtung. He was a second degree graduate during the Kuang-hsü years and was the organizer and leader of the 1898 Reform Movement. After political reform failed, he became the leader of the Monarchist Party. One of the writings that represents his ideas is Ta t'ung shu. Although the theory of this book derives from Confucius, the book already reflected the ideological decline of the clan society. It was a Utopian theory of agrarian socialism.

10. Sun Yat-sen (1866-1925) organized the small revolutionary corps called the Revive China Society [Hsing Chung hui] in 1894 in Honolulu. In 1905 he combined two [other] anti-Ch'ing organizations — the China Revival Society [Hua hsing hui] and the Restoration Society [Kuang-fu hui] — and organized the United League [T'ung-meng hui] in Japan, coming out with a bourgeois revolutionary program to "expel the Tartar caitiffs, restore China, establish a republic, and equalize land rights." During the period between 1905 and 1911, Sun Yat-sen

joined with secret societies and the New Army and launched many anti-Ch'ing armed uprisings.

11. In 1903 the Ch'ing government ordered Yüan Shih-k'ai to create a modern army (the origin of the Peiyang Army). It subsequently followed this up by ordering the governors and governors-general of each province to recruit youths from the age of twenty to twenty-five and organize them into three chen of the New Army (a chen was equal to a division). Hunan set up and trained the Thirteenth Chen. At this time there were a great number of youths animated by anti-Ch'ing patriotic ideas who joined the New Army. The United League and the revolutionaries from various areas all made the New Army the target of their activities. Thus the New Army was one of the forces that brought about the 1911 Revolution.

12. T'an Yen-k'ai was from Hunan. He was a Han-lin scholar of the Ch'ing dynasty and originally advocated constitutional monarchy. Later, in his capacity as a representative of the landlords and bureaucrats, he opportunistically threw his lot in with the 1911 Revolution. After the Wuchang uprising, the revolutionary leaders of the Hunan secret society and the New Army, Chiao Ta-ling and Ch'en Tso-hsin, led the masses in response to the call and were selected as military governor [tu-tu] and vice governor, respectively. In this new government T'an Yen-k'ai was head of the Ministry of Civil Affairs. After a couple of weeks, making use of a piao-t'ung (equal to a regimental commander) in the New Army, T'an murdered Chiao and Ch'en and became military governor himself.

13. These were all classics of eighteenth and nineteenth century bourgeois social and natural science. For the most part, they were introduced to China in the late Ch'ing and early Republican period. Before the May Fourth movement the new culture of the bourgeoisie and the old culture of the feudal class were locked in a struggle that was growing steadily more violent. These books were representative instances of the so-called new learning.

14. Yen Fu (1835-1921) was from Min-hou, Fukien. He was educated in England as a youth and was one of the progressive Chinese in the 1890s who sought a truth from the West by which to save his country. Rather systematically, he introduced Western bourgeois academic thought. The Darwinist point of view that he disseminated had a great influence in intellectual circles at the time.

15. Chang Shih (1133-1180), of the Southern Sung dynasty, lived in Heng-yang and called himself Nan-hsüan. With Chu Hsi, he cherished the goal of making Confucianism flourish and engaged in teaching and transmission to disciples. He wrote Lun Yü chieh [An Explanation of the Analects] and Meng Tzu shuo [On Mencius].

16. Chu Hsi (1130-1200) was the apotheosis of Sung dynasty Confucianism and also a famous educationalist. The feudal ethical theory that he advertised, the Study of the Tao [Tao hsüeh — better known as "Neo-Confucianism" in the West. — Tr.], was totally unconcerned with either speech or action and was an aid to generations of feudal rulers who came after the Southern Sung dynasty.

17. New Youth was published in September 1915 and was edited by Ch'en Tu-hsiu. The primary contributors were Li Ta-chao and Lu Hsün. Before and after the May Fourth period this periodical was the leader and organizer of the Chinese people's New Culture and New Enlightenment movements (which advocated democracy and opposed feudalism, advocated science and opposed superstition, and advocated the use of the vernacular language [pai-hua] and opposed the use of the

classical language). It was the most treasured reading material at the time among all progressive intellectuals and the broad masses of young people through-out the country. All told, nine volumes of New Youth were published. Beginning with volume eight it became the organ of the Shanghai-based promotion organiza-tion [fa-ch'i tsu] of the Chinese Communist Party. When the Party was founded in 1921 this periodical was also used on one occasion as its organ. From 1922 to 1924, four quarterly numbers appeared.

18. T'an Ssu-t'ung (1865-1898) was from Liu-yang, Hunan. He was the most forceful thinker of China's old democratic revolutionary period before the advent of Sun Yat-sen and was one of the six martyrs of the 1898 Coup d'Etat. From childhood he was fond of the writings of Wang Fu-chih. His ideological theory appears primarily in his Jen hsüeh [Study of Benevolence]. Although in his thinking he was still incapable of divorcing himself from Confucianism, T'an par-tially reflected the national bourgeoisie's demands for development after imperi-alist aggression had penetrated China. Jen hsüeh boldly advanced the slogan of "bursting the net" on the ideological plane, breaking all the traditional shackles, and fiercely attacking the so-called "school of names" with its "Three Bonds and Five Constant Virtues" [relationships between prince and minister, father and son, husband and wife; benevolence, righteousness, propriety, knowledge, and sincerity — Tr.] that was part of China's several-thousand-year-old feudal, clan society. Jen hsüeh advocated "people's rule" [min chih], opposed the hypo-critical virtue and political autocracy of Chinese feudalism, and expressed a fu-rious and bitter hatred for the Ch'ing government. The philosophical thought of Jen hsüeh was quite muddled. There were some serious idealistic and meta-physical points of view; there were also certain materialist and dialectic ele-ments. But because he was unable to merge with the people's struggle and un-able to embody accurately the interests of the people, in the end T'an traveled the road of reformism in his political practice. [This last sentence is quite ex-traordinary, even on Li Jui's part. There was no serious revolutionary, as op-posed to reformist, movement which T'an could have joined in the last decade of the nineteenth century, and in the end he "traveled the road" of voluntary martyr-dom for his ideas, thus earning the respect of all progressive Chinese, including Mao. — S.R.S.]

19. T'ang Ts'ai-ch'ang (1867-1900) was from Liu-yang, Hunan. He was a forceful modernist of the late Ch'ing. After the 1898 Coup d'Etat, he returned to China from Japan and joined with members of secret societies to organize an Independent Army [Tzu-li chün] and planned to start uprisings throughout Hupei. Because news of this leaked out, however, he was arrested and killed in 1900 at Hankow. His activities had a great influence on the late Ch'ing revolutionary movement.

20. Wang Hsien-ch'ien (1841-1917) was from Liu-yang, Hunan. His hao was K'uei-wan. He became a graduate of the third degree [chin shih — the highest] during the T'ung-chih period [1862-1874] and was an eminent sinologist who emphasized textual criticism in the study of the classics.

21. Yeh Te-hui (1864-1927) was from Changsha, Hunan. He became a third de-gree graduate during the Kuang-hsü period [1875-1907] and was a famous scholar, devoting a lifetime of effort to collecting and collating ancient books. He was also a famous powerful gentry in Hunan. When Liang Ch'i-ch'ao was teaching in Hunan at the School of Current Affairs [Shih-wu hsüeh-t'ang], he was very much opposed to the writing of K'ang Yu-wei and Liang, calling it a "collection of heresy," and

considering himself a defender of the Way [wei tao — i.e., tradition], and he
resolutely opposed institutional reform. During the First Revolutionary Civil
War he was judged and executed by the Revolutionary Government in 1927 because
he had subverted the peasant movement.

22. Huang Hsing (1874-1916) was from Changsha, Hunan. In 1901 he went to
Japan to investigate education, and he leaned toward revolution. He returned to
China in 1903 and joined with other returned students from Japan in Changsha to
form the China Revival Society and was elected its first president. In 1904 he
joined with elements of secret societies to found the Revolutionary Army, himself becoming the generalissimo. His plans for uprisings were unsuccessful,
and he fled to Japan. In 1905 he joined with Sun Yat-sen to organize the Chinese
United League in Tokyo. From 1906 to 1911 Huang Hsing was the organizer and
commander of a series of uprisings initiated by the United League in Kwangsi,
Yunnan, and Kwangtung and was known as a practitioner. He was a member of
the revolutionary party whose reputation was second only to that of Sun Yat-sen.
After the 1911 Revolution, Huang Hsing vigorously advocated a compromise between the revolutionary party and Yüan Shih-k'ai. After the failure of the Second
Revolution in 1913, he split with Sun Yat-sen and separately organized the Society
for the Study of European Affairs [Ou shih yen-chiu hui], which became a small
rightist faction. In October 1916 he died of illness.

23. Sung Chiao-jen (1881-1913) was from T'ao-yüan, Hunan. He was an intellectual who came from a background of poverty. When he was studying in 1903
at Wu-chang, he devoted his efforts to the formation of a revolutionary organization and together with Huang Hsing participated in the revolutionary activities of
the China Revival Society and the United League. After the 1911 Revolution he
became one of the eminent political activists. He was intoxicated with the notion
of China realizing parliamentary government, joined up with a few small parties
and reorganized the United League into the Kuomintang. In order to win over a
majority in the National Assembly, he founded the so-called responsible cabinet.
In 1913 he personally went out on the hustings, delivering election speeches
everywhere, and he was assassinated in Shanghai by Yüan Shih-k'ai's men. Sung
Chiao-jen was a sincere defender of bourgeois parliamentary government. He
proved with his own blood that this system was unrealizable under the rule of
the warlords.

24. Wang Ch'uan-shan (1619-1692), whose ming was Fu-chih [by which he is
better known] was from Heng-yang, Hunan. When the Ming collapsed he raised
troops and opposed the Ch'ing, but this proved unsuccessful. Thereafter he fled
and hid on Heng-yang's Shih-ch'uan-shan. He wrote books for a period of forty
years, in all producing over seventy. Referred to by later generations as "Mr.
Ch'uan-shan," he has been known, together with Huang Tsung-hsi and Ku Yen-wu,
as a great late Ming-early Ch'ing patriotic thinker. His philosophical thinking
contains materialist elements. In politics he opposed the resurrection of ancient
institutions and proposed to return land to the tillers' ownership. In classical
scholarship he emphasized skepticism and self-reliance, ruled out superstition,
and stressed evidence. Those people who utilized their learning as a tool to get
food and clothing he attacked with all his might. He encouraged a fighting spirit,
a goal of emphasizing "nature" and attacking "habit" — esteeming man's individual nature and the changing of his environment. Progressive intellectuals
attached great importance to Wang's theory during the late Ch'ing-early Republic
period. Its influence in Hunan was particularly great. Praising Wang Fu-chih,

T'an Ssu-t'ung said: "In the past five hundred years Ch'uan-shan has been the only person who has really comprehended the affairs of Heaven and of Man."

25. Fang Wei-hsia was from P'ing-chiang, Hunan. In his early years he was a student in Japan, and during the early years of the "Republic" he was a member of Hunan educational circles who favored renovation. He was a member of the Provincial Parliament in the government of Chao Heng-t'i (provincial governor of Hunan from 1920 to 1926). In 1925 he joined the Chinese Communist Party. During the First Revolutionary Civil War he was the divisional Party representative with the Second Army of the Northern Expeditionary Army. During the Second Revolutionary Civil War he was head of the Central Democratic Government's General Affairs Department. In 1935 he was martyred while working along the Hunan-Kuangsi border.

Hsia Hsi was from I-yang, Hunan. He was one of Comrade Mao Tse-tung's principal associates during the period when the latter led the early revolutionary activities in Hunan. After 1923 Hsia was one of those who bore responsibility in the Hunan provincial committee of the Chinese Communist Party. During the First Revolutionary Civil War he presided over the work of the revolutionary Hunan branch of the Kuomintang. During the Second Revolutionary Civil War he participated in the leadership of both elements of the Workers' and Peasants' Red Army. In 1935 he was martyred on the Red Army's Long March. The rest of the martyrs will be given special attention below in the various sections.

26. Following the "April 12" counterrevolutionary coup of 1927 at Shanghai, the Chiang Kai-shek counterrevolutionary faction immediately directed the Northern Expeditionary Army and the Kuomintang right wing, which were under Chiang's influence, to actively arrange throughout the country a great massacre directed against the revolution. The warlord Ho Chien, commander of the Northern Expeditionary Army's Thirty-fifth Army, who was entrenched in Hunan at the time, thereupon rose up and played his part in the overall plan. On the night of May 21, Ho's regimental commander, Hsü K'o-hsiang, suddenly surrounded all revolutionary organs in Changsha and launched a frenzied massacre. The reactionary wing of the Kuomintang followed this up with a counterrevolutionary massacre on a provincewide scale. This fateful event was the signal of open cooperation between the counterrevolutionary Wuhan Kuomintang faction, headed by Wang Ching-wei, and the counterrevolutionary Nanking faction, headed by Chiang Kai-shek. The day rhyme for the twenty-first was "ma" [horse], hence the name "Horse Day Incident."

27. Ts'ai Yüan-p'ei (1868-1940) was from Shao-hsing, Chekiang. During the late Ch'ing he was a member of the Han-lin Academy, and he had also studied abroad in Germany. He was an eminent democratic educationalist of modern China. In the winter of 1904, with T'ao Ch'eng-chang and others, he organized the Restoration Society. In 1905 he joined the United League, and in 1911 he was the first minister of education in the provisional government of the "Chinese Republic." In 1916 he was the president [hsiao chang] of Peking University. He advocated academic freedom and invited the progressives Ch'en Tu-hsiu and Li Tao-chao to come and teach. He was very closely connected with Peking University's emergence as the center of the New Culture movement. For a time in 1927 he supported Chiang Kai-shek against the Communists, but later out of opposition to Chiang's policy of massacre against the revolution, he organized in 1930, with Messrs. Sung Ch'ing-ling and Lu Hsün, a "Great Alliance for the Preservation of People's Rights" [Min ch'üan pao-chang ta t'ung-meng]. After

the September 18 Incident, he endorsed the political proposal put forth by the Chinese Communist Party for "Internal Solidarity and Joint Halting of Foreign Insult."

28. Chou Shih-chao, "Ti-i shih-fan shih-tai ti Mao chu-hsi" [Chairman Mao in the First Normal Period], Hsin kuan-ch'a [New Observer], II, No. 2.

29. Ethics (or the theory of morality) is the science of dealing with moral norms. Heretofore, the idealist and metaphysical theories of ethics (or morality) of the feudal and bourgeois classes all placed primary emphasis on the study of eternal moral concepts and norms of behavior that stood above classes. But in reality there is no unchanging and eternal moral truth at all. Therefore, ethics is a kind of historical science, and it should study the changing moral forms that accompany classes, class struggle, their ideologies, and this psychology.

30. Ch'eng refers to the brothers Ch'eng Hao and Ch'eng I of the Northern Sung dynasty (also known collectively as Ch'eng Tzu). Chu is Chu Hsi of the Southern Sung. The scholastic thought of the Two Ch'engs and Chu Hsi was different but they were all idealists who advertised the Confucian and Mencian theory of human relationships and who studied the principles of "rectifying the mind, sincerity, self-cultivation, managing the family, ruling the country, and bringing peace to all under Heaven." At the same time, they drew on the mystical Taoist theories of yin and yang, li and ch'i [roughly, principle and matter], and the Buddhist approach to cultivation that was divorced from reality, that of sitting quietly and nurturing one's nature [ching tso yang hsing], so that "Confucianism" now had a great many new variations. Chu Hsi systematized all of this and in the areas of study, self-cultivation, handling affairs, and social intercourse also set down a great deal of strict dogma, which was quite useful in safeguarding feudal ruling power. Thus Chu Hsi and the Two Ch'engs have always been praised as great Confucians by the feudal ruling class, which has encouraged their theories on a broad scale.

31. Mr. Yang Ch'ang-chi died on January 17, 1920. At that time, educational circles in Peking and Hunan held memorial services for him. The "death notice" signed by Ts'ai Yüan-p'ei, Comrade Mao Tse-tung, and others read: "Mr. [Yang] was pure in action, earnest in ambition, and fond of study.... Our country's learning is not prospering, and scholars of merit are as few as morning stars. Certainly Mr. [Yang] was fond of study to the end of his days, but because [Heaven] did not grant him a longer life, he did not achieve [even] one of the many ambitions he had when alive."

32. The basic aim of the Sung-Ming School of Ethics [li-hsüeh] was to prove that the Three Bonds of Confucianism (the prince was bonded by ties to his minister, the father to his son, and the husband to his wife) and the Five Constant Virtues (benevolence, righteousness, propriety, knowledge, and sincerity became transformed into the Five Relationships; prince-minister, father-son, husband-wife, older brother-younger brother, friend-friend) were eternal truths and that the Five Constant Virtues were subordinate to the Three Bonds. At the same time, it advocated "quietude" (the nature of Heaven is that man is born and is in a state of quietude) and held that if one moved, this was having human desires. (When man's desires are extreme, he offends superiors and rebels.) The most fundamental time of this so-called cultivation was spent in "overcoming desire." Thus this theory fully corresponded with the needs of the ruling class: obedience and submission to superiors and a prohibition against offending them. During the height of Chu Hsi's teaching there was another group even more influenced

by Buddhism, that of Lu Chiu-yüan. He advocated the position that one came to an understanding of subjective judgments through "practice," that a lot of book study was unnecessary. He held that the Chu school spoke only hollow words and paid no attention to real work, that it had not the least significance. During the Ming dynasty, Wang Shou-jen [Wang Yang-ming] developed the school of Liu Chiu-yüan and overthrew the Ch'eng-Chu school that had shackled man's mind and body. He advocated an "unbridled" (advancing in accordance with truth) style that freely developed the individual. The aim of Wang's school was to "reach intuition," his method was the "unity of knowledge and action," holding that "knowledge, this is action," "knowledge is action." In substance this was the subjective idealism. The theories of the Ch'eng-Chu, Lu-Wang schools can be taken as representative of the Sung-Ming School of Ethics.

33. Immanual Kant (1724-1804) was an eminent German bourgeois philosopher and the founder of German idealism. Kant used the argument of the unknowability of the world to arm the whole body of bourgeois philosophy that came afterward. The fundamental characteristic of Kant's philosophy was the idea of amalgamating materialism and idealism so that the two theories would be brought into harmony and the two different, contradictory philosophical ideologies would be united into one philosophical system. He admitted the existence of a "thing itself" beyond us; this is a materialist point of view. But he also denied objective laws, causation, time, and space, thus becoming an idealist. His philosophy was, therefore, a contradictory dualism, a philosophy of compromise.

34. This diary was obtained from the home of the martyr Chang K'un-ti in I-yang. The diary was an eleven-column, self-made "class diary" dating from that year at First Normal. On the upper right-hand side of the cover was inscribed "July 31 to October 2, the Sixth Year of the Republic [i.e., 1917]." In the middle was written "No. 9," and in the upper left-hand corner were also written the four characters "correct mistakes, renew the self" [kai kuo tzu hsin].

35. This so-called "mindfulness and cultivation" was based on a phrase by Mencius, who argued for the natural goodness of man's nature: "preserve in the mind and cultivate the nature." This was advocating that man should often reflect inwardly and carefully study and perfect his cultivation, preserve the roots of goodness of his nature, and not be influenced by the evil customs of society. Put more concretely, it was advocating self-control and limited desires, to be content with little and to make clear one's ambition, not to seek worldly fame and fortune.

36. That is, T'an Ssu-t'ung. T'an was from Liu-yang, Hunan. To honor a person in China it was a traditional practice to refer to him by the name of his birthplace or long-time residence.

37. The Shen yin yü was written by the late-Ming scholar Lü K'un (whose hao was Hsin-wu) and consisted of six chüan divided into seventeen sections, such as Ethics, Discussions on the Tao, Self-Cultivation, Questions on Study, Meeting Emergencies, Maintaining a Livelihood, Changes of the Times, Sages, Study of the Tao, Human Feelings, and Nature. In the Introduction to the Shen yin yü, Lu Ch'i-lung wrote: "In Shen yin yü Mr. Lü Hsin-wu examined self-control. The reason he called the book Shen yin yü [Tortured Words] was that he saw himself as if in constant sickness, groaning constantly and at everything; he examined himself severely and controlled his conduct bravely, yet was unable to put an end to it [human desire]."

38. Hsi ming [The Western Inscription] was the work of the Sung dynasty

scholar and educator Chang Tsai (1020-1077). The opening paragraph of the
"Cheng meng" section, numbering over two hundred characters, was an important
piece of writing that gave a general description of Confucian ethical thought. In
the area of a universal view, Chang Tsai's theory contained a materialist point of
view. The scholastic theories of Wang Fu-chih were much influenced by the thinking of Chang Tsai. Wang wrote a piece entitled "Annotations to Chang Tsai's
Cheng meng."

39. Hsi T'ang (Li Hsiao-tan), "Yang Huai-chung hsien-sheng shih-shih tsai
chih," Changsha Ta-kung pao, January 20, 1920.

40. Han Yü (768-824) was an eminent essayist of the T'ang dynasty. He had
an extensive understanding of Confucianism and opposed parallel prose (a purely
formal style of writing that was popular from the Wei, Chin, Northern and Southern dynasties period [386-589] to the Sui and T'ang), which was very popular at
the time, and Buddhism. He proposed to "record the Way with literature (Way —
the instructions of the Confucian school), to "unite the Way with literature" (the
revolution of the ancient style of writing against the parallel prose style). His
essays showed an understanding of the style of Ssu-ma Ch'ien and Yang Hsiung's
classical writing (ordinary essays dating from before the Wei, Chin, Northern
and Southern dynasties period), and he created a particular style all his own,
known by later generations as "Han writing."

41. This was edited by crown prince Hsiao T'ung (501-531), Liang Chao-ming,
during the Northern and Southern dynasties period. The collection included poetry and essays dating from the Ch'in and Han periods [221 B.C.-A.D. 222] up to
the date of editing and comprised sixty chüan. This collection of selected essays
is famous in Chinese history.

42. K'ung Jung (153-208) was a man from the Eastern Han period who had a
talent for writing since youth. During the reign of Han Hsien-ti, K'ung Jung held
the position of minister [hsiang] of Pohai. He was killed as a result of attacking
Ts'ao Ts'ao. He is the author of K'ung Po-hai chi [K'ung's Pohai Collection].
Ch'en T'ung-fu, whose ming was Liang, was from the Northern Sung. He had a
rich and flourishing literary talent and was fond of exploring politics and military affairs, often delivering himself of patriotic utterances. Yeh Shui-hsin,
whose ming was Ch'ien (1150-1223), was a Northern Sung graduate of the third
degree and a famous patriotic scholar with a "bountiful ambition." He is the
author of Shui-hsin chi [Collected Works of Shui-hsin].

43. Ssu-ma Kuang (1019-1086) was from the Northern Sung. He attained the
post of chief minister and in the field of politics was a conservative. He was
given an imperial order to write an annalistic history of China that would cover
the period from the Warring States to the Five Dynasties [403 B.C.-A.D. 960].
Taking the position of the ruling class, he stupidly applied the concepts of good
and evil and of teaching and warning to all matters concerned with the rise and
fall of states. For this reason, [the emperor] Sung Shen-tsung entitled the work
the Tzu chih t'ung chien [The Comprehensive Mirror for Aid in Government].
The old historians of China revered this book as an orthodox piece of historical
writing. Ku Tsu-yü (1624-1680) was from the late Ming period and was versed
in historical and geographical studies. When the Ming fell, he went into the
mountains to live in seclusion, devoting his efforts exclusively to writing. In his
book Tu shih fang-yü chi-yao [The Essentials of Geography for Reading History]
he gives a detailed record of the geographic regions of China, the mountains,
rivers, passes, and open spaces as well as the traces of ancient and modern

battles, victories and defeats, gains and losses. Moreover, this is all accompanied with full discussions.

44. Chou Shih-chao, "Ti-i shih-fan shih-tai ti Mao chu-hsi" [Chairman Mao of the First Normal Period].

45. Ch'en Tu-hsiu (1880-1942) was from Huai-ning, Anhwei. During the May Fourth period he was a radical democrat, an active promoter of the New Culture movement, and one of the founders of the Chinese Communist Party. Because of his fame gained in the May Fourth Movement, and also owing to the immaturity of the Party during the period when it was being created, he was the person who held primary responsibility in the Chinese Communist Party during the early period. During the First Revolutionary Civil War, rightist thinking within the Party, represented by him, formed a capitulationist line. In 1927, after the failure of the Revolution, he became an anti-Party Trotskyite and was thus expelled from the Party in 1929.

46. Li Ta-chao (1888-1927) was from Lao-t'ing, Hopei. He was one of the founders of the Chinese Communist Party and a direct organizer and leader of the May Fourth movement; at the time he was holding the position of professor at Peking University. Very early on he disseminated Marxism in the periodical New Youth. He played a great part in bringing about the Nationalist-Communist [i.e., Kuomintang-Chinese Communist Party] cooperation of 1924 and in having Sun Yat-sen embrace the "three great policies" that were advantageous for the Revolution. During the First Revolutionary Civil War he led the revolutionary activities in the north. In April 1927 he was arrested by the warlord Chang Tso-lin in Peking, and on the twenty-eighth he was martyred. Two essays, "Ch'ing ch'un" [Spring of Youth] and "Chin" [Today] were separately printed in New Youth in Vol. II, No. 1 (September 1916), and Vol. IV, No. 4 (April 1918). His essay "Ch'ing ch'un" pointed out that China was already in an historical period of substituting the new for the old. The spring of youth evolved, without beginning and without end. Thus the progress of China should also be without limit. He called upon youth to "break through the old historical net," to smash all the old, decayed theories and to remake an old China that was about to meet its death into a new nation of the spring. "Chin" means now. The essay pointed out that the present time was an historical stage. "The past and the future are both the present." "Today," in relation to yesterday and tomorrow, has the function of carrying on the one and beginning the other. Thus we must take the present as our foothold and as our starting point to advance forward. "We cannot dislike 'today' and only think about the 'past' and dream about the 'future,' thereby squandering and neglecting efforts in the present. Neither can we be self-satisfied with the limit of 'today,' and take up no effort in the 'present' to plan for the development of the 'future.'"

47. Wu Yu-ling is Wu Yü (1874-1943). He was from Chengtu, Szuchuan, and was a revolutionary democrat. In 1896 he went to Japan to study, and there he embraced bourgeois-democratic thought. Because his book Sung Yuan hsüeh-an ts'ui yü [Pure Words on the Sung Yüan hsüeh-an] criticized Neo-Confucian theory, it was banned by the Ch'ing Board of Education. In 1913 he founded the paper The Waking Masses [Hsing ch'ün pao] in Chengtu, which encouraged the New Learning, and it was forced to stop publication. From 1917 onward he published serially in New Youth the anti-Confucian articles entitled "Ju chia chih-tu wei chuan-chih chu-i chih ken-chü lun" [On the Confucian System as the Basis for Despotism] and "Ch'ih jen yü li chiao" [Exploiting People and the Teaching of

Propriety]. He was called the "hero of Szuchuan who single-handedly brought down the Confucianists." Afterward he was a professor at Peking and Szuchuan universities. In his later years he lived in seclusion and wrote the Wu Yü wen lu [The Literary Record of Wu Yü] and the Wu Yü wen hsü lu [Sequel to the Literary Record of Wu Yü].

48. Meaning the theories of Confucius, Mo Tzu, Yang Tzu [i.e., Yang Hsiung], Lao Tzu, Mencius, Hsün Tzu, and Han Fei Tzu, all from the Chou period.

49. The first number of the Ch'uan-shan Journal [Ch'uan-shan hsüeh-pao] was published in August 1915. The director of this periodical was Liu Jen-hsi (from Liu-yang, Hunan. He had held the position of principal in the Central Circuit Normal School, the predecessor of First Normal. When T'ang Hsiang-ming fled in 1916, he became military governor in Hunan for a few months.) In the first sentence of his "Explanatory Preface (Hsü i) to the Ch'uan-shan Journal" he wrote: "Why is the Ch'uan-shan Journal being created? Because we grieve for the Chinese Republic." The journal included the printing of Wang Fu-chih's "Last Testament" with notes and corrections as well as discussions on politics and current affairs and special articles devoted to philosophy, literature, and history. This was an ecclectic journal written in the classical language that encouraged "national studies" and whose contributors were all old-style literary men and well-known scholars. When Yüan Shih-k'ai proclaimed himself emperor, this journal was critical of the move. From its inception until August 1927 it published a total of eight numbers. During its second period of publication, from the end of 1932 to the end of 1937, it published altogether fourteen numbers. After this it ceased publication. Later, this magazine only exerted some influence on a small number of conservative literary men in Hunan.

50. Yüan Shih-k'ai (1859-1916) was the boss of the Peiyang warlords at the end of the Ch'ing dynasty. After the 1911 Revolution, relying on the support of counterrevolutionary military forces and on that of imperialism, he further utilized the compromising nature of the bourgeoisie who were leading the revolution at the time and seized the post of president, organizing the first Peiyang warlord government, a government that represented the big landlord comprador class. In 1915, in a bid to become emperor, he sought the support of imperialism and acknowledged Japan's Twenty-one Demands, demands whose purpose it was to gain exclusive control of China. On December 12 of the same year he proclaimed himself emperor. An uprising broke out in Yünnan, and Yüan Shih-k'ai was forced to abolish the title on March 22, 1916. He died in June in Peking.

51. Ku Yen-wu (1613-1682) was a famous patriotic thinker of the late Ming-early Ch'ing period. He had raised troops and resisted the Ch'ing but failed. Later, he left his native town in K'un-shan, Kiangsu, and traveled through a great number of places in the country (primarily in the north; in his later years he settled in Shensi), all of which is recorded in his Jih chih lu [Record of Daily Knowledge], a compilation in 120 chüan; dealing with material in local gazeteers on military, political, economic, and social institutions and history, geography, villages, and water conservation was the T'ien-hsia chün-kuo li ping shu [On the Good and Ill of the Commanderies of the Realm] and another work entitled Chao yü chih [On Grave Boundaries] in 100 chüan. He also wrote several dozen other works. He advocated the creation of a spirit and attitude of searching for the truth, crying out: "In the rise and fall of the Empire, the common man has a responsibility." With a patriotic spirit he ceaselessly carried on propaganda against the Ch'ing dynasty and for the restoration of the Ming.

52. Yen Hsi-chai (1635-1704), whose ming was Yüan, was from the late Ming-early Ch'ing period and had been fond of study since childhood. He studied military science, engaged in productive labor, and was filled with patriotic thought. He was very much opposed to the Ch'eng-Chu, Lu-Wang schools of thought and was an advocate of restoring the ancient institutions, practicing the Six Arts [of the gentleman: propriety, music, archery, charioteering, writing, and mathematics] and studying the school of practical statesmanship. He maintained that "the more one studies books, the more one is misled, and the more one will be ignorant in judging the opportune moment for doing things and the more incapable of managing a family." In his later years he was a lecturer at the Chang-nan Academy of Fei-hsiang. Reflecting his criticism of the uselessness of the Sung-Ming Confucian school with its empty theory, he founded courses at the Academy in expository writing, armaments, classics, history, and artistic skill. His theory stressed carrying things out in practice, and he maintained that the way of study was not in "lecturing," but in "practicing." He advocated that one "repress his lust, weary his strength, talk about the affairs of this life, all for the use of the world and the state." He wrote Ssu ts'un pien [Four Inquiries] (politics, study, Man, and Nature).

53. Ssu-ma Ch'ien (145-86 B.C.) was from the Western Han dynasty and was the author of China's famous historical work, the Shih-chi [Historical Records]. After the age of twenty he traveled everywhere; his footsteps led throughout the empire. His mind was broadened and his knowledge greatly increased. Later, he carried on the office of Grand Historian and Astronomer [T'ai-shih ling] that had been held by his father [Ssu-ma T'an] and completed the Shih-chi, a work in altogether 130 sections with over 520,000 characters that covered the history of China from the inception of civilization up to the Han dynasty [206 B.C.]. The Shih-chi created the "biographical system" in which individual people were taken as the center of interest. The writing style was not only pure and simple, it was very free and flowing; it made the most tortuous things seem natural and was especially strong in description. Not only was the content concerned with political phenomena and the recording of the emperors, it also paid attention to socio-economics. He even dealt with riffraff, assassins, and diviners as social problems and accorded them their proper positions.

54. Li Kang-chu (1659-1733), whose ming was Kung, was a student of Yen Hsi-chai and a person whose name was as important as that of Yen. He was also a late Ming-early Ch'ing thinker and educator who was opposed to the Sung-Ming School of Ethics. Later ages called this the Yen-Li School.

55. From an essay written at the time by Comrade Mao Tse-tung on the subject of physical education. [English translation from Stuart R. Schram, The Political Thought of Mao Tse-tung, p. 154. — Tr.] [ Published in Hsin ch'ing-nien, Vol. 3, No. 2, April 1917. — S.R.S.]

56. Yen Tzu is Yen Hui, a student of Confucius. He was intelligent and fond of study, content with poverty, took pleasure in the Way, and died at an early age. Chia Sheng is Chia I (200-168 B.C.) of the Han dynasty. At the time, he was an outstanding publicist and essayist. Han Wen-ti prized his ability very highly, and he later became the Assistant Grand Tutor to the Prince of Changsha. He died at the age of thirty-three. Wang P'o (647-675) was from the T'ang dynasty and even as a child was known for his ability as an essayist. He was one of the four outstanding men of the early T'ang. He died at the age of twenty-eight.

57. In the local dialect of Hunan: pa man.

58. See note 55 [Schram, The Political Thought of Mao Tse-tung, p. 157].

59. See the essay "T'i-yü chih yen-chiu" [A Study of Physical Culture].

60. The thinkers and writers of the late Ming-early Ch'ing whom the notes touch upon include Ku Yen-wu, Yen Hsi-chai, Wang Fu-chih, Hou Chao-tsung, Wu Mei-ts'un, the Three Wei from Ning-tu, Wang Yao-feng, Wan Yü-yang, as well as the T'ung-ch'eng School and the Yang-hu School. Throughout Chinese history, every time China was invaded by a foreign race, patriotic scholars would very often become full of anger and sorrow and go to live in seclusion, reading and writing with the hope that their writings would be circulated, that men's spirits would not die, and that there thus would be a day for the revival of their people. For this reason the combining of study with resistance against the Ch'ing and the identity of writing and practice among the scholars of the early Ch'ing period was particularly prevalent. Hou Chao-tsung, whose ming was Fang-yü, did not serve in any official capacity after the fall of the Ming. His attainments in poetry and classical writing were very high, and generations have said of him: "In his poetry he followed Tu Fu, in prose he imitated Han [Yü] and Ou [-yang Hsiu]." The Three Wei of Ning-tu refers to the three brothers Wei Hsi, Wei Hsiang, and Wei Li of Ning-tu. After the fall of the Ming they all lived in seclusion in the mountains and forests, passing on their essays to those scholars of the time who possessed moral courage. Wei Hsi was particularly well known. After the fall of the Ming, Wu Mei-ts'un was forced to submit to the Ch'ing. He became a third degree graduate during the Ch'ung-chen period [1628-1644]. Later, he felt very much ashamed and pained and turned his attention to poetry and literature, which was very melancholy yet vigorous. Wang Yao-feng's ming was Yüan, and Wang Yü-yang's ming was Shih-chen. The former was an essayist and the latter a poet. Both were third degree graduates from the Shun-chih period [1644-1661]. The T'ung-ch'eng School was a name given to a school of [writing] of the Ch'ing period. Fang Pao, Liu Ta-k'uei, and Yao Nai were all from T'ung-ch'eng. Their classical writing was very direct and pure, and they came to form a particular school, known by later generations as the T'ung-ch'eng School. The Yang-hu School was contemporary with the T'ung-ch'eng School and was composed of Yün Ching, from Yang-hu, and Chang Hui-yen, from Wu-chin. They wrote with great boldness and were known as the Yang-hu School.

61. Caesar was a great general of ancient Rome. He was also a politician. In the middle of the first century B.C. he conducted both northern and southern expeditionary campaigns, establishing the Roman Empire. Later, he was assassinated in the Roman Senate by his enemies, the men of the Republican Party. Fukuzawa Yukichi was a Japanese educator. During the Meiji Restoration he was the most energetic in the introduction of European capitalist culture. He was referred to as the prophet of the Meiji intellectuals.

62. Yen Tzu-ling, whose ming was Kuang, was from the Han dynasty. He had traveled about for information with Emperor Kuang-wu, Liu Hsiu. After Liu Hsiu became emperor, Yen changed his name and lived unseen in seclusion. Liu Hsiu repeatedly sought him out for office, but he would not accept and continued as before to live in the country, reading and tilling the fields until the end of his days.

63. Fan Chung-yen (989-1052) was a third degree graduate from the Northern Sung dynasty who advocated the reform of the bureaucratic system as it existed at the time. He often took the universe as his own responsibility. His famous saying was: "Put first the worries of the world and put last its pleasures." For

a time he was in charge of guarding the frontier pass at Shensi and Kansu. He issued strict and specific orders, had a great affection for his troops, and saved a dangerous situation at a time when foreign peoples were making aggression against China. To this day there is still a stone wall at the foot of Mt. Pao-t'a in Yenan which bears an inscription of his words: "In my bosom I myself have a million brave soldiers" [i.e., he was a great strategist].

64. Chang Liang was from the Ch'in dynasty [221 B.C.-206 B.C.]. After the state of Ch'u had exterminated Han, Chang Liang took all his family possessions and used them to get men to [help him] avenge this grievance for Han. He got hold of a strong man to make a sneak attack on the emperor, Ch'in Shih-huang. The attack was unsuccessful but was of utmost importance in giving encouragement to the anti-Ch'in movement. Later, when Liu Pang [the future first emperor of the Han dynasty that would replace the Ch'in] rose up in revolt with his troops, Chang Liang was his most powerful counselor.

65. I Yin was the "virtuous Prime Minister" of the Shang dynasty so much praised by the Confucians. When King T'ang attacked King Chieh and destroyed the Hsia dynasty, thus unifying the empire, I Yin acquired a great deal of credit for the part he had played. Mencius referred to him as the "sagely officeholder."

66. That is, T'ao K'an. From P'o-yang, he was skilled in military matters and was a great general. He spent over forty years in the military, had great fortitude, decisiveness, and great prestige. There is a famous story about him when he was in the army in Kwangtung: he transported glazed tiles in order to practice hard work. He also urged people to be careful in their use of time. When a boat was being built he would collect and store away all the wood and bamboo odds and ends, which would later all have their individual uses.

67. A System of Ethics [ed. and trans. by Frank Thilly (New York: C. Scribner's sons, 1899)] was written by the German Friedrich Paulsen. It was translated by Ts'ai Yüan-p'ei and published in 1913 by the Commercial Press.

68. Chou Shih-chao, "Ti-i shih-fan shih-tai ti Mao chu-hsi."

69. The two essays by Comrade Li Ta-chao, "Shu-min ti sheng-li" [The Victory of the Masses] and "Bolshevism ti sheng-li" [The Victory of Bolshevism] were published in New Youth, Vol. V, No. 5 (November 15, 1918). It was not until May 1919 with Vol. VI, No. 5, that a special issue devoted exclusively to the discussion of Marxism was put out.

70. Snow, Red Star over China [pp. 148-49].

71. Chou Shih-chao, "Ti i shih-fan shih-tai ti Mao chu-hsi."

72. When Liang Ch'i-ch'ao was managing the New People's Journal [Hsin min ts'ung-pao] he created a kind of "new writing style." This style of writing still used the classical language, but it was "simple and clear, mixed with slang and foreign words, and let the pen fly wherever it might without constraint." At the time, the ancient literature school dismissed him as a "wild fox meditator" [ye hu ch'an] [i.e., one who does not know his own ability and attempts to imitate others: from a story of such a person who made a mistake while talking about meditation and was forthwith turned into a wild fox. This term is used by Buddhists in criticism of outside imitators.], but he was welcomed by the broad masses of intellectual youth.

73. After the defeat of Chang Hsün and Fu Pi in 1917, Tuan Ch'i-jui held the power of government in Peking and refused to revive the National Assembly as prescribed by the provisional constitution. Sun Yat-sen led the navy southward and in Kwangtung organized a military government, setting up the flag of "Pro-

tecting the Constitution" (the "provisional constitution" that had been promulgated in the first year of the Republic [i.e., 1911]). The southern warlords from Kwangsi and Yünnan, T'ang Chi-yao and Lu Jung-t'ing, were in an antagonistic position vis-à-vis the northern Peiyang warlords, and they too joined in "protecting the constitution." In a bid to seize Hunan, Tuan Ch'i-jui sent his vice commander of the army, Fu Liang-tso, to Hunan to take up the post of Tuchün. This led the troops under Lu Jung-t'ing of the Kwangsi Army to "aid Hunan." This war was known as the "War for the Protection of the Constitution."

74. Li Yu-wen later became head of the Department of the Army in the War Office for the warlord Chao Heng-t'i. In the beginning of 1922, on orders from Chao Heng-t'i, he murdered the leaders of the strike at Changsha's No. 1 Cotton Mill, Huang Ai and P'ang Jen-ch'üan. For this reason he was executed by the Revolutionary Court during the First Revolutionary Civil War.

75. Fu Ting-i was the principal of Hunan First Middle School in 1914. When T'ang Hsiang-ming was Tuchün of Hunan, Fu was vice chairman of the Provincial Education Society. When Yüan Shih-k'ai proclaimed himself emperor, Fu initiated the "Hunan Branch of the Peace Planning Society" [Ch'ou an hui] with Ye Te-huai, the two of them being chairman and vice chairman of the Society respectively.

76. In the fall of 1916 First Normal organized a student volunteer army in order to carry out the order for "national military education" under which students received simple military training. The entire school was made into one battalion. Beneath this were companies, platoons, and squads. The positions of company commander on down were filled from the student body.

77. During the 1951 land reform, three record books of the First Normal Student Society that dated from 1917 to 1918 were found in the home of the former principal of the school, K'ung Chao-huan. The K'ung family residence was one of long standing in Changsha. There was one book entitled Hsüeh yu hui chi-shih lu [Records of the Student Society] and two volumes of the Ye hsüeh jih chih [Night School Record]. A portion of what is recorded in these three volumes was personally written by the hand of Comrade Mao Tse-tung.

78. Ch'en Shu-i, Chai Shih, "Mao chu-hsi ku-shih shih-ling" [Miscellaneous Stories on Chairman Mao], New Hunan News [Hsin Hu-nan pao], July 1, 1950.

79. Li Ming, "Chi-nien Ts'ai Ho-sen t'ung-chih" [In Memory of Comrade Ts'ai Ho-sen], in Chung-kuo kung-ch'an-tang lieh-shih chuan [Heroes of the CCP] (Ch'ing-nien ch'u-pan-she).

80. Shui-k'ou-shan is in Ch'ang-ning hsien, Hunan. It is an important lead mine.

81. Both Comrades Chiang Meng-chou and Ho Shu-heng participated in the early revolutionary movements in Hunan led by Comrade Mao Tse-tung. They were managers in both Self-Study University and in Hsiang-chiang Middle School (the regular school run by the Party in Changsha in 1923). In January 1929 they were martyred in Changsha. During the First Revolutionary Civil War, Comrade Wang Ling-po was the head of the Hunan Branch Secretariat of the Kuomintang left wing. Later, he engaged in underground work in Shanghai and was twice put in prison. At the beginning of the War of Resistance against Japan he presided over the work of the Eighth Route Army's Hunan Office, and in September 1941 he passed away in Yenan.

82. Hsieh Chüeh-tsai, "I Shu-heng t'ung-chih" [On Comrade Shu-sheng], Liberation Daily [Chieh-fang jih-pao], May 18, 1942 (Yenan edition).

83. Hsiao San, "Mao Tse-tung t'ung chih ti ch'u-ch'i ke-ming huo-tung" [The Early Revolutionary Activities of Comrade Mao Tse-tung] (originally printed in the Yenan Liberation Daily).

84. See note 82.

85. The Ta Hsüeh [Great Learning] was originally the name of a section in the Li Chi [Book of Rites] and was set up by Chu Hsi as the first and foremost of the "Four Books." (The others were the Chung Yung [The Mean], the Lun Yü [Analects], and the Meng Tzu [Mencius].) Chu Hsi spent a lifetime of energy in annotating the Four Books, and from this time onward the Four Books became the fundamental textbooks for educated people in feudal society.

86. The "T'ang Kao" is the name of a section in the Shu Ching. "Kao" means command: the words of the emperor that he declares to the people.

87. Hsiang Ching-yü was from Hsü-p'u, Hunan, and was the earliest and most capable woman leader in the Chinese Communist Party. After the May Fourth movement, she went to France as part of the Diligent Work and Frugal Study program. She returned home in 1922 and was elected a member of the Central Committee at the Second Congress of the Chinese Communist Party. She was also responsible for leadership work in the woman's department of the Party Central Committee. In 1925 she went to study in Moscow at Eastern University. After she returned home she undertook work in the propaganda department of the Wuhan General Labor Union and the propaganda department of the Hankow municipal Party committee. After the failure of the First Revolutionary Civil War, she kept up the struggle at Wuhan and was responsible for work in the Hupei provincial Party committee. In the spring of 1928 she was arrested by the Kuomintang reactionary wing in league with the police station of the French concession at Hankow. On May 1 of the same year, at four o'clock in the morning, she nobly died for the cause. This incident shook the entire nation.

88. Snow, Red Star over China [p. 148].

89. After the imperialist countries coerced the Ch'ing government into acknowledging a certain number of places as treaty ports, that is to say, forcibly occupying what they considered suitable places and making them into their "leased territories" [i.e., the so-called "concessions"], they put into operation a ruling system within the "leased territories" that was completely independent of China's administrative and legal system; this was imperialism's colonial system.

90. That is, counsular jurisdiction. This was one of the special privileges set up in the unequal treaties that the imperialist countries forced the government of old China to make. It began in 1843 with the Sino-English Treaty of the Bogue and in 1844 with the Sino-American Treaty of Wanghsia. This special privilege was that every country that enjoyed the right of counsular jurisdiction in China had exclusive jurisdiction when its own nationals were accused in civil cases and that the Chinese courts had no right of decision.

91. See the Manifesto of the Second Congress of the Chinese Communist Party.

92. Hsi-k'uang-shan is in Hsin-hua hsien, Hunan. It is the world's leader in the production of antimony. During the early period of World War I when production was at its peak, the number of workers reached one hundred thousand.

93. Excerpted from Changsha's Ta-kung pao, March to August 1918. This is all original material, but some has been abridged.

94. Mao Tse-tung, "On the People's Democratic Dictatorship" [in Selected Works of Mao Tse-tung, IV (Peking: Foreign Languages Press, 1967), p. 413 —

Selected Works of Mao Tse-tung hereinafter referred to as SW.]

95. L. N. Tolstoy (1828-1910) was a great Russian writer of the latter half of the nineteenth century. He severely criticized capitalist exploitation, mercilessly exposed the ruthlessness of Czarist government, ripped off all the false masks of the ruling class, and conveyed deep-felt sympathy to the oppressed masses. Nevertheless, because he was unable to unite with the people's revolutionary movement, his theory and point of view could not help being filled with contradictions. He propagated the idea of nonresistance against force and called for a "self-perfection in morality," speaking of "conscience" and of an all-embracing, human "love." He preached "asceticism." Lenin said: "Tolstoy reflected that deep hatred, that ripe hope for 'what is better,' and the desire to shun the 'past.' He also reflected an immaturity in his illusions, his lack of political training, and in his softness toward revolution." Romain Rolland's biography, La Vie de Tolstoï, opens with the phrase: "Russia's great spirit."

96. Mao Tse-tung, "Oppose Stereotyped Party Writing" [SW, III, pp. 54-55].

97. During the feudal examination period the spiritless literary men were unwilling to engage in labor production. Some relied on the writing of scrolls for other people. This was known as "traveling about to acquire education." It was popularly referred to as "raising the autumn wind." [Actually, "traveling about to acquire education" is quite different. This tradition, yu-hsüeh, has deep roots in Chinese history and is particularly evident in the person of China's first great historian, Ssu-ma Ch'ien (as was pointed out in a previous note). "Raising the autumn wind," on the other hand, does refer to making small presents in hopes of receiving some recompense. — Tr.]

98. Mr. and Mrs. Pan Wei-lien, Hsin hsi hsing man chi, chapter XVI.


## 2. REVOLUTIONARY ACTIVITIES BEFORE AND AFTER THE MAY FOURTH PERIOD

1. This was the so-called recruitment of "Chinese labor" during World War I. This operation was managed at the time by the Hui min ["benefit the people"] Company of Liang Shih-i, minister of finance in the Tuan Ch'i-jui government. Liang became very rich as a result of this venture.

2. Wang Jo-fei was from An-shun, Kweichow. He was a member of the Chinese Communist Party. At the Fifth Party Congress he was elected a member of the Central Committee. After the Sixth Party Congress he was sent as one of the representatives of the Chinese delegation to the Comintern. In 1931 he returned home and took up the position of secretary of the Chinese Communist Party Central Committee's Northern and Central China Work Committee [Chungkung chung-yang Hua-pei — Hua-chung kung-tso wei-yüan-hui]. He was also secretary of the Chinese Communist Party Central Committee. At the Seventh Congress of the Party he was elected again and continued in his post as a member of the Central Committee. In 1946 he attended the Political Consultative Conference as a representative of the Chinese Communist Party. On April 8 he met his death in an airplane accident on his way back to Yenan.

3. Wu Chih-hui was a famous Kuomintang politician. In the late Ch'ing period he had joined the "Patriotic Society" [Ai-kuo hsüeh-she] that had been organized by Chang T'ai-yen and Ts'ai Yüan-p'ei and regularly published political essays in Shanghai's Su Pao, fomenting an anti-Ch'ing revolution. In 1903 Chang T'ai-

yen, Tsou Jung and others were arrested and the Su Pao was closed down. Wu escaped to France and joined the United League, publishing the paper New Century [Hsin shih-chi], which championed anarchism and advocated revolution through assassination. After the 1911 Revolution he returned home, dropped anarchism, and with a flick of the finger became a politician. During and after the First Revolutionary Civil War he changed once more, this time into an anticommunist, anti-people mouthpiece for Chiang Kai-shek.

4. Snow, Red Star over China [p. 151].

5. Hsia Chia, "Pei-jing ta-hsüeh ti Mao chu-hsi ho Li Tao-chao t'ung-chih chi-nien shih" [The Commemorative Room of Chairman Mao Tse-tung and Comrade Li Ta-chao at Peking University], June 29, 1951.

6. Teng Chung-hsia was from I-chang, Hunan. He was a member of the Chinese Communist Party and an outstanding leader of the Chinese labor movement. During the first high tide of strikes from 1922 to 1923 he participated in and led the strikes at Ch'ang-hsin-tien, the K'ai-luan Coal Mines, and the Peking-Hankow Railroad. In 1924 during the second high tide of the labor movement he was one of the leaders of the anti-Japanese strike of forty thousand workers at the Shanghai Japanese cotton mill. After the Second Party Congress he became a member of the Party Central Committee and continued in that position until his death. After the failure of the First Revolutionary Civil War, he was secretary of the Kiangsu provincial Party committee, of the Canton provincial Party committee, a special member of the Chinese Communist Party Central Committee, a member of the political committee of the Second Red Army Regiment, and the chairman of the Mutual Benevolence Society [Hu chi tsung hui] (which led the work of revolutionary relief). He was arrested in the French concession in Shanghai in May 1933. He was then extradited to Nanking and there bravely sacrificed his life. He wrote Chung-kuo chih-kung yün-tung chien shih [A Short History of the Chinese Trade Union Movement].

7. Shao P'iao-p'ing is Shao Chen-ch'ing. He was a reporter at the time who had a sense of justice. On April 26 he was executed by the Fengtien warlord Chang Tsung-ch'ang in Peking.

8. Kropotkin (1842-1921) was a Russian. Influenced by Bakunin, he joined the anarchist movement and became a world-famous anarchist. During World War I he blindly protected the nationalists of his country [tsu-kuo p'ai]. After Russia's February Revolution, he advocated that the socialist revolution should rapidly destroy the state, law, and the means of production, and even go so far as to destroy the private ownership of commodities. He opposed all forms of the state and thus also opposed the dictatorship of the proletariat. He was nothing short of a petty bourgeois dreamer who gave no thought to reality.

9. Mao Tse-tung, "On New Democracy" [SW, II, p. 373].

10. Ibid.

11. Ibid.

12. P'eng Huang, whose hao was Yin-pai, was a student leader of Hunan during the May Fourth movement. He died in 1922.

13. Liu Chih-hsün was from Changsha, Hunan. He was a member of the Chinese Communist Party. At the time, he was studying at a church-related university. During the First Revolutionary Civil War he was secretary of the Hunan Peasant Association. After the failure of the First Revolutionary Civil War, he worked in the white [i.e., noncommunist] areas. He was sacrificed in 1933 in the revolutionary base area of Hung-hu.

14. The Weekly Review [Mei-chou p'ing-lun] began publication on December 22, 1918, and on August 30, 1919, it was closed down by the Peiyang warlord government. Altogether it published thirty-seven issues. This periodical fully reflected the Chinese political thought of the May Fourth movement. In the beginning, this periodical was a publication for the expression of political views that was jointly run by communist intellectuals, petty bourgeois intellectuals, and bourgeois intellectuals. Comrade Li Ta-chao was the editor.

15. See The Weekly Review, No. 36 (August 24, 1919): "New Publications."

16. Chou Shih-chao, "Wo so jen-shih ti Mao chu-hsi" [The Chairman Mao I Knew], New Hunan News, July 1, 1950.

17. At the time, Clemenceau was the premier of France. He was chosen as chairman of the Paris Peace Conference. Lloyd Goerge was the prime minister of England and was England's chief delegate to the Conference. Wilson was the president of the United States and was the chief American delegate.

18. Hsiao Ching-kuang, "Tao Pi-shih" [In Memory of (Jen) Pi-shih], People's Daily [Jen-min jih-pao], October 31, 1950.

19. See "Ch'ang-sha she-hui mien-mien kuan," New Youth, VII, No. 1. Women's Bell had not yet been found.

20. Ch'en Tu-hsiu, "Tzu-sha lun [On Suicide], New Youth, VII, No. 2 (January 1, 1920).

21. In 1917 the secret struggle between the Chihli warlord Feng Kuo-chang and the Anhwei warlord Tuan Ch'i-jui was very fierce. In Peking Tuan organized the "Anfu Club" in Anfu Lane and pulled in politicians with him. For this reason the Peiyang warlords were also referred to as the Anfu Clique.

22. At this time Feng Yü-hsiang was brigade commander and was part of the Chihli Clique. In 1926 he announced at Sui-yüan that he was pulling out of the Peiyang warlord system to join the Revolution. After the revolt of Chiang Kai-shek and Wang Ching-wei in 1927, Feng joined in anticommunist activities, but all along there existed clashes of interest with the Chiang Kai-shek bloc. After the September 18 Incident he endorsed resistance against Japan, cooperated with the Communist Party in 1933, and organized the Popular Allied Army of Resistance against Japan [Min-chung k'ang-Jih t'ung-meng chün] in Chang-chia-k'ou. In his later years he continued to adopt a cooperative position vis-à-vis the Communist Party.

23. Ch'en Shu-i, Chia Shih, "Mao chu-hsi ku-shih shih-ling" [Anthology of Stories on Chairman Mao], New Hunan News, July 1, 1950.

24. On July 22, 1920, T'an Yen-k'ai sent out the so-called "Ma Telegram" ["Ma" is the name of a sacrifice made to the god of war before a military campaign. — Tr.] in which he announced the aims and purposes of Hunan autonomy: "The reality of a republic lies solely with the practice of people's rule; the realization of people's rule lies most of all with the organization and practice of local government by the people of the various provinces.... We believe that unless we divide the government of Hunan among the entire body of Hunan citizens, we will be unable to relieve quickly their pain and suffering or rapidly restore their original vigor."

25. Chu Chien-fan was from Changsha and was the person who founded Chou-nan Girls' School in the late Ch'ing period. He was an enlightened person and was famous in Hunan educational circles. During the First Revolutionary Civil War he was a member of the Kuomintang left wing and participated in the leadership of the Hunan branch of the Kuomintang and its Changsha municipal branch.

After the failure of the Revolution, a warrant was issued for his arrest by the reactionaries and he fled. He died in Shanghai in 1935.

26. See Changsha's Ta-kung pao for October 7, 1920. The newspaper material used in this section all comes from this paper.

### 3. ACTIVITIES SURROUNDING THE ESTABLISHMENT OF THE CHINESE COMMUNIST PARTY

1. Hsiao Tzu-sheng was a student in the second class of First Normal. When he was in school he showed a progressive attitude and was extremely talented. In 1919 he went to France and participated in the Diligent Work and Frugal Study movement. Afterward he frequented the doorsteps of the Kuomintang bureaucratic politicians Li Shih-tseng and I P'ei-chi. He held the position of vice minister of agriculture and mining in the Kuomintang government.

2. Proudhon (1809-1865) was a French petty bourgeois thinker and one of the fathers of modern anarchism. He dreamed about making the system of small private ownership last forever and opposed class struggle and the dictatorship of the proletariat. He advocated the organization of a kind of "people's bank" that would extend noninterest loans in order to help workers become handicraft entrepreneurs. He advocated the reform of capitalism, the abolition of the "bad" aspects of capitalism, and the establishment of "good" capitalism. Marx's famous The Poverty of Philosophy dealt a fatal blow with its criticism of Proudhon's "impoverished philosophy."

3. Bertrand Russell [1872-[1970]) is an English philosopher and one of the leading intellects of modern idealism. He has always been opposed to revolutionary theories dealing with class struggle and socialism. He is an anti-Soviet and anticommunist fomenter and a bellicose imperialist thinker. Recently, owing to the spread of the world peace movement, Russell has also begun to advocate peace, and in 1955 he stated his opposition to nuclear war. [The reference here is to the now largely forgotten articles of the early 1950s in which Russell advocated a tough line with the Soviet Union in order to defend the "Free World." For Mao's comment of December 1965 on Russell's change of heart, see Mao Tse-tung Unrehearsed, p. 239. — S.R.S.]

4. Ch'en Tzu-po was from Hsiang-hsiang, Hunan. He passed away from illness in 1923.

5. The Wen-hua shu-she she-wu pao-kao was printed from lead type and was not for sale. Only issue No. 2 has been discovered so far; this was obtained from the home of the revolutionary martyr Ho Erh-k'ang.

6. Hsiao Shu-fan was from Ning-hsiang, Hunan. He was a member of the Chinese Communist Party. During the First Revolutionary Civil War, he held the position of secretary of the Hunan committee of the Communist Youth Corps. He died from illness in 1927.

7. Hsieh Hsüeh-tsai, "Ti-i tz'u hui-chien Mao Tse-tung t'ung-chih" [My First Meeting with Comrade Mao Tse-tung], New Observer, 1952, No. 11.

8. Hsiao Ching-kuang, "Tao Pi-shih."

9. These essays were printed in the Changsha Ta-kung pao from November to December 1920 and in the beginning of 1921.

10. This man's ming was Chang Wen-liang. Later, he never did join the revolution but became mentally deranged. This diary was obtained from the home of the martyr Ho Erh-k'ang.

11. Hsieh Hsüeh-tsai, "Ti-i tz'u hui-chien Mao Tse-tung t'ung-chih."

12. Liu Shao-ch'i, Lun tang [On the Party]. [Translation from Collected Works of Liu Shao-ch'i, 1945-1957 (Hong Kong: Union Research Institute, 1969), p. 14.]

13. Ibid [p. 17].

14. Comrade Ch'en Yu-k'uei was sacrificed in 1928. At the time he was secretary of the Heng-yang Special Committee.

15. Li Yao-jung was from Changsha, Hunan. In 1923 he joined the Socialist Youth Corps and was secretary of the Corps branch at the Kuang-Hua Electric Light Company. He was murdered in September 1927.

16. Hsieh Hsüeh-tsai, "Chiang Meng-chou t'ung-chih chuan" [Biography of Comrade Chiang Meng-chou], in Hu-nan ko-ming lieh-shih chuan [Biographies of Revolutionary Heroes of Hunan], Hu-nan Jen-min ch'u-pan-she.

17. Ibid.

18. Ho Erh-k'ang was from Hsiang-t'an, Hunan. He was a member of the Chinese Communist Party. After he graduated from Hsiang-hsiang School, the Party sent him to do work among the peasants. During the First Revolutionary Civil War he was responsible for the work of the Hsiang-t'an Peasant Association. In 1927 after the Horse Day Incident he was arrested, and in April 1928 he sacrificed his life. His diary and essays were obtained from his home in Hsiang-t'an.

## 4. THE EARLY LABOR MOVEMENT IN HUNAN LED BY COMRADE MAO TSE-TUNG

1. Hu Ch'iao-mu, Chung-kuo kung-ch'an-tang san-shih nien [Thirty Years of the CCP] (2nd ed.), pp. 5-6.

2. Ch'en Po-ta, Mao Tse-tung lun Chung-kuo ko-ming (2nd ed.), pp. 6-7. [Translation from Chen Po-ta, Mao Tse-tung on the Chinese Revolution (Peking: Foreign Languages Press, 1953), p. 9.]

3. Mao Tse-tung, "On New Democracy" [SW, II, p. 371].

4. Kuo Liang, Hu-nan kung-jen yün-tung ti kuo-ch'ü yü hsien-tsai [The Past and Present of the Hunan Workers' Movement]. This small pamphlet was published in Changsha in February 1927 and has long been out of print.

5. Ch'en Po-ta, "Wu-Ssu Yün-tung yü chih-shih fen-tzu ti tao-lu" [The May Fourth Movement and the Road of the Intellectuals], Jen-min jih-pao [People's Daily], May 4, 1949.

6. Mao Tse-tung, "The May Fourth Movement" [SW, II, p. 238].

7. Mao Tse-tung, "Oppose Stereotyped Party Writing" [SW, III, pp. 59-60].

8. Mao Tse-tung, "The Orientation of the Youth Movement" [SW, II, p. 246].

9. Mao Tse-tung, "Talks at the Yenan Forum on Literature and Art" [SW, III, p. 73].

10. The Political Study Clique was formed in 1916 by a group of Progressive Party members (the political party organized by Liang Ch'i-ch'ao and his group during the early years of the Republic in agreement with Yüan Shih-k'ai) and a group of Kuomintang Party members. It was an extreme right-wing political clique. The members of this clique followed a path of opportunism with respect to the northern and southern warlords in order to seize official positions. During the Northern Expedition in 1926 and 1927 some members of the Political Study Clique began to conspire with Chiang Kai-shek and use their political experience

to help Chiang establish a counterrevolutionary regime.

11. That is, Tseng Kuo-fan, Tso Tsung-t'ang, P'eng Yü-lin, and Hu Lin-i. They were central figures who helped the Ch'ing government suppress the peasant revolutionary movement during the Taiping Heavenly Kingdom period [1851-1864]. They loudly sang the praises of the fallacious Neo-Confucianism of the Ch'eng brothers and Chu Hsi, greatly extended local gentry power, and created ways to support and strengthen feudal rule.

12. With regard to the shortcomings of the other labor unions existing at the time throughout the country, Teng Chung-hsia has written in Chapter III of his Chung-kuo chih-kung yun-tung chien shih: "Generally speaking, the unions of that time had only upper-level organization, they had no lower-level organization." "The comrades in the trade union movement at the time never did develop a Party organization within the union." [italics in the original] Also, in an article entitled "Kuan-yü kung-hui nei-cheng ti chung-yao wen-t'i" [On the Important Question of the Union's Internal Government] that appeared in issues Nos. 5 to 8 (May to June 1923) of the Canton Lao-tung chou pao [Labor Weekly] we read: "The reason that the Canton labor movement is in eclipse is (1) no one has given any attention to the problem of leadership, (2) no one has given any attention to the problem of discipline. Members freely withdraw from the union; group activities are undermined because of individual interests; there is a mutual clash of opinion that leads to splitting."

13. V. I. Lenin, The State and Revolution [The Collected Works of V. I. Lenin, XXV (Moscow: Progress Publishers, 1964), p. 484].

14. According to the recollection of Mr. I Li-jung.

15. Teng Chung-hsia, Chung-kuo chih-kung yün-tung chien shih, Chapter III.

16. Huang Ching-yüan, then vice chairman of the Anyüan Workers' Club, was murdered in October 1925 in Anyüan by the warlord Fang Pen-jen.

17. When Wang Hsien-tsung was leading the peasant movement in Suchou in November 1925 he was murdered by the troops of Chao Heng-t'i.

18. Teng Chung-hsia, Chung-kuo chih-kung yün-tung chien shih, Chapter III.

19. Chien Ch'ü-ping was a member of the Chinese Communist Party. During the First Revolutionary Civil War he held the position of secretary of the Hunan General Labor Union. He was sacrificed in 1928.

20. P'ang Jen-chien was the older brother of P'ang Jen-ch'üan and a member of the Chinese Communist Party. He was sacrificed in 1927.

21. P'eng Chiang-liu, "Tsai Mao chu-hsi ling-tao hsia ch'ien An-yüan mei-k'uang ti kung-jen yun-tung" [The Anyüan Coal Mine Workers' Movement before Coming under the Leadership of Chairman Mao], Kiangsi Daily [Chiang-hsi jih-pao], July 1, 1951.

22. Mao Tse-min was from Hsiang-t'an, Hunan, and was the younger brother [ch'in ti] of Comrade Mao Tse-tung and a member of the Chinese Communist Party. After working at Anyüan, he was transferred in 1925 to the position of manager of the Party Central's Department of Publications and in Wuhan, Changsha, and Shanghai personally established a publication network for Party propaganda — the Ch'ang-chiang Book Company. In 1931 he came to the Fukien-Canton-Kiangsi Revolutionary Base Area and took up the position of head of the Department of Management for the Military Region (equal to today's head of logistics). In 1932 he was president of the National Bank of the Central Revolutionary Base Area. He joined the Long March, and after arriving in the revolutionary base area in northern Shensi, he became minister of National Economics. In 1938 he

turned toward Sinkiang to do work. Later, he was head of the Sinkiang Department of Finance. In 1942 when Sheng Shih-ts'ai went over to Chiang Kai-shek and became an anti-soviet and anti-communist, Mao Tse-min and other comrades were arrested and thrown into jail. Soon thereafter they were killed by poisoned wine given to them by the enemy.

23. Teng Chung-hsia, Chung-kuo chih-kung yün-tung chien shih, Chapter III.

24. P'eng Chiang-liu, "Tsai Mao chu-hsi ling-tao hsia ch'ien An-yüan mei-k'uang ti kung-jen yün-tung."

25. For this essay as well as for the proclamation of this strike, related letters, and other relevant reports quoted in this section, see the Changsha Ta-kung pao from August 10 to October 27, 1922.

26. Yüan Fu-ch'ing, "Hui-i Mao Tse-tung t'ung-chih ch'in-tzu ling-tao hsia ti Hu-nan ch'u-ch'i kung-jen yün-tung" [Remembering the First Hunan Workers' Movement under the Personal Leadership of Comrade Mao Tse-tung], New Hunan News, June 20, 1951.

27. For this proclamation and the relevant material quoted in this section, see Changsha's Ta-kung pao from September 10 to 17, 1922.

28. Liu Ya-ch'iu, "Ti-i tz'u kuo-nei ko-ming chan-cheng ch'ien-hou Shui-k'ou-shan ti kung-jen yün-tung" [The Workers' Movement in Shui-k'ou-shan during the First Revolutionary Civil War], New Hunan News, May 1, 1952.

29. See the relevant reports in the New Hunan News of May 1, 1952 (first page).

30. Mao Tse-t'an was from Hsiang-t'an, Hunan, and was the young brother [yu ti] of Mao Tse-tung. He was a member of the Chinese Communist Party. He was the Military Region secretary of the Twelfth Army in eastern Fukien and the secretary of the Central Bureau in the Central Revolutionary Base Area. In the spring of 1935 he died in battle at Ch'ang-t'ing, Fukien.

31. Changsha Ta-kung pao, November 22, 1922.

32. Miu Chung-k'un, "Hui-i Mao chu-hsi ling-tao ch'ang-sha ch'ien-yin huo-pan kung-jen pa-kung tou-cheng" [Remembering the Strike Struggle of the Changsha Type Machinists and Typesetters Led by Chairman Mao], Yangtze Daily, July 1, 1951.

33. Ch'en Po-ta, Mao Tse-tung lun Chung-kuo ko-ming [Mao Tse-tung on the Chinese Revolution] (2nd ed.), p. 38. [Translation from Chen Po-ta, Mao Tse-tung on the Chinese Revolution (Peking: Foreign Languages Press, 1953), pp. 49-50.]

34. Mao Tse-tung, "Analysis of the Classes in Chinese Society" [SW, I, p. 14].

35. Teng Chung-hsia, Chung-kuo chih-kung yün-tung chien shih, Chapter III.

36. Changsha Ta-kung pao, October 3, 1922.


CONCLUSION

1. Liu Shao-ch'i, Lun tang [On the Party]. [Translation from Collected Works of Liu Shao-ch'i, 1945-1957 (Hong Kong: Union Research Institute, 1969), p. 14.]

2. Ibid [p. 34].

3. Ibid [pp. 21-22].

4. Ibid. [My translation. I have been unable to locate this sentence in the official English translation of 1954. Li Jui gives no page number for the 1953 Chinese edition that he uses. — Tr.]

5. Ibid [pp. 29-30].
6. Ch'en Po-ta, Ssu-ta-lin ho Chung-kuo ko-ming [Stalin and the Chinese Revolution], Jen-min ch'u-pan-she, 1953.
7. Ch'en Po-ta, Tu "Hu-nan nung-min yün-tung k'ao-ch'a pao-kao" [Reading "Report on an Investigation of the Peasant Movement in Hunan"], Jen-min ch'u-pan-she, p. 43.


APPENDIX: THE HUNAN PEASANT MOVEMENT DURING THE PERIOD OF THE FIRST REVOLUTIONARY CIVIL WAR

1. During the first period of cooperation between the Chinese Communist Party and the Kuomintang, Comrade Mao Tse-tung was elected as an alternate member of the Central Executive Committee of the Kuomintang at the first Kuomintang Congress in 1924.
2. Mao Yüan-yao, "Tsai Mao chu-hsi ch'in-tzu chiao-yü hsia ti Shao-shan nung-min" [The Peasants of Shao-shan under the Personal Teaching of Chairman Mao], in Chung-kuo kung-ch'an-tang ling-tao Hu-nan jen-min ying-yung fen-tou ti san-shih nien [Thirty Years of the CCP Leading the Heroic Struggles of the People of Hunan] (Jen-min ch'u-pan-she, 1951).
3. The Ox Prince temple and the Horse Prince temple refer to the courts of justice of the landlord tyrant camp. The "three potato rice" refers to the fact that the peasants of the Tung-chiang region around Canton, because of the excessive land rent, regularly ate a mixture of three parts sweet potato and one part unhulled rice. Most of the children were so starved that they suffered from edema.
4. "Chi Mao chu-hsi tsai Kuang-chou nung-min yün-tung chiang-hsi so ti erh san shih" [Remembering Several Matters Concerning Chairman Mao at the Canton Peasant Training Institute], in Hua-nan ko-ming shih-chi [Records of the Revolution in South China] (Hua-nan Jen-min ch'u-pan-she).
5. P'eng P'ai was from Hai-feng, Kwangtung. He was a member of the Chinese Communist Party and an outstanding leader of the Chinese peasant movement. During the First Revolutionary Civil War he led the peasant movement in Tung-chiang, Kwangtung. At the Fifth Party Congress he was elected a member of the Central Committee. After the failure of the First Revolutionary Civil War, he joined the August 1 Nan-ch'ang Uprising and after this organized the Peasant Self-Defense Army [Nung-min tzu-wei chün] in Hai-feng and Lu-feng and established China's first soviet government. In 1928 at the Sixth Party Congress he was elected a member of the Central Committee and a member of the Central Politburo. In 1929 he participated in leadership work in Shanghai in the Kiangsu Provincial Party Committee. On August 24 of the same year he was arrested as the result of the work of a spy, and on the thirtieth was sacrificed in Lung-hua, Shanghai hsien.
6. "Ti-liu chieh nung-min yün-tung chiang-hsi so pan-li ching-kuo" [Experience of Running the Sixth (Session of the) Peasant Training Institute], in Ti-i tz'u kuo-nei ko-ming chan-cheng shih-ch'i ti nung-min yün-tung [The Peasant Movement during the First Revolutionary Civil War Period] (Jen-min ch'u-pan-she), pp. 20-32. [Translated in Day, Mao Zedong, pp. 307-311. — S.R.S.]
7. See SW, I, p. 19.
8. Warrior [Chan-shih], No. 19 (September 19, 1926). (At the time, this was

the organ of the Hunan provincial Party committee.)

9. Hunan People's Gazette [Hu-nan min pao], August 29, 1926.

10. Mao Tse-tung, "Report on an Investigation of the Peasant Movement in Hunan" [SW, I, p. 26].

11. Chang Shih-chao, whose tzu was Hsing-yen, was from Changsha, Hunan. Before the 1911 Revolution he had joined the anti-Ch'ing revolutionary movement. After the May Fourth movement he was a restorationist. From 1924 to 1926 he was minister of justice and minister of education in the administration of the Peiyang warlord Tuan Ch'i-jui.

12. "Hu-nan nung-min yün-tung chen-shih ch'ing-hsing" [The True Circumstances of the Hunan Peasant Movement], in Ti-i tz'u kuo-nei ko-ming chan-cheng shih-ch'i ti nung-min yün-tung.

13. Quoted in Joseph Stalin, "Foundations of Leninism" [in Problems of Leninism (Moscow: Foreign Languages Publishing House, 1945), p. 91].

14. "Ma-jih shih-pien ti hui-i" [Recollections of the Horse Day Incident], in Ti-i tz'u kuo-nei ko-ming chan-cheng shih-ch'i ti nung-min yün-tung.

15. Mao Tse-tung, "Introducing The Communist" [SW, II, p. 292].

# Index

345

Hsien-chu. See Vanguard
Hsin ch'ao. See New Tide
Hsin Ch'ing-nien. See New Youth
Hsin-min hsüeh hui. See New People's Study Society
Hsin-min ts'ung-pao. See New People's Journal
Hsin shih-tai. See New Age
Hsin-wen-hsüeh yen-chiu hui. See Peking University Society for Journalism Research
Hsiung Chen-lü, 314
Hsiung Hsi-ling, 139
Hsü K'o-hsiang, 212, 314-315
Hsü T'e-li, 13, 42, 46, 50, 85, 92 105, 110
Hsüeh ch'ih hui. See Society for Avenging Shame
Hsüeh-sheng lien-ho hui. See United Association of Students
Hsüeh-sheng chou-k'an lien-ho hui. See United Association of Student Weeklies
Hsüeh-yu hui chi shih lu. See Records of the Student Society
Hu Shih, xxvi, xxix, xxx, xli, 23n, 111n, 117
Hua-Fa chiao-yü hui. See Sino-French Educational Society
Hua hsing hui. See China Revival Society
Huang Ai, xxi, 146, 155, 179, 192, 194-200, 221, 229, 266
Huang Ching-yüan, 168, 170, 188, 198, 202, 212, 287-289, 340n16
Huang Hsing, 12, 323n22
Hunan, modernist movement in, 3; educational system, 8, 10; political history, 11-12, 79-81, 278; conditions under warlord rule, 46-48, 50-51, 59-60, 63-64, 79-81, 96, 98, 101, 111, 121-127, 135-146, 179, 188-189, 214-215, 286-287; movement to Expel Chang Ching-yao, 49, 103, 110, 115, 126-135, 140, 148, 163, 179, 192, 195, 198; youth to France, 91-92, 134; movement for the boycott of Japanese goods, 103-104, 106; autonomy movement,

xvi, xxxi, xxxii, 137-146, 148; peasant associations in, 279-282, 285, 288, 293-295, 297-298, 300-306, 310, 310n, 311-312, 314; Northern Expedition in, 290-293, 295, 302, 306-307, 314
Hunan All-Circles Foreign Affairs Reinforcement Association (Hunan ko-chieh wai-chiao hou-yüan hui), 270
Hunan Association for the Support of National Goods (Hu-nan kuo huo wei-ch'ih hui), 103-104, 106
Hu-nan ch'üan-sheng kung-t'uan lien-ho-hui. See All-Hunan United Association of Labor Organizations
Hu-nan ch'üan-sheng tsung-kung-hui. See All-Hunan General Labor Union
Hunan Daily (Hu-nan jih-pao), 247-248
Hunan Educational Society (Chiao-yü hui), 103
Hunan Industrial General Assembly (Hu-nan kung-yeh tsung-hui), 191
Hu-nan jen-min lin-shih wei-yüan hui. See Hunan People's Ad Hoc Committee
Hu-nan jih-pao. See Hunan Daily
Hunan Journal (Hsiang pao), 12
Hu-nan kai-tsao ts'u-ch'eng hui. See Association for the Promotion of Hunan Reconstruction
Hu-nan ko-chieh lien-ho hui. See Hunan United Association of All Circles
Hu-nan ko-chieh wai-chiao hou-yüan hui. See Hunan All-Circles Foreign Affairs Reinforcement Association
Hu-nan kung-yeh tsung-hui. See Hunan Industrial General Assembly
Hu-nan lao-kung hui. See Hunan Labor Union
Hunan Labor Union (Hu-nan lao-kung hui), 192-194, 196-198
Hunan People's Ad Hoc Committee (Hu-nan jen-min lin-shih wei-

# About the Contributors

Anthony W. Sariti received his Ph.D. in Chinese history from Georgetown University and was on the faculty of Temple University from 1969 to 1976. He is presently associated with a project at Brown University to collect, translate, and annotate all of Mao Tse-tung's post-1949 works.

James C. Hsiung is Professor of Politics and Director of the Modern East Asian Program, Department of Politics, New York University. His publications include Law and Policy in China's Foreign Relations (1972) and Logic of "Maoism": Critiques and Explication (1974), and he is currently editing a book on Competing Models of Communist Politics and coediting (with Samuel S. Kim) a volume entitled China in the Global Community.

Stuart R. Schram is Professor of Politics (with reference to China) in the University of London, School of Oriental and African Studies. His many writings on Mao and contemporary China include Mao Tse-tung (1967) and The Political Thought of Mao Tse-tung (1969), and he is the editor of the book Mao Tse-tung Unrehearsed (1974).